Warriors of the Continuum
Part Two
DECEPTION

Warriors of the Continuum

Part Two

DECEPTION

Roger P. Heath

First Published in 2025 by LifWynn Books
welcome@lifwynnbooks.com
www.lifwynnbooks.com

ISBN 978-1-0684136-4-3

10 9 8 7 6 5 4 3 2 1

Cover design by Ken Dawson
Cover illustrations by Paola Andreatta

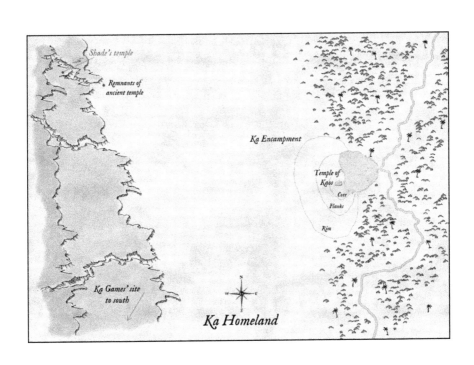

Shade's temple

Remnants of
ancient temple

Ka Encampment

Temple of
Kaos

Core
Flanks
Rim

Ka Games' site
to south

N
W   E
S

Ka Homeland

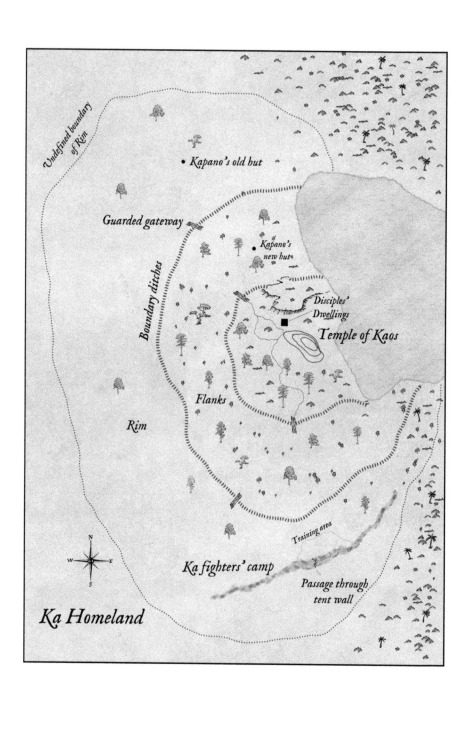

Undefined boundary of Rim

• Kapano's old hut

Guarded gateway

Boundary ditches

• Kapano's new hut

Disciples' Dwellings

Temple of Kaos

Flanks

Rim

N
W   E
S

Training area

Ka fighters' camp

Passage through tent wall

Ka Homeland

DRAMATIS PERSONAE

THE TIME OF LANKY & JESSICA

Lanky, Warrior, finder of the Staff, car mechanic
Jessica, Guardian, twin sister of Eshe, trainee firefighter
Beth, Warrior, soldier, youngest lance corporal in her unit
Erin, college student
Fletcher, local police officer
Tricia, aspiring artist
Mr. Robert Martin, local bookseller, mentor, and family friend to Lanky
Eshe, twin sister of Jessica, killed by a white-haired shaman of her time
Professor Khaled Tadros, professor at Qahir University, colleague of Robert Martin
Asim Adom, mute companion of the professor, a Keeper
The burnt man, unknown shaman of Jessica's nightmares
White-haired shaman, servant of the Dark, killer of Jessica's sister

THE TIME OF THE IYES & THE KA

Iyes tribe
Bear, leader of the Iyes
River, Warrior, shaman, Mother of the Iyes tribe, sister of Sheba, adopted daughter of Bear
Rind, leader of the White Crags camp, hunter, fighter
Amber, healer
Spider, scout, hunter
Knuckles, experienced hunter, fighter, Shield
Shorty, experienced hunter, fighter, maker
Svana, scout, hunter, twin sister of Rind
Gravel, experienced hunter, fighter, Shield
Sheba, skilled weapons maker, sister of River, adopted daughter of Bear

Dune, maker, twin brother of Scorpion
Scorpion, maker, twin brother of Dune
Freya, hunter, scout
Darius, hunter, fighter
Naga, shaman, previous Mother of the Iyes, assassinated by Nefra
Heba, fighter
Tarla, maker

Ka tribe
The Ensi, leader of the Ka
Shadow, Disciple of the Ensi, executing clandestine operations with the Shade
Sy, warrior monk allocated to Shadow
Growl, Shade of the Ka, adherent of Kaos
Cobra, Disciple of the Ensi, camp administrator
Xerses, Disciple of the Ensi, military leader
Qiax, Disciple of the Ensi, spymaster
Rathe, a captain of the Temple Guard
Harg, head of the Temple Guard
Cleft and Hands, hunters, brothers
Karnt, guard, fighter
Tarq, guard, fighter
Scowl, fighter of the southern Rim
Skits, fighter of the southern Rim

The Islanders
Parig, leader of the Islanders, adopted father of Rind
Davak, military advisor to Parig

Meso tribe
Krull, shaman of the Meso tribe, chosen of Kaos
Nefra, daughter of the Meso tribe leader, proposed to bond with Shadow

The Warriors within
Dysam, the spirit of an ancient Warrior, one Lanky suppresses
Bethusa, the spirit of an ancient Warrior, one Beth fights to suppress
Revri, the spirit of an ancient Warrior, one aligned with River
Jalu, the spirit of an ancient Guardian of another world

Daemons bonded with the Warriors
Garrion, daemon in form of a black horse
Fen, daemon in form of a white wolf
Iolaire, daemon in form of an eagle
Afari, daemon in the form of a lioness
Balena, daemon in the form of a whale
Melapis, daemon in the form of a swarm of bees

Shamans of Kaos
K'zarz, ancient shaman, brother of Shaydu
Xehalla, ancient shaman, wife of K'zarz

Daemons of the Dark
Alkazar, free-roaming daemon, servant of Kaos
Ereboz, daemon of Kaos assigned to Growl
Nergai, original daemon of Krull
Angram, original daemon of K'zarz, later acquired by Krull
Ereshki, daemon of Xehalla

Further players
Kapano, recently arrived from the far south, a Keeper of his tribe's stories
Inyana, granddaughter of Kapano, hunter, singer
Streak, black wolf, companion of Growl
Rakana, a dragon, one of the Ancients deemed allies of the Ka
Hydrak, a dragon, ally of Rakana
Stealth, servant of Rakana
Cyrene, mage of the Islanders, sister of Sylander, serves the god Taran
Sylander, mage of the Islanders, brother of Cyrene, serves the god Taran
Zaidu, ancient Warrior, Warden of the Geddon's prison
IY, god of the Iyes, of the Light
Kaos, god of the Ka, of the Dark
Taran, god of the Islanders

PROLOGUE

The snake thought he knew. But he misunderstood.

$\mathcal{T}$he young woman hurried down the dust-laden steps of the hand-hewn passageway and out onto the boulder-strewn banks of the broad, steep-walled river gorge. Impervious to the growing heat of the day, she clambered over the scattered rockfall from the heights above, weaving her way towards the cool blue waters of the river, where the precious log boat lay tethered beside a flat-topped rock. On that rock stood the one aiding her. The one who had always aided her. *The one who has kept my daughters hidden from those who would harm them.*

She smiled as the two young toddlers suddenly noticed her. They made to run towards her, but the round-faced man beside the boat held them back, dropping to their side and murmuring something while pointing to the slippery rocks. She hurried on, lightly stepping through the shallow pools of water swirling between the boulders before stepping onto the flat granite slab.

The round-faced man released her daughters, and they tottered, arms aloft, towards her. Embracing them in her strong arms, she hugged them close, blinking tears from her eyes.

The man cast a sorrow-filled gaze towards her. "We must leave."

The young woman hugged her daughters tightly to her chest. "This isn't fair," she whispered.

"Yet it allows them to live."

A savage anger coursed through her. "I didn't want this. I didn't ask for it."

"And yet, it is your fate."

My fate? Who chose this for me? Who decided it should be me?

1

Trembling, she strove to push the anger away as she saw the sudden worry in her young daughters' eyes. *They sense my rage. I don't want them to remember me like this.* Drawing a deep breath, she smiled and tapped each of them lightly on the nose. "On a boat today," she said, keeping a lightness to her voice. She reached down to the water, wetting her hand, then flicked her fingers at their faces.

The youngest screwed up her face. The other laughed and tried to reach down to the river.

"Oh no, you don't," the young woman said, smiling.

The child laughed and tried again. The young woman wrapped her arms around them, then stood, lifting them into the air. "Right, into the boat you go."

With the youngest burying her face into her neck, and the older squirming to get to the water, she moved to step into the boat, but stopped, frowning. Two unfamiliar bundles lay beside the man's pack. "What is this?"

The man came to her side. "Twins. Another two of the Flanks who must leave this place." He reached up and adjusted the hair knot at the back of his neck. "A curse of our people's beliefs, one that not even you will be able to break."

The young woman turned to him, a green flash in her eyes. "This cannot compromise my daughters."

The man shook his head. "It won't. And be happy that two more lives are saved." He gestured to the boat. "I have to leave. Now."

Her heart hammering in her chest, the woman stepped into the boat and lowered her children into the hull. The youngest held up her arms. "Up," she said. The other looked around, suddenly uncertain, then grasped tightly on to her mother's legs.

Tears rolled down the young woman's face.

The boat rocked as the round-faced man stepped in. "Look," he said, bending down and placing a selection of soft berries on top of his pack.

The two children looked up at her. She smiled. "For you," she whispered.

The man took their hands and guided them to his pack. As they each grasped a berry, the man glanced up at her. "Go now," he whispered.

"Will I see them again?" the woman breathed.

The water lapped against the side of the boat, and she thought she would receive no answer. "Nothing in life is ever certain," came the man's quiet voice, "but always hope remains." He gave a small smile. "And I am a great believer in hope." His smile faded. "You must go."

Struggling to breathe, the woman nodded. She took a final look at her most beautiful daughters, then turned and climbed out of the boat. As if in a dream, she walked to one end of the granite slab and unwound the tether, throwing it into the boat. She repeated it with the other. Then, tears rolling down her cheeks, she stood with her back to the river, unable to watch as her beloved daughters sailed away from her to a destination unknown, untold.

Some indeterminate time later, the sky darkened, and a cooler breeze cut through the heat of the morning as a bank of clouds passed over the sun. She slowly turned, then let her gaze follow the path of the glistening river as it wound its way through the deep gorge.

The boat had long gone.

Her daughters were gone.

She slumped to her knees, staring at the swirling waters, forlorn and alone. Yet for the briefest of moments, a spark of resistance flared. *One day, I will find you. One day, you will be once more by my side.* She looked up to the overcast sky. *With or without you, Kaos, I will build my empire. And then I will find them.*

Then, head bowed, she let her grief flood in.

*

Treading lightly along the animal trail through the darkness of the wood, the round-faced man caught his first glimpse of the flickering lights of the enemy camp ahead.

Good, they're still here.

Halting in the deep shadows at the fringes of the wood, he waited a moment, listening, sensing, quickly scanning the moonlit clearing. The compact rounded dwellings of the camp lay scattered before him, the closest bathed in the subdued light of an adjacent fire. The camp occupants slept, save two silent guards: one who sat beside the fire, the other who kept watch from the shadows of a hut.

Satisfied, the round-faced man withdrew silently back into the wood, then picked up the trail, following it the short distance back to where he'd left the two toddlers. As he approached them, the girls scampered towards him, each grabbing a leg, trembling. *Too young to know what is happening, yet, as we all, they easily know fear.* But there was nothing he could do to ease that distress. *This must be done. They will be safe here.* He adjusted the strap of the papoose on his back, where the babies slumbered in an unnatural sleep. *They will all be safe here.*

With no reason to delay, he drew energy from the A'ven and cloaked them. Then he set off confidently towards the enemy camp, the two sisters clinging to his legs.

Moments later, he entered the camp, and keeping to the shadows as best he could, he made his purposeful way to a very particular hut. Stopping by the hut's entrance, he untied the straps of the papoose, then lowered it gently to the ground.

Still kneeling, he turned to the two toddlers who cowered by his side recoiling from the darkness around them. "One day, you may reunite with your mother," he whispered, knowing they would understand nothing of what he said. "That lies in the hands of fate now. But at least you will have a life here."

As the sisters looked up at him, lips quivering, the man heard movement from within the hut. *Good, the one known as Naga awakes.*

He stood. Then, adjusting the hair knot at the back of his neck, he reached for a Cord.

The Iyes camp vanished. He travelled home.

I. BETRAYAL

CHAPTER ONE

Their enmity was born long before,
but this explains a part of it.

The two fighters slowly circled one another, muscles tensed, eyes unflinching, each searching for the slightest weakness in their opponent's stance, both tiring in the baking, dry heat of the midday sun. A flicker of doubt crept into Brak's mind. How many lightning-fast strikes had he made on the other, only to be viciously repulsed? How many times had the crowd erupted into wild cheers, believing he'd finally broken through, only to be silenced as his opponent skilfully repelled the attack, striking with her own ruthless blow? *Too many*, Brak thought, wracked with fiery pain from the deep, savage cuts lacerating his stricken body.

Forcing himself to keep moving, Brak circled the other, but he saw no weakness, no lessening of the fearsome intensity in the formidable woman's eyes. A terrible fear rose. *She's stronger than me. I can't let this go on much longer.*

Continuing to circle, he twitched his blade hand in a vain attempt to draw her attention. The woman's cold eyes never flinched. *She's too good. I must act!*

He made a sudden lunge, and the crowd – set in a wide, ragged ring around the fighters – roared him on, straining forward to catch the killing blow. But Nefra swayed easily, avoiding his crude strike … yet, to his astonishment, she stumbled and fell, crashing facedown to the sandy ground. With the crowd roaring on in wild delight as an unexpected victory unfolded before them, Brak took his chance. He dived in for the kill, striking hard for his opponent's neck—

Which was no longer there!

His blade struck the ground, and he staggered, trying to keep his feet …

Searing pain tore across his calf.

Grimacing, he tried to turn to face his opponent, but dropped to one knee as his left leg gave way. A chill crossed his soul as he looked up to see Nefra standing above him, her blood-smeared blade clenched in one hand. She flicked her bound hair back over her shoulder and smiled.

The crowd grew silent.

Brak watched, understanding.

Breathing heavily, Nefra sauntered towards him, her lean, toned body glistening in the desert sun.

"I plead mercy," he whispered. *But I know none will be given.*

"Today," she said, "I will oblige."

Stunned, his heart leapt as she walked past him. *I will see my children today. I—*

He felt the sharp point of the blade at the back of his neck.

"I will oblige," she repeated. "It will be quick."

Pain exploded in his head.

He felt himself falling, no chance to think of his life, his children, only darkness …

*

Shadow watched the tall warrior walk away, the crowd of onlookers parting to let her through, all silent, several with death in their eyes. But these were downcast eyes, carefully averted from the dangerous warrior striding through their midst. *None wishes to catch a deadly glance from this warrior.*

Nefra's head swung his way, and her sharp eyes caught his. She smiled and changed course, angling towards him with a relaxed, confident gait. She was clothed in the same simple strips of tight-fitting leather as most other fighters for the Games. Beads of sweat rolled off her sculpted body. "You like what you saw?" she said, brushing his arm as she came to a stop. Her dark eyes locked onto his. Striking eyes, but eyes that seldom smiled.

"You didn't need to kill him," the young man said simply.

She held his cold gaze. "No, but it's expected of me. I have a reputation to keep."

His anger flared. "Curse your reputation. You'd won. Fairly. That was enough."

A small smile played on her lips. "That's the difference between us, Shadow. Oh, you're good." She tilted her head. "Very good. But you're losing your ambition. I want more. I want it all." She ran a finger down his arm. "All …"

"Well, that won't happen," he growled. "Good day to you." He turned and strode away.

He heard Nefra laugh. "It will, my Shadow. Oh, it will."

That is a dangerous woman, he thought as he passed the numerous scattered tents of the Games' contestants, heading towards his own secluded camp. During the Games, he'd kept her at a safe distance, especially in the evenings, but his patience with her was wearing thin. Yet he couldn't lose control, couldn't say the things he really wanted to say. That could prove a perilous mistake.

He scowled and walked on. Most of the crowd, Games contestants themselves, had dispersed, returning to their shared tents if they held such status, else to their chosen patch of ground cleared of scrub and scorpions. He acknowledged several fighters as he passed, but kept moving, in no mood to be drawn into discussions of the fight. His lips pressed to a thin line. And why were they all here, anyway? Wasn't there a war to be fought? Sure, these Games were a valuable, if brutal, training regime. But right now? *Kef! Just get them into battle!* And the greatest irony? *I have to oversee this grand distraction.* He grimaced. He was stuck in this wilderness for half a moon more. And why? *Because I've been asking too many questions.* Head down and muttering to himself, he walked out of the dusty encampment and on southward towards his own camp, still some distance ahead.

It was now many days since his return from his mission, delivered home in style on the back of the ice dragon; days since his meeting with the Ensi, imparting the news of a Staff safely delivered, and of a Warrior dead in the frozen north. And during those many days, his fellow Disciples had relentlessly quizzed him, seeking to eke out every morsel of information on the ice dragon, on the Hidden, on all he could tell them.

And then he'd asked some questions of his own.

And I found myself here.

He reached the edge of the sandy plateau, meeting the steep trail leading down the escarpment to his basic camp below. Sitting on a broad terrace, elevated above the green river valley beyond, the camp nestled between two tall pillars of rock, providing the occupants welcome shade from the blistering summer sun. A home to five Ka, and luckily for him, not Nefra. She'd been told that as a contestant, she had to stay in the Games' main encampment.

As he descended the steep slope, he saw Sy standing by the camp's fire. *I hope he's prepared something good today.* But he wasn't that hopeful.

Not that Sy couldn't cook – the man cooked as well as he fought – but their diet was limited by how little time they had to hunt. And their unwanted companions in the camp were plain lazy.

Reaching the base of the escarpment, he walked on into the cooling shade cast by the rock pillars. As he approached Sy, a now familiar, if unwelcome, smell greeted him. *Ah, wonderful! Fish! What a delightful surprise. Only the seventh day in a row?* Approaching the fire, he thought his friend hadn't seen or heard him, but then Sy put out his hand and flashed a quick message. Shadow laughed. Walking around to the other side of the fire, Shadow signed a message back – Sy encouraged him to sign when he could. "No, I didn't bring Nefra back for lunch. Or for dinner." He glanced around. "The others?"

Sy shrugged.

Shadow frowned. He hadn't seen them up at the Games. They were probably down in the valley, stealing food off the locals again. "Any news from home?" he asked, then reached up to untie the binding of his short ponytail. His hair fell loose around his ears.

Sy shook his head, then removed two blackened parcels from the coals, setting them on the sandy ground beside him. "Fetch the dates," he signed.

Shadow crossed to the hut he shared with Sy. Sturdy, low roofed, and with a frame anchored with limestone blocks, it offered shelter from stray sand-laden gales and escape from their irksome companions. Drawing back the entrance hide, he reached inside and pulled out a woven reed container. Allowing the hide to fall back in place, he walked back over to Sy and handed him the dates. "Another gourmet meal of dates and fish. My friend, I believe I may soon start sprouting palm leaves, and I've a strange inkling to spend the rest of the day swimming in the river."

"Be quiet, and let's eat."

Ever the supportive partner. Grabbing a scorched parcel from the ground, he unwrapped it to reveal a steamed slice of catfish. He sighed. *Maybe I gather food tomorrow.*

They sat and ate in silence, looking out over the river valley below. The flood season had arrived; muddy waters encroached far into the grassy plains to either side of the swollen river. A good time to be a fisher stalking the catfish idling in the shallows, but also a time when rising waters, locally at least, displaced the wild cattle and wildebeest, removing a source of dinner for Shadow's bowl.

Soon, he was finished. "Well, Sy," he said, wiping his mouth. "Even though I'm growing tired of our fishy friends, that was gratefully received. It's a pity our other fishy friends are not proving so helpful."

Sy's fingers flashed. "We could ease our burden there."

Shadow shook his head. "It seems I'm already suffering a … reminder, shall we say, to not pry into the wider realm of our leader. I wouldn't want to extend my stay further by executing three of the Temple Guard."

"Maybe they deserted?" Sy offered.

"Deserted in the desert? Yes, that is a pleasant thought. But no, I doubt anyone would believe Rathe would run. That man would try to halt the flow of the river if he thought it would further the cause of the Ka."

"If we stay much longer, then—"

"Then, yes, your patience will break." An event as rare as a hiding of the sun. *And one I've seen only once.*

They'd been training in the mountains for a full moon under the baleful eye of their loathsome instructor, Lok, a man who'd already abused two of their group. One evening, sitting by the fire, they saw Lok leading one of their friends away from the camp. Sy had quietly climbed to his feet, pulled a blade from his tunic, then followed Lok. Moments later, they heard a scream. Then more screaming. Then silence. Sy returned with his friend and sat back down beside Shadow, tending the fire – and cleaning his bloodied blade.

Shadow glanced at Sy. He was one of the cleverest people Shadow had met, but he saw life in a simple way. What was right, was right; what was wrong, was wrong. If action was needed, take it. Maybe that was what enabled him to function so efficiently. And it seemed Sy believed action was needed now. But killing Rathe was not an option. That would bring the wrath of the other Disciples on them.

He studied Sy a moment longer. This warrior-monk was not a man who searched for danger. *No, he's the one who stops me stepping into those murky waters – until I ignore him and ask too many questions.* But being stuck here with the other imbeciles was driving them both mad. "I'm sorry, Sy. I shouldn't have dragged you into this. But I have to say, I still don't know why I'm here."

"Because of you and your foolish questions," Sy signed, glaring at him.

"All I wanted to know was—"

"You don't question the Ensi."

"I have in the past," Shadow said firmly. "That's why I'm there. I am a Disciple who asks questions."

"Not those questioning leadership."

"Now that's not fair. I asked about the leavers. I asked—"

"About them being killed – by the Ensi's Temple Guard. That's an accusation you can't make."

"Well, in fairness, I didn't make it face-to-face with the Ensi. I only spoke with Xerses."

"Which means you spoke with the Ensi, as you four Disciples share everything."

"Ah, well …"

"Don't you?"

"Honestly?"

Shadow did his best to withstand Sy's glare. "Well, not everything. It pays to keep some things to yourself."

"Pays, as in ending up here?"

Sy had a point. *Back up.* "How could I ignore what Stealth told us?" Shadow said, throwing fish bones into the fire. "How can I ignore an ex-Ka member? One handpicked by our ally, the Ancient, as his trusted servant?" A ripple of unease crossed his features. "And what did he tell us? That he didn't return to the Ka because we were killing leavers. That a member of the Temple Guard was personally involved. That—"

"It was one story. One incident. Nothing more."

"Stealth had more to tell, but we didn't get the chance to hear. We had to leave." Shadow blew a sigh of frustration. "Look, I only wanted to know if others knew of this dragon's servant – of what he had to tell. Tell me, why is that wrong?"

"Because you decide to question the Ensi on the back of one man's words. This is why I tell you to keep your mouth shut. You think too much, then you let your mouth spew out your thoughts before checking how they might sound." Sy paused his furious signing to wave his finger at Shadow, then: "Keep your mouth shut!"

Shadow raised an eyebrow. A severe lecture indeed by Sy's standards. A veritable haranguing. He shifted his weight and gazed out to the valley. "That may well be true, Sy, but I tell you, something's not right."

Sy cast him a frustrated glare, then collected the debris from the meal and threw it on the fire. Then he grabbed a waterskin and took a long draught.

Shadow looked to the northern horizon, where the Ka encampment lay a few days' march away. He understood Sy's reticence – the man had his duty to protect him – but there was a foul stench rising from his homeland, one he couldn't ignore. And unknown to his friend, he'd been asking even more questions, subtly, quietly, following his intuition; casual conversations from the Rim to the Core. And that quiet and most secret questioning of the last half-moon had revealed hints of a concealed network buried deep within the Ka, buried beyond the eyes of the Disciples.

His eyes narrowed. But maybe not beyond all. Maybe not beyond the snake.

A repulsive taste tainted Shadow's mouth as remembered words of one he'd met crept back into his mind – the cryptic, yet brutal words of a woman he'd been asked to meet by an informant.

"They kill our children," the gaunt woman in the Rim had whispered, her shaking voice betraying her fear. Those few fraught words spoken, she'd quickly backed away and fled into the shadows.

What had she meant?

I don't know, Shadow thought angrily, kicking at a stone, which skittered into the fire, raising the eyebrow of Sy. He didn't know because he'd been sent here to the Games, away from the homeland, unable to probe deeper into the woman's words. *But somehow the snake is involved, I'm sure.* Because that slippery Disciple, Cobra, had slowly and imperceptibly grown in power. He had slithered his way into all those mundane areas of administration that no one else wanted to touch: tracking supplies to and from the homeland; hunting and gathering rotas; monitoring the peoples living in the Flanks and the Rim; tallying the tributes paid by the outlying empire tribes; all those deathly boring tasks that someone had to do, but that none wished to take on. And the more the snake grasped, the greater his web of influence grew. And his ambition. *And the Ensi doesn't see how much power the snake now has. I didn't see it.* And now a stench permeated his homeland.

He glanced again to the northern horizon. Something was wrong, but how had he missed it before? *Too long spent away on missions for the Ensi, that's why.* He scowled. *I need to find out what's going on, find out what Cobra is doing behind our backs.* And then he needed to find time with the Ensi alone, to share his worries, unfiltered by the machinations of others. He felt a restless frustration. Too much to do, and too little time. *And I'm stuck here.*

He noticed movement in the valley to his right. He signed to Sy. "Here comes the cheerful trio. I'm heading back to the Games. You want to come?"

Sy nodded.

They stood, and leaving the smouldering fire, walked together to the escarpment. Reaching the trail leading to the Games, Shadow paused. *Nefra, or Rathe and the two fools?*

It was a close call, but he walked on towards the Games.

*

The day's Games long finished, Shadow and Sy climbed carefully down the steep cliff trail back to their camp, the flickering light of their torch guiding their way as they descended through the gloom. Shadow sighed as he saw the dimly lit figures sitting around the small campfire below. *Oh joy. They're still here. Another delightful evening in the company of these three.*

They reached the base of the trail and walked on to the group at the fire.

"Good evening, all," Shadow called out to the grim-faced men as they reached the fire's glow. "Glad you could make it tonight."

"You'll be glad, all right," said Cleft, a scrawny-looking man sitting on the far right of the three, who seemed to Shadow to be permanently sick. And who now sported an ugly gash on his left cheek.

"Why?" Shadow said. "You leaving?"

"No, I'm staying. I—"

"So, what happened to your face?" Shadow asked, pointing at the man's head. "I take it one of the locals took exception to your advances?"

"I—"

"Not that I'm bothered, you understand," Shadow continued lightly, spearing the end of his torch into the sand beside the fire. "Just making conversation."

"Your mouth will turn around to bite you one day, you know," murmured the lean, muscular man sitting between the other two men. A faint smile played on his lips.

Shadow eyed the man with suspicion. *What's Rathe looking so pleased about?* And why was a captain of the Guard here, anyway? "Don't you have better things to do than stay here? Like protecting the Ensi?"

Rathe gazed at him with a cold glint in his eye.

Sy signed in the background.

Yes, I know. I should back off. "So, what did happen to your face?" he asked jovially to the injured Cleft.

Cleft spat into the fire. "Someone paid for their insolence."

Shadow's disgust for the man deepened. Which innocent had suffered today from Cleft's arrogance and stupidity? "It seems misfortune follows you closely." He turned back to Rathe. "Maybe you should stay closer to this unlucky soul to help prevent further … misadventure."

Rathe merely smiled at him with a smug detachment edged with contempt.

Anger flaring, Shadow bristled. *Maybe I should listen to Sy's advice – maybe we do need to act. These are not the behaviours of a Ka.*

"How were the Games today?" Rathe asked, still smiling.

Shadow's eyes narrowed slightly. *What is going on here?* "The same as usual," he said, smiling and keeping his voice light. "Some of our best fighters maiming each other in preparation for our battles ahead. Another useful day."

"*Best* fighters?"

Okay, here it comes. What smart idea does he have now?

Rathe cocked his head. "It seems to me that we're missing some of our best fighters."

"Such as?"

"You," Rathe said with an infuriating grin.

Shadow ignored a shiver of unease. "Well, that's true, Rathe. And for that matter, also Sy. But luckily for the others up there, we are down here, enjoying a fascinating conversation with delinquents."

"Delen Qwents?" muttered Hands, the equally scrawny, blunt-featured brother of Cleft. "Who's that?"

"He means you're stupid," Rathe said, his eyes alive. "And in your case, he's right."

"Hey, I—"

"But, no matter, Hands. Tomorrow, you can watch your better in the Games."

What!

"I believe you're scheduled in the morning," Rathe continued.

"I don't think—"

"It seems it's true," said a familiar, silky voice. Shadow turned to see Nefra standing in the shadows of his hut. "I heard the runner myself. The Ensi has stated her pleasure in announcing a special guest partaking in our Games – for one contest only." Nefra tilted her head. "You can imagine what a stir it will create when your name is declared."

Shadow looked back at Rathe. "And do you have proof of this?"

"Hands, fetch the Ensi's mark."

Moments later, he held the amber in his hand. He turned it over – and there was the eye. He held his expression flat, hiding his shock. No doubt remained; no one would bring death and destruction on their family by falsely carrying such an object. And no one would alter its message. Especially Rathe, a devotee of the Ensi.

"A privilege for sure," Rathe said with an irritating smile, "for both you and those watching. Who will they choose as your opponent, I wonder?"

Yes, plenty of volunteers for sure, including those reaching the peak of their abilities and seeing the chance of a lifetime to show their worth, a chance the very best wouldn't let slip through their fingers. He studied the amber a moment longer. But why? Why had the Ensi done this? *Does she want me dead? Does she send me another warning?* He frowned at another unsettling thought. Had some unknown player taken a most deadly risk and faked the amber, someone who wanted him out of the way? *A snake, maybe?*

"A word, Disciple," came Nefra's quiet voice.

His reverie broken, Shadow glanced to his hut. A word? Yes, and more if she could snare him. But he had survived this long and would take his chances rather than suffer another moment of Rathe's infuriating grin. Settling his expression, he looked around the seated Ka. "Well, I will say good night to you all. It has been a wonderful evening, and I can't wait to repeat it tomorrow."

"We shall watch your fight on the morrow," Rathe drawled, prodding the fire with a scorched twig. "And I do hope for a good end for you. Sleep well."

As Shadow walked towards his hut, he quickly signed to Sy. His friend acknowledged him with a barely perceptible nod. Reaching the hut entrance, Shadow pulled back the hide, draping it up onto the roof, then ducked inside.

"I shall be comfortable in here tonight," Nefra murmured, sitting on his bed of furs, the soft light of the fire outside playing across her face. "Come, sit beside me."

Crouching, Shadow manoeuvred himself over to Sy's bed and sat down. "What is it you want, Nefra?"

"You still have to ask?" she whispered.

"That is not to be," he said, hardness in his voice. "We are not to be."

He thought he caught a spark of anger in her eyes, but her expression seemed amused. "I know you desire me. You can't hide that from me. So, why resist? It's what you want. And it's what the Ensi requires." She cocked her head. "The Ensi? Is that it? You rebel because you're being told what to do? How to act? You would lose me for that?"

"My heart and head are not ruled by desire, Nefra. We are simply not compatible."

Nefra tilted her head. "I think we would be most compatible," she said softly. "A perfect fit." She leaned forward and crawled towards him. "The smartest and most liked Disciple of the four together with the daughter of the leader of the most powerful tribe outside the Ka – a greater fit could not be imagined."

15

"That would appear so to some. Not to me."

Nefra moved closer, her face now beside his, her breath gently caressing his neck. "Let us not talk now of heart or head, but of desire …" Her lips brushed his cheek and her hand—

The hut darkened, and with a loud rustling, Sy fell into the hut.

"Kef, Sy!" Shadow exclaimed, twisting around, his arm swinging out and striking Nefra's face, rocking her backwards. "What are you doing?"

"Sorry," Sy signed. "I slipped."

"What's he doing here?" Nefra growled, sitting up and nursing her face.

"Well, he does sleep here. I guess he's tired."

"Get him out!" she grated. "We have more to discuss. Privately."

"Well, I can't just turf him out," Shadow said in a pained voice. "Look, let's move over there, then at least he can get to his bed. He looks tired, falling over like that."

As Shadow crawled past Nefra, Sy dropped to his bed and lay down.

Reaching his own bed, Shadow turned to see Nefra's dark eyes glowering at him. *Now there's the real Nefra. The eyes of a heartless, selfish killer.* "You do still want to talk, don't you?" he asked with a smile.

Seething, Nefra half stood, stooping under the low roof, and took a step towards him. "This can't go on," she said in an ice-cold voice. "We must unite. Our tribes must unite. I would wish it to be you, but if not, then …" Before she looked away, he saw death in her eyes. She took a step towards the entrance, then paused and bowed her head.

He waited, watching her breathe deeply, composing herself.

She turned and looked back at him, her eyes softening. "We still have a chance. I … desire it."

Shadow was shocked. This was not an act. *She truly wants this.* "I …" he began. *I what?*

She stepped towards him, then gently placed her hand on his arm. "It is what I wish for," she said, her eyes pleading. "With all my heart."

His defences trembled. *It would cement the bond between two great tribes and would double our empire in an instant. It would—*

He winced. *Don't crumble now! This woman isn't for you.* He hardened his heart. "I don't desire it. It will not be."

Her hand tightened on his arm. And was that a tear in her eye?

Without saying a word, she released his arm, turned, and walked out of the tent.

He waited until the sound of her footsteps faded into silence, then looked at Sy, who sat up, facing him. "Thanks, Sy, that could have been messy without you."

"And you think this isn't a mess already?" Sy signed.

"True. Very true." But at least he'd avoided – yet again – being lured into a lifetime of misery. Given the status of both, either could claim consummation as cause for a bond to be declared. *And that would be tragic. For both me and for her.*

"She will react."

That was certain. *Someplace, sometime, her vengeful fury will strike.*

*

Stepping out into the warm evening air, Cobra stood for a moment at the threshold of his dwelling, savouring the strangely hypnotic burr of the cicadas and the rich, sensual scent of jasmine. It provided the briefest of moments to pause from the day's meticulous planning – most covert planning – and reflect on the fruits born of his cunning mind. *Like my home,* he thought with pride, turning to the neat stone building behind him. Set into the lee of a low limestone ridge beside the temple rise, it was one of only four such dwellings constructed in the Ka homeland, only the Disciples and their families worthy enough citizens for such a technological luxury.

Apart from one, of course. But who knew where the Ensi actually slept?

He looked east to the darkening waters of the lake, whose flood-enhanced shoreline provided rich pickings for the fishers – and for hunters stalking those animals seeking refuge in the grassland bowl around them. A perfect location for the homeland of the Ka.

Or was it?

Cobra grimaced at the remembered words of the tribe's Shade, telling of a time many generations before when the entire land around them, even the desert to the west, had been far, far richer. A time when the seasonal rains had sustained vast grasslands teeming with life.

A bountiful land.

A land where the Ka had flourished.

His lips curled into a snarl. Until the devils of the enemy had weaved their apocalyptic spell, driving the ice far to the north, stripping the rains from the land, that most precious lifeblood sustaining his people. Cobra spat. The hated Iyes and their cursed goddess, IY. In this enemy festered an abhorrent and unfathomable hatred so deep, so unwavering, that all sense had been lost. *They destroy their own lands by their actions. They will destroy* all *lands.*

Yet all was not lost. Thanks to the greatness of his god, Kaos, the ice now held. Soon, it would push southward once more, returning the rains to the desert, bringing life to his people. And this time, they would destroy these defilers of the land, these zealots of the devil, IY.

Because this time, we are stronger.

Our god, Kaos, is stronger.

A thin smile crossed his lips. See how quickly the defilers had been hurt. One of their prized Warriors destroyed, another banished from the land, and their cursed shaman killed. His brow furrowed. The killing of the shaman surprised him the most. How had Nefra achieved this so easily? With no battle, no loss on their side. Was this a sign the Iyes were weakening?

He stood taller, a rush of pride sweeping through him. Whether the Iyes were weakening or not, the Ka were gaining strength. A strength nurtured and earned. A strength wrought by maintaining a single-minded discipline and focus to support Kaos in his fight against the enemy. No weakness shown. No deviation from the path.

No questioning of the path.

Especially from the Disciples.

A delightful pleasure arose at the course of his thoughts. Yes, a Disciple trod a fine line – serving the needs of both the Shade and the Ensi was a delicate task requiring both skill and discretion. But it was not for a Disciple to understand why something must be done. They just had to do it. And to the standards expected of the Ka.

And no questions.

No overt questions.

He giggled at the joyous memory of his discovery of such loose, overt questioning. *Ah, Shadow. You lack the finesse to become a true leader. A great leader.*

Unlike someone like … me.

He smiled. Yes, serving the Shade and the Ensi wasn't easy. Each Disciple knew their own role, but not each Disciple knew the full roles of others …

Unlike … me.

He had played his game well, played his role as a loyal Disciple with great skill. He giggled again. And no one knew what was coming, what he had planned. Not even the Shade and his pet, Shadow.

Cobra's lips widened into a thin smile. *Yes, Shadow.* With exquisite timing, the smug fool had stepped across a boundary – *and into my territory.* A step most pleasing. A step providing opportunity. *Now we shall see. Finally, we —*

He flinched at the sound of a familiar, deceptively friendly voice. "Good evening, my friend. We think we should talk."

CHAPTER TWO

To turn and face again terrors once faced,
that indeed requires true courage.

*O*rin's gaze followed the pod of minke whales as they continued to feed in the bay, the calm waters broken by occasional sprays of mist from the violent exhales of a deep diver emptying its lungs before drawing breath and returning to the depths. This was one of her favourite spots on the island, quiet and stunningly beautiful; and with the sun on her back, it afforded a clear, crisp view across the stretch of water before her.

Lulled by the restful sight, she soon lay down, resting for a moment. She rested, and yet she dreamed.

In her dream, she swam in the cool waters of the deep sea, exhilarated by the sleek company around her. Darting this way and that, she and two others harried the shoal, snatching those fish that turned too late and herding others into the waiting mouths of her pod. And all the while, singing her song, her voice carrying far into the waters beyond.

Feeling her air stale, she flicked her tail and drove for the surface—
Then a panicked pulse of alarm!
Danger!
A cry heard, yet immediately silenced.
Fear swept through her. Orcas!
She pulsed her own alarm.
But too late. Approaching at speed from her flanks, a killer arrowed towards her!
She turned hard, but the attacker turned faster, closing fast. Arching and twisting, she drove for the surface, but a second orca swept in, riding up over her back and forcing her down. Again, and again, she

fought to regain the surface, but the merciless harrying of the fearsome animals denied her air.

I have to breathe!

In desperation, she dived deeper, hoping her surprise move would escape their trap – but to her horror, three more orcas swam into view.

A frantic battle for survival was joined.

One she fought bravely until her young body grew so weak that she could swim no more.

Held down and now truly helpless, her life began to ebb.

And into her mind came horrifying visions of hell: her beloved pod dying on a blackened beach; her sister choking on a ragged ball of plastic; and the beautiful voice of her mother turning to rasping, cruel laughter. *'You are nothing,'* her mother said in a baleful drawl. *'Your life is unworthy … unneeded.'*

Wretched despair filled her soul. *'I am dying, Mother … Don't abandon me …'*

Yet at this nexus of utter despair, a powerful voice swept through the waters – powerful, yet melodic and otherworldly. *'Enough. It is time to wake.'* In a swirling storm of violent eddies, an enormous whale swept from the depths, scattering the orcas and releasing her to the surface. Crashing through the water's surface, she emptied her lungs of the stale, toxic air, and drew in the glorious fresh air from above.

The commanding voice spoke again. *'It is time to waken. Aid your friends. Find the Keeper. The traitor will aid you.'*

Keeper? Traitor? As an image of one she recognised flashed into her mind, Erin woke with a start, gasping for air.

"Are you okay?" came a concerned voice from nearby.

Drawing deep, ragged breaths, Erin pushed herself up and sat, head bowed.

"Are you okay?" the voice repeated.

Steadying her breathing, Erin looked up. A man stood a short distance away, binoculars hanging from his neck. "I'm okay," she managed. "A coughing fit."

The worry slipped from the man's face. "I was watching the drama out there when I heard you call out. But you seemed to be sleeping. A nightmare?"

Erin slowly climbed to her feet. "Must have been, I guess. What drama?"

The man gestured out to sea. "A pod of minke whales attacked by orcas. And then, incredibly, a few passing humpbacks came to their aid – at least that's what it looked like from here." He shook his head. "Never seen the like before."

A chill settled on her. *Not again.*

"It's amazing what goes on out there, isn't it? Three quarters of our planet covered by this stuff, yet we know so little of its life. But one thing's for sure, these whales are pretty smart."

Erin nodded slowly, echoes of her dream fogging her thoughts.

"Well, if you're sure you're okay, I'll be on my way."

"I'm fine. Thanks."

The man smiled, then gestured to the sea. "They're still out there if you want to see them. Have a good evening."

Evening? "Okay, will do. Bye."

As the man picked up his bag and walked off, Erin glanced at her watch. *I've been out for hours.* She looked back out to sea, and, as though it had waited for her, the misty jet from a larger whale rose from the waves. A humpback, the man had said. In the silence of the moment, she was suddenly sure of one thing. *I can't ignore this. This is really happening.*

She stared out at the calm waters, set a deep, inky blue by the evening light. Weeks had passed since she had travelled here, finally given the okay by the police sergeant to leave a holiday cottage in the south. *Holiday?* No, it had been an ordeal from hell, one in which her best friends had vanished along with a lad called Lanky from the village; an ordeal in which she had been assailed by foul horrors she never wished to cross again. She had retreated to her gran's house here in the northern isles, believing the warm, calming environment would be far better than fretting alone in her own home, and far, far better than her squabbling parents' place. And so it had proved. The time spent in this, her early childhood home, had finally broken those weeks of sleepless, nightmare-wracked nights.

Or so she'd thought.

For yesterday, in this very same spot, she'd dreamt of swimming beside three adult humpbacks and a young one – and that melodic, otherworldly voice had told her to return to the traitor and find the Keeper.

She glanced out to sea. *And now again today.*

Running her fingers through her hair, she frowned. She had no idea what was meant by a Keeper, but when the voice had spoken of a traitor, an image had instantly sprung to mind.

The image of a bespectacled grey-haired man.

The image of the bookseller.

Robert.

Her chest tightened. Beneath the simmering terror of the memories of that terrible night at the mountain – a terror she had feared to face these past weeks – a part of her already suspected the bookseller had more to tell. But she had been too scared to face him; too scared to go back to that village. *Too scared ...* That and guilt had followed her these last weeks. *Too scared to meet again with the bookseller. Too scared to have followed Jessica, Beth, and Trish into the mountain. Too scared to ...*

She pulled away from the guilt-ridden thoughts. Jessica had clearly and forcefully told them not to follow her, to stay away and let her do what was needed. *I did what you said, Jess, but then I heard nothing from you ... From anyone.* She glanced out to sea, where the pod of whales was heading into deeper waters. *Until now.*

As the remembered melodic voice of the whale lingered, it triggered the memory of the grief-stricken aftermath of her friends' disappearance into the mountainside. For in that moment when her soul had been tainted by the deadly caresses of a malignant evil, another presence had entered her mind. A calm, ethereal presence, she remembered, not the commanding, otherworldly sense of this whale. *And it told me my friends were alive. It told me I would be needed.* During the weeks of convalescence with her gran, she had begun to dismiss that ethereal voice as the bizarre creation of a tortured mind. But as her gaze followed the departing whales, she knew she couldn't ignore these eerie visitations. *I've seen horrors I never knew existed, but I must also believe there are those beyond my sight who can help my friends.*

Her keen blue eyes hardened. She'd been hiding away for too long, ignoring the nagging questions swirling at the edges of her consciousness. It was time to forget the pain, the sorrow, the fear. It was time to act. *Because I want my friends back.*

Casting a final glance to the ocean, she turned away, striding with a purpose back to her grandma's cottage. She needed to say her goodbyes, then face the realities of what she'd seen. *Visit the police officer first.* He would listen.

Because he'd also seen and felt the evil on that night.

*

Fletcher walked wearily through the glistening, rain-soaked streets of his village, his young face aged and drawn from many fraught days and nights of restless worry. But inside burned a fierce – even joyous – relief to finally return home after escaping the weeks of draining grilling from those at head office about the tragic events at the mountain. He knew how it worked, but even he'd been frustrated by the repeated interrogation of his story. *"So tell me again ..."* and *"Can I just clarify ..."*

Didn't they trust him?

23

Trust? No, they had every right to challenge him. After all, how many lies had he actually told them?

Too many.

Oh, part of what he'd told was true. Erin and Tricia persuaded him to travel to Mount Hope in his search for missing persons; they'd met with those missing persons, Jessica and Beth; then the cliff side had subsequently collapsed, sealing three of the girls within. A strange, uncomfortable tale to tell but one hiding a far more fantastical – no, horrific – tale that no one would have believed.

And so, the lies, the cover-up, one saving him from being declared insane.

For how did you explain what he'd witnessed? From the attack by some malevolent evil that had driven him to attempt murder, to their defence by two women wielding magical axes, women who then departed this land via a hidden cave.

How on earth did you explain this to anyone?

You didn't.

You lied.

And so, a fabricated story was told of a kidnapping, a secret ransom attempt, and the collapse of a mountain tunnel that had buried not only Jessica, Beth, and Tricia, but the local missing lad, Lanky. All four were now presumed dead. No mention of malevolent forces, of things beyond his ken, just an unknown kidnap group and a tragic ending. One that would end his career, of that he was sure. *"You went after them alone,"* they would say. *"You screwed up, big time,"* they would surmise.

And Robert? The man who appeared broken by the loss of his friend Lanky? No. No mention of the bookseller's role in this. *And broken? Yes, but not for the reasons people think.*

Fletcher walked on and found himself passing the aging bookshop, which had remained closed despite Robert's return to the village. Glancing to his left, he looked down a side street to a row of terrace houses, and to one house in particular. A dreadful pang of sorrow struck him as he thought of Lanky's mum sitting inside, alone, clinging to some forlorn hope that her son would be found alive. Sorrow and guilt. Because this would be his hardest task. Continuing to pretend her son was still missing, presumed dead, when he'd been told by the young woman called Jessica that Lanky was still alive.

But not in this time.

He exhaled softly as he bore left onto a narrow street. And the truth? That was not easily seen or understood. But what had been clear was that Jessica had insisted she could save Lanky. *And I gave her that chance. Her and her formidable allies.* He turned that thought over as he strode on down the narrow road. Formidable allies, yes, but also some terrifying enemies. That night had shown him a part of his world he did not want to see again. *And I will not see it again. I will rebuild my life. My promise has been kept.*

His promise to Jessica that he would help Erin as he could.

I played my part. He'd helped Erin with her tale – her lies – of what had happened, and she'd eventually been freed to leave the area. She'd travelled north to her family home, gaining much-needed loving care. He felt a peculiar pang of regret. *But far better she's there than here.*

Reaching the end of the road, he rounded the corner to his house ...

He stopped, staring in disbelief at the forlorn figure sitting on the steps outside his house, her short blonde hair lying across her face, her head in her hands. A tumult of emotions whipped through him: surprise, confusion, and a disturbing foreboding that his world was about to be upturned yet again.

And yet a strange sense of anticipation tingled inside.

He took a deep breath and walked on.

Erin looked up as he approached. "Hi, Fletcher," she said quietly.

"Hi, there," he said with genuine warmth. "I suppose you'd like to come in?"

*

"How are you?" he asked, looking over at Erin, who'd just dropped her bag beside the couch.

"Improving," she said with a smile as she dropped down into the chair, her blonde hair bobbing around her ears. "Definitely better. How about you?"

"Hmm. Not sure," he said, squatting on the floor. He gestured around the sparsely furnished room. "As you can see by my unusually tidy place, I've only just returned – haven't really had time to stop and think."

"Do you still have a job?" she asked carefully.

"Today, yes. Tomorrow? Probably not ..."

"I'm sorry."

So am I. I liked my job. I was good at it. Until the horrors at the mountain. He studied Erin, seeing a renewed strength in her face; this was not the anguished woman who had left the village weeks before. "Why are you back?" he asked, absently stroking his goatee. "I'd have thought this the last place you wanted to be so soon after ..." *After that hell.*

Erin sat back in the chair, scanning his face as though considering her answer.

Nice eyes, he thought. His breath caught. *I didn't say that aloud, did I?*

25

Erin seemed to catch something in his expression. "You okay?"

"Fine," he said, feeling foolish. "I think you were about to tell me why you're here."

She held his gaze for heartbeats longer, then looked down, suddenly nervous. "Now that I'm sitting here, it seems harder than I imagined to say what I wanted to say."

"Try me."

He saw her hands clasp tightly together. "Someone – something – asked me to come back here."

Fletcher frowned. "Something? What do you mean, something?"

She hesitated, then glanced up. "A voice spoke to me. It said I needed to help my friends. It asked me to visit the traitor."

"A voice?"

Shifting uncomfortably, she nodded.

Fletcher sensed he was about to cross back into a territory he hadn't wanted to revisit. Ever. "Are you sure that …?" He glanced at her, uncertain whether he should head down that path.

Erin leaned forward, her eyes flaring. "Am I sure of what, Fletcher? That I'm sane? That I'm not just hearing imaginary voices? You saw what I saw that night. You heard and felt the same things. There is a world out there we never knew existed – but it is there, it is real. And now a part of it seeks to help me."

Fletcher inwardly groaned. Despite his strange nervous delight at Erin's unexpected return, her brief few words threatened to derail his own carefully planned and much-needed rehabilitation. Over the weeks since she'd left, he'd forced the horrors of that evening to the furthest reaches of his conscious mind. *But at night …* He shuddered. The darkness of the night unleashed memories that terrorised his mind and shredded his dreams, leaving him spent and exhausted, fighting for the slightest semblance of sleep. And now, with a much-needed respite at hand, he was faced with this, the risk of being pulled back towards things he didn't understand. *Which scares the hell out of me.*

Erin studied him for a moment, then spoke in a softer voice. "I know my hearing voices is hard to accept – weird even – but I truly believe someone is trying to help Jessica and the others. I can't ignore it. I have to take the chance."

Seeing the fearful tension in her eyes, his gut twisted with a pang of guilt. She was here for his help. *And I want to help.* But to do what? He fought to wrap a hold on his own churning unease. "Who sent you this message?"

She looked down, suddenly seeming unsure, uncertain.

"Do you know?" he pressed.

"I'm scared to tell you. Scared it won't make any sense to you."

Fletcher gave a short laugh. "And the rest of it does?" He saw her tense, and immediately regretted his words. "I'm sorry," he said quickly. "That didn't come out right. Look, tell me what happened, and …" He hesitated, his hands suddenly cold and clammy. "And I'll help you as I can."

She looked up, eyes shining with a desperate hope. "Are you sure?"

He stood and walked over to the couch and sat down beside her. "Tell me what you know."

Breathing a sigh of relief, she leaned forward and began.

As she told her tale, a harsh, cold reality swept over him – his recuperation was over before it had begun.

"So, I decided to return here," Erin finished, turning to him. Her eyes hardened. "Robert says he can't remember his time inside Mount Hope, but I don't believe him. I want to speak with him and find out what happened in there." She reached out and placed a gentle hand on his. "I think we both need to know what happened."

And there it was. Despite the storm of confusion Erin's words had seeded – *she heard the voice of a whale?* – she had just spoken a simple truth: he needed to understand what happened at the mountain.

When Robert had unexpectedly arrived back at the car that fateful night, it was clear he'd suffered more severely than either himself or Erin. How that was possible, Fletcher didn't know, and Robert had not answered their questions. He looked a broken man. As they'd driven to a place where he could make the dread call for police backup – backup he knew wasn't needed – it had taken all of his powers of persuasion to make Robert understand they needed to talk, to discuss what had happened and what to say to the police when they arrived. Tired and hungry, they'd formulated their story, with Fletcher hammering home the importance of simplicity. No embellishments, no additions, stick to the simple lie. Over and over again, he'd asked them to repeat their stories. When Erin had called enough, he'd then prayed to whoever was listening: *Let it be enough.*

And so it had proved; for these past weeks, it had been enough, a story sufficient to hide the truth. But what was the truth? Before she had left for the northern isles, Erin had revealed to him more of the tale told by Jessica and her strange friend River. A tale too absurd – too deranged – to be believed unless you had witnessed the events of that night. And if to be believed, then a tale yet unfinished, the stories of Jessica and the others still to be told.

He grimaced. What *had* happened inside the mountain?

I need to know.

And one person *did* know.

Fletcher squeezed Erin's hand. "Let's go and see Robert."

*

Standing at the door to Robert's house, Erin's courage wavered. Back at Fletcher's place, their path had seemed clear. For her, to better understand the path her friends had taken, and to aid them as she could; for Fletcher, a chance to seek comfort that his decisions – and lies – had not been in vain, that his soul had not been left buried under a mountain of shattered rocks.

"Shall we do it?" came Fletcher's quiet voice.

Erin nodded, not trusting herself to speak.

Fletcher knocked on the door. And again. And again.

No answer.

"He's not in," Erin said, her bitter disappointment tainted by a guilty relief.

"Or not answering."

Fletcher walked to the weatherworn multipaned window and peered in. "He leaves his coat on that chair, so given it's not there, we can assume he's out. But I've an idea where he might be."

A few minutes later, they arrived at Robert's shop, the *Closed until further notice* sign still hanging in the door. Fletcher didn't hesitate and knocked on the door, gently at first, then increasing in strength, until he hammered so hard Erin feared the door would collapse. Passersby gave them a wide berth or glanced at them with suspicion.

"I know you're in there, Robert," Fletcher shouted. "I won't stop until you answer the door." He continued to pound on the door.

"I'll call the police if you keep doing that," an older man said, stopping to glare at them. "I'll … Oh. Hello, Fletcher. I didn't recognise you. What are you doing? You won't get in. He's shut."

"It's okay, Harold, I know he's in. He just can't hear me."

"Well, okay. But careful of that glass," the man said, gesturing with his walking stick. "It will break, the way you're going. It—"

"Thanks, Harold. See you later." Fletcher pounded again at the door. "Quite a crowd out here now, Robert," he shouted, raising his voice. "Let's see how many—"

The door opened. "Go away, Fletcher," said the weary-looking man, his grey stubble now thick, his metal-framed glasses perched at an angle on his nose. The door began to close.

Fletcher stuck his foot in the crack, jamming it open. "I don't think so, Robert. Erin and I thought we should check in on you, to check you're okay."

"I don't—"

"And given Erin has travelled a fair way to see you, it wouldn't be polite to simply turn her away." Fletcher gently pushed on the door.

Robert stared at him for a moment, then, without saying a word, he turned inside.

Fletcher gave a wry smile to Erin. "It looks as though we've been invited in."

Taking a deep breath, she stepped through the door, quickly followed by Fletcher, who closed the door behind him. As she entered the shop, she heard Robert walking up the wooden staircase to the second floor.

"Come on," Fletcher muttered, walking past her. "Let's see what he'll tell us."

She followed him past bowed shelves stacked high with disparate objects of all shapes and sizes – bric-a-brac to some, antiques to others – and then up the staircase to the upper floor. It was a while since she'd visited, but as she walked out onto the floor, she saw the familiar, tightly packed bookcases, their shelves jam-packed with a bewildering array of books: tall ones, thin ones, ragged ones; bestsellers, first editions, and editions long forgotten; books on poetry, children's books, sci-fi and fantasy books; a myriad of prose awaiting their perfect reader and companion. This was a place she could lose herself in, searching through the worlds of others' minds, waiting for the spark of a connection saying, "Yes, right now I need *you*."

But today was very different. As she rounded the last aisle, she was faced with the pitiful sight of Robert sitting with his back to one of the shelves, his head in his hands, a selection of discarded food wrappings beside him. A battered kettle sat in the corner of the aisle.

She glanced at Fletcher, who gently shook his head before walking slowly over to Robert. The sergeant sat down opposite the bookseller. "Do we get a cup of tea?" Fletcher said as Erin stood watching them.

Robert didn't respond.

"I see you still have the shop closed. You have any thoughts on when you'll reopen?"

Robert sat in silence, his head in his hands.

Fletcher looked over at Erin and shrugged.

Girding herself, Erin walked down the aisle towards them. "Robert," she said softly. "We're all hurting. We all suffered that nightmarish evening. And me more than most – those were my friends that vanished."

Robert still didn't move.

"But it's important we talk," she continued. "That the three of us who were there talk to each other about what happened. Because we can help each other." She paused, then seeing no response, felt her anger rising. "I know you say you don't remember what happened," she said, unable to keep her irritation from her voice, "but maybe by talking, there's something you can recall. Anything."

Robert said nothing.

Her anger flared. *I don't have time for this.* "Why are they calling you a traitor?"

The bookseller stiffened. "What?"

"I said, why are they—"

"Who?" he said, looking up with red-rimmed eyes. "Who is saying that?"

"Beth called you that. On that night. And I heard it – from someone else. Why are they calling you that?"

Robert's flat gaze lingered on her, then he turned away, his shoulders slumping.

Erin glowered at the bookseller. "You can't sit here and ignore us forever! You can't ignore what happened. Talk to us! My friends need help."

Robert didn't move.

How far gone is he? He must—

"I betrayed them," Robert whispered. "I betrayed my own …" He fell silent.

Own who? She pushed that thought aside. *One thing at a time.* "How did you betray them?"

Head bowed, Robert wrung a handful of hair. "You see, I believed the voices. I believed all they told me. Even to the end, I believed."

Voices? What was this? "What did you believe?"

"That my parents were alive. That I could bring them back."

This made no sense. *But keep him talking.* "And how could you get them back?"

"The Staff. That was always the key. But years wasted, searching. Until … Lanky …" He fell silent.

The Staff! Jessica had told them about the Staff. That it was the Staff that had triggered their disappearance from this time, their travel to another land. *And I saw them disappear from the trail in the woods.* And then on her return, it was the Staff again that Jessica had sought at Mount Hope. A Staff she hoped would return her to a past age to rescue Beth and the lad Lanky. *But Beth was at the mountain. Someone like Beth.* "You helped Jessica. You travelled with her to find the Staff. Did she find it?"

Robert's laugh was bitter. "Helped? Yes, I helped. For decades, I helped. All to find the Staff. So I could take it for myself."

"What!"

He looked up, a faint smile on his mouth. "Ahh, now you see. A traitor? Yes, of the highest degree."

"But why?" she breathed.

"I have already told you – to bring my parents back. To save my parents."

Then ... "So, you stole the Staff," she whispered, her heart in her mouth. "And Jessica and Tricia?"

"I was prevented from reaching the Staff. And almost killed by one of your friends." He cast his eyes down. "But someone came. They saved me."

His words made little sense. *But he didn't get the Staff.* "What happened to Jessica and Tricia?" she demanded. "And Beth?"

Robert sighed. "I don't know. I was told to leave." Fear flitted across his face. "On pain of death if I didn't – she meant it."

Erin's mind raced. Robert had clearly betrayed her friends, but what had happened to them after the cave had collapsed? The voice at the mountain had told her that her friends still lived, so had they managed to return to that past age? But where exactly was this other place, this ancient time? How did that work? She tried to calm her thoughts. She had to believe that Jessica, Beth, and Tricia remained alive. And maybe they walked in that ancient place. *And I may need to seek it out ...*

Fletcher leaned closer to Robert. "You really don't know what happened to Erin's friends?" he said, steel in his voice. "Forgive me if I'm a little sceptical of a proven liar – and a traitor."

Robert's smile was taut and pained. "That is indeed what I am. What I became." He looked over at Fletcher. "But it seems you now join me as a liar and as a—"

Fletcher surged forward. Grabbing Robert by his shirt, he raised his right fist—

"Stop!" Erin cried. "Fletcher, don't!"

Shaking, Fletcher glared at Robert ... then released his shirt and sat back down, scowling at the man opposite.

"Answer him, Robert," Erin said, standing over the bookseller. "You don't know what happened to my friends?"

Robert's thin smile faded. "I don't."

A cool numbness travelled through her thoughts. All this because he had listened to voices. Acted on voices. What dangers lurked in

31

those voices? *For I hear them too.* "Who told you to do this?" she asked, fearful of his answer.

"A god. Or that's what he told me." Hands clasped, his fingers absently rubbed against knuckles. "I ignored those voices for years, you know. I thought I was going mad, then I realised I always heard them in the same places. That seemed too ordered for a crazed brain to create, and so, I went back – and listened."

"And?"

"And over time, they convinced me. Convinced me that my parents were alive. That there were artefacts hidden in this area that could help find them. And do you know how long I searched, how long Lanky searched? Each failed day was as a lifetime."

"And then you were invited to our cottage, and you heard Jessica's story."

"I heard. And I gave an excuse to leave the cottage for a while. To hear my instructions. I needed to reach the Staff before them. To take the Staff. Then my parents would return to me. I almost made it."

"A traitor indeed," Erin said coldly. "And what would have happened to them – to my friends?"

"Those here would not have left this land, and those who had would be returned. They were on the wrong side, but my god was a lenient god."

"And you believed this?"

He hesitated. "I did … But now …" He fell silent, his eyes dulled by resignation.

"Which leaves a question," Fletcher said, the anger still clear in his voice. "Whose side are you on now?"

Robert turned away from Fletcher's scathing glare and dropped his head once again. "I don't know," he murmured. "I don't trust anyone. I don't trust—"

"Don't speak of trust," Fletcher growled. "I don't think you have that right."

"Myself," Robert finished in a whisper. "I don't trust myself." He seemed to shrink in on himself. "I hear voices again. But not in this place. Here it is quiet. I prefer it here."

Erin tensed. *And I hear voices. And I listened to them.* "What voices do you hear?"

Robert shook his head. "I ignore them."

"What do they say?" she insisted.

He looked back up at her. "To speak with you. To tell you things. Of a place to go."

Erin gasped. "What place?"

The bookseller's features twisted in discomfort.

"What place?" she demanded.

"Didn't you listen?" Robert said, his voice rising. "I can't trust myself. I can't trust anyone. I can't trust anything!"

"What place?" she yelled, grasping his shirt in a haze of anger. "Tell me!"

He looked up at her, anguish etched on his face. Yet he answered. "Misr. They said I should take you to Misr."

"What!" Fletcher exclaimed. "You're not taking anyone anywhere. And who's telling you this? Your god?"

Robert winced. "I *am* going mad, remember. Quite insane. A god? No, not a god this time. Only a daemon. A whale daemon …" He gave a harsh laugh and looked back up at Erin. "Daemons. Whales. Quite mad, you see."

Stung by his words, she released his shirt and stepped back, hands trembling. Insane? If so, then so was she. She glanced at Fletcher – his expression was one of disbelief. Her thoughts a tumbling confusion, she walked a few paces down the aisle. Robert had heard the voice, the voice of the whale. *He calls it a daemon.* It was a voice from Jessica's veiled world, a world both alien and terrifying. And one she somehow knew she'd felt only the faintest touch of.

Yet it was there. For all she may fear it, it was real.

And in that moment, she felt the smallest spark of hope. The whale – the daemon – said she needed to help her friends. That she needed to find the Keeper.

Then my friends are still alive.

Her face hardened. *They need my help. And I* can *do something.*

She turned to Robert. "What do you know of the Keeper?"

He stared at her as if disbelieving of what she asked.

She stepped toward him, her eyes boring into his. "What do you know?"

He shifted uncomfortably. "It was a long time ago. And it wasn't me, it was another."

"What are you talking about?" Fletcher said.

"A professor. Khaled. One I worked with."

"Go on."

"I don't know … I never met the child. Khaled … he was the one fixated with him."

"What child?"

Robert's gaze flicked back to Erin. "A troubled child. Khaled called the child a Keeper."

Erin stared at Robert in amazement. Then a wave of utter relief swept through her. *The voice didn't lie. I'm not mad.* She slumped to the floor and sat with her back to a bookshelf. The daemon had said she needed to find the Keeper, and now she had a chance to do so. But what was a Keeper? And how could this Keeper help them? She didn't know, but ... "I need to find this person," she said, her voice steely. "You have to take me to this professor of yours."

"What!" Fletcher exclaimed.

"No," Robert said firmly. "That isn't going to happen."

Erin glared at him, her resolve growing. "You *are* taking me to Misr. I want to meet this Keeper." *I have to try to help my friends.*

CHAPTER THREE

*I wonder what the Shade knew of the
plot – and of the daemon within him.*

With Sy at his side, Shadow walked easily across the gravel-strewn wadi floor towards the Games encampment, the rising sun casting a warm glow on the multicoloured layers of the canyon's eroded sandstone walls.

Shadow's fingers flashed. "There's more to this than simple punishment for unwanted questions," he signed. "Someone has made a move to remove me. And the players in that dangerous game are few."

"A Disciple," Sy signed, his sharp eyes flicking to Shadow. "Or our leader."

"Indeed, my friend. And if the Ensi? Then why am I not already floating facedown in the river, food for crocodiles?" He kicked a stone, which skittered off across the dusty ground and sent a scorpion scurrying for cover. "No, not the Ensi. But I see one too many snakes slithering in our camp these days."

Sy's eyes narrowed. "Cobra?"

Shadow nodded. "Each time I return, he stays as far away from me as he can. When we do meet, he can't hide his growing hatred for me. He's—"

"He hates you," Sy signed, "because you treat him like a child."

"Because he is a child," Shadow grunted. "But a sly child, one with a devious mind." His jaw clenched. "He's up to something, I'm sure, but I can't figure out what."

"We spend too long away. You lose touch with the games being played."

"I serve the Ensi. I fix problems in the Ensi's empire. No time exists for games."

"You should make time," Sy signed. "Else you won't see the blade before it stabs you in the back."

Sy's right again, Shadow thought wryly. *But I serve the Ensi. I can't just ignore direct commands.* "I have my orders for now, Sy. Oversee the Games." He eased the tension of his pack's shoulder strap as he walked. "Let's get these Games out of the way, then we can seek out and understand these other games you talk of." *Games? That woman said they kill the children.*

Sy flicked his gaze to Shadow. "The game has already sought *you* out. You have a fight to win this morning. A fight that was not needed."

A fight against some poor innocent who would die unless he could convince them to surrender. A poor innocent? No, he suspected it would be the ugly face of Rathe he would find waiting for him. "Let's just get this over with."

Climbing up and out of the wadi, then out onto the flat plain above, they walked on towards camp, the occasional sharp crunch breaking the silence as their feet broke through thin patches of the gypsum-rich crust. Soon, expectant murmurings drifted through the air, and beyond a slight rise, the Games camp came into view in the depression below.

Closest lay the confused clutter of the fighters' quarters, a haphazard array of dwellings, some large and well built, others mere strips of hide on the ground. All a hotchpotch of material sourced from the river valley beyond. Beyond the camp lay the arena: several simple circular fighting rings, cleaned of stones and covered with sand. *Bloodied sand is easier to remove. Just hopefully not mine.*

They quickly dropped into the fighters' encampment. The largest dwellings belonged mostly to those of the elite Ka warriors who had arrived by raft from the homeland, bringing their valuable supplies with them: weapons, toughened leathers, and various healing lotions and potions. Of the other fighters, maybe over half had arrived by raft, and the rest on foot, with some journeys taking two turnings of the moon. Shadow wasn't surprised by the efforts some made to reach this place. The Games drew keen, aspiring fighters from many distant lands – non-Ka fighters of disparate tribes, drawn by legendary tales of glory and opportunity. Opportunity to show their worth to the mighty Ka. Opportunity to show their talent and be accepted into an elite group of warriors.

Shadow glanced at several fighters talking together in low voices as he passed. The chances were low to nonexistent that any of them would be taken. And for good reasons. *Our supplies, our food, is limited. We can only take the very best.*

And, of course, many wouldn't survive the Games. Survival of the defeated lay in the hands of the victor, a simple yet often cruel verdict delivered at the peak of battle lust. If fighting your friend, then some hope remained – although not a certainty. If fighting an enemy, then your life lay in your own hands – you must win. Of course, an adjudicator judged, but what use was that when you were dead?

He sighed as he walked on. It was brutal. It was not how he would have it. But the Games were the Games. Maybe, in time, he could change how they did this, but for now he wouldn't waste the opportunity. He would keep his eyes open. Who were the fighters who, having the chance to deliver the fatal strike, stayed in control, containing their killer instinct? Who were those fighters who, having won their fierce battle, saw life as precious and not to be casually discarded? Who were those who showed restraint in their victory? Those were the people he could work with. *People like Sy.* Those who could defend the Ka's people and resources and empire – but also defend its values.

Because we will only succeed if we honour our ancestors.

He frowned. And yet something wasn't right. He sensed a taint in the air at his homeland, a breath of decay. And the longer he'd had to think about it, stuck at this desert outpost, the more he was sure. There was a threat within. His lips thinned with frustrated impatience. He needed time with the Ensi. *Yet the Ensi asks me to stay here and fight.*

As they neared the fighting rings, he saw a large crowd had already assembled.

"It seems the word is out," Sy signed.

Forcing back his dark thoughts, he strode on. Cheers erupted as he and Sy approached.

"It seems you're more popular than I remembered."

"Or," Shadow said with a wry smile, "they dislike my opponent."

Sy gestured to a vacant lean-to shelter to their right. "Shall we prepare?"

Shadow shook his head. "I'm ready. Let's get this over with."

As they approached the fighting ring, the crowd parted …

And Rathe stepped into his path.

"So," Shadow said coldly, "my opponent, I presume?"

Rathe grunted a knowing laugh. "I wish it were so, believe me, I do. But today, alas, I am a mere adjudicator, here to ensure fair play in the ring. To ensure skill alone wins this fight, and that the best fighter wins. And the loser?" He shrugged.

Frowning, Shadow glanced around. "And so, who do I fight?"

Rathe laughed again. "It seems the camp was unanimous in its vote. And it has chosen wisely – a fairer match could not have been imagined."

"Who?" Shadow growled, wearying of Rathe's juvenile games.

"Someone so keen to fight that they arrived well ahead of you, preparing themselves most carefully to face such a skilled opponent. And being the Games' chosen, they had the right to select weapons."

Shadow hissed a sharp breath, suddenly knowing who he'd be facing. "Kef!" he muttered, pushing past Rathe and on through the crowd. "What madness is this?"

"Ah, good of you to arrive," Nefra said, smiling, her body glistening with a sheen of sweat, a blade held casually in each hand. "And on time."

Shadow strode up to the tall woman. "We don't have to do this. We're being used."

"No," Nefra said, her dark eyes hardening. "You failed to do the duty asked of you by your leader. That's why you're here."

"And you?"

"I asked to be considered," Nefra said, flicking a blade over in her hand. "It turns out that wasn't needed. I'd been chosen already." She gestured to the crowd. "It seems people like me."

Shadow's laugh was harsh. "You can't really believe that? They hate you. They wish to see you dead."

Nefra's eyes flashed in anger. "You can't accept others being liked as much as you, can you?" She made to walk away, then paused, a harsh smile on her lips. "As you can see, we fight with blades. And to the death." She strode away through the crowd.

Sy tapped him on the shoulder. "You should refuse. We should leave."

Shadow shook his head. "No, that way lies ruin. But whoever has played this, has played it well. If I die, then they win. If I kill Nefra, then her people will want revenge, and I may have started a war with the Meso tribes." *Who we need with us, not against us. Assimilation by stealth, not force … and with a quiet assassination where needed.*

"So, we walk," Sy repeated. "You lose, but you keep your life."

Shadow's frown was dismissive. "A Disciple who turns? One who flees from the Ensi's Games? I'd lose everything, and whoever planned this would've won. No, the Ka are my life, my family. I can't lose that. I won't lose that." He glanced towards the fighting ring. "The only way is to fight. She's good, but not good enough."

"Win, but spare her life?"

"Yes, and then get to the Ensi. Something's wrong, and I want to find out what."

Sy grasped his shoulder. "Then fight and trust to Kaos this ends well."

Shadow grimaced. "It seems Kaos's eyes have been elsewhere in recent times. Today, I prefer to trust in my skill."

*

Her long black hair tied with a leather thong behind her head, Nefra strode into the prepared fighting ring with a confidence that would unsettle many a seasoned fighter. This was no tactic, Shadow knew. This was the natural gait of a woman at ease with her surroundings, assured of her victory. He also knew the excitable, expectant crowd would see the same calm confidence in him. They would marvel at two proven killers, unbeaten in battle, masters of the ring. He sighed. A perfect mirage, of course. None of those watching had ever seen him fight, none had seen his deadly and silent work. A killer yes, but not one seen.

A shadow indeed.

He licked his lips, acknowledging his nerves. Nefra was strong, quick, and with an extremely long reach. Hence her weapon of choice, the blades. Blades of the latest design, carved obsidian with integral handles. Light, easy to wield, and sharp as hell. *And lethal in her hands.*

And he was unprepared. He had told Sy he was ready, but he wasn't. He tried to dismiss the distracting thought; what could he have done a few minutes before the fight? Disciplined preparation took him weeks, irrespective of who he would fight. But he couldn't shake the truth. "Always prepare for the unexpected" was his common refrain. *Well, this was unexpected; why aren't you ready?* Too wrapped up in pitying himself for being stuck here, that's why.

Nefra stopped in front of him, then set herself into a fighting crouch, her right hand held loosely by her side, her left raised, a vicious blade swaying menacingly from side to side. A guttural roar erupted from the crowd, and they began chanting his name. Nefra's gaze sharpened – and her *right* hand twitched.

Shadow smiled and crouched.

"To the death!" Rathe cried.

Nefra immediately sprang forward, driving the blade in her left hand with blistering speed towards his head – but at the same time she thrust her right hand through behind, arcing the second blade to his heart. The twitch he'd seen saved him, and he was already leaping to his right – both strikes narrowly swept by.

Shadow spun around to face her. Her surprise attack thwarted, Nefra reset her stance and slowly circled him. Mirroring her movements to form a mesmerising yet macabre dance, he flicked his single blade from one hand to the other, scanning his opponent's eyes for any hint of distraction. But her eyes stayed glued to his, as a hawk eyeing its prey.

Don't wait, Shadow, your move.

Switching the blade to his right hand, he flicked his eyes to the ground to the right as though planning to step there and strike. Nefra took the bait, launching herself to his left side and driving her blade for his chest. Anticipating the strike, he twisted away from her strike while sweeping his own blade towards her body as it passed.

Nefra's blade swept through thin air.

His blade hit! A nick to her side. The crowd roared in delight.

Steadying himself, he half turned …

Then grunted at a searing stab of pain in his arm. Facing off to Nefra, he winced as her thrown blade fell from his left arm to land by his feet. A stream of blood ran from the wound. He silently cursed. It didn't seem deep, but enough to become a problem. He gritted his teeth. He couldn't let this fight last too long. But that was easy to say, difficult to achieve. He forced a smile. "Already desperate, I see. You've now lost a blade." Having no use for it, preferring a free hand, he kicked it away. It landed on the ground by the crowd, then quickly disappeared. A bonus for one fighter.

As they circled once more, eyes scanning the other for any slightest slip in concentration, he heard the crowd baying their disapproval, howling for the adjudicator to intervene. He gave a wry smile. *No chance there.* While throwing was rarely used, being an unwritten understanding between the Games' fighters, it was allowed. And it could have been worse – she'd been turning and unable to throw the blade with much weight.

"That must hurt," Nefra said, smiling, her remaining blade in her left hand. "You want me to look at it more closely?"

Shadow smiled back. "Are you offering to submit? So early in the game? I'm sorely disappointed." He gestured to the crowd. "They'd be happy, though, to see you lose. Yes, I think they might even cheer."

Nefra's smile vanished, and she took a stride forward.

Shadow took a step back. He felt softer sand beneath his feet. *Now this could be useful.*

Nefra took another stride.

And he backed off again, drawing her into the looser ground. *This will slow her.*

40

"Scared, my Shadow?" she breathed with a smirk. She took another step towards him.

Realising he'd backed close to the crowd, Shadow held his ground. *This will do. This ground—*

Nefra attacked, hammering her right foot into his wounded left arm, sending an agonising lance of pain through his body. Muscles tensed, he waited for the coming attack to his right, but she struck again to his left with another vicious and well-aimed kick. And again. Each time, he was too slow to move – hampered by the soft sand. *Kef! That wasn't such a smart move.* And he struggled to see an easy way out. The crowd curved behind him, blocking his escape path, and Nefra held her ground in front of him.

Holding his defensive crouch, he suddenly felt tired, weak. How much blood had he lost? *It must be worse than I thought.* He clenched his hand tightly around his blade. *I need to finish this.*

Readying his blade, he made to drive forward—

His foot slid back in the sand, and he stumbled …

Nefra struck down at his head …

His foot bit on firmer ground, and he launched towards her, striking her hips with his right shoulder – her blade narrowly missed his head but raked along his back as he surged forward. His momentum sent them both crashing to the ground. Ignoring the flare of pain in his back and arm, he somehow sprang to his feet first, and scrambling on top of her, he pinned her to the ground. Dropping his blade from his left hand, he struck Nefra in the face with his right. Then he grasped her shoulders and headbutted her hard in the face.

The crowd roared its approval.

Don't listen to them, he told himself, crippling exhaustion sweeping over him. *Focus.*

But his vision blurred, fog clouding his mind.

As his hold on her weakened, the shocking truth gripped him. *Poison! She put poison on the blade!*

He struggled to focus on her swirling face. *How did she think she would get away with this? How—*

A sharp blow struck his back, rocking him forward. And another blow. She was striking him with her knee. He saw a blurred shadow, then his head exploded with a tremendous pain. She'd headbutted him. His head spinning, his hold on her slipped, and with a defiant grunt, she heaved him away.

Rolling onto his back, Shadow lay on the ground, groaning. Defeated. Through his dazed confusion, he heard the eerie silence of the crowd. *I wonder what's happening.*

A shadow fell over him. *Ah. The delightful Nefra is visiting again. Oh, joy.*

She straddled him.

No escape this time.

She raised her hand.

It seems she wants to give me something. Makes a change. She always wanted something from me.

Her hand struck down—

"Stop!" a voice commanded.

No, more than a command. An intervention.

A foul taste in his mouth, Shadow's muscles froze. *No movement allowed*, he thought dreamily. The daylight seemed to fade. *I wonder ...*

*

He became aware of ... something, but he denied his awakening. *Ignore it. You escape the pain in here.* But as he drifted through hazy mists, a faint voice sounded from the distance. A calm, ethereal voice. *'It won't be long. Soon, you can aid us.'*

'Aid who?'

Silence answered him.

Good. Leave me in peace.

Drifting on, he realised the gloom was lifting, a cold glow growing around him.

Go away. Bring back the darkness.

The darkness did not come. But the pain did. In his back, in his arm, in his head. "I hurt," he mumbled through parched lips.

"Ahh. A shadow appears as the Shadow returns," came a maddeningly familiar voice. "And pain? Pain is good. Yes, pain brings life. Open your eyes now."

"No."

"If we help with the pain, will you open your eyes?"

"Yes."

A stabbing pain lanced up his leg. "Aahhh! Stop, that hurts!"

"But it relieves the other pains, yes? We think so, yes, indeed we do."

Shadow forced open one eye. Next to him sat an older man with a neat grey beard, his silvery-grey hair drawn back and tied behind his head. The man's eyes were black, flecked with specks of silver. "How's Streak?" Shadow murmured.

Growl's thin lips curled into a smile. "Ah, pleased will Streak be that he is first in line. Oh yes. And Growl thinks Streak is well. Down in the valley, making new friends. Oh yes, Streak is well."

Shadow doubted those new friends would be pleased to meet that great beast of a wolf.

"But maybe those friends are not glad to see him," Growl said, his eyes twinkling. "But we are pleased to see you, my friend. And we shall talk. But later. Rest now. Not long. No, not too long. Too long would be too long, we think. We shall see you in but a heartbeat."

The shaman stood and strode out.

With a familiar sense of bemusement, Shadow shook his head – and instantly regretted it. Lying still, waiting for the throbbing pain to subside, he absently chased a thought. *Why was Growl here?* Why would one of the land's most redoubtable shamans – the Ensi's Shade – decide to visit the Games? The man openly detested the event, believing, as he did, that no fighters of the Ka should be wasted in this way. *Why does …*

His thoughts were distracted by a hand on his arm and the tapped signal of Sy. He opened both eyes.

"How are you?" Sy signed immediately.

"I feel terrible. I …" Shadow frowned, reassessing his planned answer. Beside his throbbing head, the acute pain in his body had eased to a dull ache. A wry smile crossed his lips. Growl had been at work. "Actually, considering what just happened, I don't feel too bad."

"Just happened? You've been out for two days."

"What!" Shadow exclaimed. Staring at Sy's impassive face, memories flooded back: of the last moments of the fight; of his attempt to disarm and subdue Nefra; then the fog of confusion, the slowing of his thoughts. "I was poisoned …"

Sy nodded.

"Then why am I not dead?"

"You came close. Twice. The poison almost killed you, and so did Nefra's blade when you lay defenceless before her."

"What stopped her?"

"Growl. Immobilised all within an axe's throw."

"Impressive," Shadow murmured, the vague taste of a remembered wielding of the land's power lingering on his tongue. "And the poison?"

Sy shrugged, his fingers flicked. "A Ka blade, and according to Growl, a Ka poison. He fixed it."

Shadow's eyes narrowed. "But there's no cure for such a poison."

Sy shrugged again.

No cure. Hence the ban on its use on a fellow Ka. And if used, then a vicious and disproportionate retribution would fall on the assailant, their family – their tribe. His mind flashed back to his brief encounter with the enemy Warrior, the one later captured by the Ancient. He had used a poisoned blade against her – and somehow, she had survived. He licked his dry lips. There were powers at work here beyond his understanding. "Pass me a skin," he said, propping himself up on his elbow.

Sy unstoppered a waterskin and passed it to Shadow. He lifted it gratefully to his lips and took a short drink. He passed the bottle back to Sy. "Why did Nefra use a Ka poison?"

"She claims she didn't."

"And does she still live?"

"Growl stayed her execution. He's allowing her to meet you."

"Well, that's nice. Will she bring any blades?"

Smiling, Sy shrugged.

A sudden weariness swept over Shadow. Growl had clearly helped him, but it seemed his body wasn't yet ready to play. He sighed. "Is it possible, Sy? Could someone have tampered with her blades?"

Sy shrugged. "Much is possible."

"Well, that's helpful," Shadow said, frowning and yawning at the same time. "What's Growl doing here anyway?"

Sy shrugged.

Reaching the Sy shrugging phase generally meant his trusted yet brusque companion had taken what he needed from the conversation and had no interest in continuing. It was time to move on. He glanced up. This was not their hut. "Where are we?"

"Still in the Games encampment. It was thought better not to move you." Sy gestured to the corner of the hut. "Our packs are over there."

Shadow yawned again. "Well, Sy, I've had a tough day today talking to you. Think I'll rest awhile. Wake me later when you have food." He laid his head down and closed his eyes. Sleep came quickly.

*

"You'll make yourself sick."

Ignoring his friend, Shadow scooped up more of the steaming, meaty stew, then poured the brimming ladleful into his bowl.

"You must see Nefra now," Sy signed. "The Shade believes you're sleeping, but he won't wait much longer for your answer."

Shaking his head, Shadow gestured with his spoon to his bowl. "I'm finishing this first."

Sy gave him a hard, searching look. Then he climbed to his feet, his head brushing the hides of the roof, and walked purposefully to the entrance. As Sy left, Shadow muttered to himself. "Why does no one listen to me?"

He turned his attention back to his food. Upon awakening, his body had demanded instant nourishment, and who was he to gainsay his own body, to ignore himself? No, that would be foolish. So, let them wait.

As he took another quick mouthful, the entrance flap swung inwards.

Nefra walked in, guided by two guards.

With another deep sigh, he put down his bowl, then looked up at her, smiling. "What a pleasure it is to see you, Nefra. And how has your day been? Or rather, your days? It seems I had the luxury of catching up on my sleep, which, looking at you, I'd surmise you didn't?"

Dressed in a ragged tunic, hands tied behind her back, her bruised face was tired and drawn. He recognised the jagged cut above her eye, one inflicted by his vicious headbutt in the fight. The bruises on her arms and face? *Someone taking revenge?* A prisoner, and one so disliked, might easily receive some quiet retribution. A small part of him was sorry for her – *it shouldn't happen* – but not the part that had seen her own brutality in action. Like yesterday, or whatever day it had been, when she had given no mercy to the man she'd defeated in the ring. She had a heart somewhere – *and maybe truly holds some part of it for me* – but it was buried deep within a cold killer.

A sardonic thought was quick to mock. *And what are you?*

He quashed it. *I serve my Ensi, but I take no pleasure in killing.*

"That was not my poison," Nefra said quietly.

One of the guards behind her scowled and muttered something under his breath.

Shadow flicked his fingers …

Sy moved in a blur, the blow hardly seen, and the impertinent guard collapsed to the ground. His fellow guard stood, unmoving, eyes fixed resolutely ahead.

Impressive, Shadow thought, glancing at the young man. "Take your friend outside," he grunted, "and remind him of his duty. Then send him to Dun; he can help shift waste for a few days."

The young guard gave an almost imperceptible bow, then immediately bent down and dragged his colleague outside. Shadow waited until they'd left. Standards were dropping. Discipline was waning. He needed to speak to the Ensi.

"That was not my poison," Nefra repeated, her jaded eyes locking onto his.

Shadow tilted his head. "That would be hard for many people to accept."

"Even so, it is true."

"But you wanted me dead."

"I *want* you dead," she corrected, a flash of contempt crossing her face.

Sy's fingers flicked.

"A good point from my friend," Shadow murmured. "The blades you used in the fight were your own, were they not?"

"They were."

"So, when did they leave your possession? To allow another to add the poison?"

"They didn't."

Shadow looked at her in surprise. "Well, I think at this point you would lose any supporters you may have had. So, how do you expect me to accept it wasn't you?"

She held his gaze. "I don't. I just wanted you to know it wasn't me."

"And why would you want that?"

"I choose who I kill," she growled, her hard features sharpening. "And how I kill. No one else."

Shadow laughed. "You could have come here with just about any other set of words but these – and if you had, you'd leave here to your death. But this?" He shook his head and laughed again. "This is so perfectly you."

He signed to Sy. The warrior-monk walked up to Nefra, took her arm, and guided her away. Before exiting, she stopped, still facing away from him. "I'd have wished it to have been different between us," she said in a hushed voice. "It *could* have been so different." Sy pulled her forward, and they ducked out of the hut.

Shadow gazed at the entrance flap as it swayed in the gentle breeze. What had Growl wanted to achieve with this? To show him it wasn't Nefra who'd used the poison? To get him to forgive her? Or some other message he couldn't yet fathom? What was going on?

His thoughts tumbling and churning, the image of the Ensi flashed clear. The Ensi had ordered him to fight; was that the source of the poison? But no, else why would the Shade have intervened in the fight? He rubbed his forehead, another face looming. The face of the sly snake. *It's him, I'm sure of it. He's at the centre of whatever's going on here.*

He looked up as Sy reappeared.

"We must go to the Shade," Sy signed. "And that means now. It seems we may be needed elsewhere."

Shadow grunted a curse. Now? With all that was happening? "What does the madman have planned now?"

Sy shrugged.

Shadow released a resigned sigh. Having run many missions with the Shade, he knew he should give up trying to unravel the man's thinking. And mad though Growl was, he was impressively efficient and dedicated to the cause of the Ka. *Mad? He's being pushed to the edge of insanity by that foul daemon of his.* He shuddered. The life of a Shade was not one he'd ever want.

And Nefra?

He glanced up at Sy. "Do you believe her?"

"There's talk of a fighter that died suddenly with no obvious cause. His body disappeared."

"Poison?"

"It may be. He was also seen close to Nefra's tent before the fight."

"Whose man is he?"

"An unknown, not from the Ka. I am … talking with others."

Sy's talking could be very persuasive. "Keep talking, Sy. That poison didn't come from Nefra. Not a chance." *I'm sure of it.* "A killer she may be, but she's no fool; she wouldn't risk using the Ka poison on me."

Sy nodded, then signed. "We have to go."

Shadow stood and stretched his legs. "Fine. Let's see what our friend wants." *But best I don't walk out of here undressed. Seems there's someone out there who doesn't like me.* He crossed to his pack and bent down to retrieve a blade, slipping it into the belt of his tunic. Picking up a spear, he smiled at Sy. "That's better."

Outside, Shadow paused, surprised by the number of guards on duty. The young guard he'd spoken to before peeled away from the others, moving to stand silently behind him.

"You can stand down," Shadow said to the man.

The guard gave a brief bow of acknowledgement – and remained where he was.

"Orders of the Shade," Sy signed. "We need to go." He walked off.

Shadow stared at Sy's departing back for a moment, then he gestured to the guard. "Fine. The sun's high and it's as hot as hell, so, let's go for a walk. We can burn to a cinder together."

As they set off, he heard a raucous cheering. Looking around, he saw a group of young fighters walking past. They punched the air and shouted his name. "They're confusing me with someone else," he said to the guard. "I don't remember my fight being that good."

The guard remained silent.

Shadow glanced at the man. Lithe, fresh-faced, and clearly with a sharp mind. And a sense of discipline – only talk to a superior when asked a direct question. "Can you talk?" Shadow asked as they walked on. The guard nodded. "Well talk, man. What's your name?"

"Karnt," the man said.

"Why can't you?"

"No. My name's Karnt."

"Well, that's unfortunate. Why are you called that?"

"I … well," the man began, for the first time looking uncomfortable. "Was a problem with … women."

Shadow raised an eyebrow. "And now?" he said lightly.

"Well, now it's different."

"Then you should change your name to Can."

The guard let slip a small smile.

"Good," Shadow said. "You have a sense of humour. And a good one to recognise mine. Why are you here?"

"I pushed a council member off a raft."

"Well done. Why weren't you promoted?"

Karnt laughed, then caught himself and walked on.

Ahead, Sy stood waiting for them outside a high-roofed hut, by far the largest construction in the camp – and one that Shadow had not seen two days before. Approaching the hut, Shadow handed his spear to Sy, then pulled back the entrance hide and entered.

"Ah, at last!" came Growl's grating voice. "Our displaced and distracted dissident Disciple. Please sit. You know Cobra, of course, your fellow Disciple and camp overseer."

"I do," Shadow said evenly, looking across at the thin, sharp-featured man seated to the right of Growl. "Your hair gets shorter every time I see you, Cobra. Why not shave it all off? Or is that a sign of your age? I still like mine like this," he continued, reaching back and running his hand down his ponytail. "No need to take a sharp blade to it each day and risk slicing myself." He frowned. "Is that how you lost your ear?"

Cobra glowered at him through hooded eyes set beneath a thin brow.

Shadow ignored him and continued. "I keep plenty of sharp blades to hand, though. You never know when snakes may be close." He dropped to his haunches. "But I guess you're not here to compare hairstyles. Or snakes. To what do I owe the privilege?"

With a smile that could greet a friend most warmly, while slipping a blade in her gut, Growl cast his black eyes on Shadow. "Our discordant Disciple, we don't think we are a privilege, oh no indeed, no privilege at all. Don't you think, Overseer, good friend?"

Cobra's eyes flashed with anger. "Well, I—"

"No, not at all," Growl continued, holding Shadow's bemused gaze. "And you start this day with a question. Questions, questions – what is hiding in the shadows, we think?"

Was that actually a question for me? Shadow thought, struggling to make sense of what was happening.

"What is hiding in the shadows?" Growl asked, his keen eyes locking onto Shadow's.

Ah, so he's about to reprimand me. For asking those questions. "Well, not much at this time of day," Shadow answered. "The sun rides high."

Growl laughed. "Very good, very good. Yes, we like humour. It banishes those deceitful shadows." His smile faded. "Or deepens them. Why are you here, at these Games?"

Shadow studied the Ensi's most dangerous Shade with suspicion. *Why do you ask this? Surely you know … Don't you?* "Another question," Shadow observed, choosing his words with care. "But a good one. And not one I can answer fully. But my assigned, Sy, has graciously warned me many times that my curiosity could be the undoing of me." He shrugged. "Maybe I grew too curious."

It was almost unnoticeable, but he'd been looking for it – the faintest of twitches in Cobra's sly face. *You are a snake indeed, Cobra. What game have you been playing?*

"Curious about what?" Growl murmured.

Shadow's suspicion deepened. Here sat the most powerful Shade the Ka had known for generations, a Shade loyal to the Ensi, and one who would know all that the Disciples discussed. *So why does he ask me these questions?* He girded himself. *I've no idea what's happening here, so in with both feet.* "I asked about the killings of leavers. And about the history of the dragon's servant, Stealth." *The man who left the Ka because of what he'd seen.*

"And we wonder, why would that send you here? A *Disciple* to look over the Games?"

Shadow flicked a glance at Cobra. He saw a single bead of moisture glinting on the man's forehead. Under his facade of anger, Cobra was nervous, afraid. *And his eyes …* The story was always told in the eyes. What was going on? Why was Cobra here? "I'm not sure I can answer that question," he said, his eyes meeting Growl's.

The Shade's piercing black eyes bored into him. Shadow forced himself to hold the searching – almost menacing – gaze.

Growl suddenly smiled. "So be it. If it is said a Disciple is needed here, then we cannot gainsay that, oh no."

Shadow noticed the minute easing of tension in Cobra's body.

"And so, tomorrow," Growl continued, turning to Cobra, "you shall take over and oversee the Games, Overseer." His head cocked a fraction. "If that is amenable to you?"

"I ... I ..." Cobra stuttered, his eyes widening.

"Good. Then it is agreed." Growl turned back to Shadow. "We leave now. Your monk will join us. Collect what you need and be back before the shadows lengthen."

Move now? Kef! What's happening now?

"We suggest you take what little time you have," Growl said, studying him carefully.

"Yes. Right. I'll tell Sy."

Shadow quickly stood, curtly nodded at Cobra and Growl, then made his way out of the hut. Once outside, he drew a deep breath. Everything seemed to be happening at once. What exactly was Cobra up to? And what was Growl's game? *I should have asked where we're going.* "This is the problem with Growl," he muttered to himself. "The man never tells me anything until it's too late to change it." He needed to have a quiet talk with the Shade.

A frown marked his brow. That was easier said than done.

He walked over to Sy. "You were right. It seems we're relieved of our duties. Our Shade has found a better man to oversee these Games."

"When do we leave?"

"Now."

Sy immediately turned and walked off towards their hut.

Shadow shook his head. *That man has no patience – no wonder he's so thin. And he's taken my spear. Doesn't he know people are trying to kill me? Maybe I should replace him.*

He glanced at the young guard.

And had an idea. "What are you doing until the next turn of the moon?"

*

Cobra sat in his hut, fuming. What right did that cursed devil have to demean him like this, transporting him here against his will, leaving no time to inform his friends of his leaving? The Shade was straying even further out of the Disciples' control – out of *his* control. And to cap it all, Nefra had failed to kill Shadow. He clenched his fist. *So close!* Could he have somehow pulled Nefra to the cause and told her about the blade? He cast that thought aside. Her sole aim was an alliance between her Meso tribe and the Ka. She could not be bought. He cursed. The Shade was growing too unpredictable. *I must move faster than I'd planned.*

He heard the sound of voices outside. The entrance flap opened, and a heavyset, bearded man ducked in.

"Sit!" Cobra commanded in a low voice. "And keep your voice down. These walls have ears."

Smiling, the scarred, blunt-nosed captain walked over and sat opposite him.

"And wipe that smile off your face, Rathe," Cobra hissed. "You failed."

"It would have succeeded," Rathe countered, reaching for a date from the bowl, "if you had not brought that cursed shaman here."

Cobra seethed. "If I had not ..." He quivered with rage. "I was kidnapped, you fool. Brought here against my will."

"Either way, the Shade arrived," Rathe observed, spitting out a stone. "And just a moment too soon. Pity. We lost a good man."

"What are you talking about? What man?"

"A trusted fighter, Pep. Nefra's second for the fight. It was thought a coating of poison on his hands would get it unseen to the blades – unfortunately for him, he wasn't careful enough. And he had no shaman to aid him."

"I hope you disposed of him?"

"He got into a fight." Rathe smiled. "And the dagger struck his heart. The guards bought the charade." His smile faded. "But a shame – like I said, he was a good man."

"He was nothing," Cobra spat. "He—"

Rathe shot forward, grabbing Cobra by the throat. He could smell musty date on the man's breath. "You sit in your tower of stone, drink your fine wines, sleep with your chosen for the day," Rathe said calmly as Cobra fought for his breath. "While out in the land, men – like Pep – create and preserve our grand empire." The captain bared his teeth. "Do not forget this, because the day you forget will be the day this empire starts to crumble, beginning its descent into chaos." His fingers dug deeper. "Do. Not. Forget."

His eyes bulging from their sockets and a darkness closing around his thoughts, Cobra panicked. He hit Rathe in the side of his head – the man just smiled. *He's going to kill me! He—*

Rathe released him and sat back, picking up a second date.

Gasping, Cobra sucked in lungfuls of air, his hands shaking uncontrollably. His breathing ragged, he glared at the scarred face in front of him. *You wait, Rathe. I will see plenty more scars added to that face. You will see.*

Fighting to calm himself, he breathed deeply. *Patience.* Yes, patience, because how many sun-cycles had he most carefully manoeuvred the pieces, biding his time, weaving the disguised web of deceit? And now, how close to striking? *Close. Very close.* A fierce shiver of elation coursed through him. A new shaman was coming, a new beginning.

And then Growl would see.

Growl! His anger flared at the stark impudence of this mere captain in the Guard to treat him this way, displaying an utter contempt for Cobra's position as a Disciple in Kaos's temple. The man was out of control, a danger to both him and all he had prepared. But what could he do? He silently cursed. *Nothing yet. But soon …*

He glanced up at Rathe, who sat watching him from keen, brutal eyes. Straightening, Cobra steadied himself. *Stay calm. Hold firm.* "Forgive me. You are right. Men like … like …"

"Pep," Rathe offered, his eyes cold.

"Men like Pep are to be remembered. They serve our cause well."

"Kaos's cause."

Cobra nodded. "But do not forget, Rathe, we cannot grieve over those who have failed. And we cannot afford to fail as we did here. We must move ever onward, else our enemy will overwhelm us."

"I do what I can. If that's not enough …" Rathe shrugged.

"So, you would choose to step down?" Cobra said in a low voice. "Several men in your section would be pleased to take your place as captain."

"That's not what I said. I serve the Ensi. I protect—"

"You serve the Ensi?" Cobra sniped, a cold smile on his lips. "Even to you, that must sound hollow."

"I serve the Ensi – that doesn't mean I support who's sitting in that chair."

"Weak and incompetent, I've heard you say."

"Until a change comes, I serve."

Cobra stared at the man. *A perverse loyalty indeed.* "And when I sit in that chair?"

"I will serve you as the new Head of the Guard."

But maybe not support. No matter. Gain the prize. And the power. A surge of elation coursed through his veins. *And what a power to wield! And you, my small-minded Rathe, will be able to talk with Pep all you like.* "Will the Guard support you? Will they allow Harg to be disposed?"

"They are my men and my women now."

Cobra scowled. Women! Why Harg had insisted having women in the Guard, he knew not.

"They will follow their leader," Rathe continued. "And Harg?" His lips curled. "The man is weak. It's time for a change."

52

Cobra suppressed a sudden urge to snigger. *Long overdue changes, Rathe. Beyond your imagining.*

But that was to come.

Focus on the now. We failed to kill Shadow, but the plan remains. "Prepare yourself to leave. Growl will not stay long at the temple. We will travel there at nightfall. It is time to—"

"We? Did you hear the Shade? *You* are stuck here for the duration of the Games. You—"

"Ignore the old fool," Cobra spat. "It's time to act. It's time to bring Krull out of hiding." He saw the captain's eyes narrow. *Yes, Rathe, who is in control here? You will see.*

Rathe stroked his beard, studying Cobra. "The shaman from the Meso tribes? Can he be trusted? You have more than the word of Nefra, I hope?"

Now it was Cobra's turn to smile. "I spread my sources far in this land. Of that, have no doubt."

"An answer to one question. And trust?"

"I trust no one. Least of all shamans."

Rathe's distaste was clear. "I don't like it. We should expand the Guard, recruit more fighters, get on the ground and destroy the defilers. When I command the Guard, this will be so. It is people—"

"Yes, people like Pep, I know."

"It is people," Rathe continued, glaring at Cobra, "who will defeat our enemy. Not these daemon worshippers."

Is he really that ignorant? Or wilfully blind. *I don't want – or need – this conversation now.*

He said nothing.

"So, what about the Disciple?" Rathe grumbled after a while.

"For now, nothing. He will travel with Growl." His thin lips tightened. "Which is why, my friend, the time to strike is now." He nodded to the entrance of the tent. "Many fighters are here, away from the homeland. Growl and Shadow will be travelling. And the new shaman is ready." His lips curled into a smile. "It is our time. Are *you* ready?"

"I'm ready. And so are my people. Where and when?"

"That, we will discuss later. For now, prepare to leave. To avoid suspicion, choose someone from the Guard to oversee the Games – others of the Guard come with us. When Growl leaves, we make our excuses and leave for the temple." *The new moon is coming. And I know where the Ensi will be.*

The stars aligned.

A glorious pleasure coursed through him. The new Ensi would soon be unveiled. *I will be unveiled.* And then things would change. For his leader had become weak. Too lax on their empire tribes, too meek within their own walls, listening to too many feeble voices pleading for fair treatment. And too many foreigners coming into their homeland, too many mouths to feed. His lips curled in disgust. *And too many women.* Too many women taking the work of men, too many women thinking themselves above their station. He put his hand to his head, feeling the ragged scar of the missing ear. *This will be repaid one hundredfold.*

He started as he realised Rathe was standing before him, glaring down at him.

"It will be as you say," the captain said in an icy voice. "And with Kaos's help, we will prevail." He leaned down towards Cobra. "But remember Pep. Remember all those who have died for the Ka. We will use your new authority to destroy our enemy. To destroy all those who do not bow to the Ka, all those who would seek to destroy us." He leaned closer. "Do not disappoint us," he whispered, patting Cobra's cheek.

Smiling, Rathe drew himself up, then walked to the entrance, where he pushed through the hanging hides and disappeared from view.

Cobra glared at the swaying hides. *I will enjoy hearing you scream. And scream.* As artifices of revenge played in his mind, a smile played on his lips. That was the problem with these small-minded men. They just didn't see it coming.

He giggled.

Yes, these imbeciles were all so desperately ignorant. Of all he knew. Of what he had found. But for that, he could forgive Rathe, for neither Growl nor even the Ensi were aware of what he was planning.

And when they saw it coming, it would be far, far too late.

His smile grew. *Yes, my time comes, Ensi. A new leader comes. And my revenge will be oh so sweet.*

*

They followed Growl along the heights of the rocky escarpment, gaining a brief yet expansive view of the lush green river plain beyond before dropping steeply down into a narrow and shaded ravine, where scattered scraggly trees and spindly bushes gained what water they could from the dried, cracked soils.

"Where's he taking us?" Shadow signed to Sy as they strode over the hard ground. "Does he forget I've been ill, caressing the edges of the life beyond? I should be resting for the day, not trekking through parched desert wadis."

Sy ignored him and continued walking.

Shadow sighed. *At least it's cooler down here.*

A little while later, he noticed Growl had disappeared. Walking on, he saw a break in the ravine wall to the left. Rough-hewn steps led steeply upwards. Sy turned into the opening and began climbing. Shadow paused, glancing back down the ravine. After a moment, he waved. Then he turned to the opening and followed after Sy.

Halfway up the rent in the cliff, the eroded steps levelled out into a sandy trail cutting through a narrow, shaded crevice. Following the trail, they soon emerged into bright sunlight. Blinking, Shadow glanced around. He stood beside Sy within a small amphitheatre, its sheer walls of rugged black rock looming over them, indented in places by several sharp-edged caves.

In the centre of the arena stood Growl holding his Black Staff.

And beside him stood Nefra.

"Why is she here?" Shadow grated.

"I could ask the same of you," Nefra said, her voice cold.

Growl stepped forward. "Was she the purveyor of the poison?"

Shadow scowled but said nothing.

"And so, our happy team is complete."

Shadow turned to Nefra. "I take it they've removed your poisoned blades?"

A flash of anger crossed Nefra's face.

You play a dangerous game, Shadow. He flashed his fingers at Sy. "Watch my back."

Sy nodded.

Turning, Shadow glanced around the amphitheatre, his eyes coming to rest on the gloom of a cave. "What is this place?"

With an unsettling smile, Growl scanned the black walls surrounding them. His eyes seem to burn with a black fire. "It is a place of Kaos, born of the cauldron of the deeps. It is why the Games are held here, so Kaos can watch."

"A place of Kaos," Shadow murmured, a strange unease settling on him. "As the temple at our homeland?"

"The temple serves our people, but not Kaos's true adherents." Growl swept his arm around the arena, his eyes afire. "This is a site of Kaos's true presence. Can you feel it? What power! A bounty freely given."

"No, I don't think—"

His breath caught as a crawling sensation erupted over his body and the first waft of a sickening odour fouled the air. A delicate pressure impinged on his mind, as though fingers softly caressed his brain—

His Disciple training kicked in, and he slammed up his barriers. A lingering foul taste in his mouth, he glanced over at Growl – who studied him intently. "I feel it," Shadow said, "but I'm not sure I like it."

Growl continue to watch him. Then he smiled. "Not a place that many come to enjoy. And not one for you to tarry too long." He snapped his fingers. "We leave."

"And where are we—"

Shadow spun around at a noise, dropping into a crouch, his blade already in hand.

"I suggest you put the blade away," Growl said as a huge black wolf wandered out of the cave. "Streak may misunderstand."

A low growl lent weight to the Shade's words, and Shadow straightened, slipping his blade back inside his tunic. His uneasy gaze followed the wolf as it walked silently across the amphitheatre to join Growl and Nefra. He hated wolves, but particularly *this* wolf, and had a feeling it didn't like him. No, he knew it didn't like him. *We're on the same side, but I wouldn't want to be left alone with it.*

As if reading his thoughts, the wolf growled. He watched it warily as it stalked past him towards the crevice through which they'd entered. He suddenly realised what the wolf had sensed. "Ah, yes," he said, lightly, turning to Growl. "I need to tell you something. Can you call your wolf back?"

"Can't," Growl said with a mocking smile.

Shadow regarded Growl with a sudden uneasy sense of misgiving. Did this man know everything? *I should have mentioned this to Growl.*

"At ease, Streak," Growl murmured, his voice easily carrying to the wolf. "We should let our friend's friend enter."

"It's okay, Karnt," Shadow shouted. "It won't harm you." *I hope.*

Karnt appeared from the narrow crevice. He glanced around, then steadied himself – *remarkably well* – and walked over to Shadow.

"Why is he here?" Nefra growled.

"I'd like an extra set of eyes on my back," Shadow said, nervously eyeing Growl. "If you'd allow it?"

Growl smiled. "This we will allow. But …" His smile vanished. "Do not presume again, shadow of ours. This is no game."

No game? There are many games at work. But he saw the anger burning in the Shade's eyes. He nodded. "Maybe now you'll tell us where we're going?"

Growl glared at him for a moment longer, then lifted his Black Staff. "We are tasked with another mission, but first we travel home. And for us, my Disciple, there is a meeting with the Ensi. Prepare yourself." He looked to those around him. "Stand close."

With a twinge of fear, mixed with keen anticipation, Shadow walked with the others to stand beside Growl. *We meet the Ensi. Good. Our leader needs to hear what I have to say.*

An acrid taste fouled his mouth, and the arena vanished.

CHAPTER FOUR

*Youth was no barrier; she was strong. But she
was unprepared for what was expected of her.*

Standing, rain-soaked, in the cloying mud by the cave entrance,
Jessica watched the desperate battle growing ever closer as the
defending Iyes fighters were slowly forced back by the relentless and
frenzied attack of the enemy. In the distance, Beth and Rind tackled
two of the oncoming attackers, Beth's Axe cleaving a man's skull in
two while Rind's spear drove into a tattooed woman's belly. Yet on the
savage marauders came, streaming into the gorge, seeking the
destruction of all who stood against them. And also seemingly intent
on reaching the cave behind her.

"They seek to destroy our Sacred Chamber," the Iyes healer, Amber,
had said. "They believe we draw a power from the Spirits contained
there."

Jessica grimaced. She'd sensed no aid from those Spirits during this
battle – and still nothing from the Iyes's Mother.

"To me!" she heard Rind command.

Most of the reserve group around Jessica immediately rushed to
their leader, bolstering the defence within the gorge entrance. Others of
the Iyes and their allies remained locked in ferocious, brutal fighting
with those who had bypassed the core of the battle, attacking from the
flanks or with the enemy group approaching from the narrower upper
reaches of the gorge.

We are stretched too thin. We—

Jessica flinched as an arrow whistled past her ear.

"Get inside," Amber hissed. "Now!"

Rain trickling down sodden strands of hair plastered to her cheeks,
Jessica shook her head. "I may be needed."

"You'll be of no use with an arrow in your head." Amber grasped Jessica's shoulder. "Come with me. Join River."

Jessica's face hardened. "No. We stay." *And River should be here, fighting beside us.*

She looked out at the frenzied battle. *How do they keep finding us?* Three times the Iyes tribe had been forced further south as they waited for their envoys to return with news of their allies. But each safe haven they'd reached had been discovered, and the Iyes tribe forced to flee again.

And now we're hurting.

And we have no time to plan, to understand what we must do.

An ear-shattering blast echoed from the cliff tops above, then a scream rent the air as a body fell from the heights. Lanky was at work. For someone who didn't consider himself a Warrior, he was quickly mastering the use of the Land's energy – the A'ven, as the god of the Iyes, IY, called it – and he'd reached, and maybe now surpassed, Beth's skill and knowledge. A shadow crossed Jessica's face. Maybe not so unexpected, given Beth hadn't reengaged with her daemon – or with Bethusa – since returning to the Land after the battle at Mount Hope. *She fears what she can't remember. She's terrified of what she might become.*

Her hand clenched tightly around her Staff. *And me?* After contact at Naga's funeral, IY had spoken to her only twice more, and then a silence, one both worrying and infuriating. Yes, IY had guided her wielding of the energy of the A'ven – the wielding of the power of the Light – and of the use of the Land's Cords, but she'd expected to learn more. More of the Kade, of the Dark, of how to defeat Kaos. More of the secrets of this mystifying world from her past that the Iyes called simply 'the Land'. But IY had remained silent. *We delayed agreeing on our next steps, waiting for that contact. See where that has landed us.*

There was a cry from her left, and she turned to see Dune being pulled from the melee and dragged towards her. Behind the injured Iyes, the line of defence was weakening fast, while the attackers' numbers continue to swell. She grasped Amber's arm. "Go to River and tell her we need her help now, else Rind's group will be lost."

Amber immediately turned and ran back inside the gorge.

With an aching sense of hopelessness, Jessica watched as Dune was hoisted onto a man's shoulder and hurriedly carried inside. IY had told her she was the Guardian, that she walked beside the Warriors as they defended the Land from the hordes of Kaos. But was this what was expected from a Guardian? To watch as comrades were injured or killed? She felt the Staff in her hand and the latent power of the A'ven surrounding her. *I should be fighting beside Beth and Lanky.* But Lanky had been insistent; she had to stay by the cave entrance as a final defence. Her lips thinned. *Because he thinks I'm weaker than him and Beth. He thinks I can't fight.* But her spark of anger faded as quickly as it had flared. *No. Because he wants to protect as many as he can.*

Another deafening blast sounded high above as Lanky continued his lone attack on the enemy on the ridge. He was proving a most fearsome fighter. Despite Lanky's stubborn resistance to bonding with Fen, the daemon had continued to support and train him. Yet the precarious tension between the two remained. *A tension that will at some point explode.*

'Lanky,' she pulsed, reaching out with her mind.

'I'm pretty busy, Jess,' Lanky replied instantly. 'Can it wait?'

'Our defence is being forced back. Bethusa's not here, and River won't fight.'

'Damn! I can't leave these up here – they'd pick us off one by one. Can't you ask IY for help?'

'I still can't contact her.'

'Still? What use are these supposedly great beings when they're not here when we need them? They wanted our help, after all!'

She felt his frustration. He was right.

'Try Beth again,' came Lanky's voice. 'See if she'll release Bethusa.' A ripple of unease swept through the connection. 'If not, you'll have to engage.'

Despite her earlier frustration at being held back from the fight, her gut twisted. Lanky and Beth – even without Bethusa – were both proving stronger than her. *If they are failing …*

She clenched her fist more tightly around her Staff. *I will fight. I must fight.* 'I'll contact Beth. Keep safe, Lanky.'

'I'm trying,' he said, his grim resolve sweeping over her. 'I am trying.'

*

Lanky darted between the gnarled boles of the ancient trees, arcing his path to intercept an enemy group making their way towards the cliff edge, seeking a place to launch another rain of arrows and spears into the fighters below. Closing in fast behind them, he released pent energy from the A'ven.

A wave of virulent power exploded from the Axe—

Cries of raw terror erupted from the unsuspecting group as they were swept off the cliff edge into the abyss below.

His face grim, Lanky paused and listened.

There!

Turning from the gorge, he sprinted back through the trees to greet the next party. He leapt over a fallen tree … and landed on a steep slope, falling, then tumbling into the midst of a group of startled enemy fighters. Leaping to his feet, he deflected a thrown spear, then released the A'ven's power, casting its energy as a scythe.

The four fighters fell, screaming, bodies afire.

Shaking, Lanky stood, listening for sounds beyond those of the dying. He sensed nothing close by. Hands trembling, he looked down at the ravaged bodies before him, their cries cutting to his soul. Three men and one woman. *They didn't want to be here, any more than I did.* A pang of horror – of grief – held him in place. Which of them had families they would never see again, their lives extinguished by the force of his will?

His head bowed as the cries slowly faded, a terrible darkness closing around his heart. How could he do it? How did he bring himself to do it? He stood for a moment, wishing he was anywhere but this cold, brutal world. Yet the cruel reality could not be escaped. *I am here. I must protect Jessica, Beth, and Tricia. I must protect the Iyes. I must protect Rind.*

Forcing himself to move, he glanced at the four slaughtered enemies. *They had no way to defend against me.*

Hence his quiet words as he passed. "I am so sorry."

*

'Beth!' Jessica called.

'What!' Beth shouted.

'You need to risk Bethusa – you're being pushed too far back.'

'No!' Beth snarled. *'And go away.'*

The connection was cut.

Jessica swore. They needed all the aid they could get. If they couldn't escape the murderous jaws closing around them, nothing else would matter. Yet she couldn't hold her anger. *You know what Beth has been through … You know more than Beth.* For IY had revealed to her the unimaginable truth. That Beth had been taken against her will, imprisoned within Mount Hope for millennia, protecting the Staff, awaiting the time to reunite with her. *Imprisoned within the mountain? No, she fought at a Gate – she defended the Gate – because that's what Warriors do.* She winced at the ghostly memories seemingly not her own. She licked her suddenly dry lips. But that was not all that Beth had done. She had killed the bookseller in a single act of brutality. And that Beth also didn't remember. *Because I corrected it. I reset the Continuum.* Yet only fragmented memories of Beth's savage actions remained in her own mind. *But I know it happened. I used the power of the Staff.* At that thought, the Staff tingled in her hand. Her fingers clasped more tightly around the smooth golden-hued wood. *My Staff.* But a Staff that IY had told her not to use again. *Not until IY understands more of what happened. Not until one called Jalu comes to aid me.*

She forced her racing thoughts to settle. She had to accept it. Beth would not use Bethusa; she would not risk allowing that one from the mountain back to the fore. She looked out at the ferocious battle raging within the gorge. Her heart wrenched as she saw another body being pulled away. *Heba.* A woman she'd spoken with only this morning, but now passed on to the ancestors. Cold dread washed over her. This attack was far more sustained than the previous skirmishes – the enemy seemed to have pushed a large force into these northern lands. How this had been achieved, she knew not. But they were here.

And they're defeating us.

They pulled another body clear, a young man – a boy – his brother sheltering inside with the young children. Then another.

Hearing a noise behind, she turned to see Amber returning.

Alone.

The healer shook her head. "She is … occupied."

Jessica's heart sank. A Warrior – the shaman and Mother of the tribe – refusing to fight. And refusing to talk. She silently cursed. *Can't you see what's happening, River? Your people are dying.* She looked out into the gorge and saw Beth, bloodied hands glistening, Axe sweeping in merciless arcs as she cleared a space around her – but a moment's relief only before the relentless press of the attackers surged again.

And then Beth slipped.

Two attackers leapt forward, striking with their spears—

An Iyes defender flung himself over Beth's body and then spasmed as the spears pierced his back. Screaming a battle cry, Rind surged forward with her fighters, surrounding the fallen man and Warrior. Jessica saw Beth scramble back to her feet and the fallen fighter pulled out of the heaving mass of bodies.

The Iyes's defensive wall buckled and began to fall back in the face of the resurgent enemy.

We can't win, Jessica thought, the numbing reality chilling her soul. *Without Bethusa and Revri, we can't win.*

And I can't save them.

Like my sister.

She shuddered at the memory of that horrific night. Of walking with her sister on a rainswept night. Of a sudden cry and being knocked to the ground. Then of turning to see her sister convulsing on the ground, a knife in her neck as a hooded assailant strode away. *And I did nothing. I let her die. I—*

'Jess!' came Lanky's strident voice. *'What's happening down there?'*

Her nightmare shattered.

Gulping a lungful of air, she cast aside the dark thoughts. *We still live. This isn't over.* She looked up to the cliff top. *'Lanky, we need help! Now!'* And I have to get River to this battle, even if I have to drag her—

Bloodcurdling cries erupted in the distance. Turning, she saw the terrifying sight of a fearsome horde sweeping up the gorge towards them. All hope seemed to vanish in an instant. *We're too late. I'm too late.*

But as the horde reached the battleground, she looked on in stunned amazement as these new fighters hammered into the ranks of the enemy.

What! These are friends?

Blindsided, the rear of the enemy force turned to face their new, deadly assailants. The seething mass spread out across the gorge, panicked fighters frantically seeking to escape the vice in which they were now trapped. Jessica caught movement above, and looked up to see a shining figure plummet from the cliff top, careening into the midst of the chaotic enemy force—

She shielded her eyes as a tremendous explosion rent the air, rocking the ground on which she stood. As the blaze of light faded, she looked out on a scorched, smouldering field of shredded bodies lying scattered around the Warrior – around Lanky. The bloodied and torn fighters left standing were scrambling over each other to escape the terror that had descended into their midst.

They were met by the unknown allies, who seemed in no mood to show mercy.

Within minutes, silence fell over the gorge, not even the birds having the appetite for song.

*

'You are learning,' the warg said. 'But still as a child. Bond now and become a man.'

'Go to hell,' Lanky replied, his head bowed as he stood within the field of death. He pushed the presence back deep within himself.

"Lanky?" came a familiar voice.

He roused himself to see Jessica, Beth, and Rind all standing, watching him.

"I thought I was doing the right thing," he said, wiping his brow. With eyes filled with wretched guilt, and even deeper sorrow, he scanned the scorched bodies of the broken enemy lying dead or dying around him. "But this … this makes me not so sure." *This was hell. This was …* "Fugazi," he whispered in a voice almost unheard, the brutality of the moment suddenly overwhelming.

There was a stretch of pained silence, then Rind spoke, her words quiet yet firm. "If you hadn't acted as you did, Warrior, more of us would have died. More fathers, mothers, sons, and daughters. You – and the Islanders – saved us. For that, we are grateful. Again."

Lanky glanced at Rind, her heartfelt words dulling a little of his pain.

"This is a war," she continued, "where we face dread forces rising against us, forces that threaten to corrupt our Land." Her eyes flashed. "And the Iyes will always stand against such evil … whatever the cost."

Lanky studied Rind's dirt-streaked face, seeing the unyielding determination of the young Iyes leader – the de facto leader in Bear's absence. *She warns me that this is just the start. That more will die. But that we cannot yield.* What cruel gods had drawn them into this?

His hand tightened on his Axe. *In this moment, it matters not. We are here.* "I stand beside you," he said quietly. A keen, visceral surge of emotion coursed through him. *And I will protect you. I will …* He slammed a halt to those tantalising, yet unsettling thoughts. *Remember who you are. Remember you want to get home. This is not your age.*

Rind tilted her head, her eyes questioning.

He shook himself from his reverie. "How many did we lose this time?"

"Maybe six. Probably more."

The answer distressed him in many ways. For the heart-wrenching loss of life. And for the stark fact that they couldn't sustain this. Not when the enemy seemed able to find them at will. *We run, but we can't hide.* Brushing a strand of his lengthening hair from his brow, he glanced at Jessica. "And River?"

"She wouldn't join us."

His mood darkened. How long now had she been absent from her tribe, unable, or unwilling, to fight? A confrontation was coming, especially after the sickening losses of today. He glanced around the battlefield, then frowned as he saw a figure striding towards them – a huge mountain of a man with thick, unruly hair and a bloodstained beard; a man he didn't recognise.

He instantly tensed.

"Relax," Rind said, turning to the new arrival. "This is Parig, the leader of the Islanders." She walked forward to greet him.

Rind was small, but still, this man's towering frame dwarfed her. Ignoring her hand, the mountainous man grabbed her in bearlike arms, sweeping her off her feet, the bright yellow beads scattered around her body clattering loudly. It was a moment in stark contrast to the horrors so recently witnessed.

"I take it they know one another then," Jessica said.

"Maybe," Lanky grunted. He noticed Jessica's eyes on him. "What?"

Jessica tilted her head. "Did I sense a note of disapproval? What some may even call jealousy?"

Lanky scowled. "Don't be stupid. I don't know him."

"But you know Rind," she said carefully.

He shifted uncomfortably.

"Hmm. This is unexpected."

He tried to ignore her, but even within the darkness of his mood, a burgeoning truth couldn't be ignored. *I do like Rind.* But jealous? "Don't be stupid," he muttered again, then walked off towards Parig and Rind.

"Put me down, you fool." Rind laughed, still trapped in the mighty man's embrace.

"You heard her," Lanky growled as he walked up to them.

Parig gave Rind a last crushing hug, then dropped her unceremoniously to the ground. "And who do we have here?" he grated from a throat sounding as though it crushed rocks.

Lanky looked up into the older man's rugged face, noting the ruthless intensity in the man's deep brown eyes. He held out his hand. "Lanky."

"And what do you do, boy?" the man said, ignoring the proffered hand.

"What is needed," Lanky said simply, still holding out his hand. "And," he continued easily, "greeting a friend."

The man leaned forward with a crooked grin, his broken teeth, gaps and all, looming in front of Lanky's face. "Do I look like a friend?"

Lanky smiled. "You look like an old man, and smell like a dead rat. But you may still have your uses."

The man lifted his head and roared with laughter. "Good," he rumbled as he looked around at those watching. "I detest a man who cannot smile." He grabbed Lanky's arm above his wrist, and Lanky did the same. The man's grip was immense, but Lanky responded in kind. They held for a moment, and then released.

"Now, daughter," Parig said, turning to Rind. "I have an army needing fed. Lead on!"

65

Rind, her short curls scattered wildly by her father's enthusiastic greeting, scowled at the mountainous man. "I am not your cook. Follow me and I'll show you to our stores. I'm sure you'll know what to do with them."

Parig laughed riotously and followed Rind towards the gorge entrance.

Lanky watched them walk away. *Daughter …*

Jessica glanced at him. "Well, that's lightened your mood." Her eyes flicked to the mountainous man striding away. "That may explain why he's brought so many of his tribe – and so quickly."

Lanky nodded. Islanders. The allies of the Iyes from Eil'an, the westernmost land before the Great Sea. *And our saviours today.* He looked around and saw Gravel and Beth in the distance, both barking orders as the tribe regrouped. They would head out of the gorge to the razed encampment beyond, to rebuild what they could for the night ahead. And with the heavy rain bombarding them for days, they needed the shelter.

And we can't keep running. We need a plan. We need to act.

He faced Jessica. "Let's find River. This can't continue."

*

"I can't let you past, Warrior," Darius said. "The Mother is not to be disturbed. I am sorry."

"The time for apologies is long past, Darius," Jessica said, walking on with Lanky at her side.

The young hunter stepped into their path. "I can't allow it," he said, his voice shaking.

Scowling, Lanky removed his Axe.

"Hold!" Jessica said sharply.

Lanky paused, holding his position, but Jessica knew that wouldn't last. He was angry. *But we can't spill blood. Not between us. And yet we can't afford to tread lightly.* Things needed to change. "Do you know what happened out there?" she said, looking directly into Darius's troubled eyes. "Do you know how many people died, fighting to save others?"

"Too many," Lanky spat, glaring at Darius.

"Too many," Jessica agreed. "While both River – and you – sat in here doing nothing."

"I—"

"Don't give excuses!" Lanky snarled. "You're a coward."

Darius's face darkened. "I'm not a—"

"A coward. Nothing more – but probably less."

Darius took a step forward, baring his teeth. "You will take that back. I am not a coward."

"Stop!" a voice commanded, echoing from the tunnel within.

At last! I feared she wouldn't intervene.

"Let them past, Darius," came River's distant voice from within the cave. "And thank you. You may go."

Darius glanced down the tunnel, his face pained as though not fully believing he should obey the command. Hands shaking, he turned back and glared at Lanky. Jessica saw tears in his eyes. The young Iyes pushed past them and stalked out.

Jessica sighed. *That friendship will take a few days to mend.* But as she walked down the rough-hewn passageway towards the inner sanctuary of the cave, Lanky's footsteps echoing behind her, she knew things had to change. Because during weeks of constant hiding from the enemy, they had achieved nothing, while those adherents of the Dark grew stronger. *Those adherents of Kaos.* Recent words of IY returned with stark clarity. "Kaos seeks this Land's destruction," the spiky-haired woman had said. "He seeks the annihilation of all Life. Life is his antithesis, an abhorrent disease that must be eradicated at all costs. But Life is resilient. The Light is resilient. It resists him and his agents of the Dark – you and the Warriors resist him. But always the threat of the Geddon looms over us all. If Kaos releases the Geddon, all is lost." The woman had placed her hand on Jessica's shoulder. "Find the Kade. Find the source of Kaos's power and bring it to me."

Her heart chilled at the memory. So much contained in IY's words to her, yet so little understood. *She talks of life – Life – as much greater than the life I know. She talks of the Kade but explains nothing.* And the Geddon. "A destroyer of worlds," IY had said. "An unstoppable force of the Dark that if released, we would not defeat." *This Kaos seeks all life's destruction. All life, across all time.*

The horrific truth sank its twisting roots deeper. All she wished for was to return to her own time, her own life, to be as they had once been, innocent of these evils lurking beyond her sight. But the truth had been laid bare. *I have no choice. I must do what I can to stop this evil.* Those roots binding her tightened. *Because I am the Guardian.*

Biting frustration welled. Yes, she and the others now knew they had become reluctant, ignorant players in an unfolding, apocalyptic nightmare. Players who needed to find the Kade, this source of Kaos's power. But they spent all their time running from the enemy, defending the Iyes as best they could. *We have no time to search for this Kade.* And IY? Where was she now? She cursed softly. In this moment of need, IY had vanished. Yet so many questions needed answers. Glancing up, she saw they were approaching the soft glow of the Sacred Chamber. *And through all this, River hides away.*

Entering the Iyes's sacred place, she tensed, feeling the unnerving presence of others within the ether. The Spirits of the Land. Masters of the daemons aiding the Warriors. Companions of IY. *Players in the game, but beyond my reach.*

Eddies swirled around her as the Spirits brushed her mind, intrigued, curious, agitated … and afraid. *Why troubled?* Because of the horrors of battle outside? Or because of actions taken – or not taken – over these last weeks? *I don't know, but answering those questions will have to wait,* she thought as she studied the girl squatting on the ground in front of her. *A girl or a young woman?* She sighed. What the hell did that matter? What she saw was the stalwart face, the youthful face, of the youngest shaman of the Iyes in generations, one impelled to carry the weight of her people's Story after the brutal death of Naga. And one whose young features bore the unrelenting strain of the unimaginable burden thrust upon her. *The people of this ancient Land lose their innocence early in life, but this …*

Suppressing a shiver, she glanced at the two green-hued Axes lying by River's side. She sensed the now familiar aura of River's Axe, but the other beside it remained unclaimed. *Lanky, Beth, and River hold three of the four Axes of the Iyes tribe, and I hold the Staff. Then who will carry this Axe?* But that would not be known until the fourth Warrior was revealed to them – and none knew when that would be.

She glanced back to River. The shaman of the Iyes sat unmoving, staring intently at the wall ahead. Jessica followed her gaze. Covered with a myriad of dynamic sketches and drawings of animals and people, the wall appeared as a vivid tapestry of life, its rich hues and textures bringing a vibrancy and honesty to the subjects painted, a vibrancy enhanced by the flickering light of the torches. But this was more than art, this was the means with which the tribe connected to their ancestors, to the Spirits.

And to IY.

Following the thought, she reached out, questing … but nothing. No sense of IY here either.

"She is gone," River murmured, still staring at the paintings.

Jessica turned to the girl. "Where?"

"That, I do not know."

"Is that why the Spirits are upset?"

River glanced at her. "You sense that?"

Jessica nodded.

River gazed back at the paintings. "Something is wrong. I know this. But I cannot find out what."

"Is that why you're here?" Jessica said, a sudden bite to her voice. "Why you abandon your people?"

River faced her, eyes flashing with anger. "Do not try the same with me as you did with Darius. That would not be wise."

"Well, in that case, I will try," Lanky growled. "Why are you sitting, contemplating your navel, when your tribe is being slaughtered right outside your front door? I've heard what you did at Mount Hope. I—"

"Enough," River said. "I—"

"Enough?" Lanky shouted, his eyes blazing. "Enough? Yes, of you sitting here feeling sorry for yourself when others are dying." He took a step forward, his head angled as though a wolf eyeing his quarry. "What would Naga think of you now? What is the shaman and Mother of the Iyes doing now to honour her ancestors and preserve her Land for the future? What—"

"What future!" River hissed. She quickly stood and faced them, eyes blazing. "Your future?" she demanded, her face hardening. "You forget, Warrior, I saw your future! I saw what you have done! Is that what my people lay down their lives for? Is that it?" She shook her head. "No. That is not the future I want. It has to change." She looked away. "And Naga tried to warn me. About the future. Something is not right."

Jessica was shocked by the vehemence of the outburst. *Is this what this is about? About her glimpse of my world?* "But you don't know my land. Not really. You saw only a fraction." She felt a sudden unease at her own words. Compared with the pristine lands of this age, maybe River had glimpsed enough of the future's inexorable reshaping of the planet.

River spun around. "I saw enough, Warrior," she insisted as if hearing Jessica's thoughts. "And I listened. Listened to the stories of Iolaire. Your people ignore the life of your lands, ignore all but yourselves. You destroy the land that feeds you, the air that you breathe, and the water you drink." She looked back to the flickering images on the wall. "There *must* be a better future for our people," she said in a quieter voice. "There *must* be a better path to tread. And until I find it, until the Spirits help me find the way, then I cannot trust what we do next. I cannot help you."

Lanky's bitter laugh mocked River's words. "Well, isn't that a change in tune? From Naga the overly helpful shaman, to River, the stand-back-and-let-you-drown shaman. Well, thanks for nothing. Your people are dying. You—"

"Okay, you've made your point," Jessica growled.

"I—"

Jessica held up her hand. "Give me a moment, Lanky," she said more softly.

Lanky scowled. "Pah! I've had it with her." His shoulders taut with pent rage, he stormed out of the chamber.

Jessica sighed, then walked over to River. "You're making a terrible mistake."

River snorted. "The mistakes are not mine. They—"

"And you're playing with fire," Jessica continued. "You sit here, alone, and consider the future – you plot to change the future."

River's eyes flicked away, downcast.

"Do you think it's right that one person alone takes this decision?" Jessica continued in a softening voice. "That you alone sit over all life to determine its future? If so, what makes you any different from this Enemy we fight – any different from Kaos and all those who follow his commands?"

River flinched.

Jessica moved imperceptibly closer. "And if you can alter the future, what then? You may make it better … but you may make it worse. Can you be sure which it will be?"

The girl's shoulders slumped.

Jessica reached out and gently placed her hand on River's arm. "Your people are dying. How much blood can you let spill trying to win such an uncertain game?"

Silence fell in the chamber as a storm of conflicting emotions raged across the girl's face: anger, fear, bitterness, guilt … and a crippling exhaustion. Jessica waited, shadows dancing on the walls in tune with the flames, until the storm calmed.

Until before her stood a frightened and lost soul.

River dropped to her knees. "I don't know what to do," she whispered. "I am lost."

Her heart wrenching, Jessica knelt beside the young Mother of the Iyes. "After what you've been through, I believe you."

River turned to her, tears in her grief-filled eyes.

Jessica brushed River's cheek. "You've become the tribe's Mother, the tribe's shaman, and also a Warrior. But underneath all that, is River, a young and terrified girl. How can you not be lost?"

River bowed her head, tears streaming down her cheeks. Jessica reached out and pulled River gently towards her, hugging her in a close embrace. She said nothing – and nothing needed to be said.

She held River close, feeling the desperate grief in the girl's trembling body, until her sobs slowly died. Wiping her eyes, River looked up. "What can I do now?" she whispered, her voice catching.

"Now there's a question that could be tricky to answer," Jessica said, holding River's hand. "River as a *Warrior*, I can help – Lanky and Beth can help. Just talk. Share your fears, your worries, your hopes. We have to – we will – support each other, staying aligned and focussed, unbreakable."

The slightest tension eased from River's face.

"As the tribe's *Mother*, well, even through all that's happened, you have retained the heart of the tribe out there, a tribe that wishes to help you." She saw River's face betray a pang of anguish. *She fears she has lost the tribe. But my words are true. The tribe will never abandon their Mother.* She squeezed River's hand. "And as a *shaman*? Well, that one isn't easy for me to answer." She smiled. "But I think I know someone who can help."

River stared intently at Jessica. "Who?"

"One called River. I believe she's a smart girl. Touchy at times, but not too bad, I hear."

A faint smile broke through River's tear-stained face.

"Listen to yourself, River. Trust yourself. But also listen to us. We can help you. We want to help you."

Wiping her cheek, River nodded. Then the girl tilted her head slightly. "You speak wisely," she murmured, still holding the faint smile on her lips. "For one so young."

Jessica's smile broadened. "But the young become wiser. And why not today?"

River breathed the lightest of laughs, then her smile faded. "My tribe is suffering. I must change. I must change what I say, and what I do. I *must* help."

And that's what I needed to hear, Jessica thought, relief flooding through her.

"But," River continued, her expression hardening, "I meant what I said, Jessica. I do not like the future I saw. I will still seek answers."

Jessica nodded. They could cross that bridge later. She climbed to her feet and offered her hand to River. "Let us greet the Islanders." Helping River to her feet, she tensed as the wretched images of battle returned. It was time to agree on a new way forward and escape the cycles of slaughter.

River swept up her Axe, then faced Jessica. "I am ready."

We have River back, Jessica thought as they walked out of the chamber together, *but we also have the Mother, the Warrior, and the shaman.*

A potent combination?

Or a catastrophic burden for such a young soul? *One that could break her.*

As they followed the cave's tunnels to the exit, her dark thoughts led to a memory hidden deep. Of a conversation with IY, who had revealed that a suspected traitor was amongst them, one IY secretly tracked. A traitor who sought the Iyes's destruction. A traitor who had helped Kaos banish Jessica from this world. *But IY doesn't trust me with a name.* Nor had IY allowed her to tell anyone else, not even Lanky or Beth.

She glanced at the girl by her side, seeing River's stern, determined face bathed in the tunnel's torchlight. The burden River carried was great. Could it have broken her? Could this be the reason she'd withdrawn herself, hiding herself away from the Warriors and her tribe? Had this led the girl to do the unthinkable and betray her own tribe? *Could she be the traitor?*

Jessica forced the horrific thought away. No. This couldn't be. River – as the Warrior, Revri – had saved their lives at the mountain. *She could never betray us.*

They walked on towards the light at the end of the tunnel.

But I will watch her all the same.

A traitor is here.

Somewhere.

CHAPTER FIVE

No one in the Land knew the truth of Kaos. How could they?
None knew but I. And I was bound by the game of my masters.
Only the release of the Geddon would allow them to see.

Beth's weary eyes surveyed the scattered huts of the firelit encampment. "At least we have shelter for the night. And just in time, because here comes the rain again."

"How are we for supplies?" Lanky asked, pulling up the collar of his tunic.

Gravel glanced at him. "Sufficient for a few days more. Mostly smoked fish and meats from our camp a few days past. If our enemy pauses in their pursuit, we may hunt tomorrow."

Beth studied the weary Shield. "You should get that tended to," she said, pointing at the wound on the veteran's neck. Yet another battle scar added to the story carved into the warrior's leathered skin. "You need a stitch – or three."

Gravel's sharp eyes met hers. "It's nothing. Many others paid a much greater price." His shoulders straightened. "But their ancestors will greet them warmly for their brave actions."

Lanky grimaced. "It would have been much worse if the Islanders hadn't arrived when they did."

"True. But what is also true is we wouldn't have held without your assistance, Warrior. It was … impressive."

Beth glanced at Lanky, who had cast troubled eyes to the killing fields. Yes, without him, they'd have been in dire straits. She wondered, yet again, how this car mechanic and part-time relic hunter had morphed into this efficient killing machine. Especially as he hadn't yet bonded to the daemon Fen. She glanced at his Axe. Some of it lay there, she knew. The power of the Axe enhanced you, stimulated and invigorated you, endowing skills, abilities, and a prowess beyond your wildest dreams. But the Axe alone did not make a Warrior. Someone was teaching him. Had Fen relented in his stubborn insistence that Lanky bond with him before he would aid them?

"It was a slaughter," Lanky said, turning back to them.

"I don't care what you call it," Gravel said sharply. "All I know is, without it, they'd have slaughtered us." He looked at Beth. "A pity all Warriors would not engage. Some would still be talking with their families had that been so."

"I'm sorry, Gravel," Beth said with a grimace. "I can't. Not yet." *I don't trust myself.*

She shivered, recalling her release of the one called Bethusa when the enemy had first descended. Bethusa had stormed to the fore, and a whole flank of the attacking horde had been destroyed in an instant. *But I can't describe what I did ... what she did.* But she did remember the vibrant taste of death, the sweet smell of her enemy's destruction.

And that had terrified her. Now, she held herself back, not releasing the full Warrior within her. Not releasing Bethusa.

Gravel's penetrating gaze lingered, then, shaking his head, he turned to Lanky. "I see our Mother has left the caves. Is *that* Warrior now joining the fray?"

"You still haven't spoken with her?"

"I believe she wishes a change in the Shields. Knuckles is gone. And I abandoned Naga. That is hard to forgive."

"Now hold on," Lanky said, bristling. "I was there, remember? Naga commanded you to travel on with me."

Gravel sighed. "Even so."

Beth glanced at the man beside her. They said that Gravel held himself responsible for the old Mother's death, but she couldn't help but feel from Lanky's description of Naga's last words to him that the old woman had known her death was coming. But why had the shaman handled it that way? Why not have kept Gravel and the others close beside her as they travelled to the White Crags camp? To save others' lives? To sacrifice herself to pass on her knowledge and powers to River? Or a terrible misjudgement?

Beth suppressed a sigh. Neither she nor any other would probably ever know the truth of that moment. But Naga was no fool, and the fact remained that sending Lanky on ahead had saved the Sacred Site from destruction – and most likely many lives within the camp. Gravel may still be hurting from Naga's death, but abandoning her? No, no one should blame the Shield for that.

She caught movement and glanced around to see two weary Iyes walking past, carrying another slumped body between them. "When will we bury the dead?" she asked, knowing the tribe would wish to pass them to their ancestors before they moved on from this place.

His face grim, Gravel watched the group walk by. "First light. Then we should travel to our other allies to spread the word that the enemy moves against us." He paused. "At least, that is what I think."

Lanky grunted. "And there lies another problem. We run, we fight, we run again. But we run blind, with no plan. We need a clear leader. With Bear still not returned from the failed mission north, we ..." He trailed off, flicking a glance at Beth.

Not returned and not seen since I was captured by the dragon. The memory of that terrifying moment flashed through her mind: the Ancient's shocking arrival out of the valley, grasping her in its monstrous talons, the rest of the group forced back by the beast's deadly fire; then a harrowing journey north, her body growing colder and colder in the bone-chilling air, pushing her to the brink of unconsciousness.

I remember mountains ...

But then nothing more. Not until waking, confused and bewildered, at the White Crags camp with Jessica, River, and Tricia. And the rest of the group? *Bear, Svana, Knuckles, Shorty, Scorpion ...* A familiar pang of guilt returned. *I failed them.* A single moment's lapse had been enough to allow the dragon to approach unseen, grasping her in a vicelike grip before spraying the surrounding area with a searing blaze of fire. What had been their fate? Had any survived? The worry – and the guilt – was constant, but despite this, she hadn't abandoned hope. She was certain it had only been her the dragon had sought, and the rest had been far away from the beast's fire. *I have to believe they survived.*

"Beth?"

She looked up, pulling herself back to the moment. "You're right, Lanky. We spend all our time fleeing from the enemy, barely surviving. The time is slipping through our fingers. We can't continue like this." Anger flashed. "And we *have* been too easy on River. Her period of mourning, or whatever it's been, needs to end."

"And end it will."

The three turned in surprise.

"You move quietly," Lanky said evenly as River approached.

"Too quietly, for too long."

As River stopped before them, Beth studied the drawn face of the girl – a girl who'd attempted to kill her at their first meeting. She looked nervous and uncertain, though tried to hide it by standing tall and proud. Her short-cropped hair retained scattered remnants of curls, the unusual side-effect of the vicious, energised battle River – or Revri – had fought at Mount Hope, defending Jessica against a daemon of the Dark.

And I was there, I'm told.

But she remembered nothing.

"I would like to say thank you," River murmured, her strained eyes not quite holding theirs, "for your efforts to defend my people." She cast her eyes down. "But I feel that is something I have no right to say. That, I will leave to my tribe."

No one said anything.

Because she's right – we don't need her thanks. Beth noticed River's shoulders drop a little as the silence grew. *This hurts her. Give her something.* "I accept your thanks," she said simply.

Lanky and Gravel remained silent.

River glanced at each of them in turn, clearly uncertain what to say. "I look forward to your valued advice at our meeting later," she managed, then turned and walked away.

"How many dead?" Lanky said under his breath.

His voice clearly carried, as River tensed as she walked away.

Beth watched her for a moment. Nothing more could be said on this right now. Time – and actions – would be a bigger healer than words. She glanced up, squinting against the rain. "This is getting heavier. I suggest we get under shelter and take the chance of some rest before we meet the others."

"Good idea," Lanky muttered, already turning. "See you later."

Gravel grunted something unintelligible, then also walked away.

Beth sighed, then made her way towards her hut, striving to settle her thoughts. But they remained a chaotic jumble, an anarchy of distractions, as stark memories cried out to be heard. Memories of their violent, unexpected arrival to the land of the Iyes. Memories of her joining with the daemon Garrion, who had acted as though she knew Beth from a time before. And fraught memories of violent skirmishes as the tribe attempted to elude their enemy's grasp.

And through this disturbing turmoil welled other fractured memories not her own. Of violent, bloody battles in storm-lashed mountains. Of shadowy creatures sweeping out from a swirling rent fouling the sky. All ragged, blurred tapestries of unknown landscapes, unknown ages, each riddled with death and destruction yet suffused with a desperate hope. These were from the mind of Bethusa, she was sure. The one the daemons knew. An ancient Warrior, they said. And one who sought to break free from Beth. To become Beth.

I'm told I was at Mount Hope.

Me? Or Bethusa?

She had no memory of it. All she knew was that she had returned to this age with a fractured knowledge not her own.

But I am Beth.

I wish to remain Beth.

Yet the one known as Bethusa was growing stronger, and though Beth resisted the sweet temptation of the rich power of the Land, she feared what else lay undiscovered within the swirling, translucent mists of her mind.

Was this madness?

A memory returned of her sitting under the stars at White Crags camp, Lanky beside her. What had he said? *Talk to us.* But what was she doing? She was acting like River, burying things deep and hiding them from her friends. Her allies. *I need to talk. Else I think I will go mad.*

Or worse.

Reaching her hut, where the heavy rain hammered off the hide roof, she yawned as she pulled back the entrance covering and ducked inside. She desperately needed to rest awhile. But was she brave enough to face the unguarded dreams of her sleeping mind? Unstrapping the Axe from her back, she yawned again as she dropped it to the ground. *I've no choice. I'm exhausted.* She pulled off her wet jacket and tunic, then unlaced her leather trousers. With a deep sigh, she lay down on her bed of furs, pulling them around her, feeling the softness of the grasses beneath. Closing her eyes, she let sleep overtake her.

*

"Your shoulder seems to be healing well, Spider," Amber said, kneeling beside him, warmed by the crackling fire by their side. "It's come on well since the stitches came out. But," she continued, jabbing him gently in the ribs, "still only light work until it fully heals."

"Ow, that hurt," Spider moaned, holding his hand to his bare chest, feigning a grimace. "My ribs are still sore, you know."

Amber brushed a strand of damp red hair from her cheek, then reached for her pack. "So, as I said, light work. Keep up those exercises, stay out of trouble, and you'll be back to full duties soon enough."

"Well, thank IY for that," Spider said with feeling as Amber helped him pull his weaved vest over his head. "I'm going crazy stuck on camp duties. And today ..." A pained look crossed his face as he looked out beyond the overhanging canopy into the driving rain sweeping across the camp. "I felt so helpless. I couldn't help them. Heba, Drake, the young lad Art." *And so many others from our allies.*

As Amber helped him on with his tunic, Spider noticed the heavy look in her eyes. *She's worked miracles today, and yet she's suffered her own recent loss.* "And thank you," he murmured. "I know there's many worse than me today."

Reaching for her pack, Amber said nothing.

Spider sighed. His physical injuries would quickly heal, but Amber's hurt ran far deeper. And she had no time to grieve, no time to allow the memory of Eagle to find rest in her thoughts. He picked up a stone and hurled it into the rain. "Something's wrong, Amber. We're drifting. Where are our leaders? We're running from one disaster to another." *And River – where is the woman I love? Why has she abandoned me? Abandoned us?*

He heard a quiet sniffing by his side. Turning, he saw Amber, head bowed, her face partly obscured by falling strands of hair. Grimacing, he placed his hand gently on hers.

"I miss him," Amber said, her voice catching as she spoke.

Spider felt a sudden chill inside. Eagle. Her intended. The one killed trying to protect Naga after she had sent her best fighters away. *Sent to find me,* he thought, his stomach churning. And there it was. The truth. His stupidity in trusting the traveller, Growl, had led to Naga's and Eagle's deaths. "I'm sorry," he whispered. "So very sorry."

Amber looked up at him, her damp hair clinging to her high-boned cheeks, her tear-stained face glistening in the fire's light. "Don't go there, Spider," she said, an edge to her voice. "Eagle died protecting our Mother, not by your hands. Don't make me argue this again."

Don't go there. Don't add to her torment. He nodded.

Amber wiped her eyes. "I miss him," she whispered. "His voice, his words, his smile, his touch. Each day, I wish I could walk out at dawn and see him laughing with his friends, or sit in the evening light and share – with joy or with sorrow – what the day had brought." She looked around at Spider. "But the hardest?" she said, a tear in the corner of her eye. "Thinking of those things I wished I'd said but never did. That's the cruellest thing of all."

As silence fell, Spider found his next words came easily. *Because I saw the light in his eyes.* "I don't know all that you wished you'd said, but I do know Eagle was entranced by what you *did* say." He heard her breath catch. "You could have led that man out into the darkest depths of the Great Sea, and he would have followed your every step. He would have crossed the driest of deserts and the highest of snow-laden mountains to have listened to but a single word from you." He squeezed her hand. "Don't think of what more you could have said, because Eagle heard every word you spoke, and each lifted his heart. You brought him joy and helped him live. Do not regret. Simply remember."

Amber leaned into him, sobbing gently.

They sat for a while, remembering.

*

Beth awoke, body aching but mind refreshed. She could hear the torrential rain had stopped – unexpected, but welcome – and the camp lay quiet, all resting from the crushing exertions of battle. Kicking off the furs covering her, she slowly stretched, easing her strained muscles into motion. Then she lay for a moment, allowing her thoughts to settle on the upcoming meeting. *No more running. We must act. We ...*

She frowned, a sense of unease crawling across her skin.

She scrambled into a seated position, then listened, turning her head slowly.

Nothing – not a sound.

No voices, no low whispers, no coughs – and no birdsong. Had she slept so late? She crawled over to the hut entrance and pulled back the hide.

She gasped as she looked out into the emptiness of a deep black void!

Stunned, she dropped the hide and scrambled back into the refuge of her hut. What was happening? Where was she? Thoughts racing, she reached out for her Axe, pulling it close. *What the hell is out there?* Heart hammering in her chest, the unnatural silence stretched on. *I can't just sit here. Move!* Reaching for her clothes, she quickly dressed, then crawled back to the entrance. Rising to a crouch, her hand tightly clenched around the haft of her Axe, she pushed the flap aside, then cautiously stepped outside.

She froze at the sight before her.

The black void had given way to a scene of utter devastation. All around her, the land lay scorched and blackened, tendrils of acrid smoke rising from the charred bodies lying strewn across the camp. She struggled to breathe. *This can't be ...* Her chest tight, her disbelieving eyes ran over the broken bodies, the burnt scrub, and the charcoal-black trees ...

Catching a blurred movement in the corner of her eye, she swung around to the gorge—

An amorphous, oily black morass swept from the ravine, filling the ether with a ferocious hatred, an overwhelming desire for destruction.

Swamped by a glacial terror, which closed like tentacles around her soul, Beth felt herself drop to her knees, the head of her Axe falling limply to the ground by her side. *What hell is this? I can't face this. No one can face this.*

'*Your friends are dying,*' said a chilling voice in her mind. '*Your Warriors are dying. And like theirs, your death will be slow. Here, see their pain.*'

Anguished cries twisted her gut in a chorus of death as visions from hell assailed her: Lanky and Jessica hanging head down, nails through their feet, their skinned bodies dripping blood onto broken bodies below; River impaled on a stake, writhing in agony, her mouth open with a scream, but no sound being emitted; Sheba's young baby being torn apart by wolves—

"No!" Beth screamed, her whole being utterly defiled.

The world shimmered …

Then disappeared.

She flailed, falling; disorientated and lost; floating in a void.

'*Beth,*' came a distant voice, almost lost in the void. '*Reconnect with Bethusa, else all will be lost.*'

The world shimmered, and the ghastly visions stormed back into her ravaged mind, accosting her with the sickly stench of death.

She retched and threw up.

Head bowed, her stomach heaving with waves of nausea, she glanced up through tear-filled eyes. The rapacious wall of death was almost upon her.

'*For you, I reserve the best,*' the chilling voice rasped. '*I give you an eternity to die.*' A tendril of the darkness swept out towards her—

The world shimmered.

And she knelt in the void.

'*Beth,*' the distant voice urged. '*Release Bethusa!*'

'*Fen?*' she whispered, the harsh tone of the voice familiar.

'*Release Bethusa!*' Fen commanded.

A nameless dread engulfed her. '*I can't do it,*' she said in despair.

'*You fool! You fear Bethusa more than you fear Alkazar? Release her!*'

'*It's not … I—*'

The world shimmered, and the tendril of death reached for her—

A blinding flash of white light exploded around her, and a deafening blast hurled her backwards through the air. Slamming her into the muddy ground with a harsh grunt, the blast echoed in her skull like a drum. With explosions continuing to thunder around her, Beth covered her head, curling into a ball in a vain attempt to escape the nightmare engulfing her. Yet as she cowered in the mud, the malevolent presence surrounding her suddenly weakened, drawing itself away from a burgeoning force crackling in the ether, a force she recognised as one wielded by Warriors.

Lanky … River …

Beth's stomach twisted as deep within, something stirred – a feeling of guilt, of deep, deep shame. *Others fight for me, others defend me, and I do nothing.*

A thunderous crack rent the air, and the fog suddenly lifted from her mind, the clawing sense of despair vanishing from her soul.

The loathsome evil had gone.

Confused, ashamed, relieved, she lay still, the foul taste in her mouth slowly fading. Rain hammered down on her cheek. *Rain. It's still raining.*

The murmur of familiar voices drifted through the air.

Forcing herself to move, she looked up to see Lanky walking towards her, his resolute frame set against the driving rain. She pulled herself up from the mud, then stood, shivering against the sudden cold.

Lanky approached, his face twisted in concern. "Are you okay?" he said, putting a hand on her shoulder. "Are you hurt?"

Hurt inside … Ashamed … She shook her head. "What was it?" she managed.

"Alkazar, a daemon of the Dark. One River fought in another time." He held her eyes. "And one you've fought before – and defeated."

"But … but that thing was an evil from the depths of hell. I couldn't fight this."

Lanky shook his head. "And yet you already have."

She struggled to believe. How? How could she have fought one such as this?

"There's much to discuss," came Jessica's voice behind her. "But first you should get out of these clothes. Let's get up to the rock shelter and you can dry off there."

"I'll catch up with River, then see you there," Lanky said. He made to go.

"Lanky," Beth called. He glanced at her. "Thanks," she murmured.

Rain dripping from his nose and mass of sodden hair, Lanky smiled. "It wasn't only me. It took River and Jessica to keep it at bay."

Beth's eyes widened. She turned to Jessica. "You?"

"It wasn't much, but I did what I could to help."

"Don't knock yourself, Jess," Lanky said. "Seems IY has a fast-learning pupil. You surprised me."

Jessica pushed a strand of her rain-soaked hair from her face. "Not as much as it surprised me." She gestured to the gorge. "Come on, let's get out of this rain."

As she strode beside her friend, a simmering frustration taunted Beth's mind. How had it come to this? That she needed her friends to save her? The frustration lit a spark of anger. *I've become weak, frightened by those things I can't see. And that could get me killed. It could get my friends killed.* Her head bowed against the driving rain, she knew now that she couldn't keep running from her fears … *From Bethusa.* Things needed to change. *Things* will *change.*

*

Lanky crouched in the lee of a dome-shaped hut, looking out across the rainswept camp, where runners were crossing from hut to hut, calling the all-clear. Yet his unease remained. The attack was over, but for how long? "What was that thing?"

"A creature of the Enemy," River said, sheltering beside him, "a free-roaming daemon of the Dark." Her young face took on a harder edge. "Alkazar was born with the Land within a poisoned abyss. A corruption of Kaos, it exists to destroy, all life its antithesis."

The muscles of Lanky's jaw tensed. *Kaos. Always Kaos.* "I asked this question of Naga. What truly is this Kaos?"

River's weary eyes met his. "No one can be sure. At least not I, or Naga, or the line of the shamans. We hold only echoes of frightened whispers about this terror of the Dark. Nothing truly seen. Little understood."

"That still shocks me. How can you know so little about your nemesis, one whose shadow has been cast over the history of your tribe?"

"Because those half-heard whispers talk of a life unlike ours. They say that Kaos is an unassailable energy, enduring and ordered. Life, but not as you and me. Not as the animals, the trees, the plants of this Land, but a life, nonetheless. And Kaos remains hidden, cloaked within the darkness." Her expression turned grim. "And this life has cunning and intent. An intent to destroy us, to tear our Land apart."

A flash of lightning lit up the heavens, followed moments later by a sharp crack of thunder and a deep, rolling rumble.

The rain lashed across the camp, storm driven.

River spoke, her voice hushed. "I am sorry, Warrior."

Lanky knew immediately what she meant. *Sorry? And so, you should be. People have died whilst you examined your navel.* "As am I," he murmured. *I can only speak the truth.* He regarded her, settling his thoughts. She had now left her place of hiding – *of escape?* – and had a chance to make amends. *And she fought bravely against the evil that came against us tonight.* He needed to move on from what had been. "That daemon is something I don't want to face again in a hurry. We were lucky you arrived when you did."

River studied him for a moment, then turned her head from a swirling gust of rain. As the gust swept by, she turned back. "The luck lay in how it attacked. And its target."

"Why's that?" Lanky said, water dripping from his hair and running down his neck.

"It materialised at the entrance of the gorge. If it had attacked our caves and rock shelters deeper within the valley, we'd have had many more deaths on our hands."

"A bloodbath."

"But it focussed on Warrior Beth. Maybe the daemon sensed her weakness, believing it had a chance of a quick kill."

"Could be." He flicked his hand through his hair in a vain attempt to stop the water streaming down his neck. "But whatever its target, it failed, and now we've bloodied its nose and hopefully bought us time before it returns."

Another crack of thunder rent the air, and the rain swept around the lee of the hut.

Grimacing, Lanky turned to the hut. "I don't know whose this is," he muttered, searching for the entrance, "but we're borrowing it."

He quickly found the entrance hide, and pulling it aside, he and River ducked inside. Edging forward in the dark, he stumbled and almost fell.

"Aargh. Who's that?" a familiar voice shouted. He heard the frantic scuffling of someone sitting up quickly. "You better talk fast, else you'll get kicked hard where it hurts!"

"Calm down, Tricia," Lanky said quickly – he'd heard from Jessica how hard the woman could hit when disturbed in her own bed. "It's only me and River."

"What are you doing in here? You interrupted a beautiful dream. And this is not your tent, it's mine and Jessica's. Are you trying to sneak a private moment? Use Beth's next door, she's—"

"Of course not," River said, an edge to her voice. "We were caught in the rain."

"Well, what were you doing out in that?"

Lanky frowned. "Hold on a minute. First, didn't you realise this camp was under attack? And second, how did you understand what River just said?"

"First," Tricia said, mimicking his voice, "I've been sleeping. And second, River helped me."

She slept through that? And River helped her?

"Jessica asked me to help," came River's voice by his side. "And so, I asked Iolaire for help – she gained support for Tricia from another daemon."

Dumbfounded, Lanky stared into the darkness. "You're a Warrior?" he managed.

"What?" came Tricia's suddenly terse and challenging voice. "You think I couldn't be a Warrior?"

"I …" Lanky hesitated, realising the difficulty of dealing with this in the dark.

Tricia grunted. "You think Trish couldn't be a great Warrior – a Protector of Freedom, a Breaker of Chains? You really think that?"

"I—"

"I could be. And a great Warrior too. I'd kick your ass."

"Well, I—"

Tricia laughed. "Relax. I'm no Warrior. Just have a hidden friend helping me understand what's being said."

"So, who's helping you?"

"That's a good question. I'm sure I asked that earlier but didn't get an answer. Who *is* working the magic in my head?"

River sighed. "A daemon named Mede."

"Well, that's a nice name," Tricia said from the dark.

"And who is Mede?" Lanky asked.

"One who aids the spirit of millipedes," River replied.

"What!" came Tricia's indignant voice. "I've millipedes stuffed down my ears?"

Lanky grinned. "Don't knock them. They've been around for millions of years."

"Not down my ears, they haven't," Tricia muttered. "And a millipede? Why not a lemur, or a starfish?"

Lanky sensed River tense beside him. "You do not pick and choose," she said firmly. "These are not your servants. Mede has offered to help. If you do not wish it, then he will leave."

"No," Tricia said quickly. "I *am* thankful for Mede's help. Relying on Lanky and Jessica to translate was a pain – humour doesn't work with those two standing in between."

Peering into the darkness, Lanky's smile faded. No, and this one needed her humour to keep her sane in a land where her friends were slowly drifting away from her, drawn ever deeper into a tangled web spun by unseen enemies – *and by supposed allies*. It would have been better if Tricia had stayed in their own time, because here she was proving … *Worthless? A distraction?* He suppressed a sigh. *She is here. Live with it.* "Well, it's good to know you're sorted, Trish," he said, keeping his voice light. He turned to the shadowy presence of River by his side. "I can hear the rain easing. We should head to the rock shelter for the meeting."

"I agree," River said. He heard her moving to the entrance.

"Do I come?" Tricia asked, hope in her voice.

Lanky hesitated, then: "It's a limited group this evening, Trish. But why don't you come up to the gorge? There's no point in you sitting here by yourself."

"Okay. Yes, I'll do that. Give me a moment to put on some clothes."

Clothes? Lanky shook his head, replaying the conversations he'd just had with a naked Tricia. "Okay, just let me turn away."

"Very funny."

A short while later, they left the hut, running through the light rain from the passing storm clouds up to the gorge.

*

The black wolf watched them for a while, its deep yellow eyes blinking against the persistent rain. Then it turned and silently padded away into the gloom, gradually picking up speed as it headed east to rendezvous with its waiting master.

CHAPTER SIX

*Even in the vastness of the Continuum – and
of the Void beyond – small things matter. A
single life may change all. If it can survive.*

*T*hankful to have left the sweltering taxi behind, Erin followed the
black-jacketed porter into the wonderfully cool air-conditioned
hotel lobby. The wiry man had insisted he carry her bags, and given her
Araci consisted of about four things she'd learnt off a talkative Misrian
man on the plane, she was in no position to argue. She was just glad to
get out of the searing North Frykan heat, too much for an
unacclimatised body like hers – a long, cold drink was what she
desperately needed now. *And a moment of calm.* It had been a short
journey from the airport, but the manic city and its people had crashed
into her like a train, a dramatic assault on the senses, overwhelming,
unnerving, yet powerfully intoxicating. From the chaotic transit
through the mystifying vagaries of airport officialdom, to the rich,
pungent aromas drifting on the late summer air, to the deadly mayhem
of the city's overcrowded, seemingly unregulated roads, where cars
and pedestrians alike fought for dominance – a short journey, maybe,
but a typical thread in the rich tapestry of this North Frykan country.

As she walked up to the check-in desk, the receptionist looked up
and smiled warmly. "Welcome to the hotel and welcome to Qahir," he
said, correctly guessing her language. "Is this your first visit?"

Tension eased from Erin's shoulders. "It is," she said, returning his
smile. "I'm looking forward to my stay."

"I hope it is a good one," the receptionist said, tapping on the
keyboard in front of him. "Could I take your name? And your
passport, please – we need a copy for the police registration."

"Erin Catran," she said, reaching into her pocket for her passport. Realising it wasn't there, she suddenly remembered she'd put it into her day sack, which the porter had collected from the taxi. She looked around and saw her suitcase by a coffee table in the centre of the lobby. "I just need to get my bag."

The receptionist acknowledged her with a nod, and she turned and walked over to the suitcase. *Now, where's my bag?* she thought, glancing around? *Where did he put it?*

It wasn't there.

A sinking feeling rose in the pit of her stomach.

Looking up, she scanned the lobby for the porter, but the man had gone. Her unease deepening, she returned to the check-in desk. "Where did the porter put my bag?"

"The porter?" the receptionist said with a puzzled frown. "The porter is over at the concierge desk. But he did not bring your bags. Your driver carried them in."

"My driver? No, no, the taxi driver didn't come in. It was your porter."

The receptionist reached over and hit a bell on his desk three times, then waved across to the concierge desk. A tall, stout man acknowledged him and walked over. "Yes, Bakar?" the stout man said as he approached.

"This lady said you brought in her bags. Did you—"

"No, not this man," Erin interrupted. "The porter."

"This is the porter, madam."

Erin stared at the receptionist, an awful truth looming.

The receptionist spoke a few words to the porter, who nodded, then left. The receptionist faced her. "So, you did not know the man who brought in your bags?"

"I thought … I thought it was the hotel porter."

"And you don't see the man here?"

She shook her head.

"Please wait a moment, madam. I will report this immediately." He turned to a colleague, spoke briefly in Araci, then reached for a phone.

Erin silently berated herself for her stupidity. *Fool. You've been here moments only, and you've let a stranger steal your bag.* She stood, frustrated and angry, as the receptionist spoke on the phone.

A familiar voice sounded behind her. "Hi, Erin."

Erin turned, relief flooding through her as she saw the young man walking towards her.

"How was your trip?" Fletcher said with a smile as he stopped in front of her. "How … Hey – are you okay?"

"Madam Erin," the receptionist said, behind her.

Erin pursed her lips. "Hold on a second, Fletch. But stay right there." She turned to the receptionist.

"I have called the police, and they will arrive soon," the man said.

"Police?" Fletcher said behind her. "What—"

She held up her hand to forestall his questions.

"You can make a report to them," the receptionist continued, "including the description of the man." He coughed. "But to be honest, madam, I hold little hope for any valuables you may have had, or for the police being able to track this man down." He gave a casual shrug. "The thief won't want your passport, so that may be found, but best you call your embassy to arrange things with them. I will give you their number."

Erin nodded weakly. "Thank you. Shukra."

The man smiled. "Awan," he said in reply. "It is good. You speak Araci. A few more days and you will be Misrian."

She forced a smile.

"The best I can do now is to check you in – is that okay?"

Erin nodded, and the man began to tap at the keyboard.

She faced Fletcher, who stood shaking his head. "Two hours here and you lose your passport?"

"It was stolen."

"Well, I think the receptionist is right. Given how long it might take to get a new passport, I think you'll become a master of the language."

"Not helpful, Fletch," she said, flicking him a hard glance.

"Sorry," he muttered. "What happened?"

She relayed the story, then cursed under her breath. "I can't believe I let that man take my bag."

Fletcher sighed. "Well, it's done now. At least you're safe and well." He stepped closer. "And Robert – is he still on track to arrive tomorrow?"

Harsh, unyielding reality swept back. "He promised he'd be on that flight, but I still won't fully believe it until I see it. It would've been easier if he could have travelled with us."

"With all the questions we've already faced at home, best we did it this way." Fletcher gestured to the check-in desk. "The receptionist is ready for you again. Look, check in and drop your bags – your bag – to your room and then come straight back down. I'll stay with you while you talk to the police."

"Thanks." She put a hand on his arm. "And the rest of it – why we're here – I know it seems crazy, but I'm grateful for you coming, really I am." *Because we may be able to help my friends.*

Fletcher smiled, but she saw the doubt still lingering in his eyes. *He doesn't really believe we should be here.*

She forced her own unease to the shadows of her mind.

"Madam?"

She glanced at Fletcher. "I better get this done. I'll drop my bag and come back down." She squeezed his arm. "And thank you again."

"I'll meet you over by those couches." With a departing smile, he walked away across the lobby.

Erin faced the receptionist once more. "Okay. Let's try this again."

*

"Would you like a drink, sir?"

Robert looked up. "No, thank you, I'm fine." The flight attendant smiled and pulled her trolley to the next row of the plane.

Fine? Really? No, I'm not fine! Nothing is fine!

He drew deep breaths to quell the rising panic. *Why am I doing this? Because you're slowly going mad.*

Mad? What was madness? *Who is mad and who is not? And who decides?*

'Robert,' came a firm voice in his mind. 'Remember who you are and what you are doing.'

All other thoughts instantly shattered. It was back. The voice of the daemon. The voice of a whale. 'Go away.'

'No. I am here. Remember Lanky. Do not forget Lanky.'

A sudden surge of emotion welled inside, a violent coursing of fire within his veins. *Lanky! My son!* Hands suddenly trembling, he put them to his head. What had he done? How could he have forsaken his own son?

'Few could have resisted the strength of the daemon who found you,' came the firm voice. 'One who serves the god of the darkness.'

Yet how had he been so weak? He'd believed some ancient, forgotten god would aid him, aid a simple bookseller. *And Lanky … Rebecca …* Love, lust, a brief affair … *And I walked away. Even when her husband left, I wouldn't commit.* His hands clasped tightly on his temples, the memories too painful to bear.

'Yet these memories are real,' the voice insisted. 'As is your love for Lanky.'

'Why do you still haunt me?'

'You think I am a ghost?'

A ghost? A fabricated creature of a frightened imagination? No, this voice wasn't a ghost. 'Few resisted,' Robert said grimly, 'but I should have been one of them. I was weak.'

'That may have been true,' the voice said. 'But believe me when I say now you are stronger.'

'Strong? I feel that evil's presence surrounding me. I can't escape its claws.'

'It is true, the Enemy maintains its attack on you; but, with my help, you are resisting – and resisting well. But you cannot lose focus, drowning in self-pity. This is what the Enemy waits for – what it feeds on. It is creating this despair you feel.'

Robert dropped his hands from his face, clasping them tightly in his lap as he tried to make sense of his febrile mind.

'You do still want help, don't you?' the voice asked.

He shuddered. What he so desperately wanted was to have never lost his parents, to never have lost those incredible souls from his life. For a time after their shocking disappearance, seemingly into thin air, he had drifted, lost and distraught, unable to accept they'd gone. But finding their incredible work, their meticulous studies, had given him a purpose, and for years, he'd followed in their footsteps, chasing their belief of veiled powers in the land, of ancient artefacts awaiting those who could wield them. And those studies – and the calm oasis of his bookshop – had saved him … until the tainted promise of the false god. With his weak, delusional acceptance of the false god's lies, that rebuilt life had been thrown away in an instant, discarded by the wayside along with the rest of the useless detritus of his life.

'Robert,' came the voice. 'That path leads nowhere but to pointless despair.'

He fought to stave off the darkness tainting his thoughts. Maybe his life had been destroyed, but … *I had to try to save them. I had to try to save my parents.*

'You can still save your son.'

Lanky.

Yes, there was still a chance to save his son.

That stark, visceral truth sliced through the fog of his mind. 'I want to help my son.'

'Then continue to fight! Resist the Enemy's attack and focus on saving Lanky.'

'Why is it doing this to me?'

'The Enemy is worried. It fears you.'

'That makes no sense. What can I possibly do against that … thing?'

'I do not know how you can harm them,' admitted the voice. 'I am not a spirit or a god. I have my place in the Continuum, and there are things I know and things I do not. But I sense their fear of you.'

'Why? You tell me to travel, and yet –'

'The Keeper. Let Erin speak with the Keeper. Something is concealed, something I cannot see.'

Something hidden? His jagged nerves twisted as he thought of the hell which had lain behind beguiling spoken words before, words of a false god. What else might be hidden now? Could he trust that this whale daemon spoke true?

But maybe this time, he could. Because this time, another heard it. The young woman Erin. *One not as weak or as evil as me.*

'Will you take Erin to the Keeper?'

"I will," he whispered.

And those few simple words lit a small fire inside. A weak, pitiful fire, yet one whose embryonic flames pushed back against the fear, settled the angst of his disturbed mind.

'You have started the journey,' the voice said. *'And in this journey, I will aid you as I can. Where it will take you, that is not clear, but at the right place and the right time, you will know what to do. And at that time, listen to no one but yourself.'*

Robert sat, eyes closed, his hands clasped tightly in his lap. His thoughts calmed, settling around one single goal. To save his son. *This is all that matters to me now, and this path may give me that chance.* Within moments, the world around him drifted away, gaining him welcomed respite from himself – and from his conscience.

*

Fletcher took another swig from his bottle of beer – his third – then glanced across at Erin, who was gazing at something across the hotel bar. It had been her idea to come here. And a good one. A brief respite from the manic stresses of the past weeks. *Else we'll go mad.* Yet maybe they were already mad, coming to this chaotic city on foreign soil at the words of some unseen, mystical being. *The words of a daemon …* He sat for a moment, staring at his bottle, the chatter of the bar drowned by his churning thoughts. Then he sighed. This was an evening to escape, even if but for the shortest of moments, the gnawing unease that had settled on him since that fateful night at Mount Hope.

He leaned forward in his chair and raised his bottle. "Well, here's hoping for the best with your passport," he said, keeping his voice light, "and to us dealing with whatever else is heading our way over the next few days."

Erin turned to him. "You've said that already."

"Even so." He tilted his bottle towards hers.

A faint smile crossed her lips, and she raised her bottle, clinking the glass against his. "Cheers."

"Cheers."

They both drank deeply.

He studied her face. "You think he will turn up in the morning?"

She cocked her head. "You've also asked that about five times."

"But you think he will?"

"Yes, about nine thirty, God willing."

He took another drink. "Do you believe in God? Or is that too pertinent a question?"

Erin's blue eyes flashed. "If it is, then you've already crossed the boundary. That phrase allows people to ask dumb questions, then use it as an excuse to get away with it."

"Ah. Sorry. You're probably right." Fletcher looked down at his bottle. "It's just with what we saw that night at the mountain – what we felt – I can now believe there's such a thing as pure evil. A devil, if you like. Something I thought only existed in stories and films, and in the words of your parents when they were scaring the living daylights out of you, teaching you right from wrong. It—"

"How many of those beers have you had? Can't we have a couple more before you start on religion, politics and … well, those two?"

Despite the tension inside, Fletcher smiled. "I already had a couple more. But this is relevant," he continued quickly. "That battle at the mountain; was that a god-versus-devil fight we saw? Right versus wrong? Light against the darkness?"

Erin frowned. "What's taken you down this path?"

He hesitated, a familiar ache returning to his gut. "I wondered whether you'd thought more about that night. About what happened." *Because it haunts me. Because it terrifies me.*

Erin took a sip of her beer, studying him closely. She ran her hand through her short blonde hair, pushing strands back behind her ear, then tilted her head. "Light against darkness? Yes, that's a good enough description. But the intervention of God? Or a god?" Her jaw tensed. "Who could truly answer that?"

"So, you believe in different gods – ah, sorry," he said, seeing her frown. "Let me rephrase that." He ran his fingers through his short goatee. "I understand people worshipping many gods – in fact, I understand that people may worship none, one, or many gods – but surely, behind it all, there must be one … something? An ultimate being, an overarching entity or energy that ties it all together? Wouldn't you think?"

Erin shrugged. "Maybe. But that comes back to what you believe, what faith you have, or have not."

He leaned forward. "Have you ever seen the 'pale blue dot' picture? You know, the shot of Earth taken way out past Jupiter – the Voyager picture?"

"Should I have?"

"It was the last shot before the camera powered down. And what a picture. A tiny insignificant dot floating alone in the vastness of space. But on that dot's surface, life! When you see that image, it's truly mind-blowingly stunning for anyone with half an ounce of soul. All of life's joys, delights, disasters, triumphs, all contained on that minute blue dot. Billions and billions of life-forms swimming, walking, crawling, and flying over its surface—"

"Okay, Fletch, I get it," Erin said, putting her bottle on the table beside her. "I believe you. A fantastic picture, and it stirs your soul. But what's your point?"

"My point is, why are we here? Why on that small blue dot? And what else is out there? What else lurks in the shadows, watching and waiting for the unwary …" Like the terror that had descended on them at the mountain.

Erin's keen eyes scanned his face. "What is it you really want to ask, Fletch?"

Was it that obvious? "You say we need to help your friends, but what does that really mean? Let's say you meet this professor that Robert knows from his past, and maybe you meet this mysterious Keeper, whatever, whoever, that is. Then what? What do you actually plan to do here? And all this because of voices …" He caught himself, not wanting to tread that path. He took a swig of his beer.

"Because of voices in my head? Is that what you mean?"

"I didn't mean it like that."

Erin tilted her head, her eyes narrowing. "Do you think I'm crazy?"

"No," he said fiercely. He glanced around at the tables near them, then looked back at her. "No," he said more quietly. "You're no crazier than me."

Her brows rose.

"I mean, no, you're not crazy," he said quickly. "That voice you hear … well, maybe it could be … I mean, I think …"

He floundered as more than simple irritation clouded Erin's face – she was pissed off.

Fletcher silently kicked himself. *I'm messing this up.* And he didn't want to do that.

Because I want to help her.

And there it was, the simple, honest truth. Despite enduring an horrific assault on his senses that he never wanted to experience again, he wanted to help. Because whatever had come to them that night had been truly evil. *And I can't walk away and leave Erin to face this alone.* But he needed to know more. "This is all hard to take in," he said softly, "and yes, including the voices in your head."

Erin's steely eyes watched him, waiting.

He took a slug of his beer, then: "None of it makes sense to me, and I've a million and one questions storming around my head. Like why is it happening, and why is it happening only to us, a bunch of insignificant people on this insignificant pale blue dot? And what actually are these things we've seen? Ghosts? Devils? Deranged spirits?" He grimaced. "And to top it all, we're relying on Robert to help us, a man who betrayed a friend, one who had trusted him for most of his young life. If I stop and think about this too much, I struggle to believe it's all happening …"

He waited for her to comment, but she said nothing. He downed the last of his beer, then looked around and caught the attention of the waiter. "Another beer, please. And you?" he asked, turning to Erin.

"I'm fine."

As the waiter walked away, he saw a quiet frustration still simmering on Erin's face. "The daemon that spoke to you," he said. "That whale daemon. What is it?"

She was silent for a moment, then, as though accepting she had to offer something, she sighed and leaned forward. "A daemon called Balena."

Fletcher tensed. She'd deftly sidestepped his previous efforts to find such an answer.

"Balena serves a spirit of the sea, and once aided another from a distant age."

"Do you know who he helped, and why?"

She shook her head.

"But it's not like that thing we saw at the mountain?"

"Would I be talking to it if it was?" There was an edge to her voice.

"Okay, okay," he said, raising his hands. "Fine. It's not." He frowned. "So what is this Balena exactly?"

She looked down at her beer.

"You don't know, do you?"

Glancing up, she said, "In the way you mean, no, I don't know what this daemon is. But I sense no evil from it. I sense … I sense the same surge of hope in my soul that I felt from Beth and from the other woman at the mountain that night." She hesitated. "Yes, there is fear. Yes, my head aches from a strange presence in my mind. But I trust it."

He saw the belief in Erin's eyes. *But others have believed.* "Robert trusted those guiding him in the past. He sensed no evil in them either."

Erin winced. "I've thought of that too. Maybe Robert didn't see the evil in the one that spoke with him. Or maybe he did and ignored it, the pull of finding his parents too great. All I can say is, I sense no evil in the one that spoke with me."

Sense no evil ... Was that enough? Was her belief that this whale daemon sought to aid them enough to be sure they weren't striding into mortal danger? He saw Erin watching him closely. And he saw the desperate yearning in her eyes. *She wants my help.* Something shifted inside. He didn't know enough to be sure of the right path, or what might be lurking in the shadows, but it didn't matter, he realised. He would continue to help Erin as he could, honouring his promise to her friend Jessica.

A warmth kindled deep within. *And I want to help Erin. I ...*

Before the distracting thought could fully land, the server appeared, placing a paper coaster on the table, followed by an ice-cold beer.

"Thank you," Fletcher murmured, signing the paper chit and handing it back. The server gave a brief nod, then walked away.

He picked up his beer, then sat back with a sigh. "Okay. I believe you. I trust you." He smiled, holding up his bottle. "But maybe I need a couple more of these to fully understand it."

Erin's face visibly relaxed, tension easing from her frame. "Thanks, Fletch. That means a lot."

He took a slug of beer. "Now, for the rest of the evening, I suggest we steer clear of talk of daemons and such like. Agreed?"

She smiled. "Agreed."

Frazzled, he took another swig of his beer.

And during the evening, took several more to hold the swirling doubts at bay.

*

Erin groaned as she glanced at the clock on her bedside table, her pounding head punishing her for their overlong stay at the bar. *Ten o'clock!* What time had she agreed to meet Fletcher? And Robert should have arrived by now. She pulled the sheet off her and—

"Good morning," came Fletcher's deep voice from across the room.

Erin yelped and hauled the sheet back over her. Eyes peeping over the top of the cover, she saw him standing at the bathroom door, a towel wrapped around his waist. "I wondered when you'd wake up," he said, smiling. "I told you whiskey was a bad idea."

"What … what are you doing in here?" she stumbled.

He looked at her, his head tilting to one side. "You don't remember?"

She stared at him. *Remember what?*

"Well then," Fletcher said, stepping into the room. "This is rather awkward."

"Stay where you are," Erin said quickly. Through the fog of her hangover, she desperately tried to remember. *We left the bar together. We came to our rooms together. And …* "I remember last night just fine. I went to bed. Nothing …" She glowered at him. "Why are you here?"

Fletcher smiled. "You sure you don't remember?"

Glaring at him, her anger rose. "It's not a joke. Why are you in my room?"

"Probably because this is *my* room?"

Erin stared at him for a moment, then turned to look at the room. She knew immediately. This was not her room. *I followed him, and …*

She heard a chuckle from Fletcher. "After we left the bar, you wanted to finish that story you were telling. You followed me to my room, sat on my bed … then fell asleep."

She remembered. *I was so tired.* A sudden dread thought flashed through her mind. *Where are my clothes?* She pulled the covers closer around her.

"That wasn't me," he said, raising his hands. "At some point, I heard you get up, walk into the bathroom, then come back and climb back into bed. I guess that last whiskey was enough for you to think you were in your own room." He pointed to the floor. "That was my bed for the night."

Erin, you're an idiot, she scolded herself. *A stupid fool. Cut out the whiskey next time.* "I—"

The bed shook as a tremendous blast thundered from within the hotel.

"What the hell was that?" Erin gasped, eyes wide. "What's—"

A piercing siren sounded in the corridor outside.

"That's the fire alarm!" Fletcher exclaimed. "We've got to get out of here!" He grabbed his bag. "Aah! Where are my pants?"

"Where are my clothes!" Erin yelled, still holding the sheet around her as the siren continued to ring.

Fletcher grabbed his trousers from the floor and struggled into them. "Come on. You have to move."

Head throbbing, Erin stared at him in dismay. *This can't be happening. It—*

"What's that?" Fletcher hissed, looking up at the air-conditioning unit. "That's smoke!"

Holding the covers up to her neck, Erin pushed herself up. "Are you sure?"

Fletcher reached over and yanked the covers from the bed. "Move!"

Erin yelped. She grabbed a pillow, covering her body.

"Look," Fletcher growled. "Forget your modesty, just get dressed! We need to leave!"

Her gaze flicked from him, then to the smoke drifting into the room, and then back to him.

"Aargh!" Fletcher exclaimed, picking up his bag. "Look, I'm dressed. I'll see you outside this door in thirty seconds."

He ran to the door, wrenched it open, and left.

Erin immediately leapt out of bed and frantically grabbed her scattered clothes.

Moments later, she ran from the room, a small bag in one hand.

Thick black smoke swirled above her head.

"Let's get to the stairs," Fletcher snapped, already striding down the corridor.

"What's happened?"

"I don't know. An explosion … or worse."

Worse? "Like what?"

Fletcher didn't answer.

And yet an alarming answer came to her, one not unheard of in this North Frykan country. *A bomb?* "What do we do?" she said as they hurried through the fire exit into the emergency staircase.

"Get out. Get to the muster point."

Muster point? "Where's that?"

"Out front, across the street, on the pavement by the river."

As they quickly descended towards the ground floor, frightened guests from other floors rushed into the stairwell, adding to the sense of acute panic. Dropping another level, they came to an abrupt halt as they met a stationary crowd on the stairs. Several people were shouting to those below, but no one was moving.

"What's going on down there?" Fletcher shouted.

A bearded man a few steps down looked up at them. "The exit door won't open." Erin heard the distress in his voice.

Fletcher spat a curse, then glanced at Erin. "Follow me." He pushed his way through the crowd on the stairs below them, ignoring the irate curses from those reluctant to let him past. Holding on to his t-shirt tightly, Erin followed closely behind, her fear growing.

"What's the problem?" Fletcher said as they reached the fire door.

"The door won't open," a stocky man by the door said, sweating profusely. "It's unlocked but blocked from the other side."

Fletcher stepped up to the door and gave it a push, then a shove with his shoulder. It didn't move. "We'll have to go back up and find a different way. Can you—"

Erin shrieked as another tremendous blast sounded from within the hotel, and a wall of heat rushed down the stairwell. People screamed and Erin saw smoke streaming into the stairwell from the floor above.

"Stop pushing!" she shouted, the press of people around her growing as those above fled from the smoke.

"We have to get out!" a man shouted from above. "Get that door down there open!"

Erin looked up. A torrent of black smoke poured into the stairwell – for now, it streamed up and away from them to the floors above.

"Is everybody okay up there?" Fletcher shouted.

"Does it look okay to you?" the same man answered.

"We can't close the fire door up here," came another panicked shout. "Please, open the door!"

"Give me a little space," Fletcher grunted, pushing towards the exit door. People shuffled out of the way as best they could, then Fletcher stepped back and launched himself at the door.

It didn't move an inch.

A woman pushed her way to his side and hammered her fists on the door. "Can anyone hear us?" she shouted. "Is anyone there? Open the door!"

Erin heard someone shouting in Araci, and another speaking softly as if saying a prayer. Hands shaking, she turned to Fletcher. "What can we do?"

"We'll have to go up and see if there's another way out. We can't stay here – this place will fill up with smoke in no time."

But as Erin looked up, she saw the thick black smoke pouring into the stairwell had already formed a dark, deadly cloud, its swirling base seeming to reach for those clogging the staircase as they strove to escape. "We can't get back up there," she whispered, already feeling the oppressive pressure of the seething crowd around her.

"This can't be happening," Fletcher hissed by her side. She felt him struggle to turn back to the fire door. "Why the hell won't it open?"

As she watched him push his way to the door, the crowd behind her surged – the stifling crush of heaving bodies around her intensified. "Let us pass," shouted a man. Another shouted – pleaded – in Araci, the terror in the woman's voice slicing through Erin's soul.

"We can't move," Erin shouted with growing despair as the crush of bodies inexorably tightened around her. "You have to stop pushing. We can't breathe."

"We can't stay where we are!" a man shouted. "We need to get out!"

Another surge swept through the crowd, and the sweat-drenched bodies jammed even tighter around her.

Unable to move, she suddenly struggled to breathe.

A glacial dread flooded through her. *We're not going to get out of this.*

Someone screamed, and the crowd surged again.

A body – man or woman, she didn't know – pressed with chilling force against her chest.

She fought for a breath – but it wouldn't come.

In that moment, she knew true terror. *We're going to die.*

A flurry of images flashed through her mind. Of her mother and her father. Of Jess, of Beth, of Trish … and of the friend they'd lost, Eshe.

And of Fletch.

I don't want to die. Please don't let me die here.

And yet, she was unable to take even a single breath of life.

This can't be real. This—

A crash of breaking glass sounded beyond the fire-exit door.

"What's happening?" cried an anguished voice.

"Help us!" cried another by the door.

Yes, help us, cried Erin's fractured mind. *Please, someone—*

The harsh sound of grating metal cut through the air …

Then a blaze of light flooded into the stairwell.

Instantly, a flood of frantic humanity surged towards the light, and Erin was swept outside on a wave of stunned disbelief. Gasping for breath and fighting to stay on her feet, she lurched over the dusty ground, carried along in the crowd's panicked bid for freedom. Struck in the shoulder, she stumbled out of the crowd and onto clear ground. Staggering onwards for several steps, she then came to a halt, unable to believe she'd escaped. She fell to her knees, sucking in deep lungfuls of wondrously fresh air. *I'm alive! We're alive!*

She knelt, head bowed, savage relief flooding through her as others streamed past. *We almost died. We—*

"Erin!"

She looked up, her breathing ragged, searching for Fletcher.

"Over here!" she heard him shout.

Turning, she saw him standing a short distance away, waving her over.

She quickly climbed to her feet, then hurried over to him. "We could have died in there," she whispered, fighting back tears.

Fletcher nodded, visceral relief etched on his drawn, sweat-ridden face. He laid a gentle hand on her arm. "Are you okay?"

Wiping an eye, she nodded. "But that was hell."

"I thought ... I thought we wouldn't make it."

She licked her dry lips. "We almost didn't," she whispered.

Fletcher glanced back to the hotel, and she followed his gaze. As people ran from the back of the hotel, smoke poured from a jagged rent in the wall above.

"That's our floor," she said, hands still trembling.

Fletcher said nothing.

Her thoughts returned to that fraught, moment when they'd heard the explosion. Had it been an accident? Or ... "Was it a bomb?"

His expression grim, Fletcher gestured towards the fire-escape door. "That car was parked across the door, that's why it wouldn't open. Someone moved it out of the way just in time."

Scanning the wall, Erin saw a car sitting a short way from the fire exit. Its passenger window was smashed, and the car door open. "Why would someone ..." Her breath caught. "Someone parked it there on purpose? Why—"

"Fletcher!" a voice called.

They turned to see a bespectacled, grim-faced man walked towards them.

"Robert?" Fletcher exclaimed. "What are you doing here?"

"I was invited," he said, scowling. "By you, remember? We need to go. Follow me."

"Hold on," Erin stammered, her stressed mind twisting further. "What *are* you doing here?"

Robert glared at her. "They bombed the hotel. It's not safe here. Follow me, I'll explain on the way." He walked away, weaving a path through the melee of people scattered across the open ground.

Erin stared after the retreating bookseller in disbelief. She turned to Fletcher, her heart hammering in her chest. "When did he get here? And how does he know it was a bomb?"

Fletcher's narrowed gaze followed Robert. "I've no idea. But I've no idea on anything that's been happening here."

Glancing back to the burning hotel, Erin ran her fingers through her sweat-drenched hair. What hell had they landed in here? *And who do we trust?* As she glanced along the wall of the hotel, she froze. A familiar, wiry man in a black jacket was watching them from the far corner of the hotel. She grabbed Fletcher's arm. "Look! That's the man who stole my bag."

Fletcher spun around, but as she pointed, the thief drew back, then slipped behind the wall of the hotel. He frowned. "You sure it was him?"

"I'm sure," she hissed. "It was the thief." Her gut clenched. *A simple thief? Or something more?* She turned back to Fletcher. "That man ... a bomb ..."

"And the exit door blocked. Yes, this stinks." He faced her, his features grim. "You should rethink what you're doing here, Erin. Maybe this wasn't aimed at us, but that thief coming back here ..." He shook his head. "You're entering a dangerous world, one that's almost killed you." He laid his hand on her arm. "Are you sure of what you're doing – what we're doing? Maybe we back off this plan, and just go to the police and tell them the thief is here. Let them figure out what's happened."

Erin stared at him, confused, uncertain. After what had just happened, should they abandon their quest and go to the police?

Of course, shouted a fearful part of her.

Follow the Keeper, said a quiet yet potent voice deep within.

Fletcher's troubling question harried her. *Are you sure of what you're doing?*

No. I'm scared. Terrified.

She glanced back to the bookseller, who'd crossed the open ground, heading towards a side road beyond. How had he found them? How had he known they'd be there? *Can we trust him?* The remembered words of the whale daemon, Balena, drifted through her mind. *The daemon said we needed him to take us to this Keeper, to one who may help my friends.*

Her gaze on the bookseller, she strove to quell the cacophony of her thoughts. Because despite the terrors they had faced, she was sure of one thing. Whatever hell they needed to pass through, she had to help her friends – and the bookseller might be the only one to allow her to do that. "We need Robert. I don't like it, but we have to follow this through."

Fletcher nervously rubbed his goatee. "Someone planted a bomb. You could have died. Do you understand that?"

She saw the deep worry in his eyes. "I know," she whispered, ignoring the terrible churning in her stomach. "But we came here to find this Keeper. That's still what I want to do." *It's what I have to do.*

He studied her, doubt – and fear – clear in his eyes. Then he sighed. "Then I'll go on with you." A grim smile crossed his lips. "But I must be mad."

A rush of relief sweeping through her, she stepped forward and hugged him. "Thank you, Fletch. Thank you."

He held her close for a moment, then stepped away. "Thank me when we get back home. Then buy me a cold beer."

Forcing a smile, she took his hand in hers. "I do need to do this, Fletch. I'm sure it's the right thing to do."

His face hardened. "Then let's find out what Robert has to say for himself."

Hands clasped tightly together, they set off across the square.

Crossing the dust-laden ground, she glanced back. The black-jacketed man at the far corner of the hotel was gone ... but through the distorted, heat-hazed air, she saw a faint image of a tall man with long white hair. Her breath catching, she slowed to a stop, a harrowing vision returning. A vision of the white-haired man who'd confronted her and Tricia in what seemed an age past in the lakeside village. "Where is the Guardian?" that man had demanded of them. Then another memory of their journey north to the mountain where this man had demanded of Fletcher the same information. *He'd been looking for Jess.*

She was aware of Fletcher coming to her side. "What's wrong?" came his concerned voice.

She blinked.

The vision was gone.

"Erin?"

She stared at the empty space at the end of the hotel. "I thought ..." *I thought I saw another horror in this unending nightmare.*

"He killed Eshe. That man slaughtered my sister." Those overheard words of Jessica's slipped into Erin's mind. Words Jessica had spoken to River at Mount Hope before they'd driven the daemon away. In the terror of the moment, the words had been lost. *But I hear them now. Jess believed this white-haired man killed her sister.*

Fletcher gently held her arm. "You okay?"

As Erin scanned the vacant area, doubts crept in. Had she really seen that terrifying man? Or were the horrors of the day creating their own haunting daemons? *And if he was there, what can we do? Does it change what I need to do now?* She turned and glanced at Fletcher, who was studying her, frowning. *I need Fletch with me. Don't worry him with this right now.* "I'm okay," she answered. "Just fighting the nerves."

"You sure?"

"Sure," she managed. *Keep moving, else I'll turn and run.* "Come on. We're losing Robert."

Ignoring Fletcher's doubtful gaze, she pulled him away.

With Fletcher muttering to himself, they quickly crossed the dusty square in pursuit of Robert, who was turning a corner into the neighbouring street. Reaching the corner, they saw the bookseller standing beside a large vehicle, some kind of 4x4.

"Hurry," Robert urged. "It's not safe here."

"Whose is this?" Fletcher eyes narrowed on the car. "Where are we going?"

"Get in. I'll explain on the way." Robert walked around the car and climbed into the front passenger seat.

As Erin hesitated, the smiling face of an older man appeared at the driver's window. "Hello. My name is Professor Khaled. I am most pleased to meet you."

"We'll do the introductions as we drive," came Robert's impatient voice from inside. "Get in."

As the professor's head pulled back, Fletcher cast her a questioning glance. She girded herself. *This is my choice.* She gave an affirmative nod. His expression grim, Fletcher opened the back door and held it for her. She climbed inside, sliding along to the middle seat of three and manoeuvring next to a young man sleeping in the seat beside the far window. Fletcher climbed in beside her and closed the door. Moments later, they were driving down the quiet side street before swinging out into the heavier traffic of a main road.

With gut-deep unease and swirling unanswered questions, Erin stared at the back of the professor's head. So, this was the man they'd come to meet? Robert's old acquaintance, the one who could know more of the world her friends had entered.

The one who may lead them to the Keeper.

She glanced at the man sleeping on the seat beside her. *A cool one to be sleeping while we barge in here.*

"What's this all about, Robert?" came Fletcher's voice beside her.

"Someone may have tried to kill you," Robert said, his eyes on the road ahead.

The image of the black-jacketed man came to Erin's mind. And the white-haired man.

"And why do you think that?" Fletcher pressed.

Robert glanced in the car's mirror, catching Erin's eyes. "I was told there was a threat to you. To us."

Erin licked her lips. "Told by who?"

"By a mutual friend of the sea," Robert replied, wiping his brow. "We've been ... in contact."

The whale daemon had spoken to Robert? *Why didn't the daemon speak with me?*

"Our friend knew some people here in the city posed a threat," he continued. "But not who or when. I'd just arrived at the hotel to meet you when the bomb exploded. We were led out to the muster area, where I met you."

Her unease deepened. Robert had appeared after the explosion. Could he have been involved? *No, he couldn't have turned again. Not after all we've spoken of.*

"Our friend tried to contact you," Robert was saying. "Last evening and this morning, but said you were otherwise engaged and that your mind wouldn't receive him."

The daemon *had* tried to contact her. *To warn me.* But the drinks in the bar … *And then …* "I … I …"

"You were nursing a hangover is what you're trying to say," Fletcher said smoothly.

"It's clear someone planned it carefully, knowing which rooms you were in, and which escape route you would take when they triggered the fire alarm. They'd parked deliberately across that exit."

"Who tried to kill us?" she managed, her mouth dry.

"Agents of the enemy," Professor Khaled said, beeping the horn at an errant driver.

Erin glanced at the professor. "Which enemy?"

"*The* Enemy," Khaled said, turning the car into a busy street. "The one commanding those your friends have already fought. The one commanding those you saw at the mountain."

The white-haired man. And that hellish creature that tore at our minds, the creature that Beth drove away. What did this professor know of those events?

"I've told him what he needs to know," Robert said, his eyes on her in the mirror, his words seeming to answer part of her thoughts. "He's been a friend for a long time."

Her heart beat a little faster. *A friend of yours, but is this professor a friend of ours?* A part of her chilled. Why had she thought that? *Because a cold finger runs down my back when I look at this professor.*

"Who's this?" Fletcher asked, gesturing to the sleeping man beside her.

"Asim," the professor said, beeping his horn again at a car cutting across them. "A young man I met when he was a child. He has stories of another land. Stories few believe."

Erin's eyes widened. Was this the one? Was this the Keeper?

"He sleeps now," the professor said. "You can speak with him when he awakens. That will be … interesting."

Erin gazed at the peaceful face of the young man, his head resting on his hand, his short, dark hair ruffled by his fingers. His sleep seemed calm and still, the sleep of one at ease with himself, his surroundings. And yet, a prickling sense of something suppressed, hidden, seemed to play on the man's serene features. *And his aura ...* At the half-formed, poorly understood thought, a sudden certainty gripped her. *This* is *the Keeper. This is the one I was sent to find.* Her thoughts leapt on. *He can help us. He can help my friends.* But where there should have been elation, doubt rushed in. What did that really mean? How exactly would this Keeper help them? Her stomach twisted as her thoughts spiralled. What could he do? What did she expect him to do?

She realised she was wringing her hands. *Calm! Calm yourself.*

She felt Fletcher's hand on hers.

"I'm scared," she whispered, seeking refuge from her twisting thoughts from the one person here she trusted.

"You and me both," he said in a low whisper. "Let's see what these people have to say, then we'll decide what to do. It's why we're here, right?"

It is. But I'm still scared.

She nodded.

Fletcher squeezed her hand, then turned to look out the window.

Erin drew a slow, silent breath and relaxed her hands. *Remember why you're here. You wanted to find the Keeper, and now you have.* She glanced at the sleeping young man by her side. *Hear what he has to say. Understand how to help my friends.* Her gaze lingered on Asim for a moment, then shifted to the professor and the bookseller. And she needed to find out what these two had been doing. They were friends, they were partners in study, but what had they studied? *And what have they found?*

Unsettled, uncertain, she closed her eyes, and the world disappeared.

But the sense of foreboding grew.

CHAPTER SEVEN

Could the Guardian have been told more by now? Yes. Should we have told her more? Maybe. But this game had many ears.

"Explain that again, Warrior," the mountainous man growled, standing by the ember fire within the cavernous rock shelter. "Because it still makes little sense."

Lanky glowered at the leader of the Islanders. "What don't you understand? We can't fight our way south to the enemy heartland. It would take months. We need to be smart, act quickly. The Warriors have to find a way to cripple the power of Kaos soon, else—"

"The Warriors must do what we brought them here for," Parig growled, his massive frame looming over the surrounding group as he scanned their strained faces. "To fight. To push these devils of Kaos from our lands. To—"

"No, we won't do it that way," Lanky retorted. "That isn't going to happen."

"Well, then this is a waste of our time," Parig grunted. His gaze levelled on River. "We will leave for our own homeland in the morning, and I suggest you and your tribe are with us." He gestured dismissively to Lanky. "If these are not the promised Warriors, then each should look to their own – we must defend our own people and families." He turned to go.

"Sit down!" came a strident voice. "This meeting isn't yet finished."

Parig faced his daughter, glowering.

Rind glared back, unbowed. "Sit. When did you ever turn your back on your allies?"

Parig stood for a moment, his massive hands clenching and unclenching. Then grunting something unheard, he strode to his place in the circle and dropped to the ground. He flicked an angry glance towards Lanky.

Save for the rain, which was again hammering on the weather-beaten rocks outside the shelter, relentless in its efforts to reach inside, silence fell around the ember pit. Ten select of the Iyes and their allies searched for answers in either the weary faces of one another or the pulsating, fiery glow of the embers.

This isn't going well, Jessica thought, her fingers caressing the golden-hued wood of the Staff by her side. After an encouraging start, where each group had shared updates on what they knew about such things as enemy movements and allies' readiness, they'd reached an impasse on what to do next. For Parig, it was clear. He had seen the destructive power of the Warriors in battle and was now certain they would prevail if the Warriors led them into battle, obliterating their enemies as they marched south to challenge the Ka. But both Lanky and she disagreed. *IY told us we need to find the Kade, find the source of the enemy's power.* And they'd already delayed too long. Yes, they'd been continually harried by enemy forces – *and we thought IY would have returned by now* – but in hindsight, they should have acted sooner.

Sudden anger flared. Where were those who were supposed to help them? Where were the daemons? Where was IY? *We're doing what we can to understand this world – to help this world. Why aren't you with us?*

Eyes hardening, she glanced across at the scowling Parig. Now that the Islanders were here, the Iyes had allies to help protect them. The Warriors – some Warriors – were needed elsewhere. *We can no longer wait. We must act.*

"Look," came Lanky's tired voice into the silence. "We Warriors didn't ask to be here, we didn't want to be here, but here we are, caught in a hellish struggle for survival that we're fighting to understand. A struggle that's somehow dragged the fate of you and your people into its grubby maw." He glanced up, eyes locking onto Parig. "Yet we have agreed to help, and yes, using what powers we can. But I repeat, I will not blaze through the land wreaking death and destruction on whoever steps in our way. That's not going to happen."

"Then, I repeat," Parig said, "you are useless to me."

A flash of anger darkened Lanky's eyes. "How can you say that? You've only just arrived. You—"

"If you will not fight," Parig rasped, leaning forward, baring his teeth, "you have no use to me or my people."

"Now, hold on," Lanky said, bristling, "I didn't say I won't fight. I—"

"Stop!" Rind commanded, standing swiftly, then stepping over to the two increasingly fractious men. "You will cease now!"

Jessica silently applauded. *Good work. This is getting us nowhere.* And wasn't Lanky originally sent south to be their ambassador, paving the way for the Warriors' triumphant arrival? *Now, that was a good choice.*

She glanced at Lanky, who was still glaring at Parig but remained silent. *He listens to Rind. He likes Rind.* A flicker of unease ran through her. What would the Continuum make of a burgeoning love between two souls born millennia apart? With a sudden, unexpected wrench in her heart, she glanced at Beth. *But who am I to advise on love? My heart once lay with one who could not accept it.*

Rind's firm voice cut through her distraction. "I'd like to hear from one who has not yet spoken." She gestured to River. "Mother …"

Drawn back to the moment, Jessica steadied her wandering thoughts. *Be happy for Lanky.* Maybe love could come from the most unexpected places, the most unexpected times …

She watched as River slowly regarded those around the circle, her gaze lingering on each face as if considering their worth. "I have questions," the girl said, a coldness to her voice.

Jessica saw puzzled looks on several faces.

River turned to Lanky. "Why do you not connect with the daemon freely offered by our Spirits?" she said, an edge to her voice. "Do you reject our Story?"

Jessica took a sharp intake of breath as astonished eyes fell on Lanky. She leaned towards River and said in a low voice, "Is this something you want to talk about here?"

"It must be asked."

Jessica stiffened. *What is she doing?*

Lanky held River's challenging gaze, unflinching. "Because I don't trust him," he answered evenly. "I will take the power. I will use the power. But on my terms only."

"So, you may not be aligned with the will of IY?"

Does she doubt his commitment to her tribe, to their cause? Jessica thought, watching Lanky consider his answer. *After what he's given to defend her tribe.*

Lanky eventually shrugged. "That may well be true. But—"

"And so, how do we trust you?"

Before Lanky could answer, River's gaze shifted to Beth, who sat by his side. "And you," the Iyes's shaman said in the same quiet, challenging tone, "why do you not unleash your true power?"

It was barely noticeable, but Jessica saw Beth tense – from anger at River's challenge, or from her own deeper fear? Beth's next words gave

Jessica her answer. "I'm scared of what it will do to me, of what I may do." Her eyes briefly flicked to Jessica. "And I fear for what I may have done." She looked back at River, her face hardening. "I want more time to prepare for what I might become, but still, I fight."

"And you," River said, turning to the lean, dark-eyed man opposite her as though instantly dismissing Beth's answer. "What are your thoughts on what you've heard here today?"

Spider, who had been sitting quietly, his keen eyes sparkling in the firelight as he prodded the glowing embers with a bent twig, glanced up. Jessica couldn't help but notice the scout's matted hair was as unkempt as usual. "Helps me blend into the undergrowth," she'd heard him once quip. The scout nervously cleared his throat—

"Now hold on," Parig said loudly. "That one has no voice here. He—"

"Silence," Rind rasped, her voice carrying effortlessly around the circle. "I asked him here as the representative of Bear, the leader of this tribe. You will not insult me again, Father, or you will leave."

Jessica saw a flash of anger on Parig's face as he tensed. The torrential rain beyond the shelter sounded as thunder as all waited for the mountainous man's temper to flare. Then the Islander grinned. "That's my daughter," he grunted, jabbing his elbow into the ribs of Artur, the young leader of the Mancs tribe beside him, who grimaced in obvious pain.

"Spider?" Rind prompted.

Dropping the twig by the fire, Spider glanced apprehensively around the group. "Well," he began, hesitantly, "it seems to me I'm hearing questions of trust. Simple questions they may be, yet they're important questions lying at the heart of each tribe – at the heart of our shared history." He rubbed his clean-shaven chin, then sat a little taller. "And if I remember that history well, all leaders of our alliance pledged their fealty to IY ..." He glanced at the leader of the Islanders. "Even you, Parig, one reluctant to commit to any but Taran."

Parig glared at him, muttering under his breath.

"That alliance between our tribes preserves the hard-won commitment made so long ago, one carried through generation after generation by our brave ancestors. An enduring commitment to defend this precious Land from the Enemy's foul grasp." Spider glanced at Jessica. "And – as I believe we all accept – in those times of our people's direst need, the Warriors can be called to deliver our salvation."

He paused, then looked around the attentive group. "And this is what our late Mother decided was needed. Seeing the rising threat of

Kaos, Naga made the Request for aid … and these three travellers answered that call. And then another from these lands was revealed as a Warrior," he continued with a glance at River. "But it appears none of these four wished for, or desired, this terrible burden thrust upon them. Even so, here they remain. Whether through choice or necessity, whether with a driving passion or with pained regrets, they stand by our side."

He scanned the silent faces arrayed around him, the hard glint in his eyes throwing out a challenge. "Trust? Yes, you owe them your trust." He glanced at Parig. "We *must* trust them. We must *listen* to them."

No sooner had Spider's words drifted out into the rain than a slow clapping echoed around the shelter. "Very good, little spider," Parig said. "Soothing words you have spoken, a tale fit to be told to our children. But such words do not defeat our enemies. Only decisive actions, driven home by the powerful fists of the brave, will clear our lands of the scum of Kaos. And I still see no one willing to act."

"River, please finish," Rind grated, glaring at her father.

Parig's eyes blazed. "Pah!" he grunted, turning away.

Jessica looked across at River, seeing the girl's strained face staring intently into the fire …

The young shaman suddenly glanced up and caught her gaze. It was if a ripple of cold air had swept over her. *I can feel her, taste her.* She instinctively latched on to River's cast emotions, and tasted an acute, restless fear. A deep-seated fear of someone unknown and unseen, of someone hidden and dangerous. *The traitor! She is still searching for the traitor.* Holding herself steady, unmoving, Jessica sensed something more. She pushed her mind further, slipping past the projected fear, and encountered a calming aura of strength, of unwavering trust. *She trusts me. She trusts the Warriors.*

"I know what you did for me in your land, Jessica," River said. "You returned me to my home, and for that I am grateful. You know how grateful," she said pointedly.

With sudden understanding, Jessica simply nodded in acknowledgement. River was clearly still searching for the traitor, but in those pulsed emotions, the Mother of the Iyes had conveyed her trust in the Warriors. But with the others, it seemed she was treading a careful path, allowing some things to be said, and some things to be held close. *Only she and IY understand precisely how they are planning to draw the traitor out.*

"And I have seen and heard what you have done," River said, turning to Lanky. "Your growing mastery of the energy of the Land is impressive and commendable. And," she said to Beth, "I have seen how you fought to defend us, both here and in your land. And I understand your torment. I too …" She broke off, her face betraying a flash of regret.

Jessica felt the girl's pain. *I know your own torment.*

Settling herself, River scanned the seated group. "But all this being said, something is not right."

"Finally!" Parig grunted. "That, I can agree with."

"Yes, something is not right," River repeated, "something I cannot yet see." Her expression showed a sudden determination, a certainty of path. "But despite that, what is clear in this moment is we cannot continue as we are."

"We all agree on that," Parig said. "What I need to know is where these Warriors will fight."

River held Parig's louring gaze for a moment, then turned to Jessica. "We cannot wait any longer for IY and the daemons to return to us. You should act now." Her sharp eyes delivered more than her words.

The Kade. IY told us to recover the Kade.

River switched her attention to the others. "Warriors, Rind, and Parig, stay to hear what will be said. I thank the rest for your patience, and we will talk again later."

With a quiet rustling of clothing and shuffling of feet, Gravel, Spider, and the others at the meeting quickly left the shelter, acknowledging River as they passed.

Jessica, Beth, and Lanky sat, watching River with quizzical gazes. Parig scowled.

River turned back to Jessica. "IY told you to recover the Kade?"

"She did."

"And that it lies hidden in the Ka homeland?"

Jessica nodded.

"Then that is where you should go."

Lanky frowned. "And how precisely do we enter the heartland of the enemy?"

The faintest curl of a smile crossed River's lips. "You walk in."

Jessica heard Beth's intake of breath.

River leaned forward. "Listen well, then decide."

*

Jessica watched as River pulled her jacket closer around her before hurrying out into the rain after Parig. Rind stood, as if to leave.

"Could you stay a moment?" Jessica said.

Rind looked at her, then nodded and sat back down next to Beth and Lanky.

"Thank you," Jessica said, then glanced to the rear of the shelter. "You can come out now, Trish."

"At last," Tricia said, peeling out of the shadows. "Do you know how cold it is back here?" She walked up to the warmth of the ember fire and held out her hands. "You should give this fire a poke. It's going out."

Jessica glanced at the fire, which Freya had been tending during the meeting, bringing fresh fuel from the camp's two sheltered stock fires out in the gorge. It was yet another learning of the realities of life in this age. An active camp like this could not survive without fire on tap. "It's perfectly fine," she said with a faint smile. "We only need the embers, unless you want to smoke us out?"

Tricia muttered something unintelligible and continued to warm her hands.

Jessica turned to Lanky and Beth. "What are your thoughts on River's idea?"

Lanky stroked, then scratched, his short beard. Allowing it to grow had been easier than trying to remain smooth-chinned, and now a sharp obsidian blade kept it in the trim style he said he'd often thought of trying. To Jessica, it had now become part of him. But it seemed the beard came with a price. Lanky relieved the present itch, then glanced at her. "Just walk in? It sounds completely crazy, but the more I think about it, that could be the cleanest way. IY said we wouldn't succeed with brute force on the battlefield, but by stealth and quick minds. If you want stealth, this is it."

A frown creased Beth's brow. "But we know nothing of the Ka – not really. How can you expect to land in their midst and walk around unchallenged?"

"Many new people appear at the Ka's camps," Rind said, fingering the bright yellow wooden beads around her neck. "Some abandoned by their own tribes, others whose tribes have dwindled to an unsustainable level. All these seek the protection provided by the empire of the Ka." She dropped her hands to her lap. "Then there are the greedy, the ruthlessly ambitious, those who hear of the power they might attain if they join the Ka." She pursed her lips, then nodded. "It could work."

Beth glanced at Jessica. "You're forgetting something. That Ka who kidnapped you, the one who took the Staff, he knows what you look like. He knows what the Staff looks like."

"That's not forgotten, but yes, it's a risk. But if he's there, he's only one person within a sprawling camp. If we cross his path, then I get us out, fast." She held up her Staff. "And this?" The embedded crystal vanished, and she held a simple wooden Staff in her hand.

Beth tilted her head. "Where'd you learn that trick?"

"The warg," Lanky grunted. "Seems he has some limited use after all."

Beth regarded the Staff a moment longer. "Fine, they may not recognise you for a while, but we still don't know what this Kade looks like."

"We've been over this," Jessica said, a note of impatience in her voice. "IY says we'll sense it."

"Hah!" Beth snorted, sitting straighter. "And as I keep saying, that's fine for this goddess to say, but—"

"She's not a goddess," Lanky muttered.

Beth glared at Lanky. "My point is this. How long do you plan to wander around in the hornets' nest, prodding things and searching for this Kade, before you get stung?"

"Drop it, Beth," Jessica said in a low voice, glancing at Rind, who watched them carefully. "If IY says we can sense it, I believe her. And remember, you're not going."

Beth glared at Jessica for a moment. Then her shoulders relaxed. "Okay," she said in a quieter voice. "If it's there, and you sense it, what then?"

"That, we will work on. All of us."

Beth's eyes narrowed, but she said nothing.

Lanky cleared his throat. "Like you say, Jess, we need to figure out what we'll do if we find something there, but first, we have to be sure we can get to this site, and quickly." His sharp eyes studied her closely. "*Can* you get us there?"

Jessica's hand closed around the Staff lying across her lap. *Could I? Am I confident enough to take this next step?* A shiver of fear ran through her at a sudden stark vision: of wraithlike creatures of the Dark swarming around her, of her holding the seething masses at bay with a shimmering shield. Her Staff tingled in her hand. *They are creatures of the Void beyond the Continuum,* came a swirling thought from a great distance. *I take us out of the Continuum and into the Void, and then return us to the place and time I wish to be.* She fought to hang on to the ephemeral thread. *I am able to travel into the Void, into the place of the Dark. But it is also the place of the Light.*

"What is the Guardian?" she had asked IY at Naga's funeral.

"The one who can travel the timelines of the Continuum, guarding Warrior companions journeying by her side," IY had answered.

Because the creatures of the Void strove to kill them.

113

And I defend us as we travel.
Because I am the Guardian.
I wield the power of the Light.

Indistinct memories swirled in fragments: the forced journey back to her own time after she'd been challenged by the malignant yellow eye when first attempting to meet the daemons; her spontaneous undoing of Beth's shocking killing of the traitorous bookseller, a correction of the Continuum even IY did not understand; and her reluctant return back to this time with Beth, River, and Tricia. All remembered, yet details vague and confused. But all unbelievable demonstrations of the instinctive wielding of that virulent, febrile power of the Land.

"Jessica?" came Lanky's voice through her swirling thoughts.

She blinked.

Refocussing, she saw him studying her, concern in his eyes. She forced a smile. "I'm okay. Just fighting through this murky fog of confusion."

Lanky scowled, running his hand through his lengthening hair. "Welcome to the club. That isn't going away anytime soon." His gaze sharpened. "So can you get us there?"

She pursed her lips, considering. Despite the confusion of her thoughts, she felt a growing certainty. Unlike those remembered times she had wielded the Land's power, this move to the Ka lands involved no movement through time, no dramatic entry into the hell of the Void beyond the Continuum. Just a simple move within the Land, like the jump from the mountain lair to Rind's camp at the White Crags. *Using the Cords.* Those strings of quivering energy in the ether that IY had shown her were the pathways to the Glades. *And then onwards to a chosen place in the Land. Or a Gate.*

But with others ...

Her eyes narrowed at the remembered words of IY before the goddess of the Iyes had abandoned them. "It will take time to teach, but soon your fellow Warriors will be able to use these Cords to travel within the Land. But even then, the risk of them taking others with them is great."

"And the risk to others when I move them?" Jessica had asked.

A heartbeat's hesitation only, then IY had answered, "You have the skill."

And now, in this moment, it was Jessica who hesitated as Lanky awaited her answer. She reached down for her waterskin, and undoing the stopper, took a mouthful of the cooling liquid. *Do what is needed.*

Resealing the skin, she held Lanky's eyes. "I can get us there. Leave that to me."

Lanky's gaze lingered on her for a moment, then he nodded. "Good."

His face thoughtful, he stood, then walked a few steps from the fire. He turned back to them, his eyes narrowing. "How is this going to work? Who is going? And what do we do when we get there?"

"I will go," Rind said. "Aside from escaping my infuriating father, I can play one of the roles needed. In addition, I suggest two Warriors and probably a fourth person." She glanced at Jessica. "As a witness. To allow word to be sent back to the tribe if …" Rind shrugged.

If we fail.

"Two Warriors?" Lanky said, looking at Jessica.

"You and me," she said firmly. "River should stay here and …" She glanced at Beth. "If it comes to a serious fight down there …"

Beth's expression was pained. "I know. Right now, I'd be a hindrance. I just need to—"

"You don't need to explain," Lanky said quickly. "And considering what the enemy's thrown at us here, you and River are going to be hard-pressed enough on your journey south."

Beth glanced at him, then pursed her lips and nodded.

Rind, spinning one of the beads on her wrist, settled her gaze on Jessica. "You and I won't stand out too much from the crowd – apart from being attractive women, of course." She winked at Jessica, then turned to Lanky. "And so, my friend, you take the role of apprentice – an attractive apprentice, of course."

"Hold on," Lanky said, scowling. "Does that mean general workhorse?"

"I don't know that term, but if that means you prepare the camp and food, carry extra packs for us, that sort of thing, then yes, that's what you are."

His brow furrowed. "I see you aren't joking."

"Someone has to do it."

"So, explain again what you two will be doing."

"I am a tribe emissary, and this is my protector, my guard, if you like."

"Why can't I be the guard?" Lanky asked, standing tall.

"You, a pale northerner, are the odd one out, and in Ka society, you're close to the bottom of the pot – the dregs, you might say. One of the other niceties of Ka culture."

"My dislike of these Ka grows and grows," Lanky growled.

Jessica stood and stretched, her fingers brushing the shelter roof above. The tension eased from her shoulders. "So, we're agreed that we three travel." She glanced at Rind. "But you think we need a fourth?"

"We need backup. Or to say it more clearly, *I* need backup. For that, I suggest Spider."

Lanky grunted in agreement. "A good choice. One I hope we don't need to use in anger."

"That makes two of us, Warrior." Rind looked back at Jessica. "When we arrive, we separate. Spider stays close but not as part of our group. If for some reason I fail, then you find him and join him. As far as others see it, you've simply switched allegiance to another."

Jessica tensed. Failure. They had to plan for it, but she couldn't dwell on it. It was time to act. They had to find the Kade and prevent the release of the Geddon.

The Geddon. She quailed at the name. A destroyer of the world, Fen had said. What horrors could the mind imagine for this? But what *was* this Geddon? What evil force was this that could destroy their world? None could say. *Or won't say.*

And if they found the Kade, what then? *Where does this end?*

She forced the doubts away. For now, they had no choice. *Focus on the Kade. Deliver the Kade to IY.* And try to understand.

She looked out into the gloom of the night. "The rain has eased. I suggest we turn in." She faced the group. "Sleep on it, and we'll regroup in the morning. We'll pool the tribe's knowledge, then prepare ourselves to leave."

"And be crystal clear on the mission target," Beth said firmly. "What do you do if you actually find the Kade? How do you get it out of there?"

Jessica nodded. "Agreed."

But as they moved out into the darkness, her suppressed doubts crept to the fore. How to plan with so little information to hand. A location, a description of a sacred temple, and a statement from IY that she would recognise the Kade when she sensed it. *But where are you now, IY, when we need you the most?*

As fear, her constant companion, struggled to break free, an unbidden image swept into her mind – of a tall and beautiful girl, laughter shining in her striking brown eyes. An image of her wonderful sister. *Eshe. How I wish I could speak to you now. How I wish I could hear your wonderful voice.* But it would never be. That fateful night had taken her most beloved sister from her side. *She cried out for me to save her – and I did nothing.*

Remembering the pain of that night, a loathsome vision returned. Of a shaman, his white hair streaked with black. The shaman who had killed her sister. A shaman of the Dark. *One day, I will find you, devil. And on that day, my revenge will be sweet.*

Holding on to the wonderful image of the sister she loved, she noticed a flickering light approaching from their left, and a moment later, Tricia appeared from the gloom holding a small torch. The three walked silently down the gorge to the camp beyond.

As the image of her sister faded, the doubts returned. *Where does this end?* she asked herself again as they walked through the gloom. *We are not the first Warriors. Will we be – can we be – the last?*

The slightest tingle in her Staff hand, then a sudden chill settled on her.

She glanced around, feeling as though another had arrived by her side – but she saw only her two friends. *Calm yourself. You jump at shadows.* She needed to stay strong, to listen and learn. *For I'm certain there is far more to this than we can see.*

*

The rains had blown over, and sitting in the faint glow of the fire beside her, Jessica could see a myriad of stars scattered across the clear night sky. She was alone, save for the occasional movement of a guard at the distant edge of the camp or the silent flight of an owl gliding through the crisp evening air in search of its next meal. Sleep lay beyond her, her mind unable to break away from the horror of the day, the horror of so many days. Of so many deaths. *And yet we're here to protect them. To save them.*

Yet how quickly had that burden descended? And how long ago? It seemed like only yesterday they'd been simply four close friends reunited, revelling in their cherished time together, sharing their lives, their joys, their worries … *And honouring the memory of my sister.*

That all seemed an eternity ago.

She caught a bright streak in the sky as an alien speck of dust ended its vast interstellar journey in a brief final farewell. *All journeys end.*

But not all were witnessed.

Who will witness us, the Warriors?

She let out a quiet gasp as the sudden reality of that thought hit her. Despite the doubts, despite the fears and uncertainty, they'd accepted it.

We are Warriors.

A ripple of unease ran through her. *And I am the Guardian.*

Her unease deepened. But the Guardian of what? Of the Warriors? Of the Land?

Of the Continuum?

Gazing into the starry sky, her thoughts drifted to that stunning concept Bear had first shared with Beth, and that IY had later described to her. The Continuum. The past, the present, and the future naturally entwined; constantly in flux, yet fully synchronised; compatible, and aligned, any changes seamlessly adjusted, unseen and unknown to all those who lived within.

Life lives, and the Continuum flows.

No matter how it was described, she still struggled to grasp the scale, the mind-bending enormity, of such a thing.

And for a god observing this all-encompassing temporal realm? All that had happened, was happening, and would happen would be seen, all aligned and smoothly flowing as one. Something changed there, in that time and place, and the Continuum would simply adjust, preserving its sublime consistency and alignment.

No paradoxes needed or allowed.

How such a thing could exist, she knew not, but it seemed this was indeed the wondrous yet quietly terrifying place in which she lived. In which she could travel. *A Continuum I could change.*

She absently ran her hand through her tangled hair, her last thought reverberating with sharp, chilling tones. When you had the godlike power to move within the Continuum, whether small moves or gargantuan leaps, what unintended and devastating impact could she have? One simple move to another time may prove immaterial, for it may already be written within time's tapestry of life. But to move and create conflict? How might the Continuum react? How might life react? It might write them out of its story. Their friends and family may not exist. *Forget friends and family – future life might not exist!*

And therein lay a most monumental and spine-chilling thought. Maybe those other Warriors before her *had* changed the course of the Continuum. Maybe the world she lived in now was a product of their actions. *But we may never know that. We could change the course of history – the course of life itself – and no one may ever realise it.* Because she was certain of a stark truth. The Continuum she walked in now was the only current reality. *The Continuum adjusts. Unseen. Unknowable.*

Yet while that instinctive knowledge seemed solid and inviolate, other hazy visions flickered, part-formed, as though ghostly memories at the edges of perception. Of the Void. Of the Cords. Of the Guardian. *Of things I feel I should remember …*

Her breath caught at a staggering thought. *Was there a different me that once existed?* In some turning of the Continuum, had she already walked these lands? She baulked at the enormity of the question. *How could I ever know that?* She glanced up at the starlit sky as if the answers lay there. But the heavens remained silent.

She sat for a while, allowing the storm of her thoughts to ebb. But other questions swirled in its wake. *Was there a different me? One who found someone I loved to walk by my side? One such as Beth? Or another?* She savoured the intoxicating vision for a moment, then, with a heavy heart, released it. If that had been so, then that Jess was now gone, eradicated in a shifting of the Continuum. *Today, I walk alone.* The lament evoked remembered words of Beth: "There's someone out there for you, Jess. And you'll find her – or she'll find you."

Jessica sighed. *But when?*

Her thoughts shifted. Alone? She wasn't truly alone. *I have friends around me. Friends who are by my side. Friends who ...*

Friends who were changing.

That was the truth. Neither Beth nor Lanky – *nor me* – was still the innocent who'd first arrived in this Land. The energy of the Land – the A'ven – was changing them, changing something deep within them. *And that scares me. Terrifies me.*

And what lay ahead of them? Naga and the Iyes's Story had told of an evil that had to be stopped.

Stop the spread of the Dark, the growing reach of Kaos.

Prevent Armageddon.

'*And protect Life,*' came a voice from deep within her.

Jessica started. '*IY?*' She reached out – but sensed nothing.

She cursed, anger flaring. '*Where are you? We can't do this alone.*'

No answer came.

Frustrated, she pulled her fur closer around her as the chill of the night crept past the fire. She, Lanky, and Beth had changed from those innocent arrivals to this age, but just as they'd sought more answers to the threats they faced, all those who'd promised to aid them had vanished: IY; the daemons; the ancient Warriors within; even the Spirits had abandoned the Mother of the Iyes. *No one guides us. But why?* Her frustration deepened. Always the question why, but seldom a useful answer given.

The remembered words of IY returned: "Jalu will aid you." But who was Jalu? *The daemons call me Jalu.* But why? "Because they say Jalu is the Guardian," Lanky had said after his last heated encounter with the daemon Fen. "The Iyes's Story tells of others before us. Other Warriors. It seems these daemons still hark back to those they knew. But I trust no one, Jess. Especially one who wishes to push me aside." And she could understand that completely. There were dangers here beyond their comprehension. *Just look at Beth.* There was an entity within her friend seeking dominance, one who was quick to act, asking questions later. Only River seemed to have accepted the other within her, accepted Revri. *And yet even she fights other hidden battles.*

She pulled her thoughts back to the name IY had spoken. *Jalu.* She lifted her Staff, the purple stone glistening in the glow of the fire's embers. *The daemons call Jalu the Guardian. Did she hold this Staff? Did she know what to do?*

'*I once knew,*' came a gravelly voice.

Jessica sprang to her feet, sucking in energy from the A'ven as a faint apparition appeared on the far side of the dying fire. "Who are you?" she demanded, licks of white energy swirling around her Staff.

"I am Jalu," the ghostly figure said.

Heart pounding, Jessica peered through the gloom to see the form of a strong-featured, dark-haired woman staring back at her, her silvery eyes glinting in the darkness. "What are you?" she said, taking a tentative step forward and cautiously reaching out to sense the energy around the ghostly figure.

"I was once the Guardian. Of another time, another place."

Jessica gasped. Then the daemons were right. Weren't they?

And yet she says she was once *the Guardian. Then what is she now?*

Calming her breathing, she reached out and probed the aura of the ghostly figure. She tasted no foul threat of the Dark, no threatening ripples of energy – but she held herself ready to strike. "Why are you here?"

"You grow in strength. There is a chance you will be the one. I seek to aid you." The woman tilted her head a fraction. "I *have* helped you."

Jessica studied the silver-eyed woman for a moment, then cast a quick glance to the camp. All remained quiet. She looked back at the apparition, still sensing no threat. "If you wish to aid us, then others should hear this. I—"

"No!" the woman hissed softly. "I have little time, and we cannot alert the traitor."

"You know of this?"

Jalu nodded.

"Then I'd be a fool to speak with you. One I don't know."

"I am Jalu," the apparition said. Her next words slipped into Jessica's mind. '*I protected Life, as now you must, Guardian. This is your duty.*'

Jessica's eyes widened. *Protect Life?* A ghost of a memory, a faint and distant recollection, tugged at her mind. Of her hearing these words before. But if so, her memory or another's? Or something planted by one before her? "Who sent you here?"

"I arrived here long ago," Jalu said, glancing to the sky. "From another time, another place." A flash of anger crossed her face as she looked back at Jessica. "Who sent me? Those I served."

"IY?"

"The Light."

Was IY not the god of the Light? *Move on.* "Why are you here?" Jessica asked again.

Jalu frowned. "Why? That is a question for the Light. But I *am* here, and I try to serve. To protect Life and to aid you as I tried to aid the others." She held up her hand as Jessica made to speak. "You grow in strength, Guardian, but you are as ignorant as all the others the Light has chosen. And yet I see within you a hope, and so will aid you as I can."

Jessica's frustration flared. "Many say they seek to aid us. And yet we're fighting here alone. Why should I believe you?"

"You will. In time, you will. For now, listen. Follow the Kade. Protect the Kade." The ghostly woman's eyes locked onto Jessica's. *'And protect Life. Protect the Seed of Life.'*

Protect Life? A Seed? Jessica struggled to fathom the meaning of the woman's words – of her purpose. "You mean prevent Armageddon? That, I've been told already. That—"

'Protect the Kade, prevent Armageddon, and *protect Life,'* Jalu said firmly. *'Others do not see this. Others cannot see, cannot know.'*

The woman took a step closer.

Jessica's Staff crackled as she prepared to defend herself.

Jalu's silvery eyes blazed. *'In your hands, I have now placed a secret unknown in this Land. Do not reveal my presence, do not speak of what I say here. Else you may destroy Life.'*

The ghostly woman began to fade. "Follow the Kade."

Then she vanished.

Jessica stood, staring into empty darkness.

Then she hammered her Staff into the ground in frustration. "Damn it!" She looked up at the night sky. "Damn you all!"

There was a rustle behind her, and she turned to see Tricia's head appearing from the gloom of the hut's entrance. "If you're going to sit out here all night, can you at least do it quietly?" Her friend withdrew back inside, strung hides falling back into place behind her.

Jessica's gaze returned briefly to the smouldering embers, then she scanned around the silent camp. "Jalu will aid you," IY had said. "Is that the help I was promised?" she muttered to herself. "What can I believe?"

Jalu's words rang in her head. "Protect the Kade, prevent Armageddon, *and* protect Life."

She speaks as though there's another threat to life. But a threat beyond Armageddon?

It suddenly seemed as though a vast weight had been thrust upon her shoulders, one impossible to bear alone. *I need to talk this through with Lanky and Beth …*

But no sooner had the thought formed than a numbing dread stabbed through her heart. "I can't," she whispered. *I can't speak of this to another.* She stared blindly into the gloom of the camp. *There is a secret here I cannot release.*

The Seed of Life.

She stifled a cry of frustration. But what was this Seed? Why had IY not spoken of it?

Faint, tantalising answers murmured in the darkest recesses of her mind.

But she could not hear the words.

She put her head in her hands. What terrible burden had this Jalu placed on her? *And do I carry this burden alone?*

In the dying light of the embers, an intense loneliness swept over her.

They call me the Guardian, but what does that truly mean?
And who will stand beside me and comfort my soul?

*

River sat alone in the chamber, warmed by the heat from the embers of the small fire. The meeting had gone as well as could have been expected, and she was confident her plan would be accepted. Two Warriors would leave on the mission for the Kade, which would leave an inviting weakness in their defences at the gorge. *Will that be enough to tempt the traitor?* She looked to the Spirit art on the wall ahead. *We play a dangerous game, but—*

A movement behind interrupted her thoughts. She turned to see Spider standing in the entrance. "May I come in … Mother?"

Has it already come to this? she thought sadly. "Please, join me, Spider. I would enjoy your company – and your thoughts. It has been too long."

Spider walked in slowly, then sat beside her at the fire.

122

"How are your injuries?" she asked, smiling. "You seem to be moving well."

"Good," he answered with a nervous smile. "Amber is a skilled healer, and I'm grateful for her time, but she has many more seriously wounded to tend." His smile faded. "And she has her own loss to deal with."

As have too many of our tribe. And this is only the beginning. "Eagle's death and the death of all others will be avenged in time." *This, I must believe.*

Spider nodded, then studied her in silence.

My own silence hasn't helped things between us, she thought sadly. *I haven't explained how I feel.*

"Rind spoke to me just now," Spider murmured after a moment. "She revealed the secret mission in the south and asked if I'd join her and the Warriors."

"And what did you say?" she said, fingering the bracelet on her wrist.

"Yes, of course."

Of course. Spider was ever faithful to the cause. "You don't have to go." *I wouldn't want to lose you.*

Spider hesitated. "If that's where I'm needed, then I must go." He looked up, meeting her eyes. "Unless …"

Unless I need him here, she knew he wanted to say. *Unless I need him beside me.* She drew a quiet breath. "I love you, Spider," she said softly. She saw a flash of hope in his eyes. "I love you as a brother." She saw the sharp pain that her swift blade had delivered. "And that love runs deep, deeper than you may realise." She reached out and gently placed her hand on his knee. "But right now – in this moment – I can't go further. I …" A tightness ran across her chest as she struggled to continue. "I hold too many things within; too many worries; too much conflict."

"I can help," Spider said quickly, his deep brown eyes eroding her defences. "If you'd allow me closer to your heart."

I can't. Not right now. I have to be sure. I must know who I am. "I know," she said, forcing her voice to remain steady. "But I need your help as a friend, a brother. As we've always been." *Until this fight is over.*

Spider winced, unable to hide the pain. He drew himself upright and nodded. "I understand," he said, forcing a smile. "I don't like it, but I understand."

No. No, he doesn't. He just tries to hide it. "I'm sorry," she said.

Is that all! Tell him more. Tell him …

Tell him what? What else could she say right now?

Spider looked around, clearly uncertain what to do next. He sighed, then placed his hands on his lap. "I have to go." She could hear the hurt in his voice. "But first I must return this." He reached out and placed an object next to her feet.

Her heart wrenched as she saw what lay there. Her most precious bone horse carving.

"No!" she exclaimed. "Please keep it, Spider. It is yours now."

He slowly climbed to his feet. "It was a wonderful gift, River, and I thank you for it. But this is not for me ... It is for another." It seemed he might speak further, but then he turned and walked out of the chamber.

River stared after him into the now silent chamber, distraught. *I do love you, Spider, I do. But ... but ...*

As everything seemed to crumble inside, she leaned forward and cried, deep sobs from the depth of her being.

She cried until she could cry no more.

Eventually, she looked up, wiping her eyes. Glancing down, she saw the bone carving, her heartfelt gift to the one she loved. She forced herself to reach out and take it in her trembling hand. Then she held it to her heart, tears once more running down her cheek.

CHAPTER EIGHT

The snake was most clever indeed. And the rest of the Disciples? Too distracted by the demands of the Ensi, who in turn had looked too far from home. As had many of us.

Walking south through the scrub of the northern Rim, Shadow wiped his brow. The few scattered, scrawny trees of this outer sector of the Ka homeland provided little respite from the rising heat of the fringe-desert sun. But at least he had escaped the distraction of the Games. *Escaped with my life.* He glanced at Growl, who strode, grim-faced, a few paces ahead. *Thanks to this one.* His eyes narrowed. But the Shade's intervention had been no altruistic protection of a Disciple of the Ensi. *He came to collect me for a mission.* Yet since arriving on the outskirts of the encampment, the Shade had remained tight-lipped. "First the Ensi," Growl had said, a fire in his eyes. "We must see if it is true. We must see if we can strike now."

"Strike who?" Shadow had asked. But to no avail; the Shade did not answer.

Shadow brushed away the frustration. No matter, this was a chance for him to speak to the Ensi. And to catch up with friends. *Life is for living as well as serving.*

Continuing on, they weaved a path through a particularly densely packed quarter of the Rim, many of the makeshift shelters simply a shared roof, shade from the blazing sun. The sight was worrying. The place grew too crowded. He was certain they couldn't sustain these growing numbers. Access to food was good for now, but the wildlife moved ever further from the encampment as the intensity of hunting grew – and the thought of eating catfish every day was not appealing. The council knew of his concern, but they didn't see anyone starving, most certainly not themselves. And so, the Rim grew. *But let it grow too*

125

far and you will see people stressed. And stress them too much, and those privileged in the Core might be welcoming in the angry hordes for dinner. If they could only get the animals to stay closer to the encampment, but he knew not how this could be done. *They're too scared of us humans.* And rightly so.

Glancing around, he saw that as usual for this time of day, most occupants of the Rim were scattered out in the valley, hunting within the rich, fertile plains or fishing on the margins of the lake to the east. Those people remaining eyed them with suspicion, wary of these high-ranking personnel of the Ka walking amongst them. And he knew their caution was prudent. A few words from one of his rank, and they and their families could be expelled from the camp. Not that he had ever done so. *And why would I? These people are needed.* But he understood their caution. There were those of the Ka hierarchy who liked to flex their muscles when others were not watching.

His thoughts momentarily soured. *Like the snake ...*

Even so, as he and Growl walked on, the bravest – or most stupid – of the Rim approached them, giving thanks for their good fortune at being allowed into the Rim, grateful for their security and easier access to food and supplies ... and all with a chance, one day, of moving into the Flanks, and even to the Core. But nothing came free. Without their acceptance of the weekly levy of meat and grain to be supplied to the Ka stores, these people wouldn't be here. And for the true citizens of the Ka homeland, those privileged occupants of the Flanks and the Core, the presence of the Rim provided other benefits. Predators took the easier pickings of the unwary or unprepared of the exposed outer sector, and many of the snakes and scorpions failed to make it through. But most importantly, the Rim provided a buffer, a first line of defence, against those occasional futile raids from a vassal tribe, one growing restless and thinking to test their strength against their masters. *Forgetting the retribution that would follow.* Annihilation proved an ultimate deterrent.

As they walked on towards the Flanks, Shadow couldn't doubt the value of his homeland's design – or his people's aspirations for a better future for their children. *But to preserve that future, we can't overreach ourselves. We cannot become too greedy.* He sighed. Maybe he should raise this again with the Ensi. And yet how far had he already pushed with his previous challenging questions? A wry smile crossed his lips. *When did that ever stop me?* Shaking his head, he walked on.

A short while later, they approached the boundary ditch marking the outer limits of the Flanks. No resident of the Rim would risk their lives crossing that threshold. Growl strode ahead, ignoring the suddenly tense guard at the entranceway. Shadow acknowledged the guard with a nod and a smile, receiving a sharp bow and the faintest hint of a smile in return. A childhood friend remained a friend at heart, no matter the gulf in status between them. *And this empire of ours relies on all such as Ciate.*

As Shadow crossed the earthen walkway across the deep trench and on into the outer Flanks, an intense calm fell over him at the familiar sight of the vegetated landscape of his childhood home. Walking on with a smile, he scanned around, recognising several weatherworn, sun-bleached huts, somehow unyielding survivors over the many sun-cycles since they'd been built. Set against those rooted relics of his childhood stood many new builds, displaying a bewildering array of sizes and shapes, some seemingly as large as the greatest in the Core. *Our homeland prospers,* he thought as they passed under one of the many magnificent, wide-canopied trees that had been so carefully cultivated over generations and now cast their cooling shadow over grand dwellings beneath.

As he approached the area of his old family hut, some of those around greeted him warmly. An old thin-haired man mending a leather tunic hailed him by name; a stooped, one-armed woman using a pestle to crush grain in a black-stone mortar wedged between her thighs gave him a wave. He greeted each in kind, but though he would have liked to have stopped and exchanged news, he was carried along in Growl's wake.

They continued south through increasingly verdant ground, each hut now lying within its own clearly demarcated parcel of land, until, at last, they reached an entranceway to the Core. Stepping through the guarded gateway in the low boundary wall, he walked into his home of the last two sun-cycles, his home in the heart of the Ka's homeland.

An unusual sense of pride rose as he walked on to the temple. Maybe it was because his walk from the outlands beyond the camp and through the Rim and Flanks to the Core had mimicked the journey of his family. *My grandfather arrived at the Rim with nothing, and now see where I am.* He had attained the Core. He held the ear of the Ensi. *And I was the youngest Ka to get here.* He grunted a wry laugh at the thought, gaining a sharp sideways glare from Growl. Was that really a good thing? What else had he sacrificed to achieve it?

Not much, he answered himself, feeling the truth of that answer. *I like what I do.*

I serve the Ka. I serve the Ensi.

And you serve yourself, he admitted, with a faint smile. *Particularly wine. I serve plenty of that.*

Walking on, he lifted his head, savouring a sweet fragrance in the air. He glanced to his left to see thick bushes of purple flowering desert sage. *Nice, but not a patch on my vines from the north.* He grinned with sudden joyful anticipation. He'd planted those choice vines in the dry soil adjacent to his home and was sure there lay the secret to surpassing Stealth's mountain wine. *The next time we meet, I will repay your hospitality, my friend.*

Reaching the short rise to the temple, he saw a familiar woman appear at the entry to a prominent stone house to his left. A house of a Disciple. He halted to greet her. "Hello, young Asta. I hope you're feeling as wonderful as you look."

"Hah," the older woman muttered, glowering at him. "I see your wit has not improved. And why are you here? Don't you have the Games to run?"

"It seems I'm relieved," he said, gesturing to the rangy figure of the Shade climbing the rise to the temple. "In more ways than one. Is Xerses in?"

Asta waved an arm in the temple's direction. "Up there. With the others. And the Ensi, I believe."

"Hmm. Well, this might be interesting. Wish me luck." He turned and headed after Growl.

"Use your head now," she called after him, a sharp edge to her voice. "That luck of yours won't last forever."

He waved, smiling as though casually dismissing her words, but as he climbed the rise, Asta's not-so-subtle warning – clearly one coming from her husband – brought reality crashing home. The reality that someone had tried to kill him. The reality that something wasn't right in his homeland. He had to unravel what was happening, and soon. Yes, it was clear someone wanted him out of the way, and that someone was Cobra, he was sure. The overseer had nefarious roots creeping throughout their home camp, sucking out the nutrients needed to pursue his selfish ambitions while tightly binding those who would support him. But who else was involved? Another Disciple?

He immediately dismissed Xerses. If not a friend, he felt certain Xerses was still his ally. And the general was too busy overseeing his forces in the far reaches of the empire, ably supported by Growl, who sent reports from the remotest of areas, which would take many moons to reach the homeland by other means.

Then what about Qiax, the one who also avidly awaited the narratives from afar? The one who needed the Shade's roving eyes to quench his relentless thirst for detailed intelligence of … well, of everything and anything; nothing discarded or filtered; nothing wasted or ignored. Could he be a possible ally of Cobra's? Knowing the quiet spymaster, Shadow doubted it very much. The man from the east said little, but when he spoke, Shadow listened. *I like him, and though he hides it, I believe he likes me. And I believe he hates Cobra.*

His brow furrowed. Then who else could be allied with Cobra? And what was their plan? His unease deepened. *The snake is planning something, I'm sure of it. But what?* He had to speak with the Ensi. Alone.

Reaching the top of the rise, Shadow stepped onto a stout wooden walkway. Bordering the entire perimeter of the crest of the temple, this privileged vantage point afforded a select few a sweeping view of the entire domain of the Ka's homeland. He paused to glance towards the glistening lake to the east, that sustaining lifeblood of the encampment. Fed from the main river channel, the deep, expansive water allowed this desert fringe to thrive with a rich diversity of plant and animal life. It supported the life of the Ka in an otherwise inhospitable land. He frowned. A land devastated by the cursed Iyes. *They push our water ever northward. They seek our destruction.*

Pushing that flash of anger aside, he shifted his attention to the temple. Within the expansive inner area enclosed by the wooden walkway lay a great circle of smooth white marble, gleaming in the late summer sun. Seemingly of one piece, only a most careful inspection would reveal the finest of joints between precisely cut blocks of crystalline marble, a testament to the wondrous skill of ancient makers. Allowing his gaze to drift to the centre of the gleaming white circle, his eyes fell on the pyramid of Kaos, which loomed over all. *A reminder that Kaos protects us ... and watches us.* So straight were the carved lines of the glasslike obsidian, so symmetrical the construction, that it might have been forged by Kaos himself. *And maybe it was ...* But Shadow knew he would never get close enough to know its true design – to step on the white marble would be his last step in this land.

Flicking his gaze to the side of the temple bordering the lake, he marvelled again at the sight of the coils of smoke issuing from a concealed vent. For in those wispy tendrils lay the evidence of the simple yet ingenious system devised by the ancient makers, which used airflow from an inlet vent on the far side of the temple to sweep foul air from the underground chambers and tunnels. *Yet our makers today cannot match this skill. We have lost—*

He flinched as his skin suddenly tingled, his head throbbing with a gentle, pulsating pressure. His wandering thoughts disrupted, his gaze settled on the gleaming crest of the temple. While many of the Ka's inhabitants might appreciate the tremendous skill of the makers, only a handful would be capable of sensing the unnerving energy suffusing the air as Shadow did now. The energy of the Dark. The life force of the shamans. *An energy I occasionally sense but cannot wield.* No, of the Ka, only the Ensi and the Shade had that gift.

The Ensi and the Shade ... Hauled back to the task in hand, and with an acrid taste in his mouth, Shadow turned and headed along the wooden walkway towards the regimented guards standing by the distant entrance to the temple interior. And to the waiting Growl.

"We suggest you step aside," Shadow heard Growl rasp to one of the guards as he approached. "My patience is wearing thin."

"Problems?" Shadow asked with a smile, halting before the sharp-nosed guard who had stepped from the ranks to challenge Growl.

"You don't have, um, an appointment, my lord," the guard said nervously. Nervous, but seemingly relieved to be speaking to anyone else but the Shade.

Shadow raised an eyebrow in genuine surprise. "Since when did we need appointments?"

"For the past two days, my lord," the guard answered, his brow sheened in sweat.

Scowling, Growl muttered as if to himself. "A mistake, it seems, allowing that snake to speak to another before leaving for the Games."

Ah, so the work of Cobra. But what does this serve? Shadow shrugged. "No matter. Tell the council we're here. And quickly."

"I, um, that has been done, my lord."

"And?"

"They are, um, busy. You must wait."

"No, we must not wait," Growl rasped, striding forward.

Four of the six guards stepped into his path.

The sharp-nosed guard cast fearful eyes at Shadow. "Please. If you attempt to pass, we'd have no choice, and then ..." His panicked eyes flicked to Growl.

And then, you would die. Shadow glanced at the Shade. Not one of the Ka could stand in this shaman's way. Only the Ensi. Probably. He sighed. "Growl. A quiet word, please."

Growl continued to glower at the guards, clasping his Black Staff with tight knuckles. The guards held their ground. *Impressive. These men have sturdy spines.* "Growl," he said again.

The Shade spat a curse at the guards, then with a face like thunder, he turned and strode to Shadow. "Yes?" he snapped.

"Do you know what's happening?"

"You need to ask that?" Growl hissed, flicking a hateful glance at the guards.

"Not them. What's happening within the council? Has a threat been found?"

Growl eyed him for a moment from hooded eyes. "A threat to who?"

To me. "To the Ensi," Shadow replied.

"You suggest treachery?" Growl said, his voice dripping with sarcasm. "Surely not."

"I suggest things are not as they were. That—"

"Things most certainly are not as they were." The Shade studied Shadow as though he were a fool. "You were there at the arrival of the enemy Warriors in the Iyes's lands?"

"Clearly, I was," Shadow said, confused. "I—"

"Really?" the Shade said, sarcasm colouring his voice. "You noticed them? And so, learned friend, why did you let them go? That seems a poor choice indeed, yes it does."

This again? Was this the real problem for him? Not his perceived loose questioning, but that two of the Warriors had been within his grasp? *And that I left them with Krag, and they escaped.*

Was that his fault?

It was, he answered himself.

"I've explained it," Shadow said testily. "There could have been another way to deal with it, but I was there, and I did what I thought right. And I captured the Staff, and I killed … well, almost killed, a Warrior." He rubbed his neck. "Anyway, she died later."

"That Warrior is alive and well, enjoying her life in the enemy camp, and—"

"What!" Shadow exclaimed, staring unbelievingly at Growl. "I saw her, she was—"

"And you will be most pleased to hear, reports arrive of the Staff of IY being seen in the enemy's hands."

Shadow stared at Growl, stunned. "No," he whispered. "That can't be possible. The Ancient—"

"So," Growl continued, the curl of a harsh smile on his lips. "You can see how this might appear to our council friends. How your version of your tale might be doubted."

"But Sy … the council have spoken with him, and surely, they can see he's not lying."

"He is your warrior-monk. A loyal ally."

"But the man is incapable of lying, he—"

"Enough!" Growl hissed. "No matter what the truth, the facts – yes, the facts – can all be used against you. And against the Ensi."

131

"What does the Ensi have to do with my actions?" But of course, he knew. The Ensi had sanctioned his mission. Even with an apparently unassailable position, those coveting the Ensi's power could exploit the faintest of cracks, chipping away at them until they widened far enough to force open and break.

"You ask yet another pointless question," the Shade said with a snarl. "Yes, there is a threat, and as you can see by these actions behind us, that threat is real, and it is imminent." The lines on Growl's face deepened. "The full scope of this threat is not yet revealed. This will take—"

"I am sorry, my friends," came a deep voice behind them. "It seems our new protocol has been enthusiastically adopted."

"It seems so," Growl snapped, immediately turning and striding past the wary guards to start his descent into the gloomy temple interior.

Shadow turned to see a heavyset, broad-shouldered older man approaching, his familiar shock of dark, curly hair grown even wilder since their last meeting. Shadow noticed the general still wore the polished bone earring his wife had made for him. *He serves his Ensi in war, but his soul walks with Asta.*

"I see our Shade is in a good mood," Xerses said, smiling at Shadow as he stopped by his side. "How are you?" His smile faded. "And who gave you permission to leave the Games?"

Shadow smiled. Typical Xerses. *To the point.* "I'm fine. And Cobra was kind enough to volunteer to take my place."

Xerses raised a thick eyebrow. "Is that so? I wasn't aware the council had sanctioned that change. Has your role expanded?"

"I hope not," Shadow said, laughing. "I think the persuasive powers of our beloved Shade convinced Cobra to take over the running of the Games. But I expect the overseer will quickly grow bored of his overseeing and soon return to ensure his homeland isn't falling apart in his absence."

Xerses stepped closer. "Take care," he growled. "Your way of working and your lack of discipline – and your friendships – are testing the patience of the council. Including me. And removing yourself from the Games was not a good idea. It was better for you to be out of the way for a while. There is nothing wrong with mundane delivery now and then, Shadow. It reminds people you still serve at the Ensi's behest and not your own."

"Maybe. But exhilarating as it was to be close to death, I prefer to be in a place where an assassin might be noticed more quickly." *And I note your reference to my friends, Xerses, but I'm happy to have those friends in the Flanks – it keeps me sane.*

Xerses's penetrating gaze studied Shadow. "What assassin?"

You sound surprised. Shadow scanned the general's face, searching for hints of masked intentions. But this Disciple revealed only what he wished to be seen.

He relayed the events of the last few days.

Xerses frowned. "You have enemies in the ranks, as do we all, but this ..." His eyes flicked to the temple entrance. "It is unfortunate you were targeted, but fortunate indeed the Shade was on hand."

Is that suspicion I detect? Maybe.

Of me? Maybe.

Of Growl? Maybe.

It seemed that in these times, suspicion was rife. "Are you joining us inside?"

A purposeful edge sharpened the general's features. "I have what I need. I travel to the northeast region to meet several tribe leaders, including the Kutr and Azgoths, to assess our next moves." He grimaced. "Growl will take me there, though with each passing sun-cycle, my aging body complains more vociferously of the Shade's mercurial means of transport."

"When do you leave?"

"First light tomorrow, before your group leaves."

Casually, Shadow sought an answer to a most pressing question. "And where is my group going?"

"For that, follow the Shade." A small smile played on Xerses's lips. "Did I tell you that the Ensi sits awaiting you? You know our leader doesn't like guests to be late."

So, some games continue. Shadow held his smile. "No, you didn't say. Then I should say both goodbye and that I look forward to meeting you upon our return."

Xerses gave a curt nod and seemed about to leave ... then he paused. "Watch your back, Shadow. Or at least make sure Sy has it covered. You never know who you can trust." Then he set off along the walkway towards the trail down to the Core.

Watching Xerses walk away, Shadow's mood darkened. People – smart and intelligent people – were moving. People who had gained a taste for the trappings of power and who were clambering over others, driving them into the mud, even stabbing them in the back, in their efforts to grab more. His heart railed at the injustice. What had happened to working for the good of the Ka, striving for an equal and fair society for all? *Hah, very good,* answered his cynical head, *but have you met humans? Equal? Equal until I can take a little bit more for me. Fair? Fair until I explain why I need to move ahead of you – just for now, you understand.*

He sighed. *Come on, snap out of it.*

But it was hard to push back the creeping malaise as his swirling thoughts dragged in other remembered words. The words of the Rim woman: "They kill our children."

His shoulders tensed with growing frustration. Little things were beginning to ripple around him, and those ripples were expanding. *What am I missing? What is the Ensi missing?* Because if they weren't careful, these ripples would soon rise into towering waves, then thunder down upon them, smashing them against mocking cliffs of ignorance, leaving no trace. He shook his head and sighed. He'd been on such a high when he'd first returned from the last mission. *Why am I being targeted? Why this suspicion of me?* He clenched his hand. *Because life isn't fair, you idiot. Stop feeling sorry for yourself and find out what's happening. Now.*

Plagued by bitter thoughts, he strode over to the temple entrance.

"I'm sorry we had to stop you, Sh … my lord," said the guard who had challenged them. Wilder was his name, a friend of his and Sy's when they'd been younger.

Shadow looked around the faces of the other five men, none of whom he recognised. Several looked sourly at him – those in Rathe's pocket, he thought. "You and your men did well," he said evenly. It wouldn't do to acknowledge his recognition of his old friend. "Carry on."

He walked past them and onto the worn steps leading down into the temple interior. As he passed the last guard, he heard the man mutter something under his breath. At another time, in another place, the man would now be dropping to the ground, clutching his ruptured throat. But this was a sensitive time and a sensitive place – killing the guard here would complicate Shadow's already increasingly unsettled life.

But elsewhere …

He committed the face to his memory and walked on down the steps.

CHAPTER NINE

The deception was simple and effective.
So much lay hidden in plain sight.

Shadow gathered the loose strand of hair behind his neck and reset the binding, then sat back, drumming his fingers on his leg. He felt on edge. Not because they still sat in the spartan chamber waiting to be admitted to the Ensi, but because of Growl's restless pacing – up and down, up and down. The Shade's anger put even the seasoned temple guards on edge.

"Why don't you take a seat?" Shadow asked for the second time, pointing to the furs set around the edges of the chamber. "It would benefit us both."

Pacing towards him, Growl cast a fierce glare before turning and pacing back across the chamber.

Well, this is going to be a fun day.

"Good morning to you," came a calm, silky voice from the inner entrance. A short, round-faced man walked towards them, clothed in a long-armed, knee-length tunic tied at the waist with a twisted twine belt.

"We find nothing good about this morning," Growl replied, gaze furious. "Why delay our mission? The opportunity could be missed."

"And good morning to you," Qiax purred, looking over at Shadow. The man reminded him of a slightly older version of Sy. It was the shaved sides of the head and long, tied-back hair. Men from the far east, so Qiax claimed. A fair rarity here.

"Always pleased to see the spymaster," Shadow said. "And even happier if I don't."

Qiax smiled. "I—"

"Enough of this," Growl growled, walking to the inner passageway. "We go to see the Ensi."

Moving imperceptibly, Qiax glided to the entrance, blocking the Shade's path. "I don't believe I heard you being called," the spymaster murmured, smiling as he stood face-to-face with Growl – or rather his face to Growl's chest. "Sit for a moment. There is something the Ensi would have me ask of her Shade."

Growl glared at the spymaster a moment longer, then, with a scowl, he averted his gaze. "Ask what you need to ask."

"This I will not do before you face me."

Shadow hid his surprise. This was serious. An unprecedented demand of the Shade – at least as far as he knew.

"You are certain of this request?" Growl said in a glacial tone. "We do not forget."

"And I do not ignore the commands of my leader."

Growl slowly turned.

If eyes could kill, Qiax would now be a smouldering pile of ashes heaped on the ground.

But Qiax stood, unperturbed. "Did you order Cobra to leave and join you at the Games?"

Growl glared at Qiax. "Do not try another of your own questions, sly one," he spat, "else that will be your last."

Qiax shrugged. "I had to try," he said with a smile. "But, if you will not play, then here is the question from our leader. Who do you serve?"

"Our leader," Growl replied instantly. He stood taller. "And Kaos."

The spymaster regarded Growl with a relaxed gaze. "Hmm. And in the event of a conflict, who do you serve?"

"There should be no conflict."

"And if there is?"

"I warned you," Growl said, raising his Staff.

"No!" Shadow commanded. "Growl! Stand down!"

He could see a gleeful rage rippling on the face of the Shade. Growl, but not Growl. *The daemon inside him grows ever more forceful.* Ereboz, wasn't that the name he'd heard? The daemon of the Shade. No choices, no refusal, this daemon of the Dark came with the position of the Ensi's Shade. *Of Kaos's servant.* A bitter taste fouled his mouth. No, not for all the treasures of the lands would he ever accept that deal. "Stand down," he said, more softly. "We have a job to do – or so you tell me."

The Shade continued to glare at Qiax, who stood observing the glowering shaman as though holding a casual exchange amongst friends.

That man has the nerves of granite – and a ruthlessly efficient mind.

"Does the Ensi now have an adequate answer?" Growl spat, swaying his head as though a snake considering a strike.

"It is sufficient," Qiax said, stepping aside. "You may enter."

Growl immediately stepped forward – then stopped beside Qiax. "We do not like you, little man. And this is the only time we will tolerate your questions, oh yes, it is. But if you see fit to try again, we will be pleased to answer you appropriately. Most appropriately indeed. Come!" he commanded, and he strode out of the chamber.

As Shadow made to follow, Qiax glided back to block the entrance. Looking down on the man, Shadow saw several almost imperceptible beads of sweat glistening on his forehead. *So, he is human after all.*

"Life has become quite complex and intriguing," Qiax purred. "And I find this most welcome and exhilarating – a chance, hmm, to show my best work."

To yourself, maybe, Shadow thought wryly. *Not many see your work.*

"But," the spymaster continued, gesturing with one hand, "I also sense some growing threats to our, hmm, foundations. And I dislike being undermined. It may be some corrections are necessary." He stepped closer to Shadow. "I like you, Shadow. It would be good if you lie on the right side of the corrections."

Intriguing indeed. "What did you see?"

Qiax examined Shadow's face. "A question for a question?"

A most dangerous game with this one. "Agreed? Answer me first."

"I saw a dangerous man. And one not to be trusted."

Shadow raised an eyebrow. "And yet you let him through?"

"Corrections require risks." Qiax's gaze locked onto Shadow's. "Who do you serve?"

Shadow felt the faint probing. "I serve the Ensi. And Kaos."

Qiax continued to stare into Shadow's eyes, his face impassive, unmoving.

Except ...

Except Shadow had seen the minutest of twitches in the spymaster's hand, partly obscured below the man's cloak. But not if you were watching so very carefully as Shadow always did. *So, what did he see that was not in my answer?* There had to be something – the spymaster missed nothing when you answered to his face.

"Good," Qiax murmured, relaxing his gaze. "I believe we understand each other."

He knows I saw his reaction. But what did that mean? Shadow's disquiet grew. *He might understand me, but right now, I don't understand him.*

"I wish you well on your mission." Qiax gave a small bow. "And if you change your mind, please call on me when you return." And with that, he casually walked out of the chamber.

Brow furrowed, Shadow stared after the departed spymaster. *He wished me well on my mission. I wish I understood what he was talking about.*

'Shadow!' Growl's voice echoed in his head.

"I've told you before, don't *do* that!" Shadow muttered, shaking his head. He sighed and strode on to the meeting with the Ensi.

*

The slightest twist of apprehension in his gut, Shadow watched his leader rise from the rough-hewn stone throne, then walk across the dais by the far wall of the chamber before stepping down the two low steps to the pentagonal marble slab where he and Growl stood.

"You may leave us now," the Ensi murmured.

Shadow flicked a glance to the dark alcoves set into the ancient clay-brick walls of the pentagonal chamber, where several shadowy figures were silently leaving through shrouded exits. The Ensi's personal guard. So, no ears allowed for this meeting.

He turned back to the person standing before him.

Not tall, not short. Not young, not old. Shortish hair. Maybe a nondescript person if seen from a distance walking through the camp. But that watcher would be making a potentially fatal mistake.

This woman was the most powerful human he knew in their lands.

The Ensi. The leader of the Ka. The leader of a growing empire.

And as usual, he couldn't help himself – he gazed at her emerald-green eyes.

From a distance, nondescript she may appear, but close up, those emerald eyes were mesmerising. Not another wore these eyes – only the Ensi. They were rich eyes, deep and sultry eyes that warmed you, excited you, drew you in, setting your heart racing, your mind engaging—

He felt a sharp blow on his left arm.

He blinked. *Where am I?* He looked around. *Kef! The Ensi. I have to stop doing that.* "Thanks," he grunted to Growl.

The Shade simply scowled.

Shadow's gaze drifted back to the Ensi, focussing on the small smile on her lips. *Stay away from the eyes.*

"A pity," the Ensi said, drawing out the words in her gravelly voice, "you have an intriguing soul."

"That may be so," he said, keeping his eyes fixed on her mouth, "but yours is kind of frightening."

"You scare so easily?"

"No – and that's the problem."

"But I thought you found last time … exhilarating?"

Shadow flicked a glance to Growl – his deep black eyes were glaring at the Ensi – then turned back to his liege. She was right. The last time he'd gazed fully into those eyes had indeed been exhilarating. An unexpected moment of passion that had not been repeated. Or mentioned again. He looked back to the Ensi. "I—"

Growl took a step forward. "Not wishing to intrude on your affairs, my liege, but we suggest—"

"No!" the Ensi commanded, her face hardening, her narrowed eyes bearing down on the Shade. "Only *you* are welcome at this meeting."

Growl glared at the Ensi. "We would—"

"Just you," the Ensi commanded, taking a step towards him.

Growl stood, unflinching. Shadow held his breath.

Then something flickered in Growl's eyes. He bowed his head. "As you wish," he said in a low voice. He straightened, his now silvery eyes looking up at the Ensi. "*I* am now at your service."

The Ensi gave a curt nod.

Shadow glanced at Growl. His affliction was so familiar, it sounded strange on these recently rare occasions when he referred to himself in the singular – on these rare occasions when his companion left.

The Ensi sauntered forward and slowly made a complete circuit around them. *Is she ensuring the daemon is gone?* She came back into view and studied Growl. "Is everything ready?"

"As the sun crosses to the west, preparations will be complete. The group will travel."

"And the way is clear?"

"It is."

"And are you ready?" she asked, turning to Shadow.

His brow creased. "Well, my liege, you have an advantage over me. What am I supposed to be ready for?"

"They have not been told," Growl interjected. His sharp eyes flicked to Shadow. "I waited until they needed to know."

Shadow raised a brow. "Well, maybe now is a good time?"

The Ensi smiled. "You will strike at the heart of the enemy, my loyal Disciple. With the blessing of Kaos, you will remove another Warrior from our lands." She moved closer to him, her green eyes boring into him. "I say 'another'," she murmured, "but it seems the one you claimed dead has arisen." She reached up and stroked the nail of her finger slowly across his neck. "That would seem strange, would it not?"

Unease settled in his stomach. "I saw her," he breathed. "She was dead."

"And the Staff. It has returned to the hands of the enemy. This also seems counter to your story."

"I … I delivered it as promised," he stammered. "The Ancient held them both – the Warrior and the Staff." He frowned. "I don't understand …"

She moved her hand around to the back of his neck, then pulled his head gently towards her. "Look into my eyes. I must see the truth."

He shivered. "I cannot."

"I will save you the worst, my Shadow, but I must do this – you have no choice."

He knew it was true. He had to obey. *I must look into those eyes.* Eyes that saw into a person's soul. And while controlled and precise, protecting her victim, what leaked from *her* soul was hard to erase. *But I must accept.* Else she would take what she needed by other means. And that could kill him. Or worse.

He looked up – straight into the devilish beauty of those beguiling eyes.

A warmth swept over him. Such wondrous eyes, such depth of feeling, welcoming him into a glorious place of calm understanding and deep compassion, enticing him ever onwards to accept her warming embrace, those gentle caresses so tender and soft.

'You have suffered, my loyal servant. Tell me your tale.'

Onwards he was drawn, crossing the emerald portal, and passing within.

And he talked. He shared his hopes and his dreams; he revealed his doubts and his fears; he spoke of travellers and a Staff – and he spoke of his foolish, unforgiveable mistakes.

He told her his tale.

And ever deeper he was drawn into the emerald realm, that vast and illimitable void.

I am lost!

'Have no fear, my Disciple, your tale is not yet told. I must hear it all. Continue.'

On he spoke, her eyes now lost in a growing darkness; *his* eyes desperately searching the gloom, fearful at what lay beyond.

Then the darkness became bleaker.

And the screaming began.

Screaming of babies seeing a terror not understood. Howling of old men seeing their life's nightmares become real. Shrieking of young women not believing what was being done.

And the screaming of a scared woman, who held this inside.

I can't—

'The story must be told.'

A baby with green eyes trying to scream under water. The girl with green eyes being held down against her will. A woman with green eyes slicing a throat with a smile. A woman with green eyes waving goodbye to unknown children on a boat. A woman—

Standing before him once again.

Shadow collapsed to his knees, weeping.

"Things are not what they seem," he heard the Ensi say.

How! How can she hold this within? He looked up, wiping his eyes. "How?"

She looked down on him, her smile gone, her expression grim and determined. "You serve me well, Disciple, and you speak true. No fault lies with you. But it seems the game has changed." She faced Growl, her eyes afire. "The word we have been waiting for has come. You strike tomorrow."

"The Iyes spy?"

The slightest nod answered him. "I expect visitors soon. You will leave once they have arrived."

Growl scowled. "Then you will kindly let me know when they've arrived?"

The Ensi paused. "No. No communications. You will wait – concealed – within the canyon by the old temple of the ancients to the west. You will know when to leave."

Growl bowed. "It shall be as you say."

"And Growl," she said in a low voice. "You shall not intervene. They must be allowed to enter. Do you understand?"

"We do," Growl said, a smile on his face, his black eyes afire. "Oh yes, we—"

The shaman collapsed to the ground, violently spasming, his face hideously twisting. But his gaping mouth emitted no sound.

"Disobey me again, and you die," the Ensi snarled, her eyes blazing. She sauntered up to her tortured Shade. "I know you can hear me, daemon," she said with quiet ferocity. "You are trapped, and – most delightfully – can feel this pain."

Shadow stared on in horror. *What about Growl? Was this his fault?*

The Ensi regarded the convulsing figure for a while longer, then turned and strode towards her throne. "My commands are not optional, Ereboz. Leave while you still live."

Growl's movements abruptly calmed, and moments later, Shadow heard him groan.

He rushed to the Shade's side.

"I don't need your help, boy," the Shade rasped, pushing Shadow away. He clambered to his feet and stood rather unsteadily.

Shadow saw the acute pain etched in Growl's face. *But he used 'I'.* Ereboz had gone. "Do you really need that thing?" he whispered.

"He wouldn't be my Shade without it," the Ensi answered from her throne. "Leave us, Growl. I would speak with my Disciple."

Adjusting his patchwork tunic and standing taller, Growl faced the throne, then bowed. "As you wish." Turning to leave, he cast a harsh gaze at Shadow. "Meet me at the forum when you are done here." Then he strode out of the chamber.

Shadow stood for a moment, allowing his fractured nerves to settle, then girding himself, he walked slowly over to the throne. The Ensi watched him approach. "What did you see?" he asked.

"That you told me truthfully what you saw."

"Why did you send me to the Games?"

The Ensi raised an eyebrow. "I did not send you – you think I have time to worry about the Games? My attention has been elsewhere."

He hid his surprise. She knew nothing of him being at the Games? Then what of the Ensi's seal? *The one that almost got me killed.* It was unthinkable anyone else would dare to use it without her knowing. Shadow studied her face – was she lying to him? Or was someone else playing an extremely dangerous game? "Why did you want to see me?" he asked, focussed on a point by her left ear.

"You have been asking questions. Questions that cause disruption. You must stop."

"What happens to leavers?"

The Ensi's eyes flashed. He remained focussed on her ear. "You push yourself too far, Disciple. You—"

"Only to better serve—"

"Do not interrupt me!" she stormed, surging up from the throne.

Shadow tensed at a sharp pulse of pressure in his mind. "I apologise, my liege. But something isn't right. Cobra is—"

"Cease!" she hissed.

Shadow cursed himself for his loose tongue. He could hear Sy berating him. *Time to close that mouth of yours.* He said nothing more and saw the tension slowly ease from the shoulders of the Ensi.

"My attention has not been on the Games," she said in a quieter voice. "Nor should it be. But your actions forced it there." Her head tilted a fraction. "Why have you not accepted the bond with Nefra?"

Because she is a cold killer. Because she sees no value in others' lives. "We are not … compatible."

The Ensi scowled. "What is compatible is the union between our tribe and the tribes of the Meso people. You facilitate that. In this, you have no choice. You *will* accept Nefra."

"I—"

"It is decided. Upon your return from this mission, you and Nefra will be joined."

He heard the finality in her voice. *I need to back off.* Else his relationship with the Ensi would suffer. Permanently. Inwardly he sighed. Despite his rejection of Nefra, he understood why the Ensi was right to push for the pairing – while a disaster for him, it made sense for the tribe. *Yet still I have to find another way. Step back now and live to fight another day.* He bowed. "It will be as you say. Upon my return, I will seek to join Nefra as soon as I am able."

"You play with words, Disciple. It *will* happen, else you can join those leavers you show such great interest in."

Now he knew it was no time for games. And little chance of escape. The one sure thing he knew about the Ensi was that she worked tirelessly for the good of the tribe, for the progression of the tribe. She was set on the alliance with the Meso tribes, and so it would happen.

With a disconcerting reality looming before him, his brow furrowed at the sudden echo of a so-recent thought. *For the good of the tribe …* He slowed his breathing. Yes, the Ensi fought constantly for the security and wellbeing of her people, but what about the leavers? What of the accusation by the dragon's servant, Stealth? *And by the Rim woman?* He felt a sudden chill. What was the Ensi's part in this story? What did she know? What cloaked orders might she have given?

With the cascade of questions, a wall began to crumble …

No! He forced back the heretical thoughts. *She is my Ensi. She is the rock on which the Ka stand.* Fierce certainty coursed through him. It was Cobra, he was sure of it. *He lies hidden in the grasses, ready to strike.* He had to find out what the snake was doing; he had to find time to dig into the snake's nest.

Frustration welled. *But I never have time. I'm always away.*

And now a new mission. Growl had mentioned an Iyes spy. *So we travel north?* He glanced up. The Ensi was watching him with an unnerving intensity. He cleared his throat. "The mission, my liege. It seems I'm the only one who doesn't know what it is."

"You will be told when needed," the Ensi grated.

He quickly scanned her face; it brooked no challenge on this. *But she needs to know my concerns.* "My liege, I would ask that you hear me. Cobra is planning something, I'm sure. He—"

"This meeting is over, Disciple. I wish you success in the mission and may Kaos be with you." She clapped her hands twice. The shadowy figures reappeared in the alcoves.

Shadow hesitated. He had served in this place for several sun-cycles now, with a bittersweet edge between him and the Ensi, a challenging tension that had been needed. And until this point, she had allowed him that space. He glanced at her stern face. *Then where am I going wrong here?* "I—"

"Enough!"

Shadow looked up at the Ensi, a desperate frustration welling. *I can't push it any further. I just can't.* With a flash of anger, he bowed. "It is a pleasure to serve you and the Ka," he said curtly, then turned and walked away.

As he crossed the central pentagonal platform, he glanced left and right at the austere surroundings, the gold-veined marble beneath his feet the only pattern or colour breaking the monotony of the grey chamber. At the sight, his anger quickly faded. Where did she live? Where did she sleep? He knew nothing of the temple beyond this chamber. *And that pleases me.* The place set his nerves on edge. *And yet this is her home. Alone.*

Navigating the familiar passageways to the exit, he sought to make sense of his confused jumble of thoughts. *She wouldn't listen to me. Why?* Surely, she would want to know why he'd been banished to the Games without her knowing? And why the Shade had left Cobra at the Games. *And why I wish to talk of the leavers.* Wouldn't she? He pursed his lips. She'd heard him say the snake's name. Maybe that was enough. And maybe she had concerns herself, concerns that she kept from him and her Disciples.

But if so, why keep them hidden?

He searched for answers as he walked on, then eventually sighed, recognising the futility of his question. She was the Ensi, a leader who ruled an empire. What did he really know of what it was like to hold command over such an empire, to drive an empire ever onwards? Of what troubles, tensions, horrors she continually faced. Of what sly treachery she constantly battled. *Of what she chooses to keep secret.* At the thought, disturbing images from his bonding with the Ensi flashed into his mind. *Maybe I know a few of those horrors she hides.*

No, he didn't envy her position at all. Or her life and ascension to power.

Reaching the guarded exit, he climbed the steps into the welcoming daylight and stepped out onto the wooden balcony. He drew a welcome breath of the wonderfully fresh air, then looked out over the sprawling encampment. *I try to help,* he thought, fighting back a creeping sense of failure. *I try.*

He looked east to where Growl would be waiting for him. *Krez! Let him wait. This foul mood of mine has to be lightened.* He glanced south. He needed to see friends. He needed to partake of a drink or three. *I need to escape my duty, if just for a short while.*

He forced a smile. Friends and a drink – what more pleasure could you want from life?

His smile slipped. But it seemed that for some, this wasn't enough.

CHAPTER TEN

What is true evil? Some suggest it only exists in the
minds and actions of mankind. But what of the gods?

uy one, get one free, missus," an animated man cried from the
colourful stall to her right.

"Everything free today – come see," shouted another.

Erin pushed her way through the sweltering, crowded alleyway,
struggling to keep Robert in sight. A sprightly old man jumped in front
of her, holding a chain of threaded beads in his hand.

"Look! Only here can you buy such gems. Special price for you
today."

"Shukra," she said firmly, walking on past a white-robed, bearded
man, who she heard try his luck with Fletcher behind her. *Shukra. A*
strange word. Used one way, it thanked the person, but if used as she
had, it became a polite decline. And it was becoming an oft-used word
as they ran the souq's gauntlet of energetic traders.

Hurrying after Robert, she flicked glances at the haphazard stalls
and single-paned stores as she passed. On her left, a stall was stacked
high with multicoloured rugs and carpets spilling out into the
walkway. To her right, a gleaming window displayed a dazzling array
of intricately worked glass bottles, some with finely worked stoppers,
others filled with a variety of rich, vibrant liquids. And all goods
touted for sale at a special price by each of the enthusiastic stall
holders. "Please! Come inside and see! Today, a fabulous gift, free."

She walked on.

And ever the twisting turns, the thriving alleyways, the animated
sellers and their endless wares. Over there, pale and delicate alabaster
vases, lit from within by faint, flickering candles. Opposite, brightly
coloured dresses hung high from densely packed rails attached to the

canopy above, all dangling over the traditional lanterns and arcuate lamps arrayed haphazardly on a bench below. It was a bewildering assault on her senses, and she was certain that if left alone, she'd be unable to find her way out of this fantastical maze.

But as they walked deeper into the depths of the souq, the alleys became quieter. The profusion of shops and sellers seemed the same, but she was not so aggressively accosted. As they passed a shop laden with shining copper goods, the grizzled old man outside briefly raised his head, smiled, then returned to his conversation with the moustachioed man beside him.

"I guess we've left the tourist areas," Fletcher said as he came alongside her, something he'd been unable to do in the thick crowds they'd left behind.

Erin wiped her brow. "Well, I'm happy for the breathing space. That wasn't pleasant."

"I kind of liked it," he said, flicking his eyes to the stalls on either side. "It's alive."

She grunted. "I like life, but I prefer a less intrusive shopping experience – one with fewer people and less heat. And I seemed to be targeted a little more than you."

"They seem to have good taste."

Erin glanced at him, her eyes narrowing. "Flattery will get you …" She stopped herself. She didn't want to go there.

Fletcher grinned. "Hmm, sounds interesting."

She ignored him.

"Robert's just headed into that alley on the left," Fletcher said, looking ahead. "Let's not lose him now."

Erin nodded and they hurried on.

They'd left the car in a busy side street outside the market, then the professor had asked them to split up and take different routes to his house. "Merely a precaution," Khaled had told them as he and Asim had left the car. "I've seen no one following us."

Those words had triggered Erin to furtively glance behind them, searching for the black-jacketed thief. Or the white-haired man. But she'd seen neither as she and Fletcher had followed Robert on their trek through the crowded warren of the busy souq, a path seemingly very familiar to the bookseller.

And now, as they entered a narrow gap between two shops to follow Robert into a dimly lit alley, a recurring thought returned. *A strange place for the professor's home.*

"Up here," came Robert's voice from above.

Looking up, she saw him climbing the last section of a wooden staircase before disappearing into an elevated passageway between the buildings.

"This is one hell of a maze," Fletcher muttered. "But I guess we've arrived to …" His brow furrowed. "To wherever this is." He gestured to the staircase, smiling. "Beauty before age."

"I think I can take that," Erin replied, returning his smile. She stepped past him and made her way up the stairs.

Reaching the top, sweating profusely in the heat, she saw elevated pathways running along and between the chaotically constructed buildings. She turned into the gap Robert had entered and walked on through the gloomy passageway before exiting onto a well-lit wooden walkway. *Actually, a balcony,* she thought as she looked over the battered railing to her left into the courtyard below. The elevated balcony she stood on ran around all four bounding walls of the surrounding buildings. Walking on along the walkway, she came to the end of the building to her right and found herself entering a separate square courtyard, higher up and offset to the courtyard below. *It's like a three-dimensional puzzle.* Maybe if you wanted to hide, this was not a bad place to be.

Following Robert, they crossed the courtyard, passing a man seemingly sleeping, his hat drawn down over his forehead – but she saw the glint of his eyes beneath. Reaching a door in the building beyond, she heard Robert's voice from within. "Up here," the bookseller called.

Where on earth are we going? she thought, wiping her brow as they followed Robert's voice up the stone staircase. She heard the grate of a door above, and light flooded down the stairwell. She continued climbing, then passed through an open door and walked out into the glare of the sun.

"Welcome," came a richly timbred voice.

Shielding her eyes from the sun, she saw the professor sitting at a table shaded by the wide canopy of several large-leafed potted trees. Robert stood to one side of the professor, and the young man, Asim, sat in a chair to the other side. His dark eyes calmly studied her.

"Please," the professor said, smiling. "Take a seat. We have much to discuss."

*

Erin pulled her gaze back from the sand-coloured rooftops of Qahir, then took another sip of her ice-cold drink. "That's good." She sighed, the terrors of the morning momentarily subdued. She placed her glass on the marble-topped table by her chair, then sat back with a quiet sigh. "I could drink that all day."

"From a good friend of mine," the bespectacled professor said. "I can of course make it myself, but why, when you can drink such perfect lemonade as this?"

Erin watched the man – *in his sixties* – run his hand over the bald pate of his receding hairline. Taken together with his grey-flecked hair and glasses, it painted the perfect image of what she expected a professor to look like. She wiped her brow. "It's perfect for this heat. It will take time to acclimatise, I think."

The professor clasped his hands on the paunch of his stomach. "I expect you will soon wish you were back in the cool shade of my home."

The words shattered Erin's brief moment of calm.

Fletcher looked over at the professor. "So that brings us back to where you want to take us – and why."

Khaled glanced at Robert. "What have you told them?"

"Nothing. There hasn't been time."

Khaled studied Robert for a while, as if waiting for him to expand, but the bookseller remained silent. Khaled turned back. "Well, this is really Robert's story, but maybe I should provide some background from my side. Then I'd like to hear more from you – from the little Robert has told me, it seems you have most interesting acquaintances."

Tense anticipation ran through Erin. *As do you*, she thought, glancing at the young man in the chair beside the professor. *Unassuming. About my age.* And the Keeper she been asked to find.

Khaled adjusted his spectacles. "Well, I'll be brief, as there will be much to do." He leaned forward, one arm resting on his knee. "I've worked with Robert for many, many years. In fact, at the start of my career, I knew Robert's parents – it was they who triggered my passion in my subject." A smile played on the professor's lips. "A subject not well liked by my colleagues."

"And that is?" Erin prompted.

"I study anything relating to ... hmm, the devil, you may say. At least as far as it relates to this part of the world, the Suma region."

"A pleasant occupation, I'm sure," Fletcher muttered, his brow furrowing.

Khaled laughed. "Luckily for me, enough people in the world are willing to help pay for my research." He gave a casual shrug, holding his hands palms-up. "It has allowed me to live comfortably enough." He glanced over at Robert. "But this meeting is not about me."

He paused, seeming to collect his thoughts. "When I became connected with Robert and his views – and those of his parents – I was able to provide input from ancient writings I'd been studying. Writings from here, from ancient Mesotania, from any such work they hadn't yet accessed or were unable to interpret themselves. Over time, we formed the view of a late ice age power in the region, predating the supposed start of civilisation by several thousand years." He smiled. "Preposterous, most said, dismissing the idea that late Palaeolithic man could organise themselves in this way. But think, how long had humans developed over the tens of thousands of years prior to this? An incredibly long time," he answered himself, a fire in his eyes. "Early humans adapted supremely well to living on this planet. They were smart, skilled, socially aware, and with the same human impulses as you and I."

His smile faded. "And for Robert and me, these ancient people would most definitely have had their tyrants, those who would seek to dominate others, often most viciously, in their desire for power, for wealth." He tilted his head slightly. "Think only of those most hated leaders in our own recorded history to see what humans are capable of inflicting on others. Or maybe also of those most venerated heroes." He studied Erin intently. "A conquered people seldom consider themselves treated in a fair and just manner, don't you think?" He paused as if waiting for a reaction.

What does he want us to say? Erin thought. *And what's the point of this?* She glanced at Asim, who sat silently in his chair, his hands resting on his lap, his sharp eyes looking back at her. What did this have to do with the Keeper?

Khaled straightened in his chair. "My point is this," he said as if reading her thoughts. "Smart and intelligent humans, whether now, or thousands of years in the past, can decide – for what might be just or unjust reasons – to dominate others. And they can most certainty be influenced by the gods of their time." He picked up his glass and took a sip. Then: "And my belief is that most formidable gods exist beyond our sight, gods who have engaged with the people of this land for a long, long time."

"What sort of gods?" Erin asked, thinking of the evil she had encountered on the mountain that fateful evening.

"Ones of many flavours," the professor answered, his sharp eyes locking onto hers. "Those I focussed on – the ones I label devils – these have been seen in earliest recorded history. Of course, the concept of evil has changed. That of a 'devil', separate from God, is a more recent concept, but the notion of evil, or of an uncontrollable chaos, has always been there. And do you think this concept merely happened to be coincident with the first keeping of records? Of course not! Complex societies and beliefs have existed for many tens of thousands of years. Evil did not appear because man could write."

With a sudden gleam in his eyes, he looked out over the dramatic vista of jumbled rooftops of the historic city. "No, I believe there has been a constant root evil throughout humanity's existence. Possibly beyond. A core evil transcending all those religions that have come and gone since. One existing here in those Palaeolithic times, and one still existing here today." His gaze shifted to Robert, whose face remained unreadable. "My friend abandoned the search, but I kept looking. Then I met Asim ... and that made me certain."

Erin glanced back to Asim, who had been flicking his eyes between her and Robert as the professor spoke. Asim smiled at her. Despite the growing tension, she smiled back. "And what did you say that made the professor certain of his theory?" she asked him.

Asim held a hand up to his mouth.

The professor cleared his throat. "Unfortunately, Asim has no voice. At least none I have heard. Why this should be so is still not clear to me. I believe it is a product of his treatment."

Shocked, she looked back to Khaled. "He was ill?"

"He was considered so by those doctors who examined him – and by those psychiatrists who analysed him."

"What was wrong with him?" she asked, glancing back at the young man, uncomfortable having this conversation with him sitting right there.

'They thought I was mad.'

She almost jumped out of her chair as the voice sounded clear as day in her mind.

"Ah," the professor said, staring at her intently. "I'm pleased. This is a welcome sign."

Frowning, Fletcher turned to her. "What is? Did I miss something?"

"I think I heard Asim speak – in here." She tapped her head.

His face strained, Fletcher stared at her and then at Asim.

Erin reached out and laid her hand on Fletcher's. "I know it's not easy to believe," she whispered. "But believe me, hearing voices isn't so comfortable either."

Fletcher fell silent for a moment, then his drawn-out sigh was heavy. "I guess not."

She squeezed his hand, then turned back to Asim. *They thought he was mad.* "So, you had – or have – beliefs not accepted, not understood by others?"

Asim smiled and nodded.

"Not only not understood," Khaled said. "Show them, Asim."

Asim stood and pulled up his shirt.

"Oh my God," Erin gasped, her hand rising to her mouth. The young man's chest and stomach were crisscrossed with the scars of ... of what? "Who did this? What did they do?"

"People who thought he was crazy," Khaled said. "People who should have cared for him."

The young man pulled his shirt down and sat back on his chair.

Sickened, Erin's gaze was drawn back to the professor. "What were these beliefs? Why did they think him mad?"

"He wrote of many things. He wrote of a coming Armageddon. He wrote of an evil god." He tilted his head a fraction. "And there was another with him who claimed to hear Asim's voice in his head."

They thought him mad. So what does that make me? "Robert said you call him the Keeper. Why?"

"He is the Keeper of a story ... But I think that story is incomplete." He leaned forward slightly, his eyes glistening with a fierce intensity. "Maybe on this, you may be of some help?"

She shifted uncomfortably on her seat. *Why is it I don't trust you?* "How did you find him?"

"In a city of over seventeen million people? Either with great good fortune or with help. I will let you choose which."

The answer to that was clear.

But who had helped the professor was not.

Her mouth suddenly dry, Erin detached from the professor's intense gaze and looked at the young man.

'You can speak to me this way,' came Asim's voice in her mind. *'No one else will hear.'*

Startled, she managed to hold a steady gaze on Asim, revealing nothing of her shock. *Speak with my mind? How—*

'Yes, like that.'

'You heard me?' she asked incredulously.

'It seems you are blessed with this gift.'

A gift? No, talking with someone like this was not a gift. It was a curse. *And yet, you've already done this. With a daemon.* She steadied herself. *It's happening. Deal with it. What can you learn?* She thought of the scars. *'Who were the people who did those things to you?'*

'People who did not understand. People who did things they did not fully understand. But IY supported me, told me someone was coming who could help me.'

'Who is IY?'

'One who seeks to protect life.'

'From who?'

'The Dark.'

She fought to understand what she was hearing. *'Are you the Keeper? What is the Keeper?'*

'I am the Keeper. I hold the memory – the Story – of those before me. The Keepers wait for those who will come.'

'Wait for who?'

'For you. And for another I cannot reveal here. It is not safe.'

Stunned, Erin stared at Asim. *'You waited for me?'*

'The Story is carried through the Continuum. The Story tells of you.'

'I don't understand,' she stammered.

'There is much neither I nor you can understand of this,' Asim murmured. *'That is for the Guardian. But I know the Continuum adjusts, it aligns. And it holds the Story. Maybe you will understand once we meet the other who comes.'*

'But you will not tell me who?'

'Not in this moment. But soon.' His gentle smile belied a tension beneath.

Erin licked her dry lips. She'd been sent to find the Keeper, and now the Keeper said he waited for her. *This makes no sense. I am nobody.* And yet she was here. She felt the professor's eyes boring into her. *'Do you trust these men? The professor … and Robert.'*

'I will not risk an answer here.'

He'd deflected the question, yet she heard his answer. The trust wasn't there. *But for one, or for both?* Steadying herself, she held the fear from her face. *'Do you trust me?'*

Asim smiled, deep warmth in his young eyes. *'You ask me this question? You who are a friend of the Warriors. You who are told of in the Story. Far more important is, do you trust me?'*

There was that word again. Trust. But who to trust? She picked up her glass and took a sip of the cooling drink. *I have to trust somebody.* 'I think so,' she said simply, placing the glass back on the table.

'That is good enough for now. We must travel south, and there we will speak again. But for now, please excuse me. I must sleep.' He laid his head back in the chair and closed his eyes.

"What did he say?" came Khaled's voice.

She turned to see the professor's sharp eyes scanning her face. "He said he holds a story," she said, choosing her words carefully. "And that he waits for something. He said we should travel south, then said he needed to sleep."

Khaled studied her for a moment, then smiled and sat up in his chair. "It seems to be a necessity. When he requires sleep, he sleeps. I have no control over this, and neither, I suspect, does he." He shrugged. "It is no great matter. We just don't let him drive."

Erin forced a smile, then sat back into her chair, trying to grasp a hold on her thoughts. It was clear that the world Jessica and her friends – and now, she and Fletcher – had become involved in was a complex and dangerous one. A world containing entities – could she say gods? – beyond her ken. But why had she and her friends fallen into this? *These are things beyond our understanding. These are not things for us.* Yet she knew those words rang hollow. She couldn't turn away, couldn't pretend this wasn't her problem, because she'd already seen and felt the fearsome presence of an entity wielding a diabolical power, an entity that threatened both her and her friends. She'd already crossed the threshold from an unbeliever to a … to a what? To one who would end up in the same institution as Asim if she declared it. *But to help my friends, I can't deny what I've seen and felt.*

She glanced at Robert, and then the professor. *Asim wouldn't say if he trusted you two. So where does that leave me?*

She focussed her gaze on Robert. "Is there more you know of the Keeper?"

Robert shook his head, his face unreadable. "Nothing more than I've told you. My attention was elsewhere. I had no contact with Khaled for many years. Not until …" A shadow crossed his features. "Until recently."

She saw Khaled glance at Robert, his eyes scanning his friend's face. *Does he know what Robert did? Did Robert tell him he tried to betray my friends?* Realisation dawned. *Robert has not told the professor all. Why?*

Khaled turned to her. "Asim shares what he can, but many things remain unclear." He reached out and laid his hand on the sleeping man's shoulder. "That he's connected to the cause your friends now fight for, I have no doubt. His story runs parallel to the one Robert has related and to all we have discovered over the years. He protects a certain knowledge that will be needed. By whom, and when? This is not something he will tell." An intense look came into his eyes. "But he's been clear on where we should go. And we must go soon."

Erin held her breath. "Where?"

"A place to the southwest. An ancient site I have worked on for years. Yet a place where I've found nothing of genuine interest, at least nothing of an age that interests me. But no matter. We will try once again. And it is not far, a few hours' drive, no more." He glanced at Robert. "Is all ready?"

Robert, a sudden weariness in his eyes, pulled himself up to his feet. "Almost. We'll be ready to leave in the morning." He looked over at Erin. "If you're refreshed, we should use the time we've left today to finalise the supplies."

Erin glanced at the sleeping Asim. They had to travel south, that's what he had said. Well, for now, she would keep moving and find out more from Asim; find the true reason why the whale daemon, Balena, had told her to find the Keeper. "Fine," she answered in a firm voice. "Where will we stay tonight?"

"Here," Khaled said, lifting himself out of his chair. "There are rooms below. I'll show you now before you leave with Robert."

Somehow holding an external calm, Erin climbed to her feet. She glanced out over the city's chaotic rooftops – a strange, exotic cityscape in its own right.

"There is always something new to see and hear," the professor said, catching her gaze. "A sparkling oasis despite the appearance of chaos. Yes, this city has its own order, its own delights. When the wind blows, you will see the children out on these rooftops flying their ragged kites. On most days, wind or not, you also see the women, such as that one in the red robes, hanging out their family's washing to dry. Flying their own kites, it might be said."

He turned to her. "But I know the ferocious intensity of this city is not for everyone. To some, it is a poor and infested concrete jungle, devoid of adequate living space for the majority – not a future to be aspired to. But for me, I enjoy the company of others. I enjoy the intensity and diversity of the life. The sounds and sights of my city's streets make me feel alive." He sighed, then offered a wry smile. "But I am privileged – I have two houses, one in the city, and one out in the country. So maybe I am not the best judge." His smile broadened. "Come, let me show you your rooms."

As they crossed the rooftop terrace to the entrance back into the building, Erin stopped and glanced back, realising Asim still slept in his chair.

"Don't worry about Asim. He will find me when he awakes." Khaled smiled at her. "He clearly trusts you. To my knowledge, you are only the second person he has spoken to. And that makes you most fascinating – most fascinating indeed." He gestured for them to follow, then stepped through the doorway and on into the gloomy interior.

As Fletcher and Robert followed the professor, Erin studied the sleeping young man. What terrors had he endured? And how enduring his will to have come through those horrors and appear so composed? Who had helped protect his soul?

She grimaced. *And how am I supposed to help one such as this?*

She turned to the shaded doorway, the dying echoes of her questions replaced by the sharp footsteps of the men below. *Listen to the Keeper,* she told herself firmly. *In him you must trust.*

She stepped inside.

CHAPTER ELEVEN

The Keeper knew enough. He played his part.

"We turn off about two kilometres ahead, on the left," Khaled said from the passenger seat. Beside him, Robert nodded, both hands on the steering wheel and his eyes fixed firmly on the empty desert road ahead. Seated in the back of the car, Erin strained to catch a glance out of the rear window. The road behind was clear. Breathing a sigh of relief, she turned back, settling in her seat, hearing the gentle snores of the sleeping Asim beside her. Could the bag thief have given up? She doubted it.

It had been soon after meeting up in the morning that she had spotted the bag thief standing in the distance beside a nondescript white car. Just the thief, no sign of a white-haired man. *Was that white-haired man real? Or a figment of my fear?* Hurrying to their own car, Khaled had driven off at speed into the rush-hour traffic – though rush hour seemed a mocking misnomer in that unsleeping city, as chaos reigned at all hours. Taking a random route and several illegal turns, they'd appeared to lose their stalker. But an hour south of Qahir, as they switched drivers to allow the professor to navigate, she'd watched the thief's white car drive past them. And a while later, a few kilometres along the road, they in turn had passed the white car parked by a dusty roadside shack. The thief had been sitting at a table, his back to them.

Since then, the thief's car had not been seen. *But he doesn't need to stay close to follow us now.* Khaled had said the desert road continued, unbroken, for over fifty kilometres south until the next junction.

But the professor was not intending to travel that far.

Erin brushed a strand of her short blonde hair over her ear. What could she do? What could she and Fletcher do? The thief was trouble;

of that, she was sure. *And he may have tried to kill us already,* she thought, wincing at the memory of their frantic escape from the hotel fire. She wiped her sweaty hand on her cotton trousers and stared out of the car window. They were in too deep to back out now. *Trust the Keeper. See what Asim wants to show us at these ancient ruins.* She licked her dry lips. *But I'm scared. Terrified.*

"Prepare yourself," came Khaled's voice. "When I tell you, pull off the road, then climb the railway embankment, cross the rail tracks, and drop to the other side and stop." He waved a finger at Robert. "And drive steadily – not too fast, not too slow. I don't wish to be betrayed by clouds of dust swirling in our wake."

Her heart thumping, Erin saw Khaled check his GPS, then stare out of the front windscreen. "Not far. Not far now."

Erin looked back out of the side window next to Fletcher, seeing the embankment streaking past. They had followed this raised rail track for most of their journey, occasionally seeing the glint of the tracks themselves, but mostly the sand-strewn embankment, which hid the bleak desert beyond.

"There!" Khaled said suddenly. "Follow those tracks."

Robert slowed the car, then turned to the left.

"Steady. A little slower, please."

The car slowed, then bounced a little as they crossed the rough verge of the road.

"Good – a little to the right."

Light dust kicked up from the verge. *This wind should move it – I hope,* Erin thought, pushed back in her seat as they climbed the rocky embankment. As they levelled out at the crest, she twisted to look back down the road. "I don't see anything," she said as they rumbled over the tracks. But as they began their downward descent to the desert plain, to her dismay, she caught a brief glimpse of a distant car ... then they were over the crest and out of sight of the road – out of sight of their pursuer.

"I saw him," she said in a breathless voice as they dropped down the far slope of the embankment. "He's still following us." She turned to Fletcher. "Did he see us?"

His face drawn, Fletcher said, "Not sure."

"Stop here," Khaled said quickly as they reached the sandy, gravel-strewn ground beyond the embankment. "We don't want to kick up dust. And kill the engine."

Khaled opened his door and climbed out. Erin, Robert, and Fletcher followed.

Then they waited in silence, listening.

A distant noise reached them, slowly growing louder as they anxiously waited. As the drone of the car approached, Erin tensed. What would they do if it stopped? She glanced at Khaled – and stifled a gasp. Was that a gun he'd slipped inside his jacket? Khaled's eyes caught hers. He smiled and put his finger to his lips. Wincing, she looked away. Her mistrust of the man was quickly turning to dislike.

Switching her attention back to the car, she held her breath as its drone grew louder … but moments later, she heard the drop in pitch as it sped by. Hearing the car gradually fade into the distance, she allowed herself to breathe. "He won't stop chasing us," she said in a low voice.

"Yes," Khaled answered. "This thief you spoke of seems more than a simple pickpocket. I suspect this is the very group Robert was warned about. Agents of the Enemy."

"What do they want?"

"Us – our knowledge." Khaled gestured to the car where Asim slept. "His knowledge."

"Then why target me and Fletcher?"

The professor's gaze sharpened. "If this thief is indeed an agent of the Enemy, that should be clear to you."

She bristled. "No, nothing is clear to me. Maybe Fletcher and I have seen a little of this crazy world, but what do we truly know?" She gestured at the bookseller, who was staring east across the flat expanse of gravel-strewn desert. "*He* told you what we know. You two know more about what's going on here than us."

"Maybe you know more than you think … or have told."

She saw the faintest flicker of anger deep within the professor's eyes. *He thinks we hide something, something of value to him. He's trying to flush it out.* Her unease of the man deepened. Whatever little she knew, she would tell him nothing. "If that's what they think, they're mistaken."

"That doesn't help us," Fletcher said to her side. "Whoever they are, and whatever they think, they're clearly following us. And they're getting good information on our movements. The hotel … This morning …"

Erin glanced at Khaled, whose glinting eyes still studied her. *Could he have been involved with these others? Could he—*

Khaled cleared his throat. "I can see the question in your eyes," he said, tilting his head and smiling. "I wondered how long it would take to point a finger of suspicion on me." He shrugged. "And I don't blame you, my dear, but you think I – one who supports one such as Asim, and is trusted by him – would work for his enemy? No, I fight for those in the right, of that you can be sure."

Trusted? No, I don't think you are. And don't call me 'my dear.'

Khaled strolled a few paces away from them, then turned back. "Who knew you would be at that hotel? The hotel staff, the airport staff, the police, immigration, the travel agency. All those that place their secret cookies on your computer. Should I go on?"

Erin said nothing.

"No one can claim their movements are unknown. A 'Big Brother' is alive and well." He smiled. "You know that book?"

She nodded.

"That writer was reacting against despots who sought to capture and devour people's freedom and liberty, stripping them of their privacy and laying them bare. And now? People freely invite these devils into their homes – let me buy a cheap television and I will give you my soul. So, no, it was not only Robert and I who knew you were at the hotel."

Erin held her neutral expression. *Nice speech. But I don't trust you. I'm sorry, I just don't.*

The professor sighed and walked back towards them. "Forgive me. I hold a particular hatred of aspects of our modern world. It is one of the reasons I like my home in the souq. Everything is transparent and real. And no one knows what I do." He stopped in front of her. "I hope we are still friends."

No, Erin thought. *We are not.* But she forced a smile. And forced a lie. "Friends," she said, holding his eyes.

"Excellent." He pulled out a handkerchief and wiped his brow. "I would think our pursuer is well past now. It will be safe to travel on."

"Are we sure about that?" Fletcher muttered to her side. "These people following us could be pretty dangerous folk."

'We must go on,' came Asim's voice in Erin's mind. *'The one pursuing us will soon realise his mistake and turn back.'*

'Who is he?'

'I don't know, but if he had wanted to stop us, they had opportunity enough on this road.'

'So, he wants to find out where we're going?'

'It seems so, but that is out of our hands. We must go on. The time is approaching.'

'Time for what?'

Asim fell silent – yet Fletcher's question still echoed in her mind. *Are we sure …?*

She ran her hand through her hair and glanced around – both Robert and Khaled stood to one side, watching her. Struck by sudden doubts, her gut twisted. What was she doing, heading deep into a desert desolation with an enemy behind and an unknown destination ahead? Her furtive gaze lingered on Khaled. *And travelling with someone I don't trust.* Her eyes flicked to Robert. *And with another who failed the trust of others.* She glanced east to the gravel-strewn, desert plain, beyond which lay the place Asim wished her to visit. *Do we still go on?*

With a gnawing dread in the pit of her stomach, she felt Fletcher and Asim by her side. Their comforting presence seemed to draw a soothing cloth across her brow, dampening her fear. *In these two I trust.* The waves of panic settling, her resolve returned. *Keep moving. Trust in one who knows something of the world of my friends. Do what you can to help them.*

She turned back to Fletcher. "We need to go on, Fletch. We have to see what lies at these ancient ruins they speak of." *See who it is that Asim awaits.*

Fletcher edged closer to her. "You're sure of that?"

She forced a thin smile. "As sure as any of us can be."

A flurry of emotions crossed his face, then he sighed. "Okay. We go on."

"Thank you," she whispered.

Fletcher faced Khaled, whose lips held a faint smile. "Where do we go from here?"

"The way you face," Khaled said, turning away and walking to join Robert. "East to the lake, where the ruins lie. Not too far, and a most pleasant view on the way. You'll see." He laid his hand on Robert's shoulder, and together, the two men walked back to the car.

Fletcher glanced at Erin. "I hope these voices of yours know what they're doing."

She gave a pained smile. "So do I, Fletch." *So do I.*

*

Standing on the crest of the escarpment, Erin could see now why they needed the off-road car – the descent down looked treacherous.

"Remnants of ancient lava flows," Khaled said, looking down over several broad terraces which stepped down to the distant plain. "Worked by the ancient people of the K'Met, but probably from long before that."

"K'Met?" Fletcher asked, coming alongside Erin.

161

"The ancient name of this land. The Black Land. Maybe because of the black soil of the floodplains beyond."

Erin's gaze shifted from the plains vista to the wide, jagged rent slicing through the stepped terraces and sharp-edged escarpments, its sheer walls revealing the multicoloured layers of the ground beneath their feet. This was the canyon that would serve as the path to their destination. She followed the great chasm to the final terrace, where it broke through to the great plain beyond. The vast expanse of golden sand and gravel of the plain was broken in the distance by the vivid blue waters of a large lake.

"Arun Lake," Khaled said, seeing her studying the lake. "And beyond, the town of Fym." He swept his arm to the right. "But on this side of the lake lies our destination, the ruins of Dyma."

"And they are?"

"Once a great Olemaic city, later occupied, then destroyed by barbarian invaders. That lake is fed from the great Iteru River and once reached the very edges of the old city. Some people, possibly the Olemies themselves, dammed the inlet to the lake – the result we see before us."

Erin scanned the distant horizon. *And what else lies waiting for us?*

Khaled smiled. "Come, let us see how Robert handles the drive down."

The path to the plain was as difficult as she'd feared – several kilometres of perilous driving, the car sliding precariously close to the canyon's many sheer drops as they navigated slowly down the treacherous ravine. But finally, with deep sighs of relief from all, they descended the last ridge and drove out of the canyon.

"Good work," Khaled said as they drove out onto the sandy plain before turning to track the front of the final escarpment. "Keep your speed up now. We don't want to get bogged down in soft sand."

Moments later, Erin noticed a stone structure at the mouth of a smaller canyon cutting through the escarpment. "What's that building over there to the right?"

"Kasr Agha," the professor said. "An ancient temple of K'Met. Dedicated to a local deity – a crocodile god." He shook his head. "It is amazing how much those people forgot – how much they lost."

How much they *forgot?* Surely, he meant how much *we* forgot?

Khaled gestured ahead. "That's our destination over there in the distance, on that low rise."

Looking to the south through the windscreen to the distant hill just visible on the horizon, Erin saw a jagged profile of sandstone pillars.

162

As they drove on, she scanned the pillars for evidence of buildings. "I can't see the ruins yet."

"Surely you can," Khaled said in surprise. "Their profile is clear from here."

"I can see eroded sandstone pillars, but no building."

Khaled laughed. "Those pillars *are* the buildings – or what is left of them two thousand years later."

"Impressive," Fletcher murmured by her side.

A great sight for a tourist, maybe, but they're making me cold.

A short while later, they pulled up at the base of the steep rise to the ruins.

"We're here," the quietest of voices breathed in her ear.

Erin turned, eyes widening.

Asim put a finger to his lips. *'Shall we go?'* he pulsed in her mind. Then he opened the door and climbed out.

She stared after him, shocked. He could talk? Then why the silence? Why the subterfuge? She saw the professor open his door and quickly climb out, hurrying after Asim.

"Not now, Asim," she heard the professor call after Asim. "We need to set up our camp and equipment, then we can search."

Erin's gaze followed the professor. *Maybe Asim's silence is to hide things from you.*

"You okay?" Fletcher said beside her.

"Fine," she replied, managing to hold her voice steady while gesturing surreptitiously to Robert and putting a finger to her lips. "Just taking in the sights."

Fletcher's eyes narrowed … then he gave a slight nod. He reached for his water bottle. "Is this where we're staying, Robert?"

"The odd tourist visits this place, so I think we'll camp a short distance away over there." He pointed over to their right. "Keeps our belongings out of the way. And fewer questions. We'll move when Khaled gets Asim back in the car."

Erin glanced out of the window. Khaled had caught up with Asim. She opened the door. "Come on, Fletch. I want a quick look at this place."

She heard him sigh as she jumped out, but then he scrambled out of the car.

As they climbed the rise, Khaled was already walking back down with an arm around Asim's shoulder.

"Going to have a quick look up there, if that's all right," Erin said as Khaled walked Asim back to the car.

"Please be brief. We must set up camp. We will have time to look around later when it's cooler."

Erin and Fletcher scrambled up the sandy slope to the nearest crumbling wall. Fletcher picked up a shard-like fragment from the ground. "Look at all this broken pottery. Someone really trashed this place when they left. And over there, do you—"

Erin gasped as a loathsome nausea ripped through her stomach.

"What is it?" Fletcher said, quickly coming to her side. "You okay?"

Her gut twisting, cold fear engulfed her, and she almost turned and ran.

"Erin, what's wrong?"

She glanced up at the ruins. "There's a terrible evil here. Can't you feel it?"

"No," he breathed, glancing around nervously. "But you look as though you've seen a ghost."

"Worse than that," she whispered, fighting the urge to flee. "Far worse."

"What is it?"

"I don't know."

She jumped as Asim's voice whispered in her mind. *'It cannot hurt you. Already it is passing.'*

Fletcher gripped her hand. "Erin – we should go back to the car."

"A moment, Fletch," she said, already feeling the churning nausea easing. "Give me a moment."

He fell silent, watching her.

'What is it?' she replied to Asim as moment by moment the sense of dread seemed to lessen.

'Ancient entities who should remain locked within their prison. Luckily for us, they are shielded – we do not suffer their full effect.'

'A prison? Is the other you await here?'

'It is told the one who comes will enter this place, but no, they are not imprisoned here.'

'Who is?'

'That, we shall not speak of in this moment. And do not mention this to the others.'

'Fletcher knows I've felt something.'

'He is your friend.'

Her hands cold and clammy, Erin looked down at the car. Khaled and Robert stood by the bonnet, looking up at them. At her. These two could not be called friends. Especially the professor. But was he an enemy? Had he some connection to what had happened at the hotel? Another image came to mind. She reached out to Asim. *'At the hotel, I thought I saw someone who I've seen before. A white-haired man who seeks the Guardian.'*

She sensed a flicker of dismay from Asim. *'One who serves Kaos. One who does not know who I am.'*

'Then he is here?'

The hesitation was barely perceptible. *'We cannot be distracted by him. We must do what is needed. I will call you when it is time.'*

She felt Asim's presence leave.

"Erin," came Fletcher's voice. "What's wrong?"

Enemies are close. "Asim says this is the place we should be. But we need to take care. Stay close – please."

A strained smile broke on his drained face. He squeezed her hand. "Don't worry about that. There's much about this I don't understand, but one thing I do know is that we're in this together."

Despite the lingering sense of something foul in the air, she managed a small smile. Glancing down the slope, she saw both men were back in the car. "Then let's keep moving," she whispered. *And pray that Asim knows what he's doing.*

*

"You are certain you felt nothing?" the professor asked, sweat dripping from his brow in the heat of the midday sun as he carried the last box from the back of the car to his tent.

"Maybe something – I'm not sure," Erin said, searching for the right response as she dropped a bag into her and Fletcher's tent. "Those ruins are an amazing sight sitting isolated in the midst of this vast desert. I guess that's enough to trigger an emotional response in most people."

"And you, Robert? Still nothing?"

Robert closed the back of the car. "I've already told you, Khaled, expect nothing from me. She's the one who was told to come here. I just agreed to help – and thought you could help them."

Hold on, Erin thought. So Robert hadn't revealed to Khaled his connection with the whale daemon? That he also was told to travel to Misr? She watched Robert walk over to his tent and crawl inside. What game was he playing?

"An interesting man, don't you think?"

She jumped at the professor's voice by her shoulder.

"He … yes, amazing the work he did for all those years," she said, trying clamp hold on rattled nerves.

"We lost touch for quite a while," the professor said in a low voice. "This saddened me because I knew we were onto something. I couldn't believe he had actually given up and often wondered whether he continued to work in the background. Did he ever say anything to you?"

"I … I didn't know him at all," she said, alarm bells ringing. "Other than as a bookseller."

"What happened to him at the mountain?"

He knows a lot, she thought, scrambling to figure out how she should respond. *But clearly not everything.* "Well, I guess he told you all about that," she said in an even voice.

Khaled stepped closer. "He told me something, but it is clear he has changed from the confident man I knew. He seems broken in some way."

A part of Erin bristled. "Look," she said in a quiet voice, holding his gaze. "I'm not comfortable talking about him like this when he's just over there. Aside from him hearing us gossip, I'm not one to pry into another's business. I think we should drop this."

Khaled smiled and dipped his head. "Quite right. Forgive me. My concern for Robert has exceeded my sensibilities. Consider the subject closed. Now," he said in a louder voice, "our last task is to assemble this canopy – and I for one will be grateful for the cooling shade it will offer. And then lunch." He patted his stomach. "The most accurate timepiece on the planet. Never fails to sound an alarm around midday."

Erin smiled … on the outside. For inside, her unease of the professor was deepening.

Or was it the lingering smell of evil from the ruins?

She suppressed a shiver. *Maybe both …*

CHAPTER TWELVE

Never give up, never cease your wondrous endeavour to reach your goal, for when you arrive, it may offer far more than you could ever have dreamed.

A disgruntled voice swept out of the swirling winds of the blizzard. "Azar! This cursed snow! We might walk straight past the peak, and we'd never know."

"You'd struggle to navigate yourself off the top of a mountain on a calm sunny day, Shorty," Knuckles called, trudging wearily over the snow-laden ground behind his tall friend. "But for once, you're right – we're in danger of becoming separated. We should find some cover and let it blow out. Let's wait for the others."

Knuckles halted beside Shorty, then glanced back. Shielding his face from the biting gale, his keen eyes caught sight of a bowed figure in the whiteout. Battered by the wind, the figure struggled inexorably onward through the drifting snow. He grimaced. Reaching the northern tip of the land and turning east along the coastal escarpment into this bleak, icy landscape, they'd thought this part of the journey would be easier underfoot. And before the storm, it had been. Dotted with hardy trees, bushes, and patches of thicker scrub, these undulating foothills had proved easier going than the coastal mountains to the south. But though the vegetation clung to life on these frozen, northern shores, it all bowed down to the vicious, snow-laden northerly howling in off the Great Sea.

"Just like us," he muttered, turning his back to the blizzard.

He waited beside Shorty, his body braced against the gale, until the weary-looking, snow-covered figure of Svana walked up to him.

"What's up?" she said, pulling down her hood and scanning around through squinted eyes.

"Well, in case you hadn't noticed, it's snowing."

She turned and looked down on him, snow already catching in the ragged curls of her dark hair. "And?"

"And that makes it tricky to see where we're going. It's two days since we turned in from the coast, and we'll be in danger of missing the peak if we keep going in this weather."

"Agreed," came a deep voice behind Knuckles. "We'll break before this weather if we keep going."

Bear's heavyset frame appeared by Svana's shoulder, immediately followed by Scorpion, both men plastered with snow.

"I've seen boulders up ahead that might provide some shelter," came Shorty's muffled voice, his face still buried under his hood.

"Okay, lead on," Bear grunted, his solid face standing resolute against the driving snow. "Let's see what shelter we can find."

Forcing his weary legs to move, Knuckles took his place behind Shorty, trudging on in the tall man's wake. "Don't walk on past that refuge you saw, Shorty," he muttered. "For once, keep your eyes peeled."

If Shorty answered him, he didn't hear it.

But soon enough, he heard the words he'd been waiting for. "Over here," Shorty called.

Glancing up, Knuckles caught sight of snow-laden mounds to their right. "Those will do fine," he muttered to himself, and followed on after his friend.

As he entered the lee of the snowcapped boulders, the numbing chill of the wind instantly cut off. Despite his mood, he grinned. "Well, this does look a good spot, Shorty. Seems you occasionally have your uses."

As the others entered the shelter, Knuckles dropped his spear to the ground, undid the straps on his pack, then twisted it off his back to the ground, taking care not to displace the smaller spear strapped to the top. He turned to Svana, who was already removing her pack, bow, and quiver. "If you search for fuel with Shorty, we'll clear the ground."

"Come on then, big man," Svana said. "Let's see what we can find." A moment later, Shorty followed her back out into the gale.

Knuckles began shifting packs of snow with his gloved hands, shovelling it as best he could outside the sheltered area. Bear and Scorpion joined him, and they quickly cleared an area large enough for them and the fire.

"That will have to do," he said, dusting the snow from his gloves and surveying the rough shelter. "We can't shift it all."

Switching his attention to the boulders behind them, Knuckles pulled out a stone blade from inside his tunic and scraped off small pieces of cold, dry moss from the snow-free face. Once satisfied with the bundle in his hand, he glanced out to the driving snow. "Now let's hope they find some fuel for us."

By the time Shorty and Svana returned, each carrying an armful of dead scrub, juniper branches, and several broken tree-branch fragments, a coldness had crept into his body.

"Good job," he said, quickly reaching for the greenest juniper branches and laying them on the cleared ground. He passed the bundle of moss to Scorpion, then both knelt, sheltering in the lee of the largest boulder. As Scorpion held out the moss within a cupped hand, Knuckles took out his flint and his most treasured pyrite. *Our saviour, many times over,* he thought, tenderly handling the valuable nodule. Working quickly, several measured, sharp strikes saw the first tendrils of smoke rising from the bundle of moss, and within, the magical orange glow of an ember. Svana leaned in with a handful of dried bark shavings taken from their dwindling stock, and Knuckles carefully placed the moss and its precious ember within the shavings. Blowing gently, Svana breathed life into the nascent cinder, spawning a flurry of fresh sparks. A warming glow grew within the shavings, and then, with a flash, Knuckles saw it burst into flame. *Each time I do this, I'm thankful for the god who gave us this miracle.* He watched as Svana carefully carried the fiery bundle to the prepared fire site, shielding it in the shelter of her body. Taking great care, they placed scraps of tinder and kindling around the flaming bundle, then once alight, they added the main fuel of scrub and dead wood. Within moments, the fire crackled and popped, their heat – and survival – for the next short while assured.

We still live. Hope remains.

They sat in a close huddle, warming nicely, Bear and Scorpion already dozing. Watching the swirling snow stream over their heads before arrowing off into the distance, Knuckles's thoughts drifted back to their mission. *The mountain we seek can't be far now, and at least this snow is keeping the dragon off our tracks.* Long unsure whether they had made the right call to continue north, they had now seen the ice dragon several times in the distance. Each time, they had hurriedly found a place to hide; each time, the dragon had passed them by.

A raw wound opened yet again. *Why didn't we see it when it first attacked Beth?*

The answer remained unclear. The hurt endured.

169

Over half a moon had passed since the Warrior had been taken on the flanks of the great canyon – a sea in the Warrior's time, she had said – and the memories remained raw. *I let her down.* In the immediate aftermath of her capture, there had been shock, then despair. Only Svana had kept her head, galvanising them to continue their mission to find the stolen Staff. *And stolen Warrior.* But as the fire of Svana's words had died, the self-recriminations began, each blaming themselves for failing to protect their ward, each believing they should have acted differently. *I shouldn't have agreed she drop to the rear of our group. My eyes were not on her.*

And then, so soon after Beth's loss, the devastating sense of grief from the south. *It was Naga, I'm sure.* The Iyes's Mother had always told him she carried a part of them in her heart – to look over them and protect them – and he had believed he held part of her in return. On that particular day when they'd all stopped and looked south, an emptiness in their very souls, he was certain some foul deed had wrenched that part of Naga from his body; he was certain that their Mother lay dead.

Yet over the days that followed, he had felt something growing in its place, something feeling its way in the Land, unsure yet of its path. A young soul, one raw and untested. *River? Was River their new shaman?* If so, what a formidable challenge for one so young. The weight of the tribe's future, and what unknown burdens of the line of the shamans? But therein lay things he knew nothing of. And he was thankful for it. *But for River …* He held his hands to the fire, seeking its warmth and its comfort as his guilt resurfaced. *I should be there, helping her. We all should be there.*

With Beth.

He leaned back, resting his tired and aching body against his pack. They would find the captured Warrior. They would rescue her from the grip of the beast. For the mountain lay close, he was sure, and when the blizzard eased, they would see it. Their destination. The Mountain of Hope.

There, we will find Beth and the Staff.

We will *find them.*

With the warmth of the fire blanketing him, he closed his eyes and withdrew from the tensions of the Land, if only for a moment.

*

Knuckles woke and looked around. The fire was almost out and the group still sleeping, but the blizzard had finally stopped. He stood and walked away from the sheltered fire, heading out into the open land.

The view north was incredible, a majestic, sweeping vista over the deep blue waters of a calm sea. A calm between storms.

And so, the mountain?

He turned to face inland …

And his gut twisted as he stared, unbelieving, across a flat, barren plain to the far horizon. He could see nothing! No mountains, no hills, no hint of a distant range. The mountain they sought was not here.

An unbearable despair washed over him. *How is this possible?*

Scanning the barren landscape, the cold truth slammed into him. *Because the Mountain of Hope doesn't exist.* Staring blindly at the shocking scene, he felt numb inside. How could they have been deceived like this? How could they have endured days and days of pain and hunger, all on a false trail. And his friend, Beth? Dead, he was sure.

A furious anger ignited. *Because we've all been fools!*

He turned back to the fire, glaring at the one who had led them on this fool's mission. *Bear.* There lay their great leader, resting in peace. What other lies had the deceiver told? What sly game did the traitor play?

In an instant, it struck him; here was the presence of the Enemy within, drawing this group far away from their people, from their allies, from the protection of their Mother and shaman, Naga. *And from the Warriors we should be aiding.*

His rage growing, he drew a blade, and strode towards Bear, death writ across his face.

'Stop!' an ethereal voice commanded.

No, he must die.

'Stop and think.'

No, the time for reason is over – he must die.

'Without reason, we are nothing.'

No, he must … I must …

Knuckles gasped. *There is nothing I must do.*

He fought against the strange fog in his mind. *Wake up! Wake up, you bloody fool!*

*

Knuckles's eyes snapped open. Licking his dry lips, he glanced around. The fire was almost out, and the group still sleeping …

All except Scorpion, who advanced on Svana with a drawn blade!

Knuckles immediately sprang up and launched himself at Scorpion, crashing into the lithe man as he was striking out at Svana. As Scorpion fell, his killing strike brushed past Svana's ear, striking the rock behind her head. Both men grunted as they hit the ground – and both sprang back to their feet, facing each other in a fighter's crouch, a light flurry of snow swirling around their heads. Scorpion, his long, dark hair swaying in the breeze, held his blade before him, switching it from hand to hand as his glazed eyes locked onto Knuckles.

"Strike! What are you doing?" Svana yelled, leaping up and turning to face them.

"Wake Bear and Shorty," Knuckles said quietly but firmly, his eyes not leaving Scorpion. "And prepare for a fight. There's an evil here—"

Scorpion sprang forward, and Knuckles barely swayed out of the deadly arc of his blade.

"You're dreaming, Scorpion! Wake up!"

Scorpion tensed his left arm to strike – but Knuckles's eyes were locked on the blade in the man's right hand. Ignoring the feint, he hammered his foot into Scorpion's blade hand. Grunting in pain, Scorpion stepped back, once more flicking his blade from hand to hand.

Knuckles caught a movement to Scorpion's right. *Svana. He hasn't seen her.* Swaying to Scorpion's left, Knuckles led the man away from the silent figure gliding in. Scorpion turned to follow him—

Svana leapt forward and struck Scorpion in the temple.

The young man collapsed to the ground.

The fight was over.

"Are they okay?" Knuckles panted, looking over to Bear and Shorty. His eyes widened as he saw Shorty lying on the ground.

"Bear will be fine. And Shorty …" Svana shrugged. "Well, I wasn't sure what was going on."

"So, you laid him out?"

"Like I said, I wasn't sure he was himself."

"Hmm," Knuckles murmured, looking back at Shorty's prone body. "I guess his hard head can take it." He glanced down at Scorpion, his face wrinkling in distaste. "Something attacked us, attacked our minds. And I … well, I almost did something I would forever regret."

Svana's sharp eyes scanned his face. "But you didn't."

"I didn't," he breathed. He looked up at her. "And you? Did you feel its attack?"

She cocked her head. "Something irritated my dreams. But I kicked it out of my bed."

Knuckles raised an eyebrow.

Svana shrugged. "They're my dreams. I can do there what I want."

He smiled. "Fair enough. It seems our minds were not so well protected as yours." He studied her, his smile fading as she knelt to check on Scorpion. *What tricks do you hold? Certainly, an impressive one, if you brushed off that attack so easily.*

"It seems some of us are not so fortunate," came Bear's voice. Knuckles turned to see the stocky man slowly standing. "So, what were *your* dreams of, Knuckles?"

Knuckles ran his hand through his short, thick hair, cringing at his imagined rage at Bear. "Ah," he mumbled, reluctant to delve into the strange workings of his mind. "I'd rather not say."

"Well, I was being persuaded to strangle your little neck," Bear said evenly. "But it's not the first time that idea has come to mind."

Knuckles laughed, bringing a welcome easing of tension to his frazzled mind. "Well, I'm glad you decided not to. I like my neck."

"Any ideas what this ... entity was?" Svana asked, standing.

Bear shook his head. "It's clear, as Knuckles said, that we were under attack, but we have no shaman or Warrior here to help us understand it." He frowned. "Why now, and why here, I don't know, but it is a sobering reminder of the Enemy's growing power and reach." He straightened, a strength to his stance. "It tells me we remain a threat. And that is valuable to know."

"Valuable indeed," Svana said, her eyes burning brightly.

Shorty groaned.

"Yes, indeed," Knuckles said, grinning as he looked down on the sorry figure on the ground. "Those who stand against us don't realise what skilled fighters they're about to face. Good job you didn't kill our secret weapon, Svana."

She scowled. "I might grow to regret that."

Knuckles laughed. "You'd be lost without him. Who else would you squabble with?"

She glared at him, but he saw through the facade to the faint smile beneath.

"Okay," Bear said, glancing at the sky. "The snow is finally relenting. As soon as these two clear their heads, we move." He looked back at them. "We don't know what triggered this attack, but while we have the light, we should move as far from here as we can." He stepped closer, his eyes hardening. "And keep an eye on Scorpion. We relieve him of guard duty, and from now on, we double up. We cannot – and will not – be defeated this close to our goal."

*

They continued east along the northern coastline, hugging the gale-swept, lightly snow-dusted ground beside the sea cliffs. The storm had blown over, and Svana saw scattered patches of blue sky appearing

173

between the fragmenting clouds. The sight lifted some of the gloom that had befallen them, raising the hope that this might be the day they would finally catch a glimpse of the mountain peak. She glanced to the rise ahead where the arc of low-lying inland hills to the south met the cliffs of the Great Sea. *From that rise, we'll get a better view inland.*

Walking on, she saw they were not the only animal to have come out of hiding after the storm. The occasional large white bird scurried away into shrubs as they passed, and clean, sharp tracks in the snow marked the path of small animals, probably hares. All good signs, she thought, thinking of the last of the smoked meat in her pack. They could survive – and already had on their brutal journey – for days without food, but in these bitterly cold conditions, just staying warm burnt most of their energy. Tomorrow, if the weather held, they'd make the time to hunt. *Unless we see the end of our journey …*

Striding onwards on the easy ground, they soon approached the low rise where the dying inland hills hit the coast. As they climbed the gentle slope, the startling blue waters of the ocean slowly came into view. Where the ground flattened out, she saw the rugged cliffs of the coastline running off to the east, forming a jagged divide between the snow-covered land to the right, and the vivid blue of the cold waters to the left. She paused for a moment as stark memories of Beth's capture returned. It had been cliffs such as these that the dragon had used for cover on its silent approach to capture the Warrior.

"Better progress today," Shorty said as he came up beside her.

"So far," she agreed, her legs welcoming the easier ground. She glanced up at the tall, bearded man. "How you feeling?"

"My head's a little sore – you caught me pretty cleanly." His smile was wry. "But don't try that again. I won't be caught twice."

"Then stay on your guard. Whatever attacked us could try again."

Shorty grunted. "I wouldn't want those foul thoughts in my head again. Seems your head was thick enough to keep our unwelcome visitor out."

She glanced away, hiding a sudden unease. Shorty was right, she hadn't suffered like the others.

And yet still I suffered …

Because a long-forgotten – a long-suppressed – dream had returned, one that had haunted her youth. A dream of a mother who had abandoned her. A dream of a mother who had walked away from her and her sister, Rind.

I thought that terrible nightmare had gone.

I was glad it had gone.

For it ripped through her soul and tore at her heart.

Forcing the dread thoughts away, she faced inland, and from the heights of the rise, scanned the horizon. "We should make good progress today, the …"

She paused midbreath as she caught sight of a distant peak.

Shorty frowned as she pushed past him. "What's wrong?"

Standing on the terminus of those inland hills that had blocked their view south, a wonderfully clear vista now opened up towards a distant mountain range, a range holding a very distinctive peak, proud in its isolation, exactly as Warrior Beth had described.

She stared at the peak, not quite believing what she was seeing.

Shorty came alongside and followed her gaze. "Is that it?" he whispered.

"That's it," she breathed. "The Mountain of Hope."

"I thought … I doubted …"

At times, so did we all, she thought, her heart mirroring Shorty's astonishment. *And yet there it stands.*

In the moment, nothing more needed to be said. The two simply stood in awe at the extraordinary sight, no thought of what would happen next, only the dawning realisation that they had finally arrived at this place that Warrior Lanky had said would be here. *The last mountain of the land before the sea.* Soon, one by one, the others arrived, each looking to the mountain with the same widening eyes.

"Utterly incredible," Knuckles murmured. "That lad Lanky knows some things."

"Knows far more than you, that's for sure," Shorty said. "You—"

"What's that?" Scorpion interjected, gesturing to the south.

As Svana squinted skyward, Bear rasped a sharp command. "Drop low!"

Instantly, Svana dropped with the others, crouching down but keeping her eyes fixed on a dark object moving low in the sky.

"It's a big beast to be able to see it from here," Knuckles whispered beside her. "I think this is it."

Though its shape remained indistinct, Svana had no doubt as they watched it sweep rapidly from right to left, keeping low to the horizon. They had found the dragon.

"It's heading for the peak," Knuckles whispered.

Svana watched it drop lower and lower in the sky until it disappeared behind the distant mountain. She released a slow breath. "This must be the place we seek."

Bear clambered to his feet. "Yes. It seems our final objective is in sight." As she and the others stood, Bear glanced to the west. "We've still plenty of light, and if we're lucky, the weather will hold.

Depending on the terrain, it's possible we could reach that range today. But I wouldn't like to set a camp too close to the mountain – we should find a secluded site along the way, then make our push at daybreak."

"Sounds like the better plan," Knuckles said. "Now we know this mountain really exists, we can figure out what it is we're actually going to do when we get there. Getting past that dragon won't be easy."

Bear scanned the southern skies. "Let's move on while it's out of sight. I'll lead. Svana, you take the rear." Adjusting the strap of his pack, their leader walked away, heading for the southern flank of the rise.

Svana waited to let the others past: first Knuckles, then Shorty. As Scorpion walked towards her, she could sense his unease. Maybe now he would finally speak of what had happened earlier.

Sure enough, as he walked by, he halted, his long hair spilling over the ruff of his jacket. "How was it able to turn me?" he said, forcing himself to meet her eyes. "Am I that weak?"

What torment each of the men had suffered during the strange attack on their minds, Svana couldn't truly know. Somehow, she had been immune to its sly caresses. Unlike Scorpion. *And a dreadful guilt eats away at him.* "I don't know," she said, with brutal honestly. "But after that attack, you now hold an advantage that you didn't before – you know what it can do, you know what it feels like."

Scorpion winced.

Svana stepped to his side. "You're a smart man, Scorpion, and a good man, better than many. Now, you need to prove your resilience." She punched him on the shoulder. "My advice? Don't let it get you again."

He seemed to consider her words for a moment, then a tension eased from his shoulders. "Thanks, Svana. I doubt any of the others would have been as plain honest as that."

"Well, my honesty comes with a price. I want to see your head held high and no more moping. Redeem yourself."

Scorpion stood a fraction taller. Then he glanced to the distant peak. "My salvation lies on this path we take, I'm sure of it." He flicked a weak smile at Svana, then walked on.

She watched him walk away. Knuckles had joked many times on this trek that she favoured Scorpion. And maybe the Shield was right – she saw a simple honesty in the tribe's maker, an honesty some would see as an innocence. *And maybe that's something that cannot survive easily in these times.* She sighed. But, if it did, and if Scorpion proved his strength of will ... well, she would think on that some more.

She walked on.

CHAPTER THIRTEEN

There comes a time when all deceptions
must end. If not, the head becomes buried in
the sand while the body is slowly destroyed.

*P*eering around the edge of an ice-capped boulder, Svana jumped
at a sudden, sharp crack of breaking ice beyond the glacier front
down below. Breathing heavily, she leaned forward, listening intently.
A series of deep crunching noises carried on the still air, as though
something heavy moved through the frozen snow beyond the ice
sheet. She quickly backed behind the boulder, then signalled to the
others up the hill to get out of sight. Then, squatting, she pushed
herself as tightly as she could into the hollow behind the boulder.
Hidden from view from the south, she waited. *Now we may finally see*
where this beast hides.

After enduring a cold, fireless night on the far side of the valley, they
had risen early in the predawn light, then cautiously crossed the icy
valley floor, tracking as best they could the flight of the dragon they'd
seen the day before. Making good progress, they had soon reached the
southwestern flank of Lanky's mountain peak before slowly climbing
to the head of the ice sheet on which they now stood. Offering a wider
view of the barren landscape, it allowed them to quickly scan for
possible locations of the dragon's lair.

And now something large moves down below us.

Her heart pounding, Svana settled even further into the hollow.
Could the dragon's lair be concealed below? And if so, was the dragon
leaving? Her tense anticipation grew. What an unexpected yet
incredible chance could be unfolding to enter the beast's lair and
search for Warrior Beth. *If she's here.* She pushed the grim thought away.
They had to believe. *And we must grasp this chance.*

177

Still and silent, she waited.

But moments only, then a rhythmic beat cut the air.

Keeping as low as possible, ice-fractured ridges of the icy boulder digging into her back, she glanced westward. "Come on, where are you?"

Two thumping heartbeats later, the dragon swept into view.

Hardly daring to breathe, Svana watched as the shimmering blue-hued beast climbed steeply into the cloudless sky before arcing away from her, streaking westwards over the icebound land. Holding still, she followed the dragon's path until it passed into the haze of the distant horizon. As the beast faded from view, she drew deep, relief-filled lungfuls of air. Yet still she held her gaze on that distant horizon, waiting, ensuring the beast had really gone.

As she watched, her thoughts drifted, a connection half formed. The beast that had taken the Warrior Beth, had that one been blue? But the memory was indistinct, fogged by the terror that had engulfed them all. Forcing stiffening limbs to move, she pushed herself up out of the snow-filled hollow, then, glancing up the hill, she gave a low whistle. As the rest of the group emerged from hiding, she waved them to join her.

"Did you see where it came from?" Knuckles said breathlessly as he approached, the rim of his hood crystal-white with ice.

"Not clearly. But it definitely came from the plateau in front of the ice sheet. Its lair must lie down there somewhere."

Bear stepped forward, gazing down the snow-laden glacier. "Well, we can't afford to spend any more time up here – there's virtually no cover. We'll move down to the plateau and see what we can find." He studied the hillside, then glanced at Svana. "It's open ground from here down to the glacier edge. You go on and check if all's clear."

Making a quick adjustment to her pack, she headed off down the glacier. Keeping to the right of the main ice sheet, she picked her way between the drifts of thicker snow, weaving towards the ice front. With the brilliant white of the ice surrounding her and the storm-washed, vivid blue of the sky above, a vibrant energy seemed to rise from these most northerly lands. She felt alive, invincible even, a feeling like the moment battle was joined. Similar, but richer …

"Don't move," came a calm, deep voice behind her.

Stifling a cry, she heard a shout from Knuckles from the hillside above.

"And tell your friends to stay where they are," the calm voice continued. "Or you die. And I would prefer that you didn't have to die today."

Something in the man's voice told her he wouldn't strike immediately. She wouldn't die yet.

"Turn slowly to face me, then you will tell your friends to stay where they are."

Bow in tense hand, she slowly turned to face a hooded figure. The man stood in a crater, snow-white flakes falling off thick winter clothes. *He hid in the snow!* She was grudgingly impressed. The man must have seen them, then hidden. *But we didn't see him.*

"Talk to your friends," he said firmly.

She held up her hand and shouted. "Stay where you are! Stay back!" She saw Knuckles hesitate, then talk with Shorty – and then continue to advance. "Strike! Stay, I said! Stay!"

They halted – and watched.

"Good," the man murmured, pushing back his hood to reveal an etched, weather-beaten face, offset with long grey hair and a short white beard.

An old man, Svana thought, subtly shifting the weight on her feet. *I wonder —*

"Many have thought to better me in battle, my girl," the man said, his sharp eyes narrowing. "And they are now dead. Do not make the same mistake."

"I'm not your girl … old man."

He laughed. "Good – a sense of humour." He stepped closer, staring into her eyes. "And your name?"

She held his stare. "Svana. And yours, old man?"

The man smiled. "Stealth," he said, proffering a slight tilt of the head. "Now, please drop your weapons and pack, then head down there." He gestured to the steep slope to the right of the ice sheet.

"That doesn't seem a good option to me." She stepped towards him—

The man loosed an arrow, and it hammered into her left arm.

She stifled a scream at the sudden, intense pain.

"It is your *best* option," Stealth said, another arrow already nocked in the bowstring. He glanced up the hill. "And remind your friends not to move – the next one goes through your right eye."

Pain searing through her arm, dread twisted her gut. *I can't die like this. I must keep our mission alive.* Calming herself, she drew a slow breath. *Think.* The dragon had left. Who else was here? *If it is just you, old man, you will not defeat all four of us.* But for now, she would follow his commands. *Wait. A chance will come.*

Seeing Bear and the others moving down the hill towards them, she held up her right hand. "Stay!" she shouted. "Else he'll kill me."

The group halted, and she heard their quiet yet urgent voices debating what to do.

Stealth gestured to her weapons. "You won't need those."

Svana dropped her spear, then unstrapped her bow and pack, letting them fall to the ground.

He gestured down the hill. "Now move."

With no other option, and with her left arm held limply by her side, she headed down the slope, the man following closely behind. She knew the others would soon follow, but what was not clear was what this man would do about that. Her foot crunching through a patch of frozen vegetation, her jaw clenched. Who was this man? An ally of the dragon's? And if so, were there others here? A glimmer of hope rose. *For now, he only seems to want to deal with me.* So, maybe he had no backup. She steadied herself as her foot slipped on ice beneath the thin snow cover, then continued on cautiously down the hillside. She had to give the rest of her group a chance to complete their mission. *Let them do what they need to do, and you focus on what's before you. Then act when the chance comes.*

They soon reached the base of the hillside, where a short, painful scramble down a jagged ridge led her onto the small plateau below. She glanced to the broad icebound valley beyond the plateau. There lay their fastest route away from this place. *If we survive.*

The man tapped her shoulder. "This way. Towards the ice cliff."

The main glacier they'd skirted on the way down now loomed ahead in the form of a sheer, glinting cliff face at the ice-sheet terminus. Prodded by the man behind, Svana walked on over the frozen ground of the plateau, the ice cliff to her left steadily growing higher and steeper. Surprisingly solid with few fissures and tinged blue in the morning sunlight, the towering glacier front seemed an elemental feature cut by gods. *Or by a dragon?*

As she walked on, a darker shadow soon appeared within the ice cliff ahead. *An entrance,* she realised as they approached. *So, this is the beast's lair.*

"Head inside," Stealth directed as they approached the rough-hewn entrance.

She hesitated only a heartbeat as a sudden desire to see what lay within this long-sought lair drew her on. *Is Warrior Beth here?* Entering the glistening, smooth-walled tunnel, the brilliant snow-scattered light of the frozen exterior gave way to fantastical twisting shades of startling blue. Despite the throbbing pain from the arrow's blade in her arm, the strange beauty of the place beguiled her. *A place suited to our Spirits, not to this cursed beast.*

"Keep walking," came the man's voice. "Not too far now."

His voice rekindled her anger. *One mistake, and you're mine.*

On they journeyed, travelling first through the entrancing light of the ice-walled tunnel, then through the eerie gloom of the wide, dimly torchlit, rock-hewn passageways of the mountain itself. Then, upon passing through a grand open gateway of a construction she'd never seen, they finally emerged into a massive arched chamber, the polished white stone of its gleaming walls and ceiling dancing with yellow and red light.

In the centre of the chamber stood an imposing circular dais, its granite edge scored and fractured … and on that dais lay a sleek silver-scaled dragon, its massive head held proudly high, one baleful eye focussed on Svana as she halted, wide-eyed.

"But …"

"But you saw a dragon leave?" Stealth said, walking over to her. "Maybe you can't count. You—"

Driven by a surge of fear, Svana acted. All pain drowned by the fire raging within, she swung her foot – hard – at the back of the old man's knees. Her attack connected cleanly, and the man's legs buckled, collapsing him to the ground. She immediately lunged towards him, striking hard with her fist at the man's head …

With lightning speed, the man rolled to the side, and an intense pain shot through her arm as her fist slammed into the solid ground. Then a hammer blow rocked the side of her head.

All around her darkened …

*

Aware of a dull ache in her head, she groaned.

"Ah, good," came Stealth's voice. "I worried I might have killed you."

"Not a good start," boomed another voice, echoing around the chamber.

"Not so loud," Stealth murmured. "I think this one's head may be delicate."

Svana blinked against the light, then forced her eyes open. Wincing, she turned her head. She lay in the dragon's high-arched chamber. But something felt different.

My arm.

Lifting her left arm, she saw the arrow was gone, and the wound covered in a neat poultice bound by leather strapping.

Stealth studied her. "A flesh wound only, but you'll be hampered for a while. It would've been more helpful if you'd listened to what I had to say."

Girding herself, Svana hauled herself upright, then sat for a moment, allowing her pounding head to settle. "Where are my friends?" she muttered as the throbbing eased.

"Probably trying to figure out how to get through the entrance doors. Which they'll be unable to do. But they're safe. For now."

"Safe?" she spat, glaring at the man. "No one is safe with you scum."

"That's no way to speak to a stranger," Stealth said, stepping towards her.

"You are no stranger, Ka. You devils are all the same." She faced the dragon with a defiant stance. "Where's the woman you took?"

The dragon's monstrous head turned. Long, bony ridges arced from its nostrils and jaw, sweeping up the sides of its massive head before flaring backwards and outwards like bladelike flames. Within a whorl of those harsh ridges, a menacing, fiery eye locked onto her. 'What is she to you?' came a rumbling voice in her mind.

As part of her recoiled from the beast, another glared back at the dragon's eye. "Don't try any tricks with me, evil one. Where is she?"

"I repeat," came the dragon's booming voice into the chamber. "What is she to you?"

Svana scowled. "My friend."

The dragon's massive sculpted head swung towards her. "Is that all?"

"It's all you need to know."

"So not a Warrior? And you are not a member of the Iyes tribe come to recover her and the Staff?"

Svana stifled a gasp. *The beast knows all. It—*

"I know many things," the dragon rumbled. "But all? No, no one knows all."

Licking her dry lips, Svana suddenly realised the power of the beast she faced. *It sees into my mind.* "What do you want with me?"

"I wish for you to listen."

"Listen?" Svana spat, her anger flaring. "To what? To the lies of an ancient enemy? To the—"

'The Warrior is safe,' came the dragon's voice in her mind.

She froze. "What did you say?"

"I said the Warrior is safe," the dragon rumbled.

What trick is this? She looked over at Stealth.

"It's true," the grey-haired man said calmly, holding her gaze.

Unable to accept what she was hearing, she flicked her suspicious gaze between the man and the dragon. Looking back to Stealth, she slowly walked over to him. "Who are you?"

"I am what you see. A man serving my master. Who in turn serves IY."

"What foul lies do you speak now?" she hissed. Shaking her head, she glared at Stealth. "You are Ka scum, old man, that's what you are. And you are Kaos's thug," she snarled, turning to the dragon.

"I told you she wouldn't believe it," Stealth said with a resigned sigh.

The dragon lowered its massive head, swinging closer to Svana. "A game is being played here that is not what it seems. And for good reason. At stake lies all life in this Land."

Svana scowled. "Well, now you speak a truth. But you're on the wrong side of the game."

Stealth stepped in front of her, shaking his head. "To those beyond this mountain, it must appear this way. And it must stay this way awhile longer yet. But we *do* fight for the same cause. We fight for IY."

"How stupid do you think I am? We—"

"They stand at the door," the dragon rumbled. "Please greet them."

Stealth gestured to Svana. "Follow me." He turned and walked out of the chamber.

What trick is this now? Glancing at the dragon, she subtly flexed her injured arm. *But if I can get away from this beast, I can escape the old man.* She hurried after Stealth.

They soon reached the impressive gateway of unknown construction they'd passed earlier. Massive doors now sealed the way. Her muscles tensed, she watched as Stealth crossed to the wall beside the right-hand door and reached out, placing his hand palm-down onto a smooth section of rock. Immediately, the doors began to swing open—

Svana ran hard, aiming straight for the widening gap. "Get ready!" she yelled, storming through the opening doors. "Enemy following behind me!"

But emerging into the tunnel beyond, she was shocked to find the muted group milling in silence, staring up at the doors behind her.

"Move!" she yelled as Bear turned to her. "Only one man stands against us!"

Bear held up his hands. "It's okay, Svana. Stand down."

"What are you talking about!" she snapped, glaring at the silent group. "He's coming—"

"On the door. The symbols on the door."

Breathing hard, she glanced back, scanning the partially open doors in confusion. Prominent on the upper section of both doors was a cleanly carved intricate symbol. It displayed two circles, one enclosing the other, between which lay complex – and to her, meaningless – markings. In the centre of the inner circle were carved two upright coiled snakes, tightly interlocked as though one.

Shaking her head in frustration, she turned back to Bear. "What is this? What—"

"Those are the protective symbols of IY herself," Bear said, relief etched on his face.

Svana stared at him, open-mouthed.

Bear looked towards the passageway beyond the opening doors. "This means that the agents of Kaos cannot pass this gateway. Whoever stands within has IY's blessing."

Stealth appeared in the doorway. "You are welcome to enter, friends. But I suggest you control your feisty friend over there. I'd prefer no more harm befall her today."

*

Bear regarded the monstrous dragon on the dais, his mind reeling. Their ancient enemy was in fact an ally? How had this been hidden from them? How had their ancient Story been so wrong? *Naga died believing these beasts were killers of our ancestors.* And yet here stood the Ancient under the protective shield of IY.

His hand tightened around his spear. *Unless we are being deceived. Tread cautiously.*

He walked forward, trying to quell the rippling fear within him. "It is an honour to meet you, Ancient One," he said, holding his voice steady as he halted in front of the raised dais. "This is an outcome that is … unexpected."

A rumble of deep laughter rolled around the chamber, and the dragon flexed its massive neck. "You are a master of your emotions, Leader of the Iyes – a truly human trait." Its massive eye flicked to Svana. "Occasionally, a valuable thing."

Knuckles stepped out in front of Shorty and Scorpion, the strain of the last days eased from his robust weather-beaten face. "Well, I for one am glad to avoid meeting you in battle. That would—"

"You would have been obliterated, little human," blasted a harsh, commanding voice into the cave.

The hairs on the back of his neck rising, Bear watched in fearful awe as a second massive dragon stalked into the cave. Far larger than the Ancient on the dais, this dragon barely squeezed through the chamber's entrance, shards of glistening ice clinging to its head and body. The fearsome beast stopped by the side wall of the chamber, then lowered itself to the ground, ice-free patches of its body shimmering with vibrant flashes of silvery blue. Swinging its giant head towards them, razor-sharp teeth glinting in the torchlight, it settled a single fiery yellow eye on them.

Bear licked his dry lips. *Indeed, we would have been slaughtered if facing this beast alone.* He turned back to the silver dragon. "I should introduce—"

"That is unnecessary. I know you, Bear, and I know these others. The Iyes tribe is well known to me."

"And may I know your name?"

"I am Rakana," the Ancient said. "And behind you lies Hydrak."

"It is an honour to serve you, Rakana. I—"

"You will serve me, fool," boomed the voice of Hydrak.

"We'll serve no one who tries to force us," Svana said in a cold voice, glaring at the ice-blue dragon.

"Hold, Svana," Knuckles said quietly. "Let us hear what shall be said."

"Wise words, little human. You will serve me well. I—"

"QUIET!" Rakana thundered, the deafening sound echoing around the chamber. "Remember your pledge, Hydrak. Do not break it before we have begun."

A low rumble came from Hydrak's chest, thrumming through Bear's body.

"And if you continue arming, I will consider it an act of war."

The rumble continued for a moment longer – then abruptly ceased. "Humans annoy me," Hydrak thundered, rivulets of melting ice dripping from its head. "They spread like a plague. They must be controlled."

"Then you know nothing of us," Svana grated. "You—"

"Svana," Knuckles grunted. "Remember I'm still your Shield. Do not dishonour me."

Svana flashed him a furious glance, then fixed her hard eyes back on the silvery-blue dragon. She said nothing.

Bear glanced at Svana. It was rare for Knuckles to reprimand this one, but while her anger was understandable given they were facing what they'd believed until moments ago to be their feared enemy, that anger needed to be held in check. *Because this Hydrak seems unpredictable.* His gaze returned to Rakana. *And there is much here still unknown.* "Forgive me if I seem confused, but the last time we saw you,

you captured our Warrior." He glanced at Svana and her bandaged arm. "And here your servant almost killed one of my party. I also—"

He flinched as a sharp hiss sounded from his left. A cloud of steam from the blue dragon jetted down the side of the chamber and out into the tunnel beyond. *Ignore the other. Concentrate on Rakana.* "I also remember our first encounter, when you attacked others of my tribe and left with our hallowed Staff. Taken together, these seem unusual actions of an ally. If it were not for the signs of IY on the doors, I …" He hesitated, his mouth suddenly parched.

Rakana's fierce eye raked him. "You believe I could still be your enemy? You think followers of Kaos could have passed IY's defences?" A deep rumble issued from the dragon. "No, that power is not yet theirs to wield."

Bear held the dragon's frightening gaze. "But how would I know that?" he managed.

'You have one in your midst who can tell you,' Rakana replied in his mind. *'One receptive to IY's power – ask her what she feels.'*

She? He frowned, then realisation struck. Svana? Did Rakana mean she was a Warrior?

Rakana's wry laughter echoed in his head. *'A Warrior cannot be foretold until revealed, so to that question, I cannot answer yes or no. What I speak of is the shaman within her.'*

A shaman? Did the Ancient speak true? Of this, Naga had said nothing.

'She did not know,' Rakana said. *'The strength lay in the one known as River. That one was Naga's focus, and rightly so. But ask this woman here what she senses … when she truly listens.'*

'I hear you, Ancient One,' came Svana's harsh, yet strained, voice. *'But I'm no shaman.'*

'No, not as River or Naga,' Rakana rumbled. *'Yet still, you hold a gift within you. What do you sense here?'*

Bear flicked his gaze to Svana. A shaman? How was this possible? No sooner had the question formed than he grimaced. In these times, it seemed many things were possible. "What do you think? Has IY's defence been breached?" *Is the Enemy within?*

Svana's expression was wary. "I don't see how I can help. What am I supposed to feel?"

"Anything. It may help us."

Bear caught Knuckles looking quizzically at them both. He gestured to the Shield to stay silent.

Beside him, Svana shrugged, then slowly looked around the chamber. She blinked. "I sense the Spirits, but not the Spirits. I sense IY, but not IY."

Bear struggled to understand her words. "Do you sense Kaos?"

She said nothing, seeming to stare blindly at the walls of the chamber.

"Svana?"

She blinked. Her brow furrowed as her gaze returned to the dragons. "I don't know why, but I sense no evil here."

"So, you think the defences of IY hold?"

She glanced at Stealth, who stood impassively, watching her. "I believe they do."

Bear studied her for a moment. *So the Iyes have another with shamanic skills.* Turning back to the Ancient, he looked into the depths of the beast's eye. *And it seems the Iyes also have a most unexpected ally.* "What is happening?"

"A game is being played," Rakana rumbled. "For life."

Bear moved closer to the dragon, seeing himself reflected in its fiery eyes. "And the Warrior?"

"She is safe. For now."

Bear heard a gasp from Scorpion. "Here?" he asked.

"No, she stands with your tribe in the south. And the Staff is with the Guardian."

A wave of unbridled elation swept through him. *The Warriors live. We have a chance!*

"And your Mother lives," Rakana continued. The dragon's voice then sounded in his mind. *'But Naga is dead.'*

Bear froze as the wound – so tightly closed since they had sensed her passing from afar – ripped open, unleashing a tide of agony which swamped his burgeoning joy. *Naga! We couldn't say goodbye!*

Fighting to hold back the wretched pain inside, he bowed his head. *'Tell your companions later – in your own way,'* Rakana said softly.

His gut wrenched. Naga was dead. Yes, they'd known, they'd sensed her passing, but hearing the stark words spoken made it so very real. *The others will hurt too when they hear.*

"Bear?" came Knuckles's questioning voice from behind him.

Bear forced back the pain and turned to the Iyes Shield. He, Scorpion, and Shorty would be struggling to follow what had been said. "I'll explain in a moment," he said, holding his voice steady.

Knuckles frowned but gave a nod of acknowledgement.

I must harden my heart for now, Naga, but I will speak to you soon. He glanced at Rakana. "What happens now?"

A light rumble rolled from the Ancient. "Now, I will leave you in the hands of this old human. Those very few who visit this place speak of his kind hospitality." There was a grunt from Svana at this. "But I advise you to beware his offers of a drink – we must regroup tomorrow with clear heads."

Bear looked up at the silver dragon. "So, we will rejoin my tribe?"

"Not in the manner you expect," the Ancient said, swinging her massive head away. "But that is for tomorrow. Stealth."

Stealth walked towards them. "Let us collect your packs and weapons, and then I'll have time to answer more of your questions."

So, this audience is clearly over, Bear thought. He glanced back at the Ancient. "We travelled far in our efforts to recover our Warrior and the Staff, but it is not yet clear to me what we have gained. I hope tomorrow you will show a clearer path to allow us to engage and avenge."

But besides a low rumble, no answer came.

Bear's gaze flicked to Stealth. "I hope for further answers, my friend."

Stealth smiled. "Then follow me."

The dragon's servant walked away under the menacing regard of the dragon, Hydrak, whose whole body, now absent its layer of ice, shimmered with a rich blue hue.

Bear walked back to his party and kept his voice low. "There is more to be told and more to be learnt, but Warrior Lanky has been proved correct – both the Warrior and the Staff were indeed delivered to this place. But it seems we have entered a bigger game, one we cannot yet see."

"A game we need to flush out," Svana grunted.

Bear regarded each of them in turn. "We are here, together, and within the domain of IY with a new ally. Whether this is fate, or intended, it matters not. We should grasp the opportunity and ensure we join the fray. We must keep moving on. We *will* keep moving on. And whatever it takes, we will aid the Warriors in their fight."

With a chorus of agreement, the group followed Bear from the chamber, quickly joining Stealth, who led them to their quarters.

And later, and into the late evening, a tale was told of a quite stunning deception.

CHAPTER FOURTEEN

*The complexity of human emotion is staggering and made
more so by the contorted workings of their stressed minds.*

*W*alking past another empty hut, Tricia sighed. *Empty.* Her
feelings exactly. She kicked a fragment of fire-blackened wood
from her path. What was she doing here? "Stuff, plenty of stuff," she
muttered dryly to herself. Harvesting and processing wood for their
fires, fires that were tended twenty-four seven; processing animal
carcasses for materials for the tribe's makers; helping corral the smaller
children at busier times for the tribe – and comforting them during the
sickening battles; in fact, assisting grateful tribe members with any
number of other tasks. *Not bad for a humble aspiring artist.*

Except none of it was enough. None of it seemed to take the load off
her friends' backs, friends she saw less and less of as the weeks went
by. *They just don't seem to have the time for me.* And now her best friend
was about to embark on a crazy mission into the enemy's heartland.
She'd heard the debate and the reasoning, but it didn't make it any less
crazy. *What hell have we entered here?*

Grimacing, she walked on through the cold, barren camp. The rain
had eased, and most of the tribe were out in the surrounding land,
stocking up on food or scouting for signs of enemy movements. *And I
remain here, waiting for the next task.* Familiar, nagging questions
needled her. Why had she come here? On that fateful night, why had
she followed Jessica into the unknown? *And will we get back? I really
want to go back.* But as she sauntered on through the camp, she knew
that wouldn't happen soon. It seemed her friends were intent on
stepping deeper into the dark, dangerous places of this harsh land.
Stepping? *Striding,* she thought grimly. Striding forward, but into
what? Did they really understand what they might meet within that

ominous darkness? Because she didn't. *I see and feel the growing nightmare around me, but I don't understand it.*

She knew now she'd been a fool to come here. She'd seen the appalling power wielded at Mount Hope, and yet had blindly thought she'd somehow be able to help. *Yet I can do nothing.* And worse, her friends were drifting further away from her. Oh, they still spoke to her, but there was less and less she could offer them. *This place is too far from what I know.*

A few steps later, she stopped and drew a deep breath. Her morose thoughts were leading her to places she didn't want to go. *Just focus on what's in front of you, Trish, and help as you can.* Gritting her teeth, she walked on, trying to ignore the niggling ache tickling the pit of her stomach.

A few moments later, she heard quiet voices ahead. Passing around the next hut, she saw a small group sitting around a fire. She made to walk on, not wishing to intrude.

"Hi, Tricia," called the jet-black-haired young woman sitting beside Amber, Dune, and Freya. "Come and join us."

Tricia stopped and glanced over to Sheba. With child – *and with the battles ahead* – the weapon maker spent a fair amount of time in camp; and, like she did Amber, Tricia found her easy company. *But I'm not sure I'm good company today.* "Are you sure? I don't want to interrupt you."

"Sit down," Sheba urged. "What are you doing?"

"Erm – not much," Tricia muttered, walking over and dropping to her haunches. "How are you feeling today?"

Sheba put her hand to her belly. "All well. The little one clearly enjoyed my breakfast; she's dancing around in there."

Tricia smiled. "She must take after her mother. So, you still think it's a girl?"

"I do. And she's special, I can feel it."

"Maybe that's just your breakfast," Dune quipped, a smile on his tired face.

The short, curly-haired woman by the maker's side thumped him.

"Ow, Freya, that hurt." The lithe man held his hand to his bandaged side. "I'm still injured, remember."

Freya cast him a mock frown. "That scratch? I've had worse from scrabbling for berries."

Tricia smiled, tension easing from her. She looked back at Sheba. "It's getting close now. Another two moons?"

"Yes, it's that soon." Her smile fading, she looked down and stroked her belly. "But I wish I could keep the little one safe in here for a while longer – until this war is over."

The healer, Amber, placed a gentle hand on Sheba's. "Trust in the Warriors, Sheba. They will find a way to win this war, and soon. Until then, we'll keep protecting you and your little one." Amber studied Sheba's face. "You sure you don't want to leave with the others?"

Sheba held Amber's gaze. *She's seriously thinking about it*, Tricia thought. To join a group of women and small children leaving for the east to join the refuge of an allied tribe. *But her sister is still here. She won't leave River.*

"Weapons must be made. I'm needed here."

Tricia saw the formidable strength of will in Sheba's face. *These are a tough people. If that was me, you wouldn't see me for dust.*

Sheba smiled. "I'm needed and I have friends around to help me."

"You live a life of luxury, Sheb," Dune said, winking at Tricia. "It's a wonder – ow!"

Freya looked away, a picture of innocence. Dune rubbed his arm and feigned a scowl at the girl beside him.

Tricia glanced at the young man, yet again amazed at the resilience of these people. Though injured, Dune continued with camp duties, and somewhere in the north, his twin brother, Scorpion, remained lost with Bear and others. Yet somehow he, like so many of the others with their own terrible scars, took the briefest of moments to relax with friends. *I guess else you go mad.*

Like me?

She forced the thought away. "How is the injury, Dune?"

"It *was* doing fine," Dune growled, brushing a strand of his flowing dark hair behind his ears.

Freya grinned.

"It's thanks to Amber as usual," Sheba said, glancing at the tribe's healer. "I don't know how you do it – you're stretched so thin."

"I can help," Tricia blurted before she even knew what she'd said.

Amber raised an eyebrow. "You have the skill? You haven't mentioned this before."

"Ah, no, I can't say I'm skilled. No. But I can strip a whole carcass in a single morning."

Freya laughed.

And a hint of a smile crossed Amber's lips. "Well, I don't know …"

"Look," Tricia said quickly. "That didn't come out right. In fact, I didn't know I was going to say it at all." Freya laughed again. "But what it has shown me is I'm not afraid of blood – of cutting things to

191

pieces." Her brow furrowed. "Which would be quite worrying back home."

Amber tilted her head, her brow rising higher.

Tricia slumped. "To be honest, I'm feeling lost. I need something meaningful to do. Not that gathering wood is unimportant, but …" She glanced up at Amber. "Helping you – if I can – would be better."

"It sounds as though you have a willing volunteer," Sheba said. "And a hard worker, from what I've seen. I think you should take her."

Amber hesitated, then: "Well … I guess I could use the help."

Sheba smiled and gestured to Tricia. "Say welcome to the tribe's newest healer."

Tricia grinned. "Wow, that's great. A proper job!"

"You can begin your butchering tomorrow," Dune said with a grin.

"Yes," Freya muttered. "And you can start with him."

Genuine warmth filled Tricia. She could finally really help these people. "Wait till I tell …"

She broke off, harsh reality kicking her in the guts. *Tell who? My friends who are leaving me?*

"When are they going?" Sheba asked in the sudden silence.

Tricia sighed. "They're keeping that a secret. Even from me."

"Then I guess there's a very good reason for it," Sheba said.

Brushing a wandering spider from her tunic, Tricia considered Sheba's words. Deep down, she knew they were true. *They must be hurting as much as me.* She had to leave them – *the Warriors* – to do what they thought had to be done. *And me?* She glanced at Sheba and smiled. "Well, I'm a healer now."

"A healer's helper," Amber said, the faintest hint of admonishment in her voice.

Tricia grinned. "That's what I meant to say."

"And a wonderful helper she will be," Freya said, turning to Amber and wagging her finger.

Amber ignored her.

Sheba leaned forward. "So, you were not a healer in your time. What did you do?"

"I was an artist. Well, trying to be."

"An artist!" Dune exclaimed. "You've never mentioned that before." The tiredness in his lean face had vanished. "When we get time, you can show me and my brother your work, your technique."

"You're now trapped," Freya said, grinning. "This sculptor won't let you go until he's learnt something new."

"Are we still talking of art?" Tricia asked, smiling.

Freya laughed. "Are you, Dune? What *are* you thinking about?"

"Leave him be, Freya," Amber said.

"What about me?" Tricia quipped.

"You too, my friend. The boy wouldn't stand against you both."

"It's okay, Amber," Dune said, smiling. "I'm hardier than my brother."

"How hard?" Freya asked, leaning closer.

Tricia winked at Freya. "That sounds like an offer you can't refuse."

Dune feigned a grimace, then glanced at the healer. "Okay, Amber, maybe I do need your help."

"It seems so," Amber said, climbing to her feet. "However, for now, you're on your own. I've people to treat."

Sheba held out her hand. "Help me up. There's stone waiting for me to release their blades."

As Amber helped Sheba to her feet, Dune also stood. "You want any extra help today, Amber?"

"Think I'm fine." Amber gestured to Tricia. "Especially with my new healer. Are you ready to start now?"

"Too right I am," Tricia said, quickly climbing to her feet. "Ready to go, boss."

"Leaves me and you, Dune," Freya said, smiling up at the maker. "Sit back down and you can show me your sculptures."

Dune pushed back a lock of hair from his cheek. "Ah, sorry, Freya. I should get back to the gorge. Firuz wanted help to clear a damaged shelter."

"That's good," Freya said, standing. "That's where I was heading."

"Ah, good. Well, let's go up together then." He glanced at Amber. "You heading that way?"

"No. I – we," she said, glancing at Tricia, "have to visit one of Parig's men on the far side of the camp."

Freya grabbed Dune's arm. "Let's go." Pulling the hesitant man away, she flicked them a backwards glance. "See you later. And eat with us tonight, Tricia. By the main fire."

As Freya and Dune walked away, Tricia glanced at Amber. "He has a thing for you, you know?"

"Who? Dune? No, his sight is on Freya."

"Freya has eyes for him. His eyes roam elsewhere."

Her face suddenly grim, Amber looked out across the camp. "No matter," she said, the slightest waver in her voice. "My heart lies with another – and there it will remain." She reached for her pack. "We have work to do."

With a pang of guilt, Tricia watched the healer walk from the fire. "Maybe I shouldn't have said anything."

"Maybe not," Sheba murmured by her side. "Eagle's loss was devastating for her. It will take a long time to heal. But you were right. Dune has always liked Amber. Time will tell where that one will go." She glanced towards the gorge. "But now I need to find my sister. She's not been the best company of late. She hides away. And she hides something from me. I ..." She shook her head. "No matter, that one is not for you." She smiled. "I suggest you catch up with your new teacher. Just avoid matters of the heart."

Parting company, Tricia walked on after Amber. Maybe she shouldn't have said anything, but that was a problem for another time. *I have a new job – a purpose.* She smiled. Yes, a purpose. To help save lives. To keep the tribe on their feet during the troubled time ahead. A chance for her to finally contribute to the tribe.

And to keep my mind off the nightmares.

She hurried on after her new teacher.

*

"But when do I get to help you with a patient?" Tricia asked, carrying a bundle of wood to the fire. "So far, my job hasn't changed at all."

Amber sealed off the new bandage on the woman's wounded leg. "That should be fine for now," she told the prone Islander. "Leave it three days, then find me again." She helped the woman up, then turned to Tricia. "You *are* helping. This gives me more hands-on time rather than ... well, doing that."

"Hmm," Tricia muttered, dropping the wood by the fire. "Thought I'd be doing a little more than this."

"Hi, Amber," came a subdued voice behind them. "Hi, Trish."

"Good day to you, Spider," Tricia said with a smile. "Here to see the new surgeon at work? Any problems we can look at for you?"

Spider scowled. "Not the kind you can help with."

"River?" Amber prompted.

The scout grunted a sound that may have been a yes, then, walking up to the fire, he kicked an errant fragment of smouldering wood into the glowing embers.

"Hey," Tricia complained. "Don't mess with my fire. We need it for ... healing and stuff."

Spider looked up. "Stuff? Stuff like what?"

"Like ... like ... you tell him, Amber."

"Just stuff," Amber muttered.

Spider shook his head.

"So what's so bad you need to kick fires? Problems of the heart? Talk to Auntie Trish."

He frowned. "Have you been eating those mushrooms again?"

No, that won't happen again, she thought, recalling the hazy memory of that evening when she'd thought to cook for herself, using ingredients she'd found herself. "No, think I'll leave those in Amber's capable hands. So, what's the problem?"

His shoulders dropped. "Not sure I want to talk about it."

"Maybe not, but it will help. Sharing your problems usually does."

"On this, she's right," Amber said. "It is better to talk, Spider."

Spider shuffled his feet, then sighed and dropped to his haunches, staring at the fire. "I love her," he said in a hushed voice. "And thought she had feelings for me. But it's changed, all changed, since she became the tribe's Mother. Or shaman. Or Warrior. Whatever she is." He looked up. "The waiting was the hardest. Not able to see her. Too busy, she said. And then … well, then it was over so quickly."

Amber crossed over to him and knelt beside him. "I'm so sorry."

Tricia replayed Spider's words. "What did River actually say?"

"That she loves me as a brother," Spider muttered.

Ah, Tricia thought. *Then not the love he wanted.* "Anything else?"

"No. Just words. Not now, she said. Too much stuff going on, she said." He scowled. "It was quick. We didn't say that much."

"Not now," Tricia said. "What did she mean by that?"

Spider's look was pained. "I don't know. It doesn't matter."

Amber's eyes narrowed. She glanced at Tricia, then back at Spider. "Of course it matters. She must have explained. What else did she tell you?"

"Not you as well!" He looked dejectedly into the fire. "I don't know. I can't remember. But I know what she meant. It was clear."

Amber stood and looked down at Spider, sudden fire in her eyes. "You're a fool. Do you think you can read a woman's mind? Were you able to study River's thoughts and see exactly what she was thinking? No! I doubt you even understood what was going on in your own stupid head! You're going to tell us exactly what she said, or I'll hand you over to Tricia as her first patient."

It took a while, but they forced it all out of him – words, gestures, looks and all.

As he finished, Tricia sighed. "Amber's right. You're a fool."

Spider looked at them, bemused. "What am I missing?"

Amber glared at him. "She's confused, overwhelmed, struggling to know what to do."

"You just need to give her time," Tricia said. "We're all struggling at the moment."

Amber glanced at Tricia, then back at Spider. "Talk to her again," she said in a calmer voice. "Tell her you understand. That you'll give her space."

"So there's still a chance?"

"Yes!" Tricia and Amber said in unison.

A short while later, Spider left, preparing himself to visit River once more.

"It seems you may have your uses after all," Amber said, smiling at Tricia. "Drawing information from people can be valuable in our work."

As Amber reached for her healer's pack, Tricia felt a rising pride.

"Now I need you to fetch more water – this next one will bleed."

"Will do, boss. Water coming up."

Quickly collecting the water carrier, she headed off for the stream with a smile. Yes, today was a much better day.

*

"Hey, Spider," Lanky shouted, seeing the scout walking away from camp.

Head down, Spider trudged on towards the gorge.

"Spider!" Lanky called again.

He saw the young man stop and look around.

"You have a minute?"

Spider glanced towards the gorge. Seeming to sigh, he walked towards them.

"Good," Lanky said, turning to Rind and Jessica. "We can sort this out now."

Spider walked up to them. "What's up?" he asked, his matted hair pushed back behind his ears.

He looks tired, Lanky thought. *But he's not the only one; we're all exhausted.* He cleared his throat. "We tackled most of what was needed this morning, but I want a final check that the four of us are sure of what we're planning tomorrow." He looked around the small group. "That we're absolutely sure."

Spider frowned. "Has anything changed?"

"Jessica's now adamant we should retrieve the Kade if we find it. So not just a scouting mission but a find-and-retrieve mission. I don't need to tell you that makes it a little trickier … and certainly more dangerous."

Spider considered for a moment, then turned to Jessica. "Why so certain of this when we're not even sure what it is? Could we even take it away if we find it?"

Lanky caught the flicker of unease in Jessica's face before it was quickly hidden. His eyes narrowed a fraction. She'd told him there was another who would help them, but not who or why this entity had suddenly appeared now. He inwardly grimaced. In truth, she'd told him nothing. And yet he trusted her implicitly. *There will be a good reason for what she's doing, and she'll tell me when she's ready.*

"There is one who seeks to help me," Jessica said slowly. "Help us."

Spider waited, but Jessica said nothing more. "You trust this one?" he pressed.

Jessica hesitated. "Trust? That's difficult to answer. But IY told us the same thing. Retrieve the Kade and take it to her. I believe that if we see the chance, then that's what we should do."

Spider scanned her face. Then he shrugged. "You are the Warrior. You understand this better than me."

Lanky saw the tension in Jessica's eyes – a tension he knew so well. Understanding was relative. *There is so much of this we don't understand.*

Spider turned to Rind. "To me, it makes sense. We're taking a massive risk entering the Ka homeland – don't we want a big reward to make it worth it? But I'll follow your lead."

Rind smiled. "I appreciate the vote of confidence, Spider, but in this, we all must agree."

"Then I agree."

Rind faced Jessica. "I'm confident I can lead us through the camp, and I've confidence you will find this Kade. And recover it."

Jessica acknowledged Rind with a smile. "Then it's your call," she said to Lanky.

Feeling a twist in his gut, Lanky took a few steps away from the group, the sun a welcome warmth on his face. *I can't be responsible for others' lives.*

Too late, he told himself with a cold, unwelcome certitude. *You already are.*

He tensed at the increasingly fell burden weighing on his soul. The burden of an emerging Warrior. The burden of one expected to save the lives of the peoples of this Land. *To save the Land from Armageddon.* Grimacing, he ran his fingers through his short beard. He hadn't asked for any of this. And yet here he was, in this time, in this moment. Wherever here really was. Because what truly was this Continuum he walked within? How could he be living here in this past time while his friends, his mother, all those others he knew, all lived in another time? *How the hell can that work?*

He let out a slow breath. Did it really matter how it worked? Whatever this Continuum was, it was real. *I stand here, living and breathing. And I can die here.* An unexpected stab of fear cut through him, drawing desires buried deep. *I want to see my friends again. I want to see my mother again.* His chest tightened. *Let me get home. At the end of this, please let us all get home.*

Unnerved by the dark turn of his thoughts, doubts found their voice. If he agreed to this plan to capture the Kade – *something we still know almost nothing about* – all four of them would be taking a horrendous risk. Could he allow Jessica to be exposed to that? Spider? *And Rind … Can I really allow this to happen?*

As though hearing her name in his thoughts, Rind appeared by his side.

She reached out and held his hand in hers.

A sudden warmth lit inside.

"Being a leader is hard," she murmured. "It's lonely. But you should continue to do what you believe is right. Don't be ruled by your heart, even if your heart wishes it."

A lock of her soft curls brushed her face in the breeze.

"But how do we know?" he whispered. "How do we know we make the right decision?"

"What have you known for sure during these last hellish days? To fight in the way you have? How?"

I don't know. "I just do it," he whispered.

Rind released his hand and stepped in front of him. "You're becoming a true Warrior. And you've felt the influence of the terrible evil rising in my Land, an evil Jessica saw in your own time. You now have a chance to stop it before it destroys us and all those around us. Before it destroys your own land."

"When I stop and think, it terrifies me."

"We have lived with this hanging over us for longer than you."

He turned to her, seeing a gritty determination shining on her face. But her fingers caressed twine-strung beads on her wrist, and a faint shadow of fear tainted her keen eyes. *I need to get home, but right now I'm here. These people need me. Do what must be done to help us* all *survive.* "Thank you," he said softly.

She acknowledged him with a smile.

Gathering himself, he walked back to the others. "Okay," he said, a strength in his stance. "If the Kade is where IY thinks it is, and if we see a chance to capture it, we'll take it. But if at any stage, Jess or I think we should abort, we call it. Agreed?"

"Agreed," Jessica said immediately.

"Agreed," Rind and Spider both said together.

Lanky flicked his eyes over them, searching for any glimmer of doubt, but was met with steadfast gazes. Only Spider seemed distracted, casting sidelong glances to the gorge. *I think I know who he wishes to see.*

His gaze returned to Rind. "The timing … You said this morning we should arrive at the outskirts of the Ka camp – the Rim, you called it – as though travellers from afar."

"We should. So, we should plan to arrive after the sun passes to the west, seeming as though we travelled a good distance that day."

Lanky glanced at Jessica. "You still think this place is what we know as Misr?"

"From the descriptions we've been given, like the great inland sea to the north and a seemingly endless river running through a dry land, it's my best guess."

"Then that will have to do." His brow furrowed. "Midday will be a couple of hours ahead of here, so we should leave late morning tomorrow to arrive there after midday."

"That should work," Jessica agreed.

"Good." He looked around. "So, what next?"

Spider coughed. "If you've finished with me, I'll head off. I've … something to do."

Lanky glanced at Jessica. She nodded. "Fine," he said. "We can regroup later, down by the main hut."

Spider immediately turned and strode off.

Lanky flicked a glance at Jessica. She shrugged.

"Best you two come with me," Rind said. "We should prepare our packs. And our clothing – remember, the south will be warmer than here. Then we need to ready our stories, and practice. Then practice again and again. And again."

"Acting has never been my thing," Lanky muttered.

"But your life has never depended on it before," Rind said softly as they walked off towards the gorge.

That's true, he thought with a shiver. *And neither has yours depended on me …*

*

"Are you stupid, woman!" Parig exclaimed, as a group of bemused Islanders looked on. "A Warrior must travel south with me. And we must move now."

"My name is Beth, *man,*" Beth said in an icy voice. "And what can't you understand? We need to protect this place until the others return."

199

His eyes blazed in fury. "What we must do is take the fight to those scum who invade these lands. And if you won't fight, then stand aside and let those who will defend the innocent."

"You are a fool," Beth grated.

Stepping away from the others, Parig stormed over to Beth, towering over her. "And you are weak. But if you wish to remain here, cowering in the caves, then do so. I and the others here march south." He made to push past her.

She stepped into his path. "You are not in command here. Stand down."

Parig's mouth curled into an infuriating smile. "In my land, the strongest command." His smile broadened, baring twisted, broken teeth. "Do you think to stop me?" He shoved her hard in the chest, pushing her backwards.

"Hold!" a commanding voice shouted. Beth glanced around to see Rind striding towards them, Lanky and Jessica following closely behind.

"Don't interfere, woman!" Parig roared. "Stay out of this!"

Beth caught Rind's eye – and winked.

Rind came up short, her brow furrowing. Then a faint look of recognition flashed in her eyes. "Well, I guess it is *your* business," she said to her father. She took a step back and folded her arms.

"What!" Jessica said. "You—"

Beth turned and launched herself at Parig, hitting the unprepared man square in the chest, taking them both to the ground. Immediately, rolling away, she sprang to her feet, setting herself into a low crouch in front of the spluttering man.

Parig stood slowly, climbing to his full mountainous height. "I will—"

Beth struck out with her right leg, hammering her foot into Parig's left knee. As the great man howled in pain, she spun around, smashing the heel of her left foot into the side of his massive head, rocking him backwards. Continuing her fluid movement, she smashed her right forearm into the spot her foot had just left.

Howling again, Parig dropped his head …

It was enough. Leaping up, she grabbed the back of his head and yanked downwards with all her might – there was a satisfying crack as his chin met her right knee. Releasing her grip, she stood back as the man collapsed to the ground. As a few Islanders moved towards them, she held up her hand. "Stay where you are," she growled, then stepping closer to the fallen man, she crouched down beside him. But not too low and not too close.

She waited.

After a while, his eyes opened, and he groaned. He pushed himself up from the ground. "Cursed woman!" he grunted.

She kneed him in the head.

"Beth!" Jessica shouted as Parig collapsed like a stone.

"Leave her be," Rind said, holding Jessica back, a note of humour in her voice.

Once more, Beth waited.

And once more, Parig finally stirred, groaning.

Beth watched as he slowly pushed himself up to a seated position, head bowed.

She tensed, readying herself.

Arm shaking, he put up his hand. "Enough," he whispered. "You win ... Warrior."

Beth knelt down beside him. "We are equals," she whispered. "Try to bully me again, and I'll cut off your balls and serve them to you for dinner. Now, shall we get back to the meeting?"

Hearing him wheezing, she was worried she might actually have broken something in the man's thick head. But she realised he was laughing. "If you don't mind, Warrior, I think I will stay a moment. For some reason, my head aches."

Beth climbed to her feet and glanced at the hesitant group around them. "We're taking a break. When you see the flag raised, return." As the group of Islanders dispersed with low murmurs, she walked over to join Rind and her friends.

"Well?" Jessica said, hands on hips. "What the hell was that about?"

"He was annoying me."

"Well, you may find that's not the way to make friends."

"It is with my father," Rind said, grinning. "Excellent work, Warrior."

"What triggered this?" Lanky said, watching the subdued Parig wipe his bloodied nose on the back of his hand.

"He wants me to travel south with him – he wants a Warrior with his people. But we can't leave until you finish your mission. We—"

"If we finish it," Lanky muttered.

"I understand the risks ... but we have to plan for success. We should wait for your return."

"But how long do you wait?" Jessica said. "One day? Two? Seven? We agreed lingering overlong in this place is not an option, so if Parig has ideas, let's listen to them."

"I get that," Beth said with a scowl. "But he wants to go now. Today. The man is a force of nature. He can't sit still for a moment."

"Not sure about that," Lanky quipped, looking over at the dazed man.

"The tribe can't leave immediately," Beth continued. "We can't leave the Sacred Chamber unprotected, else it could be attacked and destroyed, cutting your link back. Or you could return to a camp occupied by hostiles. No, we need to remain for the length of your mission." She glanced at Jessica. "But I agree, we can't stay long."

An uneasy silence fell.

Then Lanky spoke. "Scouts have seen no other enemy forces close by, and after the defeat they've suffered and the presence of the Islanders, they may take time to regroup. But nothing is certain, so we make this mission as short as we can." He cocked his head as he glanced at Jessica. "Two days? Three?"

"How long is a piece of string?" she answered.

Rind frowned. "I don't understand."

Lanky smiled. "An expression – who knows what the answer is?" His amusement quickly died. "But I can tell you, if we haven't found our answer in the Ka camp within a few days, we get out – it's scaring the hell out of me thinking about it."

"I agree," Beth said. "Each day in enemy territory is a day too long. But the reality is, you'll need enough time within the camp to execute the plan safely. Rushing it risks blowing your covers." She hesitated, fearing her next words. "Three days?"

Lanky and Jessica looked at each other. They both nodded.

"Three days," Lanky said. "We'll be back within three days."

And if they're not back? Beth pushed that dread thought away. *Plan for success.* "So, when do you leave?"

Silence fell.

She frowned. "You still haven't decided?"

"We have," Lanky muttered, scratching his beard. "It's just ..." He glanced at Jessica.

Beth's eyes narrowed. "It's just you're not telling anyone? Not even me?"

Jessica sighed. "Tomorrow," she said in a low voice. "But we'll leave unseen."

"I understand that," Beth grunted, glaring at Jessica. "But I want to be there when you go."

Jessica made to answer, then turned at the sound of approaching voices. "We can discuss more later."

They waited as Amber and Tricia approached.

"Amber," Jessica said, acknowledging the healer. She smiled at Tricia. "And a new assistant, I see?"

"She is," Amber answered. "And I think I've found the first victim for her to work on."

There was a loud groan from Parig.

"Either your patient is still hurting," Lanky said, "or he's not too impressed by the new healer."

"Ha, ha," Tricia muttered, casting a scowl at Lanky as she walked with Amber over to Parig. "Wait until you're sick. Then you'll be begging for my help."

*

As Tricia and Amber tended Parig, Jessica turned to Beth. "Three days then. From tomorrow."

Her face strained, Beth nodded. "But don't push it, Jess. Any signs you've been discovered, get out of there."

Jessica's gut twisted. How much easier it would be to remain with the Iyes and the Islanders and seek a safe refuge here in the north. *Or use the Staff to flee the terrors of this Land. To return home …*

Steadying herself, she forced back the lure of the siren. *I wish it so much, but I know there's no escape yet.* For she was the Guardian. She was needed to prevent the release of an evil they called the Geddon. *Find the Kade. Deliver it to IY.*

And the Seed of Life spoken of by the ancient spirit Jalu? What of that? *Another unknown. Another secret to hide.* But that was for another time. *First the Kade.*

She glanced at Beth, who was watching her closely. "We have to push hard. IY needs us to secure the Kade."

"I know. But take care. This is beyond anything we've attempted so far."

Jessica laid her hand on Beth's arm. "But we're developing beyond anything we've been before. And we need to keep developing, keep understanding." *For there's far more to this than we can see. I feel it. I sense it.*

She squeezed Beth's arm. "We'll make sure we see you before we go. Promise."

Jessica saw the relief in Beth's eyes. "You better," her friend growled. "Else there'll be trouble."

"Think we've enough of that without annoying you."

A flicker of a smile crossed Beth's face.

"Come on," Jessica said, turning to Lanky and Rind. "Think we should all head to the kitchen to eat."

"Sounds good," Rind said, grabbing Lanky by the arm. "If we get there early, Warrior, the choice cuts of meat are ours."

Jessica watched the two walk away. *Something's developing there. Slowly.*

The thought triggered a sudden pang in her heart ... jealousy? She forced it away. She was genuinely happy for him. *We could all do with someone by our side.* She turned to Beth. *But we don't always get the one we want.* "You coming?"

"You go on ahead," Beth replied, her gaze on Tricia, who wiped a thick black tar on the gash on her groggy patient's nose. "Think I need a quiet chat with our friend over there."

Jessica smiled. "Okay, but give him a break. Remember, he is the leader of our allies."

As she walked away, cold fear stirred once more. A constant fear, an unwanted companion. She breathed deeply. *Accept it. Use it. Focus on what's in front of you.*

The Kade.

Secure the Kade.

*

"What are you doing?" Darius asked.

Spider looked up. "What?"

"I said, what are you doing?"

"I ... I'm heading to see Firuz. They're repairing a shelter."

Darius stepped away from the entrance to the cave. "You've walked up the gorge seven times. You've walked back here seven times. And Firuz is right over there." He pointed to the opposite wall of the gorge, where Firuz and several others ferried blocks of stone up to a shelter.

"Ah ... yes. I—"

"I don't need to know, Spider, but whatever you're trying to do, can you please get on with it? It's driving me mad watching you."

Spider glanced towards the entrance to the cave, to the entrance leading to the Sacred Chamber where River was resting. *Do it.*

He took a step forward.

And then stopped. What if Amber and Tricia were wrong? *They weren't there. I can't put her in that position again ... can I?*

"Hey, Spider! Can you help us for a while?"

"There you go," Darius said brightly. "Firuz has found *you*. That's saved you any more walking up and down trying to find *him*."

Spider scowled at Darius, then glanced towards the shelter where Firuz stood waving at him. He released a deep sigh. *Fine, I'll help them for a while. Later ... Maybe I'll see her later.*

With a heavy heart and a confused mind, Spider walked towards the shelter.

River gazed at the smooth bone carving lying in her palm. Though devastated to hold it once more, her soul still stirred at the glorious sweep of the horse's head as the graceful animal raced ever onwards towards its distant goal. How long ago had she carved it? Several sun-cycles ago now. The image of her sitting beside her sister, Sheba, floated into her mind. "No, gently, River," she heard her sister say as she ran the gleaming edge of the stone flake along another line of the carving. "The bone wishes to be carved, but slowly – take your time."

Sheba had always been a natural sculptor, the stone, bone, or wooden cores effortlessly evolving within her gifted hands into beautiful works of art – or deadly weapons of death. *Reflecting our lives,* River thought grimly, their love for one another balanced against their constant fight for survival.

And now Sheba carried another reason to fight to survive. *She carries her child. She carries a most special child.* It had taken time, but River had finally found that knowledge buried deep with the inherited memories of the old Mother. *Naga knew, but she didn't tell. But I see now, it's why she kept Sheba close.* River ran her fingers gently over the bone carving. *It's why I now watch over you, my sister, even from afar. We must preserve the line of the Iyes's shamans. We must protect you and your child from the evils of the Ka and their god Kaos.*

As she turned the cool bone in her hand, the ache in her heart deepened. She had wanted Spider to keep this most cherished part of her life. She had wanted him to hold it in his hands and think of her. She bowed her head. *Then why not follow your heart? Why not embrace the love you feel?* The Mother inside her quickly answered. *Because my people need me. Because in this moment, I cannot be distracted.*

Wincing, River raised her head and looked blindly at the richly adorned walls. Did it have to be this way? *You know it doesn't. IY told you this.* And yet in the memories of Naga, she could find no Mother who'd shared their life with another. *Why?*

It doesn't matter, you fool. Follow your heart.

She clenched her hand tightly around the carving. She couldn't. Not yet. Powerful forces of the Dark were rising in the Land, bent on its destruction, and she was at the centre of the fight to resist that evil. To force it back. To destroy it.

I cannot commit all of myself to him. And he deserves that from me.

Stay as a friend for now, Spider – and then we will see.

She opened her hand and looked again at the carving. *But I want him to take it on his mission. It can help him, protect him.* For she felt the latent power within the carving – a power the Spirits had gifted her. "This is a great work," Sheba had said when the carving was nearing completion. "This, you should complete before the eyes of the Spirits." River had been so proud to receive such praise and recognition from her sister, and to complete such a work in the presence of those who watched over them was a rare privilege. *It was my proudest achievement,* she thought, remembering her keen concentration during those final delicate lines she'd etched within the sanctity of the Sacred Chamber.

And I felt their blessing.

She'd felt the breath of her ancestors on the carving.

It became a talisman of the tribe.

And I want Spider to have it for his journey. He will *have it. I need—*

The hairs on her neck stood on end as a forbidding presence swept into the chamber.

She sprang to her feet, drawing from the A'ven.

A woman with short, spiky hair stood before her, her face grim.

"IY?" River stammered. "Where have you been?"

The spiky-haired woman stepped forward. "I have little time. We have discovered the traitor. Listen well, we must act."

CHAPTER FIFTEEN

Whether your life is short or long, do not
waste it; spend time with those you like.

*Y*ou know, friends, I like this place. I like it a lot. I like the people. I
like the conversation. I like—"

"You like wine," Sy signed. "A lot."

"Yes, I like wine, but it's early," Shadow said, pointing through the
branches of the tree towards the burning sun, still riding high to the
west, "and so I'm treating her with respect."

"Her?"

"Well, yes, for me that's true. A man doesn't provide such comfort
and joy. With this," he said, raising his cup, "I can relax in her warm
embrace and forget my worries for a while."

Tomas, a broad-nosed man sitting with his back to the tree, laughed.

"You don't ever accept my offers of embrace," Kat murmured. She
lay beside Sy with her head propped in one hand, her long hair
draping down the swell of her muscled arm, and studied Shadow
through playful eyes.

Shadow laughed. "I'd never leave. And I've still so many things to
do and to see."

"I could show you plenty of things to do and see," Kat teased,
winking at Sy.

"Well …"

She pushed a strand of her black hair from her cheek. "Who are you
waiting for, Shadow? Who is the perfect woman for you? Or man?"

"Sy is the perfect man for me," he said. "We're a match made by
Kaos himself."

"And woman?"

"Ha," Tomas said brightly. "There's no woman in our lands that could compete with—"

"His lack of ambition, poor wit, and pitiful choice in companions," a cold voice snarled behind Shadow.

Immediately, Kat and Tomas pulled themselves to their feet. They acknowledged their superior with a slight tilt of the head.

"You're late for the meeting," Nefra growled as she walked into Shadow's circle of friends. She glared down at the Disciple, who sat cross-legged, his cup of wine nestled in his hands. "And I don't like being used as a messenger."

"Please sit and join us, Nefra. We still have time before we leave. Sy, grab another cup and fill it with this interesting brew. It—"

"I will say this only once more," Nefra hissed, glaring at him. "Get up and join us for the meeting. And if you don't, it will not be taken well – for you or your friends."

Kat immediately placed her cup down on the ground. "I know when a party is over," she said, casting a warm smile at Shadow. "When you get back, see me – before you see that wine. Come on, Tomas, more blades to be made." She gave Nefra a slight bow, then holding Tomas's arm, she walked off, out of the shade of the tree.

Shadow climbed angrily to his feet, then strode to Nefra. He leaned close to her face. "Don't ever threaten my friends again."

Nefra smiled, her stance relaxing. "But it worked, didn't it? Your friends have gone, so now you can join the meeting." She leaned in herself, her breath brushing his face. "While part of me wished for the Shade to follow me here, you would have suffered his wrath. And that wouldn't do – this mission needs you." She tilted her head a fraction. "The Ensi was quite clear on that."

"You saw the Ensi?"

"I did. It seems you had a change of heart." She placed a hand on his chest. "I look forward to hearing the new beat."

Shadow grabbed her wrist, gripping it tightly. "It seems you – and the Ensi – are mistaken." He pushed her arm away.

Nefra's breathy laugh sounded irritatingly confident. "No, not this time, my Shadow. Not even you could be foolish enough to gainsay your leader again." She leaned into him. "You worry about my game with your friends? The Ensi plays no such games. No, I believe you understood her very clearly; fail her on this, and no friend of yours will exist in any of these lands." She ran her finger up his chest and neck, and to his lips. "And you do need your friends, don't you?" With a knowing smile, she stepped back. "The Shade awaits. And bring your new pet from the Games – it will be amusing to see him battle a Warrior."

With a final guileful glance, she turned and walked off towards the Core.

Shadow stood, shaking with growing rage, the joy of his friends' warming companionship already lost. Clenching his jaw, he reached into his tunic and closed his hand around a blade. He walked forward …

Sy jumped to his feet and leapt in front of him, grabbing his arm and clasping him firmly. The warrior-monk glared at him, shaking his head. Shadow stared after the retreating Nefra, fighting against the tide of anger washing over him.

Sy's fingers dug deep into his arm, and the pain sliced through his cold rage. Trembling, he knew Sy was right. *She's not worth dying for.* He nodded to Sy, who immediately released his arm.

Closing his eyes, Shadow took deep, slow breaths. Whether it had been pure anger, or a rage fuelled by his drinking, he would have made a fatal mistake if Sy had not intervened. *Am I losing control?* Of himself, of his relationship with the Ensi … of his life? "What am I doing wrong?" he muttered.

Sy's fingers flashed. "I've told you again and again, stop asking questions of the Ensi. But you don't listen!" He jabbed a finger into Shadow's chest. "This is no game. I've *my* life to consider – and *my* friends. If you continue, I will—"

"What?" Shadow said sharply. "You will what? Leave me?"

Sy held a finger to Shadow's mouth, then jabbed him in the chest again. Then his fingers flashed. "Keep your mouth shut! Just do your job!" He glared at Shadow, then shook his head. "We need to find this new friend of yours. Another stupid move."

Shadow glared after Sy, watching him gather their drinking cups, then take them across to his Flanks' hut.

His rage quickly dissipated.

Sy was right. And Sy was wrong. *I'm a Disciple. I need to ask questions.* But he needed to get smarter at how he did it. He recalled Xerses telling him he was too young to be a Disciple. *I'm not. But, yes, there are things I should learn.*

He watched Sy return. "I heard you," he said as a way of clearing the air.

Sy's stern eyes regarded him for a moment, then his fingers flashed. "It's behind us. We move on."

Shadow acknowledged him with a relieved nod. He needed his friend on his side.

Sy picked up his pack and spear. "Let's go," he signed, then walked away towards the Rim.

Shadow reached down and swung his own pack onto his back. Picking up his fighting staff and spear, he strode after Sy. *The time for play is over. The Ensi has a task for you.* He needed to execute the mission – when he finally found out what it was – then return and sweep through his homeland. For a stench was rising, and it needed cleaning whether the Ensi saw it or not.

*

The men stared in disbelief at the timeworn knucklebones lying on the dusty ground, the second roll to all land face-up.

"He's cheating us," Tarq growled, baring his teeth.

"I don't see how," said a wizened, weather-beaten man in the ring. "These are my knuckles – and you scramble them. He has either the skill of a shaman or Kaos on his side. Either way, I'm out. I can't afford to lose another of my best blades."

"He still has a throw left, you old fool," Tarq growled.

The old man flicked a weary glance at the temple guard. "And as I said, I can't afford to lose again. I'm out."

The heavyset man beside Tarq threw in a blade. "I'm in."

"And me," another said.

Scowling, Tarq picked up the knuckles. Hiding them from sight, he churned them around in his hand. "Throw," he snarled, holding out his fist to the young man opposite.

Karnt tentatively held out his hand—

Tarq smashed his fist down into Karnt's palm. "Throw wisely," he hissed, throwing down an obsidian dagger. "I want this weapon back."

A calm acceptance settled on Karnt. He needed to play again. He glanced up at the sun. But he needed to leave soon; the Disciple was expecting him. And he couldn't miss that – the chance of a lifetime. A rush of excitement ran through him. Rumours abounded of the long-haired Disciple and his companion: that they held veiled powers gifted from Kaos; that they fought terrifying dragons in distant lands; that they were invincible in battle. Karnt glanced back at Tarq. *And I'm playing knuckles with this fool.*

He suppressed a sigh. He'd tried leaving the game when he saw how many blades he'd won, but Tarq had insisted he stay. So he'd stayed – and won more blades. But this Tarq was a dangerous man, Karnt had realised too late. *But I have no time for trouble here.* He caressed the knuckles in his hand, feeling the rougher edges of those the temple guard had just switched into the game. Fine, losing was now the easiest way out.

He looked to the sandy ground, then closed his eyes and threw.

A gasp from the players told him all he needed to know.

With a resigned sigh, Karnt opened his eyes and glanced at Tarq. The temple guard's face was as dumbfounded as the rest – until it contorted with sudden fury. His face seething, the guard climbed to his feet and pulled out a blade. "You cheating scum! You die!"

The guard sprang across the sand, driving forward with his blade arm …

Already moving, Karnt rolled to the side as the deadly strike passed through thin air. Grasping an object from the ground, Karnt leapt to his feet – Tarq's obsidian dagger fit comfortably in his palm. "It feels good," he said, brandishing the gleaming weapon. "Thank you for your gift."

As intended, Tarq's face exploded with unbridled rage, and he launched himself forward with a guttural roar. Swaying easily from the guard's clumsy strike, Karnt flicked the dagger from one hand to the other, then delivered his own vicious thrust under Tarq's chin. With a terrible scream, the guard's heavy weight clattered into him, and they both collapsed to the ground. But Karnt knew he'd delivered a killing blow.

With a grunt, he pushed the twitching body away, then climbed to his feet, brushing himself down.

"I think these are yours," the weathered old man said, holding up a handful of blades. With a tilt of his head, the man gestured to the worn knuckles lying spilled from Tarq's hand. "He thought taking those from the game would change his luck. Seems he was wrong." The old man looked back at Karnt. "Take them. They've been with me a long time, but it seems they like you."

"And him?"

"Let me deal with that. They hated him here in the Rim, but he was a man with friends within." The old man shrugged. "I suppose they may not like the message – or messenger – but you dealt with our problem, so I will help you with yours."

"I'll vouch for you, old man, don't worry about that," came a calm voice. "It saved me the effort."

*

"My liege!" Karnt exclaimed as the old man and others of the game bowed their heads in deference. "I can explain what—"

"Nothing to explain, my good friend," Shadow murmured. "I witnessed this foul man's unprovoked attack, as did all those here." Each man muttered their agreement, but each took an involuntary step backwards. "And I expect each of you to make a statement in support of this man," Shadow continued, halting the men's movements.

He glanced at the dead guard, one who'd been due a visit tonight to repay the fool's treacherous jibe at the temple entrance. An insult Shadow could not ignore. He shifted his attention to the old man. A brave man to have offered his help to Karnt. "What's your name?"

"Kapano, my liege."

"And do you have a family here?"

"Just my granddaughter, my liege. She's away hunting right now."

"And where are you from?"

"South. Far to the south where the lands are rich and green." His eyes flicked to the dead man. "And where maybe the people are friendlier too."

"If that is so, why are you here?"

The weatherworn man glanced at him. "I didn't know how green my land was and how friendly my own folk were, till I lived here."

Shadow smiled. "You see that, Sy? An honest man, as well as a brave man. And what do you and your granddaughter do, aside from hunting and playing knuckles?"

"My granddaughter is the finest singer and player of the flute you would ever meet," Kapano said earnestly. "Unfortunately, she would as soon kill you as sing to you – which is why she refuses to bond."

Shadow laughed.

"And I am merely a holder of stories and a teller of tales," finished the old man.

"I like you and your granddaughter more and more, by each word."

Kapano inclined his head. "Thank you, my liege."

Shadow studied him. Bright, intelligent eyes, and a warmth about him. And courage. His heart lifted. This was the type of citizen they needed. One who sought to do the right thing, despite the threat they may face. It was as though a sparkling stream of clear fresh water had come and washed away the grime. *These are the people I fight for. These are the people we must reward.*

He looked around at those cautiously watching him. "By the word of a Disciple of the Ensi, and borne witness to by those present, I promote this man, Kapano, and his granddaughter to the Flanks." He looked back at Kapano. "Stay in this very spot and someone will visit you soon. You will have a place by my old family, and when I return, I will hear your tales of your green land and your warm people."

Kapano reached out with a shaking hand. "There are few words I can find for this wonderful gift. Thank you."

Shadow grasped the man's wrist in a firm grip. His flesh felt like the hide of a rhinoceros. *Matches his crinkled, sun-wrinkled face,* he thought, amused. Releasing the man's leathery skin, he turned to a grinning Karnt. "Right. We're off to see a shaman – a particularly angry one – but we now travel with a much lighter heart." He glanced at Sy. "This day is turning for the better."

Sy shrugged and walked off towards the Flanks.

"Yes," Shadow said, smiling. "A good day indeed."

CHAPTER SIXTEEN

As Kaos's influence deepened in the Land, his daemons grew stronger, exerting greater and greater control of those minds who used their power – and delivering swift retribution on any who sought to tread their own path.

River tasted the nervous tension cutting the air of the Sacred Chamber as the group made their final checks on their packs. A Guardian, a Warrior, and two of the tribe's most trusted members about to begin a bold foray into the heart of the Ka's homeland. Watching them, she wiped a sweaty palm on her tunic, hoping she had taken the right path. She glanced at Jessica. *I must speak with her now. I owe her this.* But it had to be done carefully. She stepped closer to the group.

Lanky was eyeing his bulging pack. "That looks heavy," he muttered. "Explain again why I had to play the servant?"

Rind winked at Jessica, then turned to Lanky. "Stop complaining, else you'll feel the back of my hand."

Lanky glowered at Rind. "Well, this is going to be fun."

Spider laughed, but despite the light tones, River heard the edge to their voices.

The humour fading from her eyes, Rind adjusted the strap of the light pack she carried, then straightened her bloodred tunic. "There's no point in prolonging this," she said, picking up an ornately carved staff. "We're ready. We should go."

Silence descended as each member of the group looked at one another.

River stepped forward to face Jessica. "You have the image clear in your mind? The ruins of the stone circle by the escarpment?"

Jessica nodded.

"And you remember the Cord to use to get there?"

The memory of the complex taste, smell, and vibration of the quivering strand of energy that River had shown her snapped into her mind. The Cord. Their path to the fringes of the Ka camp. "I do, but using it to get us there? That's not so certain."

"Keep a calm mind and clear purpose. You are the Staff Holder – the Guardian – you wield the power within the Continuum."

Jessica glanced at her Staff, now appearing as a simple wooden staff. "I know. I just wish I knew more."

"You know more than any in this Land. Stay resolute, firm in the belief you will succeed."

"If only we didn't have to take the Staff," Lanky muttered. "You two worked hard to get this back. If—"

"Don't go there," Jessica said firmly. "We can only play the cards we have, and this is a strong one."

"But you managed to take yourself and River back to the future. You did that without the Staff."

"I had no conscious role in that, I was just trying to get away from the burnt man. And IY believes Kaos was at work, somehow banishing me. No, the Staff remains with me. I need it."

River saw the doubt in Lanky's face, but this was Jessica's call. He sighed and turned to Spider. "You ready to go?"

Spider glanced her way. She smiled. He smiled back, holding her gaze for a moment before turning back to Lanky. "Ready," he said, picking up his pack.

River watched Spider set the pack on his back. There had been no time to meet since the words of yesterday. Should she talk to him again? There were many things she would like to say. *But not here, not in front of the others.* The chance had passed.

She glanced at Jessica. *But this I can't delay.*

Catching the tall woman's eyes, River gestured her to follow, then stepped a few paces away.

With quizzical eyes, Jessica walked over to her. "What's up?"

River glanced at the others, who were talking quietly amongst themselves. "First this," she whispered, clasping the Warrior's hand. "Please pass this on to Spider. Discreetly. I will feel better knowing he has it." She released the bone carving into Jessica's hand.

"Consider it done," Jessica murmured, her hand closing around the carving.

Let the Spirits protect him. Breathing a little easier, River stepped closer to Jessica. "We are moving against the traitor." She saw Jessica

215

stiffen. "And a trap is set for the Ka's shaman, the one they call the Shade. We draw him here."

Jessica drew a sharp breath.

"Do not yet speak of this to anyone," River continued, voice low. "Only when you've left this place. Drawing the Shade here will aid you on your mission – it removes a key defence from their homeland."

Jessica stared at River, her eyes wide. "What about you? What about all those here? How do you plan to defeat the Ka's shaman?"

"I cannot tell you more. I just can't. Even this ..." Dread curled around her. *If the traitor learns of this ...* She held Jessica's challenging gaze. "It is your choice whether you proceed, but ..." *But we would lose this chance.*

Jessica pushed a strand of hair behind her ear, uncertainty writ across her face. "Who else knows?"

"IY and one other. And now you. Your mission remains as it was, only now you will have one less power standing against you."

"And Beth?"

"She will be told soon," River said evenly.

Jessica grimaced. "Damn it, River. Why like this?"

"We can't alert the traitor. We can't destroy this opportunity." She could see the confusion – and anger – darkening Jessica's face. "It's the best chance you'll have. It's the best chance *we* will have."

Jessica glared at her. "If the Shade is coming here, I hope you're truly ready for him."

They were as ready as they could be after only a day's preparation. "We are," River said in a low voice. "The Shade of the Ka will be ours."

Jessica shook her head. "I hope you know what you're doing. I hope IY knows what she's doing."

Fear trickled down River's spine. *We know as much as we can in these dread times.* She said nothing.

"If their Shade comes," Jessica whispered, "then I can see how it will help our mission. But I don't like how this has been done. We're supposed to talk through these things together."

The weight on River's shoulders grew, but she stood unbowed in the face of the Warrior's anger. "I agree, but in this, I had no choice."

"There's always a choice."

"Yes, and I chose to take the opportunity that presented itself. To help save my Land."

Jessica's gaze raked River's face a moment longer, then her anger slowly slipped away. She glanced to the rest of the group, where Lanky stood looking at them. "We can't back out now," she murmured as if to herself. She turned back. "Okay. You've told me. I've heard. We'll play it your way, but don't work this way again – we don't know what we might be missing."

"Risks exist in all we do," she reminded the Guardian.

"Even so ..." Jessica's gaze lingered on River, then she straightened. "We should get going." An anxious urgency entered her voice. "If you need us, reach out for me. Immediately."

"I will."

River saw the tension ease from Jessica's shoulders, then the young woman raised her clenched hand halfway. "I will deliver this."

River smiled. "Thank you. And may IY travel with you."

"And with you."

A short while later, the travelling group was assembled.

"How do you want to do this?" Rind asked.

"Stand closer," Jessica said, her jaw set tight. "It will help me focus."

Rind shifted between Lanky and Spider, then Jessica stepped in to complete a tight ring.

"Ready?" Jessica said.

"Yes," the three answered.

The energy in the chamber surged, and the group before River vanished.

Staring into the empty chamber, faint echoes from the wielding of the Land's energy still rippling around her, River felt a sudden keen sense of loss. She girded herself. "No time for regrets. Keep moving. And be ready."

Her thoughts on the trap that had to be set, she strode from the chamber.

*

Shadow looked on in dismay. It couldn't be. Not again. What was happening? He glanced down at the ground again and counted ... three, four, five. Yes, five knuckles lying marks up. "Give me those!" he hissed. "Let me try again."

Karnt picked up the knuckles and handed them to Shadow.

"Okay," Shadow said, peering at the bones intently. "Place them in my hand just as you had them. Okay, like that? Are you sure?"

"That's how I held them."

Shadow steadied himself, then threw the knuckles, copying Karnt's style. He watched expectantly as they fell to the ground and scattered, but as they came to rest, his face fell even further. Five – but five with no markings! He sat back on his haunches, shaking his head. "These things are cursed! Cursed by the god of Karnt who won't let anyone else win."

Beside him, Growl hissed in irritation. "I won't tell you again, Disciple. Keep quiet."

Wiping his brow, Shadow turned to the Shade in annoyance. "Look, we've been cooking behind these rocks for hours, watching what? The odd scorpion crawling over the sand and the sun crossing overhead. Maybe the Ensi was wrong about visitors. And what visitors anyway?"

He saw Growl grimace, but the Shade didn't reply.

He doesn't know. I keep asking, but it seems he really doesn't know. Shadow raised his head a fraction, glancing over the top of the boulders they hid behind, quickly scanning the fractured circle of stones in the plain below – stones of a long-forgotten temple to some long-forgotten god. He frowned. So, what game did the Ensi play here?

Shaking his head, he began to lower himself down—

A flare of light lit up the circle of stones, then vanished as quickly as it had appeared. Several figures staggered, then collapsed to the ground.

Shadow quickly dropped out of sight. "Well, what do you know," he breathed. "Seems the Ensi was right after all."

Nefra immediately glanced over the top of the boulders. "The fool's right. We have visitors." She was silent for a moment. "They lie still, unmoving." Dropping back down, she glanced at Growl. "To travel here in this way, they must be aided by a powerful shaman. If we move now, we could assess the threat – then act."

Growl's face creased to a half frown, half smile. "We are thinking the same. Yes, we are."

"Not so fast," Shadow whispered. "The Ensi told us to ignore them."

"Are you certain of that?" Nefra growled. "Did she say they would be accompanied by a shaman with the power of our Shade?"

Shadow glared at her. "I know what I heard." He glanced at Growl. "And so do you."

Growl bared his teeth. "We heard, but to miss this chance. We should … We should …" His face twisted with uncertainty, and his eyes burned black with bright flashes of silver.

A tremor of disquiet ran through Shadow. *He's fighting his daemon friend.*

The silvery black flames danced in Growl's eyes, then the fire dimmed. "We should, but we cannot," the Shade continued in a strained voice. "Observe only. That was the command. Once they have gone, we leave."

"I didn't get that order," Nefra hissed. "We can't miss this chance." She started to rise—

And was roughly pulled down by Growl. "We have our orders. We hold."

"Too late anyway," Karnt whispered.

Shadow peered through a crack between the boulders. Karnt was right; two of the unknown arrivals – a tall, imposing woman and a lean man of the north – were on their feet. Nefra's recent words echoed: "To travel here in this way, they must be aided by a powerful shaman." He knew of only their Shade who could travel the land in this way, and that sparingly used. Sparingly, because not all survived that journey through the darkness. *And yet, still I'm foolish enough to accept these missions afar.* He studied those below, seeing the lean one rubbing his temple. There were tales of the power of the Iyes's shaman, but it seemed likely to him that at least one of these visitors had the skills of Growl …

He froze as the figures half turned. It couldn't be!

But as his widening eyes flicked between the two, he couldn't deny what he was seeing. *The two who carried the Staff – the two I left with Krag.* Twisting around, setting his back to the boulder, he glanced at Sy and signed. "Do you see what I see?"

"Two of the Iyes tribe and the two travellers we captured."

Shadow sat, stunned. What were they doing here? How had they escaped Krag? The chaotic swirl of his thoughts triggered the remembered words of Ensi: "… it seems the one you claimed dead has arisen." He winced at the memory of the feisty woman who'd faced him in battle after he'd captured the Staff. *The one I poisoned. Then the one I saw lying lifeless in the snow at the lair of the Ancient.* Yet the Ensi said that woman still lived. And now these two companions of that unkillable woman – two he'd left to their fates in the foul hands of Krag – were here. Alive.

A terrible realisation churned his stomach. *I didn't see what was before me.* He shifted closer to Growl. "I know two of those down there," he whispered. "Travellers who arrived to the Iyes. Travellers who I now believe are Warriors."

Wringing his hands, Growl's silver-flecked eyes narrowed. But he said nothing.

Did Growl already know this? He leaned towards the Shade. "Are these the travellers the Ensi expected? Did she—"

"Quiet, Disciple! That is not ours to question before others."

Shadow saw a tangle of confusion on the Shade's face. *Whatever he knows of these below, he doesn't know all. He doesn't know what the Ensi is planning.* He replayed Growl's last words. *And he doesn't want me to dig deeper in the presence of Sy and Nefra.* He glanced at the swirling chaos in

Growl's eyes. Or was it his cursed daemon, Ereboz, that the Shade feared to hear the Ensi's secrets?

Shadow studied the Shade's unsettled features. The daemon's influence was growing, but the man, Growl, remained dominant. *He still seeks to protect the Ensi.* And that was the way of their leader; she inspired trust in all around her. *Because she has led our people well.* But still, a ripple of unease ran through him. The Ensi wasn't a god; she could make mistakes. *Like the snake. She didn't listen to me. Cobra is a threat.*

But that was for another time. "What do we do now?" he whispered. "They will sense us."

"You take me for a fool," Growl muttered. "We are shielded."

He then heard Growl mumbling under his breath. He strained to hear. "... good, yes, excellent. We can see how this helps us, yes, we can. Our path to the devil shaman is cleared, yes, it is."

The devil shaman? Shadow's heart raced with a sudden fierce anticipation. *So that was it? We attack the heart of the Iyes?* He glanced at Growl. So, when was their Shade planning to tell them the details?

Growl turned to him, his eyes a deepest black. "Soon, Disciple. So very soon."

*

Her head pounding, Jessica slowly climbed to her feet. With the disguised Staff held loosely in one hand, she squinted against the intense glare from the desert sun. They had most definitely left the lands of the White Crags camp, but had she managed to get them to their destination?

Shielding her eyes, she scanned the ether but felt no unusual energy close by; there seemed no imminent danger. Glancing down, she saw she stood on the eroded remains of a stone floor. Once probably ornate, it was now fractured and broken, only a few faded blocks remaining intact as laid by its makers, builders who were now long gone together with those who had worshipped its forgotten god.

But a place known to the Iyes's shaman. *We've arrived at the place River described.*

Jessica looked out across a flat plain of golden sand and mud-brown gravel to a haze of green on the distant horizon. *The river valley of the Ka.* But, as far as she could see, no people. No threats.

Dropping her shielding hand, she turned to the stepped escarpment behind her. A narrow canyon cut deep into the cliffs, revealing multicoloured layers of ancient rock – rocks that could tell of other long-gone times to one who could decipher the tale locked in their grains.

Again, no threat. A worst-case scenario was gone.

Breathing more easily, she felt the throbbing pain in her head easing already. The move via the Cord had been painful, but nothing like the trauma of those first hellish travels through time. *Because I didn't pass through a Gate. I didn't enter the Void.*

She shivered. The Void beyond the Gates. The Void beyond the Continuum.

The realm of the Dark.

And of the Light.

She sensed other clouded, ephemeral memories hovering at the fringes of perception. Unseen memories that loomed with palpable dread yet remained beyond her reach. *I am the Guardian, but what else lies hidden beyond my sight?* She knew that soon she would need to touch that darkness and truly face what roamed there. But right now, in this moment, that was a journey too far. *Focus on what's before you.*

And what was before them was a half-day's walk from the very heart of the Ka homeland, a half-day's walk from beginning their dangerous quest to find the enigmatic Kade. What lay ahead of them? What defences of the Ka would they need to pass?

The memory of River's words hammered back into her mind: "… a trap is set for the Ka's shaman, the one they call the Shade. We draw him here." Jessica's brow creased in frustration. *Why this way, River? You didn't engage us. What might we have missed?*

Hearing groaning behind her, she turned to see Lanky climbing slowly to his feet. "That hurt," he said, shielding his eyes. "I thought you said it wouldn't hurt."

Not yet. I can't tell them of River's words yet. "We're here," she said, keeping a lightness to her voice. "And not yet dead. I'll take that as a win for now."

"Well, you set your bar high, I see," Lanky grunted. But he didn't refute it. "This is coming off," he said, stripping off his tunic, revealing his vest.

"You'll burn."

"I can't change my skin." Then he frowned. "But that's a fair point. I don't look like a man who's been travelling through these sun-scorched lands for weeks. That could be a problem. Why didn't we think of that before?"

"Because it's always the simple things we miss. Now put the tunic back on – that's not a good look."

221

"Hey, this is the only body I have. I can't change it. And anyway, it's getting toned. Look." He flexed his arm.

"I've bigger muscles than that," came Rind's unsteady voice. "And put that tunic on. You look out of place."

"Now hold on," Lanky began. "If—"

"Put the tunic on, Lanky," Spider muttered, slowly drawing himself up to a seated position. "This journey will be far easier if you just do what they say. And you are supposed to be their servant, remember?"

Jessica smiled. "I'm growing to like you, Spider." She walked over to him and helped him up. She stumbled as she did so but caught herself on his tunic. The carving dropped neatly into his tunic pocket.

"Easy," Spider said, steadying her with his outstretched hand. "Don't want an injury before we've started."

Jessica's thoughtful gaze returned to Lanky. "So, what do we do about this?"

"I am here, you know."

Rind considered Lanky's body, her brow furrowing. "If someone asks, we'll call it an affliction. That's how he is – and that's how he stays." She glanced back to his face. "Keep out of the sun."

"Well," Lanky said, making a show of looking around the sun-drenched desert plain. "That could be tricky."

Jessica glanced to the plain, shielding her eyes. The green haze resolved into a distant band of vegetation, running as far as the eye could see. And off to the right, a sliver of blue glittered in the sunlight. "The encampment lies beside the lake. It's not that far to walk."

"And there's scattered cloud cover," Rind said, casting a wry smile at Lanky. "We won't be in direct sun all the way."

Lanky scratched his beard, then adjusted the straps on his pack. "Okay. Guess there's no reason to delay this. Let's get moving."

Rind turned to Spider. "You'll wait awhile before following?"

"I'll find shade somewhere up there," he said, gesturing to the canyon.

Jessica glanced at Rind. "Are we certain we want to separate? We could just—"

"Let's stick with the plan," Rind said firmly. "It gives us one extra knuckle to throw if things go wrong. But remember, Spider, if all hell breaks loose in there, I want all of us to get back here. All of us."

Spider nodded. "I can handle myself. And you can be sure I'll be keeping you in my sights."

"Okay," Lanky said. "Let's get moving. We—"

"Hold on," Rind said firmly. "From now on, get into character. You don't give your master orders. And anyway, you can't speak. Remember that ... boy."

Lanky muttered something unheard.

Spider walked to his side. "Good luck," the scout said. "See you on the other side."

Lanky grasped the scout's wrist. "Good luck yourself, Spider, and take care. And I look forward to seeing you – on whatever the other side is."

Rind and Jessica walked over to say their goodbyes.

After giving Spider a warm hug, Rind stepped away. She reset the beads around her neck, then straightened, standing tall. *She stands with a pride about her*, Jessica thought. *With an air of arrogance. She will act the part well.*

"Jessica, we leave," Rind said in a calm yet commanding voice. Ignoring Lanky, she turned and strode with an easy grace onto the gravel plain.

"Hey, you forgot your pack," Lanky shouted.

"I don't think she did," Jessica said with a smile. "Come on. You can't let your liege wander in the desert alone."

Shaking his head, Lanky checked his own pack and Axe holster before picking up Rind's smaller pack. He dropped the strap over his head, then let the pack settle against his chest. "All the best, Spider," he called as they walked away. "And may IY travel with you."

"And with you, Warriors," Spider called after them.

Jessica stepped in beside Lanky as they strode on after Rind.

"Is this what all those other Warriors had to go through?" Lanky muttered beside her. "Heroes and heroines, the lot of them."

As they walked on, she heard his mutterings turn to a quiet humming. Discordant, nervous humming but an attempted tune, nonetheless. *I haven't heard that for quite a while.* She grimaced. *It shows what hell we've been through.* Glancing ahead, she looked to the distant lake. *And what else awaits us here?*

*

"They're leaving," Karnt whispered in a tense voice. "Hold on – three of them are leaving." He cursed. "The fourth one is heading up here."

"We leave!" Growl commanded. "Move! And keep low."

Moving quickly, Shadow dropped into the gulley behind the boulders, then followed it around to the mouth of the canyon. Once inside and around the first bend, they'd be out of sight. He stepped up on to the next ledge ...

His foot slipped, and he fell, triggering a rockfall into the gulley.

"He's seen us!" Nefra hissed.

"Run!" Growl rasped.

Back on his feet, Shadow quickly scrambled up onto the ledge. Looking down, he could see the man climbing up towards them. Shadow quickly stepped onto the smoother ground of the wadi, then ran hard, chasing after the others.

"Here!" Growl hissed from a blackness within the canyon wall to his left.

Shadow ran to the cave and entered.

"Follow me." A faint, eerie light issued from Growl's Black Staff.

They hurried after the Shade, who guided them on through a complex web of intersecting passageways, and as Shadow rounded another corner, he knew the Iyes would have no chance of finding them in here. And if he had found them, what had the man expected to do against the five of them? *Unless he only saw me?*

As the way became steeper, they dropped deeper and deeper into the cave network. Shadow felt a growing unease.

"What's that smell?" Karnt said, glancing back at Shadow. "It's making me feel sick."

"I don't smell anything." But he felt sick all the same. This place was not at all to his liking.

A short while later, Karnt halted. "I don't think I can go on." He leaned over and threw up.

"How much further?" Shadow shouted.

But the group ahead kept moving.

"You can't stay here," Shadow said as Karnt wiped his mouth. "It shouldn't be far now."

Looking miserable, Karnt nodded, and they walked on.

And as Shadow had guessed, rounding the next corner, they walked out into a spacious chamber, where Growl, Sy, and Nefra stood in the glow of the Shade's Staff. Glancing around, he caught his balance, suddenly disorientated. Peering out beyond the Shade's light, he saw no walls to the chamber, no roof.

Only blackness.

"Welcome to another of this land's delights," Growl crowed. "Beauty in its purest form."

The Shade's eyes appeared as pits of unrelenting darkness that sought to swallow you whole. The daemon within him had stormed to the fore.

Growl walked up to Karnt. "Come," he said, a cold smile on his face. "Greet your god."

Karnt cast a questioning glance at Shadow.

"What is this place?" Shadow said, taking a step towards Growl.

The Shade's Black Staff thrust towards Shadow, and he staggered back as pain ripped through his chest.

"Look!" Growl commanded to Karnt as though nothing had happened. "There. What do you see?"

Dazed, confused, and gasping for breath, Shadow watched Karnt cautiously edge towards the place Growl pointed. Shadow shifted his gaze to that place but could see nothing. Literally nothing. It was as though he looked into a void that devoured the light.

He watched Karnt edge forward, peering ahead in confusion.

And then Shadow saw a faint ripple, a flicker of ... something. Leaning closer, his brow creased as he sought to understand what he was seeing. He gasped as a roiling wall of intense blackness suddenly emerged, its oily surface a violent storm, chaotic waves crisscrossing from every direction. As an overwhelming sense of dread swept over him, he forced himself to move. "Karnt! Stand back—"

The wall flexed violently, morphing into a grotesque, manic face, and a rippling, black-clawed hand reached towards Karnt, who stood, frozen in terror.

"Get away! Run—"

The cascade of blood was sudden and gruesome as the claws raked down, shredding Karnt's body from head to toe. Shadow stared in transfixed horror as blood flooded the ground where Karnt had once stood. The roiling, oily blackness sprang outward, its vacuous maw engulfing the bespoiled remains of Karnt. Then – as suddenly as it had appeared – the unhuman visage melted away and the oily surface settled into a gently rippling bloodred wall.

All trace of Karnt had vanished from sight.

The chamber fell silent.

Shadow stared, unbelieving, at what he'd just seen. *Karnt didn't scream.* There had been no time to scream. He tried to take a step, but instead staggered. "What did you do?" he breathed, fighting to still his trembling body.

No one spoke.

Shadow slowly turned.

Both Nefra and Sy stood unmoving, eyes wide, faces strained.

Growl stood relaxed, eyes deepest black, a faint smile on his face.

Rage poured into all parts of Shadow's body. Pulling out a blade, he leapt forward—

Then collapsed in agony, all muscles of his body violently contracting as the pain swallowed him whole.

He heard Growl speak. "We suggest – most humbly – you do not attack a Kaos adherent, in Kaos's own temple."

Shadow could do nothing but endure the intense, crippling pain piercing every nerve of his body.

"You feel the pain? You feel how the Ensi treats us, Disciple? But you feel only a fraction of that inflicted on us, yes you do. No, this is what we feel ..."

The breath burst from Shadow's lungs, then he spasmed uncontrollably as his body lit up in indescribable agony, fire stabbing deep within his skull. His mind lay fully open, forced to attune to each searing lance of pain in his body. He screamed in silence.

"It is exquisite how well our mind can focus when directed so. But ..."

The torture mercifully ceased.

Shadow lay shaking, drawing deep, shuddering gasps.

"But we are most loving and kind to our fellow devotees of Kaos," came Growl's voice above him. "But please remember, never, ever, try to attack us." He felt Growl's face move closer. "And never seek to carve your own path – that Karnt be allowed. Do you understand?"

His breathing ragged, Shadow glared up at the daemonic Shade. He forced himself to nod.

"Good," the Shade murmured, his black eyes cold. He stepped away and spoke curt words to the remaining group. "Rest. And prepare." Then he walked to the bloodred wall and eased himself into its rippling surface.

The Shade disappeared from view.

His body trembling with a burning pain, his mind reeling from the horror of Karnt's horrific slaughter, Shadow stared blindly at the fell wall. He became aware of Sy beside him.

"Are you okay?" Sy flashed.

No, I'm not okay. He spat out blood from his bitten tongue, then forced himself to his feet, grappling the pain into submission. This was a savagery he'd not seen before from Growl. The Shade was tough, often brutally tough, but always aligned with Ka values. Yes, people died, but those were the enemies of the Ka. *Not this. No, not this.*

It is the daemon, Ereboz, a part of him said. *He grows too strong.*

It was the man who had led them here, Shadow thought angrily, glaring at the rippling wall. It was Growl who had allowed it to happen, allowed an innocent to be slaughtered as an offering to ... to who? To Kaos? He cast that thought aside. *We offer none of our people in this way. None!* He stood taller, fists clenched. *This is the way of barbarians, the way of the damned, not of our god.*

Not of Kaos.

Shadow turned and found Nefra staring at him, the horror still clear in her eyes.

"Why?" he breathed. "Why?"

"I don't know," she said, her voice shaking. "But clearly he was a threat to the Ka."

"What!" he rasped, his voice ragged. "How was that boy a threat?"

Nefra shook her head. "It was not my act, Disciple. Ask Growl."

Shadow's distraught gaze found Sy. "He was a boy, just a boy."

Sy nodded, his face drawn.

With a glance over to where the young man had died, he saw several small objects lying on the ground. He walked slowly over and bent down, a tear forming in the corner of his eye as he recognised what they were. "A boy who liked knuckles," he whispered as he looked down on the five knuckles. All five lay with no mark showing. *His luck finally ran out.*

Gathering them up, Shadow held the cold knuckles in his fist and stood in silence, a dark emptiness opening inside. These were not the actions of a Ka, not the actions of an adherent of Kaos. *These are not the actions of a man with a soul.* He turned to Sy. "We execute this mission, and then we return home and find out what's happening out of sight." *We find the source of this stench pervading my home.*

The strain in Sy's face seemed to deepen. He flicked his fingers. "What must be done, will be done."

At Sy's words, a whisper of something brushed Shadow's mind. Yet he couldn't grasp it. He felt the knuckles in his hand. "I will avenge you, Karnt," he whispered, his fist tightening. "Somehow, someday, I will avenge you."

*

As Spider had made his way closer to the escarpment to find shade, he'd heard a clatter of rocks from above – something had moved there, he was sure. But what? Had someone seen them arrive? He'd readied his spear in one hand and moved quickly up the slope …

Then froze as he heard a faint noise.

Looking up, he'd seen a man climb onto a ledge and pass from view into the canyon.

"Krez!" he muttered. "What's he doing here?"

Picking up his pace, Spider had climbed up the rubble-strewn slope, quickly reaching the ledge where he'd seen the man. He'd clambered up and walked out onto the wadi floor, then, hesitating only a heartbeat, he'd run on into the canyon, scanning around for the vanished man. *Krez! Our mission may fail before it has even begun.*

But running on, he saw no one.

Now, reaching a great rockfall blocking the way ahead, he accepted the man had escaped. Either he was well hidden behind any of the hundreds of boulders of the rockfall, or he'd missed his hiding place on the way.

Grimacing, he turned and ran back to the canyon entrance.

Looking out over the plain, he saw his friends in the far distance, but no sign of the unknown man. Knowing there was little more he could do, he moved into the shade and sat down on the ledge, laying his pack beside him. *I have to wait awhile, anyway. Let's see if a rat emerges from any of these nooks and crannies.*

He rested – with one eye open.

CHAPTER SEVENTEEN

Who is your enemy? Really, who are they?
Do you know? Did you ask them?

"We have followers," Jessica murmured under her breath as they walked past another group of ramshackle wooden shelters. "It seems some of those who refused to help remain interested in what we're doing here."

"More likely in what we're carrying," Rind said, following behind the tall Warrior, her head held high. "Keep walking. We need to find a way to access the interior of the camp."

The interior of the camp, and the Kade …

With Lanky at the rear, they walked on through a myriad of roughly made huts and shelters, the lake far to their left, tailed at a distance by three grim-faced men. Those others who were in camp at this time of day hid from the burning sun in the shade of their shelters. Many slept. Some eyed them suspiciously as they passed. None spoke.

"Over there," Rind whispered as they passed into a patch of more open ground, a deep trench beyond. "To your right. There's someone guarding that path across the ditch. Head over to him."

Seeing the still figure standing in the shadows of a broad-limbed tree, Jessica veered towards him.

"Remember to announce me."

"I know, I know," Jessica muttered, her stomach churning.

As they approached the earthen walkway across the deep ditch, an armed man dressed in a clean-cut tunic stepped out of the shade of the tree, relaxed but eyeing them carefully.

"Good day," Jessica said, holding her voice steady as she came to a stop some yards from the man. "I am pleased to introduce my master, Raki of the Natu tribe, who comes bearing news for the Ka leaders. My master seeks an audience with your tribe's council to share this news, and to offer our tribe's services to the Ka. We—"

"That's enough," Rind muttered from behind.

The guard walked closer to Jessica, his eyes scanning her disguised Staff, then lingering over her body before finally glancing at the pack on her back. His face impassive, he moved to pass her …

Jessica stepped into his path. "That is close enough to my master," she growled, hoping she wasn't pushing it too far.

The young man looked up at her, raising an eyebrow. Tilting his head a fraction, he rested his spear on his shoulder. "You're lucky to have met me today, my friend, and not Laugar, else you would now be lying screaming on the ground."

Jessica forced a smile. "I doubt that. I—"

"Stand aside," came Rind's order from behind.

Relieved, Jessica stepped to the side, bowing her head.

"I apologise," Rind said in a softer voice. "Our journey has been … eventful."

The young guard studied Jessica for a moment longer, then his keen eyes shifted to Rind. "You've arrived in good shape – where did you say you travelled from?"

Rind smiled. "I didn't." She took a step forward. "We have travelled from a land to the north, east of the Great Water. Six set out. Three remain."

The guard cocked his head. "And what do you offer the Ka, aside from news?"

"We will make this known to your council. But," Rind continued quickly, seeing the man frown, "I will tell you this. We seek a trade alliance with the Ka. And I have word of the enemy. Of their Warriors …"

The guard looked at her sharply, his eyes widening a fraction. Then, quickly hiding his surprise, he grasped his spear and walked slowly around her. "Many claim news of our enemy, but I hear few impress our leaders."

Rind said nothing.

Stepping away from her, the guard walked over to Lanky. "This one is strange. Where's he from?"

"From the far north, we believe," Rind said, looking with disdain at Lanky, "but no one knows for sure. And he cannot speak. He is a freak, that is clear, but he is loyal, works hard, and seldom needs beating." She gestured to the Axe strapped to Lanky's back. "And his axe has deterred many who might have troubled us."

With a calm confidence, the guard walked around Lanky—

Then hit him hard in the side.

Lanky fell to the ground, holding his ribs – but uttered no sound.

Jessica held her breath.

The guard glanced down at Lanky, who was breathing hard. "Interesting."

As the guard regarded Lanky with apparent curiosity, an old weather-wrinkled man crossed the earthen walkway across the trench. The guard flicked him a quick glance as he passed, then turned back to face Rind. "Return at sunset. I'll let you know whether a meeting has been accepted."

Jessica let out a silent sigh of relief.

"I thank you," Rind said, her head held high. "I am sure your council will be greatly pleased with what I can impart." She bowed respectfully.

As though disinterested with her words, the guard merely grunted something unintelligible, then walked back towards his station.

Rind cast a peremptory gaze to Jessica. "Lead on."

"Where to?" Jessica whispered.

"Back to the Rim," Rind hissed. "Just walk away."

As Jessica turned, she saw the old man who had passed, standing close by, watching them.

"Good day," he said, cautiously. "It seems you have recently arrived."

Jessica hesitated, studying the old man's wrinkled, weather-beaten face. He seemed harmless. *But in this place …*

"Talk to him," Rind whispered behind her. "Else it will look strange."

Sighing, Jessica walked to meet the old man. "Indeed, we have," she said, halting before him. "My master has recently arrived at this great tribe's homeland, and we're awaiting an audience with their leaders to discuss trade between our peoples."

The old man's sharp eyes flicked over her and her friends. Then he nodded gently. "One good deed deserves another," he murmured as though to himself.

What deed? Jessica thought, watching him carefully.

"Do you need somewhere to rest?"

She thought quickly. "We were just considering what we should do," she said evenly. "But yes, a place to rest would be welcome."

The old man cleared his throat. "I have just moved into the Flanks," he said, gesturing to the land beyond the ditch. "A stroke of great fortune. And generosity." He smiled. "A friend will take my old hut, but for a day or two, you can take it if you so wish."

A day or two? It seemed, today, the gods had weighted the die in their favour.

Rind appeared by her side. "That is a generous gift indeed. I am in your debt …" She looked at him expectantly.

"Kapano," the man said, holding out his arm.

"Raki," Rind said, grasping his upper arm and holding his gaze.

Kapano smiled. "Follow me. But be prepared. We might need to clear out a few rats."

*

Sitting outside Kapano's old hut in the Rim, Lanky cut off his low humming as he saw the three men passing close by. Again. The scavengers – the rats, as Kapano called them – had fled as soon as they'd approached the old man's hut, but these three, who had tailed them all day, looked far tougher men and seemed set to cause trouble. *And I'm sleeping outside tonight.* He'd prefer them gone.

But what could he do? It would be easier if he could talk. *Or if I could use the Axe.* But even the minutest pull on the energy of the A'ven could alert the Ka's shaman. *I'm on my own. And I'm no street fighter.* Watching the men out of the corner of his eye, he made a show of lifting the Axe into his lap …

He breathed a sigh of relief as the men walked on by. *Yes, walk on by.*

Turning towards the distant lake, he saw Jessica and Rind returning from their short foray towards the boundary ditch of the Flanks, where, away from the prying eyes of the surrounding huts and watching thugs, they'd sought time to discuss their next steps. Grunting in frustration, Lanky gripped the shaft of his Axe more tightly. It was hard playing dumb. *But we need to talk now.*

He acknowledged them with a grim smile as they approached.

Rind looked straight past him, a frown on her face. Jessica's face hardened.

Lanky turned around.

The three men stood glaring at them. He saw a fight in their eyes. *Damn it!*

He climbed to his feet, hefting his Axe.

Jessica strode past him, her Staff in hand. "Stay there," she whispered.

Lanky watched, bemused, as Jessica strode up to the largest man of the three. "What do you want?" she growled, glaring down at the heavyset man, his face scarred by an ugly gash down his cheek.

"This is our hut," grated a scrawny man by the larger man's side.

Jessica smiled.

The scrawny man frowned.

Lanky hardly saw Jessica move, but her Staff lashed out in a vicious arc, then the scrawny man collapsed in a heap. Jessica stepped back from her fighting crouch to stand calmly in front of the heavyset man. "I think your friend made a mistake. This is our shelter."

The heavyset man looked her up and down, then Lanky saw the faintest of twitches in the man's eye. "Maybe he did," the man growled. He gestured to the third man, who'd stood nervously watching. "Bring him with you," he muttered, then walked away.

The third man bent down and, grunting, lifted the scrawny man over his shoulders and staggered slowly away.

"Impressive," Lanky whispered as they watched the men walk into the distance.

"They'll be back," Rind said to his side.

"Let's hope not too soon," Jessica said.

Glancing at her, Lanky noticed her hand shaking. *Warriors maybe, yet still this is hard.* Releasing a low sigh, he casually scanned their surroundings. Only one gazed their way from another hut, yet even he returned to his chores. *I guess there are squabbles over housing here all the time.* He pitied those at the bottom of the pecking order.

Turning back to Rind and Jessica, he squatted down to his haunches. He half covered his mouth. "What are you two thinking? About what we do next?"

Jessica glanced to the camp's interior. "That we need to get into the Flanks and then into the Core. And then into the temple."

"What?" Lanky exclaimed. "The temple?"

"Quiet, you fool," Rind hissed. "You can't talk, remember." She glared at him. "And I hope you've not been croaking those awful songs of yours to yourself."

He scowled but said nothing.

"The temple is the diseased heart of the Ka," Rind said, relaxing her stance. "Their place of worship for their cursed god. And it's where I'd keep those things most valuable to me. Like the thing you seek."

"Maybe," he muttered.

Jessica glanced towards the Flanks. "If this guard gets Rind an audience with someone deeper inside the camp, then this will be working out far better than I'd expected. I half expected we'd already be fighting our way out." She turned back, absently rubbing her cheek. "But if we get to the Flanks, we could get to the Core. And if there … well then, maybe, if needed, we can get into the temple."

Lanky ground his teeth as he considered her words. They had come here to get the Kade, and if it lay in the temple, then that's where they'd have to go. *If it's there* ... He ran fingers through his beard, hand covering his mouth. "You sense anything ... unusual out there?"

"Nothing yet," Jessica answered.

"Neither have I," he muttered behind his hand. *So we still don't know where this damned Kade is – or if it's actually here.* Keeping his head still, he glanced at Rind. "How many people in the Core?"

"Resident? About fifty. Aside from the Ensi's immediate entourage, they're the most trusted members of the Ka."

"And the Temple Guard?"

"Unknown. But many. Both inside the temple and out in the Core."

Lanky rubbed his beard. "So, this is going to be easy."

Jessica stepped closer. "From what I've seen of the camp so far, there are virtually no guards on the boundaries between the camp zones. And the barriers are nonexistent. Look at what we saw today. That ditch surrounding the Flanks wouldn't stop a child. I think we should plan to slip over the ditch after dark, then see what we can sense further in."

Rind shook her head, fidgeting with a band of beads in her hand. "Step over that boundary without the blessing of one of the Core, and it will be your last step in this place." She spun an ochre-stained bead with her fingers. "Why? Because that step takes a misguided Rim dreamer closer to the supposed privileged life of a true Ka of the Core. And who of the Rim and the Flanks would want to see another scramble to that place ahead of them? No one. It would be one less space for them." She looked up at Jessica. "We can't see them, but believe me, people will be watching, people who are the eyes and ears of the Ka and who would report their own family if it gained them a progression. No, we can't cross unseen."

"Not all as friendly as this Kapano, then," Lanky grunted.

Rind placed the band over her hand and onto her wrist, tying it in place. "Let's see what happens when I return to the guard at sundown. In the meantime, I suggest you two scout close to the Flanks to see if you can sense anything there."

Lanky glanced back to where the thugs had gone. "I'm not sure it's a good idea to leave you here alone."

"I doubt we'll see them again today," Rind said. "And anyway, I'm hungry. We should eat." She straightened. "I'm your liege, remember? Go and see what you can find."

"Don't push it," Lanky muttered.

"I'll come with you," Jessica said, smiling. "See if I can keep you out of trouble. We'll try the lake; I saw folk fishing down there."

Lanky looked to the distant water. "Well, that's not a bad idea." He climbed to his feet. "A swim and wash at the same time."

"You do know crocodiles hunt in the lake?" Rind said, a note of exasperation in her voice. "And please remember, you can't speak."

"Argh," Lanky muttered under his breath.

Jessica winked at Rind. "Come," she said in a louder voice. "There's work to be done, boy." Then she set off for the lake, her Staff in one hand, a spear in the other.

Lanky glared after her.

"Hurry!" Rind commanded. "Before you lose the light."

Glowering at her, Lanky picked up his Axe and spear, then stormed after Jessica. "This is the one and only time I play this game."

*

Jessica stood motionless, keen eyes fixed on her victim, her spear primed and ready to strike. Most catfish in the shallows were huge, and she'd let many swim by, waiting for something smaller. *Like this one.* This one was dinner. If she could catch it.

They'd watched others fishing nearby, and like them, they weren't concealed from the fish. It didn't seem to be a problem, so long as you remained still. True, many of the nearby fisherfolk had an advantage: They used nets. But not all. And anyway, some were using their nets to catch unwary waterfowl, not the fish.

Jessica watched – and waited. Then struck.

She made a clean hit.

"Got one!" she called to Lanky, who stood out in deeper water. The fish wriggled and splashed in the shallow, muddy water but remained firmly skewered by her spear. Lifting the fish, she hauled it out of the shallows and onto the dry bank.

"Here, I'll hold it," she said, straddling the main body of the fish as Lanky waded out of the water. "The cleanest way will be to take off its head."

Within seconds, Lanky wielded his Axe, and the fish lay still, bleeding out.

"Okay," Jessica said. "At least we'll eat today." She glanced to the west, where the sun was dropping. "Let's get this back. We should eat before Rind has to head back to the guard."

They gathered up their kit and headed back towards Kapano's hut, alert for any strange ripples in the ether. But, so far, neither she nor Lanky had sensed anything unusual about the camp, at least not in those places they'd travelled through. *We need to get closer to the Core.*

Walking on, she surreptitiously scanned the threadbare huts and shelters as they passed and noticed the Rim was filling quickly as people returned from their tasks outside of camp. Good. It meant she and Lanky blended more easily into the background. Just another group returning with food. Passing a haphazard circle of shelters, she saw a larger group in its midst preparing a meal. Fish, several small birds, and an array of plants all lay on palm leaves waiting to be cooked. People talked, they laughed, and to her right a couple broke out in argument. A scuffle followed.

Glancing to the next huddle of shelters and the men and women around them, a nagging thought finally crystallised. She had seen very few children here in the Rim. Not in the shelters, not outside, not within the flux of people returning from their day's tasks. *Why?* One thought immediately crossed her mind; possibly the long, arduous journey to reach the Ka's homeland deterred those with families. But the people of this land were travellers. Maybe not every day, or every week ... *but they are mobile.* And yet it appeared they brought few children. With a strange disquiet lingering, she let the thought drop. If they saw Kapano again, maybe she'd ask him about it.

She glanced ahead, seeking Kapano's hut, which couldn't be far now – and saw a familiar figure approaching. *Spider!* He was walking towards them from the western fringes of the Rim, angling across to the lakeshore. Holding her path, she and Lanky passed within hailing distance of the Iyes scout. Neither said a word, but seeing Spider scratch his neck with his right hand – the agreed signal – she breathed a sigh of relief. *He's not in any trouble.* And she guessed the sight of her and Lanky walking through camp with a freshly caught catfish would trigger no worries in him!

She glanced back at Lanky, who winked, and they continued on their way.

As they approached their newly acquired hut, she saw Rind had visitors: the old man, Kapano, and an unknown girl with a bold white feather in her hair. She heard a faint grumble from Lanky; the presence of guests would prolong his forced silence.

"Ah, I see you've brought food," Rind said as they approached. "Good. Join us, Jessica." She then gestured to Lanky. "Fetch wood for the fire."

"No need. No need," Kapano said, smiling. "You see the hut over there? Tell them Kapano sent you, and they'll provide what you need for now. You can repay them tomorrow."

"That is kind of you, Kapano," Rind said. "Unfortunately, my servant has no voice."

"Ah. In that case, my granddaughter Inyana will help—"

"No, Inyana will not help," the girl said with a scowl, adjusting the white feather in her hair. "Inyana is tired."

"Don't worry," Jessica began. "I'll—"

"Inyana," Kapano said, his wiry bowed frame turning to his granddaughter. "Please help these people. This will be our thanks to Kaos for his great gift to us. I would not like him to be displeased."

Inyana held her scowl a moment longer, then released a frustrated sigh. "Fine," she muttered. She turned to Lanky. "Follow me."

Jessica watched Lanky walk after Inyana. *She may be impetuous, but she listens to her grandfather.*

"Will you stay for dinner?" Rind asked.

"I thank you for the offer, but no. It is wise for us to return inside to eat … and to make new contacts." He looked down. "Which may prove difficult," he murmured as if to himself.

"Well, I wish you luck." Rind gestured to the hut. "And I thank you again for your kindness."

Kapano smiled as he looked back at his weathered wooden hut. "This was my home for many sun-cycles. But finally" – a note of prideful excitement entered his voice – "we have made it inside. To a new beginning. To a new future."

"What brought you here?" Jessica asked, warming to the man.

"The Ka. Many travellers brought us stories of the Ka. Of the better life they offered. Of the security they provided." He gestured to them. "No different to you being here, to better your tribe's lives." His inquisitive eyes settled on Rind. "Part of the Meso tribes, you said?"

"The Natu tribe," she said, the faintest touch of anger in her voice. "Not yet conquered and subdued."

"Ah, then I heard wrong." Kapano scratched his wiry neck, thoughtful. "I admire your wish for independence for your tribe, but the Meso tribe – and the Ka – will come."

"Then it would make our tribes enemies. That is not a pleasant thought."

Kapano smiled. "You are here, you tell me, to treaty for trade with the Ka. If you are successful, you will become part of the Ka empire. You will not be an enemy. You will be part of my new tribe."

"And if I don't wish to be part of the Ka?" Rind said, her eyes briefly flashing in anger.

Jessica willed Rind to hold her temper. *We need this man.*

Kapano shrugged. "You can leave to go elsewhere … or fight them and die."

"Fight *them*?" Jessica said, confused. "Not fight *us*? Are *you* not of the Ka?"

"I am," Kapano said, looking past them towards his granddaughter. "But I am neither a leader nor a fighter, and I hold no enmity for others." He sighed. "I understand more of the Ka day by day. I don't agree with all they do, but I wish for a better life for my family. And the Ka are the future, Kaos willing."

Jessica saw Rind bristling. With Kapano's attention on his granddaughter, she caught Rind's eye and gently shook her head. *Let me handle it,* she mouthed. Rind frowned but pulled her vexed gaze from the old man.

"I hear much of the Ka," Jessica said lightly. "What could they offer me?"

He turned to face her. "The same as the rest of us. Stability. Discipline. Organisation. Like-minded people." His expression clouded. "And protection against the devils who would destroy us – destroy our lands."

He means the Iyes ... "I've heard of those people. Why would they seek to do this?"

Holding up his arms in a gesture of bewilderment, Kapano frowned. "It seems madness, I know. Why destroy the very land they live in? And why seek to destroy others, who simply wish to live in peace? But it is their gods driving them to this destruction – their people see nothing of what will come of it."

"And have you witnessed this destruction?"

"You don't need to stand out in the rain to be sure the water will drip from your nose. We know what is true. From the Ka. And from our Story. The Iyes are coming. It is sad, but at least the Ka do something to stop them." He straightened – as much as his bent frame would allow. "And in this, I will help them. I ..." He turned at a noise. "Ah. It seems my granddaughter has been successful."

Jessica followed his gaze and saw a mountain of wood walking towards her – accompanied by Inyana carrying a handful of moss and kindling. Despite the tension in the air, Jessica smiled as the mountain staggered towards her. "About there is fine."

The mountain collapsed as Lanky dropped his load. Inyana placed her handful beside the pile, then stepped over to her grandfather.

"Prepare our meal," Rind ordered. "I leave before the sun goes down."

As Lanky turned away with the faintest of scowls, Jessica muttered a silent curse as Rind stepped closer to Kapano.

"How do your people know these stories of the enemy?" Rind asked. Jessica heard the brittle tension beneath her voice.

Kapano smiled. "We preserve them. In our stories and in our songs."

"My father is the greatest teller of our tribe," Inyana said, staring at Rind as though expecting to be challenged. "The last Keeper of the songs."

Jessica felt a memory stirring. "A Keeper?"

"You don't have a Keeper? One who holds the stories of your tribe?"

Stories. Like the Iyes's Story held by Naga? "I … We …"

"We do," Rind answered. "But of simple songs and simple stories."

"Not ours," Inyana said, her eyes shining. "Ours tell the story of a time before the Ka, of a great god before Kaos, of—"

"Forgive me," Kapano said, stepping forward and taking his granddaughter's arm. "You need time to ready yourself for your appointment. My granddaughter is proud of her old tribe and their history. She would hold you here until the moon rises."

Inyana glanced at her father, suddenly uncertain. Then she nodded and drew back into his shadow.

Jessica studied the girl. What story did she have that her grandfather didn't wish to be told?

Kapano smiled at his granddaughter. "Another time, maybe. You tell the tales well." He turned his smiling eyes to Rind and Jessica. "But now, we must leave you. As I said, we should attempt to meet our new neighbours inside. Please use this as your home for as long as you need it."

Jessica could see Rind holding her emotions in check. "Thank you," the Iyes said, bowing respectfully. "And I wish you luck in your new home. Maybe we will meet again soon."

Kapano bowed, then walked away, his granddaughter by his side.

Jessica watched the two figures head south for the Flanks. *The old man's people hold a story, one of a time before the Ka.* What did it tell? What was *their* story?

Questions unanswered, she turned back to the hut, where Rind sat in the shade. Lanky pulled a few logs closer to the hut, edging closer himself.

"We were damn lucky meeting that guy," he whispered, reaching to his side and grabbing a handful of moss. "This will work well as a base for us."

Rind grunted. "He has helped us, that's true. But he's misguided."

"Not the enemy I expected," Jessica murmured.

Rind's eyes narrowed. "What does that mean?"

Jessica looked down. "These people seem … well, they seem like the Iyes." She glanced up at Rind. "Not what I expected," she repeated.

Rind leaned forward, her expression stern. "What did you expect? A fiery band of cutthroat warriors and shamans? A seething horde ready to storm our lands? Here in the Rim, these *are* normal people. Foolish, deluded people, but not yet evil." She gestured south towards the Core. "But in there? Step closer and closer to that temple and that's where you'll find the true Ka."

She sat back and sighed. "One thing that old man has right is that it *is* the gods driving the people. But from where he stands, he can't see it's his god bringing the death and destruction."

Troubled, Jessica looked down at her Staff, gently running her fingers over its disguised plain surface. Kapano believed the Ka to be a peaceful people, but the Iyes saw them as their mortal enemy. *And I've seen the Ka and their allies attack and kill Iyes innocents.* Then why the whispers of doubt? Doubt that now morphed into disturbing questions. *Is there any truth in Kapano's words? What else about this ancient conflict remains hidden from me?*

Unsettled, she wrapped her fingers around the Staff—

'We have to enter the temple,' came a woman's voice, a gravelly voice she recognised.

Jalu.

'I sense it,' Jalu said, an urgency in her voice. *'The Kade is here. Find a way into the temple.'*

Jessica stilled her breathing. *The Staff. She is in the Staff.*

Allowing her mind to reach towards the Staff, she slipped beneath its subtle defences, feeling the rippling streams of energy flowing within and tasting the warming vibrations of the A'ven's energy. She pushed deeper, travelling towards the core of this enigmatic tool of the Light – of the Guardian – a core explored before, but understood only as the energy cache for the Staff, a store to be drawn on in times of need. *But what did I miss?* Her senses now heightened, she carefully, meticulously, scanned the core, yet still sensed nothing but the energy of the A'ven. No life-form. No daemon—

She froze at the most subtle change in vibration, the most imperceptible variation in taste.

She sensed the spirit of Jalu.

'How long have you been here?' she whispered.

'Aeons beyond your imagining,' Jalu answered.

'You are of the Light.'

'I served the Light.'

Then she could be trusted … couldn't she?

'It matters not in this moment,' Jalu said, reading her thoughts. *'What you seek is in the temple.'*

The minute blemish within the core vanished.

In the sudden, harsh silence that followed, a hesitant truth came to the fore. *She lies deep within the Staff in a place the Dark can't enter. She* must *be of the Light.*

Mustn't she?

She fought a numbing confusion. *I feel I'm just a pawn. And I don't see the hand moving me.*

Who can I trust?

And who is the enemy?

"Jessica?"

Jessica blinked, her gaze refocussing on Rind and Lanky, who were watching her closely. "Sorry," she said, Jalu's words ringing in her mind. "What did you say?"

"Did you two find anything else out there today?" Rind asked. "Apart from fish."

Jessica forced a grip on her thoughts. The Ka were a hostile and aggressive tribe, of that, she had little doubt. But more lay hidden beyond her sight. She needed to search harder, understand more.

And Jalu?

She glanced at the Staff. Whoever she truly was, in this moment, their thoughts aligned. Her gaze shifted back to Rind and Lanky. "We need to get inside the temple."

"You sense it?" Lanky whispered.

Jessica tensed. *Tell him about Jalu.* And yet that spirit had asked to remain concealed. *I can't take that risk. Not yet.* "The temple," she repeated, her voice firm. "We have to find a way in."

Lanky seemed to consider her answer for a moment, then he returned his attention to the small bundle of moss in his hand. Striking a flint against a piece of gold pyrite, he created a spark that landed in the moss, and the seed of their fire was born. "Okay," he whispered, dropping the moss carefully into the tinder. "How?"

Jessica glanced at Rind.

"Step by step," Rind said. "Let's see if our meeting is accepted, then we plan the next move."

Lanky watched the moss quickly burn, igniting the tinder. He put his hand to his beard, obscuring his mouth. "Fine. But before that, we've fish to cook and eat. An army marches on its stomach, and this one is growling."

Spider sat, his back to the low sun, seemingly resting as though a weary traveller taking the weight off his legs; but he kept a close eye on the distant hut where Rind and the Warriors were eating. He'd entered the Rim late in the day and almost immediately encountered Jessica and Lanky returning with their catch from the lake. Signing 'all's well', he'd continued on, setting about a brief reconnaissance of the northern Rim. He'd been surprised by how wide an area the Rim covered and by the sheer number of dwellings haphazardly scattered within – it was the largest settlement by far he'd seen in his young life. Completing an initial surreptitious scout of the Rim and the guarded entranceways into the Flanks, he'd retraced his steps and, after a brief search, found the Warriors and Rind occupying a weathered old hut. As the sun dropped lower in the sky, taking with it the burning heat of the day, he'd watched and waited …

And now, he realised three men had gathered nearby. Snatches of their conversation drifted to him.

"… will pay for what she did."

"… like to see that …"

"… they leave, then we will see what they have in there."

Spider turned to the men. "You looking to get something from that hut over there?"

"What's it to you?" grated a scrawny-looking man, scowling.

"I don't want any trouble," Spider said easily, turning back to look at the hut. "But you'll find it here if you want it." His back to the men, he let his words hang, then: "All I want is some of that fish they're cooking." He was partly serious – he was hungry. *They better leave some for me,* he thought, his stomach rumbling.

"I'm sick of fish," the scrawny man whined. "He can have it."

A heavyset man, an ugly gash on his cheek, glanced at Spider. "Don't touch anything else," he muttered, then resumed his nefarious vigil.

Spider smiled and settled to see what happened.

*

Rind reached for her water bottle to rinse her hands. "Not bad – a bit firm, but okay."

"Well, yours may have been okay, but mine tasted like mud," Lanky muttered in a low whisper, scowling.

Rind poured a little water over her fingers, then glanced at him. "Yes. Never eat that part – it always tastes rotten."

"Well, now you tell me! Why—"

"Hush, someone's coming," Jessica said. Grasping her Staff, she stood and peered out into the fading light. "It's our new friend, Kapano." She watched the old man approach, then greeted him with a smile. "So, you do want to share our fish after all?"

"No, no, but thank you again," Kapano said breathlessly. "No, the reason I'm here – and you will not believe it – is that they've granted you an audience with the factor!" He stood, beaming at them.

"Who's the factor?"

Looking confused, Kapano turned to Rind. "The trading agent for the Ka … this is the one you wished to see, yes?"

"Indeed, it is," Rind said, smiling at Kapano. "And how came you by this news?"

"Ah, yes. Remember the guard you spoke to at the Flanks' gateway? It turns out he is a neighbour of mine – well, close enough to be called a neighbour. Of course, he lives in a much larger—"

"So, he's your neighbour," Rind summarised. "And?"

"Well, he was passing by," Kapano continued, "and he stopped to ask how we were doing. I suspect he has eyes for my granddaughter. That usually—"

"He stopped by …" Rind prompted.

"Yes, he did, and I told him we'd left the hut here and given it to you. That's when he asked if I wouldn't mind bringing a message to you. And here I am." Kapano beamed. "The factor can see you now but leaves by sundown – the guard thought you may want to take this chance while it is there."

Rind stood. "Good news indeed. And a good thing we chanced upon you today, Kapano. Do you know where I can find the factor?"

"He resides in the temple." The craggy wrinkles on Kapano's brow deepened. "At least, that is what I am told. The temple is not a place one like me could ever—"

"You can take me there?"

Kapano's eyes brightened. "I can." He opened his hand to reveal a small marked stone. "And here is your pass from the guard." He held the stone almost reverently, then handed it to Rind. "It allows us access to the Core. I can guide you all there."

"We can go with my master?" Jessica said in surprise as Rind examined the stone.

Kapano shrugged. "The guard said it was a pass for you all. But that is your decision, I think."

Jessica studied the old man, her suspicion growing. He'd been generous to them, but this *was* the enemy camp – what might he be planning? She tensed at the remembered words of River before they'd left; River and IY planned a trap for the traitor. And for the Ka Shade. Now standing in the enemy's homeland, did this old man lead her, Rind, and Lanky into a trap of the Ka's making? *You should have spoken to us earlier, River. What might we have missed?*

She caught Rind's gaze and saw the question clear in the Iyes's face: *Do we go with him?*

Despite the fear of betrayal, she knew they had to try. They had to take the chance to get inside the temple. She carefully and cautiously reached for the A'ven – and tasted its reassuring latent power. *If needed, I can get us out of here.*

She answered Rind's unvoiced question with an almost imperceptible nod.

But I need to talk to Rind and Lanky. I have to tell them what River revealed.

Rind faced the waiting Kapano. "This is an opportunity not to be missed, for which I thank you." The old man seemed genuinely pleased. Rind turned to Jessica. "You both will accompany me. Bring what is valuable. Leave the rest."

Jessica gave a slight bow in acknowledgement. *And prepare for a fight.*

"Since you all plan to leave," Kapano said, "I'll arrange for someone to watch over the hut." He put his fingers to his lips and whistled: two high notes and one low. He waved to someone unseen. Seemingly satisfied with what he saw, he turned back to Rind. "It is done."

Rind inclined her head. "Thank you. Again."

The group readied themselves. Lanky secured his Axe to his back, then looped a skin of water over his shoulder. Rind patted her tunic – checking her blades – then picked up a spear. Jessica grasped her Staff.

"You look as though you are preparing for battle," Kapano said, smiling.

Rind smiled back. "Always prepared. You know how tough these traders can be."

Kapano laughed. "Well, let us hope your traders have eaten well today. If you are ready, let us go."

Following Kapano away from the hut and towards the Flanks, Jessica tightened her grip on her Staff. *Let's hope there are indeed traders to meet us, and not Ka fighters.*

*

Spider watched Rind and the Warriors gather their weapons, then leave together with the stranger. As soon as they were out of sight, he stood and walked purposefully across to the hut.

244

The three Ka scavengers followed him.

At the fire, Spider reached down, grabbed a loose chunk of fish, then immediately walked off. As he did so, someone shouted. Spider picked up his pace. He smiled. *Fools.* Those scavengers hadn't seen what he'd seen; they were being watched by people at a nearby hut. He risked a glance behind and chuckled. The three men were being chased by three others; Rind had somehow arranged a guard on their hut. And it had worked.

And I have fish!

He quickly picked up sight of Rind and the group and cautiously followed at a distance, savouring mouthfuls of the delicious fish. A short while later, the final morsel devoured, he watched in astonishment as the group passed quickly through a guarded entrance into the Flanks. *Krez! Who is this old man? And where's he taking them?*

Veering away from the gateway, Spider walked a little further, then stopped, dropping to his knee as though tightening the strapping on his legs. He glanced towards the Flanks. *Well, they're in. That's what we wanted.* Even so, he felt a flutter in his stomach. *That's because I'm wandering about in the midst of the enemy's camp.* With a wry shake of the head, he carefully scanned the Flanks' border. No barriers, no visible guards except those at the path across the border ditch. But that lack of defence meant nothing. *The Ka will have their eyes, their ears.* Later. He'd cross after dark.

He finished his pretence, then stood facing west. *Use the time wisely; continue scouting.* He adjusted his pack and set off at an easy pace.

*

The unfamiliar guard had scowled as they'd approached, clearly ready to send them away, but upon Kapano showing the marked stone, the man had waved them on. With a mixture of relief and trepidation, Jessica now walked beside Lanky and Rind through the vegetated Flanks, the tops of the scattered trees lit by the dying rays of the sun. *We're heading to where we want to be.* But that didn't stop the unsettling feeling that they were heading where *someone else* wanted them to be.

She glanced around as they walked on, and despite her unease, she couldn't help noticing that from what she'd seen of this land, this place called the Flanks appeared a pleasant place to stay. The dwellings' appearance remained basic to her eyes but were larger than those in the Rim. *More permanent.* And there was greater space between huts, with more vegetation. Aromatic scents drifted to her from the many plants around the dwellings. To live here, Kapano had clearly proved his worth in some way.

Hearing excited voices close by, she caught sight of several children running between low bushes. *Children ...*

Lengthening her stride, she caught up with Kapano. He glanced at her and smiled.

"I see many more children here," she said as they walked on. "In fact, I'm not sure I saw any in the Rim."

Kapano's smile vanished. He walked on in silence.

Well, that went well. Why—

"It is a thing that has to change," Kapano said in a subdued voice. "Somehow it must change." He glanced around, as though checking who was around them. "I didn't know," he murmured, walking on. "And I still don't understand all. It's best not to speak of this here."

Unsettled, Jessica dropped back to rejoin Rind and Lanky. "I asked—"

"I heard," Rind said. "That was unfortunate. We need to keep him on our side."

"What the hell is the problem?" she hissed.

Rind frowned. "The Ka wish to form a society built on the best. The best as they see it. So they choose who passes through the Rim. Those who are chosen are the people allowed to have children – the people around you now."

Nausea crept into Jessica's stomach. "What happens to those who arrive here with children?"

"We believe few do, because of what they hear. And if they do ..." Rind's expression revealed her disgust. "Work it out."

Jessica stared at Rind in horror. *No!* Were these people that brutal? She thought of those she'd seen in the camp, the majority just normal people eking out a living. *No, not those.* She glanced ahead towards the centre of the camp. *But their leaders?*

"We walk through a land thirteen thousand years before our time," Lanky whispered. "It seems humanity constantly throws up some pretty twisted people. People who should be resisted at all costs."

"Lanky speaks true. Don't be fooled by what you see around you. Gird yourself for what lies in wait."

They slaughter children? What depraved barbary was this? It seemed these Ka were indeed an evil in the Land. *We must prevent the Geddon from being released, and we must end the tyranny of the Ka.*

They walked on towards the Core, to the temple of the Ka's god, Kaos.

*

The guard waved them on, and they passed through the entrance to the Core. As they continued on, Jessica's unease deepened. *This is far too easy.* She waited until they rounded a large wooden dwelling, passing out of sight of the guards at the entrance, then tapped Rind on the shoulder.

Rind stopped. Lanky walked up beside them.

"We're being played," Jessica said in a whisper.

"That's clear," Rind muttered, wiping her brow.

"You think they know who we are?" Lanky whispered, waving as if at a fly to obscure his mouth.

"*Who* we are? Unlikely. But suspicious of us? Almost certainly."

"So at best, suspicious," Lanky whispered. "At worst, a trap. Do we go on?"

Jessica's stomach churned. A trap? Maybe. But the one in the Staff who sought to help her – Jalu – said the Kade lay inside the temple.

But is she part of the trap? Maybe the Staff is false, tainted in some way?

Then all they thought they knew would vanish in an instant. *And I can't go there. I must believe in something.* She had to believe that Jalu was aiding them. She had to believe that the Kade lay within the temple, and that bringing this Kade to IY would remove the threat of Armageddon … *And that eventually we will all get home.*

Home.

The thought echoed, reverberating with a now familiar refrain: *I am the Guardian … so what is home?*

Seeing Rind and Lanky studying her, she girded herself. In this moment, all that mattered was that she needed to go on. But a harsh truth twisted her heart – she had concealed something from those who trusted her. *I should have said something before. Now I'm as bad as River.* She stepped closer to them. "I need to tell you something. You need to hear it now before we decide what to do."

She quickly relayed River's words to her just before they'd left, telling of the hidden traitor within the Iyes and of an imminent attack on the Iyes camp.

"And you thought it best to wait until we're in the midst of the Ka before telling us this?" Lanky hissed as she finished.

"Quiet," Rind whispered. "Kapano's watching us. You don't speak, remember?"

Lanky shifted slightly, putting his back to Kapano. His angry gaze remained fixed on Jessica.

Rind faced Jessica, her eyes ablaze. "But Lanky's right, you've left this a little late. River had no right to do what she did without us knowing."

Jessica knew they were right, but … "River's doing what she must. And you don't repeat that kind of information until you absolutely have to." She studied them, her gaze unflinching. "You know it now. What do you want to do?"

Rind glared at her a moment longer, then ran her hand through her short curls. "You wanted inside the temple – this gets us in." She looked towards the Core's interior. "If it goes wrong, can you get us out?"

"I can," Jessica said, remembering her sensing of the A'ven.

Rind cast a quick glance to Kapano, who was patiently waiting for them, then her gaze flicked to Lanky. "It's your call. But be quick – he'll be wondering what we're up to."

Lanky rubbed his beard, his hand covering his mouth. "I think I'm crazy, that's what I think. What was River thinking of?" He glanced at Jessica. "But we're here, and I agree with you. If this temple is as important to the Ka as Rind believes it is, then this Kade could well be there. So, we go on, but be damn ready to get us out."

Jessica nodded.

"Then it's agreed. We go on," Rind said. "Remember to stay calm – only react if we're threatened. We don't want to trigger any aggression if it's not warranted."

They walked on to catch up with the waiting Kapano.

"Any problem?" he asked, looking at Rind.

"All good," she answered lightly. "Just wanted to make sure I'm prepared. Important to have your story straight."

The old man smiled. "It's the same before a telling." He walked away, gesturing for them to follow. "Past these trees, we will see the temple."

Skirting around the small clump of trees, they followed a clear trail between widely spaced dwellings, then soon gained a clear view of a looming rise ahead. She studied it, trying to make sense of what she was seeing. But aside from a wooden platform at the crest of the rise, little else could be seen. Was the temple inside? *If so, it's a massive structure.*

Drawing closer, she noticed several stone structures lying in the lee of a shallow ridge to their left. Dwellings, she realised as they grew closer. And for important people if that was indeed the temple ahead. Movement to her right caught her eye – an armed group moving as a unit heading their way along a side trail.

She stopped as Kapano held up his hand.

"They look serious," Lanky whispered behind her.

Men and women dressed in yellow tunics, each carrying a sleek spear in their hand and a bow on their back, moved in unison led by a tall man in a black tunic.

Jessica reached out for the A'ven—

"Hold," hissed Rind to her side, clearly seeing her tensing. "Do nothing yet."

Her mind still tensed for action, Jessica relaxed her grip on her Staff.

As the group approached, the tall man in black barked an order. A man from the front row peeled off, and as the group marched past, he strode over to them. Jessica saw the alarm on Kapano's face.

"Where are you going?" the man barked.

"We have a meeting with the factor," Rind said, stepping forward and holding out the marked stone.

The man took the stone. His eyes narrowed briefly as he examined the mark, then he passed the stone back. He gave a curt bow, then strode away without another word.

Allowing the coiled tension in her mind to ease, Jessica turned to Kapano. "I take it these are not regular guards."

Kapano shook his head. She noticed a bead of sweat on the man's brow. "No. These you do not want to meet. Ever."

He's shaking. So people fear these yellow-vests.

"Not regular at all," the old man continued. "These are part of the Temple Guard." His nervous eyes scanned ahead. "I'll take you as promised, but I would like to return to the Flanks. I'm not sure this place is for me." He walked on.

"Not for me either," Lanky whispered.

"Quiet," Jessica hissed. "You trying to get this mission to fail?"

Lanky scowled at her but said nothing more.

"Come on," Rind said, nervously pushing a strand of hair back behind her ear. "Looks as though we're almost at the temple."

They continued, seeing several other groups of yellow-tunicked fighters.

"This Core is well organised," Lanky whispered. "And these fighters look disciplined."

"Each would be difficult to beat in a one-to-one battle," Rind said under her breath. "You would need help from ..." She left the rest unsaid, but Jessica saw her glance at Lanky's Axe.

They finally reached the end of the trail and stood at the foot of the broad, low rise facing rough-cut steps, which climbed the gentle slope to the wooden platform Jessica had seen from afar. The platform skirted the entire flank of the rise, disappearing from view as the rise curved away out of sight.

"The temple of Kaos," Kapano said in a low voice, and he began to climb.

They ascended the rise and stepped onto the wooden platform. Now standing at the crest of the great mound, Jessica saw an expanse of smooth white marble lay atop the mound's interior. Towards the centre lay a pyramid of black stone upon a disk of midnight-black rock. There was also something else, something inconspicuous to most. It was a quiet sense of a powerful presence nearby, like the humming heard beneath overhead power lines – subdued and indistinct but revealing the presence of a tremendous energy, one not accessible to you directly, but invaluable to others. The Kade? Possibly. Or some other energy of Land like the A'ven? Maybe. Whatever it was, it seemed to be emanating from within the mound – and it made her skin tingle with a strange anticipation.

Glancing ahead, she saw Kapano walking briskly on – as briskly as the old man could probably walk – his head bowed, shoulders tensed. *He doesn't want to be here,* Jessica thought as they walked after him. *And I can understand why.*

They followed Kapano along the wooden walkway, then halted at the top of a steep stairwell, which cut into the white marble interior, descending to a dimly lit passageway below.

The entrance was guarded by a group of yellow-tunicked men.

Kapano approached the guards, speaking in a low voice.

A single guard stepped out and walked towards them. "Who is the trader?"

"I am," Rind said in a confident voice. "I was told to meet the factor." She showed the marked stone.

The thin-faced guard examined it, then placed it in his tunic pocket. "You are expected, Emissary. Follow me." The guard walked to the top of the stone steps, where he spoke in a low voice to his fellow guards.

"This is as far as I can come," Kapano said in a low voice. "Or wish to come. May your meeting bring you success, and maybe I will see you again, sometime."

Rind gave a short bow. "Thank you, Kapano. I will remember your kind hospitality."

The old man bowed in acknowledgement, then walked quickly away.

"Follow me," repeated the guard, his voice sharper.

Rind gestured for Jessica and Lanky to follow, and they crossed to the entrance, then followed the guard down the steps into the gloomy interior.

As the guard moved a little distance ahead, Lanky came close up behind Jessica. "Nothing about this smells right," he whispered. "Would you let armed strangers walk into your homeland's temple?"

No – unless I was prepared.

Rind glanced back to them. "Your call to abort, remember," she whispered.

Jessica heard faint mutter from Lanky. "We know," she whispered.

The guard led them deeper underground, the way turning and twisting, passing side chambers and narrow passageways, until they stopped outside a well-lit chamber. The guard gestured towards the chamber. "The factor awaits, Emissary of the Natu tribe. My apologies, but this meeting is for you and the factor only. Your guards may wait for you along here."

We've no choice but to accept. "Is this acceptable, my master?"

As Rind cast a quick glance at her, Jessica gave a barely perceptible nod.

Rind drew herself up. "It is acceptable. Our guests have shown great courtesy in allowing you to accompany me. But do not stray far."

Jessica gave a shallow bow.

"You may enter," the guard said to Rind, gesturing to the glowing chamber.

With no hesitation, Rind walked proudly into the chamber. Jessica heard someone speak from within: "Good day to you, Emissary. I hear you have news for us."

The guard outside turned to Jessica. "This way." He gestured to a continuing passageway.

Are we fools? Jessica asked herself, glancing back at the chamber Rind had entered. She clenched her fist around her Staff. *Maybe we are, but we are prepared fools.*

She forced herself to turn away, then, accompanied by Lanky, followed the guard down a long passageway, the mud-brown bricks of its walls bathed by torchlight. Glancing at the walls, she realised that the bricks, like such things as the marble-clad roof and the black pyramid above, were unlike anything she'd seen in the northern Iyes lands. Was this the work of the Ka? Or of others before these people? She cast the questions aside. Those were for another time.

Reaching the tunnel's end, they passed through an opening on the right and walked out into a large chamber. Eyes narrowing, Jessica immediately saw its most obvious feature: a stark limestone throne set against the far back wall of the domed chamber. Between her and the throne lay a low marbled platform, a pentagonal centrepiece accessed on each side by shallow steps. This was not a place she'd expected to wait for Rind. *Then what did you expect?* she mocked herself.

"Wait here," the guard commanded. Then he strode away around the platform's perimeter before turning into a dimly lit alcove, one of four set into the side wall of the chamber. He disappeared from view – and then shadowy figures appeared in all four alcoves.

Her mouth suddenly dry, Jessica watched the figures settle into place, some catching the light of the chamber's torch, others remaining shrouded in darkness. Those she could see were clothed in black tunics with black strappings around their legs and arms, their faces dyed with red and black stripes. They carried sleek wooden shafts tipped with blades of jagged obsidian, edges glistening with menacing intent.

Hearing a noise behind, Jessica whirled around, her hand readying her Staff. She felt Lanky step to cover her back as another group of soldiers marched into the chamber. The soldiers strode past her and Lanky, stepping up onto the raised platform and continuing on to the back of the chamber, where they halted in front of the throne. She heard more soldiers arrive behind them, blocking their exit.

"Get ready to leave," she whispered.

"No!" Lanky hissed, abandoning any effort to remain silent. "We can't leave Rind."

"Then prepare for a fight out of here."

Three of the soldiers in the group at the throne moved away—

And a woman stepped forward.

Heart pumping, Jessica quickly assessed her: light clothing, tattooed upper arms, short hair, and around twice her age.

"Welcome, Warriors," the woman said as she reached the centre of the marble pentagon. "I am pleased to finally meet you."

"Who are you?" Lanky grunted.

But Jessica knew.

"I am the Ensi, the leader of the Ka. And you are Lanky, a Warrior." Her eyes – her fierce emerald-green eyes – shifted to Jessica. "As are you, Jessica." Her head tilted slightly. "Or are you something more?"

Eyes widening, Lanky turned to Jessica. "The traitor," he grated in a low voice.

What's happened, River? Jessica thought, despair flooding through her. *I trusted you.*

The Ensi smiled. "Your daemon has been most helpful."

"The warg," Lanky accused. "Has he betrayed us?"

I don't know. But I know we can't stay here. "We need to go. Ready?"

"Ready."

Jessica reached out for the A'ven—

To find nothing! She could sense none of the energy of the Land.

The Ensi took another step forward, her hard eyes studying them in turn. "Unlike you, I prepared well. And unlike you, I understand this land." Her green eyes flashed. "Because you have been misled, told a false story, and are about to commit a terrible mistake."

CHAPTER EIGHTEEN

*Shall we say the re-entwining of the
timelines began here? Yes, we shall.*

They'd gone and hadn't told her. Beth slammed her Axe into the stripped log, sending a splintered chunk flying towards Dune, who was shaping the end of a freshly made spear.

"Hey! Watch it!" the young maker exclaimed. He rested his flint axe on the ground, then wiped his brow. "You don't need to help me, Warrior. I'm sure you've better things to be doing."

Beth hammered her Axe into the log, cleaving it in two. *They said they would see me before they left, but they didn't. They just left without speaking to me.* Dropping her Axe, she reached down, then picked up one half of the log and threw it over to Dune.

"I think we've enough now," Dune muttered, looking at the growing pile beside him. "Else I'll be here whittling spears until the turn of the moon."

"Bring another," Beth growled to Firuz, who stood by, bemused.

Firuz looked over at Dune. Dune sighed, then nodded. Firuz and Darius headed off towards the cutting area.

Picking up her Axe, Beth looked towards the gorge, her rage still simmering. *They could've told me. Why didn't they tell me?* And yet she was the one who'd made the call not to go with them, the one still scared of what might happen if she lost control of the other within. *I need help to harness Bethusa. I need Garrion.*

But their daemons kept away. *Why? Why are we abandoned?*

As she waited for Firuz and Darius to return with a fresh trunk, she saw a figure heading towards them from the gorge. *Amber.* And the healer was in a hurry. Hefting her Axe, Beth slotted it into the holster on her back, then walked towards the approaching woman.

"You need to meet with River," Amber panted. "Now! She's in the Sacred Chamber."

"What's happened?" Beth said, already striding towards the gorge.

"I don't know," Amber said, breathing hard. "But she said you're needed. Urgently."

What the hell? Beth thought as she began to run. Had something happened to Jessica? To the others? Leaving Amber in her wake, she quickly reached the caves. Still breathing easily, she ran inside, passing through the dimly lit passageways before finally entering the Sacred Chamber.

She saw River sitting on the ground, staring at the artwork on the walls. Beside the Iyes's Mother and Warrior lay her Axe and the unclaimed fourth Axe.

Beth felt the close presence of the Spirits.

They were back.

"What's going on?" Beth growled. "Why—"

She cried out as a tremendous pain exploded in her head. Staggering, her hand tightened on the haft of her Axe, and she reached out for the A'ven …

But it wasn't there.

The intense pain in her head quickly faded, but a cloying pressure clouded her mind. *The Spirits surround me. Why?* "What the hell is going on?" she snarled, hefting her Axe and glancing around, searching for a threat.

River turned to Beth, her youthful face strained beyond her years. "The Spirits are shielding this place. Nothing can get in. Nothing can get out."

"Why?"

"We have a chance to catch the traitor. And to destroy the Ka's Shade."

She stared at River in disbelief.

"I suspected something was wrong for a while. Since the attack by the Shade on White Crags camp."

"We've all suspected something," Beth muttered, shocked and feeling naked without the comfort of the A'ven around her. "The enemy finds us too easily."

"And the daemons have been absent. The Spirits have been absent."

"And IY," Beth growled, still glancing around her, unsure what was happening.

"She was … but she came to me just now."

Beth frowned. "And said what?"

"She gave me the name of the traitor."

Beth's breath caught.

"Garrion," River said. "The traitor is Garrion."

A glacial chill ran down her spine. "It can't be," she whispered. "No, not Garrion ..."

"She's been watched for a while, but only yesterday did she finally make a mistake, exposing her bitter betrayal. She is a traitor and most likely has been so for a long time." River's gaze seemed to drift to another place. "Maybe she even betrayed the location of the Arrival site to the Ka. Maybe she allowed Kaos into the Sacred Chamber to banish the Guardian." Her gaze pulled back to Beth, her expression cold. "She has done untold damage, and I didn't see it."

Her breathing ragged, Beth dropped her Axe to her side, struggling to comprehend what was being said.

River climbed to her feet and walked towards her. "I was not ready, not attuned to the Spirits." She slammed her fist into her hand. "I see now the true damage inflicted by the Shade at White Crags before Lanky drove him away. It was the breach of our defences the Enemy needed in its attempt to subvert you – to allow the power of the Dark in."

Why? Why did Garrion do this? A savage knot twisted her stomach at a sudden dire thought. *Was it me? Is it something I've done?* "It's my fault," she whispered. "I pushed Garrion away. She might not have managed this if I'd kept her close."

"No," River said, vehemence in her voice. "It is well you kept her away. It frustrated their plans. Imagine if you'd let the daemon close to you again, allowing her to twist you to her dark intentions." She reached out and held Beth's hand. "Though you are strong, you couldn't have withstood the combined will of Garrion and the Enemy if they'd caught you unprepared. You would have become theirs."

A puppet of Kaos? No, that would never be.

She stood, churning thoughts seeking answers. How could this be? Garrion had helped her fight off the Ka poison. *She saved my life.* "Why did Garrion do it? Why betray us? Why betray me?"

River gently shook her head. "Even the Spirits cannot answer this, and so I doubt we'll ever know the truth." She released Beth's hand, then walked back to the centre of the chamber and picked up her Axe. "Allying with these daemons carries a risk. They are not of the Spirits; they are not of IY. The daemons offer their service to the Warriors, but – like the Warriors – remain unbound. But if you ask, 'Was it you?', then no; it's likely Garrion allied with Kaos before you entered our Land. Before you became a Warrior."

The biting tension eased a fraction. *It wasn't me. It wasn't what I did or didn't do. I haven't failed yet.* "And Bethusa? Did Garrion betray Bethusa?"

River hesitated. "That, *I* don't know," she said, searching Beth's eyes.

Beth sighed. *No. That's something I should know. And yet I don't. Because I'm scared.*

Scared of Bethusa. Or scared of becoming Bethusa?

Scared of a memory that lies beyond my reach ... A dread feeling of something I did ...

Ignoring the chill in her gut, she glanced at the artwork on the chamber walls. "The Spirits are here. Their absence was a ploy?"

"All access to the Warriors was blocked. A clever deception weaved to frustrate Garrion and prevent her seeing our plans while they confirmed she was the traitor. Beyond IY and the Spirits, only Fen knew of this."

"Lanky suspected Fen." *And Jessica had concerns about you.*

"Fen was the first to distrust Garrion and was the one who finally intercepted her communication with the Ka." A calculating look entered her eyes. "The Shade plans an attack. Here."

Beth tensed, hand instinctively tightening around her Axe. "When?"

"Today. Soon."

She stared at River, stunned. "And we stand here talking! Are you mad?"

"You had to hear – you had to understand – that Garrion did not do this because of you."

"Well, I've heard," Beth said, her anger growing. A hard glint appeared in her eyes. "Did you know this yesterday?"

River nodded.

"And you let Jessica and the others head to the Ka's camp?"

"I told Jessica before they left. And she agreed. Their Shade is coming here. Can you think of a better time for the Warriors to make their attempt there?"

"Yet a dangerous move. How sure is IY of what has passed between Garrion and the Ka? How sure are you the Shade will be here?"

"We are sure – because we fed the information to the Ka."

"You fed ..." Beth shook her head in disbelief. "How?"

"After Fen intercepted Garrion's communication, Iolaire has been constantly by Garrion's side, supposedly hunting for the traitor. And in the meantime, Fen sent messages to the Ka, tuned to appear to be from Garrion. Messages that said the path to the Iyes's Mother and the Sacred Chamber would be clear."

"You've set a trap? With you as the bait?"

River's momentary hesitation was laced with dread. "We have – but also with you as bait for Garrion."

"What!"

"As soon as the Shade arrives in this chamber, then IY will remove the barrier preventing the daemons reaching the Warriors. You must let Garrion come to you. If we can draw Garrion here, the Spirits can trap her."

"What have you done?" Beth whispered.

"Taken the chance to capture a traitor and destroy the Ka's most feared shaman." River's eyes burned with ruthless intent. "We must seize this chance, Warrior. Such a confluence cannot be ignored."

Maybe, but I'm not ready. "You're certain of this? Is there no other way?"

"Garrion trusts you. When IY releases the barrier, the daemon will come to you. And it must be now. The Shade is preparing to travel here."

Beth stared at River, her dismay displaced by sudden frustration. *Why leave it so late to tell me? Why not engage me from the start?* But deep down, she knew the brutal truth was that River couldn't. Not for something like this. Not when a single word might have alerted Garrion and so the Ka. Even so, frustrated anger simmered. But anger at what? At not being told? At being used as a pawn? Or because she had remained here at the camp? *I am a Warrior. I should be with Lanky and Jess. I should be fighting this war.*

She heard River's voice: "Should you release Bethusa?"

Her anger flared. "No! Not that one. If your spirits aid us, then I will do what is needed."

"Then let us ready ourselves."

Beth glanced to the entranceway. "Have you told Gravel? The others?"

River averted her gaze, her head bowing. "I cannot," she whispered. "I can't risk losing this chance."

Through her own anger, Beth saw the tension in the girl's stance. *It hurts her.* And maybe it should. The Ka Shade was coming. Here. Today. Invited in, a path cleared to the very heart of the Iyes. Her hands clenched in frustration. *And we tell no one. We risk the lives of innocents.* And all because of the treachery of her daemon. *I trusted her. I trusted Garrion.*

258

Her face grim, she stepped forward and laid her hand on River's shoulder. "Okay, walk me through the plan. We have a traitor to catch."

*

An intense crackling alerted Shadow to the Shade's return. He looked up to see the shaman striding from the blackness, oily tendrils of darkness clinging to his body before peeling away and springing back into the wall. A wave of disgust ran through him. How could he follow this man? How?

"How do we feel? Rested and ready? We think so, yes, we do," Growl said, his burning black eyes flashing over them, his crooked teeth gleaming through his smile. "And so we should be – the time of Kaos is at hand."

Shadow bristled. *You do not serve Kaos. Our god would not condone your actions.*

"That may be so," Nefra growled. "But maybe now you can tell us where we're going?"

"To kill a Warrior, a devil shaman. To destroy the soul of the Iyes." The Shade grinned. "Killing – that is what we shall do today."

"How many Iyes will we face?"

Growl dismissed Nefra's question with a wave of his arm. "These Iyes humans are weak, irrelevant. Our mission is clear, oh yes. Selective and precise. Their shaman – and their precious spirits – *these* are what matter. These are our target."

I was right. We target the Iyes. Shadow caught Sy looking at him.

"Focus on the mission," Sy signed, his fingers flashing by his side. "That is the will of the Ensi. The rest we can face later."

Scowling, Shadow flicked his gaze back to Growl. "And how do you expect us to achieve this?"

"You? We don't expect that, our beloved Disciple. Leave those to the anointed of Kaos. You are here to remove the petty distractions and allow *our* work to be done." Growl walked over to Shadow, his black eyes boring into him. "Do not engage the devils. They remain formidable adversaries, even having lost two of their kind."

Shadow's brow furrowed. "Two lost? How?"

Growl's lips curled into a vicious grin. "Let us just say, our work has been made easier by one sympathetic to our cause."

An insider? A spy? A connection was made. "The Warriors we saw, those at the camp, they've been led into a trap?"

"Another smooths the way," the shaman growled. He half turned away. "If their daemon speaks true," he muttered as if to himself.

"What daemon?" *A traitor?*

Growl's head snapped back to glare at Shadow. "No more questions. You follow and stay close. Always close. Kill anything that gets in our way – is that clear?"

"I would like—"

"Is that clear?" Growl demanded.

"Very clear," Nefra said, adjusting her pack.

"It's clear, but—"

The chamber disappeared, and Shadow stood, head ringing, in the dappled shadows of a small glade. A wide-eyed woman carrying an armful of plants stood frozen before them. She died quickly as Nefra sprang forward, but not without releasing an ear-shattering scream.

"Follow!" Growl commanded, striding away with ferocious intent.

Sy and Nefra reacted first, chasing after Growl, leaving Shadow looking down on the dead young woman, bloodied herbs scattered by her left arm. *Is this my enemy? Is this the enemy of my god?* Cries of alarm triggered him into action. "It's war," he muttered to himself as, ignoring his pounding head, he turned and raced after the others. "She chose the wrong side."

Chose?

He pushed the wandering thoughts aside and raced to catch up with the Shade. Running out of the trees, he entered a tree-topped gorge and saw the Shade striding across a narrow stream to a cave in the cliff to their left. An enemy party rushed towards them from the right. *They could be a problem …*

In that moment, rapid movement caught his eye. Glancing down the gorge, he saw a large pack of wolves bounding across the stream, arcing around to meet the approaching force. At their head was the Shade's black wolf, Streak. Despite his revulsion at the senseless slaughter of Karnt, Shadow was impressed yet again with the Shade's reach. And his planning. *The enemy will struggle to reach us quickly.*

He sprinted on, seeing Sy disappear into the gloom of the cave's entrance. He followed Sy inside—

And almost collided with Growl in the dark. "Get down – now!" the Shade commanded, raising his Black Staff.

Shadow dropped.

There was an enormous explosion from the entranceway, and a hot, dust-laden blast of air buffeted Shadow, followed by the tremendous crashing of falling rocks.

"Come!" the Shade growled, striding past Shadow.

He knows where he's going, Shadow thought as they weaved their way deeper into the cave system. *Someone has indeed betrayed the Iyes.*

"They're coming," River whispered. "Do it now."

Beth hesitated, heart lurching in her chest. But it had to be done. And it had to seem real. *Do it!* "I'm sorry," she breathed, then feeling the cold, sharp blade in her hand, she thrust it into River's side, praying she struck cleanly.

River gasped, then sank to the ground.

Beth immediately sucked in a huge pool of energy from the A'ven, quickly weaving the bindings as IY had shown her. As she completed the final binding, she felt the coiled, latent energy humming within her.

They were ready to spring their trap.

"Ready yourself," River whispered, her hand to her wounded side. "She comes. She—"

The energy of the A'ven rippled as a new presence entered the chamber.

'Beth!' came Garrion's strident voice. *'What's happening? I couldn't reach you.'*

'We're under attack!' Beth cried, playing her part. *'Someone struck River. I need your help!'*

She tensed as a now familiar energy flowed into her Axe. *'Who attacks?'* Garrion pulsed with genuine confusion. *'Where is the attacker?'* An alarmed cry erupted from the daemon. *'You hold the blade. You lie—'*

Casting a confining shield around her, Beth released her hold on the sprung bindings. Garrion roared with bestial ferocity as the cloaked jaws of the trap snapped into place – crackling coils tightened rapidly around the stricken daemon. Forcing the immense pent energy into the bindings, Beth dragged Garrion from the Axe, driving her into an ethereal prison within her. *'IY,'* she called out. *'I have the trai—'*

With a ferocious release of energy, Garrion shattered a binding.

Desperately sucking energy from the A'ven, Beth weaved it around the daemon, strengthening the straining coils that remained. Garrion fought wildly to break free, but the bindings held. But for how long? *Where are you, IY? We need—*

"The enemy is here," came River's faint whisper.

Beth heard the approaching footsteps from the passageways beyond.

With the daemon battering ever more frantically against its restraints, she readied herself to face the Ka shaman. *Hold yourself together,* she urged herself. *The Spirits will come.*

As Shadow ducked under a low point in the tunnel, he emerged to find himself in a warmly lit chamber, its walls and ceilings covered with majestic artwork. A dark-haired young woman stood, smiling before him.

He gasped at the sight of the familiar face. *The Warrior I killed. The Warrior I saw dead at the dragon's feet. The twice-dead Warrior!* She stood, her stance easy and relaxed, over a bleeding figure on the ground – and she held a blood-smeared blade loosely by her side. He shook his head. "You don't stay dead very long," he muttered.

"You know this woman?" Nefra said, her eyes narrowing.

Shadow studied the young woman's exotic face, seeing the same keen eyes, slender frame, and small scar on the cheek. "I killed her once. Then she died again." He held her eyes. "But it seems she doesn't like dying."

Growl stepped slowly forward. "We doubted it," he said, sharp eyes scanning around the chamber. "And we prepared for the worst." He looked down at the figure on the ground. "But it seems your daemon succeeded." He glanced up at the Warrior, tilting his head a fraction. "Kaos thanks you."

The Warrior bowed in acknowledgement. "It has been … difficult." She gestured to the paintings on the wall. "The pressure of their cursed spirits was terrifying, but thanks to the support of Kaos, we prevailed."

"Who's that?" Nefra asked, gesturing to the body on the ground.

The Warrior's dark eyes swung to Nefra. "The Iyes's devil shaman. She was strong." The Warrior smiled. "But I was stronger."

Nefra looked down at the body and then back up at the Warrior. Her gaze was penetrating, but she held silent.

"Impressive," Shadow murmured. "It seems we weren't needed here."

"No," Growl said, turning to him and raising his Staff. "You are not—"

"You look stressed, Warrior," came Nefra's quiet yet inquisitorial voice.

Growl spun around, his startled gaze on Nefra.

As Nefra walked towards the Warrior, Shadow quailed at Growl's half-said words. *He thought the job complete. He raised his Staff as though he were going to strike me.* He glanced back to Sy. His friend and companion had stepped back towards the entrance, his cold eyes locked onto his. A terrible regret stabbed Shadow's heart. *So, you too, Sy?* Thoughts racing, he turned back to the Warrior. *I'm not to leave here. Is this the order of the Ensi? Did I step too far?* He fought to steady himself. *Focus. There must be a way out.*

He forced his attention on Nefra, who stood before the unkillable woman, studying her face. Nefra reached out and wiped a finger across the Warrior's brow. She smiled. "I have stood opposite many a fighter," she said slowly. "And all who know me look like this. Brave on the outside but crying inside." She tilted her head. "Why would you be scared?"

Shadow studied the Warrior, suddenly seeing what he'd missed before. *It's true! She wears a mask!*

Growl frowned and stepped towards the Warrior—

"A trap! It is a trap!" shrieked the Warrior, her voice horribly distorted.

Shadow was not sure exactly what happened next, but all hell broke loose.

An intense white light exploded into the chamber, and he fell to the ground, shielding his eyes. A tremendous crackling erupted around him, and he felt his hair stand on end. A sense of horror swept over him – then elation, then terror, his mind torn one way, then another. An immense pressure pushed him into the ground, quickly growing to an unbearable weight. He struggled to breathe—

And then, as quickly as it had begun, it was over.

Silence.

Gasping, he sucked in the sharp acrid air and glanced up.

The merciless faces of enemy fighters glared back at him.

He flicked a panicked glance behind the fighters to where the Shade stood, imprisoned. The shaman's body was covered by a black oily morass, itself tightly bound by white-hot, sizzling coils of sparking energy. Through the haze of his fraught mind came a cold-eyed admiration. *They knew we were coming. They laid their own trap.*

He released the grip on his weapons, letting them fall to the ground. This was not yet his time to die, else he would already be dead. *But how long is my reprieve?* He glanced again at the fighters, and then at the bound Shade. *And which will try to kill me first?*

*

As Gravel and his fighters escorted the subdued prisoners out of the chamber, Beth sank to her knees, breathing hard.

"Are you okay?" River said, a hand on her blood-stained side, a savage relief written across her face.

Beth nodded. "And you?"

"I'll live."

Footsteps rang down the tunnel outside, and a moment later, Amber appeared. "What the hell happened?" the healer gasped, her fearful eyes glancing at the bound shaman.

"Beth stuck her blade in me," River said, casting a wry smile at Beth.

With a furtive glance at the shaman, Amber knelt down and examined the wound.

Still on her knees, Beth looked over at the bound shaman, tasting pulses of disparate energy radiating from him and his prison. *I almost failed.* The enemy fighter had challenged her, and in the woman's simple action of wiping her brow, her concentration had cracked. Garrion had surged violently, taken control of part of her mind, and called out a warning.

But the Spirits and Fen – and Revri – had finally acted.

The explosion of energy that had ripped through her as the Spirits had blasted into being had flooded the chamber with blinding light. Revri had risen from the ground, streams of intense white energy leaping from her Axe as she struck out at the enemy shaman. The shaman had instantly defended himself, his Black Staff pouring an oily blackness over his body, shielding him from Revri's attacks. But another fearsome presence had stormed into the chamber: the wolf daemon Fen. The stream of white energy from Revri's Axe had narrowed, morphing into a sleek, sizzling snake which had coiled itself around the stricken Shade. "And now you, Sister," Fen had growled to Beth. The warg, joined by another entity, this one veiled from her sight, had reached inside her, enveloping the trapped daemon Garrion. "This task is complete," Fen had said. "This traitor comes with us." The intense glare in the chamber had vanished. Fen and the Spirits had left.

"Beth!"

Her reverie broken, Beth turned. Amber was kneeling beside River, glaring at her. "I said, give me a hand. You did this, so you can help fix it."

Beth climbed slowly to her feet and walked over to them. She looked down at the injured River. "We have to figure out what to do with this one," she said, gesturing towards the bound shaman.

"And quickly," River added. "Those bindings won't hold him forever."

"Let's get you fixed up first," Amber said, her eyes flicking nervously to the enemy shaman. She looked up at Beth. "Let's get her out of here."

They helped River to her feet, then, supporting her, slowly walked out of the chamber. As they passed the enemy shaman, waves of malevolent hatred coursed through the ether.

The battle is fully joined. This will not be easy.

II. REVELATIONS

CHAPTER NINETEEN

Was she close to me? Yes. Could I influence her? Maybe. Control?
No, she carved her own path. And that is how it had to be.

The Ensi raised her arm, dismissing her black-tunicked guards. Jessica watched as the grim-faced soldiers marched out, leaving her and Lanky alone with the Ka leader. *Was this their chance?* She quickly judged the distance between her and the Ensi – she and Lanky could easily reach and strike the woman before the soldiers could get anywhere close. But it couldn't be that easy. *What am I missing?*

Scanning the chamber, she convinced herself there were no other concealed defenders. She looked back to the Ensi. A chill settled on her as she recognised a calm yet potent strength carefully veiled behind the woman's sharp emerald-green eyes – eyes that drew you in. She *is what I'm missing.*

Lanky tensed, clearly readying to attack. Jessica quickly placed her arm across his chest. "Hold," she whispered, her eyes still on the Ensi. A move towards this woman would be a step closer to death. *Stall. Figure out how to connect back to the A'ven.* "How did you know we were here?"

The Ensi smiled. "A Warrior and her daemon betrayed you. It is good some understand the lies of the Iyes."

Stunned, Jessica somehow held the shock from her face. "Which Warrior?" she managed, holding her voice steady.

"I think you know her as Beth."

Jessica froze. *Beth?*

"You expect us to believe that?" Lanky growled, taking a step forward. "You think us fools?"

Instinctively, Jessica grabbed his arm, pulling him back. Yet she was reeling from the Ensi's words.

The Ensi cocked her head. "Whether you believe me or not, it is true. We were told the time and place of your arrival." The Ensi gestured to them with a sweep of her hand. "And here you are."

Jessica's mind raced. River had spoken of a traitor. *But not Beth. No way is it Beth.*

"Jess," Lanky whispered. "We have to take this chance while the guards are away."

"We can't," she whispered back. "Not without the A'ven." *This woman is too strong.*

"Your Iyes tribe crumbles," the Ensi said. "Their time is over. Your Warrior Beth sees the truth."

"Lies!" Lanky snarled, glaring at the Ensi. "Just what I'd expect from you vermin."

"You insult me, Warrior. Not the behaviour I expected from a guest." Her gaze was contemptuous. "And what do you know of the Ka? What do you *truly* know?"

"That you're the enemy," Lanky said with venom. "That you killed the Iyes's shaman, and that you're planning to destroy the Land."

The Ensi gave a harsh laugh. "I see you use the words of the Iyes. Not simply the land, but 'the Land'. Meaning their land, the land of the Iyes."

No, swept an emphatic thought through Jessica's mind. *Far more than that. Life, the Spirits, the daemons, the A'ven. The Land is of the Light and of the Dark. It—*

"And do we look like destroyers?" the Ensi snapped, jolting Jessica back to the moment. "Have you seen our simple camp? Have you seen the humble people of this tribe? We aim to destroy nothing. *We* are the protectors here, you fool! The Ka!"

Lanky bared his teeth. "Leave your games and poisoned words for others, devil. I met your so-called protectors. Some captured and almost killed me. Your loyal shaman attempted to destroy the Iyes's spirits. And I've heard how your pet dragon captured Beth. Your people's evil actions speak for you."

The Ensi's face clouded with anger. "You understand nothing!" she snarled. "You have heard nothing of *my* story."

"I don't care," Lanky said. He turned to Jessica. "Jess, we—"

"You hold a great power, Jessica," came the Ensi's voice, now calmer and quieter, yet seeming to ripple around them. "Far more than you know. Wielding that power responsibly, with even-handed authority, cannot rise from a place of ignorance. I ask you, please, listen to my story. Then you are free to judge."

"Jess, we need to fight. It's the only way."

Jessica glanced at Lanky, seeing the flicker of fear in his face, but also the fire of the Warrior striving to be released. But they had no access to the A'ven. *We can't fight, not here, not now.* Facing the Ensi again, she noticed a tension in the woman's stance. *Why? How can we hurt her?* She felt for the A'ven again. Still nothing. *We can't fight.* Then why was this woman nervous? And why send her guards away? Her breath suddenly caught. Had the Ensi planned all this just to talk? *Does she truly want us to listen to her?* She stared at the woman, scarcely believing. But she saw it was true. *She's waiting. She's waiting for permission to speak.* Her confusion deepened. *What's happening here?*

Yet she gave the slightest nod to the Ensi.

A spark of relief flashed in the Ensi's eyes. The Ka leader walked across the marble platform towards them, halting a few paces away. "Entities exist outwith this land that are so vast that their names are meaningless, entities so far beyond our form of life that we cannot hope to understand them. But beneath them are those who do their bidding – gods if you wish. These we can embrace, seek guidance and protection from. They become *our* gods." The Ensi studied Jessica closely. "And if you sought a god to embrace, which would you seek for your families and loved ones? Which would you seek when your people were being slaughtered by a foul enemy?" Her eyes hardened. "You would seek a mighty god, a fearsome god, one that can protect you from the evil sent against you. For us, we chose Kaos. Yes, a brutal god, but one who for millennia has served us well."

"You chose a god who slaughters innocents," Lanky spat.

The Ensi's green eyes flashed in anger. "Innocents? Let me ask you – *Warrior* – if so-called innocents attacked *your* family, what would *you* do? Would you stand in silence and watch your family and friends slaughtered? See your tribe erased?" She took a step closer, glaring at Lanky. "Would you?"

Lanky glared back but said nothing.

The Ensi held his fierce gaze for a moment longer, then turned to Jessica. "We defend ourselves," she said, her voice edged with simmering anger. "We defend others in our empire. And within that empire, we hope our families can live in peace." Her attention swung back to Lanky, and she addressed him in a deadly quiet voice. "But what happens? After generations building this safe empire for our citizens, what happens? The Warriors arrive, that is what happens. Warriors sent forth by our enemy to seek us out and destroy us. Men, women, children, babies – all these innocents wiped out in mass cullings. And all in the name of IY, the god of war and disaster."

"That's not true," Jessica whispered. "The Warriors do not ... they ..." She glanced at Lanky, her mind reeling.

"It is my people who suffer at the hand of the Iyes! My people! So when we hear the Warriors have arrived and are preparing for battle against us, what do we do? What do *I* do? I fight! I fight to save my people!"

Jessica felt her chest constricting. *What is she saying? That's not who the Warriors are. It's not who we are.*

Green eyes now blazing with a cold fire, the Ensi levelled her gaze on them. "I will not let the Iyes destroy us yet again. So yes, we killed the Iyes's shaman. And yes, we tried to destroy the devil IY's sacred place. And yes, I sent one of my Disciples to capture that Staff you carry."

The hairs on her nape stiffened. *She sees through the disguise.*

The Ensi studied them, her rage barely contained. "And tell me truly, was I wrong? Were the Iyes seeking peace with me? Had they abandoned their plans to destroy my tribe? Tell me!"

The Ensi's furious words echoed around the chamber, slowly fading into silence.

Jessica stared blankly ahead, suddenly lost. What had just happened? What was she hearing?

The deathly silence around her offered no answers.

She refocussed on the Ensi, who stood proudly defiant. *Defiant, and yet, she's hurting.*

Disconcerted by the instinctive thought, she studied the woman's face, her gaze drawn inexorably to her eyes. Such a rich emerald-green with an entrancing depth enticing you in to understand more. Inviting you in with a guiding hand, while whispering for you to dispel your doubts, your worries. To reject the lies you'd been told. To learn—

The Ensi looked down, breaking the contact.

With a sharp intake of breath, Jessica glanced away. Maybe the Ensi held a hurt inside, but she was dangerous. And with a concealed strength and power that could suck you into her shrouded world.

But was it a world filled with only lies and deception?

Despite the obvious insidious power of the woman before her, *No,* came the immediate and disturbing answer. The Iyes *were* looking to destroy the Ensi and her tribe. They themselves – Warriors – had come here to steal from the Ka. To capture the Kade. *And moments ago, I thought to kill their leader.*

Her cautious gaze returned to the Ensi. Why was this leader of the Ka engaging with them like this? Why speak like this to your mortal enemy? *Who is who's enemy here?* came the thought, unbidden. *Who are the players and who are the pawns?* The questions closed around her, suffocating and binding, answers obscured much as all else remained cloaked by uncertainty. And that couldn't be. Despite the risk, she needed to know more to be sure of what to do next. "What do you know of the Kade?" she asked quietly.

"Jess, no!" Lanky hissed, grabbing her arm. "We need to leave. Now!"

"We're here," she said softly. "Alive. We must take the chance to learn what we can."

"Not this, Jess. We didn't discuss this."

Jessica pulled her arm away and fixed her eyes on the Ensi. "What do you know of the Kade?" she repeated.

"You're making a big mistake," Lanky insisted beside her.

"It is the power of Kaos in these lands," the Ensi answered. Her gaze took on a sudden piercing intensity. "Is this what you came to destroy? You wish to destroy our god?"

Jessica hesitated. "We came seeking it," she said evenly.

The Ensi's penetrating regard seemed to strip her bare. "You speak a truth," she said after a moment, "and for that, I am grateful."

Truth? What is the truth here? "What is it you intend to do with us?"

"What do you wish to do?" the Ensi countered.

Escape from here. Go home. Then find the white-haired devil who killed my sister. But with each passing moment, each harsh encounter, the deepening stark surety was that this couldn't yet happen. *I am the Guardian. I need to understand more of this Land.* "There is an old man in the Flanks. He holds a story, or so he says. I'd like to hear that story."

The Ensi raised an eyebrow.

"Jess!" Lanky hissed. "What are you doing?"

I seek the truth. Or a version of it.

"The man's name?" the Ensi asked.

"Kapano."

The Ensi clapped her hands once. Immediately, a man in a plain, knee-length tunic ran into the chamber. He stopped at the base of the steps to the marble pentagon, then sank to his knees, bowing. "Find a man named Kapano in the Flanks and bring him here." The man stood, then raced from the chamber.

The Ensi clapped twice, and the black-tunicked figures appeared in the shadows of the alcoves. Her focus switched back to Jessica. "Consider yourself as guests in this temple. You may go where you wish, see what you wish – but you may not leave. Given your intentions, I believe you understand why this is so. We will meet again once this Kapano has been found."

The Ensi turned and walked back to her throne.

The yellow-tunicked guard who had first escorted them to the chamber walked up beside them. "This way. Follow me."

Lanky glanced at Jessica, scowling. "I hope you know what you're doing."

As they followed the guard out of the chamber, Jessica wiped her clammy brow. Did she know what she was doing? *No,* came her brutal answer. *Because I don't understand what's happening.*

The Ensi's words reverberated around her mind, with one challenge cutting deep: "Wielding that power ... cannot rise from a place of ignorance." *The Ensi believes she's the one in the right.* But how was that possible? This was the Iyes's feared enemy. A grim resolve settled on her. Too much was at stake. *I'm sorry, Lanky, but we need to know more.*

*

Lanky glared at Jessica. Nothing was going right. Their mission was a failure: Rind was missing, and the green-eyed devil woman had most skilfully manipulated Jessica.

And now they argued.

"River has messed up," Lanky growled, pacing across the dingy chamber they'd been told was their sleeping quarters. "She plotted with IY behind our back to capture their Shade and they got it wrong. Our mission was leaked."

"So you keep saying," Jessica said. "But we held this mission tight. Only those we trusted knew of what we planned here."

"Then how did the Ensi know we were coming? She knew our damn names." *And what else did she know?*

"The traitor clearly knew more than we realised."

Lanky scowled. "The traitor who's still at large."

"You don't know that. River's plan might have worked. And our mission hasn't yet failed. Look around you. We're still alive. Unbound."

"Yes, because that cursed woman in there is trying to twist you around her little finger."

She glowered at him, then, shaking her head, walked a few paces away.

Lanky rubbed his beard. He was angry, scared, and worried as hell about Rind. "She left," the guard had said when they'd questioned him. "She'll meet you at your dwelling." They'd dismissed that, saying Rind wouldn't have left without them. But to no avail; the guard's message was unchanging. Lanky had then tried to leave the temple to discover the truth, but the closed ranks of the guards at the entrance had prevented that. Guests? No, prisoners of the Ka. Of the Ensi. *And so is Rind,* he thought, his frustration growing. *But where?*

Jessica turned to face him, her striking brown eyes locking onto his. *Brown, yet a glimmer of green,* came his distracted thought.

"Those things the Ensi told us … what if she's right? What do we really know of the Land? All we've been told has been through the Iyes. They—"

"Stop! Don't even go there, Jess. You now doubt the Iyes?"

"Don't twist my words. That's not what I'm saying." She glared at him. "Stand back and think about it. We arrived knowing nothing, and the first people we met introduced us to their world – to their beliefs – and told us of a great Enemy opposing them and attempting to destroy their Land. An Enemy comprising a tyrant god, Kaos, and his agents of the Dark, and a hostile tribe known as the Ka. But now we meet this Ensi, this leader of the Ka, who says that it is the Iyes who persecute her people. That it is the Warriors who destroy her people. That, in fact, the Iyes are the oppressors."

"This is crazy. She's bewitched you."

Jessica shook her head. "There's something we're missing. Something beyond what we've seen or heard." Her gaze grew more intense. "The Iyes brought us here to help them defeat their Enemy. But who truly is the Enemy? Does it include the Ensi? If so, could you, *Warrior,* really make the decision now to execute this woman? We *must* understand more before we act."

Lanky studied her with a scornful regard. "Before I answer, let me remind you of things you may have forgotten. The killing of an old lady, on *her* orders. The harrying and killing of innocents in the Iyes tribe, by *her* fighters. Attacks by *her* daemons on us, both here and in our time. The attack on us by *her* people and *her* dragon. The stealing of the Staff by *her* peo—"

"She explained that. What would you do if your own people were about to be slaughtered?"

Lanky threw up his arms, his anger flaring. "Where's that happening? Show me! I don't see her people fleeing hordes of ravening Iyes fighters invading her borders."

"But that's just what the Iyes are preparing to do. And with our help. It's why they made their Request for our aid."

"Because these Ka are about to destroy *them!*" Lanky shouted in growing frustration. "And we're not about to massacre innocents. We're defending the Iyes, their allies, and their Land."

Jessica walked up to him, thrusting her face into his. "Here's a question for you. Who started attacking who first?"

"You know that, damn you! The Ka! They're trying to turn this world into ice. They've done it before and will do it again."

"*How* do you know that?"

Lanky's mind whirled. "Naga, Bear, the Iyes's Story …"

"But how do you *know*?"

Lanky grimaced. He knew. He just knew.

Didn't he?

An errant thought fought to be heard. *But, what if …?*

"No," he snapped, spinning away from her and prowling, head down, around the chamber. "She's crawled under your skin. These Ka – their daemons and devil shaman – are evil. Plain and simple." He stopped and glared at her. "She's done her job well – very well. But she doesn't fool me. Please don't let her fool you."

Jessica glared back at him.

His mind raced. The Ensi had played a most clever and deadly hand, weaving a beguiling web around them. And she was drawing Jessica in. *Yes, a most clever hand.* You didn't run an empire like the Ka through brute strength and ignorance. No, you needed political guile and surgical precision. And masterful deception when needed.

And this was definitely a master at work.

This had become a real mess. No sign of the Kade. No sign of Rind. And trapped by the Ensi. *We have to get out. And quickly.* But how? He'd tried reaching for the A'ven, but though he sensed its tantalising presence, he couldn't connect. *Why?* It made no sense. If he could feel it, why couldn't he access it?

Damn it! What do we do?

Not fight amongst ourselves, came his immediate answer.

He forced himself to steady his breathing. *If we fracture, we've lost. We need to stay together.* "Brothers in arms," he whispered.

Jessica's eyes narrowed.

He drew a deep breath. "Truce," he said, holding up his hands. "I don't agree with you, but this is crazy. If we carry on like this, she'll have already won."

Eyes remaining fixed on his, she said nothing.

Lanky tilted his head. "What do you want to do next?"

He saw the tension ease from her shoulders, and a moment later, her eyes softened.

"We need to know more," she said, her voice weary. "We're trapped inside this place for now, but it seems we can move freely within. Let's use the time to search for Rind and see what else we can learn of this place."

Rind. His anger quickly faded. *Find Rind, then find a way out of this mess and return to the Iyes.* "And the Kade?"

Jessica's face was drawn. "I don't know how we can find that now. Without the A'ven, we're blind." She pushed a strand of hair behind her ear. "Let's focus on finding Rind."

He forced a smile. "Then best we start now. Better than us fighting each other in here."

She half smiled and nodded.

He gestured to the exit to the chamber. "Ladies first ..."

Jessica's brow raised a fraction, then she walked towards the exit. As she passed by, she thumped him.

He rubbed his arm as he walked after her. *Less of the quips, Lanky. She hits hard.*

*

"Should we go on?" Lanky said as they reached yet another set of rough-hewn steps descending into the deep darkness of the level below. "I'm not sure they'd have brought Rind down here."

The sixth level, or the seventh? Jessica had lost count. She peered down into the gloom, her dying torch casting wavering shadows as it flickered in the slight breeze wafting through the passageway. Should they go on? There was no sign of recent activity down here, and no sign of prisoners. And no sense of anything abnormal. Severed from the A'ven, maybe that wasn't a surprise, but even so, she had held a faint hope for some sign of the Kade. Yet all they'd found were food caches of the Ka, mostly grain and rootlike plants stored in dry, cool chambers on each of the levels above. And also, water. Running water, flowing through deep channels carved into the rugged stone floors on the northern side of each level. Together with the construction of the temple itself, it showed a sophistication way beyond anything seen in the Iyes's lands.

"Jess?"

She pulled herself back to his question. "Let's try one more level before they decide to come looking for us."

As they descended the steps, her thoughts churned once more. Having allowed them unfettered access throughout the labyrinth of the temple, the Ensi was clearly unconcerned at what they may find. *She believes we'll find nothing of interest to us.* A confident woman. *Or a fool?* No, not a fool. The Ensi was a smart and powerful woman, one who'd taken a clear and calculated risk in allowing them, her deadliest enemy, to enter the temple in the first place.

Alive.

Why? Why do this?

Remembered words of the Ensi spun out of the maelstrom of her mind and drifted to the fore. "I ask you, please, listen to my story. Then you are free to judge." These were some of the first words the Ka leader had spoken. Words of a tyrant? Words of calculating killer? *Why does she seek to engage with us? What does she want us to hear?*

Lanky seemed to whisper in her ear. *Don't trust the Ka.*

Yet she'd heard the passion in the Ensi's voice. *She meant what she said.*

Disparate thoughts swirled. "We defend ourselves ..." the Ensi had said. And the old man who had helped them ... *He holds a story of a time before the Ka. He holds a story of a god.*

Reaching the base of the steps, she paused. Within the turmoil of her disturbed mind, the mantra remained. *I have to learn more. I need to understand.* She raised the dying flame of her blackened torch to a fresh one hanging on a hammered peg in the rough-hewn wall. *But one thing at a time.*

The fresh torch blazed into life.

Discarding the spent torch and lifting out the new, she walked on to catch up with Lanky, who was silhouetted in the tunnel ahead. The gentle breeze continued to brush her face. It was a breeze they'd first encountered many levels above and one they'd hoped may lead them to a possible way out. Instead, they'd found it emanated from narrow slits in several of the walls, a clever design enabling the passageways to be cleared of smoke but providing no escape route for them.

The light in the tunnel ahead dimmed as Lanky entered another chamber.

Jessica strode on ... her eyes widened as she reached the mouth of the chamber. Her wavering torchlight threw a fitful light over a chaotically slumped mound of glittering yellow stones. Mesmerised, she knelt and picked up a rugged, palm-sized piece. "This is gold!" she exclaimed, turning the gleaming nugget over in her hand. She looked up, raising her torch. Its light glittered off countless golden nuggets stacked impossibly high in mountainous piles, which swept away into the darkness beyond.

"Unbelievable," Lanky breathed.

She cast the nugget away, then stood, swinging her torch from side to side, the mountains of gold seemed to come alive as a multitude of shadows danced to and fro. It was a collection so vast that she struggled to take it in.

"This is some horde," Lanky said, eyes wide. "Where the hell did they get it all?"

She shook her head.

"Seems the desire for gold has been around for a long time, but this?" He glanced around the heaped piles. "Why do they need so much? Trade?" He scowled. "Or pay for their dirty work to be done?"

An uneasy thought pushed to the fore. "This place, this temple … there's a sophistication here beyond anything supposedly possible by peoples of this time. And see how they organise themselves: their people, their army, and the empire Rind says they hold." She looked intently at him. "Where's this in our history books?"

His eyes narrowed. "And did you ever read about dragons – or daemons – stalking the land?"

"Only in stories."

Lanky's brow furrowed. "Stories, songs – maybe that's our real history." He shook his head. "Imaginos – damn, maybe that was real."

"Sometimes I think you're crazy."

"Sometimes I wonder myself," Lanky muttered, glancing around at the mountains of gold.

Jessica watched him for a moment. Crazy? No. This car mechanic from a sleepy village was far from crazy. *He was onto our world's incredible secrets long before any of us.* Despite the tension, a small smile played on her lips. *Imaginos* … For the briefest of moments, a warmth filled her soul. *I'm on to your childish game, Lanky – but if your music keeps you sane, then keep playing.*

With a silent sigh, she looked back at the chamber's treasure and latched back on to their conversation. *Stories* … So, why weren't the tales of this age told in their history? Why did no one know of the Warriors?

The Continuum adjusts, aligns.

The sudden, breathtaking thought rocked her. Could it be that this vast, abstruse Continuum had truly adjusted? Could some innocent act of the past – *by a Warrior?* – have irrevocably changed the course of the Land's history? Who might once have lived but now never existed? What empires could have thrived that simply vanished in the blink of an eye, no remnant remaining?

And how would anyone know?

Grimacing, she tried to escape her dread thoughts. *There lies insanity.*

Yet her mind refused to let go. *What might* our *actions unleash within the Continuum?*

"Let's see what's beyond this chamber," came Lanky's voice. "There's a path through here."

She clenched her hand until she felt her nails dig into her palm. *Stay in the moment, Jess. Deal with your fears later.* She relaxed her hand and followed after Lanky.

They continued on, their torches guiding them through scattered valleys between the gold mountains and in places across steep avalanches of slumped gold. The next chamber they entered was the same … and the next. And then a chamber of different treasures: dazzling mounds of intense blue and white crystals, their sheer, polished surfaces glinting in the fiery glow of their torches.

"How much further does this go on?" Lanky said, staring at the glittering horde.

"This is a wealth beyond imagining. But it's clear Rind isn't here."

"Shall we try one more level?"

She heard the desire in his voice. *He wants to find Rind. He needs to find Rind.*

She nodded.

Lanky immediately looked back the way they'd come. "If the layout of this level is the same as the others, then the way down to the next should be back this way – past the last gold chamber we crossed and to the right."

Retracing their steps, she followed him until they reached the entrance to the golden chamber. There, Lanky halted ahead of her. "Drat, this torch is fading fast. I hadn't realised how low it …"

His voice trailed off as he peered into the chamber of gold.

"Lanky?"

"Leave your torch there for a moment and come and see this."

She inserted her torch into a wooden holder on the wall, then walked over to him.

Joining him at the entrance to the chamber of gold, she was met by a strange sight. Within the darkness of the chamber snaked a path of soft golden light, its delicate glow mapping out the route they'd taken through the heaped treasures of gold. "Was that there when we walked through?"

"I don't know," he murmured, as they stepped into the chamber. "I guess it would've been difficult to see with the bright light of the torches. But now …" He swept his arm along the golden trail. "Well, you can see."

"What is it?" She bent down to the gold and picked up a large nugget. Holding it in the palm of her hand, a gentle yellow light suffused it.

"I'm not sure. But it's clearly reacted to us passing through here. I don't know—"

"So, it is true," came the voice of the Ensi from the darkness beyond.

Jessica sprang to her feet, sensing Lanky moving quickly to her side.

The form of the Ensi emerged on the far side of the path of gold. As she moved towards them, the glow of the golden path dimmed – but did not completely die. She studied the glowing path for a brief moment, then turned and walked away. "Follow me," she commanded. "The storyteller is here."

CHAPTER TWENTY

His story surprised me. His people did well to remember.

$\mathcal{J}$essica's mind raced as she sat beside Lanky on soft furs to one side of the marble pentagon. To their right stood a quivering Kapano, head down and clearly wishing he was anywhere but here. Ahead, the leader of the Ka sat slouched against the arm of her throne, spinning a flat golden nugget between the fingers of one hand. *Gold. Why all the gold?* And why had it reacted as it had, glowing in their wake? *It sensed our presence; it reacted to us, to the Ensi.*

"You may begin," the Ensi said, eyes still focussed on the spinning nugget.

Jessica frowned. "I don't understand. Begin what?"

"You wished to speak with this man." The Ensi flicked the nugget into the air. "Explain what you want from him."

Jessica stared at the Ensi, confused. What trickery was this?

"I hope you thought this through," Lanky muttered beside her. "Whatever *this* is."

Thought this through? How could anyone have thought this through? They had come here with the intent to find the Kade, but now it felt like she was caught in a surreal dream. *It was you who asked to hear this man's story,* she reminded herself.

Her attention turned to the weathered old man. *Keep moving. Find out what you can, while you can.* "Kapano," she said softly. He raised his head and faced her. She gestured to the Ensi. "Have you seen this woman before?"

Kapano flashed a glance to the throne, then looked back to the ground.

"You may answer any question without fear for yourself or family," the Ensi said evenly, closing her hand around the golden nugget.

So, was the old man fearing a reprisal if he spoke freely? Jessica glanced at the Ensi, studying the woman's calm yet resolute face. *The culture – the fear – starts at the top.* She looked back to Kapano. "Have you?" she repeated.

Kapano shook his head.

He tells the truth, Jessica thought, carefully studying the man's face, his demeanour, every twitch of a muscle. "I thank you for your assistance, Kapano, which was freely given to strangers. You—"

"I was told to bring you here," Kapano blurted out, a spasm of guilt in his wizened face as he looked across at Jessica. "But I meant you no harm. I …" He glanced towards the throne, then he dropped his head, eyes downcast. "I was pleased to be helping our neighbour, the guard. It was …" He trailed off, looking miserable.

Jessica saw a genuine pain etched in the man's face. It seemed he had simply been trying to make new friends. Friends with contacts that may be useful. "You did nothing wrong," she said, softening her voice.

Kapano looked up. "You're not in trouble, are you?"

Aside from the risk of never leaving this place? She smiled at him. "Not by your hand." She saw an easing of his pain, but a tension remained. She realised he was a brave man to ask questions in the presence of … of who? What exactly was the Ensi to him? "Do you know who this woman is?"

The old man licked his lips. "The Ensi," he murmured, shifting uncomfortably. "The leader of the Ka. The leader of the place I would call home."

Jessica glanced at the Ensi, who calmly watched her. *He chooses to call this place his home and she, his leader. What does he see that we don't?* She turned back to the old man. "When we spoke last, you told us you hold your tribe's story. Would you tell it now?"

"Now?" the old man said in surprise. "I don't think—"

"Proceed with your tale," commanded the Ensi from her throne.

Kapano flinched.

Jessica saw the tension in the man's body. *He's a bag of nerves.* Did the Ensi strike fear into all her people like this? "The essence of the story only," she said calmly. "As much or as little as you wish to share."

"What are you doing?" Lanky hissed to her side. "This is insane."

"Following my intuition," she whispered back.

Fidgeting with his hands, Kapano flicked his eyes to Jessica. Then he nodded. "I will tell."

Jessica saw him take a deep breath, then watched in amazement as the old man stood taller, a burgeoning strength seeming to build within him. The apprehension slipped away, and he looked out over their heads as though addressing an expectant crowd.

And then he spoke. A rich, melodic voice swept across the chamber.

"The Void. A place mankind today would fear, seeing only darkness and empty space, ephemeral reflections of themselves.

"But within this darkness – within the Void – lay the A'an, the pure essence of *being*, the primordial creators."

Jessica watched, transfixed, Kapano's mellifluous voice caressing her mind.

"The sacred energy of the A'an permeated the Void. They *were* the Void. This was a place with no beginning, no end; the Void was eternal; the A'an were eternal.

"And the A'an held the Truths. The simple and wondrous Truths of all existence. Truths forming the very fabric of the Void."

Kapano paused and climbed a step of the pentagonal platform.

"As aeons passed, the A'an evolved, diversifying, creating new forms of energy, new beings. Original life in its purest form, untainted by what was to come.

"These magnificent new energies – these offspring of the A'an – permeated the Void, ever growing and evolving, yet always beholden to the A'an and their Truths.

"And in time they begat the greatest of their children: Kaos.

"The A'an were pleased with what they saw, but knew more could be done. Working as one, they drew mighty strands of a sacred energy from a cauldron of unimaginable power.

"Weaving and tightening these miraculous strands, the A'an bound them together, drawing them even closer, compressing the whole into a space no larger than this chamber.

"They created their first Continuum."

As Kapano paused, Jessica shot Lanky an astonished glance. "Pretty story," he growled under his breath. "When does it finish?"

She turned back to Kapano, who had climbed another step.

"This Continuum grew, expanded, and within its realm birthed new entities, the like never witnessed before in the Void.

"Forged within the realm of the Continuum, these simple bodies had no life, and yet were alive. Silent and noble wanderers of the A'an's new creation.

"The Continuum had birthed all we see around us: the stars, the sun – and our Land. A vast, wondrous creation of which we glimpse but a fragment in our night sky."

Kapano smiled.

"The A'an delighted in their creation, seeing a beauty unparalleled in the Void. A beauty of form and individuality, each voyager of the Continuum independent and unique, so different from the pervasive, expansive life energy of the Void.

"Yes, this new Continuum pleased the A'an, and so they travelled the Void, birthing Continuum after Continuum. None alike, yet all sharing a simple beauty, each shining brightly within the Void."

He stepped onto the marble platform.

"And still, the A'an did not rest. Each Continuum had beauty but lacked the Truths. They were barren islands floating in the Void.

"Returning to this Continuum – the original, *ours* – the A'an were reminded of its immense beauty, its wondrous simplicity. And so they created a new life – a new spark of energy – honouring the singular glorious essence of this first Continuum.

"They chose a single place, a single Land. *Our* Land.

"And they created the first Life – *our* Life, *our* ancestors – infusing it with the original Truths.

"The A'an looked upon their creation and were pleased. The Continuum glowed both from the purity of the Truths and from its wondrous beauty."

Kapano frowned.

"But this did not last.

"The A'an left this place to continue their work elsewhere in the Void. They left our Land untended.

"They made a mistake."

Kapano ran his tongue around his lips. The Ensi clicked her fingers, and a woman ran from a shadowy alcove and passed the grateful man a skin of water. Jessica watched him slake his thirst. *He talks of the Land in the same way as the Iyes.* Coincidence or something more?

Kapano's attention returned to his audience.

"The Life created within our Continuum developed and evolved and over time lost sight of the Truths. These were diluted, lost, until only corrupted remnants of the original Truths remained.

"Life had lost its meaning.

"And the corruption of the Truths spread, poisoning the Continuum and threatening to break free, infecting the Void. This single, tainted speck of sand threatened the corruption of all.

"In time, the A'an discovered what had happened, realised their horrific mistake. This could not be; this stain could not spread from the Continuum into the Void, the pure Void. But how to correct it? The A'an could not enter, else the corruption would taint them.

"The A'an needed help. And so they searched within the Void, until at last, a champion was found. One who could restore order, restore the Truths.

"The Void found Kaos."

Kapano regarded them with a fervent gaze.

"Kaos toiled night and day, through aeons and aeons, endeavouring to restore the Truths to the Continuum. But he found Life in their ignorance thwarted him, continuing to feed the corrupted Truths.

"Forlorn and alone in a chasm of despair, Kaos thought his task lost when he sensed the faintest touch of the original Truths. He detected a life-form that listened to – and heard – his message! A people willing to help him with his quest.

"He found this Land. He found followers of the Truths."

Kapano's eyes shone brightly, all tension flown.

"Kaos spoke to these people; he spoke to the tribes.

"And my tribe was such a people, countless generations in the past. 'One will come,' Kaos told them. 'The Saviour, the redeemer of your people. Wait – and be ready.'"

There was movement from the throne.

Jessica glanced up at the Ensi, who sat proudly on the throne, her glistening emerald-green eyes studying Kapano intently.

Kapano caught her gaze – his own gaze lingered, then he gasped and dropped to one knee.

Jessica frowned. *Something has been revealed to him. But what?*

"Rise and continue … Keeper," the Ensi murmured, leaning back on her throne.

Jessica glanced at Kapano, who stared at the Ensi with a mix of astonishment and awe – and a returned undercurrent of fear. *He called himself a Keeper. And the Ensi recognised it. How? Just from his storytelling?*

"Continue," the Ensi commanded.

The old man scrambled to his feet. He licked his lips as he composed himself, slowly recovering the poise he had lost.

"Kaos readied his people," he said, his voice steadying. "He readied those people who could bring the Truths back to the Land, to the Continuum."

His voice found its tone, his demeanour settled.

"Yet unknown to Kaos, another had entered the Continuum. One intent on destruction. A devil known as IY. And with him, IY brought the Destroyers, thrusting them into the Continuum to wage war on Kaos's people and to destroy the Truths."

"The Destroyers, the most contemptible evil the Continuum has seen. They slaughtered anything and everything in their path in their fervid, apocalyptic zeal to wipe out the Life of this Land. To destroy the last of the Truths.

"Only Kaos and his people stood in their path, forestalling them, pushing them back. In time, with unimaginable losses, Kaos and his people succeeded, banishing the Destroyers from the Continuum. The battle was won ... but the war was not.

"The Destroyers returned. Time and time again, they returned."

Kapano stood tall.

"But Kaos told us not to lose hope, not to lose faith. We were told salvation would arrive; we were told to wait for the Saviour."

Kapano glanced again at the Ensi. This time, he didn't look away.

"It is told a woman will come – a woman with green eyes – and together with Kaos, they will finally cast the evil from this Land. They will restore the Truths. They will rid the Land of the Destroyers."

He lifted his head high and spoke to the Ensi.

"And Kaos's people will support the Saviour."

The old man stood proud and tall for a moment longer, then his head slowly dropped, and his shoulders bent, until he became yet again a simple old man looking unsure of why he was standing before those with such power. "This is the essence of my people's creed," he murmured to Jessica. "Is there more you wish me to tell?"

She stared at Kapano, dumbfounded by what she'd just heard. How could he have come by such a story? A story casting IY as the devil and Kaos as the defender of his people?

He believes it to be true – as the Iyes believe their Story.

And the green-eyed Ensi. *He acts as though he has found the Saviour of his tale.*

She felt as though she stood on the edge of a storm-lashed cliff, swaying as surging gusts howled around her. *I could so easily fall ...*

But which way? Where did the truth lie?

I believe the Iyes.

But I heard verity behind the words of this old man.

Can both contain truths?

Her thoughts storm-lashed, she shook her head in answer to Kapano, then turned to Lanky. He was studying the old man with an intense, unwavering gaze. Then he climbed to his feet and walked towards the storyteller. Three black-tunicked guards immediately stepped into his path, their wicked obsidian-tipped spears aimed at his chest.

"Hold!" the Ensi commanded. "Allow him forward."

Lanky glared at the three guards. They relaxed their stances and dropped their spears to their sides, but their hateful gazes remained locked on him. He took another step, then looked up at Kapano, who remained standing on the low marble platform. "I have a question for you."

Kapano looked down at him in surprise. "You talk. I thought—"

"Yes, I talk. Answer me this. Do you swear on your god and your granddaughter that what you've said here is the truth of your tale?"

"I do," the old man said immediately. "I do not lie." His thick brow furrowed. "Who are you?"

The Ensi stood up from her throne. "You may go."

One of the black-tunicked guards immediately walked over to the old man. "Come."

Kapano flicked his eyes to Jessica. "Who are you?" he asked once again.

Jessica tensed, the old man's words triggering sudden inner turmoil. *Who am I? Who are we?* A cascade of vivid memories hurtled through her mind. Of Naga. Of the Warriors. Of the putrid stench of death from the daemons of the Dark. And of a primordial presence in the Staff – a presence with the enigmatic scent of the past. As if in a dream, she answered. "We seek the truth," she said, the words flowing from her lips without thought. "And we are your saviour."

She blinked. Where had that come from?

"Come!" repeated the guard, grasping Kapano's arm. Bowing briefly to the Ensi, Kapano then quickly followed the guard across the marble platform and out of the chamber. Lanky's mistrustful, sidelong gaze followed him all the way.

"I hope you found what you were hoping for," the Ensi said, looking directly at Jessica as she approached.

Within a lingering fog of confusion, Jessica found herself drawn to the woman's eyes: their beguiling beauty, their sense of mystery, of things untold. *They are alive with promise. What stories could they tell?* She took a step forward—

The Ensi turned her head, averting her gaze.

Jessica stumbled, caught her balance, then stood, uncertain what had just happened.

"Be careful, Warrior," the Ensi said, turning back to face Jessica. "You don't want to go there. Not yet."

Her heart racing, Jessica glanced up at the Ensi. She focussed her gaze on the woman's short hair. *Her eyes have an allure, a deadly attraction. Therein lies her power.*

"It is late. Consider what you have heard, and we shall talk on the morrow." The Ensi spun and walked away.

"Wait!" Jessica called, grasping for a question half formed and not yet understood.

The Ensi halted, her back to Jessica.

What was it she'd heard? What had jarred?

IY ...

She licked her dry lips. "Kapano's story ... He spoke of IY as male. Is that right?"

The Ensi spoke without turning. "Is that of importance within all you have heard?"

The IY I've met is a woman. Who is the IY of the old man's story? Her gaze fixed on the Ensi, who stood, unmoving, Jessica hesitated. Was this important? In all she'd heard and seen, did that one part of the old man's tale matter in this moment? "No, maybe not," she murmured.

"Then maybe, for now, it shouldn't matter to you." The Ensi strode towards her throne.

Two of the black-tunicked guards stepped to either side of Jessica and Lanky and gestured to the chamber's exit. Her mind spinning, Jessica glanced back at the Ensi as the guards led them away. The leader of the Ka now sat on her throne, alone within an empty chamber. What game was this woman playing? *And why am I playing it?*

Exiting the chamber, her fraught thoughts tumbled down a disturbing path. *I know why I play.* Because this leader of the Ka was not what she'd expected. Yes, she appeared to be a feared leader of her people. Yes, she was leading her people towards a murderous war with the Iyes. *And don't forget her people killed Naga and many other Iyes since.* And yet she told a story so familiar. Of an ancient enemy. Of destroyers of her people. *And the old man tells it too.*

Two enemies. Two stories. So which one was true?

And who is pulling the strings? came a distant thought as if from another.

Walking on through the passageway, she glanced at Lanky, seeing his face still as thunder. She needed time to talk with him, to decide what to do now. *Because we're still alive, and we need to stay alive. And I need to decide what to believe.*

*

Qiax stepped out of the shadows. "This is a dangerous game, my liege. Are you sure of this path?"

The woman on the throne before him sat, eyes closed, hands resting on her thighs. A woman whose life he had watched so very closely

287

before she had been chosen, a life – unknown to her – he had helped save many times.

As I try to save so many others.

But now a net closed around them, and he could see no easy way out.

Not yet.

The Ensi's eyes opened with a flash of green. "No," came her quiet voice from the throne. "Nothing is now certain."

"Krull has arrived. Cobra will make his move soon."

"That, we both know."

When she said nothing more, he tested further. "Why not act now?"

"I wish to be sure all players are revealed. And I wish to give the Warriors time. Especially this one they call the Guardian." Her green eyes flicked to Qiax. "The daemon spy has revealed much, but there is more here unseen. Unknown. And that intrigues me. What might this offer to me and my people?"

"And if you can't persuade them to join you?"

"Then they die," came the Ensi's immediate answer. "Along with Krull."

Qiax felt the first stab of unease. "Krull is strong. He—"

"Enough, my friend. We let the game play. That is all we can do tonight."

Qiax made to respond, then caught himself. Within this game within a game, he could only do so much before unwanted eyes were drawn to him. And that couldn't be. *Because while my leader seeks to save her people, I seek to save all.*

CHAPTER TWENTY-ONE

How different the Warriors through time, each striving to serve the Light. Some succeeded. Some failed. Of those I saw, one I favoured above all others. But to tell ... well, that would be unfair.

Shadow shivered as a sudden gust released a shower of droplets from the rain-soaked tree canopy above him. He was cold, miserable, and hungry. *But we're still alive, and you've been in tricky positions before, Shadow. Stay calm. The opportunity will come.*

He glanced up, peering through a jagged fork in the gnarled branches. He knew the sun must be low, but not much could be seen through the dark, ragged clouds scudding across the sky, or through the relentless rain streaking past the cliff tops into the deep gorge. *Not a pleasant place to be caught in a flood,* he thought, looking down at the swelling stream swirling past to his right. He shivered again. Why would anyone choose to live in a place like this? Cold, wet, and gloomy much of the time.

And getting colder with each sun-cycle. "The ice is finally pushing south into the lands of the Iyes," the Shade had told them. "And so the waters of life will return to our lands." Shadow grimaced. *If* they could halt the Warriors; they were proving hard to kill. "And stay killed," he muttered to himself. The woman he'd fought – aeons past, it seemed now – had first survived the Ka poison from his blade, then later somehow escaped the clutches of the Ancient. This enemy was proving a most impressive opponent. *One I'd have preferred on my side, rather than against me.*

Yes, this Warrior was impressive – and smart. She and the Iyes had known they were coming and laid a brave and aggressive trap. *So much for the brilliant plan of our Shade,* he thought with disgust. But how had the Iyes known? A traitor in the Ka homeland? But who? Who knew of the Shade's mission?

None, beyond them and the Ensi.

So maybe not a Ka traitor.

Shadow's eyes narrowed at remembered words of Growl before they left. "They have made our task easier … if their daemon speaks true." He suddenly understood; Growl had been working with an Iyes daemon, a Warrior daemon. *An Iyes traitor.*

But somehow, even with the skill and cunning of an Iyes daemon on their side, that unkillable Warrior had known what was happening. *Somehow, she knew. Krez! This Warrior even fooled our Shade.* The image of the Warrior's face came unbidden to his mind. A strange face, an exotic face. Not the face of a killer. *But then neither is mine.*

He released a slow breath. Whatever had happened – however it had happened – the reality was here in this moment. They were hated prisoners in the midst of an enemy camp. He felt the rough, gnarly bark of the tree digging into his back. *This tree might be my last close companion, and a cold one at that.*

Feeling the faintest tendrils of fear snaking within him, he quickly pushed them away. Fear stalked as hope's mortal enemy. It would not snare him. Shifting his weight slightly, he subtly flexed his arms and legs, once again testing his bindings …

He suppressed a fierce surge of elation. His ankles remained tightly bound, but finally he felt the slightest movement in the straps around his wrists. *Now we have a chance!* He stilled his hands. *Give nothing away.*

He glanced at his three captors, who squatted in a makeshift shelter, warming themselves by a well-tended fire. Talking in low voices, two guards seemed in good humour, but the third – a battle-scarred, hungry-eyed veteran, clearly the guards' leader – watched his captives like a hawk. *No chance of escape with him around. But he can't stay awake forever. So be patient. Look for the weakness.* "We'd be pleased to join you by that fire," he called, fixing his eyes on the youngest. "And if you have wine, just a small cup would suffice."

The young man scowled. "Would you like your food first, or the wine?"

"Ah, now there's a choice," Shadow said, his stomach arguing for the food. "Maybe both together. Yes, that would be best. And for my friends."

"Quiet!" the scarred veteran growled. "One word more will be your last."

Shadow cast his eyes down. *I may be loose with my mouth, but not with my life. That man would kill me without hesitation.*

290

He turned his thoughts to the events inside the cave. Whichever way he looked at it, the Iyes had fooled the Shade. But how could Growl have misread that situation so badly? A word floated past, and he grabbed it. "Arrogance," he muttered to himself. Growl had been so sure of himself, and of his plan, that he'd discussed it with none of them. His troubled gaze drifted to the driving rain. This was not the Growl he knew. The Growl he had worked with for these last few sun-cycles had been clinical and sure, the planning flawless. So what had changed?

The daemon.

And that was worrying. If Growl's daemon was indeed coming to the fore, influencing the Shade's actions, then this mission had proved it was fallible; it made mistakes that Growl wouldn't have made. *And that's a problem for all of us – it could get us killed.*

Killed? A disturbing scene played once again. Of Growl taking a step towards him with death in his eyes. But had he misread Growl's action, misread the hate in the man's face? "I know what I saw," he murmured to himself. He licked his dry lips. But why now? *Maybe because I've become a thorn in the side of the other Disciples. Maybe because I'm asking too many questions.* And why here? *Because they can say I died in action. That would appease those who support me.*

His brooding gaze flicked to Sy, who was bound to the adjacent tree, his eyes closed. Had he read his actions clearly? Would his monk truly turn against him? *For sure,* he thought grimly. It was what they were there for. *To keep us on the path, to make sure we don't stray. And he warned me to keep my mouth shut.*

He drew his gaze away and looked out into the rain. It seemed he was a marked man by his own people. Growl for sure. *And Sy?* He hoped not. He really hoped he hadn't lost his friend. But those worries were for another time; first, they had to escape. *Remain calm and focussed. Stay alive and wait for the opportunity. It will come.*

*

Amber tied off the leather strapping around River's waist, cutting the loose ends and handing them to Tricia. "The poultice will stem the bleeding. Healing? Having seen the wounds you Warriors have survived, I doubt this will trouble you for long, Mother. Even so, take care, nothing is certain."

"Of that, there can be no doubt," River replied with a faint smile.

"Are you sure that … thing is safe?" Tricia asked again, dropping the discarded straps into a blood-stained bundle of moss, remnants from Amber's work.

River looked out from the shelter and through the driving rain to the cave beyond. "For now."

Maybe, Beth thought grimly. The daemon within the shaman was a deadly threat, and the Spirits were struggling to hold it. She heard River groan as the girl shifted her position. "Sorry," she said with a pang of guilt. "Guess the blade went in deeper than I'd planned."

River managed a smile. "It had to be real – it had to be my blood."

Else the Shade's daemon would have sensed something wrong.

"So, how long had this been planned?" Tricia asked, kneeling down and washing her hands in a bowl of water by her side.

Beth grunted. "A plan? You think there was a plan?"

"You're joking, right?"

"There was a plan of sorts," River said quickly. "But only in here." She tapped her head. "No one could know." She glanced at Beth. "Until they needed to know."

But you should have told me earlier. That was hard.

"It worked, I guess," Tricia said with a grimace. "But at a terrible price."

Tarla. The young maker. Another innocent lost due to the brutal ambitions of another.

"No one could know," River repeated quietly.

Tricia looked up. "But you told Jess and the others, right?"

"She knows what she needs to know."

"But what was left unsaid? You sure they should've left?"

River held Tricia's challenging gaze. "What better time to visit the Ka than when their most lethal weapon is away?"

"Most lethal? Are you sure about that? You neutralised this shaman pretty quickly. If these people are as deadly as you say, they must have more powerful weapons than him?"

Beth glanced at River. Neither said anything.

"Well?" Tricia said, her eyes narrowing.

"The Shade is contained," River answered, "but not, as you put it, neutralised. That is proving ... difficult."

Beth tensed. The Shade fought with a fury they'd not encountered so far. *He has the aid of his daemon.* The Spirits needed help.

"And Jessica and the others?" Tricia said quietly. "Any news?"

"No, but it is still early."

No news, because we can't contact them, Beth thought grimly. It was as though they'd vanished from the Land. But in this moment, there was nothing to be done. *Three days. We agreed to three days.*

"Well," Amber said, climbing to her feet, "we're finished here. Our next patient awaits." She slung her pack over her shoulder, picked up the water bowl, then turned to River. "We'll change the dressing tomorrow."

"Thanks, Amber. And thanks, Tricia."

"No problem," Tricia said, standing then gathering the bloodied pile of moss in her arms. "Try not to get stabbed again before it heals." River gave a faint smile. Tricia glanced at Beth. A shadow of concern crossed her eyes. "I hope they're okay."

"They're smart. They're strong. We have to believe in them." *But, yes, that doesn't stop us worrying.*

Tricia's gaze lingered for a moment, then she nodded, and together with Amber left the shelter, hurrying away through the downpour.

There was silence, save for the hammering of rain out in the gorge.

"It's been a while since we spoke alone," River said, eventually. "As friends."

"A long time," Beth acknowledged, thinking of the strained tension between them since her return to the tribe and their flight south. *We've been two women, scarred by happenings beyond our comprehension.* "Not since I left with your father and the others on the mission to recover the Staff." *Bear, Svana, Knuckles, Shorty, and Scorpion – all still missing.* "Still no word?"

River looked away, gazing into the fire. "The scouts have seen nothing of them. I fear that after your capture by the Ancient, they continued their journey north. Since you and the Staff are here ... well, we have spoken enough of this already."

A wound she doesn't want to reopen right now. Beth studied River's battle-scorched face as she stared into the fire. It was a face belying the complexity of the girl beneath – *of the emerging woman.* Here sat a formidable shaman and Warrior aligned to IY – but beneath lay a girl mourning her father, and a girl scarred by the unexpected, misunderstood glimpses of her future world.

"You called us friends," Beth said, brushing a spider off her leg. "I was never sure you saw me as a friend back then. You tried to kill me when we first met, remember?"

River glanced at her. "I knew nothing. And I was young and angry."

Beth smiled. *We're all still young and angry.* "I should be careful then. That was not so long ago."

A small smile crossed River's lips, then she gazed back into the fire. "It was not. And yet it is."

"The Transfer?"

River's eyes glimmered in the firelight. "Nothing can prepare you for that vicious torrent of knowledge, that vast onslaught of alien images and voices, those raw feelings of all IY's shamans who came

293

before. It was too sudden, too soon after our discovering I was a Warrior. And too close to seeing your land."

Beth caught the sense of a deeply entrenched, visceral fear within River. *The future. She hated what she saw. She won't let it go.* And *was* it fear she saw? Or anger? Rage? "You know," she probed, "Jessica was worried that you were pulling away from us, questioning whether to support us."

Continuing to gaze into the fire, River remained silent.

So, was Jessica right?

"So much ... and so quickly," River said in a low voice. "I was not ready, not attuned to the Spirits."

She talks again of the Transfer; she avoids my question. "Don't knock yourself," Beth said, pulling back from her quiet challenge. "It wouldn't be easy for anyone to deal with what we've had to confront." *IY, the daemons, the Ka, the Ancient, the traitor ...*

And the voice within.

Bethusa.

She gasped at a sudden, startling vision. Of her striding out, a lightning storm blazing from her Axe, engulfing the roaming daemon, Alkazar, within a ferocious blaze. As the cursed daemon desperately tried to flee, she smiled, loping easily in its wake with a terrifying power rippling through her. She lifted her Axe—

River squeezed her hand. "Are you okay?"

Beth shivered as the vivid scene vanished. "I saw myself fighting Alkazar at the mountain. You were there. Is this my memory – or another's?"

River held Beth's gaze for a moment, then squeezed her hand again. "You fought well. You saved us that night. But *your* memory? For that, you should ask the other."

Beth heard the faintest of reproaches in River's tone. *She wishes me to engage Bethusa and bring her to this fight.* She turned and gazed blindly out into the driving rain. *And maybe she's right. Maybe it is time for me to understand who I am, what I've been.*

She looked back at River, who was silently watching her. "You seem to accept the one within you. Do you know who she is? What she is?" Questions asked before, but never answered. *She said she didn't know.*

River pulled her shawl close around her, drawing it to her neck. She gazed into the fire, and Beth thought she wouldn't answer. Then the girl's eyes seemed to focus on something only she could see. "Revri was of an ancient mountain people to the east," she said in a soft voice. "A woman with a child, a woman with dreams. And then the Ka came. Her home was destroyed, her people slaughtered. Her child slaughtered. All because the Ka sought the rich stone of their mountain." River leaned forward. "Left for dead, Revri escaped in the moonless night, beginning a tortuous and harrowing flight through conquered lands. For a full turn of the moon, she sought refuge in many places, but those lands were changed, tainted, suffering under the rule of those who brought new beliefs, new punishments for the disbelievers. No one would risk harbouring a stranger, and so on she fled, welcomed by no one, aided by no one, surviving day by day as she could. It was only a chance encounter, a crossing of two disparate lives, that saved her. She met a shaman."

The fire cast wavering shadows across River's sculpted face, its fiery light glistening in enigmatic eyes that gazed into the distance. *She sees her past.* Beth's brow furrowed. *River, or Revri?*

"The shaman was a lone traveller but had a destination in mind. Revri followed him; he welcomed the company. He proved a master of deception, and they travelled through those conquered lands as though they were the very Ka themselves. Finally breaking out of the Ka territories, they travelled onwards, ever westward, through deep valleys and across vast plains, the memories of her family still burning in her heart. They travelled onwards until they reached a tribe, the shaman's destination. The tribe of IY. The Iyes. They invited the young woman in. They accepted her. They healed her."

Beth watched a calmness settle on the girl's face. "The shaman also stayed and became as a father to her. He taught her many things; he shared the secrets of the shaman – of the Light. Revri listened. She learnt. And slowly, inexorably, unnoticed by others, something grew within her.

"Then one day – a fine day promising much – the enemy attacked. They attacked with daemons of the Dark. They killed the shaman … but they unleashed the Warrior. A Warrior who needed no guidance; she knew what to do."

River blinked, then smiled. "Much more remains to be told of the story of Revri, but this suffices for now, I think. Only to say, she defeated the daemons that day – and many, many more after. This was her skill: finding roaming daemons of the Dark and destroying them." River tilted her head. "And you asked what she is? She is a friend. An ally."

Beth looked at River, amazed. How did the girl do it? She was the Iyes's Mother, a Warrior, and a shaman. And she'd accepted the presence of the ancient Warrior Revri, both working seamlessly as one.

And yet I can't accept Bethusa.

Why?

Because I don't trust her. I fear her. She grimaced. *And I don't trust myself.*

She realised she sat with her head in her hands.

Frustrated anger surged. That woman from a distant age, Revri, had lost all – her home, her family, her people – but she'd embraced the Warrior she became. *So, why should I be afraid?* She raised her head. The tribe needed her help. Her friends needed her help. *I am a Warrior. I need to fight.*

And Bethusa?

Bethusa stays where she is for now. But release Beth, the Warrior.

She climbed to her feet, then pulled on the A'ven, allowing it to course into her being. Into her body and mind. Into her spirit.

I am Beth!

'*And I am Bethusa.*'

Ignoring the strident voice, she opened herself fully to the Light's energy, and a deep, rippling pleasure rushed through her, the rich life force of the A'ven flooding her veins with a strength and vitality she struggled to contain. It was a wondrous sensation, one she'd so greatly missed. *With this power, I can defeat gods.* Savouring the glorious taste of the Land's sweet nectar, she slowly calmed the surging torrent to a swirling river, then the river to a rippling stream, then the stream to a gentle trickle. Revitalised, energised, she drew a deep lungful of air. *Be ready for what is to come. Because I am a Warrior.*

"I see you have chosen your path."

Beth blinked, then glanced at River. "You need help. You need me."

River was silent for a moment. "Another has offered to bond with you."

"Another daemon?"

River nodded.

Beth shook her head. "I'm not so sure about that."

"Without it, you lose a companion in battle, one who watches your back."

Beth scowled. "Like Garrion, you mean?"

"Garrion was a traitor."

"And this new daemon?"

River held Beth's challenging gaze. "There are risks in all we do, Warrior. But the Spirits have no doubts about the one who would bond with you. And if we start down the path of trusting no one, then where will that end?"

Beth knew River was right, yet the pain of Garrion's betrayal remained keen. "Tomorrow. I'll decide tomorrow."

River inclined her head. "So be it. Then let us move on." She climbed to her feet. "We need to plan our destruction of the Shade. That will not be easy."

The cold reality of the world outside the rock shelter slammed into Beth. *The Shade remains a danger to us. He must be dealt with.* Rain splattered her face as a gust blew flurries beneath the shelter roof. "Has anyone interrogated the Ka assassins yet? What can they tell us of this Shade?"

"We have, but nothing. They will spend the night in the cold to free their tongues. If not ..."

If not, they won't be around too much longer. They killed Tarla – that will be avenged. Beth gripped her Axe tightly. "I want to speak with these vermin. And I know where to start."

*

"I hope you're enjoying our hospitality?" Beth said, walking up to the captives and stepping inside the shelter of the tree's canopy. "We even provided you protection from the rain."

The lean, hard-eyed woman secured to a tree on her left sneered and spat at Beth. Gravel immediately walked over and struck the woman on the side of the head – hard. The woman grunted as her head violently rocked to the side. She turned back, glaring at Gravel with hate-filled eyes.

Ignoring the woman, Beth flicked her gaze past the seemingly relaxed long-haired prisoner in the centre to the figure tied to the tree on her right. Tall, his head shaven save for the strip of black hair tied at the back, the man regarded her with a calm intensity. As the others, he had a lithe, powerful frame, and eyes brimming with a fierce intelligence.

All three are killers.

And all three were shivering with the cold.

She focussed on the gaze of the shaven-headed man. "What's your name?"

The man's eyes held hers, but he said nothing.

"He can't speak," said the long-haired prisoner in the centre. "At least not in a way you would understand."

Gravel walked up to him and struck him hard in the stomach. "Talk when spoken to," he growled.

"I just—"

Gravel hit him again.

"Maybe you would like to talk now," Beth said to the shaven-headed man. "What is your name?"

297

The man held her gaze but offered no answer.

As Gravel strode towards the shaven-headed man, Beth barked a command. "Hold!"

Scowling, Gravel halted, glaring at the silent man.

Beth also studied him. Could it be that he couldn't speak? She fixed her gaze on the young Ka who certainly had no problem speaking – the man who had almost killed her with his poisoned blade. Similarly attired to his silent colleague, he looked as he had when they'd fought: a neat, sculpted beard on a strong-featured face, sleek black hair bound at the back of his neck. He was struggling to catch his breath, not helped by the tight binding around his neck. Gravel was keeping them alive but showing little mercy.

"We meet for the second time, Ka," she said, walking up to the bound man. "This time, not so lucky for you." She cocked her head. "I believe I owe you something. What was it now? Ah, yes, a poisoned blade. I—"

The man rasped a cough, then: "Third," he mumbled.

"What?" Beth said, not understanding.

He hacked another cough. "Third time we meet," he managed. "May not remember the last ... Being dead as you were ... Or so I thought. You're more difficult to kill than—"

"Silence!" Gravel hissed, striding back towards the man.

Beth gently grasped the Shield's arm. "It's okay, Gr ..." She stopped herself. No names in front of the enemy, Gravel had advised her. "I'll deal with this one as needed."

"Yes, Gr," Shadow said. "This woman can—"

Beth hit him hard in the stomach.

The man grunted, then hacked a cough, gasping for breath.

"Don't play games, Ka. That won't end well. What's your name?"

The Ka sucked in ragged lungfuls of air, then: "Names are valuable," he wheezed.

"Strip him," Beth said, standing back.

Drawing blades, Darius and Firuz stepped forward and quickly sliced through the man's tunic before ripping it off him. They reached for his leggings—

"Shadow. My name is Shadow."

"You weak fool," snarled the woman to the man's right.

Beth gestured to Darius and Firuz. "Stand down – for the moment." She waited for them to walk back to the fire, then regarded the now bare-chested man with a cold gaze. "And her name?"

"Nefra." Straining against the binding around his neck, the man tilted his head towards the bound figure to his left. "And that's Sy. He can't talk – no voice."

Nefra spat at him, then muttered angrily under her breath.

"So, you are Shadow of the Ka." Beth said. "A killer of innocents." She tilted her head. "But a simple assassin or something more? What are you, Shadow?"

"Don't answer!" Nefra grated. "Don't give this scum anything."

Beth walked over to the woman and punched her hard in the stomach. Not a pleasant thing to do, but they didn't have the luxury of time. And these were not pleasant people.

Leaving the woman gasping, she turned back to the man named Shadow. "Answer. What are you?"

"I am a Disciple of the Ensi of the Ka."

She heard a curse from one of the men by the fire.

"Quiet," Gravel growled.

Beth stared at the prisoner, clamping hold on astonishment. A Disciple. One of only four or five, from what Rind had said. As close to the Ensi as the Shade. She held her voice steady. "And so, Disciple, what is your mission?"

"To assassinate your shaman – and you."

"You will desist, worm!" yelled the bound woman. "Here," she snarled at Beth. "Here is my answer!" She spat at her again.

"Gag her, then strip her," Beth growled.

The woman fought like a tiger against her leashes, continuing a raging tirade against both Beth and the one known as Shadow. *There's a history between these two,* Beth thought, watching as they secured a binding between the woman's teeth before cutting away her tunic. *Maybe this will calm her down … or maybe not.*

She looked back at the man in the centre.

He was staring coolly back at her.

He controls himself well. He's dangerous.

You knew that already. Her response … or Bethusa's?

But he seems willing to talk.

Yes, because he knows it will buy him time – to seek his escape.

But we need answers.

She made a decision. "Cut him from the tree, making sure of his bindings, then hobble him. Then fetch two more guards and escort him to the middle shelter." She turned to Gravel. "Join me and the others shortly."

Gravel walked up beside her, holding his mouth close to her ear. "Are you sure of this, Warrior?"

"We need answers," she said quietly but firmly. And if this Ka was willing to talk, then she needed to get him away from the other prisoners. What they could believe of the assassin's words, well, that remained to be seen.

Leaving the disquieted Gravel, she walked back through the rain to find Parig and the others.

*

"Why is he here, and not dead?" growled the mountain known as Parig, prowling around the rock shelter, his head barely making its way beneath its smoke-stained roof. The huge man lumbered to a stop, then fixed his fearsome regard on Shadow.

Shadow saw death in that gaze. His death. He quickly cast his eyes down. *Thank Kaos they didn't leave me alone with that one. He wouldn't have survived it. And it seems I may not survive him yet.* Eyes still lowered, he cautiously scanned around him. The Scar stood behind him, a man whose harsh life was carved into his rugged face, each scar offering another tale of this unbreakable, unbendable character. Shadow would have better luck trying to charm a rock. By comparison, the two others by the side of the Warrior were mere children – mere babies. *If I can get time alone with them …*

Which left the Warrior.

He risked a glance up.

The woman's dark eyes still studied him. But he couldn't read them. This one was dangerous in her own way, and he needed to tread most carefully. *Give a little but hold on to all else.*

And look for the opportunity to kill her.

Easier said than done, Shadow. She must be the most difficult person in this land to kill – and keep dead.

"Why?" growled the mountain again.

"Because it speaks," the Warrior said. "And while it speaks, it lives."

"Pah! Lies, lies, and more lies is what you will get from Ka scum such as these." The mountain cast a glare of burning hatred Shadow's way. "And this one befouls his soul as a vile servant of Kaos. He is a disciple of evil and deceit, corrupting the ground he crawls upon. Beware, Warrior, of the spells he weaves with that snake tongue of his."

Shadow readied himself. *Come on, give me more. I have to make this seem real.*

The mountain obliged. "Look what these Ka have done to my daughter's people," the big man stormed. "My people will be next. These Ka are a foul plague that must be wiped from our lands—"

"As you destroy my people?" Shadow said angrily – at the same time double-checking his target on the ground.

"What!" stormed the mountain, striding over and striking Shadow across the jaw.

A crashing pain exploded in Shadow's head, and he fell sprawling to the ground. The huge man jumped on his back and hit him hard in the side of the head—

Shadow woke with a sore head and fogged mind. Someone behind him hauled him back to his feet – but not before his fingers closed around a most valuable prize.

Standing unsteadily, his vision slowly clearing, Shadow inwardly groaned as he saw the mountain sitting away to his right. From the scowl on the big man's face, he could see the brute was clearly straining against some inner leash. *And if that breaks, he will smash me to a pulp.* To have a chance of leaving alive, he needed to tread so very carefully. He steadied himself but kept his eyes downcast.

The Warrior stepped in front of him. "Who else has been sent to attack us?"

"As far as I know, only those you've seen—"

"Liar!" the mountain shouted, surging to his feet – but the Warrior faced him with an impressively hard stare, and to Shadow's relief, the brute sat back on his haunches.

The Warrior turned to Shadow. "And your armies?"

"That, I don't know. They're not under my command."

A deep growl issued from the mountain.

The Warrior's brow furrowed. "I find it hard to believe that you – part of the inner circle of your leader – don't know the movements of your army."

Shadow shrugged. "Even so, it's true. Our leader is cautious. And I have been rather busy, elsewhere." He glanced up at the Warrior. "As you know."

"You're lying!" the mountain shouted, rising to his feet. "Tell us where those armies are moving! Now! Else you die!"

The Warrior stood and walked over to the big man, then talked to him in a low voice. Shadow couldn't catch what was being said, but the mountain clearly didn't like what he was hearing and kept glancing around the woman, as if to check his victim was still there. Eventually, still scowling, the brute nodded. The Warrior and the mountain walked over to Shadow.

Is this where I die?

The mountain grasped him by the neck and hauled him violently upwards. Shadow balanced on the ends of his toes as the man's face bore down on his. The mountain bared his broken teeth, and a stream of warm, putrid breath poured over Shadow's face. "You will answer the Warrior's questions, Ka scum, else I will be back, and you will answer mine." The mountain smiled – at least Shadow thought it could have been a smile – then dropped him to the ground before striding out into the rain.

As Shadow steadied himself, the Warrior stepped in front of him. "Shall we try again before he returns? Where are your armies?"

They went around and around, but he couldn't answer her question. He honestly didn't know.

"Why are you intent on the destruction of the Iyes?"

The question threw him for a moment. He shrugged. "You're the enemy."

"Why am I the enemy?"

What trick is this? He studied her, seeing an outwardly relaxed and composed woman. A woman with deep, intelligent eyes. Sharp eyes. *A woman I could trust to fight at my side. One who looks—*

Taking a sharp breath, he took a step back.

The woman's eyes narrowed.

Kef! Don't let her draw you in, Shadow. You've seen her work; she fooled the Shade. "I don't understand," he said, somehow holding his voice steady. "You're here to destroy my people, and yet you ask me why I call you my enemy?"

"Where is your leader now?"

"That, I won't tell you."

"Who does your shaman – your Shade – serve?"

"The Ensi." *And Kaos.*

"Who does the Shade's daemon serve?"

They know of the daemon. How? "The daemon serves the Ensi," he lied.

"You lie. Who does the Shade's daemon serve?"

"The daemon serves Kaos." *Maybe. I don't know.*

"Why did you come here to kill our shaman? To kill me?"

"Because you have come to these lands to kill us."

"Who are the other people with you?"

"Sy, my good friend and protector. And Nefra, a fighter."

"And a second group?"

"If there was, I wouldn't tell you that."

"How can you sleep at night?"

What! What kind of question was that? He glared at her. She held his gaze, smiling.

He felt anger building. This wasn't a game.

She tilted her head, studying him, her smile playing on her lips.

Calm down. She's trying to get under your skin. And of course, it's a game. A game for my life. He forced himself to smile back. "I usually have a comfortable bed. Tonight might be more difficult."

"I meant how can you sleep at night knowing you kill families and their children? Knowing that you have the blood of countless innocent victims staining your hands."

He felt his anger bubbling. "I do not kill innocent people," he hissed. "I do not kill families and their children ..." He hesitated. *I kill those who plot against us.* "I do not kill children."

No sooner had the words left his mouth than he heard once again the fearful voice of the woman of the Rim. "They kill our children." His heart pounding, he stared at the Warrior before him. *She's pushing you. She's riling you. I need to—*

"Your tribe kills children, and you are one of its leaders. You—"

"No! We do not kill children!" he snapped, his anger flaring. She was wrong. The woman of the Rim was wrong. He glared at the Warrior. "You, on the other hand – Warrior – slaughter innocents in a number too vast to imagine. You kill whole peoples! Do not talk to me about killing."

He grunted as someone struck him violently on the back.

"Quiet!" ordered the voice of Scar.

"Violence is all you people know," Shadow rasped. "And you think we will simply lie down and accept it. You—"

"I said quiet!" Someone struck him harder, knocking him to the ground.

"Take him back," came the voice of the Warrior. He was hauled up by Scar and roughly led out of the shelter.

"You can't defeat us by your violence," Shadow called out as he hobbled away. "The right lies on our side."

And I have my means of escape, he thought, feeling the small blade secreted in the palm of his hand.

*

Beth watched Gravel and the others leave the shelter. "What do you think?" she asked.

"He believes he is doing right," River said, stepping out of the shadows. "As do all those who choose to serve and follow the Ka. He is a threat that must be neutralised – along with the others."

"You think we should execute them?"

"We cannot release them," River said, her hand held to her side as she walked slowly over to Beth. "And we cannot keep them with us.

You've seen the woman; she would never rest until she'd broken free of her bonds and spilt blood."

"Harsh," Beth murmured to herself.

"Yes," River said, hearing her words, "but these are harsh times."

True, but can I order someone to be killed in cold blood? "It is an option," Beth said carefully.

"No!" yelled a familiar voice. A moment later, Tricia's bedraggled head and shoulders appeared in the rain beyond the shelter's edge. "You can't just kill them!" she admonished as she walked around to the steps up to the shelter. "There has to be another way."

Beth watched her drenched friend climb the steps. "How long have you been there?"

"Long enough," Tricia said, shivering as she stopped before them. She ran her hand through her drenched hair, the tight curls springing back into shape as she swept the worst of the water away.

"And what did you hear?"

Tricia's uncertain gaze flicked between Beth and River. Then she glanced at the fire. "Can I sit there?"

Beth nodded. She watched as Tricia crossed to the fire and sat, edging closer to the heat until Beth worried her curls might catch alight. "You should dry those clothes. You'll freeze."

"I'll be fine," Tricia said, holding her hands to the fire. "And you never know who might be hiding out there, watching."

There was Tricia's humour, wielded as a defence when she was hurt or upset. Beth glanced at River. The girl glared at Tricia with undisguised anger. Beth suppressed a sigh. She too should be angry with Tricia for stepping into something she shouldn't be involved in. But in all that was happening – and in all that had happened – the truth was her friend had been abandoned. They had no time to talk as friends. *Yes, because people are trying to kill us.* Even so, she knew how hard this place had been on her friend – and could understand how difficult it would be for Tricia to hear what had just been discussed.

She crossed to Tricia's side and dropped to her haunches. "So, you heard what the assassin had to say. What do you think?"

"Sounds as though you've already made up your mind."

"Maybe," Beth said evenly. "Leaders must make hard decisions. But first, I want to hear what you thought."

Tricia said nothing.

"Come on, Trish. What's bugging you?"

Her shoulders sagged. "I don't fit here," she whispered, her anger clearly vented. "I shouldn't have come with you. This isn't my world." Her thumb traced aimless patterns on her wrist as she stared into the fire. "Oh, I like helping Amber. Think I'm good at it. I'm helping to save lives. But why?"

"Why what?" Beth said softly.

"Why all this killing? Why is this all really happening? And how can people do this to each other?"

"Because the Enemy is evil," River grated, walking towards them. "Because it seeks domination over all. It seeks to destroy us."

"But you heard the prisoner. He clearly believes *you* are trying to destroy *his* people." Tricia looked at Beth and then up at River. "And he's right on that, isn't he?"

"He is a Ka," River spat. "And the Ka's aim is to destroy all who oppose them. To help Kaos blight our lands with another age of ice." She glared at Tricia. "*That* is what he fights for. *That* is what he believes in."

Beth saw Tricia flinch in the face of River's anger. And yet she was not about to be deflected. "That's not what came across just now. What did was a man who sees the Iyes and the Warriors as people about to wage a war on them. It—"

"Words of the devil," River hissed, her eyes afire, her hands trembling with anger. "Tell me. How many people of theirs have we killed? I will tell you! Only those who came here to kill us!"

"I've heard your Story. It tells of mass killings of both Iyes and Ka. It tells of—"

"Enough! You know nothing of us. And you are not a Warrior. Do not come here and judge us. Do not defend the killers of our Mother."

Tricia's face fell. "Sorry if I offended you, River. I don't condone what's been done. I ..." She glanced at Beth, worry and uncertainty clouding her face.

Beth held up her hands in a placating gesture, then stood and walked over to the seething girl. "Tricia meant no hurt by her words. She merely answered my question. Don't judge those ignorant of the Land's history, ignorant of its legacy. Let's not fight amongst ourselves."

River remained silent for a moment longer, then the tension eased from her shoulders. "She should learn. And quickly."

"We all have much still to learn," Beth murmured, looking down at her Axe.

"Yet time is against us," the girl said, her voice subdued.

Beth looked up to see River watching her. *She admonishes me for not bonding with another daemon. But she will have to wait until I'm ready.*

"We should return to the Sacred Chamber." River threw a reproachful glance at Tricia, then walked away.

Beth watched her depart. *It's one kind of truce, I guess.* At least they weren't at each other's throats. She turned back to Tricia. "Hang in there, Trish. I know it's difficult, but we will find a way out of this." *Eventually.* "And no decision has been made – I'm seeking another way." *But if not …* She couldn't let those assassins kill again.

Tricia slowly climbed to her feet, water still dripping from her sodden clothes. "There have been too many deaths," she said, her face drawn. "But I know you hate this as much as I do." She laid her hand on Beth's shoulder. "Find that other way."

As they left the shelter together, Tricia's words lingered. Hate? No, this wasn't about what she liked or disliked; this was about doing what she had to do. *Because I am a Warrior.*

'And I am Bethusa.'

CHAPTER TWENTY-TWO

Little did he know what he had invited into his home.

$\mathcal{C}$obra watched the three men of the Guard laughing by the fire. It sickened him. He never understood the pathetic games they played, wasting away their precious lives throwing bones in the dirt. Precious? He smirked; for them, nothing could be further from the truth. They were worthless scum, no more valued than the charred fish in his food bowl – a purpose in the moment, discarded waste the next. His smirk faded as he watched Cleft throw a knucklebone. Even as a child, he had hated being dragged into games, hated the mockery meted out to him at his incompetence, and hated the feeling of self-disgust at his own failure. Yet somehow, he'd drawn that hurt deep inside, hiding it from his tormentors as he'd endured their cruel derision. And over time, he had shown them, those persecutors of his childhood, and one by one they'd fallen – an accident here, an unexplained killing there, until only one now remained.

The green-eyed witch.

Older than him by five sun-cycles, she had been unfairly pitted against him. He was but a youth, and she a captive slave and fighter. But those tormentors of his had egged him on. "This is your moment, snake," they had called. "You can finally win." But each time, he had been soundly beaten. *By a girl!* And not only beaten, maimed.

He put his hand to his missing ear. How he'd hated her.

His lips curled into a thin smile. But how well he had exacted his revenge.

Over the sun-cycles that followed the loss of his ear – and ignoring those wastrels of his youth – he'd steadfastly toiled with guile, cunning, and ruthless endeavour, proving himself skilled at managing the camp's supplies. With secret favours gifted from those supplies to

307

those who might prove useful to him, he'd also grown a loose network of allies. *Allies? Let's say, those in my debt.*

And with that nascent power, he exacted his price from the cursed green-eyed witch. Stolen at night using an indebted gang, he had taken something from her she'd not wanted to give. And the beauty of it? He knew, and she did not. They had been clever with the mask – and in other ways – to ensure she did not know it was him. For two more sun-cycles, he had secretly tormented her life, pushing her to the brink and keeping her there ...

His eyes gleamed at the memory.

But then ...

Cobra bared his teeth. But then the crippled old fool of an Ensi – aided and abetted by the treacherous Shade himself, he was sure – had proclaimed that the green-eyed witch was the rightful heir to the Ka and its empire! She was the new Ensi! Even now, so many sun-cycles later, Cobra could not believe it had happened. How? How could a lowlife slut like her have climbed higher than the hardworking, devoted Core of the Ka? Climbed higher than the devoted adherents of Kaos? *Climbed higher than me!*

A cold rage coursed through him. It had to end. *It will end! My mission will soon be complete.* A mission started many sun-cycles ago. His mission to destroy the Ensi.

He had started slowly, feeling and testing amongst those beholden to him. Who was thinking the same way as him? Who was weak-willed enough to be shown the light? But far more importantly, he had embarked on a masterclass of subterfuge known only to him. He redoubled his efforts on improving the camp supplies and logistics, while letting his roots grow out, binding more and more into his domain, into his sway. And as he'd hoped, his work within the camp didn't go unnoticed by others. None of them wanted to involve themselves with that most boring of roles. It was dull and mind-numbing. "We have bigger things cooking than this," they all said. "Let this Cobra take over camp management, Ensi."

Cobra delighted in the memory. The green-eyed devil had agreed, unknowingly inviting the cuckoo into the nest. He had made it to the Ka elite. And then those questions to his chosen few continued, leading questions most carefully placed. "Why are only green-eyes chosen to be Ensi?" he whispered in those listening ears. "Surely others also have the skill and power to be leader?" No one could tell him. "It has to be," came their only answer. "It is the will of Kaos."

A smile now touched Cobra's lips. Well, it seemed Kaos had changed his mind. *And he has chosen me to do his work.* His curled smile widened. All his efforts over those many sun-cycles would now see their just reward. The fraud would be exposed. He would finally end the travesty of the 'green-eyed' Ensi. He bared his teeth. Because it had all been a lie. This lowlife could not be the Ensi. "My final revenge approaches, witch," he snarled under his breath. "I am coming for you."

Cobra looked over at the men, smirking. Throwing bones in the dirt? No, if you must play a game, play a real game. And play it big. Not one of the fools scrabbling in the dirt knew any of this – but wait until they saw what came next.

He giggled. *I need people like this – so I can watch their faces just before they die.*

As he savoured the moment, Rathe suddenly stood up beside the fire. "Who goes there?" he challenged.

"A friend," a calm voice answered. Calm, but with a whispering sense of menace.

"Well, we'll be the judge of that," Rathe said, peering into the gloom. "Approach slowly."

Cobra watched as a tall man walked confidently into view. The fire's light gleamed off the man's shaven head and cast his sculpted face – set with a short, pointed beard – into menacing relief. *Older than me. But not old.* No, this man appeared in the prime of health. Torcs arrayed with fearsome canine teeth – *most likely lion* – were strapped around the man's powerful upper arms, and a leather guard covered his left forearm. He wore a kilt of dark red, cut high on the side of the upper thigh to knee level at the front, and adorned with unrecognised golden marks and symbols around its edge. On his feet he wore sandals held firmly in place by a network of narrow leather straps around his lower leg. As the man walked closer to the fire, his rippling muscles flexed beneath an array of intricate artwork tattooed into his skin. Over his left shoulder he carried a well-crafted pack, and in his right hand, a Black Staff.

At last, Cobra rejoiced. *The time is now here!*

"And who are you?" Rathe grated, the two brothers Cleft and Hands now by his side.

"One who is expected," the man said, looking down on Rathe.

Rathe glanced at Cobra. "Is this him?"

Inwardly Cobra rejoiced. Control! He was back in control! "I wondered that myself, Rathe," he said, a sly grin on his face. "Could this be the shaman we have been waiting for, or have we here an imposter, an assassin maybe?" His gaze turned to their new guest. "If a weak man like this," he said, pointing at Hands, "wandered into our camp unannounced, what would you think—"

A sizzling bolt of jet-black flashed through the firelit air of the camp and hammered into Hands. The stricken man dropped to the ground, smoking.

Cleft sprang to his feet. "You—"

Another crackling bolt streaked through the air, and Cleft collapsed to the ground by his brother.

"Hold!" Cobra shouted, panicking. "That's enough, Krull!" Hands shaking, he stared nervously at the shaman.

A faint smile touched Krull's hard, sculpted features. "In answer to your question, I would think they could not be trusted." His gaze shifted to Rathe. "And who is this?"

"One who will get us the allies we need," Cobra said quickly. "We can't kill everybody," he added pointedly.

Krull's questioning – *or was that mocking?* – smile played on his lips, but he said nothing.

"Those were good men," Rathe said, glaring at Cobra. "That was unnecessary and a waste."

"They were scum and a liability for us," Cobra hissed, his confidence returning as he saw Krull standing quietly, awaiting orders. "They—"

"Quiet!" Cobra yelled, glaring at Rathe. "Enough!"

Rathe clenched his fist but remained silent.

Cobra's hooded gaze lingered on him. If he didn't need the captain's men for what was to come, he'd happily see him meet his friends' fate. But he did need him. "Forget these two. What I need you to do now is ready yourself for travel to the temple and prepare the way. There's a council meeting tomorrow morning, and I plan to attend."

He turned to Krull. "And to you, my friend, I say welcome. Welcome to the Ka – and welcome to your new role as our Shade."

CHAPTER TWENTY-THREE

Bravery takes many forms, but the greatest may lie in those who sense they will fail but still choose to aid those around them.

*E*rin heard Fletcher slowly unzip his sleeping bag and quietly edge over to her. She felt his arm reach over and lightly brush the side of her face. He leaned over and kissed her cheek. She put her arm around his neck and—

'Erin! Wake up! We must go.'

No, she thought, holding on to Fletcher, *I'm not going anywhere, not when—*

'Erin,' urged the voice. *'This is Asim. It is time.'*

'What! No, I'm ...' She opened bleary eyes to the dark of the tent. She lay on her side, in her sleeping bag, her arm draped over Fletcher – who slept warmly cocooned in his own bag.

A dream. Only a dream.

Confused, she carefully withdrew her arm, then lay on her back, trying to grasp the ephemeral fragments drifting from her mind.

'We must go.'

She groaned. *'It's the middle of the night.'*

'This cannot wait. Time is against us.'

Her dream lost, she rubbed her eyes, then propped herself up on one arm, trying to think clearly. *'Where do you want me to go?'*

'To the temple. Meet me by the west wall.'

'Why? Why go there now? Asim? Asim?'

She cursed as she was met by silence.

Her head fogged by sleep, she unzipped her bag, then searched around in the darkness until she found her headtorch. Setting it to a dim light, she reached for her clothes.

"What time is it?" came Fletcher's groggy voice.

"Shh," Erin whispered, grabbing her trousers and shirt. "I've no idea what time it is." Quickly, she pulled the shirt over her head. "But it's certainly not a time to be wandering around out there in the dark."

"What!" Fletcher grunted, sitting up and looking around. "Where are you going?"

"Keep your voice down!" she whispered angrily and unzipped the rest of her bag. "It's Asim. He asked me to meet him by the ruins of the temple."

"Now? You have to go now?"

"I said keep your voice down, Fletcher. And yes, now."

Fletcher grunted something unintelligible, then unzipped his bag. "Well, I'm coming too."

Erin breathed a quiet sigh of relief. It wasn't something she wanted to do by herself.

"I was having such a good dream, too," he muttered.

"Was I in it?" Erin said, intrigued. She slapped her hand to her mouth. *Did I just ask that?*

Feeling Fletcher's eyes on her, she quickly wriggled into her trousers.

Moments later, with headtorches dimmed, they unzipped the entrance flap to their tent and stepped out into the cold desert night air. She shivered, from the cold or from her rising trepidation of what Asim was doing at the temple, she didn't know.

They crossed the gravel plain in silence, casting occasional nervous glances behind them, until the dark, jagged outline of the ruined temple loomed ahead, silhouetted against the starry night sky. As they climbed the low rise to the western edge of the ruins, a figure detached from the shadows of a tall mudbrick wall.

"Hurry," Asim said in a low voice. "We don't have much time."

"You can talk!" Fletcher exclaimed as they approached him.

"When needed."

"Did you know?" he said to Erin as she came to his side.

"I did," she murmured, squinting against the glare of his torchlight.

Fletcher shook his head, muttering to himself as he cast a bewildered look at Asim. Then his brow furrowed, and he leaned forward, focussing his torch on Asim's right hand. "What the hell! Is that a sledgehammer?"

"We will need it," Asim said, walking away.

"Hey, hold on," Fletcher hissed. "Why do we need that bloody thing?"

Asim walked on through a narrow gap in the wall ahead.

"Damn it," Fletcher said angrily. "He's not helping."

Yes, Asim needs to give us more. Much more. "Come on," Erin said, walking ahead.

She heard Fletcher sigh, then the crunch of gravel beneath his feet as he climbed after her. Reaching the top of the rise, she crossed the threshold of the ruined temple—

She staggered as a deadly presence seemed to descend upon her, a putrid stench assaulting her senses.

Fletcher ran to her side, grabbing her arm. "Whoa! Careful."

"Do you sense it?" she said, steadying herself, her eyes wide. "There's an evil here."

Fletcher's fingers tightened on her arm as his widening eyes scanned the darkness. "I can't feel anything ... can't see anything ..." She felt the tension in his hand. "Are you sure we should go on, Erin? What if there's something here like that night on the mountain?"

Yes, what is it we face, Asim? Because this chills me to the bone.

"Are you okay?" came Asim's voice from the darkness ahead.

Erin looked up, her torchlight illuminating Asim, who stood within a narrow, roofless passageway. "You need to explain, Asim. What are you planning to do?"

She saw the hesitation in his face.

"I need more, Asim. Fletcher needs more."

Asim's youthful face studied her for a moment, then he nodded imperceptibly. "The one we have waited for comes."

His words stole her breath.

"The place we must go lies below, entombed beneath the surface ruins." He looked out into the darkness, a darkness mimicking the unnerving disquiet in his eyes. "There are lives to preserve. To prevent Armageddon."

Erin stared at him, dumfounded.

"What Armageddon?" Fletcher whispered, his voice shaking.

Turning to him, Asim's expression seemed haunted. "Your destruction. The destruction of your land. Of all lands."

Erin saw her own horror reflected in Fletcher's face. "How do you know this?" she whispered.

"I am the Keeper."

Asim seemed to wait for them to respond but when neither she nor Fletcher spoke, he turned and walked away. "Hurry. We have little time."

Her mind reeling, Erin watched Asim walk on through the crumbling passageway.

"Armageddon," Fletcher stammered to her side. "I wish we hadn't asked. I didn't need to hear this."

313

Neither did she. Khaled had said that Asim had written of this in the past, but for the young man to truly believe it? *What hell is this?*

Fletcher rubbed his brow and cursed. "He wants *us* to prevent the destruction of the world?" he muttered, his voice brittle. "That could be a problem."

An image of her friend Tricia sprang into Erin's mind. *She also tries to hide her fear with lame humour.* Her stomach suddenly wrenched at the thought of her friends. She wished to help them in any way she could, but she was being sucked into a hell beyond her imagining. "When we started this, I just wanted to help my friends, but now Asim talks of things beyond my comprehension – the land's Armageddon. I don't know, Fletch, maybe you're right. What will we be able to do to help the one Asim says is coming?"

Fletcher remained silent for a moment. Then, seeming to clamp a hold on his fear, he took her hand. "Don't listen to me. What do I know of any of this? What does your heart tell you to do? Do you still trust this guy, this Keeper?"

Conflicting emotions surged, a maelstrom of tumultuous thoughts. Yet in the centre of the fearful storm lay a calm, indomitable soul, one standing firm as the surge flowed past: watching, listening ... guiding her. *You* can *help*, that part of her said. *You can help the Keeper. You can help your friends.* She wet her parched mouth. "There's much I can't see, but, yes, I trust Asim. And he believes we can help."

She saw a moment of uncertainty in Fletcher's eyes, then it cleared. He squeezed her hand. "Then we go on together."

Though a sickening dread swirled in her stomach, a tremendous weight lifted from her shoulders. *Fletcher is standing with me.* She managed a smile. "Thank you."

He squeezed her hand again. "Okay, let's get after the guy with the big hammer."

Girding herself, she walked on beside Fletcher as they caught up with Asim, who then led them on through the jumbled maze of collapsed temple walls, the eerie, dancing shadows from their torchlight exacerbating the sense of menace from the lingering stench surrounding her. Stench? No, more of a crawling sensation of cold, squirming snakes slithering across her body. *I trust your intentions, Asim, but do you really know all that we face here? Do you truly sense what I sense?*

She jumped as Asim's voice cut through the silence. "Here," he said, his shadowy form dropping from view.

She stepped forward, halting at the edge of a deep depression. Swinging her torch around the sunken pit, she saw steep slopes of slumped debris, mostly shards of shattered pottery, bounding the pit on three sides. On the fourth side stood Asim, his hand resting on a large circular stone, which lay upright against a low mudbrick wall. "We need to move this."

"Why?"

"We must enter here."

"You must be joking!" Fletcher exclaimed.

Asim looked up at her. "We don't have much time."

She heard the urgency in his voice. *Keep moving.* She began to make her way carefully down the slippery slope, shards of broken pottery clinking as they shifted beneath her feet. The sound of Fletcher's grumbling followed her.

As they reached the base of the pit, Fletcher walked past Erin and examined the stone. "That looks bloody heavy." He pushed it. "It is heavy."

"It will move," Asim murmured.

Shortly, with the three of them straining hard, the stone wheel slowly turned.

"It's sitting on solid ground, thank God," Fletcher said, continuing to lean into the stone.

"Choose your words carefully," Asim admonished. "You know not which god will be listening."

Fletcher flicked a glance at Erin but said nothing. They rolled the stone as far as it would move, revealing a narrow gap in the mudbrick wall.

"We enter here." He gestured to Fletcher. "You first. I have no light."

"That was stupid. Especially if you knew we were heading in there."

Asim shrugged and gestured towards the cavity.

"You sure?" Fletcher muttered, glancing at Erin.

No. She nodded.

Fletcher stepped to the opening. "This better be worth it."

Watching Fletcher crouch down and put his head into the narrow opening, Erin's heart sank. Was now a good time to let them know she was claustrophobic? She watched, nausea rising in her stomach, as Fletcher attempted to get his broad shoulders through the tight opening. He struggled for a moment, then backed himself out. Leaning forward, he placed his right arm through the hole first, then, by twisting his body slightly, he was able to wriggle his shoulders through the ragged hole and drag himself into the interior.

"What can you see?" Erin asked, the pit of her stomach lurching.

"Not much yet," came his voice from within. "It looks as though it's just full of rubble. I don't – hold on, there's a ledge here." There was the clinking of stones, then: "Okay. I see steps over here. This area has been cleared of rubble."

"Professor Khaled and his team," Asim said, putting his head to the entrance. "Descend the steps a short way, then we will enter."

Hearing Fletcher moving inside, Asim, his sledgehammer in one hand, effortlessly pulled his slim frame through the entrance and disappeared inside. Heart racing, Erin approached the forbidding cavity. *Fletcher has a light in there,* she told herself, *and it opens up inside.* She took a deep breath. *Don't think about it, just do it.* Ignoring the oppressive sense that she would be trapped within stone jaws, she somehow dragged herself through, and moments later, stood on the upper steps of a starkly lit stairwell leading down into a dark unknown.

"Continue down, then to the right," Asim instructed Fletcher, who stood a few steps below.

Fletcher grunted a response, then she saw his silhouetted figure descending the stairs.

As Erin followed Asim down the stairwell, the surge of adrenalin from their entry receded – but the stench of evil assailed her once more.

"I feel something now," came Fletcher's strained voice. "But maybe that's because I'm scared out of my wits. Remind me not to go on vacation with you again."

Erin managed a smile. *I smile or I cry. And for Fletcher, I need to smile because I couldn't have done this without him.* "I'll check the details a little closer next time," she called down. She heard his strained laugh. In the face of adversity, maybe laughter was the strongest defence. *And he's trying so hard to stay strong.* Her smile quickly faded. Fletcher was putting his full trust in her. He was putting his *faith* in her. *Do I deserve that? Am I right to believe in those who have led us here?* But such doubts were a distraction, and in this moment, futile. They were here, and she wasn't turning back. And she had to believe those speaking to her led her on the right path, else those voices were merely a figment of ... *Don't say it. Believe in yourself.*

Distracted by her errant thoughts, she reached the foot of the stairs, then followed the hunched Asim down the narrow passageway until they encountered another stairwell descending to the left. The west, if her instinctive bearings were correct.

"What is this place?" she heard Fletcher mutter as they descended the steps.

"A section of the temple excavated by Professor Khaled," Asim answered. "A new temple built on the old. Only a few thousand years old."

"Only," Fletcher muttered as they stepped out into another mudbrick-lined tunnel.

Erin scanned the ancient walls as they walked on, recognising the skill it had required from long-gone builders – builders who had worked thousands of years ago – to have assembled such neat close-knit brickwork. *And there is an older temple below?* Just how far back in time were they heading as they dropped deeper? A staggering thought followed. Would they reach walls built in the age Jessica had visited, the age her friends might have returned to? The thought was terrifying because it somehow made Jessica's story seem so very real.

Distracted, she followed Asim through another series of twisting passages and rugged stairwells until Fletcher's voice sounded from ahead. "There's no way through." He faced them, dazzling them with his torch.

"Please step back," Asim said, hefting the sledgehammer.

Fletcher scurried past Asim to join Erin. Then, as they watched on in astonishment, Asim walked up to the wall blocking their path and proceeded to hammer against the ancient bricks with the sledgehammer. On the third blow, a crack appeared along the joints of the brickwork. On the sixth blow, a section of the wall shifted inward. And on the seventh blow, a whole section of wall collapsed.

"That will have awakened the dead," Fletcher spluttered, coughing in a cloud of swirling dust.

The dead may not need awakening, Erin thought, tasting something fouler than the dust in her mouth. *What lies here, Asim? What horror do you lead us to?*

"Now we enter the time of those known as the Ka," Asim said. "Please enter."

Fletcher peered into the cavity. "There's no room behind there. Just a rock wall."

"Look to your left. Crawl along and you will find another passageway."

"The space in there is as narrow as hell! And how do you know there's a way out?"

"I know." Asim gestured to the cavity. "Please. We have little time. The professor is coming."

Erin's stomach lurched. There was a genuine distress in Asim's voice. *He's afraid. Terrified.* "You have to move, Fletch," she said, trying to keep her fear from her voice. "We've no choice."

317

"There's always a choice," Fletcher muttered. But he pulled away another few bricks, then pulled himself into the crevice. As he crawled away, Asim followed.

Erin forced herself to move. She clambered through the rent in the shattered wall, squeezing herself into the tight space behind. She fought back a desperate urge to scream. *This is beyond my worst nightmare. This is hell.* Inching slowly forward, she was forced to twist to her side to wriggle through between the back of the brick wall and the solid stone wall behind it. She gritted her teeth and willed herself on.

She stifled a scream as Asim abruptly stopped ahead of her.

"There's no way through," came Fletcher's heart-stopping words.

She froze, a chill running down her spine.

"Look to your right and above," came Asim's calm voice. "There will be a way ahead there."

There was a pause, then Fletcher's doubtful voice. "I can see a ledge here, but hell, that's a tight squeeze."

Wedged in the base of the narrow gap, Erin sucked in ragged breaths as panic flared.

"Climb into the gap you see," Asim said, "and keep to the left. It leads down to a wider passage."

"I don't like this," Fletcher said in a strained voice. "If we get stuck, we—"

"Don't say it, Fletch," Erin called out, her whole body shivering. "I don't want to hear that."

Fletcher muttered something unheard, but his tone said it all; he was frustrated – and scared.

After what seemed an eternity of waiting, Asim moved on again—

Erin screamed as her torch went out.

She was pitched into total darkness.

'Stay calm,' came Asim's voice in her head. *'Reach out and touch me. I will guide you.'*

Hands shaking, she reached out and her fingers brushed the soft material of Asim's trousers.

'I'll move a short distance, then stop and wait until I feel your touch.'

She heard movement and the fabric pulled away from her hand.

"Wait! Not yet!" she cried, pulling herself forward in the darkness. With a flood of relief, her hand caught his foot. "Wait. Please. Just a moment."

Her hand clasped tightly around his foot, she closed her eyes and tried to still her breathing. *Just get to Fletcher. He has the light.* She drew several deep breaths, and as her panic eased, the recognition of something unexpected brushed her consciousness. *This air is fresh.* Drawing another deep breath, a glimmer of hope sparked. It was true. There was a lighter edge to the air here. *This must connect to the outside somewhere. There must be another way out.*

"We need to move," Asim said, his voice tight with tension.

Erin bowed her head. Turn back now and she'd failed. *And the professor is coming.* She looked up into the darkness, sensing again that tang of fresher air. "Okay," she whispered.

Asim instantly moved on.

Girding herself, she crawled after him, blind to all except to the sounds of his movement ahead.

They hadn't moved far before he stopped again. "There's a ledge here. Stay close and feel where I go."

In the pitch blackness, she tracked Asim's leg with her hand as it swung up, entering a gap in the rock face at hip height. Feeling around with her other hand, she felt the lip of the ledge Fletcher had mentioned. *A ledge?* More of a thin horizontal crevice, not much taller than a person's head.

No. Please, God, no.

'Stay with me, Erin,' Asim pulsed to her. 'We won't have far to travel.'

Her breathing ragged, she pushed herself up, then crouched with her head in the mouth of the crevice. It suddenly felt as though if she moved a fraction further, she would be trapped, caught in the maw of this deadly vice, sealed forever in this godforsaken tomb, her coffin. *No. I can't do this.* Yet, cold hands trembling, and riven with fear, a part of her screamed at her to move. *What else can you do!* Somehow, she found herself wriggling and squeezing into the impossibly tight hole, then dragging herself inside. Fighting back tears, she shuffled forward, urging herself on in the darkness. *You're moving. You're moving to the light.* Her legs and arms scraping against the unforgiving rock, her head catching against the jagged roof of the crevice, she inched herself onwards. *Keep moving. Just keep moving.* Yet it seemed she was crawling through her grave. That at any moment the mountain of stone and dirt above would crack and crumble, bringing the whole edifice crushing down on her—

Her shoulders caught on a jagged rock. As she shifted her weight to pass, she found herself wedged between the roof and the ground. Cold panic engulfed her. *I can't move!* Her throat tightening, she began to shake—

"I'm through!" came Fletcher's joyous cry from ahead.

He's through? The words were as a miraculous grasping hand to a drowning woman. A desperate hope surged. *There is an end to this.*

319

Hands trembling, she forced herself to breathe. *If they got through here, I can.* Ignoring the twisting sickness in her stomach, she shifted her weight, wriggling to her left …

She slipped free from the rock that had snared her.

Hardly daring to believe, she pulled away from the sickening trap, then dragged herself on, blinking back tears.

A moment later, a glorious beam of light illuminated the crevice.

"You're almost there, Erin," Fletcher called.

She dropped her head to the ground and released a slow, ragged breath. She lay still, allowing the nauseating tension to ease.

"Erin! Are you okay?"

No. This is hell. "Yes," she called out.

She lay for a moment longer, then raising her head, she dragged herself forward, slowly inching onwards. It seemed like a lifetime, but finally, shaking with relief, she emerged into a wondrous open space.

"Great work, Erin," came Fletcher's relieved voice. "Let's get you out of there."

With the aid of his guiding arm, she scrambled out of the hellhole, then stood unsteadily in a wide, torchlit tunnel.

"You okay?" Fletcher asked, drawing her into his arms.

Erin sank into him, wrapping her arms around him. "My light went out," she breathed, her body shaking. *I was terrified.* She buried her head in his shoulder, allowing the terror of the ordeal to subside.

Moments passed – how long, she didn't know – then she drew back, wiping her eyes. She glanced back at the deep shadows of the foreboding crevice in the wall. "That was horrific."

Fletcher reached into a pocket of his jacket and pulled out two batteries. "You should have come prepared."

Erin whacked him on the shoulder.

"Ow! That bloody hurt."

"Time your jokes a little better then."

"So, you don't need these?"

She glared at him for a second, then snatched the batteries from his hand.

Quickly switching the set in her torch, she glared at him again, then turned to take stock of their surroundings. The tunnel was high-roofed – even Asim was able to stand without stooping – and built in a style quite different to those passageways above, with raw, rough-hewn stone walls rather than the stacked mudbricks of the tunnels above.

"The temple of the Ka," Asim said, seeing her gaze. "What we seek is beneath us."

"Who were the Ka?"

"A people on the wrong side of history," Asim said, his face grim.

Fletcher came to her side. "How much further do you want to go?" he said in a low voice. "Because we're not equipped for this." He glanced to the dark tunnel ahead, and then back to the narrow crevice they'd emerged from. "It might not be easy, but we should head back before we run out of batteries. Then, if you really want to, we can come back when we're better prepared."

Asim stepped towards Fletcher, his face drawn. "That is not possible. If we don't act now, there will be nothing to come back to."

Erin drew an involuntary breath. *The Armageddon. Our destruction.* She saw the stark bleakness of Asim's gaze. "What is it we really face?" she whispered.

Asim held her eyes for a moment, then looked away.

Fletcher frowned, anger creeping over his face. "You don't know, do you? You don't know what we face."

"I know we should be here, in this moment. But maybe we are already too late. I ... I am not sure."

Erin's stomach churned.

Fletcher stared at Asim, open-mouthed. "After all this, you say you're not sure? What—"

"Don't," Erin whispered. "Don't, Fletch."

Fletcher glared at Asim but said nothing more.

"Nothing has changed," Asim said. "Many things are beyond my control, but I know we need to be here. I know *you* need to be here." He looked along the passageway, his face passing into shadow. "There is one here we must meet."

"Who?" Erin breathed.

"One from another time. One who is foretold by the Story I hold." Asim spun around, his eyes gazing upwards. "Please, we must go on. The professor approaches."

"And what's your problem with him?" Fletcher asked sharply.

He's evil, came the unbidden thought to Erin's mind.

"He is led by one who seeks your destruction," Asim replied, his dark eyes locking onto Fletcher's. "Your destruction and the destruction of all those who call this planet home."

Eyes widening, Fletcher gazed fearfully back at the shadowy crevice.

Asim faced Erin, his eyes beseeching her. *'Time is running out. He has entered the temple.'*

The malevolent presence within the ancient labyrinth seemed to grow in strength, ghostly tentacles seeming to slide down her neck, caress her face, and slither through her hair. She licked suddenly dry lips. "Fletch, we have to go on. We can't trust the professor. We can't go back."

She saw the tension in his stance, his face strained by the battle raging within him. *A battle I understand.*

Wincing, he wiped his brow. "I guess we really don't have a choice."

Asim immediately walked off into the darkness.

Cursing, Fletcher took her hand, and they hurried after Asim, their torches casting long, wavering shadows off the striding figure ahead. They quickly exited the tunnel, their torchlight sucked into the murk of an eerie void, the remnants of another chamber carved by a people long gone. They veered to the right, scrambling over debris from the collapsed roof to their left before entering another winding tunnel. The place was vast. Who were these Ka? Who had they worshipped here? With those questions unvoiced, they walked on, soon entering another chamber, one so extensively damaged they barely made it through the heaped rubble to the tunnel beyond.

Then a third chamber.

Where she saw the first remains of a body.

She didn't realise it at first, didn't see the significance of the tattered and decayed clothing, eerily laid out as though waiting to be seen. But as they walked on, she saw more and more scattered throughout the chamber. She finally stopped and bent down to the torn fabric by her side. Still recognisable as a tunic and leggings, it lay prone on the ground as though waiting for its wearer to reappear. "You see this?" she whispered to Fletcher, pointing to the ravaged clothing. "It looks burnt, scorched."

He nodded, grimacing.

Erin looked around, seeing a similar sight disappearing into the shadows beyond their torchlight. She felt a tightness in her chest. "These were people," she whispered in a hushed voice. "What in God's name happened here?"

"What you see is evidence of those who lived here thirteen thousand years ago," came Asim's voice. "All brave men and women, but who did not understand why they died in the temple of their god, Kaos."

"How do you know this?" Fletcher breathed.

"It is my destiny ... and my curse."

"Many of these are burnt," Erin whispered, staring at another scorched tunic. *No, not just a tunic; that was once a life.* She looked around. It was a mausoleum. To unknown dead. *Unknown?* Asim had called them the Ka.

"We must move on," Asim said. "We have little time."

Erin's gaze lingered on the remains of the dead. How many lives had come and gone through the vast passage of time since these people – these Ka – had walked this land? Each with their own joys and sadness, their loves and their losses, their own dreams for their future. So many untold lives, unremembered lives, now mere dust on the tapestry of life.

She said a silent prayer for those around her, then rejoined Fletcher. They continued on in silence, passing out of the chamber and along a narrow passageway before emerging into the largest chamber they'd seen. Flicking her torchlight around the open space, she saw in the centre of the chamber a shallow, dust-laden, pentagonal platform, and to one side, four shadowy alcoves set into the chamber's walls.

"Unbelievable," Fletcher said as they made their way up the few short steps onto the platform.

Asim walked ahead, halting at the far side of the platform, where he studied a jumble of fractured stones. "The remains of the throne of the leader of these people."

"It seems someone didn't like him," Fletcher muttered.

"Her," Asim corrected. He stepped down off the platform, then climbed several steps to the pile of rubble. Stepping around it, he walked to a small opening in the far wall. "Our journey is almost complete. Follow me."

As Erin made to follow, Fletcher grabbed her arm. "Erin. We can still turn back. Somehow, we can turn away from this."

She shook her head. "I have no choice, Fletch." Seeing the pain in his eyes, she added, "I'm sorry."

The pain was quickly hidden. "Don't apologise. This was my choice." He drew a deep breath. "Let's see what's at the end of this rainbow."

She forced a smile, and they walked quickly over to Asim.

He gestured to the opening. "Pass through and follow the steps down."

Erin followed Fletcher through the clean-cut opening, then crossed to a stairwell descending into the gloom.

"More steps," Fletcher groaned as he started downwards.

"Keep going," Asim said as they passed several openings to either side.

As they dropped deeper, Erin flinched at a sudden change in the malevolent presence surrounding them; she felt a probing, a caressing of her brain.

Then someone – something – reached out to her …

Instinctively, she slammed up barriers around her mind!

How she did this, she didn't know – but it was done. The entity was gone. Or at least gone from her mind. She reached out: *'Asim?'*

'Yes?'

She breathed a sigh of relief. *'Good. I was checking I could still talk with you. Something tried to mess with my head.'*

A ripple of concern brushed her. *'They grow stronger.'*

'They?'

"Asim, I've reached the bottom," came Fletcher's voice from below.

"Wait for us there," Asim called. *'Hurry,'* he pulsed to Erin. *'You will see.'*

See what? Wiping a clammy hand on her shirt, she followed Asim down to the base of the stairwell, where they joined Fletcher within the gloom of an expansive chamber. Several shadowy exits led away into darkness.

"There," Asim said, gesturing to a tunnel directly ahead. "Follow that passage, then enter the first chamber on the left."

Fletcher seemed to momentarily baulk, but with a shake of his head, he walked on into the tunnel, his torchlight carving an eerie path ahead.

Crossing the chamber, Asim and Erin followed him along the narrow passageway.

After only a short distance, she saw a glow in the tunnel ahead.

"We've arrived," Asim murmured.

Ahead, Fletcher stopped at an opening to the left, his face bathed in a dim light.

He stepped through the opening—

"What!" he exclaimed, staggering backwards, his eyes widening.

Erin rushed to his side. "What is it?" she said, turning to the chamber—

She froze.

She felt Asim come to her side. "This is what we must protect – and where the one will arrive."

Erin stepped forward, horrified. *I would never have imagined this. Never.*

They all walked inside.

CHAPTER TWENTY-FOUR

In success or failure, does chance play its part? The slip of a foot, the overheard words, the unexpected encounter. Whatever – whichever – the Continuum adjusts, aligns.

The western Rim had proved little different from the northern, but now, skirting the barren perimeter of the treeless southern Rim, Spider saw a very different vista. Looming in the distance lay a sprawling confusion of huts, tents, and lean-tos, each seemingly independently assembled and yet each enjoying a bizarre and haphazard joining with its neighbour. Built using hides, reeds, wood – whatever the owner had found to hand – the jumble of huts created a most chaotic patchwork village.

And one home to particularly tougher-looking individuals, hardened fighters by the look of it, none of whom Spider would wish to cross. He kept his head down and walked on along the outer perimeter of the camp within a camp.

"A new recruit by the look of it, Scowl," came a thin voice to his left.

"Scrawny looking though, Skits," came a deep voice, presumably Scowl. "He wouldn't last long, even against Huge."

Spider kept walking.

"Hey! I was talking to you!" the thin-voiced man called.

So, Skits is the loudmouth. Spider stopped and turned to see two men standing beside a group playing knuckles. Scanning them, he quickly assessed that the scrawny one of the two was most likely Skits. "From what I heard," he said, focussing on the smaller man, "you were talking to each other. But maybe you didn't hear one another – you want me to repeat it for you?"

The bigger man of the two laughed. The other stepped towards him. "You think you're funny, heh?"

"Careful, Skits, he might have a bite worse than his bark."

With a dismissive shake of the head, Spider walked away.

"Hey, I didn't say you could go," Skits called after him, and he heard the man following.

Spider slipped his pack from his shoulder, dropped his spear to the ground, and slipped a blade into his right hand. *I need to do this right.* He turned, then strode confidently up to the approaching man—

Then flashed his blade up to the man's neck. "You talk to me that way again, friend," he said fiercely, drawing blood with his blade, "and they'll be your last words to your ancestors. Understand?"

The man quickly held up his hands.

I was right. A coward at heart.

"It seems I was mistaken," the man said, eyeing the weapon.

"Good," Spider said with a smile. "I thought so." He dropped the blade from the man's neck. He'd made the point. *Now don't push it.* "Spider's the name."

"Skits."

"He knows, Skits," Scowl growled. "Go fetch some more water. We're all parched."

"Will do, Scowl," Skits said, backing away from Spider. "Water coming up." He strode away, disappearing into a gap between two of the outer tents.

"You don't look like a Scowl," Spider said, walking up to the heavyset man.

Scowl scratched his beard. "You don't want to see me when I do."

Spider nodded.

"You're new." A statement, not a question.

Spider nodded again. *Give nothing, unless asked.*

"So, are you a fighter?"

"When needed," he replied evenly.

"If you are, then you're welcome. You'll get food and shelter. And more – if you win."

"By joining the army of the Ka?"

Scowl laughed. "Now that's a good one, my friend. I—" He stopped, eyes narrowing. "You're serious." His expression grew thoughtful. "Join the game and we can talk."

Spider glanced across to the group playing knuckles. Hard faces, but no tension between them. He saw several blades on the ground. The spoils of the game. *So, a chance to learn something new about this enemy camp?* He glanced at the sun. He still had time before he needed to prepare his crossing to the Flanks. He looked back at Scowl. "I could use a new blade."

326

Scowl laughed and slapped him on the back. He led him to the game.

And so Spider played and talked ... and listened.

It seemed that most of the numerous fighters who came to join the elite of the Ka chased the same elusive dream, one only achieved by those very few who combined their great skill in battle with the greater luck of their god. Only the most skilled – and the luckiest – fighters worked their way into the Flanks. Most struggled on in the Rim, surviving in this sprawling western camp, fighting mock battles for the pleasure of those higher up the chain. And dying in those same battles. Of those fighters skilled enough to survive, many proved to have no god on their side and failed to win cleanly. Those fighters limped on to their next fight, and then the next, each injury sustained sapping their strength and power, pegging them down yet another notch, their fire not quenched, but their bodies destroyed.

"Of course," Scowl told him, while winning a blade from him, "the Ka still like us here. We are the true defenders of this homeland. We are the real Ka!"

"The Ka's backside, you mean," grunted a brute of a man to Spider's right. "The Ka squat down and squeeze us out whenever they need to shit on some new enemy of theirs."

An army at hand, Spider realised. But kept at arm's length. Only the elite allowed inside. He continued playing, picking up threads of the men's conversations, strands of the men's lives in the Rim. A grim life. A life of constant battles for position in the brutal pecking order, frequent fights flaring amongst themselves. And few women, so more fighting. *Few women*, Spider thought grimly. The perils of a system dominated by physical strength: aggression rewarded, feeding further aggression. The Rim was a hard place to live, and this fighters' camp even tougher. Not a place to raise a family for any who wished that. No, progression to the Flanks was what every man sought, and the size of this chaotic camp showed the desperate hope still burning in its residents.

He glanced at the men. Hardened men, yes, fighters trained for the battles of a militarised tribe, but in their eyes, he saw that flicker of hope when they spoke. *A false hope*, he thought grimly. It was always the leaders who drove a tribe and its people astray. *Or their gods.* And the Ka had the worst leaders and gods of them all. *They seek to destroy us.* He glanced at Scowl. *And they destroy you at the same time.*

"I'll try the Games next year," said a one-eyed man at the far side of the game.

"Why aren't *you* there, Scowl?" grunted another.

"I don't need to find yet another way to get myself killed," Scowl answered with a smile.

"Can I have your blades when you do go?" said the one-eyed man to the laughter of the others.

"I'm too slow now," Scowl said to Spider as the men returned to their game. "Not for these boys here, but down at the Games ..." He shook his head. "Fine margins matter, and I'm on the wrong side."

Shouts and jeers suddenly erupted from the far side of the tents. Scowl scowled and stood up quickly. "Let's see what's happening." He strode off towards the tented area.

Spider stood, bemused, as the other men abandoned their game and hurried after Scowl. He glanced up at the sky, seeing the sun had set whilst they'd been playing. *Time to figure out how to cross into the Flanks.* He looked over at the long barrier of tents spreading out to the east and west and saw the last of the knuckles-playing men hurrying through the only gap in the tent wall. *Guess that way gets me heading the right way.*

Picking up his pack and spear, he hurried after the men.

Entering a narrow passageway running into the deep wall of tents, he caught a glimpse of the men rounding a corner ahead and hurried on, following them as they navigated the warren. He passed a gnarly old tree growing in the very midst of the tents, and shortly after broke through the cordon to find himself standing in a wide, well-trodden area. *A perfect fighting ground for training,* he thought, scanning around. A large and noisy crowd milled at the far end of the training ground, and he saw Scowl and his fellow fighters heading that way.

Spider cautiously followed.

The crowd had gathered before one of the largest tents he'd seen in the wall. Beyond the crowd stood a man within the tent entrance, his head well above the level of the crowd. As Spider approached Scowl, he caught a glimpse of the wooden platform the man must be standing on. "What's happening?" he asked Scowl, craning his neck to see over the crowd.

"A new fighter for tomorrow, and the rumour is that it's a woman. Everybody wants this fight."

"Why?"

"A chance to be noticed. But mainly because there's a chance they'll get paid extra."

"Because they are fighting a woman?" Spider said, confused. "I don't understand."

"Neither do I," Spider heard the man mutter. "But there's even a Disciple of the Ka who always comes to watch whenever a woman's fighting. He pays extra if she's beaten, and most disappointed is he if the woman wins."

Welcome to the land of the Ka. "What does he have against women?"

But at that moment, the crowd howled, and his question was lost.

"She must be over there," Scowl muttered, and began pushing his way through the jostling crowd. Spider followed in the big man's wake until they reached the front of the gathered fighters. He could see a woman standing on a platform ...

His stomach lurched.

Rind!

His thoughts spun. What had happened? Where were the Warriors? *We've been discovered!*

His mouth suddenly dry, he stared at the platform in horror. Rind stood proudly, scanning the crowd with apparent disdain. Her eyes briefly met his before moving on to fix her scornful glare on others.

He turned away, pushing his way back out of the crowd to break through into open ground, where he stopped, his mind whirling. The noise of the crowd behind him faded into the background as panic overtook him. *What should I do! What can I do!* He was vaguely aware of the crowd quietening and a voice speaking but was too lost in his own dismay to take in what was being said. *Krez! Think, Spider, think!* Rind appeared to be as he'd last seen her, which meant she was being fairly treated – for now. But where were the Warriors? What about the mission? He fought to calm himself. For now, he needed to forget all else. *Get Rind out of there.*

But how?

A raucous cheer shook him out of his reverie, and looking up, he saw the edges of the crowd dispersing.

"Scum," an impassioned voice beside him said.

He glanced around to see a girl adjusting a white feather in her hair as she glared at the crowd in disgust. Still shaken, he looked back at the dispersing crowd. "I agree with you," he said in a low voice. "Where I'm from, we treat women with respect."

The girl gave a dismissive grunt.

"Spider! There you are," came Scowl's voice. Spider saw the man peel away from the crowd and head towards him. "She has drawn the Killer," Scowl said as he approached. "A pity. She looked as though she'd be a good fighter – small in stature, but big in heart, I would say. But against the Killer ..." He shrugged. "As I say, a pity."

Spider said nothing.

Scowl's eyes narrowed. "If I was a betting man – which I am – I'd say you know that woman over there." He smiled. "At least, she knew you. It's the eyes, you see. The eyes see everything, and everything is in the eyes."

Still Spider remained silent.

Scowl shrugged. "But no matter. Whatever lies between you both ends on the morrow. As I say, a pity." He made to go, then glanced back. "You seem the kind of person we need, Spider. If you want to join us, see me. Same time, same place, any day." Then he walked away.

Spider looked over to the corner of the open ground where, with the crowd now gone, several relaxed yet watchful men sat around, spears by their sides. *Guards.* Guarding what? *Either keeping in folk who wanted to escape, or keeping out folk who wanted in,* he thought wryly.

"Is that true? That you know her?"

He turned to the girl with the white feather in her hair. He'd thought she'd left. He nodded.

There was a moment of silence, and then: "Come with me."

*

"This is dangerous," the old man whispered, glancing nervously around the surrounds of his hut. "You should not have brought him here."

Sitting before the firelit entrance of the hut, Spider quietly studied the old man – the same old man he'd seen visiting Rind and the Warriors earlier. The girl with the fire in her eyes had turned out to be the man's granddaughter. *And I'm an unexpected and unwelcome visitor,* Spider thought, seeing the old man's discomfort. *But a grateful one.* It had gained him access to the Flanks.

And if this was a trap, it had not yet been sprung.

Yet.

"I don't have to stay," Spider said, attempting to allay the old man's fears that he'd coerced his granddaughter into bringing him here. "It—"

"We have to get that woman out of there, Patra," the girl insisted. "She's done nothing wrong and is now imprisoned by those scum."

"We don't know what she's done, and what she hasn't," her grandfather said firmly. "I—"

"You told me what happened inside the temple," the girl fired back. "Those people met with the Ensi, and they invited you to tell the Story. You've been shown a great honour."

Spider's eyes narrowed. "Hold on. *Who* met with the Ensi?"

"Your friends," the girl said to Spider's astonishment. "They and my grandfather were guests of the Ensi. They—"

"Inyana," the old man interjected, casting a fearful glance to the distant huts. "Please, keep your voice down. It wasn't so clear to me what was happening."

"What's clear to me," she hissed, "is that the woman back there has been gravely mistreated. She came here in good faith but was taken against her will – by those scum of the southern Rim."

"We can report this to the guards and leave it in their hands."

"Their hands! Phah! Their hands are only interested in one thing." Her eyes blazed. "We have to act. We have to go back and get her out."

"Now hold on!" Spider exclaimed, trying to make sense of what he was hearing. "I'm not planning to launch a full-on attack on that hornet's nest, we—"

"Why not?" Inyana said indignantly.

"Because we wouldn't last more than a blink of an eye, that's why not. That's my friend in there. I'll get her out my way, and my way only."

Inyana glared at him but said nothing more.

I should go. The girl was a blazing wildfire, a danger to his mission. Spider glanced back to the old man, who still cast nervous looks around him. What of this one? No name yet offered – *and I've not offered mine* – so a tense mistrust remained. *Yet he met my friends. And they met the Ensi?* Spider ran his fingers through his matted hair. "You saw my friends?"

The old man gave one last look around, then turned his ancient, wrinkled face to Spider. The man's deep-set eyes studied him as Inyana sat impatiently by his side. *I see a man with his life written in the lines of his face,* Spider thought. *Lines carved by the wind and the rain, and by warmth and humour, not by the blade.* This was not a fighting man – he glanced at the girl – this was a man seeking to protect his granddaughter.

But they chose the wrong tribe, he thought grimly.

The old man cleared his throat, then tilted his head slightly, furrowing his thick brow. "My name is Kapano," he said, peering intently at Spider. "But before I say more, tell me your story."

Who trusts who first? He knew the answer to that – he had too much to lose. "That tale isn't easy, or short," Spider said carefully. "And I don't trust this place to be ignorant of what we say."

"I would say it is a little late to be concerned by that, wouldn't you?"

Maybe. "Still, my story isn't for this time and this place." He brushed an inquisitive beetle from his leggings. "What do you know of my friends?"

Kapano cleared his throat. "That is not easy to say." Spider saw a tension rise in the man's face. "But I will tell you what I know."

The old man leaned forward, then spoke briefly of events that left Spider utterly shocked and bewildered. *They met the Ensi. And then they listened to this man's story?* It made no sense. "And the other wasn't with them?"

Kapano's leathery features creased with disquiet. "The one you call Rind wasn't there."

Then how had she ended up out here, captive in the fighter's camp? "My friends inside – you say they spoke freely?"

The old man nodded. "I thought them guests of the Ensi. But I was nervous. Maybe there were things I didn't see."

"You were afraid of the Ensi? They forced you there?"

"She is the Ensi. I am no one. When—"

"You are the greatest man of our people," Inyana interjected. "The Ensi will know this now. She will send for you again."

A smile touched Kapano's face, then quickly faded. He held Spider's eyes. "When you are asked to come before such as the Ensi, you do not question. It was unexpected, yes, but also a great honour. And afraid? I think most would tremble when asked to stand before their leaders."

Because they are evil tyrants, Spider thought grimly, glancing to the ground. He replayed Kapano's words. The old man had thought Rind and the Warriors were guests in the temple. *And yet Rind is now held prisoner.* This made no sense. He looked back up at Kapano. "And the story you told?"

"Not for this time and this place," Kapano answered, his sharp eyes studying Spider.

Spider peered at the man before him. A chance encounter with Rind and the Warriors, then a chance encounter with him. Was this *just* chance? Or was this the work of IY? *Or Kaos?* How had this man found himself in the centre of this web? *And do I, Spider, need to join him?* He saw no easy way forward. From Kapano's description, it seemed possible he might gain access to the Core, but not to the temple itself. A single guarded access point was not something he could tackle. *Yet.* No, the Warriors would have to fend for themselves for now. *And they don't seem to be in immediate mortal danger.* No, his focus had to be on Rind.

But what to do?

That, he didn't yet know.

He glanced at Kapano and his granddaughter. *But I've learnt what I needed here.* He climbed to his feet. "I thank you for your time, my friend. I will not keep you any longer."

"Wait," Inyana said, jumping up. "What are you going to do? How are you going to get your friend away from those scum?"

"I don't know, but I'll find a way." He turned to go.

"No!" she exclaimed. "Patra, we need to help. I want to help."

Spider turned back, confused. "Why? Why do you want to help?"

A hard glint of deepest anger – and terrible hurt – flashed in the girl's eyes. "Because they are scum," she said in a pitiless, cold voice. "And because someone once helped me."

Spider saw the hurt that crossed Kapano's face. *So, you couldn't protect her all the time.*

Kapano looked at his granddaughter, then back at Spider. "There may be a way we can help you," he said slowly. "Easier for us than for you."

Spider studied the man's face. Rind and the Warriors had sought his help, had asked him to tell his story? Why? Who was this man?

One who was offering to help. And one who was fearful of helping him. *So one I may be able to trust.* He sighed and sat back down. "My name is Spider. And I'm listening."

Kapano leaned forward. "Tomorrow morning, before the fighters emerge …"

Spider listened intently as Kapano explained his idea.

He felt it had little chance of working.

And that may be enough.

CHAPTER TWENTY-FIVE

From powerful Warriors, shamans, and mages to the simplest life in existence, all are woven into the intricate weave of the Continuum, all play their part.

ricia walked slowly through the waking camp, her breath drifting away in ephemeral coils of swirling mist through the cold morning air. *Vanishing like my good mood.* She glanced up. The rain clouds had passed, and the red sky of dawn heralded a better day. She scowled. But weren't those shepherds wary of a red sky in the morning? *Given the troubles of this age, I guess all mornings come with a health warning.* She looked to the brightening sky to the east, where the sun would soon rise above the tree line and her day would begin. But a day doing what? Helping these people she barely knew scratch out their existence here? A people preparing for deadly conflict with others from afar whom she also didn't know.

They would fight. Some would live. *Many will die.*

But the world would move on.

And then what?

Soap, rinse, repeat, came the unbidden refrain. Soap, rinse, and repeat for thirteen thousand years. People living, people dying, people enjoying themselves, people killing each other. *Soap, rinse, repeat.*

Until they reach my time.

She stopped walking, suddenly overcome by the thought. Over those thirteen thousand years ahead of her, how many tribes such as these would come together, strive for a better life – *and then vanish?* Over those thousands of years ahead, how many villages, towns, cities, and civilisations would appear, thrive, and then crumble into dust? And how many people would live and die? Each with their own wishes and their dreams, for them and for their descendants. *But only a tiny fraction to be recorded in history and remembered.* For the unimaginable number of untold others, unwitnessed by historians, not a single speck of their memory would remain.

Gone forever. Forever forgotten.

Tricia stood in silence, a darkness clouding her thoughts. What did the future hold for her? For her world? Who would be remembered thirteen thousand years on from her own time? *Will we even preserve our world for another thirteen thousand years?*

She sighed. *Snap out of it, Trish. You started with shepherds and drifted into finding the answer to life, the universe, and everything.* She forced a smile. *So, what's the question?*

She scanned around, seeing people moving all around the camp. Her smile faded. *People I'm supposed to help.* She'd been so excited to join Amber, to help those most needy in the camp – to have a purpose – but then the assassins had arrived, and she'd overheard Beth and the others talking of execution. Her world had been turned upside down. Her friend was becoming a person she didn't recognise. A person she didn't like.

That person isn't Beth. Don't walk away from your friend.

But she struggled to shake the despondent mood that had settled on her. *It's as though another walks through my mind. It's—*

The thought was lost as she saw Beth walking towards the gorge together with Amber and a man she didn't recognise. Here was a chance to engage with her friend and get back to what they'd had. *Talk to her. Help her. Be nice.* Girding herself, she set off to intercept her.

Walking towards Beth and the others, she felt the melancholic fog clouding her thoughts suddenly lifting, as though a breeze had swept through her mind. It was as though she'd woken from a bad dream, one where she'd been dragged beneath a cloak of despair. *Don't get caught there again, Trish. Focus on what's in front of you.*

She smiled as she approached Beth and the others. "Good morning, Beth. Morning, Amber. And a cold one at that." She noted the thick, warm jacket Beth wore. She'd have to find out who made it.

"Morning, Trish," Amber said. "Good to see you up and about." She held out a small pack with a smile. "Here's a set of tools Dune made for you. We'll make a healer out of you yet."

Tricia grinned as she took them. "Or a butcher."

The man next to Beth laughed. A fierce-looking man, Tricia noted as she glanced at him, but his features were softened by his smile.

"Morning, Trish," Beth said. She indicated the tall man by her side. "This is Davak, of the Islanders."

335

The man offered his arm. Tricia grasped his wrist in the Iyes way, and the man smiled, gripping her wrist tightly. "Good to meet you. Trish?"

"Trish, the butcher," she said with a smile. "And you?"

The man's smile faded. "The wrong sort of butcher," he said, releasing her hand.

"Davak is Parig's military advisor," Beth said. "Not that the fool of a man listens to advice."

Davak laughed. "It can be difficult, yes. But when it matters, he listens."

It would be good if someone would listen to me, Tricia found herself thinking. *Stop it,* she berated herself. *You said you weren't going there.*

"Walk with us," Beth said, glancing at Tricia. "It seems we're all heading the same way."

Tricia nodded, and as Beth turned back to the gorge, Davak by her side, she quickly followed. As they walked on, Beth appeared relaxed, radiating confidence and potency as she led her entourage through the waking camp. Yet there was a keen alertness in her eyes, a steely glint. *This is not the Beth I know. This woman is dangerous.* She quickly berated herself for the unguarded thought. *Stop judging. This is still Beth.*

"Is the interrogation of the captives continuing?" Davak asked Beth.

"Gravel is with them now. He'll be working them hard. Still, I'm not hopeful. One doesn't speak, and another ..." She shook her head. "That one will take her secrets to her ancestors."

"Which leaves the talkative one."

"Yes, that one is clever. He gives enough to keep himself alive, but not enough to aid us."

Davak cast a sidelong glance at Beth. "We can't talk to them all day. Scouts are returning from afar and report of tribes in conflict to the south, tribes that are allies of ours and awaiting our support. They're holding – just. But each moment we remain here is another life lost. And a chance for more assassins to find their way through."

"That's why I agreed with Parig you should leave today. But we also agreed to retain people to hold the Sacred Sites of IY – these seem to be key targets of the Ka."

Tricia almost walked into Beth as her friend abruptly stopped.

"These northern lands are prepared. Our messengers have confirmed our allies' understanding and readiness. But I agree" – Beth gestured to the south – "it's from there the pressure will come." She studied Davak closely. "Just how far does your influence hold?"

"We know many of the southern and eastern tribes as far as the great mountains – and even some tribes beyond. But influence?" He shook his head. "That's not possible over those great distances. Not for us Islanders, or for the Iyes. That's why we will march south now to meet the leaders of those tribes and aid them to gather forces to harass the Ka as they push north. It will be hard but must be done, else the enemy will overrun us."

"Who do you need?"

"I need all."

Beth shook her head. "Some of your people have to remain here. You've seen what the Ka raids have done to us. I need two of your Islander tribes."

"No," Davak said firmly. He considered for a moment. "I need the Silerians and the Hebries. You may keep the Mancs."

Tricia saw anger flare in Beth's eyes.

"This is not a decision made easily, Warrior," Davak said. "I am acutely aware Parig's foster daughter is with you."

Tricia glanced at Davak. Rind was Parig's adopted daughter? She hadn't known that.

Beth glared at Davak for a moment longer, then the anger faded from her eyes. "Tell Parig I agree to this. May our gods help us both."

He gave a slight bow. "I thank you, Warrior. I will prepare my people." Turning to go, he paused. "I forgot to ask. When is the execution planned? It would please Parig to be there – in fact he will wield the axe himself if you wish."

"Thank him for his generous offer, but I doubt we'll be wielding any axes today."

Davak gave a curt nod. "He won't like that," he said with a thin smile. "And we'll all feel the effects of his bad mood later. Some things never change." He shrugged, then bowed once more. "I bid you good day, Warrior. I wish you well until we next meet. May Taran be with you."

He turned and strode off to the east of the camp.

"Taran?" Beth whispered, turning to Amber.

"A god of the Islanders, one they turn to in battle."

"An ally of IY?"

Amber's brow furrowed. "An ally in this war, yes. But beyond that? That's a question for our shaman."

"Bloody gods," Tricia muttered under her breath. "You'd think they'd have better things to do."

"Take care with your words," Amber hissed, glaring at Tricia. "These are dangerous times."

Did I say that out loud? "Sorry. Just in jest."

Beth stepped to Tricia's side, admonishing her. "There's a time and a place. Now isn't that time." Her gaze shifted. "Now there's the man I need to see."

Tricia turned. They stood at the northern limit of the encampment; ahead lay open ground up to the gorge. The Shield, Gravel, walked towards them.

"What news from our guests?" Beth questioned as the scarred man approached.

Gravel cleared his throat, then spat to the side. "The same tune as last night. We are the destroyers of the Land, and they are the Land's saviours – at least that's what the long-haired scum said. The other has nothing to give, and the woman with a tongue of fire is itching to get to my blade – and then my neck." The scars on his face twisted as his piercing gaze locked onto Beth. "If you want my opinion – or even if you don't – we should execute them now. It's neither safe nor good for morale for them to remain in camp."

Tricia watched as Beth walked a few steps away, rubbing the back of her neck – the first obvious sign of tension she had seen from her friend this morning. "I want to speak with the long-haired one," she said, turning around to face Gravel. "Bring him to the Sacred Chamber."

"Warrior, I don't agree with this. No Ka should enter our sacred spaces."

"There is something I wish to see. If that takes us nowhere, then they die. I'll see you there shortly."

Gravel clearly struggled with the command. "My advice has been ignored before – Naga paid the price of doing so. If you want to interrogate him further, do it anywhere but there."

Beth hesitated. "That may indeed be a step too far. Return to the prisoners. I will see you there midmorning."

Gravel gave a curt nod, then strode away.

"What will you do?" Tricia asked.

Beth watched Gravel walk towards the gorge. "We'll continue to question them, then, when we're sure they've nothing left to give, they must die."

"You'll have them murdered?"

"Executed as enemy spies and assassins," Beth said, her voice hardening.

"We can bring them with us as prisoners," Tricia breathed, horrified her friend would consider murdering them.

Beth glared at her. "No. You've seen the woman – if she could free herself, she'd kill one of us without hesitation or compulsion. As would the others. No, I can't risk another death in this tribe – *my* tribe."

Tricia shuddered at the thought of the prisoners being slaughtered in cold blood. She flicked a glance towards the uncompromising figure of the retreating Shield Gravel. There walked a hard man, an unbending man of these times. Was that the answer? To leave this war to those who knew best how to fight them? No sooner had that thought run through her head than she vehemently dismissed it. *No!* Those who knew how to fight wars were not the same people who should define what was right and wrong. Wasn't this the flaw that would taint her people for the next thirteen millennia? "It's not right," she said, grabbing her friend's hand. "If it is, then *you* do it."

Beth turned her gaze towards the gorge. Towards the prisoners. "If needed, I will," she said in a quiet voice. "Now, if you'll excuse me, I need to make preparations for our move." She brushed off Tricia's hand and walked away.

Tricia stared after her, her hands shaking. She *would* do it. Her friend would kill the prisoners.

She felt someone step to her side. "She's right," came Amber's firm voice. "Those scum came here seeking our destruction. It's not safe for our tribe to have them in our midst, or safe to let them leave." Tricia faced Amber, hearing the raw emotion in the woman's voice. "My job is to save lives," Amber continued, "but not the lives of these cursed Ka." Tears formed in the young woman's eyes. "They killed my Eagle, and for that, they will pay."

Tricia could think of nothing to say.

Amber wiped her eyes. "We should go. We've many to see this morning."

Tricia followed Amber towards the gorge, her mind in turmoil. An eye for an eye? Vengeance for three assassins sent to kill Beth and the Mother of the Iyes tribe. Three killers clearly and obviously caught in the act. She glanced at Amber. Who could blame the healer for feeling this way? And who in this tribe would stop her from taking that eye?

Not many.

And yet … And yet, with a hard heart and a determined will, couldn't *somebody* say this was wrong, that this was not the way for a civilised society to work?

But this is not our age, not our people.

As the thought hammered into Tricia's mind, she felt her stomach churn. This was *not* their age. *And it's not an age I want to stay in. I want to get home.* But words Beth had just spoken scared her: "I can't risk another death in this tribe, my tribe." *My tribe?* Did Beth now see this as her tribe? Her land? She shuddered. Did Beth now *want* to stay here? That couldn't be. They needed to get back.

And we can't kill in cold blood. No, Beth. You can't do this.

She glanced to the gorge. She needed to speak with Beth and the others again. They had to hear her voice.

*

A bright glow spilled from the Sacred Chamber into the passageway down which River now walked, evidence of the Spirits' intense battle to maintain the containment shield around the Shade of the Ka. As she entered the chamber, the concern – and fear – of the Spirits washed over her. She sat down, slowing her breathing, and reached out to Iolaire.

'The Shade is growing stronger,' came Iolaire's voice, 'and building a cache of energy sufficient to shatter the bonds.'

'Can you cut off his energy source?'

'The daemon of the Shade, Ereboz, is preventing that. He is a powerful daemon, eclipsing even Garrion and Fen.'

'But I was told the Warrior Lanky broke through Ereboz's shield at White Crags camp.'

'True,' Iolaire said. 'The combined power and skill of the Warrior and Fen can match that of the Shade. But at White Crags, the Shade underestimated the Warrior – an advantage unlikely to be repeated.'

River frowned. 'Lanky and Fen? But they haven't bonded yet ... have they?'

'No. The Warrior is ever wary. But that does not prevent Fen from aiding him. His full strength may be constrained, but he is still a most prodigious Warrior.'

River looked to the far wall of the chamber, where the shaman stood cloaked within an oily blackness, itself encased in sparking coils of pulsating white energy. But the black shroud was growing outwards, pushing against the straining white coils. 'Why do the Spirits fail?'

'This is not their function. They guide and advise, aiding us in our darkest moments, showing us paths to take.' A ripple of sorrow drifted through the ether. 'Their purpose is not one of fighting, or leading armies into battle. When threatened, they will defend – and with strength – but they are not equipped to deal with the daemons of Kaos. For this they need us, their daemons. And they need the Warriors of the Continuum.' Iolaire paused, confusion swirling. 'But you must know this? Passed on by Naga.'

'I ... there is so much. At times, I think I know nothing, and then, moments later, I'm overwhelmed with a myriad of half-remembered thoughts, ideas, memories. I know so much, but I understand so little.'

'You have much to learn, this is true. But you must learn quickly. Accept all of what you are. Accept all of Revri.'

Accept what I am? She was gripped by sudden doubt. *What am I? What truly is Revri?* A swirl of fractured memories swept out of the deep well that was both the Mother's bounty and her burden. Indistinct memories of other bodies. And sharper memories of other denizens, those souls that walked beside Warriors, having once been Warriors themselves. *Denizens like Revri. Once a Warrior, and now a soul that sits beside mine.* But what of her and the Warriors of today? What truly were they? Were they as denizens too? Were they born beyond the Horizon, called to the Land by IY? Were they forced into the mind and body of an innocent, the past erased, the soul replaced by a Warrior daemon?

No. This cannot be. I know my mother. I know my father. I am River.

And the denizens, those who walked beside the Warriors?

That, I don't know. The Mothers do not know.

And in this moment, she knew some things would remain unknowable. *Accept what you are. And accept the one who walks beside me. Revri has survived in this Land for millennia. And despite my fears, together we form a potent force.*

She looked up, sensing faint ripples of cloying energy leaking from the imprisoned Shade. And they needed their combined strength to face this. *As at the Mountain of Hope.* The memory of the battle with the daemon, Alkazar, remained raw and chilling. She – Revri – had held back that foul daemon for as long as she'd been able, allowing others the time to find the way into the mountain. But Alkazar had proved too strong, and only the arrival of Beth – Bethusa – had saved them. *And this imprisoned Shade and his daemon?* Could she and Beth alone destroy these most lethal enemies, destroy those who were defeating the Spirits of this Land?

'We need the aid of both Bethusa and her new daemon,' came Iolaire's voice. 'Together we will attempt to destroy the Shade.'

'When?'

'Now.'

River steadied herself against a lance of fear. Fear of the battle to come, and fear of what Beth would choose. For Beth and Bethusa were in conflict, not yet aligned, and not yet bonded with a new daemon. She felt a moment of guilt. *I didn't share my worries, my doubts, of what Revri is. Of what I am. I let Beth see only the unity we have forged.* She cast the guilt aside. Beth didn't need any further reason to distrust Bethusa. *We need them both. As I need Revri.*

She climbed to her feet. *'I will fetch the Warrior.'*

'I will be waiting. Tell Bethusa she must not delay.'

*

For most of the miserably cold night and early morning, they'd been interrogated by the hard-nosed Scar, who was not averse to using his granitelike fist to back up his hard-bitten voice to extract answers. It proved impossible to try to influence the man. Any slightest attempt earned Shadow a vicious beating, and with his legs and neck bound tightly to a tree, it was impossible to defend himself. His brief respites came when the Warrior appeared. She was clearly no fool but engaged in a way more aligned with Shadow's plan; *she lets me talk.* So, talk he did, repeating his answers again and again, but with subtle variations and sharing only enough to show the Warrior he was cooperating, while preserving the Ka's security. A delicate balance designed to keep them alive as long as he could.

And it had been working.

Shadow felt the comforting presence of the keen-edged blade inside his closed fist. *We still have a chance.*

Nefra, wearing a tattered tunic her captors had thrown on her in the cold of the night, began to throw abuse at the guards while thrashing against her leashes. Shadow grimaced. She'd played her part so very well through the night, deflecting attention from him and Sy as they'd slowly loosened the bindings around their wrists. But it came at a terrible cost; Nefra suffered badly, bearing the brunt of the guards' efforts to quell their violent captive. He didn't like her, but that didn't mean he was immune to her suffering.

But better than being dead, he thought grimly.

With the guards' eyes once more diverted, Shadow slowly turned his head to the left and caught Sy's eyes. A pang of doubt ran through him as he remembered Sy's expression in the caves. Growl had been ready to execute him, he was sure, but Sy's part in that was uncertain. He calmed himself. If Sy had orders to kill him, the monk wouldn't act now. They needed to work together to escape. He took a deep breath. Survive in this moment, then deal with what came next.

Sy's fingers flashed behind his back.

At last! Sy's hands were free, exploiting the same sloppy work of their captors that Shadow had discovered from the start – a looseness of their binding that could prove the first step of their escape.

Shadow flashed another series of messages.

Sy acknowledged his readiness.

Shadow glanced down, straining against the binding around his neck. Cutting quickly through the neck and leg bindings was going to be tricky. *I hope this blade is as sharp as it feels.* He looked back up, tension building. Now it was a matter of timing. *But how much time do we have?*

Hearing a now familiar voice, he caught sight of the dark-haired Warrior approaching. Scar strode over to her, and they spoke in hushed voices. Was their death being sealed in those words?

A moment later, the Warrior walked over to him, stopping just out of arm's reach. As she studied his face, he studied hers. Smooth skin, marked only by one small scar on her cheek. Sharp eyes, a youthful face. Not the face of a killer. Not the face he expected of the destroyers of his people. *But have you seen many others? Have you—*

"What does Kaos offer you?" the Warrior asked.

She has a rich voice, and beautiful lilt. A voice I could easily listen to. A pity ... "Personally, nothing," he said honestly, wondering where this was heading. No matter, he would keep playing the game. "But for the Ka, a sense of trusted discipline, security for families, and the simple hope for a fair future for all. Unlike the false offering of the deceitful IY."

"Ah, yes," the Warrior murmured, her dark eyes locked onto his. "The Ka sense of discipline. One so easy to maintain when you cull those who disagree with you, don't you think? I notice a sense of justice was missing from your list."

"We 'cull' no one," Shadow said, a spark of anger firing inside.

"Taking your own people from their home at night and throwing their dead bodies in the river is not part of your culling?"

A chill ran through him at remembered words of the dragon's servant: "They killed leavers."

"Killing the children of those families that come to your camp is not part of your culling?" the Warrior said, her voice hardening.

"We do not—"

"And raping the women of the tribes you conquer is not part of your plan for the future?" the Warrior rasped, her voice as cold as ice.

"We do not—"

'I ask you again,' the Warrior snarled in his head. *'How do you sleep at night?'*

Stunned, Shadow swept the veil back across his mind as the Shade had taught him. How had she – yet again – forced his defences to drop? How did he keep underestimating this woman – this extremely dangerous woman?

"You are the defilers!" Nefra yelled to his side. "Don't lecture us, devil woman, killer of the ages."

Shadow closed his eyes, tuning out Nefra's voice as she continued to yell and scream in her efforts to further distract their guards. The Warrior had rattled him. He shouldn't have allowed it, and that annoyed him further. *Why is she getting under my skin? Ignore her. Keep to the plan.*

"You are needed," came a new voice.

Shadow opened his eyes to see the enemy shaman striding towards the Warrior. *She looks worried.* The shaman halted, and as the two women spoke, he saw a flash of concern cross the face of the Warrior. He was pleased. Anything worrying these people was something in his favour. But what was it?

It quickly became clear that the Warrior and the shaman were leaving together. But as they walked away, Shadow noticed the Warrior's almost imperceptible nod to Scar. He tensed. That was it. The Warrior had sealed their fate. Striving to clamp a hold on a rising dread, he dropped his head but watched carefully out of the corner of his eye as the two women walked away towards the entrance to the cave, the cave which held the Shade. *The Shade …* Was he fighting free? Did they—

He heard the voice of Scar to his right. Keeping his head down, he flicked his hooded eyes to the stone-faced Iyes. The man spoke in a low yet commanding voice to the two younger guards, then strode away. *This is our chance. Our only chance. We need to move now.* Pushing back the scent of death, he twisted his hand very slowly in its binding, first one way, then the other – his hand slipped through the leather binding with a tug. He turned his head gradually, subtly, to the bound figure on his left.

Sy gave the slightest of nods.

The chance remained! Now they just needed Nefra to play her part.

Shadow waited. And waited. He licked his dry lips. The Scar could be back at any moment. *As the executioner.*

He started as Nefra began another of her furious tirades, violently thrashing against her bindings. His heart hammered in his chest. *This is it!* As one of the guards walked over to restrain her, Shadow called out: "Guard! Guard! My friend over here doesn't seem to be breathing."

The young guard faced him, frowning.

"Look. He's collapsed. Something's wrong."

As the guard walked towards him, peering at the slumped figure of Sy, Shadow readied the concealed blade in his hand. "I don't know how long he's been like that," he said, concern in his voice. "Could you fetch help?"

The guard halted a few steps away, his expression uncertain.

Go on, take the bait.

The guard glanced towards Nefra, where his fellow guard attempted to restrain the snarling, spitting prisoner. He muttered something under his breath, then turned to Sy and walked across to the slumped man—

Sy's powerful hands flew from behind his back and grabbed the man by the neck, throttling him, straining thumbs compressing his windpipe. Choking, unable to cry out, the guard panicked, frantically tearing at Sy's hands to pry them loose. *He should have gone for his blade,* Shadow thought, slicing effortlessly through the leather binding around his neck before cutting the ties on his legs. The guard was a fool. *A soon-to-be-dead fool.*

The guard dealing with the screaming Nefra suddenly noticed what was happening, but Shadow was already there. He struck him a vicious and precise blow to the temple, and the guard collapsed, twitching. Sprinting to the guard's hut, Shadow grabbed a spear, then raced back and skewered the choking young guard through the spine.

Within moments all three of them were free, armed, and sprinting to the cave. *Second time lucky,* Shadow thought grimly. But why did he have a bad feeling about this? *Ignore all else. Complete the mission.*

*

"Hurry!" River called, sprinting ahead towards the Sacred Chamber.

Quelling her fears, Beth raced after her. She had finally accepted she needed a new daemon on her side to provide the potent edge in the coming battles but had wanted to engage the daemon first; to test it; to ensure it understood what she wanted from it. *But we've no time for that,* she growled to herself. The stakes had just been raised. The Ka Shade was about to break free.

As they swept into the Sacred Chamber, she saw the enemy shaman still contained within his coiled prison – but it was a prison clearly weakening. The upper coils binding the shrouded shaman were cut with intense black streaks, and his savage, malignant hate polluted the air.

Her eyes widened as she saw an Axe lying in the centre of the chamber – the final and yet unclaimed Axe of the four Axes of IY. "What's that doing here! It's not safe to have this anywhere near this monster."

"Hence, we need to be quick. Place your Axe next to the other."

"What! No! This is staying right where it needs to be – with me."

"To connect with your new daemon," River said, her voice strained with frustration, "it must first choose an Axe."

"What! Why!" She hefted her Axe. "This is mine. I chose it." *I know it.*

"We don't have time for this," River snapped. "Listen, each Axe is unique, with particular properties, distinct textures, a different essence imbued by the maker. Not seen by you, but by the daemon. Each daemon will choose the Axe that allows it to make an enduring bond with you." She leaned forward. "So put the Axe down!"

Beth glanced to the bound shaman. One constraining loop rippled with an oily blackness, while black streaks violently swirled within the others. The bindings were failing. The truth slammed into her. *I have no choice!*

She set her Axe down next to the other, then knelt in front of them.

"It is time," River intoned. "Meet the daemons."

Light breaths of energy disturbed the ether around her, and she felt an ethereal presence draw near. And then a second.

She closed her eyes and opened her mind. Two daemons appeared before her.

She turned to the first – at least, she turned to the looming presence of the first. Idling in a vast expanse of ocean beneath her swam an enormous blue whale, its sleek, elongate body seeming to glow in the crystal-clear waters, its aura overwhelming. When Beth dropped beneath the waters to regard the animal's eye, it seemed as though she gazed into the eye of a god. *There is a deep intelligence here. That could prove most valuable.*

Returning to the surface, she looked to her right. A cave lion slowly padded towards her, sleek muscles rippling with each effortless stride. *'For your sparing of one of our brothers, I stand before you, offering you my aid,'* the lioness growled. *'For our battles ahead, you will need the speed and ferocity I can bring.'* The lioness swung her head to the ocean. *'This one is for another.'*

'That's for me to decide,' Beth rasped.

The lioness curled her lip, baring razor-sharp teeth. *'Then decide before it is too late.'*

Eyes still closed, Beth reached out …

Her hand closed around the haft of an Axe.

'You have chosen well, Bethusa. I am Afari. Do you accept the bond?'

'I do.'

Adrenaline surged as the daemon's essence flooded through her and into the Axe.

'You have much to remember, Bethusa,' the lioness growled. *'But you hold enough for this battle. Are you ready?'*

Beth felt the other rise within. *'I am ready.'*

Bethusa opened her eyes, then climbed to her feet. "Revri," she said, acknowledging the other.

"Bethusa," Revri said, hefting her Axe from its holster, her eyes flashing bright.

Standing side-by-side, they watched as blackened coils fell away from the shrouded Shade until only one remained.

"Prepare to die," rasped the Shade as the black shroud around him vanished.

The last coil snapped.

And with a blazing explosion of fearsome power, battle commenced.

*

As they reached the cave entrance, a tremendous blast rocked the ground and a convulsive gale swept out from the entrance. They looked at each other, suddenly uncertain, as sharp claps of thunder echoed from within the cave.

"What do we do now?" Nefra hissed, a stolen blade in one hand, a spear in the other.

Shadow glanced along the gorge, trying to catch his breath. Enemy fighters streamed towards them. *Here we go again.* "We need the Shade," he said as another volley of sharp cracks issued from the tunnel. "We'll have to head inside and find him."

Nefra glanced to the oncoming fighters. "You go. We'll hold the entrance."

"Fine, but you can't hold against all those," Shadow said, seeing the large group heading towards them. "Remember where the tunnel narrows?" Nefra nodded. "Hold them there. I'll join you after I've seen what the kef is happening."

Without waiting for an answer, Shadow raced into the cave, passing remnants of the rockfall from the Shade's attack the previous day. He heard Sy and Nefra follow. They ran on through the tunnel network, assailed by the explosions ricocheting around the walls of the cave. It was clearly a mighty battle. The Shade fought for his freedom, Shadow was sure of it. *And we should be anywhere but in here right now.* But they needed the Shade.

Leaving Sy and Nefra to delay their pursuers, Shadow continued on, his unease deepening by the moment as he heard the deafening booms from the titanic struggle ahead. As he grew closer, he was forced to shield his eyes against the intense, blinding flares accompanying the ear-shattering cracks of thunder. And after the blinding light came flashes of deepest black, where light itself seemed to be sucked from the cave. How could he hope to achieve anything by entering that maelstrom of wanton power?

But he had to try to aid the Shade if he could. *It's our way out of here.*

He edged forward along the last stretch of the passageway, shielding from the ferocious glare as best he could, until he could finally peer into the chamber. And there, in one corner of the cavern, stood the Shade, his Black Staff held aloft, a shield of pitch-black before him – a shield being hammered by sizzling bolts of jagged white lightning from the two axe-wielding Warriors before him. He heard Growl shout a word unknown to Shadow—

The chamber plunged into darkness and a massive blast slammed into him, hurling him backwards to the ground. As a blazing white light flooded back into the cave, Shadow clambered back to his feet, gasping for breath. A ringing in his ears, he brought his fraught gaze to the Warriors, seeing the tremendous strain of their efforts etched in their faces. Their concentration was total, all focussed on the Shade. *They don't see me*, he thought, his heart racing. *There may be a chance. But what?*

Quickly scanning the chamber, he caught sight of a weapon – an axe with a green-hued blade – lying on the ground behind the Warriors. But could he reach it?

"Shadow!" he heard Nefra shout in the distance. "Be ready."

They had done well to give him this time. *I need to repay them. I—*

A section of the Shade's black shield violently flexed and distorted, and a grotesque figure leapt forward to attack one of the Warriors. The Warrior slammed up a white shield, deflecting the strike. With the enemy hidden from view, Shadow's eyes locked onto the axe. He readied himself. *I will have only one chance …*

*

She found another weak spot in the Shade's shield and switched her attack there. *'I need more,'* Bethusa demanded.

'This is all I can give,' Afari growled.

'It's not enough! Find more!'

Readying her new attack, she saw the Shade had already adjusted his defence to deflect her thunderous strikes. She immediately searched for another weak point …

And in that smallest moment of distraction, the Shade struck.

348

The chamber plunged into darkness, and she screamed as her whole body exploded in tortured pain. As a firestorm raged across the chamber, a razor-sharp stone ripped into her eyes and slowly levered them out of their sockets. Her skin was raked from her face, the bloodied strips flapping from her cheeks. A searing-hot blade slit her throat—

With a tremendous force of will, Bethusa slammed her defence back in place, then struck out with all her might at the heart of the Shade.

Light flooded back, and the horrific attack on her vanished.

But beside her, Revri screamed.

Holding her attack on the Shade, Bethusa saw Revri drop her Axe and then simply melt away before her eyes.

'Stay focussed,' came the calm voice of Afari. 'Ignore all else.'

'These games do not fool me,' Bethusa growled.

She sucked in more energy from the A'ven and forced the mirage from her mind. And once more, Revri stood resolutely beside her, unharmed and maintaining her relentless assault on the Shade. A burning rage within her, Bethusa glared at the Shade. "You'll need to try harder than that, devil," she snarled, and following Revri's line of attack, they delivered a blistering, sustained attack on the Shade's shield.

The shield began to buckle and warp.

'He's weakening,' Afari said. 'We have him.'

But in that moment, Bethusa saw the Ka assassin standing at the entrance to the chamber.

She frowned. *Another illusion?*

At this second distraction, the Shade struck again. The deformed jaws of a grotesque, alien beast thrust out from the black shield, razor-sharp teeth striking for Revri. Her partner barely managed to slam her shield in place to deflect its deadly strike.

And then the Ka assassin rushed forward, lunging for the Axe on the ground.

"Curse him," Bethusa hissed, seeing now this was no trick of the Shade. She made to switch her attack to the Ka, but the Shade's hellish creature struck out at her. Grunting, she snapped her own shield in place, then staggered as the creature hammered into her. Straining to hold, she felt the pressure ease a fraction and instantly unleashed a gout of crackling energy at the rabid beast. Buried beneath waves of lashing power, the foul creature of the Dark swept back and vanished – but behind it, the pulsating black wall of the shaman's shield crept slowly, inexorably closer. She grimaced as a tremendous strike of black lightning smashed into her shield as the Shade switched his attack.

'Bethusa! With me!' Revri shouted, swinging her shield towards Bethusa's.

Instinctively, Bethusa rotated her shield, merging it with her partner's. Their combined shield burned with a white-hot intensity, sizzling and sparking as a feral storm of black lightning tore into it.

Their shield held. Just.

Sweat pouring from her brow, Bethusa slowly turned her head—

To face the Ka standing beside her.

Holding the Axe of IY.

And ready to strike.

Unable to break away from the shield holding back the might of the Shade, it was as though death himself stood before her. A strange calm descended. *Does it end here?*

But the Ka stood, unmoving, a look of anguish on his face.

Straining with all her might to hold the shield against the Shade's frenzied attack, she stared in bewildered confusion at the Ka. *Why doesn't he attack?*

His hands shaking, sweat dripping off his brow, the Ka held the Axe aloft.

Yet still he didn't strike.

Two figures appeared at the chamber entrance, two she instantly recognised as the other two Ka assassins. As the woman hefted her spear, Bethusa felt Revri expand the shield to cover the attack from the new arrivals. The hurled spear deflected harmlessly away.

"Strike now!" Bethusa heard the woman shout to the Ka assassin.

The man with the Axe didn't move.

As Bethusa strained to hold the shield in place, the pressure of the Shade's attack grew. *Ignore this Ka. The threat lies with the Shade.* Clenching her fist tightly around her Axe, she glared towards the enshrouded presence of the foul Shade. 'Revri, are you ready!'

'Ready.'

'Drop and attack,' Bethusa commanded.

Immediately, their shield vanished, and the two women let loose a devastating stream of crackling white-hot slugs of energy, each blazing projectile slamming home with a crack of thunder, a fearsome firepower turning the Shade's shield into its own small sun.

"Surrender, Shade," Bethusa snarled as she took a step forward. "Or die."

"Shadow! Strike now!" the Ka woman screamed.

Bethusa and Revri took another step forward.

"Curse you, Shadow!" the Ka woman cried. The man beside the woman, the one who didn't speak, launched his own spear at the assassin.

Time seemed to slow for Bethusa as she watched the weapon fly through the air. *They seek to kill their own?* she thought, the faintest flicker of confusion arising amidst the heat of battle. *Why?*

The spear hurtled on—

The Ka assassin batted it away with the Axe.

Revri and Bethusa took another step. Then another.

Then as they took another step, she heard a commanding cry at the chamber's entrance. The two Ka dashed away, hiding behind the Shade's crackling shield.

"This is not over," came the Shade's snarling voice.

And then the enemy vanished – the barrier, the Shade, and the two Ka.

Bethusa and Revri both ceased their attacks.

Revri fell to her knees.

Snarling, Bethusa rushed forward, quickly searching the ether around them for the Cord the Shade had used to escape. But the distorted A'ven, screaming with the remnant vibrations of battle, masked the vibrations of the Cord she sought. Eyes blazing, she glared at the empty space. "We failed," she snarled. "How could we fail?"

She stood for a moment longer, then her fierce eyes locked onto the Ka assassin. The man, his face strained, the Axe held limply by his side, had not moved.

Gravel, together with many other fighters, poured into the chamber. Gravel scanned the chamber, then instantly cocked a spear.

"Hold!" Bethusa commanded. "I want to speak to this one."

Shaking, his arm tensed, Gravel held ready to send the spear hurtling into the Ka's head.

"I have given my command," Bethusa snarled.

Gravel, his deep eyes burning with hatred, lowered his arm, then glowered at her.

Ignoring him, Bethusa faced the assassin. "Reveal yourself," she growled.

The assassin's eyes widened as if beholding some startling vision …

Then he collapsed, the Axe falling to the ground.

As Gravel's fighters surged forward, Bethusa bent down to pick up the Axe. "Take him," she said as she stood. "Secure him in the next chamber with five beside him and five at the entrance. No one in, no one out." She turned to Gravel, holding his murderous gaze. "It seems we should have heeded your way, old man. How many killed?"

"Three," Gravel rasped. "Darius, Firuz, and one of the Islanders. I don't know his name, but I will."

Bethusa heard the unfailing intent in the fighter's voice. She tilted her head. "I will stay a while to speak to their ancestors." She glanced sidelong at the prone assassin, who was being carried out of the chamber. "Then I will send another to meet theirs."

*

Throughout the ferocious battle, Beth had hidden deep, shielding herself from the writhing waves of blistering power lashing through the ether. All the while, she watched and learned, unwilling to attempt to break Bethusa's binding on her. For she saw that the Ka Shade was too strong for her to face. Not so for Bethusa. *I couldn't have done what she did against that devil.*

But now?

I saw. I understood. I am ready.

Yet in this moment, she remained trapped by the spirit of the ancient Warrior.

Her thoughts were broken as she – as Bethusa – turned to Revri and spoke: "Stand, Warrior. Show your people your strength."

Through Bethusa's eyes – her eyes – Beth watched Revri slowly climb to her feet.

"The Shade is powerful," Bethusa growled. "But I see a weakness within him." Beth felt the ancient Warrior's attention turn to her. "As there is within me."

Her panic flared as Bethusa pushed her deeper within the darkness of the bindings.

Bethusa's attention returned to Revri. "Next time, we will defeat him. Tell me what you saw. We have time before we deal with this one."

Which one? Beth thought. *The assassin or me?*

Enough was enough. *'Afari! I need your help!'*

Immediately, the power of the A'ven streamed into her mind and into her soul. Grasping the rich energy, Beth surged ruthlessly upwards, sweeping around the distracted Bethusa, overwhelming her, dragging the ancient Warrior deep down within her.

'No!' Bethusa snarled. *'You are too weak to face what comes!'*

With the stricken Bethusa fighting to break free, Beth slammed cold-willed barriers back in place, silencing the belligerent Warrior. *At least for now.* Smelling the acrid stench of battle in the chamber, relief coursed through her at her regained freedom – together with intense waves of loss, regret, and anger from the other. *'Complain all you like,'* Beth growled. *'This is my body. My mind. I control it.'*

'The Warrior within you is fearsome,' came Afari's voice. *'You must find a way to harness your powers. To resolve your conflict. To remain you.'*

'That will not be easy.' Her thought or Bethusa's?

'Some succeed, many fail,' Afari said. *'You and Bethusa share many traits, so, yes, that makes it harder.'*

A vision of a dead man flared, an Axe buried in his head. She knew him, she was sure. And she knew the Axe was hers. But how? And why this image now?

She felt a hand on her arm. "We must pay our respects," River said at her side. "Gravel is waiting."

She pulled herself to the moment. Three more dead. *Did I make a mistake?*

A part of her reacted immediately. Yes, she'd been too slow to act. The assassins should have been executed. Her eyes narrowed. Maybe there was indeed much to learn from Bethusa.

'Yes, step aside, then you will see,' came an intemperate voice from deep within.

Beth's jaw tensed. Bethusa was of this Land, of that, she was sure. *She knows much that would be useful to me. The question is, do I dare engage?* The answer came quickly. *I have no choice. I must learn more.* Because right now she was a stranger, a novice, a dangerous imposter, one playing within a deadly game, one where she knew few of the rules.

'Yes,' came Afari's voice. *'You have no choice. Because if you don't learn, you will become Bethusa – and then what happens to Beth?'*

'The Land needs Bethusa,' came a merciless voice. *'Forget Beth.'*

*

The icy westerly wind streamed across the raging ocean, driving ever larger seas shoreward before howling up the precipitous black cliffs and buffeting the tall woman standing alone on the edge of the land. "Stand back, Cyrene," warned the dark-haired mage seated on a boulder some distance back. "You may be strong, but these winds are stronger. Don't let Eil'an take you to its bosom too early."

Cyrene smiled, an exhilaration coursing through her as she leaned into the storm-driven wind, her long fair hair streaming out behind her. This was her delight, her eager passion, immersed within the wildest elements of the land. Cutting winds, driving rains, tempestuous storms, or blinding snow; ever since she'd been a child, these had fired her blood and stirred her soul. And if their homeland of Eil'an wanted to take her now? *Then I would join my ancestors willingly.*

Except …

Except that wouldn't happen. A great task remained.

She sighed, steadied herself, then backed away from the edge of the land. The roar of the wind lessened, and she was able to turn and return to Sylander.

"Do we intervene now?" asked her brother as she approached.

"Taran wishes us to wait."

Sylander scowled. "How long? Islanders die. We are failing Parig and his people."

She looked back towards the cliff edge and saw the roiling black clouds of the storm centre moving ever closer. "There is a new entrant to the game, a quite dangerous player."

"Who?"

"The shaman of the Meso tribes. Krull."

"Him? He is weak."

"Not so. He has kept his true powers hidden." Her sharp eyes were marred by a dull edge of worry. "But hidden no longer. He is the new chosen of Kaos."

"Then we should act now before he makes his move."

Cyrene said nothing.

The wind whistled past them, and the first drops of rain spattered her face. She felt Sylander's eyes on her. "He has moved already, hasn't he?" he growled.

"He has. He is in the Ka homeland."

Sylander muttered something under his breath, his words lost in the wind.

Cyrene waited.

"This complicates things," he said eventually. "Are you certain the Guardian hasn't found the Kade?"

"We would feel it, Sylander, you know that. Once pulled into the open, it will be like a new sun floating out in the ocean."

"But she is the Guardian. She could cloak it."

"She is naive – ignorant of her powers. We *will* feel it."

"And then we move?"

"Then we move."

A violent gust of wind rocked them, and the rain stung her face.

"Time to pray?" he said, standing.

"It is time," she said, stepping into the circle of stones. It was time to converse with Taran and recharge themselves with Eil'an's energy.

The mages of the Islanders stepped into the circle, and a moment later, a shaft of vivid blue fired into the growing storm above.

CHAPTER TWENTY-SIX

*If he had truly seen who stood before him, then what
might have been? It matters not ... he didn't.*

𝒥essica stood in silence as Lanky continued to berate her, telling her
to wise up, to ignore the subtle guile of the green-eyed woman.
"Don't listen to her! She's trapping you in her venomous web of lies,
drawing you into the evil maw of the Ka." Those cutting words played
over and over in her sleeping mind, a nightmare she knew she was
riding, but one she couldn't escape.

The vision shifted. Other images flashed by, faint, blurred, and
confused.

Images of Bethusa and Revri fighting a demoniacal enemy.

Images of a colossal whale searching the ether ... *For what?*

Images of a bear and a dragon and a mountain.

And hazy shadows of creatures of the Dark.

The Dark. A simple name conjured within her dreams and redolent
with threat. And yet the Dark *felt* like no dream. *Kaos is of the Dark. The
Dark is of the Void.*

The vision shifted.

She strode with Lanky through vast fields of gold, a winding,
glowing trail in their wake. And before them a battle. A Warrior of
Light fighting a Warrior of the Dark.

The vision shifted.

She stood before the Ensi and the empty throne. The Ensi turned,
then leaned against the throne, pushing it to one side—

Jessica recoiled as the burnt man of nightmares of old burst
forward, a black haze burning within the gaping hole in his chest, his
eyes blazing with white fire. He swung a fearsome axe and sliced
through the Ensi's neck—

Jessica's eyes flew open as she awakened with a stifled scream. She pulled herself up, gasping for breath, quickly scanning around the small chamber. It was empty, save for Lanky's sleeping form beside her. Her heart hammering in her chest, she leaned forward, sitting with her head in her hands. The vision of the burnt man lingered. *The burnt man. A servant of the Dark.*

'Follow the dream,' came the sudden voice of Jalu. '*See what lies beyond the throne.*'

Pushing her hair back from her face, Jessica looked up in a daze. '*Beyond the throne?*' she pulsed from her fogged mind.

There was no answer.

Cursing, she glanced blindly around, lurid memories from her dream plaguing her still. The daemons, the Ensi, the burnt man ... *and the throne.* Jalu wanted her to search beyond the throne of the Ensi? *Why?*

Hellish images from her nightmare seared her mind.

The burnt man kills the Ensi.

But the Ensi can't die.

She ran her hands through her hair in frustration. *These are not my thoughts. These are not my memories. What's happening to me?* It felt as if her mind was tearing apart.

She forced herself still, gathering the frayed threads of her composure.

Calm yourself. You are the Guardian.

A spark of defiance lit inside – defiance against these memories, these thoughts, of another. *I may be the Guardian, but I am also Jessica.* She slowly climbed to her feet. *I came here to find the Kade. I came here to understand. I will understand.*

Driven by a sudden urgency, she reached for her Staff, then looked down at the sleeping Lanky. "I'll be back soon," she whispered. She stepped silently past his sleeping form, then strode out into the passageway and on towards the throne room. She had no idea of the time – it felt predawn – and no idea who would be around. And if she was challenged by the guards? *Stay confident. Look confident.* She walked taller, broadening her shoulders.

Reaching the entrance to the throne room, she glanced inside. It lay empty and silent. Walking quietly but confidently into the chamber, she scanned the shadowy alcoves to her right – no one. Climbing the few short steps onto the pentagonal marble platform, she paused again and listened. Hearing nothing, she glanced to the throne. She hesitated. *This is crazy. It was only a dream.* She cast aside the doubts. *Jalu wants you to see what lies behind. Just do it.*

Gritting her teeth, she quickly crossed to the far side of the marble platform and descended the shallow steps to stand before the dais of the stone throne. She cast a final glance around the chamber, then quickly climbed to the throne, which was set against the back wall of the chamber. Placing her Staff on the ground, she walked up to the throne and pushed against it as the Ensi had done in her dream.

Nothing happened.

She pushed harder – and the throne slid away from her, rotating around an unseen pivot. She glanced nervously around, but she remained alone. Heart racing, she set her weight against the throne and pushed against it, sliding it as far as it would move. Then she stood back, gazing in wonder at the gloomy opening now revealed. *Jalu knew this was here. How?* Casting a furtive glance behind her, she let that question lie. The entrance was here, as Jalu had said. *And as in my dream.* The question now was what lay within?

Quickly grabbing her Staff, she stepped through the opening to find herself standing in a narrow space at the top of a rough-hewn stairwell, which curved down into the torchlit depths below. Clasping her Staff tightly, she crossed to the stairwell and began to descend. As her weight fell on the second step, the stone shifted beneath her foot …

She froze as a low grating sounded behind her, then spun around to see the stone throne rotating quickly back into place, sealing the opening. Cursing, she rushed back and pushed against the back of the throne. It moved a fraction, followed by her sharp sigh of relief – she still had a way out.

Wiping her brow, she turned back to the stairwell and started down the worn steps. Why she chose to ignore all side exits on her descent to the base of the stairwell, she didn't know. But as she left the stairwell behind and walked out into a domed, circular chamber, glistening piles of gold heaped against its walls, she was certain it was the right path.

Because she felt the wondrous energy of the A'ven return to her.

Glorious, radiant tones hummed in the ether around her as tendrils of primordial energy licked around her Staff. Her heart leapt. With the energy of the A'ven, the balance of power shifted. *The Ensi no longer holds all the cards.* She stood, relishing the comforting warmth of the A'ven's energy. *I missed this.* The realisation shocked her. She'd missed its vibrant, fitful rhythms. She'd missed its ephemeral soothing of her soul. She'd missed—

She froze as she sensed the disturbing presence of others.

Others wielding the power of the A'ven!

Tightening her grip on her Staff, she glanced around the gold-laden chamber, scanning the numerous shadowy passageways running off to places unseen. Her gaze fell on the deep gloom of the tunnel facing her. The sense of those wielding the Land's power lay there. She hesitated. Should she go on or return to Lanky with what she'd found? Or should she try to connect with Beth and River? *No, not Beth and River. Don't expose your connection with the A'ven.* And Lanky? She sighed. Jalu's words could not be unheard. She needed to see more. What was the Ensi hiding behind her throne? *Find out what's here, then return to Lanky.*

Tightening her grip on her Staff, she quickly crossed the chamber, purposely skirting the stacked piles of gold. *Leave no trace of your visit here,* she thought, remembering the trail of glowing gold she'd left the evening before. As she entered the chosen passageway and strode on through the narrow tunnel, the disturbance in the ether grew, and disparate eddies swirled past her, ripples from those ahead wielding power. Girding herself, she snapped up a shield on her mind, then walked cautiously on towards a glowing side opening in the tunnel ahead.

She cautiously stepped inside – and gasped at the sight before her.

The marble walls and ceiling of the elongate chamber flickered with a warming yellow light cast from earthenware vases set around the edge of the black granite floor. Each vase was filled to the brim with glowing golden nuggets. Carved into the marble walls were eight deep recesses, their walls set with dazzling gems of vivid blue and brilliant white, their floors heaped with glittering mounds of lucent gold.

And within the recesses stood indistinct figures, each holding a green-stone-bladed Axe.

Jessica stood, momentarily stunned. *What was this place? Who are these people?* But as she tasted the subtle vibrancy of the rippling energy pervading the chamber, she recognised the intricate weaving of power by the potent minds of Warriors. *Warriors of IY!*

She found her hands shaking. *Warriors. Here.* Yet Naga and the Iyes's Story had told of only four Warriors. Wide-eyed, she scanned the chamber; of the eight recesses, she saw six figures holding Axes. *Six more Warriors. Six wielding the power of the A'ven.* How? How could this be? In the very heartland of the Ka!

She forced herself to move, stepping closer to the recess on her right. The Warrior inside stared out into the chamber with wide, terrified eyes fixed at a far distant place – and the woman was screaming but emitting no sound. Sickened, Jessica struggled to accept what she was seeing. *What hell is she facing?* She dragged herself away from the horrific sight and turned to the next recess. A stocky Warrior stood within, a resolute tension in his stance, his gaze also focussed on something afar. Unlike the first Warrior, a formidable yet controlled determination exuded from the man, and echoes of the wielding of immense power rippled through her. *He fights a distant battle.* She glanced to the other recesses. *They all fight an unseen enemy.*

With a suffocating foreboding enveloping her, she slowly walked on, seeing each of the six Warriors straining under the weight of their unknown battle, six Warriors locked away within the catacombs deep beneath the Ka's temple of Kaos.

How? Why?

As she approached the chamber's final two alcoves, a metallic taste fouled her mouth, and harsh lashes of energy grated against her mind. Forcing herself on, she stepped closer to the alcoves and saw two ragged figures within. Bound by six sizzling bands of silvery energy, their withered, desiccated faces set in wanton rage, they evinced a feeling of abject horror. Of a primeval fear.

As she moved, the sunken, hooded eyes followed.

These two saw her!

She took an involuntary step backwards, their hate coursing towards her. These were clearly no Warriors. *These are of the Dark. These are shamans of the Dark.*

Heart pounding, she pulled her eyes away and stepped back into the centre of the chamber, desperately trying to understand what she had found. Six Warriors held in the heart of the Ka homeland. Six Warriors that Naga had said nothing about.

Maybe she knew nothing of them.

Yet they are here.

The Warriors were here, and they were clearly held captive. She glanced to the two raging figures. And maybe those hateful shamans formed part of the Warriors' prison.

This changed their plan. She needed help. *Contact Beth. Now!*

She reached out, feeling for the presence of the A'ven …

But she failed to connect.

Alarm ripped through her gut. What had happened? Only moments before, it had been there! She reached out again for the humming strands of energy she could feel surrounding her, but yet again they slipped from her grasp, the A'ven's power remaining frustratingly – terrifyingly – elusive. *I feel the A'ven, so why can't I connect?* Something was blocking her. *But what?* Her gaze returned to the two bound figures, waves of pure hatred still streaming off them. Was it those shamans? Or was something else beyond this place? Her chest tight, she stepped unsteadily away from the bound shamans. *What can I do? What should I do?*

An answer came, fierce and unyielding. *You are the Guardian. Understand.*

Standing in the cloying silence, she forced a grip on her fear. "You wanted into this place," she muttered to herself with a cold admonishment, "and now you're in."

So, what do you see?

She glanced back to the Warriors, her gaze stopping on the stocky Warrior close to the entrance. She walked slowly over to him, halting before the alcove. Broad-faced, the man had deep, sunken eyes, which burned brightly below his proud, ridged forehead. His eyes, as with the others', focussed elsewhere. His tattered clothing hung in decaying strips over his leathery, wrinkled skin. Jessica sensed this man was old – ancient – from a people before this time.

I can't connect with the A'ven, but maybe ...

She let her consciousness reach out towards the alcove—

A tremendous force gripped her mind, hauling her towards the shrieking fury of a vicious storm. She slammed up shields to hold herself back – they were ripped to shreds as though paper. Panic swept through her as the raging vortex engulfed her. *I can't escape! I will lose my mind—*

A forceful hand grasped her, dragging her out of the wild, cascading waves of power into calmer swirls of energy at the edge of the storm. *'You cannot yet enter here, Guardian. These are not your battles – you would be extinguished.'*

'Who are you?' she pulsed, gasping for breath.

'Zaidu, a Warrior of IY.'

Though harried, nerves afire, his words jarred her. *'But how?'*

'I do not understand.'

'Six Warriors ... Only four Axes.'

A sense of confusion emanated from Zaidu. *'Four Axes? You are the Guardian. You know that not to be true.'*

Jessica felt herself drowning. *'I know nothing. I'm told nothing.'*

Zaidu's confusion deepened. *'Yet you are the Guardian.'*

Her anger flared. *'Yet I'm told nothing!'*

The mind of Zaidu grew closer. *'Why do you wait for the telling? The knowledge is within you. Listen to your memories. There, you will see the Warriors fighting at the Gates. Warriors battling the roving daemons. Warriors fighting the forces of the Dark.'*

'And you?' Jessica whispered. *'Why are you here, imprisoned with this temple of the Ka?'*

'Imprisoned? No. We bind that which must be bound. We are the Wardens of—'

Jessica cried out as pain exploded in the side of her head—

The connection severed.

Hand to her head, she spun around. Before her stood a tall, powerfully built man, his head shaved, his body littered with tattooed markings and symbols. And in his hand a Black Staff. *A shaman of the Dark!*

"I'm sorry for striking you," the shaman said with the slightest of bows. "I thought you were entrapped by those here." He tilted his head a fraction. "Were you?"

Jessica stared at him, burgeoning terror rising. That voice. She knew that voice.

The burnt man!

Hands suddenly shaking, she flicked her panicked eyes over the shaman's tattooed face and body. She saw no blazing white eyes, no blackened and scorched skin, no deep rent in his body. Not the man of her nightmares. *And yet, that voice ...* Wrestling hold of wrung emotions, she held the man's unwavering gaze. *Give him something.* "I wasn't trapped. I was ... observing."

A small smile played on the man's lips. "A strange place to come to observe. Why here?"

She frantically searched for an answer, unable to shake a clawing fear. This man showed none of the ghastly features of the scorched monster of her nightmares. *And yet why does he chill my soul?*

'*Stay calm. Give nothing away,*' came the calm voice of Jalu. '*This one also seeks answers.*'

The confident, and now familiar, voice of the one who sought to aid her brought Jessica a surge of hope. *Yes, stay calm. This shaman could have already killed you.* She held her voice steady. "Your Ensi allowed us free rein within your temple, and so I explored."

"Behind the throne of the Ensi herself?"

Jessica forced herself to stand taller. "You ask many questions. Who are you? And why are *you* here?"

The shaven-headed shaman smiled. "I am Krull. And I am a true adherent of Kaos. And you?"

"I answer only to your Ensi," Jessica said, forcing an edge to her voice.

As Krull raised a brow, she tentatively reached out with her mind. *What does this one know of this place? What—*

She stifled a cry as a searing pain shot through her body.

Krull smiled – yet within his eyes something dark was unveiled. "It seems I should apologise again. It is unclear who I can trust. My defences are ... robust."

As the pain of the shaman's blow slipped away, the edge of terror sharpened once more. *He could kill me in an instant.*

Krull flicked a glance around the chamber, then turned back to her. The smile continued to play on his lips, but now cold hatred simmered in his eyes. "It seems we may have the same questions. Shall we return and see if the Ensi can enlighten us?"

This is a truly dangerous man. Give him nothing. Follow his lead and buy time. "Shall we go?" she said, somehow forcing a smile.

The shaman gestured to the exit. "I believe you know the way."

Fear stalking her, she walked out of the chamber of Warriors, then followed the narrow passageway to the chamber of gold beyond. She heard Krull walking close behind. Who was this most dangerous shaman, and why was he here? *Whatever else he may be, this is a shaman of the Dark, an adherent of Kaos,* she answered herself. And he couldn't know who she was. *Else I'd be dead.*

And yet she'd seen the contemptuous look in his eyes.

And I felt the hate of the burnt man.

Her mouth suddenly dry as desert sand, darkness gripped her thoughts. Could it be? Could this shaman behind her somehow be the abomination of her dreams? But how? The devil of her dreams was a scorched ruin of the man she saw here. He was—

Her breath caught as a nameless dread engulfed her.

Something happens to him. This shaman becomes the burnt man.

Fighting the visceral fear coursing through her, she forced herself to breathe. *You don't know that. This is a shaman, yes, but not the man of your nightmares.*

But the cold terror refused to leave, and a bleak reality twisted her gut. Whoever, whatever, this shaman was, this was one who wouldn't allow them to leave this temple alive.

Her soul chilled. *There's no other way out of this. We'll need to fight.*

Yet what could they do with the A'ven still gone?

Clasping her trembling hand more tightly around the Staff, she lengthened her stride. She urgently needed to talk with Lanky. *But will I get the chance?*

*

His thoughts lost in a maze of false trails, Krull's shadowed eyes tracked the lithe woman as she climbed the rough-hewn steps ahead of him. As with her companion waiting in the throne room above, Krull had sensed nothing of the land's energy within her, no flickers of power, no hidden daemons. And yet her face was the same as the chimera who haunted his dreams, ruthlessly pursuing him in the darkest recesses of his consciousness.

Hunting him.

Capturing him.

She destroys me in those dreams.

The powerful tendons of his neck tensed. *And my master believes she is the enemy known as the Guardian.* The tangled web of confusion deepened. *But how can that be?* He tentatively reached out, but again felt nothing. No glimmer of the A'ven's energy within her, no pent energy waiting to be released. How was this woman – this supposed fearsome Guardian – a threat?

And yet, twice, she escaped you.

Twice, commanded and guided by Kaos, he'd thrust his mind out into enemy lands to find and destroy this woman – and twice she'd slipped from his clutches. How? She was nothing.

Yet she escaped.

And she haunts your dreams.

And still, he didn't know why.

He cast back to his encounter with the Iyes's shaman, the one called Naga. He'd scoured her mind for the secrets of the Iyes, for the secrets of these Warriors, but she had revealed little as she'd lain dying before him, bleeding out from Nefra's killing strike. *I saw much of the cursed shaman's life, but nothing of this woman called the Guardian, nothing of the others the Iyes call Warriors.* Baring his teeth, he drew in a breath of the A'ven's energy. As a renewed vigour coursed through his body and mind, his lips curled into a vicious smile. Once he understood what had been happening, Kaos's will would be done; the woman would die together with all these weak Ka.

But first, I must know what else she knows of this place.

As his eyes flashed in the gloom of the stairwell, the stunning discovery from below seared his mind. Yes, this woman would die, but what else would she betray before her soul departed? Because, beyond any hope of his wildest imagining, she had already led him to the prison of the Geddon! Even now, he reeled at the memory of the stunning sight that had faced him as he'd first walked into that secret chamber beneath the temple: the prison of the Geddon, guarded by the last six Wardens of the Light. The key Kaos had been seeking for millennia, concealed by the leader of his chosen people.

No one knew. No one suspected. Not even Kaos.

It had been a staggering unveiling of the Ensi's vast deception.

Krull's robust brow furrowed. Incredibly, there had been more – not as shocking as the discovery of the Geddon's prison, but incredible nonetheless. K'zarz and Xehalla, two of Kaos's most feared shamans of old, incarcerated beside the Wardens, hidden and shielded from all outside. Faint rumours had been spoken of their survival, but few believed. *But they were there. I saw them. I spoke with them.* It had taken only a moment to link minds with those two imprisoned shamans of Kaos. And in that moment, they'd revealed not only the sheer scale of the Ensi's deception, but also the treachery of their most long-lived ally, the Ancient, the ice dragon of the frozen north. It was still difficult to believe. His master, Kaos, had suspected traitors. *But this?*

Climbing the final twists of the stairway, Krull's mind turned, analysing, evaluating. So much revealed to him, and so quickly. But not yet all understood. *But it will be. I will know all you have concealed, my Ensi.*

His eyes shone with a sudden keen hunger. Despite the enormity of her crime, he couldn't help but admire the devastating audacity of the Ensi's deception. She had hidden the key to the Geddon from her own god. *And she hid it here, in the depths of Kaos's own temple!* What strength of will that must have taken. What incredible nerve. The Ensi had shown a most cunning and dangerous mind, one manipulating all those around her. *She manipulated her own god.* A rush of elation swept through him. And that made her a perfect ally to stand by his side.

Ally? No, more than that. Much more.

The Black Staff in his hand answered his desire with an eager tremor. So much lay now within his grasp. *So close. So very close.*

As he reached the opening into the throne room, Krull's eyes glinted with wry amusement. *And how much of this do I owe to the traitor?* So much had fallen into place because the Ka Disciple Cobra had invited him to aid his coup. The fool didn't realise what hell he'd brought to the Ka's homeland.

Me!

His expression hardened. Yes, Cobra was a fool. A fool to think he could replace the Ensi as the leader of the Ka – the snake was as a slug compared to her brilliant mind – and a fool to think he was a favourite of Kaos. *I will stand by Kaos's side, no one else.* As he stepped through the opening into the throne room, fevered anticipation swirled within him. *And the Ensi will stand by my side.*

CHAPTER TWENTY-SEVEN

I am truly sorry he died, but he played his part well.

Lanky woke from a troubling dream with a rough hand on his shoulder. Lifting his head from the furs, he saw a black-tunicked guard glaring down at him. "Come with us," the guard growled.

Frowning, Lanky pushed off the furs and climbed to his feet, looking around for Jessica. She wasn't there. Another guard stood behind him.

"Move!" the first guard growled.

"Okay," Lanky growled back. "But where's my friend?"

"Move!" the guard snarled, angling the point of his spear at Lanky's chest.

He saw the hatred in the man's eyes. *So, the last pretence vanishes. We are the enemy.* He calmed himself. *Don't do anything rash. Yet.*

He grabbed his jacket, then reached for his Axe.

It wasn't there.

His heart sinking, he quickly scanned around the chamber; there was no sign of his Axe. So the game had truly changed. *And the A'ven?* He reached out – but still he sensed nothing. He stood naked in the midst of the enemy.

A guard's spear prodded him in the back. "Move!"

"Okay," Lanky muttered. "I'm moving." *Stay calm. Wait for a chance.*

He followed the guard from the chamber and walked on in silence through the austere tunnels of the temple, his concern growing. Where was Jessica? *And where is Rind?* As they reached the throne room and passed inside, he stiffened as he saw a line of black-tunicked guards surrounding the chamber. *Something's definitely changed,* he thought, feeling the tension in the air as the guard led him through the menacing cordon. He breathed a sigh of relief to see Jessica standing on the low marble platform – a relief that was short-lived as he saw a tall, shaven-headed man standing beside her. Seeing the Black Staff the man carried, he remembered his confrontation with the Ka shaman Growl within the Iyes Sacred Chamber. He also had carried such a weapon. *A weapon the Iyes say is a gift to Kaos's chosen few.*

The guard led Lanky to Jessica's side, then stepped back into the cordon.

"You okay?" he whispered.

Jessica nodded, but he saw the strain in her face – then a flick of her fingers by her side.

The sign their mission was compromised!

"Good," crooned an unfamiliar voice.

Desperately trying to figure out what had gone wrong, Lanky turned to see a smaller, sharp-featured man standing before the throne on which the Ensi sat, arms folded, glaring down at the figure before her. To the right of the throne stood two other men, neither of whom he recognised. The thin, sharp-featured man took a step towards them. Lanky noticed he was missing his left ear. Then he noticed what the man carried in his hand. *My Axe!*

"We are blessed by your presence," crooned the man with the missing ear, smiling.

An oily voice. A snakelike face. I dislike him already.

"Please forgive us," the snake man continued. "The council and I were unable to greet you upon your arrival. We were indisposed. And my companions here were also unaware of your visit. A lapse in our internal communications, I believe."

"Enough of this nonsense," growled the taller of the two figures to the right of the throne. He was a heavyset man with thick, curly hair and beard. A slender bone ornament pierced his ear. "Who are they? And who is your new friend?"

"But here we are now," continued the snake, ignoring the heavyset man and stepping towards them. "Let us properly introduce ourselves." He stopped before Jessica. "Please tell us all who you are."

Lanky's stomach twisted. *He knows exactly who and what we are.*

Jessica held the man's gaze. "My master is here to discuss trade with the Ka. She—"

The man struck Jessica across the face, his eyes shining with delight.

Lanky surged forward, fist raised—

The shaven-headed shaman stepped in front of him, blocking his path. "That would not be wise."

His rage afire, Lanky glared past the shaman to the snake man beyond. But as a chill breath cut through the ether, he tore his gaze away, shifting attention to the shaman. Through the haze of anger, he sensed the raw power of the man standing before him. *This shaman is scary,* he thought, seeing a dangerous amusement in the shaman's dark eyes. *He could destroy me in an instant.* He glanced at Jessica. She shook her head imperceptibly. Struggling to control his anger, he stepped back. *Hold. Figure a way out of this.* Because there had to be a way. *There must be a way.*

The shaman studied him for a moment, then nodded and stepped back.

The snake man giggled, then tilted his head, his eyes locking onto Jessica. "Come now. I thought we might be friends. Shall we try that again? Who are you?"

"My master is here to—"

The man hit Jessica with the back of his hand, rocking her head to the side.

Lanky bared his teeth. *You bastard.* But he couldn't move; that would signal their death. The snake man smirked with pleasure. Lanky's eyes burnt with hate.

"Maybe you can aid us," the snake man said, turning to him. "Who are you?"

He struggled to not to strike the man. *Follow Jess's lead.* "Our master—"

Beside him, Jessica rocked as the sadistic man struck her again. She bowed her head, blood pouring from her nose.

His heart screaming with vengeful rage, Lanky tensed to strike.

"Don't," Jessica whispered, holding her hand to her bloodied nose.

Somehow holding himself back, Lanky glared at the smirking man.

"Whilst I know the pleasure you gain from hitting women, Cobra," came the voice of the heavyset man near the throne, his disgust undisguised, "I do not. And we all have better things to be doing with our time than this. Tell me what's going on, or I shall request the Ensi end this meeting."

Cobra licked his lips, his cold eyes lingering on Jessica. "I will enjoy your company later," he said in a low voice. "You will see." His gaze shifted to the woman on the throne. "The Ensi. Yes, our Ensi. Maybe *you* would like to introduce your invited guests?"

"You go too far, Cobra," the heavyset man grunted, stepping in front of the throne.

"*I* go too far, Xerses?" Cobra said, anger creeping into his voice. "Do I invite enemy Warriors to our land? Do I invite our hated enemy into the very home of the Ka?" He held up the green-bladed Axe. "Cast your eyes on the weapon of a Warrior."

Xerses's brow furrowed as he glowered at Cobra. His eyes shifted to the Axe – then widened. He turned a disbelieving gaze to Lanky and Jessica, then walked slowly towards them, intently studying their faces and bodies. His eyes lingered on Jessica's disguised Staff.

Lanky tensed. Whatever game the Ensi had been playing was over. *These men won't play with words as she did. They will kill us.* He quickly judged the distance between him and the snake man. The man looked weak. Could he take back his Axe? Even lacking access to his power, a single strike could kill the man.

A hand gently rested on his arm. "You wouldn't succeed," Jessica whispered.

At her words, Xerses quickly stepped back. He faced the throne. "Is this true?" he breathed. "My liege."

Lanky noticed the confusion in the man's voice. *He's unsure what's happening. Some other deadly game is being played here.*

The Ensi leaned forward on her throne. "You ask this question of your leader?" she said in an icy voice.

"Forgive me, my liege, but—"

"He asks what any true Disciple of the Ka would ask," Cobra snarled, glaring at the Ensi. "Please tell members of your council why you brought Warriors into our homeland. And why you hold Warriors below, within the sanctity of Kaos's own temple."

Xerses gasped. "My liege …" he stammered. "I don't understand." Seeing the Ensi glaring at him, he flicked his eyes to the third man, who'd not yet spoken. A shorter man, head shaved at the sides, hair swept back and tied back behind his neck, his rounded face seemed relaxed, but his sharp eyes fixed on Cobra.

Eyes that come from the east.

"Qiax," Xerses said. "What poison does Cobra speak? These surely cannot be Warriors? And other Warriors below? This makes no sense."

What other Warriors?

The sharp-eyed man turned to the Ensi. "It would seem the battle lust from the Games has addled Cobra's mind. I suggest we ask the guards to take him away for a much-needed rest."

The Ensi clapped three times.

Nothing moved. The alcoves remained empty.

"Ah yes," Cobra giggled. "I forgot to mention – your personal guard, my liege, is no more."

"Cobra, you go too far!" Xerses growled. "Guards, arrest him!"

No one moved.

A sturdy man dressed in black emerged from an alcove to their right.

"Xerses," Cobra smirked, "meet your replacement, Rathe."

"Guards!" Rathe barked.

Six guards detached from the cordon and surrounded Xerses.

"Take him away," Cobra ordered tersely.

"I thought you had ambitions," Xerses growled, glaring at Cobra as he was escorted off the platform. "But this? I misjudged you." As he was led away past the throne, Xerses threw a bitter glance at the Ensi. "I trusted you. It seems that too was misplaced."

Cobra clapped his hands. "Tragic," he said, giggling. "A wonderful friendship torn apart in but a few short breaths."

The snake is taking control. It's a coup. This complicated an already dire situation.

As Xerses and his escort left the throne room, Cobra sauntered over to Rathe. "I'm saddened to hear a rumour," he said, his strident voice carrying around the chamber, "that Xerses was tragically killed today, and all his family with him. Could you visit his home and verify the truth of this?"

His face grim, Rathe gave a curt bow, then walked out of the chamber.

He's signed the death warrant of that man and his family. How far does he intend … Frowning, Lanky glanced to his right as he heard the shaman beside him muttering under his breath. The shaman tapped his Black Staff softly on the ground, then a subtle ripple of energy left the chamber. Lanky studied the shaman out of the corner of his eye. *What did he just do?*

"Now," Cobra said, his voice hardening. "The pretence is over." He clapped his hands once, and two men quickly detached from the shadows and ran to the edge of the marble platform, where they threw themselves prostrate on the ground before him. "You good men of the Core have heard all that transpired here: a betrayal of the highest order." Cobra glared at the Ensi. "This woman is an imposter, an agent of the enemy, leading the destroyers from hell into our very midst." He lifted his head. "But praise be to our all-knowing, all-powerful god Kaos, the devoted protector of mankind, who saw through this woman's foul treachery. Think what countless lives have been saved from her evil designs by our liege's swift intervention." He raised his arms out before him. "The Ensi is no more, praise be to Kaos."

"Praise be to Kaos," echoed the guards around the chamber.

Cobra slowly looked about him, then stepped onto the platform. "But what about our leader, I hear you say? Are we now to be abandoned with no servant of Kaos to guide us?" He smiled. "Fear not, my friends, for Kaos has spoken." He bowed his head. "I am honoured to serve you for as long as needed, until we find the true successor."

Lanky watched the snake step closer to the throne. *So he aims for the very top.* He glanced at the Ensi. A feared tyrant she may have been, with eyes across her land, but she clearly hadn't seen this coming. He looked back at the snake. The sadistic devil had executed the coup with ruthless efficiency. The Ka had a new leader.

Cobra lifted his head and looked down on the two trembling, prostrate men. "Return to the Core – and to the Flanks and the Rim. Spread the news you have heard here this morning and let the camp celebrate this great victory. I will speak to the camp this evening."

Cobra clapped his hands. As the two men scrambled to their feet, two guards stepped out of the cordon and joined them. The four men quickly left the chamber.

It seems they'll have company in spreading their message. The right message.

"Qiax," Cobra murmured, turning to the sharp-eyed man standing by the throne. "We have always worked so well together, and long may it continue."

"I don't think so, Cobra. We are quite different you and I." Qiax adjusted the twisted cord that was his belt. "No, I think not."

Anger flashed in Cobra's eyes. Yet he smiled. "This is not your doing, Qiax," he said, his tone softening. "I know you are blameless in this most cruel and heartless treachery. You will simply pass from one master to another."

He wants something from this man, desperately wants it.

Qiax stood, calmly watching Cobra with clear disdain. "You have surprised me, Cobra. I wouldn't have said what has happened here today was possible." Lanky noticed Cobra's face light up. "For one so devoid of intelligence or wit," Qiax continued, "this really was quite remarkable." Cobra's face froze, mid smile. "I would rather try to move the entire sand of the desert with my fingers than spend a single moment of my precious time with you." Cobra's lips curled into a terrible snarl. "And Cobra … I am not blameless."

"Kill him!" Cobra shrieked, turning to the tattooed shaman behind Jessica.

"I thought this one was needed?"

"Kill! Him!"

The shaman studied Cobra for a moment, then looked towards Qiax. "Consider it done."

Lanky heard a sudden skittering of tiny feet on the stone floor of the chamber. He turned to see a sinuous black trail arcing its way around the platform towards Qiax – a trail of scurrying black scorpions, quivering tails arched, stingers primed. Then another black trail appeared. Then another. Within seconds, the stridulating mass of scorpions swept up the steps to the silent man standing beside the throne and swarmed up his legs and body.

Qiax stood calmly as his body disappeared beneath a crawling black cloak. He smiled at Cobra. "Watch and understand your own fate. It is written in the stars."

"Kill him!" Cobra screamed, his face twisted in rage. "Kill him!"

Lanky watched, horrified, as Qiax transformed into a macabre parody of a human – a heaving, rippling surface of hissing death.

Yet still the man spoke. "And the stars never lie."

Cobra ran across to the shaman. "I said kill him!" he screamed.

At a gesture from the shaven-headed shaman, the arching tails of the scorpions lanced out in unison, striking at the body cocooned within their baleful shroud.

Qiax screamed.

And screamed.

Lanky's gut wrenched. *No matter this man is a Ka, he didn't deserve this.*

Within moments, Qiax fell to the ground, convulsing, the deadly swarm continuing its voracious attack. As paralysis kicked in, his movements slowed, until finally his rippling body lay silent and still. Their murderous task now complete, the hissing coat of death slowly drew back. As the creatures scurried away, the cordon of guards broke rank, pulling back to let the terrifying killers race past.

Cobra strode over to the body on the ground. "I know you can still hear me, traitor," he snarled, kicking the body. "Your final moments in this land are with me. Enjoy them!"

Lanky turned away, disgusted. He looked over at Jessica – and a shiver ran through him as he saw the look of defeat on her strained and bloodied face. She had been the one so sure they needed to get into the temple – and the one so sure she could get them out. *But all I see in her eyes is our death.*

The full horror slammed into him. *We will die here.*

An image of his mother flashed into his mind. Then an image of Rind. *I don't want to die. I—*

"And now judgement will be passed on our treacherous leader," came Cobra's breathless voice. Turning back in a daze, Lanky saw Cobra step away from the broken body on the floor and stagger to the front of the throne. "You always think you are so clever," he spat, steadying himself. "But look – look around you now. Where are your guards? Where are your Disciples? Where have your people gone?" He giggled as he climbed the step to the throne. "But *I* am here."

The Ensi glared at him as he stood before her.

"Secrets," Cobra mused. "With you, it has always been about your secrets." He reached out and stroked the side of her face, smiling his thin, cold smile. "But you have held no secrets from me. Oh no, nothing has remained hidden, not even your ever so precious daughters."

The Ensi brushed his hand aside. "You know nothing, snake," she hissed.

But her eyes belied her shock at the man's words. And Lanky noticed the tattooed shaman beside him staring intently at the scene unfolding. *He knew nothing of this.*

"Babies so special that you gave them away. And told no one."

The Ensi's hands clenched into fists as her whole body tensed. "You know nothing."

"Oh, I know everything. You see, I had your woman followed. You remember? The round-faced cow of a woman who took your irreplaceable babies."

The Ensi glared at Cobra, her eyes cold.

Yet Lanky noticed the dismay he had noticed only moments before had eased. What had the snake done – or said – to allay it?

"I followed her. I followed her to Qiax. But you never knew where they went, did you? Never searched for them." Cobra giggled. "It took most careful – and discreet – investigation, but eventually I found where they'd been sent." He leaned forward, baring his teeth. "I know! I know where they live and breathe. And soon, your cherished daughters will be in my hands. And you will watch. You will—"

Cobra screamed, and Lanky watched in utter astonishment as the man staggered backwards, head in hands, before collapsing onto the dais steps. He lay still and silent.

Standing over the fallen snake, the Ensi glared around the chamber exuding a potent strength. Lanky was shocked. She'd struck down the snake using some aspect of the Land's energy. How had she hidden this? And why hide it until now?

"Stand down," the Ensi commanded. The guards in the chamber instantly dropped their weapons, took several paces back, and sat down on the ground. Lanky almost dropped to the ground himself.

The tattooed shaman stepped forward. "A nice trick," he said, a faint smile on his lips. "I was waiting to see what you would do. Why wait so long?"

"I needed to see who truly worked with the snake," the Ensi snarled, her eyes locked on the shaman. "And I see him now before me."

"You let your friends die."

"The stakes are far greater than friendship," she rasped, her green eyes boring into his.

"That trick won't work on me."

"No matter. But maybe this will."

The shaman staggered under an unseen assault.

She's flushed out her enemy and is taking back control. She—

The shaman steadied himself, then smiled and took a step towards the Ensi.

The Ensi's features sharpened, and Lanky felt eddies of virulent energy wash around him. The shaman flinched, his smile fading, but he took another step. And another. Step by step, the shaman walked towards the throne – and before him the Ensi's face betrayed a sudden fear.

She is strong, but the other is far stronger. She—

The Ensi's emerald eyes flicked to Lanky. *'You are released, Warrior!'* came her urgent voice in his head.

His eyes widening, Lanky felt a subtle lifting of pressure from his mind—

Then gasped as the vibrant energy of the A'ven flooded around him.

We have a chance!

But as he grasped for the A'ven, a strange, alien taste soured his mouth.

He froze, staring at the Ensi in confusion. *What is this? What has she—*

'Kill her!' demanded a strident voice, and he felt the ancient Warrior within him clawing his way out. *'Destroy the Kade!'* Dysam cried, drawing on a vast pool of the A'ven's energy. *'Destroy the Ensi!'*

All hesitation, all doubt, vanished as he recognised the threat within. Instinctively reacting, he grasped control of the A'ven and dragged Dysam back to the depths, slamming harsh barriers back in place. *I am Lanky, not Dysam. And I am a Warrior, and today is not the day to die.* He thrust out his hand. *'To me!'* he thundered into the ether.

The snake cried out as Lanky's Axe ripped from his hand and flew towards Lanky's.

The tattooed shaman spun around, his eyes afire.

'Attack!' Fen growled as the Axe hammered into Lanky's hand.

As febrile power flooded into him, he released a crackling bolt of intense white energy, which hammered into the tattooed shaman, sending him sprawling and smoking to the ground. *Time to get out of here!* He spun around and grabbed Jessica by the arm. "Run!" he shouted, pulling her towards the exit.

She pulled back against him.

"What the hell are you doing!" he yelled. "We need to go. Now!"

"We have to take the Ensi. We must—"

"What! No, we—"

A sledgehammer of a blow caught him in the side, sending him flying across the marble platform and off the far edge. A vicious pain in his ribs, Lanky scrambled to his feet to see the shaven-headed shaman striding towards him, his Black Staff raised for another strike. He snapped up a shield—

A storm of black lightning hammered into him, punching a hole deep into his sizzling shield. He dropped the dying shield and released a writhing stream of blistering energy at the shaman. His glowing Axe held before him, he continued his raking attack as he scrambled to his feet—

He flinched as a broad stream of black fire blazed narrowly past him. Cursing, he slammed his shield back in place. *He's too strong! We've got to get out of here!* Glancing to the left of his shield, he saw Jessica skirting the edge of the platform, heading towards the Ensi. *Damn! How does she think this is helping?* He made to move towards her—

The chamber suddenly exploded in a blaze of black fire, blasting him backwards towards the entrance. Grimacing at a lance of pain in his side, he scrambled to his feet and snapped his shield back in place … and was hit by hammer blow after hammer blow from the shaman, his shield lighting up in a fiery blaze as he fought to hold it in place.

'We need to bond,' Fen growled.

'This is not the time or the place to try that, warg. You—'

Another huge explosion rocked him backwards.

"Damn it, Jess," he hissed to himself as he struggled to defend himself. "What are you doing?" But he knew. *She's trying to find the Ensi.* He muttered a stream of curses. There was no way he could reach her to help her. *And if I stay here, I die.* He had to leave. *But at least I'll draw this devil shaman away.*

Immediately widening the span of his shield, he ran towards the entrance of the throne room, dragging the barrier with him. From the speed and intensity of the blasts rocking his shield, he could tell the shaman was close behind. *Okay, let's see what the range is on this.* As he left the throne room, he lodged his barrier at the entrance behind him, then raced away down the tunnel, leaving the barrier in place. *That should slow him down—*

He heard, and felt, his barrier explode. A far-flung missile whistled past his ear.

He put his head down and ran.

Racing through the twisting tunnels, lances of energy slamming into the walls, he soon saw daylight from the main temple entrance ahead. And saw a stream of people flooding down the entrance steps. *Those are not guards – what are they doing here!*

"Clear the way!" he cried, firing a warning bolt into the side of the stairwell.

People screamed – but continued to run his way!

He girded himself for battle, but as the first of the oncoming tide reached him, he quickly saw they were unarmed. And afraid. Panicked. As they streamed to either side of him and into the temple interior, he ran on towards the stairs. What the hell was happening? Why were these people here? And why weren't they scared of him? *Unless they're more scared of something outside than in here.* He grimaced. *My problem is behind me.*

He entered the stairwell and bounded up the steps, taking them two at a time. "If you touch me, you die!" he shouted to those heading towards him and fired another soft warning shot above their heads. Behind him, people screamed; it seemed the shaman had chosen a more brutal way to clear his path. Careering up the final steps and still seeing no guards, Lanky sprinted out into the morning air. He blinked to adjust to the bright light—

The thump of beating wings sounded behind him, and he instinctively dropped. A roar of flame swept above him, its raking heat scorching his back. Wincing, he forced himself up, then ran to the side of the wooden platform and leapt off, readying for the steep drop beyond. He landed with bent legs and hit the ground, rolling. *That hurt,* he thought as he got to his feet—

A bolt of black lightning hammered into the ground beside him.

Cursing, he dived to the ground, rolled to the side, then sprang to his feet, his shield back in place. He hunkered down as thunderous bolt after thunderous bolt thumped into his shield. *This guy is relentless.* Noises behind him made him turn his head. Hard-faced fighters ran towards him, and behind them a silver dragon streaked through the sky!

Lanky wiped his sweat-drenched brow. *This could prove tricky to get out of. Maybe I should have bonded with that damned warg after all.*

Crouched by the side of the marble platform, Jessica's gaze remained fixed on the shadowy opening behind the throne, through which the Ensi had just vanished. Around her echoed the ferocious sounds of violent battle as the tattooed shaman pursued Lanky out of the throne room.

The shaman. *The burnt man.*

For now, she was bone-chillingly sure that this one known as Krull was the burnt man of her nightmares. *It doesn't look like him, but somehow, it's him.*

For as the coup had played out, she'd gradually sensed the malignant taste and sickly stench of the shaman's subtle wielding of the A'ven – the same vile assault on her senses she'd suffered in those terrifying dreams of the past. And beneath Krull's composed, calm exterior she'd also sensed a well-masked, visceral hatred of her and Lanky. Cold terror had threatened to overcome her, but before it could take hold, Lanky had regained his Axe and launched a blistering attack on the shaman. Astonished that he'd regained his power, she'd reached for the A'ven herself – but it had slipped from her grasp. Then a fierce voice had sliced through her mind.

'Whatever happens, save the Ensi,' Jalu had commanded.

'The Ensi?' she had answered, as if in a dream. *'Why?'*

'You are the Guardian. Aid her.'

In that moment, Lanky had grabbed her hand. With the chamber descending into a chaotic firestorm, and her mind torn to confusion, she'd blurted out: "We have to take the Ensi." But before anything more could be said, a sizzling bolt of pitch-black energy had hammered into Lanky, tearing his hand out of hers and hurling him backwards. Acting as if in a dream, she had dived to the side, rolling off the platform, then crouched low, holding her Staff in readiness for a vain defence against the dread shaman. But the shaven-headed shaman had strode on by, streaming crackling bolts of energy into Lanky's shield. For the briefest of moments, she'd felt a savage relief. The burnt man wasn't coming for her. *I can escape him.* But that thought had been instantly swept away by a wave of fear for Lanky – and by shame at her own weakness. As she'd shifted her thoughts to what she should do – what she could do – movement to her left had caught her eye. Glancing around, she'd seen that in the confusion of battle, the leader of the Ka had pushed back the stone throne and was disappearing through the opening behind.

And now, with the Ensi having fled, Jessica stared at the shadowy opening, beset with crippling doubt. *Jalu wants me to save the Ensi, but I should get out of here. I should help Lanky against the burnt man.* But as cracks of thunder continued to roll around the cavern, she found herself scurrying towards the throne. Whatever was happening here, the Ensi lay at the heart of it. *I can't ignore this. I need to understand.* Reaching the low steps up to the dais, she paused beside the prone Ka – *the sadistic snake* – and glanced back to see Krull pursuing Lanky out of the chamber. *Keep going, Lanky! Get out of here!* Because against the might of this shaman, that's all he could do – and all she would do if facing this devil. Throwing their lives away wasn't an option. *Survive now and find another way, Lanky.*

She turned back to face the shadows behind the throne.

Images of the Warriors hidden deep below suddenly snapped into focus. Horrific images of men and woman seemingly suffering unimaginable torment in a battle only they knew. "We bind that which must be bound." That's what the Warrior had said.

Warrior? No, he called himself a Warden.

A Warden of what?

As the sound of battle receded, Jalu's urgent voice hammered in her mind. *'Follow the Ensi now, else it will be too late.'*

Acting on instinct, Jessica stepped towards the opening—

And stumbled as a hand grabbed her leg!

Steadying herself, she struck out with her Staff, cracking the sadistic Ka, Cobra, on the side of his head. The man's hand slipped from her ankle as he fell unconscious on the step, blood seeping from a wound above his missing ear. *That snake won't be moving anytime soon.* She quickly stepped through the opening, pulling the throne back into place behind her.

"Slide the locking stone down," came the Ensi's voice from the stairwell. "There, the carving of the tree. That will give us some time."

She was waiting for me!

Clamping hold on jagged nerves, Jessica quickly found the carving on a narrow, protruding section of stone. Grasping the top of the stone, she slid it down into place, then spun to face the Ensi – who immediately headed down the stairwell.

"I need answers," Jessica called after the retreating figure.

The sound of the Ensi's footsteps echoed up from below.

Despite the fevered turmoil within, cold surety gripped Jessica. "You *will* give them to me," she growled. Hand grasped tightly around her Staff, she descended the steps after the Ensi.

CHAPTER TWENTY-EIGHT

I knew nothing of Taran's gift. It was well made.

$\mathcal{A}$s a crisp desert dawn broke over the camp, Spider downed the last dregs in his bowl. "That was most welcome, Inyana. I thank you."

Chewing a mouthful of her own meal, Inyana glanced at him and inclined her head a fraction in acknowledgement.

Spider turned to Kapano. "When will they begin their training?"

"Soon," the old man replied, spinning a spindle whorl in the fingers of his left hand, his right gently pulling out a smooth thread. A simple tool, yet the quality of the twine depended on the plant fibres used and the skill of the user.

And Kapano has the skill of a master. "You're sure they'll appreciate entertainment this early in the morning?"

"Probably not," the old man said, a flicker of disgust on his face, "but they would appreciate Inyana at any time of the day." He pulled out the last of the twine, then ran it through his lips, sealing the fibres before picking up a needle and carefully threading the twine through the eye. Picking up his torn moccasin, he began to sew.

"These men would rut with the cattle," Inyana muttered, wiping her mouth with the back of her hand. "But even the cattle find them ugly."

Spider smiled.

"But you are right to be nervous," Kapano said. "There is a chance they will not want us there. And then ..." He shrugged.

And then things would be desperate.

But not lost. No, no matter how bad this situation got, whilst he still breathed, there was always a chance, always hope. Clearly something had gone badly wrong to have separated Rind and the Warriors, but thus far there was no evidence the Warriors were dead. He had to keep moving. *I need to get Rind out of there.*

"And it's straight on at that old tree?" Spider asked for the third time that morning.

"It is," Kapano said, finishing one row of stitches and starting the second.

Head the same way as Scowl and the others last night, but this time straight on at the tree. This path would seem to lead nowhere, Kapano had told him, a quirk of the chaotic building of the tented village. But unknown to most, at the end of this path to nowhere lay a slight gap between tents to the right. And this ran towards the fighter's quarters. "And you're sure it's there?"

"No one worries about an old man wandering lost around the camp. But this old man remembers what he sees when lost. It is there."

Spider scowled, remembering his encounter with Growl. "I'll remember to look out for old men in the future – something I should have done once before."

Kapano tied off the thread with a double knot, then held the repaired moccasin up for all to see. "These have served me well. I would like them to be my companion for a while longer yet." He pulled on the shoe, then smiled, his leathered face cracking into a warren of deep canyons. "Now I'm complete again." Climbing to his feet, he glanced to the east and sighed. "Well, I have no excuse to put this off any longer." He turned to Spider. "We should ready ourselves. Your companion awaits."

*

Spider acknowledged the scowling guard at the Flanks' southern gate with a slight bow as he collected his weapons. The guard ignored him, studying Kapano's pass with the jaded eye of a man wishing he were elsewhere. He handed back the marked stone and waved them on with a flick of his hand. As they crossed into the Rim, Spider waved goodbye to Kapano, simply a man parting with a friend – or so he hoped it would appear. Kapano and his granddaughter walked away, heading south directly towards the fighter's encampment.

Their plan now set in motion, Spider veered away to the southwest, heading for the Rim's scrubland. Aside from the disordered, sprawling tent wall ahead, the austere home to the Ka's loosely knit legion of fighters – *and Rind's prison* – few other dwellings lay in this thinly vegetated area of the encampment. Spider strode on, aiming for the western termination of the great tent wall.

Unchallenged and attracting little attention, he soon reached the bedraggled tip of the tent wall, which appeared to meet a seemingly invisible boundary to the Rim, beyond which no shelters could be seen. Skirting the last worn lean-to of the tent wall – a swaying lean-to that, it seemed, would not lean tomorrow – he veered east and picked up his trail from the day before, retracing his steps along the outer tent wall towards the area he'd met Scowl and his knuckle-playing friends.

Within a short while, he approached the spot and sighed in relief. No one else was around. He glanced to the tent wall – and there lay the passageway he'd passed through with Scowl to reach the fighter's training grounds inside. Praying his luck would hold, he headed towards the passageway.

A thickset, brutish looking man walked out towards him.

"May Kaos be with you this fine morning," Spider said, not breaking his stride. The man spat to the side and walked on. *Good,* Spider thought, entering the walkway into the tent wall. *Let's hope they're all as talkative as that one.*

As he moved deeper into the tent wall, he heard the familiar sounds of a camp awakening: hawking and talking; gruff laughter and coarse swearing; and scattered between, the occasional silence, the tent's occupants either already up and away or hunkering down to catch more much-needed rest. He walked quickly on, then, turning a corner, he saw the tree up ahead – the tree showing him the way to Rind. For while the main path swung left at the tree, beyond the old, gnarled trunk lay a short, untrodden piece of ground between the tents. For most, a path to nowhere. *But for me, a path to Rind.*

He quickly walked on, and after checking the path to the left was clear, he strode on past the tree, committing himself to the narrow passage beyond. His heart racing, he pushed on between the hides of the tent walls to an apparent dead end – but there, to the right of the tent blocking the way ahead, was the tight gap Kapano had promised. A gap completely obscured from view from the main path, but there all the same. He shuffled along, squeezing into the narrow gap. Now out of sight of the main pathway, he paused to settle his nerves. *No one saw me. First hurdle passed.*

He looked along the gap between the shelter walls, assessing how far he might have to shuffle along. "You will need to be guided by the sounds you hear," Kapano had told him. "And by Inyana's singing. We'll stop outside the corner tent where you saw your friend. That's where we see the fighters emerge. It's where they'll hold her. With the help of Kaos, maybe you can reach the rear of this tent while we hold an audience before it. What happens then is in your hands."

And my hands feel very slippery right now, Spider thought, still staring along the narrow crevice between the shelters. Taking a deep breath, he edged forward, turning sideways to avoid hitting the shelter walls. As he moved on, he heard shouting and laughter ahead.

And then the sound of singing.

Gritting his teeth, he hurried on as fast as he dared, trying to get a sense of where Inyana stood.

There!

He paused, sure that the singing was coming from beyond the tent before him. Reaching out, he gently touched the thin hide of the tent wall. *So, Rind was paraded in there.* Breathing softly, he moved cautiously on to the adjoining tent, the tent that Kapano thought the fighters came and went from. *But this place is a warren. How can we be sure?* He pushed back a rising unease. *Trust what you've been told. Keep moving.* Settling himself, he heard cheering from beyond the tent wall. Inyana had gathered an appreciative audience.

Take the chance now.

Gently laying down his spear, he knelt down and positioned his blade low on the tent wall. Piercing the thin hide, he made a small cut. With bated breath, he waited. Nothing. No sudden cry of alarm, no spear thrust through the tent wall. Allowing himself to breathe, he carefully sliced further, then pulled back the hide to peer through and scan the interior. *Stacks of weapons and shields, but no people.* He sliced a little further, then checked again. No one. His heart raced. *Don't wait for someone to arrive. Just do it.* Slicing a large rent in the hide, he quickly dragged himself through, reached back through the hole, and grabbed his spear and pulled it inside—

He started as he heard aggressive shouts from the crowd outside.

Calm down. They're calling for another song from Inyana.

Wiping his brow, he quietly stepped over to the weapons' pile and grabbed a shield. Returning to the tent wall, he carefully positioned it to cover the rent. *Now keep moving.*

Keeping low, he headed away from Inyana's singing and stepped into the gloom of an internal passageway within the tents.

A flood of light dazzled him.

Squinting against the glare, he saw a man, his arms aloft, pulling back a flap in the roof of the passageway. His task done, the man turned and walked towards him. "How's the singer?"

"Amazing," Spider said, fighting a gut-wrenching urge to run. "She can sing to me all day – and night."

The man laughed as he passed, and Spider heard his footsteps retreating behind him.

He stood calming himself, then glanced around. To his left was a tent doorway. He pushed aside the entrance flap, then peered inside: an empty space, save for several furs on the ground, and a pungent stale smell in the air. He dropped the flap and moved on. Another doorway and another pungent yet vacant sleeping area. As he continued on, he saw more of the same, aside from one tented chamber where a man lay sleeping. The chamber had a separate entrance on the far side leading to the training grounds outside. *A guard, most likely.*

Walking cautiously on, he heard the growing sound of voices and laughter ahead. *So now we get to it.* Reaching the end of the passageway, he stood, heart racing before a covered entranceway. Beyond, he could hear the buzz of a chamber full of people. Of fighters. *The knuckles are cast, Spider. Time to be bold.* Girding himself, he stood tall and strode on through the entrance.

He entered a spacious area, light streaming in through two openings in the roof, and pungent with the aroma of at least twenty men talking, playing games, or simply resting. But all dressed, ready for battle.

Here goes ... "Is the woman ready?" he said loudly.

He tensed as the chattering in the chamber quietened.

"She's not due on yet," said a broad-shouldered man over to his left.

Spider walked over to him. "The boss wants her shown to the crowd out there. Give them something to fire up their morning."

The man laughed, twisting the livid scar by his right eye. "Rek!" he shouted. "Fetch the woman!" He turned back to Spider. "Not seen you here before."

"Was a guard inside. Managed to annoy a Disciple. Got me a promotion here."

The man laughed. "Good on you," he said, slapping Spider on the arm. "Only the best serve in the Rim. Name's Ty."

"Spider. That her?" Spider said, looking over at Rind, who was being roughly pushed forward by Rek. But not bound. *A bonus – if we can get out of here.*

"Yep," Ty said, turning. "A shame to waste her on Killer. She'd have been good to have around a little longer. Would have taught these criminals some manners." There was laughter from some of the men close by.

"Well, given I've been promoted once this week, I'd better not do anything to deserve another. Need to get her out to the boss." Spider turned to Rind. "We're going outside, my lady," he said, half bowing, drawing laughter from those around. "I want no trouble."

Rind spat at him.

He hit her hard in the side of the face. Rind staggered backwards with the force of the blow. "I want no trouble," he growled, "and I don't care what you look like when we get out there, but outside we are going."

Rind glared at him.

I think that's real enough. But I better watch my back if we ever get out of here.

"Watch your back," Ty said, smiling. "And your weapons."

Spider grabbed Rind's arm. "Come. Your people are waiting." He pushed her in front of him, holding his spear to her back. "Move off the end of the spear and you'll feel it drive through to your stomach."

"She can move onto my spear whenever she wants," one man shouted, to hoots of laughter from others.

"Move!" Spider said firmly.

Rind walked away to a barrage of jibes and laughter.

Spider's heart leapt. *This might actually work. This—*

"Where are you going?" grunted a heavyset man as he entered the tented chamber from the walkway.

"Boss wants her outside," Spider said quickly, prodding Rind to keep moving, his heart pounding.

The man frowned. "I didn't request this." He stepped in front of Spider and drew a blade. "Who are you?"

"What?" came Ty's voice behind them. "You didn't ask for the woman?"

The heavyset man's eyes narrowed ... then his hand flashed out, driving his blade for Spider's heart—

An intense blaze of light flared in front of Spider, blinding him. He staggered backwards, searing heat scalding his chest.

Someone grabbed his spear. There was a scream.

His vision clearing, Spider saw the heavyset man lying on the ground, skewered in the stomach by the spear Rind was holding. Fear coursing through his body, Spider looked down at his chest.

Nothing. Not a scratch.

What happened? Why am I alive?

You won't be if you don't move! another part of him yelled.

He spun around to see Ty and several others staring at them in astonishment. Then Ty's face contorted with rage. "What are you waiting for? Kill them—"

A tremendous roar thundered above them, and Spider shielded his face as a searing blast of fiery light and heat ripped through the tent. The walls and roofing burst into flames. Several screams rent the air.

Horrified, he lowered his hand and glanced around the tent. The chamber erupted into a chorus of frantic shouts. "Come on!" he cried, grabbing Rind and pulling her past the stricken, heavyset man. "Run!"

As they fled, he heard shouts and yells from all directions, many panicked, some commanding. *What the hell is happening?* he thought as he raced towards the rent in the tent wall. But that question was lost as he heard loud voices approaching in the passageway ahead.

"In here!" he hissed, pushing Rind through the hanging flap of a doorway. Trying to quiet his breathing, he held the entrance flap still, then listened as the voices approached ...

They quickly passed by.

He turned and saw Rind looking down at a figure on the ground. It seemed the commotion had not stopped the snores of this sleeping man. Stepping carefully around the prone figure, he reached down and picked up the man's spear. As he stepped back, he saw Rind collect a blade from the corner of the chamber.

"What happened out there?" she whispered as she joined him.

I should be dead, Spider thought, his mind racing. "It was a dragon – I'm sure of it. But why it's attacking the Ka, I've no idea." *And I've no idea how that blade didn't strike me.* He looked down, running his hand over his tunic. There was no cut, no evidence the blade had reached him. Sliding his hands away, he froze. *That's warm,* he thought, feeling the heat from a patch of his tunic.

"What is it?" Rind whispered.

Spider reached into the pocket of his tunic – and felt the familiar shape of the warm object lying within. Pulling out the bone carving – River's carving, the one he'd left by her side – he was amazed. Both by the faint glow of the carved white bone and by the fact it was there at all. He held it gently in the palm of his hand, unable to speak.

"Was it that?" Rind whispered. "Did that protect you?"

I don't know. "Maybe." *Probably. And all thanks to the one I love.*

They both turned at the sound of someone running past in the passageway beyond. Spider took one last look at the most precious carving, then dropped it back into his tunic pocket. His desire to reunite with River burnt fiercely but their mission remained. His gaze fixed on Rind. "What happened to you?" he whispered. "Where are the Warriors?"

Her expression was grim. "They're inside the temple. At least they were. I was taken away with no explanation." The unyielding glint of the leader he knew returned to her eyes. "It may be our mission is compromised, but we are Iyes. We exist to support the Warriors. If a chance remains to find them, to aid them, we must take it."

"Then the first thing to do is stay alive." He gestured for her to follow, and then cautiously stepped to the doorway leading out to the fighter's training grounds. He carefully pulled back the entrance flap and they peered out through the narrow gap.

"It's complete chaos out there," she whispered.

Spider scanned the ground outside. "Do you see the trees over there? Towards the temple?" Rind nodded. "We head for those. I've no idea what's happening, but I hope we'll just look like two more people scattering for cover. Ready?" He saw her body tense. "Okay, go!"

They emerged from the tent into a melee of confusion. Rind charged through one bewildered group, Spider hot on her heels. Immediately, a shout went up and the people ahead of them turned … Rind simply barged right through them and sprinted on across the open ground.

Spider wasn't so lucky.

A man lunged at him and grappled him to the ground. As Spider struggled to break free, a cry of warning pierced the air. The man atop him flicked a glance up. Spider punched him hard in the side of the head, then heaved the dazed man away—

An enormous whoosh of air streamed over him, and part of the sky lit up in a fiery glow. Eyes wide, Spider looked up to see whole sections of the tents ablaze and, to his utter terror, a blue dragon streaking out of the flames. The beast unleashed another gout of roiling fire, then wheeled away, arrowing for the temple.

His blood chilled, he scrambled to his feet, then sprinted away from the burning tents towards the temple rise. He heard a volley of loud blasts from high up on the temple mound and saw flashes of pitch-black lightning shooting down into the Rim. *Krez! Now what's happening!* Crossing the boundary ditch of the Rim and the Flanks, he sprinted on, catching glimpses of Rind ahead.

"Spider!" a familiar voice shouted to his left.

Slowing, he turned to see Inyana struggling to support her grandfather. Cursing, he glanced ahead and saw Rind waiting for him in the distance. "Krez!" he muttered. *I can't leave them.* He swung to the left, racing towards Inyana.

"What happened?" he panted as he reached the girl, helping her support her grandfather. The old man was bleeding badly from a wound in his side.

"He fought off the scum who'd grabbed me," she said, tears in her eyes. "Then this daemon of the sky arrived, and the coward fled." She gestured to a blood-streaked spear on the ground. "That's his, and if I see him again, I'll feed it to him, slowly."

"Let's get him to safety." *Wherever that is,* he thought wryly.

They started towards Rind, but as Spider glanced ahead, he froze as he saw her on her knees, two men standing over her.

Then a threatening voice shouted behind him. "Spider!"

He spun around and stared in growing despair as Ty walked towards him with three men by his side. *We've lost. I tried, but we've lost.* "Move away," he whispered to Inyana as he stepped away from them, placing himself between the old man and Ty.

"I don't know what's happening," Ty snarled as he approached. "But I'm not letting the killer of my friend walk away."

Spider noticed Inyana move to his side, a blade in one hand, the bloodied spear in the other. *A brave girl.* He felt a guilty relief. *I will die with someone by my side.* Facing the oncoming fighters, he smiled. "You can't defeat us," he said, bluffing. "Walk away."

With a harsh laugh and his face cold, Ty led his fighters on. "I will walk away once you're lying dead on the ground."

Setting himself in a fighting crouch, Spider felt a strange calm settle over him. "I thank you for your aid," he said to Inyana. "We came so close."

"This is not over," Inyana grated. "My god will not let us die today."

Ty laughed an ugly laugh as his men flanked them. "I see no gods." He raised his obsidian blade and glared at her. "Only the condemned."

"You are a fool," Inyana rasped. "For Kaos sees all. You—"

"Take them!" Ty snarled.

The three fighters flanking them took a step forward ... then suddenly halted as a new presence arrived, a smell of threat descending. They all turned to see a silver dragon bearing down on them, the dread hum of its beating wings like a blade through the heart. All instantly dropped to the ground, save Spider and Ty. *A brave man,* Spider thought of his enemy as he watched the massive beast approach. *Or plain stupid like me.*

The fearsome dragon slowed as it swept in, the surging downdraft from its wings buffeting them as it loomed over them. Lowering its massive bulk to the ground, the beast furled its wings then flexed one mighty scaled leg, angling its body to one side. To Spider's utter astonishment, three familiar figures slid down from the beast's back.

"Need some help, lad?" Knuckles grunted, striding towards them, Svana and Shorty by his side.

I thought them dead, Spider thought, his eyes wide, unable to believe what he was seeing. *I hoped, but ...*

He couldn't speak.

"Good to see you too," Svana growled. She looked around. "Who dies first?"

Maintaining his relentless attack on the Warrior, one proving an infuriatingly frustrating opponent, Krull cursed his own stupidity. *I am a fool. I should have seen this one's veiled strength.* Snarling, he unleashed another stream of black-veined energy at the Warrior. How had it happened? How had the Warrior hidden his power from him?

But he knew. *The Ensi.* Once again, proving herself a master of deception.

And the other who had stood beside the Warrior, the woman who haunted his dreams? Following her down to the chamber of the Wardens, he'd sensed nothing from her, no faintest taste of the land's power. And so, seeing no threat, he'd delayed her execution, using her to discover more of the Ensi's plans.

Yet Kaos told you she was dangerous. You ignored your own god.

Continuing his ferocious attack, he embraced the frustrated anger raging inside. He knew now he'd made a grievous mistake not killing the woman – the one his god called the Guardian – in the chamber of the Wardens. *And after, in the throne room?* Once the Warrior had unveiled himself, the chance had gone. The Warrior had been too powerful to ignore. *I doubted my master. I grew too confident. But you will not escape me again, Guardian.*

Eyes blazing, he scanned the defensive shield before him, then aided by his daemon, Nergai, he streamed bolt after bolt of carefully sculpted energy at the Warrior, sensing the shield's response to one attack, then adapting the next.

And attack after attack failed.

His frustration deepened. Neither he nor Nergai could sense the daemon they battled, hampering their efforts to tune their attacks – the Warrior's shield remained stubbornly one step ahead. Whatever daemon aided the Warrior, it was clearly a match for Nergai.

Nergai. His most valuable companion. His greatest ally and advisor. Together he and his daemon had come far. *But not far enough, and that must change. That will change.* For amongst the stunning revelations of the day had been the discovery of Angram, the most venerated of the bound daemons. Hidden from all for untold ages, Angram been imprisoned together with the one he served, the ancient shaman K'zarz. Krull's lips curled into a smile. *But not for much longer.* In the brief encounter with the two shamans of Kaos, he had recognised the incredible, unique opportunity and seized it. He knew Angram's mastery of the energy of the Dark, and the daemon had seen his cunning and strength. The offer was made, and despite the vehement howling and resistance from K'zarz – who would now seek to exact his revenge – the daemon had acknowledged and accepted its new bond.

Before this day is out, I will hold Angram.

Then he would show the people of these lands what true power looked like.

It is time to change this world!

Elation coursed through him. He had found the last of the Wardens, the last barrier holding back the release of the Geddon. *Holding back the cleansing of this world.* And that final barrier would soon be destroyed. *And then my god's will can be done. We will enter the age of Kaos.*

Krull bared his teeth. *Yet this cursed Warrior distracts me.*

He unleashed a writhing wave of power, the Warrior's shield erupting into a blazing inferno as the wash of crackling energy swept over him.

And yet still the devil's shield held.

'Patience,' came Nergai's calm voice. 'Moments only, and I will unlock the shield.'

Krull scowled but instantly drew back some of his power. Nergai was right. He needed to save himself for the next battle, for the next stage of the plan: the destruction of the Ka. *For their time now ends. They—*

His thoughts were broken by the sudden overpowering presence of a new arrival.

Maintaining his attack on the Warrior, he glanced to the sky. The Ancient arrowed towards him, a silver streak in the sky. *And so, the shamans of Kaos were right. The dragon has played its own game.* So long a pretended ally of Kaos, but for so long an undiscovered defier of Kaos, thwarting his master's aims. And now, recognising the game had changed, it had finally broken cover … *Here approaches a most deadly opponent.*

Weaving a new shield, he locked the final strands in place just as a rapacious fire engulfed him. As the roiling blaze swept over him, he sensed each flame acting as a pernicious probe seeking weakness in his shield, seeking the tiniest flaw for the Ancient to exploit. But Nergai and the black shield of the Dark formed a formidable defence, resisting the foul power beyond, while ensuring little energy escaped from within – hence little was revealed. Even so, stray licks of the dragon's flame that pierced the shield were as blades driven deep into his soul. And this was but one of the weapons of the Ancient. To engage it in battle now would cost valuable time, and risk too much. He had to abandon his attack on the Warrior and withdraw.

At that very moment, as the dragon's raking blaze swept past, a piercing cry came from within the temple. *'You are needed!'*

The shamans of Kaos! The rush of elation was savage. It was finally time! With K'zarz and Xehalla free, the Wardens could be destroyed. Dropping his defence, Krull cast a hate-filled glance to the shielded Warrior, then strode up the slope to the wooden walkway. Quickly traversing the walkway, he found the Guard captain, Rathe, waiting at the temple entrance. A brave man to be standing there beneath the beast. This man would be useful. *Unlike the other.*

"My liege, I have news. The—"

Holding up his hand to silence the man, Krull glanced to the sky. The Ancient was banking tightly, sweeping back towards them. "Come."

With Rathe hurrying after him, Krull strode into the entrance and quickly descended the stairway. A flash of light lit up the stone walls, then a wall of heat swept over him. "Too late," he murmured with a thin smile as he continued down the steps.

Reaching the base of the stairway, he stopped and calmly faced Rathe. "What news?"

The man stood tall, but his eyes showed his fear. "My liege, the traitor Xerses escaped." Rathe dropped his gaze. "I know not how. But we have dealt with his family."

"By your hand?"

The man looked up, his face pale. "It was ... an order."

"An order executed well." Krull smiled. "And I know about Xerses. I protected him. In fact, *you* let him go."

Rathe gaped. "I don't understand. How—"

"Xerses is within the temple," Krull continued, ignoring the forming question on the man's lips. "He has the knowledge of this empire. We will need that." *As we wipe them all out.*

"Then his family ..." Rathe stuttered, looking sick.

"No matter." *It will fire the hate of Xerses and make him a far better servant of Kaos.* "However, I suggest you don't make it known to Xerses who pulled the blade across the throat of his wife." A small but useful hold to have over this new servant. "You are now in command of the defence of this camp until Xerses returns." He saw the man's eyes flick back up the stairway to the skies above, then he bowed in acknowledgement. *Good. This man is strong. He will be useful. For now.* "What defences do you have?"

Rathe licked his lips, then drew a stolid mask over his features. "With no obvious enemy to fight, the Core fighters are scattered, as per our drill. Maybe half inside the temple to protect our ... leader, the rest between the Core and the Flanks, awaiting the call to arms. Beyond that we rely on the fighters of the Rim – and I'm not sure what message they've received. We also have fighters at the Games to the south."

"Get this message out to all. Do not engage the Warrior. Do not engage the dragons. All fighters to retreat to the temple. All nonfighters to stay outside and hide." *And with the will of Kaos, they will all be slaughtered and help clean up this camp.* "Do you understand?"

"Yes, my liege."

"Look to the south. Aid will come. When it does, attack the intruders with force. No one may leave alive."

"Understood, my liege."

"Questions?"

He saw the man tense. *Will he ask?*

"And Cobra, my liege?"

"Unfortunately, he has not impressed my master. Do not make the same mistake."

Rathe licked his lips. "And his mistake, my liege?"

Krull smiled. A brave man indeed. "He forgot who he served."

His face drawn, Rathe gave a brief bow then started back up the stairway to deliver his message to those outside.

One of the final things they will hear.

Krull immediately strode on down the passageway, eager now for his encounter with the ancient shamans below. And for his reporting to Kaos on what he had found. *And what about that which you haven't found? Like the Kade. What do you tell Kaos about that?* Fear stirred at the disquieting thought. The Kade remained hidden, and his master was growing impatient. *But I will give him the Geddon and then he will cleanse this world of the unwanted and ready these lands for the chosen few. Ready these lands for me.* But the unease remained. The Geddon wasn't enough. Kaos wanted the Kade.

He needs the Kade.

With the Geddon, Kaos mastered this world, but with the Kade – with this ultimate key to the enveloping shield of the Continuum – his god mastered all. Hold the Kade and you controlled that shield, you controlled the flow of energy from the Void. *You become the locus for that power of the gods.* And with that power of the Dark, Kaos would become the single almighty god of the Continuum.

Krull cloaked his thoughts. *Single god? I also need the Kade.*

He forced the blasphemous thought away. That was for later. *First, deliver the Kade to Kaos.*

And the secret to the Kade lay in the Ka's temple, he was sure.

Krull's unease vanished beneath a surge of fervid anticipation. Together with the tremendous power of the daemon Angram, he *would* find the Kade. He *would* finally help Kaos purify this world. For a world it was, floating in space in an outer arm of a vast galaxy of suns, itself lying within a small corner of a vast universe of galaxies evolving within the mind-warping breadth of the Continuum. This and more – much more – Kaos had shown him. A fearsome elation ripped through him. And none of those of this world knew what was coming – *who* was coming.

The Geddon. Their Armageddon.

And me, the ruler of a cleansed world. The ruler of the people of Kaos.

Of the people of Krull.

He smiled as he strode on. It was time to complete his alliance with the Ka. *Which I doubt they will like.*

*

They'd flown in at speed from the north, and as they'd approached, the sheer scale of the enemy camp had shocked Svana. The expansive half-moon encampment sprawled across the arid land, with two deep trenches forming apparent boundaries between three half-circular zones, each truncated to the east by a glistening lake fed from the great river valley beyond. In the camp's centre, bordering the lake, rose an elevated stone edifice, glistening in the morning sun. To the north and south, along the broad river valley, a line of vegetated lands stretched as far as the eye could see. To the west lay pale, rocky ground bordering the edge of a distant desert.

As they'd swept in, there'd been no signs of battle.

Rakana's actions had changed that in an instant.

'Be ready!' Rakana had commanded as they swept over the camp.

Her stomach lurching, Svana had risen from the dragon's back as the beast dived towards the ground. Ignoring the flare of pain in her wounded arm, she'd grasped tightly onto the beast's ridge scales as they plummeted towards a chaotic array of shelters to the south of the camp. A sharp pressure had touched her mind, and then a stream of intense, raging fire had roared from the dragon's maw, raking the tops of the tents below. *This beast is as a shaman. She wields the Land's energy.* She'd burrowed down behind Knuckles as blasts of scalding air swept past the dragon's neck.

"What are you doing, you fool dragon?" she'd heard Knuckles shout.

'Stirring up the nest to see what emerges,' came Rakana's reply.

"Nothing good," Shorty responded from behind. "I can guarantee it."

Looking to her right, Svana had seen the blue dragon, Hydrak, strafing a position by the stone edifice on the rise. The temple of Kaos, Rakana had told them. They made two more sweeps around the temple before Svana realised Rakana held her fire high off the ground. *Not trying to kill those people down there,* she thought. *Just making them panic.*

Which had worked.

As they'd banked in front of the temple, she'd looked down and been startled to see Lanky emerge from a sunken entrance in the western end of the edifice. The Warrior had pushed his way through a horde of people heading inside, then bounded down the slope of the low hill. "Lanky!" she'd shouted, but her voice died in the wind as the dragon peeled away to the east. "Go back!" she'd barked at Rakana. "Lanky was there!"

'I saw him.' The dragon had banked sharply. Desperately clinging on, Svana had seen the water of the lake swing below her, and the bright blue sky rise above. The dragon straightened, then banked again, turning into a steep dive. Despite the danger, she had leaned out as far as she dared, squinting against the rushing air to find Lanky. Instead, she'd seen a shaven-headed figure walking down the rise from the temple entrance, intense bolts of black lightning streaking from his Staff and slamming with thunderous strikes into a shimmering white dome below. *He attacks the Warrior!* Each strike on the Warrior's shield triggered a blaze of crackling sparks – and with each strike, the shaven-headed figure strode closer to his target.

Then, suddenly, the figure had sensed their approach. As he looked up, a jet of fire roared from the dragon's maw. Svana had immediately pulled herself in, ducking behind Knuckles, who once again bore the brunt of the ferocious heat. As the heat switched off, she'd lifted her head and looked back at the receding temple. The tall shaman had stood, unharmed, looking up at them. Then he'd quickly turned and strode back up the hill. As they banked, she'd lost sight of him.

Rakana's command came immediately. *'We land. Prepare yourselves!'*

As they'd approached a broad, open area of the encampment, she'd gasped as she'd recognised a familiar figure below. "Do you see that, Knuckles?" she shouted.

"I do," Knuckles replied. "Move faster, beast. Spider needs our help."

No answer came, but the dragon had swept in, wings braced for landing. Once again, a sharp pressure had touched her mind as the dragon slowly lowered herself to the ground.

And now they were here with Spider staring wide-eyed at her, and beside him the unknown girl who'd bravely stood by his side. And facing them was one of the enemy Ka fighters they'd seen from above. She saw the hate in the man's eyes. *This is one who won't simply walk away from here.*

"What are you doing here?" Spider breathed. "How did you ...?" He trailed off, his gaze shifting to the dragon, disbelief writ across his face.

"Suggest we save the greetings until later," Knuckles said, glaring at the Ka. "Does this man die?"

Svana saw Spider stare at the dragon a moment longer, then turn to face the Ka, who stood defiantly in front of three others climbing warily to their feet. "You and your men have but a heartbeat to leave," Spider said in a cold voice. "Else that heart will beat no more."

He attempts to avoid the fight ... But this man won't turn away.

The Ka glared at Spider with a determined glint in his eyes. "No Ka turns from their enemy. I will see you and your ancestors die!" The Ka struck out viciously with his spear—

Before any could react, Inyana slammed down her spear, deflecting the Ka's thrust, then leapt forward, her blade flashing in the sunlight as it plunged into the man's neck.

As the Ka fell, his comrades turned and fled.

"Impressive," Svana murmured, watching Inyana pull her blade free. Her gaze levelled on Spider. "Where are the others?"

Spider turned fearful eyes to the distance. "Rind," he breathed.

*

With the shaman's relentless assault on one side, fighters approaching on the other, and a bloodthirsty dragon in the sky, Lanky had needed to batten down the hatches. With coruscating streams of glowing plasma flowing over his head from the ferocity of the shaman's attack, he'd quickly drawn his shield over and around him, then crouched within his defensive cocoon. One that the shaman had continued to mercilessly batter.

'We must move,' Fen had said.

'That's not easy right now, warg.'

'Even so, there is one who must be saved.'

'As I said, it's—'

His shield had lit up in a blistering fiery-red blaze, and he'd heard the ferocious roar of the dragon's fire rake over it. He'd cowered back from the brutally intense heat, but his shield had quickly dissipated the fire's energy. Catching his breath, he'd heard the heavy thrum of the dragon's wings pass overhead and heaved a deep sigh of relief. Then, pushing more energy into the shield, he'd waited for the shaman's onslaught to begin anew.

But aside from his nervous humming of a tune from a distant age, there had been silence.

A silence that now continued.

What was happening out there? Lanky rubbed his beard. When did the tortoise come out of its shell?

Maybe now?

Muscles tensed, he dropped the shield.

Diving to the right, he rolled, then sprang up and launched a blistering attack at the shaman's last position—

But the man was nowhere to be seen!

Lanky quickly scanned around. *Where is the next one coming from?* Yet all he saw were the smoking bodies of Ka fighters.

'*South!*' Fen commanded.

He hesitated, casting a searching glance back to the temple. '*Jessica is still in there.*'

'*She is safe for now. Others are not. Including you.*'

But the pull to Jessica was fierce. He reached out and pulsed to her. Nothing. He felt a moment of dread verging on panic. What if something had happened to her? Should he go back? *But I can't get past that bloody shaman.*

'*There's no time for this. Move!*'

Wiping his sweat-drenched brow, Lanky's gut twisted at the decision he was about to make. *I trust you, Jess. I trust you're smart enough to get out of there.* Because right now he knew he couldn't reach her. And another needed his aid. '*Where's Rind?*'

'*I told you,*' Fen snarled. '*South.*'

The choice was made. '*Let's go.*'

Keeping low, he bounded down the slope, then sprinted away from the temple, heading south. Passing burning shelters, scorched vegetation, and scattered groups of panicked Ka, he soon passed the boundary ditches of first the Core and then the Flanks.

'*Where is she?*' he asked as they passed another group of frightened Ka rushing through the Rim away from the smoking interior.

'*Close.*'

'*Well, that's helpful. What does—*'

He caught sight of a distant figure held down by two armed men. Cold terror ripped through him. "Rind!" he exclaimed, angling towards her.

'Hold, Warrior, that is not the way. She may die.'

Fen's words triggered a spasm of anguished alarm. "What then?" Lanky snapped, slowing, his mouth dry.

'Watch and learn. But this is the final aid I will provide until the time you bond. Do you understand?'

'Get on with it, warg,' Lanky growled, terrified he would be too late.

'Be precise. And have no doubts.'

A ripple of energy, and Lanky understood.

Focussing intently and hardly daring to breathe, he harnessed a precise amount of energy, shaping it into two finely tuned packets of death.

And he had no doubts.

He launched the fine projectiles towards those holding Rind.

Blood spurted from the heads of the two Ka holding her, and they dropped like stones. He saw Rind clamber to her feet, staring wide-eyed at the two men.

Lanky raced towards her. "Rind!" he shouted, bounding over a rock as he approached. "Are you okay?"

She turned, a frown on her face. "Well, you took your time. What kept you?"

CHAPTER TWENTY-NINE

Cobra knew so much, and yet so little. Babies … The fool.

Shocking visions tortured Cobra's mind as a slow, painful consciousness returned. Visions of the Warrior and of Krull – and of the brutal assault on him by the Ensi. He groaned, his head thick with confusion as he felt the cold stone steps beneath him. What was happening? Why was he still lying here? Yet through his dazed stupor, a part of him knew. His plans were being destroyed. His perfect plans honed over so many sun-cycles and set in motion a half-moon ago.

I found the Wardens! Me. I found them!

He'd entered the concealed passageway behind the throne several times since he'd first seen the green-eyed devil unknowingly reveal her secret to her most observant – and most clandestine – Disciple. A Disciple who'd found those precious few opportunities when he knew the Ensi was away to steal down to the staggering and unimaginable sights below. It had taken time to unravel the secrets, time for the two shamans imprisoned there to pierce the Warden's blockade and push through their messages to him, messages that could not break through the greater prison barriers. But unravel them he had.

And what revelations!

The deception of the Ensi, and of the Ancient. The deception of the Shade!

And his reward if he could get the message to Kaos? He would become the leader of the Ka and its empire, the imprisoned shamans had told him, to be supported by them, the most powerful shamans in all the lands.

He would become Kaos's voice across all those lands.

So, for three days following his discovery, he had visited his people's most sacred chamber and there silently prayed to Kaos, recanting his stunning tale of unholy betrayals. And on the evening of the third day, on the brink of despair that his god would not hear him, Kaos had answered his prayers! *'Send for the shaman, Krull, of the Meso peoples,'* had come the clear message. *'He will aid you in your task.'*

And, oh, the workings of Kaos! What glorious happenstance gifted him his opportunity? Because later that day, he'd overheard Nefra talking to Shadow. Talking of a fearless, ambitious man who'd become the preeminent shaman of the Meso tribes. At once, Cobra had known this was the shaman Kaos had requested! Within days he had sent a mission to the north with a simple message: Kaos needs you. He then set the rest of his plans in motion and waited for the shaman.

And after a half a moon cycle had passed, the shaman had appeared.

And not a moment too soon, Cobra thought through the throbbing pain of his pounding head.

Because the enemy had also arrived.

The Iyes's Warriors!

He'd been shocked, when, upon his secret return from the Games in the dead of last night, his trusted source had informed him that Warriors had arrived in the temple. He'd struggled to believe it until the dawn, when Krull had brought the woman to the throne room. Seeing the imposing woman and her penetrating eyes, he'd almost panicked, believing the Ensi had outmanoeuvred him. But that panic had quickly turned to elation when Krull said he sensed no great power within her.

I believed these so-called Warriors were weak, Cobra thought, his eyes now opening to the throne room. *I believed they were merely another sign of the green-eyed witch's incompetence.*

He bared his teeth as he staggered to his feet, his head pounding, his blood raging. But Krull had been wrong! These Warriors had a strength the shaman had not recognised. Cobra spat bloody phlegm to the floor. This supposed almighty shaman of the Meso tribes was a fool like all the rest.

Breathing heavily, Cobra stepped up to the throne and looked out across the marble concourse where the guards – *his* guards – stood in ragged lines, some talking in low voices, others looking towards him, suspicion in their eyes.

"Silence!" he roared.

The chamber fell quiet, aside from the quiet shuffling of feet as the guards reformed their cordon.

"Who is most senior here?" Cobra spat, craning his neck and scanning the chamber for the one who would pay for allowing his plan – his most revered plan – to descend into chaos.

A guard to his left stepped forward. "I am, my liege."

"Where is the traitor?"

"I … the traitor disappeared behind the throne, my liege. With a Warrior."

Eyes widening, Cobra quickly spun around. He rushed to the throne, grasped a corner, then pushed.

Nothing moved.

He shifted his shoulder against the stone, then pushed again. The throne stayed resolutely in place. "Help me, you fool," he yelled to the guard. The guard quickly joined him and leaned his weight into the throne. But no matter how hard they tried, the stone refused to move. *No! The green-eyed bitch cannot escape me! I will see her scream for mercy before me!* He clenched and re-clenched his hands, hands that would squeeze tightly around her neck as—

"Ah, Cobra. You are awake."

Cobra spun around, convulsive rage surging through him. "Where have you been?" he spat.

"Attempting to kill a troublesome Warrior," Krull said, smiling. "I failed."

"It seems I may have been mistaken in my choice of shaman," Cobra snarled. "It seems you have let everyone slip through your fingers."

"Not all," the shaman said, lifting his Black Staff, then striking its end to the ground. Two guards appeared from a shadowy recess, and between them walked Xerses. "This one didn't escape."

Cobra fixed murderous eyes on the general. "Why is he not dead?" he hissed, stepping down from the throne.

The shaman raised his Staff. "Watch and I will reveal all."

All heads turned at the now chilling sound of tiny claws skittering on the stone floor of the chamber. As the nearest guards took a fearful step back, Cobra watched, a harsh smile forming on his lips, as a trail of black scorpions raced across the floor towards Xerses. And then another trail. And another. Within seconds, they had reached Xerses …

Where they passed him by, spreading out in a deathly black cloud across the floor.

Cobra watched, unbelieving, as the black flood approached *him*. Unable to process what was happening, he stood transfixed. Only upon feeling their tiny claws grasping hold of his skin as they climbed his legs did the brutal reality crash home.

He was their target!

"No! What are you doing! Guards!"

The guards backed even further away.

Cobra screamed, striking out at the creatures with his hands and feet. But as quickly as he brushed them off, others filled their place. Then the stinging began. The sharp, burning pain of the first vicious stings quickly grew to an unbearable agony, his whole body afire. He dropped to the ground, arms and legs flailing in a vain attempt to halt the relentless tide. "Stop!" he screamed. "Please stop!" As the first scorpion reached his mouth, he felt his bowels release. He forced his lips and eyes shut, as tight as they would go. *Kaos help me! Please help me!*

The stinging stopped.

He felt the creatures scuttling off his body.

Was it over? Was the bestial torture over?

The pain receded from his body, and a calmness returned.

Kaos, I thank you. Oh, how I thank you.

He opened his eyes.

Xerses stood above him, a look of death on his face.

"Thank Kaos you're alive," Cobra said. At least that is what he tried to say; he heard only a mumble emerge from his own lips.

"I am thankful I didn't have to hear any more of your lies," Xerses grated. "Krull explained everything. Thank Kaos he was here to stop your foul treachery."

"What! No, he's lying! He helped me, Xerses! He is part of this." Nothing but incoherent noises left his mouth.

"The poison works fast," Xerses said, a cold smile on his face. "You will find difficulty moving, I believe."

"Please help me," Cobra said, tears forming in his eyes as he desperately tried to make himself heard. "I will appoint you Ensi – we will work well together." But his mouth refused to work. His breathing slowed, and his sight blurred.

"I don't think I have seen you cry since that girl who became the Ensi defeated you as a child – a long time ago now. And for all the evil you have done since, you choose now to cry for yourself? You are a pathetic creature, snake."

I will give you the shaman, Cobra cried. *Take him. Use him.* But his mouth lay still, his breath almost gone.

Krull appeared above him. "No one uses me, my friend," he said with a smile. He leaned closer and stared into Cobra's eyes. *'Would you like to live?'*

Yes! Please yes! What do you need?

'It seems you know many secrets, snake. The Kade. Where is the Kade?'
Kade? I know no Kade. I—
'Then face your ancestors and be ready for their wrath.'

Cobra screamed. *No! Please! I can help. I know more. The shamans below ... The Warriors ... I know—*

His mind exploded with pain as Krull clawed inside it.

All conscious thought ceased as hell descended.

*

Through the horrendous veil of pain torturing his ravaged mind, a glimmer of light appeared, then Cobra recognised the clouded form of Xerses above him. "Krull tells me you can hear me," the Ka general said. "I'm not known as a cruel man, but when a man's family is killed ... Well, that man will do just about anything in revenge."

Cobra flinched – or tried to – as indistinct shapes moved across his tear-filled eyes.

"I believe that although most of you is paralysed, parts of you can still feel pain."

Cobra didn't feel the scorpions until they reached the back of his throat.

Then he screamed – or tried to.

His consciousness fractured beneath the explosion of pain as the scorpions scuttled ever deeper down his throat, unleashing their deadly venom. All sense of being lost, his dream of ultimate power – his belief in Kaos – lay forgotten, vanished; his lifetime's efforts to destroy the green-eyed devil crumbled into dust.

He knew nothing but pain.

Even darkness, when it came, arrived behind the veil of terror.

*

Xerses looked down at the dead man. His family's killer lay dead, but he felt nothing but a void inside. *You have ripped out my heart, devil. I wish you could have suffered longer.* He turned to the tattooed shaman, the one known as Krull. "Where is the Ensi?"

The shaman's hard black eyes flicked to the throne. "She is hiding ... but not for long."

"And these were enemy Warriors she brought here?"

Krull nodded, the torchlight flickering off his shaven head.

Xerses glanced around the chamber, the silent rank of guards watching him. *Why?* Why would she do this? After all their planning, all their readiness for the coming war, why would she abandon all and bring the enemy here? It made no sense. And yet the Ensi's treachery

401

was real. He'd been told of the Warrior's murderous attack inside the temple, and of the dragons now laying waste to the camp.

His suspicious gaze found the shaman once more. "Why are you here?"

"Kaos wishes me to be here. To correct what has been done."

"And he asked you to work with this scum," Xerses snarled with a hateful glance at Cobra's dead body.

"That has been corrected – as you can see."

"What will you do now?"

"What *we* will do now, is destroy the Iyes forever."

Xerses glared at the shaman. "I don't trust you."

"Do you serve Kaos?"

"I do."

"Then I don't need your trust. I just need your continued service to Kaos."

Xerses's doubtful gaze lingered on the shaman, then he turned away, a terrible weariness sweeping over him. His life had been shattered, strewn in bloodied pieces across a land he thought he'd known. And all because of one he'd trusted. *The Ensi.* He flicked a glance to the throne. *I trusted you. I believed in you. And yet you betrayed me. You betrayed us all.*

And so who could he now trust?

No one, he thought grimly. *No one but Kaos.*

He reluctantly faced Krull. "I serve the Ka, and I serve Kaos. And in this moment, I must help them save our homeland. Once that is secure, we will talk."

"Then I suggest you find Rathe – he will need your direction. But I ask that you remain in the temple. You cannot fight dragons."

Xerses saw a calm, almost arrogant confidence in the shaman's face set against the burning intensity in the man's eyes. *An unknown. A dangerous unknown.* "And what will you be doing while I try to save my people?"

Krull smiled. "Bringing you aid. Without it, you will all die."

*

Krull watched Xerses leave, the black-tunicked guards marching out behind him. There walked a man who'd been driven by an unwavering loyalty to his people and by a boundless love for his family; but now a man crushed by their loss. *And that grief I can use.* Because he needed the Ka general to aid their cause. He glanced at the dead body of Cobra. *Especially after the disappointment of that one.*

Disappointment? Could he really say that about this Disciple of the Ka? Discovering the source of Kaos's millennia of frustration was hard to dismiss.

Wasn't it?

He crushed that thought as quickly as it had formed. Cobra had most certainly proved both cunning and sly, albeit aided by a fair slice of luck. *But not a man to be trusted to lead.* No, Cobra had been one driven by his own, hate-fuelled ambition and by a twisted mind harmful to Krull's cause. And a man thinking himself a leader, but with no one to lead, was a dangerous person to keep around.

No, Cobra had gifted him what he needed, and there was nothing more the man could give. And to be certain of this, he had ruthlessly stripped Cobra's dying mind, seeking further secrets that might be buried deep. But he'd found nothing new, only sordid memories of a lifetime of scheming and endless striving for personal power. *But he had not the mind to retain that power won, to wield it as it should be used.*

No, nothing new.

Except …

Except there had been one morsel that still swirled at the edges of Krull's mind. The Ensi's secret daughters, her baby twins. Cobra had discovered they had been taken to the Iyes tribe. But why? What threat to her daughters had she feared within her own homeland? A threat from the snake? Or something else? And why hide them within your enemy, an enemy the Ensi was preparing to destroy? No, that she wouldn't have done. So, it seemed likely she hadn't known where they'd been taken. And maybe now those children were dead, killed unknowingly by their mother in her war against the Iyes.

But maybe not.

He looked around the empty chamber. Did it matter? *Yes,* he answered himself, feeling a faint apprehension in the depths of his mind. The Ensi had run a deception so deep that even Kaos hadn't seen through the murky waters. *Whatever this Ensi does matters.* No matter how seemingly insignificant, he would report all to Kaos. *Let him decide.*

His thoughtful gaze shifted to the throne. Report all to Kaos? He most carefully shielded his mind. *No, maybe not all.* A faint smile appeared on his lips. This Ensi had proved herself a most impressive leader, not only of her own people, but of a burgeoning empire. And the woman herself? Well, by clandestine observations and now standing in her presence, he'd seen for himself the truth of her reputation: her self-belief, her strength, her poise. *She has a place by my side in my new world. We will rule together.*

403

Apart from one small problem.

She deceived our god.

When he'd followed the Guardian down to the prison and seen the hidden Wardens with his own eyes, there was no doubt. The Ensi was part of a colossal deception stretching back millennia. She had aided the Wardens to prevent the release of the Geddon, to prevent the cleansing of the unwanted. She had thought to play her own game, a game against her god.

And why? *Because she thought she could win.*

Sighing, he walked towards the throne. The Ensi had inherited an empire. Then she had expanded an empire. For her, this land belonged to her people, not to her god. But she saw no need for the Geddon, no need for the cleansing of the weak. She thought the Ka were the people of the future. He stopped before the throne. "But in this, you are wrong." She was wrong because she had failed to see that the world had grown stale; that there existed too many people – too many weak and feeble people – who had lost the original Truths of Kaos. "But even after all you have done, I will guide you back to the path of Kaos," he whispered. "I will somehow help you survive the wrath of our god."

And then you will serve by my side as we remake this realm.

Krull raised his Black Staff. And if she didn't accept the path that must be taken? "Nothing can delay what is needed," he rasped. "This world shall be cleansed. The unwanted must be destroyed." *All life, except the chosen. My people!* His black eyes focussed on the throne. *If you cannot see the Truths, my Ensi, then you also will die.*

He let the energy of the Dark flow.

CHAPTER THIRTY

What made this Guardian different from the others?
That in those times of greatest stress, she could somehow
see beyond the Horizon. And she trusted her heart.

Jessica watched the leader of the Ka stride purposefully around the chamber, seeing her pause briefly at each alcove to examine the Warrior within before stepping on to the next. As the Ensi reached the final two alcoves, in which the two ragged shamans stood snarling, a foul, bitter taste tainted Jessica's mouth. These creatures were servants of the Dark, she was sure; most likely servants of the Ensi. *They are terror that cannot be allowed to leave this place. They —*

The light within the chamber suddenly dimmed and the two snarling figures lunged forward, teeth bared, straining against their silvery bindings as they raged at the woman standing before them. No sound reached Jessica, but she saw the sizzling coils twisting and warping as they held against the frenzied struggles of the two ravening figures.

Black streaks ran through the binding coils.

They're fighting free. They're fighting free from their prison. A prison of six Warriors and two savage others. *What are —*

A blinding white light exploded throughout the chamber. Shielding her eyes, she saw the bindings of the snarling figures briefly blaze with white-hot intensity – then, as quickly as it had appeared, the dazzling light vanished. As the glare faded, she saw the black staining on the binding coils had dulled ... but the staining had not yet vanished, and the two figures raged on, heaving violently against their leashes.

Ignoring the ranting figures, and seemingly unperturbed by what had just happened, the Ensi walked to the centre of the chamber, where her sharp eyes locked onto Jessica. In the torchlight, the woman's eyes

405

shimmered with a scintillating green hue, a beguiling attraction drawing you into her world.

'I am a friend. Trust me, I —'

Jessica slammed up a defence. *She tried to enter my mind!* "Don't try that again," she hissed, her Staff half raised in reflexive action.

A brief flash of anger burnt in the Ensi's eyes before it quickly passed. Jessica saw the tension in the woman's stance ease. "Forgive me. The snake …" The Ensi sighed and rubbed the back of her neck. "No matter, he thinks he knows all." A thin smile crossed her lips and contemptuous words sounded in Jessica's mind. *'Babies. The fool.'*

Relaxing her Staff arm, Jessica's brow furrowed. *Babies? What babies?* Frowning, she cast the distracting thought aside. She needed to take care. This Ensi had slipped past her defences as though they didn't exist. "Who *are* you?"

The Ensi tilted her head and smiled. "The Ensi. The ruler of the Ka. And the sworn enemy of the Iyes."

"And these are your prisoners?"

"No. I do not hold that power."

Jessica frowned. "Then who does?"

"That is not clear to me."

"And that I don't believe."

The Ensi said nothing, her stance relaxing as though the trauma of the events in the throne room had never happened.

"These six are Warriors of IY," Jessica said firmly. "Why are they imprisoned here?"

The Ensi laughed. "Imprisoned?" She stepped towards Jessica, staring intently into her eyes. "These Warriors are not prisoners. They are the prison's Wardens."

The words of Zaidu flashed through Jessica's mind. *He called himself a Warden.* She glanced to the alcove in the wall to her right, where the ancient Warrior still stood, his teeth bared, his taut body set against an unseen adversary. *A Warden? But of what?* In her earlier encounter with him, he'd been about to say more, but the shaven-headed shaman had intervened. And now she couldn't reach him. For she'd tried and failed, the crushing maelstrom around the ancient Warrior's mind proving impenetrable. *He fights against the Dark,* came an unbidden thought. *It is what Warriors do.* And yet as she saw the struggles of Zaidu, it seemed these Warriors carried a greater burden than others.

She turned to the Ensi, who stood in silence, watching her. *Yet still this makes little sense.* "What of these two?" she said, gesturing to the two bound figures. "These that serve you."

"Serve me? No, these serve their master, Kaos."

Jessica's eyes widened. "These shamans serve Kaos?" She shook her head. "I don't believe you. Why would these be bound? You're the leader of the Ka. Your god is Kaos. Why haven't you freed them?"

The Ensi laughed, a rich sound belying the tension in the air. "Free them? That is not something any sane person would countenance."

"And you are sane?" Jessica said, her mind racing.

"As sane as you," the Ensi fired back.

And how sane am I? Jessica thought, trying to grasp the truth of what was happening. *Is what I see and hear the work of a rational mind?* She pushed the thought away. It was not her that was insane, it was this Land, this place. *This prison.*

Her attention switched back the Warriors, those that Zaidu had said were Wardens. Could the Ensi be telling the truth? Or a truth? *And if she is?* "The Warriors here are the Wardens of these two?" she asked, gesturing to the two bound figures. "Their guards?"

A shadow crossed the Ensi's eyes. "The Wardens guard far more than just these shamans. But yes, the Wardens guard them, preventing them from rejoining Kaos."

Jessica struggled to grasp what she was being told. "You know these are Warriors of IY, you know they're binding these shamans of Kaos, and yet you *allow* this. Why?"

The Ensi tilted her head. "These are Warriors, true, but of IY?" Her brow furrowed. "That is not clear to me. But yes, I allow it. These Warriors prevent the release of a great evil, one I do not wish to see unleashed across my lands."

Jessica glanced at the two snarling shamans. "These pose such a danger?"

"They are fearsome enemies – but they are not the threat of which I speak."

Jessica turned narrowing eyes on the Ensi. "Then what is?"

"The Geddon. The Wardens bind the Geddon."

Horrified, Jessica stared at the Ensi, numbness enveloping her. *No, it can't be.* "The Geddon is here?" she breathed.

"Not in the sense you ask. These Wardens access the Geddon's prison. They bind him."

Jessica's gaze flicked blindly around the chamber. These Warriors held back the Geddon? They held back this world's Armageddon? "What is it?" she breathed. What terror lay beyond their sight?

A flicker of resentment crossed the Ensi's face. "That is not known to me. I thought this something you might know … destroyer."

Jessica glared at her. "I'm no destroyer," she hissed. "And I know nothing of this."

The Ensi held Jessica's harsh gaze as if testing her worth. "I believe you," she said eventually. She cast a weary glance at the Warriors. "I asked them, you know. They won't answer."

Turning back to the Warriors, Jessica's anger quickly faded, leaving her bewildered and utterly lost. She saw once again their bodies taut with stress, their faces strained by some heart-rending burden. These were the Wardens of the Geddon? Here in the Ka temple? *This makes no sense.* "How did these Warriors get here?" she asked, watching one fight his faraway battle.

"That is also knowledge kept from me. But each Ensi before me has protected this place, ensuring it remained hidden. I have failed to do so."

The leaders of the Ka protected this place? "You serve the Ka, you serve Kaos, and yet you hold Warriors of your enemy in the heart of your homeland? You hide it from your own people?"

The Ensi's emerald-green eyes locked onto Jessica's. "Some things must remain hidden."

"But you serve Kaos!"

"I serve, but on some things, we disagree."

"You disagree with your own god?" Jessica whispered, stunned.

The Ensi was silent.

Jessica floundered, a myriad of questions half formed. Could she trust anything this woman said? *Maybe,* a part of her said. *Never,* said another. *She's already lied to you.* "Why should I believe anything you tell me? You say you knew we were coming, that you worked with a Warrior in our camp." The Ensi tilted her head slightly. "You lie," Jessica continued. "I know the person you speak of – she would never, ever, betray us."

The Ensi frowned. "Then maybe this is why we failed. I thought the Warrior was with us." She ran her hand through her short, dark hair. "Then maybe it was only the daemon who sought to aid us."

Jessica's heart leapt. The attack had failed? *But were they all okay? Was Beth—*

A piercing cry rent the air, and she spun around to see the light in one of the alcoves fading …

Then the Warrior within vanished!

She turned to the Ensi, who was staring at the alcove in disbelief. "What happened! What—"

A second cry came from the adjacent alcove. And then from the next. And the next. One by one each alcove dimmed, and one by one, each of the Warriors within disappeared, until only two remained.

'Free! Free at last!' cried a triumphant voice in her head.

Jessica spun around to see a snarling shaman straining at the single remaining coil holding him back. "Free! Free! Now you will see!" The shaman's howling flooded the chamber as he thrashed against his leash. The shaman beside him chilled Jessica's soul with a bloodcurdling screech. It seemed moments only, then they would be free.

Glancing to the two surviving Warriors, she forced herself to move. Could the Wardens help? But arriving at Zaidu's alcove, her gut twisted in a knot of anguish. Blood leaking from his nose and ears, tendons straining against some horrific burden, the Warden's once bright eyes were dulled with a wretched fear. Her horrified gaze shifted to the Warrior in the adjacent alcove – blood-stained tears streamed down the woman's face. *They see their death. And they can do nothing.* A desperate anger coursed through her. *These are fellow Warriors. I can't let them die.*

"What can we do?" she said fiercely, spinning around to the Ensi.

The Ensi was already facing the shamans, her expression a mask of concentration. Jessica felt the smallest pressure on her mind, then a blaze of darkness erupted within the shamans' alcoves, engulfing those inside.

The shamans' cries instantly died.

The Ensi walked towards Jessica, her face drawn. "I know little about these prisons, but I have done what I can. This will hold them for a moment only. They are too strong."

A shiver of dismay ran down Jessica's spine. This proud and powerful woman looked scared. Very scared. "What can we do?" she asked again.

"For these here, nothing. I—"

"Nothing! There must be something we can do."

The Ensi winced. "I thought I knew the path ahead. I thought ..." She broke off, seeming to gather herself. "We stand on a precipice, one that you cannot see. And in this moment, you walk blindly. You will fall into the abyss – we will all fall – unless you listen to me."

Her mask of defiance slipping, Jessica glanced across to Zaidu. "He's dying, and you say we can do nothing?"

"They are beyond my understanding."

Jessica stared at the distraught Warrior for a moment longer, then turned back in despair. "What can I do?"

"Help me," the Ensi said, her emerald-green eyes holding Jessica's. "And trust me."

Jessica shook her head. "You are the leader of the Ka. You serve Kaos. You—"

"You must see the truth," the Ensi said, her shimmering green eyes drawing Jessica in. "You must feel the truth. Then you may choose."

The truth? What was the truth here?

Her breath caught at her answering thought. *The truth is she hid the Wardens from Kaos.*

And there, in those simple words, was indeed the stunning reality of a staggering deception. *The Ensi protected the Wardens of the Geddon. She protected the world from destruction.*

But why?

I must see. I must understand.

Hesitating only a heartbeat longer, she freed her mind and allowed herself to be drawn into those the emerald-green eyes.

"I cannot stay here," came the Ensi's quiet voice as Jessica's world dissolved into a swirling sea of green. "If they capture me, if they find what is inside ..."

Jessica felt herself drawn deeper and deeper through the verdant ocean, her own thoughts lost within a looming sense of something ... greater. Something terrifying. With a violent wrench, she broke through the emerald ocean and into a turbulent storm of startling images and wild emotions. Some joyous, some anguished, many tragically horrific; a tempest of disparate feelings, thoughts, wishes, and desires. Of quiet reflection and of blazing rows. Of decisions made and of actions taken. Of pride and celebration, and of bitter despair and savage regrets. And fractured images of a tragic childhood, brutal images that she wished to turn away from. But on they came, raking her soul, bearing the tumultuous and torrid tale of the Ensi's life. A tale of a woman's fierce ambition to protect her people, to grow her people and her empire. A tale of her desire to resist her people's mortal enemy and the destroyers – the Warriors – they brought to the Land.

And of her desire to protect her daughters.

That evil snake man spoke true, Jessica thought, senses reeling. *They were taken away, and she doesn't know where.* The image of two young toddlers in a boat flashed into her mind. *Toddlers, not babies. The evil snake was mistaken.* And in that moment, Jessica knew that was so very, very important.

The Ensi's bloodline may be safe.

Her bloodline.

The Seed ...

Jessica reached for the thought—

And was swept away, falling deeper and deeper within the Ensi's mind, tumbling through a vast, barren desert – a darkness – until she washed up against a cold, unyielding barrier.

An ancient and impenetrable barrier.

'Look beyond,' came the Ensi's calm voice. '*You have but a moment.*'

The barrier softened, relaxed, and Jessica easily slipped through.

She entered a small domed chamber, bathed in a soft white light emanating from its glowing circular walls. In its centre lay a polished marble pedestal on which floated a slim pillar, a vortex of deep, vivid blue, a coruscating web of delicate arcs of energy crisscrossing within. Its rich, vibrant aura swept over her, a nebula of fragmented memories blazing in its wake.

An aura she instantly knew. *The Kade! She holds the Kade!*

Jessica stared at the arcing vortex, stunned. *IY said I would sense it. But I sensed nothing until now.* Unbelieving, she stepped closer, her wide eyes scanning the alien artefact. *I've seen this before. I—*

She froze as a faint discordant energy caressed her soul. An energy not of the Kade. An energy of something not wishing to be found.

She cast her mind's eye to glowing wall of the chamber.

Something else lies beyond. Something that the Ensi doesn't see.

A deep, visceral memory struggled to break free. A fractured image of two snakes standing tall. Two upright coiled snakes tightly interlocked as though one.

Snakes?

No, Life.

What—

She cried out as she was sucked out of the glowing white chamber, assailed by further tempestuous memories from the Ensi's past.

She staggered, almost falling, searing pain in her head. Dazed and bewildered, she steadied herself, shielding her eyes from the sudden harsh light surrounding her. Glancing around, she saw she stood on a golden desert plain, the sun hanging low in the sky ahead.

"A Glade," she whispered, turning to the Ensi.

The Ensi said nothing.

Jessica dropped to her haunches, her head in her hands, a myriad of barbarous images harrying her. *I couldn't hold all that within me,* she thought, fighting to make sense of what she'd seen. *How can she?* The image of the vivid blue vortex burned to the fore. She raised her head. "You hold the Kade."

The Ensi's face darkened. "A burden I must carry," she said, brittle anger in her voice. "One thrust upon me."

Fragments coalesced, and from the shadows of Jessica's mind a memory returned with a surge of fear.

Of her standing before the Ensi.

Of her saying this before.

Glacial dread twisted her gut. *No! That can't be. I knew nothing of this Kade.*

Are you sure? came another voice from within.

She struggled to her feet, aghast. "No," she stammered. "That can't be. I never met you before."

The Ensi glared at Jessica. "Of what do you speak?"

Jessica fought to control her panicked mind. *I am Jessica.*

You are the Guardian.

I am Jessica. I am the Guardian. And I haven't met this woman before.

And yet ghostly, incoherent memories swirled beyond her mind's eye. Memories that refused to be seen, merely disparate echoes of an unknown time, an unknown place.

And yet they tasted of the Kade, they smelled of the Kade. *They*—

The Ensi grasped her arm. "We have little time!"

Jessica snapped onto the Ensi's words. Steadying her shaking hand, she forced the terrifying doubts – the crippling fears – away. *Face what is before you. Understand.* "You carry the Kade? How? I thought it to be a great weapon, a cauldron of power." *A well of immense energy.*

"The Kade is the key to the energy of the Dark," the Ensi said, her voice laced with simmering anger. "The key to the A'ven."

The image of the arcing blue vortex flashed into Jessica's mind. *A key? This Kade is a key?* "I thought it would be ... Not this."

She heard a harsh laugh. "It seems your god doesn't tell you all." The Ensi's eyes narrowed. "Unless your god doesn't know the Kade's purpose?"

I don't know, Jessica thought with a sudden shocking realisation. *What do I truly know of IY?* "You hold the Kade," she whispered. "How? Why?"

A grim smile crossed the Ensi's face as she glared at Jessica. "How? Because the Light cursed me with it. Why? Because they knew I would hide it from those who seek it."

"The Light gave it to you?" she stammered, horrified. "But you are ... the enemy."

The Ensi laughed a vicious laugh. "Who is the enemy to who? You should ask yourself that, and then seek the answer." She faced the desolate landscape. "All I wish is for the best for my people." Her head imperceptibly bowed. "And for my children."

Jessica stared, shocked into silence by the incredible revelation. That which IY had asked them to find was here, hidden within the leader of the Iyes's most feared enemy. *And yet the Light arranged this?*

She flinched as she felt an energy ripple through her Staff. *'You now see the first of a great truth,'* came Jalu's voice.

Truth? Jessica thought grimly. What was the truth of this Land? What could she believe?

'You saw it within her,' Jalu continued. *'You saw the Kade. You saw the key to accessing the A'ven.'*

Of that, there was no denying. The Ensi held the Kade. But how was this possible? Why hide in one such as this?

'Why?' Jalu answered as if reading her thoughts. *'Because it worked. For aeons, neither Kaos nor IY have found it.'*

Jessica felt things slip further from her grasp. *'It was purposely hidden from IY? Why would anyone do that?'*

'Ultimate power in a single hand destroys even the strongest of wills. The Light cannot allow it. And IY is ... misguided on what to do with the Kade.'

Jessica put her hand to her head, running her fingers roughly through her hair. What crazed game was being played here?

"We are enemies," came the Ensi's quiet voice. "But allies in wishing to preserve our lands. Help me leave this place. Help me keep the Kade from Kaos's shamans."

Help her? Help this leader of the Ka?

A single draconian thought hammered into her mind. *No. But I could kill her.*

Her whole body tensed. If the Kade was the key to accessing the A'ven's energy, then kill her. Destroy the Kade. Remove the power of the A'ven from the Dark – and from the Light.

End this game.

Her hand tightened on the Staff. One blow, one brutal strike, and she could end it. End the daemons, the shamans. *The burnt man.*

She could do it. She could destroy it now.

'Destroy the Kade and you let Kaos win,' came Jalu's calm voice.

'Why?' she pulsed, her arm tensed, ready to strike as the Ensi silently watched her.

'The A'ven is an energy of the Void, untouchable by Life, unreachable by those of the Light and the Dark who roam within the protected realm of the Continuum. Only the Kade unlocks the A'ven to those within. Only the Kade allows the Warriors to access the energy they need to defend the Gates against the horde of the Dark. And only the A'ven allows the Geddon to be bound.'

Jessica froze.

'Destroy the Kade, release the Geddon.'

Aghast, she took a step back, lowering her Staff.

'And there is more,' Jalu murmured. *'You sensed more within the Ensi. Something most precious.'*

Jessica held her breath as a ghostly, barely sensed connection formed. *The two interlocking coiled snakes. Life. I sensed the Seed of Life.*

'Protect the Seed of Life,' Jalu murmured. 'You are the Guardian. You—'

"Krull comes," came the urgent voice of the Ensi. "You *must* help me escape."

Jessica felt the hairs on the back of her neck stand on end. The shaven-headed shaman.

The burnt man!

She glanced at the Ensi's strained face. *She asks for my help, but this is the leader of the Ka. This is the enemy.* Naga had told them this. Bear had told them.

'Naga and the Iyes only knew what they knew,' Jalu said. 'You are the Guardian. You guard Life. You must protect the Ensi. You must preserve the bloodline.'

The bloodline? The daughters. 'What—'

"I must return us to the Warden's chamber," the Ensi hissed. "Else we are undefended."

The golden desert vanished, and the chamber of the Warriors reappeared.

Dazed, thoughts tumultuous, Jessica's fraught gaze flicked around the chamber. The two surviving Wardens stared out from their alcoves with wild, unseeing eyes. The two shamans of Kaos remained veiled behind a dark haze.

The sound of a distant explosion from above echoed into the chamber.

"For the last time, I ask you," the Ensi said, a desperate edge to her voice. "Will you help me? Will you protect the Kade?"

In the panic of the moment, two thoughts emerged with brutal clarity from the torment of her mind.

The burnt man comes.

He can't take the Kade.

A vehement resolve flooded her veins. She didn't understand all, but in the window of the Ensi's eyes, she had seen enough. The Kade lay inside her. *And she carries something more, something she knows nothing about. A Seed. A Seed of Life.* "Protect the Seed of Life," Jalu had said. A shrouded truth was emerging from the swirling mists at the edge of her consciousness; mists forever there, but rarely parting. *I am the Guardian. I must protect Life.*

She nodded. "I will help."

"Then I release you."

She staggered as a surge of energy from the A'ven streamed into her—

'Hold the Ensi, Guardian!' IY cried in her mind. 'Do not let her leave! I will get you both out of there.'

Ignoring the voice, Jessica looked at the woman before her. "What's your name?"

"Pa'Andora," the woman answered. "But you may call me Paan."

Jessica face hardened. "So, Paan, what do we do?"

Paan glanced towards the haze-bound shamans. "Give me time." Her next words slipped into Jessica's mind. *'They must not see what we do.'* She walked to one of the vacant alcoves and stepped inside. The alcove glowed with a soft golden light—

A dreadful cry erupted from one of the two remaining Wardens – and the Warrior vanished.

Screeches of delight erupted from within the dark haze surrounding the two ancient shamans, and a foul stench flooded the chamber. The shamans of Kaos were breaking free.

'This is a mistake, Guardian,' came IY's strident voice.

'Protect me,' Paan said from within the alcove.

Instinctively facing the bound shamans, Jessica held her Staff before her. *'I need your help,'* she pulsed to Jalu. Immediately, her Staff blazed with white light. *'We must—'*

The haze around the shamans vanished as they snapped the last of their bindings. Reacting in an instant, Jessica slammed up a wall of blinding white energy across the far wall of the chamber, trapping the shrieking shamans within their alcoves – she staggered as an intense pressure wave hammered against the shield, the rabid shrieks of the shamans slicing through the air as they redoubled their efforts against her.

In that moment, a scream echoed around the chamber as the last Warden died.

Then an immense force hammered against her shield, forcing her backwards. *'We don't have much time,'* she pulsed, straining to hold the shamans back.

'I need more time,' Paan growled.

'More,' Jessica implored Jalu.

As another surge of energy coursed through her, Jessica took a step forward—

The echoing sound of someone approaching reverberated in the passageway outside.

In desperation, she peeled off a strip of energy from her shield, swinging it around to cover the chamber entrance just as the shaven-headed shaman appeared.

A colossal strike hammered on her shield.

Then another.

'I can't hold this!' she pulsed to Paan.

'Just a moment longer,' came Paan's distant voice.

Her face glistening with sweat, Jessica staggered as a concussive blast rocked the shield by the entrance, then cried out as a strike lanced through the shield holding back the shamans, its crackling energy streaking narrowly past her head.

'Thank you,' came Paan's faint voice. 'It is done.'

Straining against the forces hammering at both her shields, Jessica glanced to the portal. It was empty. *It's done. I need to—*

A massive strike shattered one of her shields and in strode the shaven-headed shaman, his Black Staff held aloft, a blaze of intense black energy streaming out from its tip.

She blinked.

Time slowed.

As the wrathful black bolt of energy from the shaman streaked towards her, Jalu spoke. *'You have done well, Guardian. You have bought us time. I will help you understand.'*

The baleful black bolt struck—

The world surrounding Jessica shimmered, and her mind exploded with pain.

She felt herself falling.

Blackness descended.

CHAPTER THIRTY-ONE

*The shamans of Kaos had proved ruthlessly efficient
in their quest to destroy Life. No one knew, but I,
how few Seeds remained. And where they lay.*

*K*rull had sundered the stone throne with a single targeted strike, the two fractured halves collapsing, shattering as they struck the ground. Striding past the rubble of the destroyed throne, he'd passed through the shadowy opening revealed, and quickly descended the narrow stairwell into the long-concealed bowels of the temple. Entering the dank tunnel leading to the prison chamber, the unbridled, manic fury of the shamans of Kaos had swept over him as the ancient ones fought to break free. Readying for battle, Krull had rushed to the entrance of the prison and briefly seen the Guardian holding back the shamans before a sizzling-white barrier had blazed in his path. He'd instantly unleashed a stream of thunderous bolts into the shield.

'*I see it!*' Nergai exclaimed immediately, and Krull sensed a subtle tuning of his Black Staff.

His next strike shattered the Guardian's shield, and without hesitation, Krull struck again at the woman now revealed.

She vanished.

Horrified, the devastating truth was revealed as he scanned the chamber.

The Guardian and the Ensi were gone.

And the Wardens were gone.

"Fool!" rasped a contemptuous voice to his side. Krull turned to see K'zarz, a shaman from ages past, step menacingly towards him. "You let her escape! You are of no use to me now."

Feeling the tell-tale harsh tremor in the ether, Krull flashed up a black shield – just in time to repel the fervid, combined assault from both ancient shamans.

So, they choose now *to test me.*

And they call me *a fool.*

He had no time for this. *'Angram, I request to serve you,'* he pulsed.

Immediately, a surge of febrile energy swept around Krull, assailing him with a dread-laden force.

'You are wise with your words,' the daemon, Angram, crooned.

His body trembling, his muscles and bones afire, a heaving power blossomed – a power to aid him conquer this world.

'It is so,' Angram murmured.

Krull smiled. *Yes, it is done.* With the potent presence of Angram beside him, he stood tall, then hammered the base of his Black Staff into the ground—

The chamber exploded into a midnight blackness, and a massive shock wave tore through the chamber. The ground trembled, and part of the roof collapsed behind him.

Then, in the darkness … silence.

Krull waited patiently for the light to return, then watched as the two ragged shamans climbed unsteadily to their feet. Both looked up at him with vengeful fury etched across their withered faces, and in their eyes, madness. Was there anything left of their original selves? He stepped towards them. "Xehalla, K'zarz, I claim you for continued service to Kaos."

Xehalla lurched forward, her steps stiff and laboured. "And who are you to claim our service?"

Her assault on his mind was swift and deadly – but Angram was quicker, flashing up a barrier to deflect her strike.

Krull smiled. "I am Krull, Kaos's chosen. You will serve me or die. You will—"

K'zarz attacked, stunning Krull with a venomous strike that sliced through one of his mind shields.

Krull flashed up another shield—

And again, K'zarz's attack slipped through his defence.

Nergai! He has control of Nergai already! And that daemon he had just released in favour of Angram knew the inside of his mind as well as him.

Krull's eyes darkened. *Enough of this!* Wielding the energy of the Dark, he drew a pitch-black oily morass up around the legs of both shamans, pinning them in place. As the oily morass swept up the shamans' bodies, K'zarz fought with deranged fury to break Krull's mind shields – with Angram's aid, Krull absorbed each attack with ease. *You have sealed your own fate,* Krull thought as the shamans vanished beneath the black cloak. With both immobilised, he held his Black Staff before him and wound tight, binding coils of energy around the two. Then, with Angram holding the coils in place, he allowed the black morass to slip away.

The two shamans stood exposed, defenceless.

Krull's eyes blazed. "Now you die!" he snarled, pouring all his vehement fury into a violent, lashing attack on the stricken shamans. Although bound, the shamans' reactions were fast and furious, and their shields snapped into place before his strike landed. A seething cauldron of fire erupted as the energies collided. Yet the shamans' desperate defence was no match for Krull's cold rage. As his attack intensified, he sensed their growing disbelief – and terror – as they realised they would die.

'Cease, my shaman,' came Angram's calm voice. *'You – we – need them. They hold the key to the red dragons.'*

Ignoring Angram, Krull increased the ferocity of his blistering attack, revelling in the sheer panic of both the shamans and their daemons.

'They cannot die. They know the secrets of the Ensi.'

Krull's lips curled into a disdainful sneer. *'I have seen her secrets. Those Warriors are now dead.'*

'Not the Warriors. The Kade. And her bloodline.'

Xehalla's shield collapsed.

Krull snapped off his attack.

Xehalla stood, gasping, her desiccated, bald head bowed, her tattered body slumped. K'zarz stood defiant but reeking of fear. He avoided Krull's eyes.

'Tell me those secrets,' Krull commanded of Angram.

'They know, not I. They hide things deep, in places I cannot reach. But those secrets are there.'

Krull took a menacing step towards the two cowed shamans. "Look at me," he commanded. Xehalla lifted her head, and K'zarz turned bitter eyes to him. "Your answers now decide your fate. Where is the Kade?"

Xehalla spat. "The Ensi—"

"Silence!" K'zarz snarled, spinning around to Xehalla. "Say no more. Tell—"

The ancient shaman cried out, then fell to the ground, screaming, his body jerking uncontrollably.

Krull lowered his Black Staff. "I ask only once more. Where is the Kade?"

Xehalla's deep-pitted eyes skittered between Krull and K'zarz, who was climbing slowly to his feet, his face twisted with both fear and rage. Xehalla licked her lips, then craned her scrawny neck towards Krull. "The Ensi," she grated. "The Ensi carries the Kade."

Krull froze. *The Ensi … The Kade …* It couldn't be. "How do you know this?" he said, somehow holding his voice steady.

"We know many things, O chosen of Kaos," K'zarz snarled, baring his teeth.

Krull glared at the man. *He will die.*

'But not yet,' came the voice of Angram. *'I sense the truth of what they say. What else do they know?'*

Krull's mind raced. The Ensi held the Kade. How was this possible? And how hadn't he known? A frustrated rage threatened to explode. The prize had stood before him. She had been within his grasp. *'Why did they not tell me? Tell Kaos?'*

'None are to blame here,' Angram said. *'The prison was hidden and sealed from all. The shamans could not reach Kaos.'*

And yet the Ensi had been here. *I was here.*

But he'd focussed on the wrong people. He'd focussed on the devil Warrior above.

'There is more to be told,' came Angram's voice. *'They know more. The bloodline.'*

Bloodline?

Eyes narrowing, he took a step towards the shamans. Xehalla retreated. K'zarz held his ground yet his gaunt frame curled a little tighter. "What of the Ensi's bloodline?" Krull growled.

"They must be slaughtered!" Xehalla shrieked. "They are a curse upon this land. They must be slain and cleansed! They—"

"Silence!" K'zarz shrieked. "Else the wrath of Kaos will descend upon you." His hate-filled gaze flicked towards Krull. "We serve Kaos, shaman, not you. We—"

"To you, I am Kaos," Krull roared, hammering his Black Staff into the ground. K'zarz staggered as an explosion of blackness rocked the chamber. Krull bared his teeth. "You obey me. Only me. There lies your single chance of redemption."

K'zarz glared at Krull under hooded eyes.

Krull raised his Staff. "I will ask this only once. Do you accept me? Do you serve me? Your answer decides your fate."

Xehalla scurried forward, her head bowed low. "I serve. Yes, I serve."

Drawing energy from the A'ven and readying his attack, Krull shifted his merciless gaze to K'zarz. "And you?"

He watched the shaman's face twist through a multitude of emotions: fury, fear, envy, then finally recognition. Recognition he was defeated. "It is accepted," K'zarz rasped.

The shaman's submission tempered a little of Krull's anger. The words spoken formed an unbreakable bond. They would try, of course, looking for a mis-said word or thought that could release them. *But I will be careful.* These two were his for a long, long time.

He stepped closer to K'zarz. "What of this bloodline?"

"We know!" Xehalla hissed. "They all must die! Their blood is cursed!"

"Who must die?" Krull growled.

"Those with the stench upon them! Those who reek of death!"

Beside her, K'zarz scowled. "She speaks true," he spat. "And the stench is within the Ensi." He bared his teeth. "But we could do nothing. No one came for us. We were abandoned!"

Krull held back his frustration, trying to unravel the man's words, trying to pick through his madness. "Who must die?" he asked again. "Why must they die?"

"They are diseased!" Xehalla cried. "They will kill us all. They must be killed."

A disease? "What is this disease?" he said, holding his scathing gaze on K'zarz.

"A disease that lives in the bloodline," snarled the tattered shaman.

"The Ensi," Xehalla hissed. "Her cursed daughters. They *are* the disease. A disease that will kill us all."

The bloodline of the Ensi was a disease? What twisted tale was this?

K'zarz licked his ravaged lips. "Kaos demanded it from us. *Our master* demanded it from us. To seek out the diseased ones. To find those that had been missed."

"There were others?"

"You know nothing," K'zarz snarled. "Others? Many others. All killed by shamans before us." Feral fire burnt in the man's eyes. "This line was missed, but we found it! The Ensi. Her bloodline."

"And you let her go!" Xehalla spat, glaring at Krull.

Krull's eyes flicked from one to the other as he grappled with the sudden unveiling of this staggering revelation. These shamans had been tasked with seeking and destroying carriers of a disease, a disease that could kill them all. A disease he knew nothing of. Why had he never heard of this? Why had Kaos not told him of this?

'Because you are not the master,' came Angram's quiet voice.

Krull grimaced; he needed to better shield his thoughts. But Angram was right. He wasn't Kaos, and he shouldn't ever forget that.

Until my time comes.

K'zarz was studying him, a sly glint in his eye. "You ask many questions, O chosen one, questions we dare not ask." The tattered shaman tilted his head, a ghastly smile appearing on his face. "Maybe you should seek your answers from Kaos himself?"

Ask Kaos? Krull's blood ran cold as a rare tremor of fear ran through him. *I once asked a question. Never again.* Forcing back that dread memory, Krull focussed on the two shamans. Xehalla shuffled back and forth, muttering to herself. K'zarz continued glaring at him under hooded eyes. Their incarceration had pushed them to the verge of insanity. And yet it had also allowed them to unmask the most incredible secret: the Ensi held the Kade.

And this disease? The Ensi's bloodline? What of that?

He turned away, his eyes narrowing as he walked a few steps across the chamber. What had the snake, Cobra, told him? A tale of the Ensi's secret babies smuggled out of the Ka homeland and sent to a tribe in the far north.

The north ...

He frowned, a spark of a connection flaring. *The devil shaman of the Iyes, the one called Naga.* He had raked her mind before she'd died, probing her vast memory for the secrets of the tribe of IY, for the Story of the Iyes. He'd seen and heard much within those stolen memories, but of the Iyes's Story, nothing. The devil shaman had buried that Story deep, somehow holding it from his grasp. Yet the other stolen memories remained within him – and something within those memories called to him now. Something linked to the Ensi and her daughters.

But what?

Calming himself, he mentally withdrew from the chamber and reached within himself, delving deep into his own mind, searching for those stolen memories of the Iyes's shaman. And so very quickly he found those memories, swirling in fresh, chaotic agitation as he entered their midst. Working quickly and carefully, he weaved his way through the ages of the shaman's life, scanning the ephemeral sights and sounds surrounding him, listening to the remembered stories of others, all the while searching for that which had drawn him here ...

And one of the shaman's memories suddenly seemed to glow more brightly than the others. Of a particular moonlit night. A night when two babies had been abandoned at the entrance to Naga's hut.

Two babies ...

Was that it? Were these the elusive daughters of the Ensi, hidden within the Iyes tribe?

Maybe.

Or maybe not.

But if they were, then these were the bloodline that Kaos was seeking to eradicate.

Because they carry a disease.

But what disease? *And why do I know nothing of this?*

His thoughts – his anger – spiralling, his hand tightened around his Black Staff. *This will not be kept from me. Nothing will be kept from me.*

Allowing his mind to once more sweep through the Iyes shaman's memories, he followed the path of those abandoned babies …

There! He heard the shaman, Naga, say their names. *Sheba and her sister, River!*

He instantly snapped his mind back to the chamber.

The two shamans of Kaos eyed him with hateful suspicion.

Give nothing away. This knowledge is mine, and mine only. Strengthening his mind's shield, a faint smile appeared on his lips. He would begin a search for those daughters of the Ensi. He would find out more for himself. *I will learn this secret. For nothing will be hidden from me in the new world to come.*

He drew back from those thoughts, hiding them deep, and his gaze drifted around the chamber. So much had happened, and so quickly, that it was only now that the enormity of what he was seeing struck him.

The Wardens of the Geddon had truly vanished.

'What happened here?' he pulsed to Angram.

'The Wardens died. In another time. How? That, I do not know.'

Staring at the six empty alcoves, fierce elation surged.

The Wardens were dead.

The Geddon could be released.

The cleansing can begin.

Krull stood tall, his taut muscles flexing against his tunic, wild pleasure coursing through him at the stunning news he could impart to his master Kaos. The discovery of the Kade, and the death of the Wardens.

'And the Ensi?' came Angram's voice. *'And the Guardian?'*

He considered the daemon's words. The Guardian he would seek out and kill soon enough. *That mistake, I will correct.* And the Ensi and her blasphemous deception? His eyes hardened. *I will give you one chance, my Ensi. One chance only.* Yes, he would tell of the deception, but he would tell of a deception commanded by the Ancient, by the ice dragon of the north. *I will place the blame there, my Ensi. I will try. But when I find you and the Kade – and find you I will – there will be one choice only. Join me and rule by my side – or die.*

'You play a most dangerous game,' came Angram's calm voice.

'Be careful how far you step into my mind, daemon. You may hold a great strength, but in this moment, you are bound to me. You serve me. Do not think to judge me. That lies in the hands of my master.'

'I do not judge,' Angram replied. 'I merely state a truth.'

'Stay out of my mind,' Krull grated.

The presence of the daemon retreated.

Reinforcing the shield on his mind, Krull cursed his stupidity. He could let no one see what he truly intended. *Especially my god.*

He straightened, muscles tensing. But in this moment, his god needed to be told of what had transpired. *He must hear of this now. From me, and no other.*

But one command remained.

"Release the red dragons," he snarled to K'zarz as he strode out of the chamber. "It is time to rid ourselves of our visitors."

To begin the cleansing of these lands, to cleanse it of the unwanted.

A savage delight rose. *My time is coming. The time of Krull is near.*

*

Qiax pulled his eye back from the fine crevice in the wall above the chamber and wiped his damp brow. Hope remained. The Guardian and the Ensi had escaped. Although Krull was proving to be far more powerful than he'd envisaged.

He leaned back against the smooth wall of the unlit passageway, allowing himself the briefest moment to pay his respects to the brave friend who had perished in the throne room above. A willing double, who had served him well over these past sun-cycles, but who had paid the ultimate price in service to their cause. Qiax released a heavy breath. But this was not the first sacrifice and would not be the last.

After a short while, he reached back and adjusted the cord holding his hair. Satisfied, he felt his way along the familiar darkness of the passage towards his refuge. What to do now? His gaze sharpened. *Do what I have done for so long.* Be patient. Pull and prod unseen. *And hope the Guardian understands.*

CHAPTER THIRTY-TWO

As I have spoken of before: to step into the unknown with terror in your soul to save others, this is true courage.

*H*er nerves still shattered after their harrowing journey deep into the ancient labyrinth of a long-forgotten people, Erin followed Fletcher around the edge of a dimly lit, elongate chamber. Stepping through the strewn rubble from the partially collapsed ceiling, her stomach churned at the macabre sight around her. Decayed and tattered bodies surrounded her, each stored upright and openly displayed in faintly glowing alcoves set into the stone walls of the chamber. She saw seven … no, eight recesses – eight bodies preserved deep underground within this ancient temple.

Within this prison.

Was this what Asim had expected? *Who are they? Why are they here?*

"What is this place?" Fletcher said, his voice shaking.

Asim turned to him. "A once impregnable fortress built to withstand the forces of evil. And to contain them."

"How old are these bodies?" Erin whispered, glancing at the withered corpse in the alcove beside her. *Once a man*, she thought. Skin stretched taut across his gaunt body, shrivelled tears revealing sinews which had dried nut-brown. Patches of long, straggly hair fell from the man's broad, heavy-browed skull. An axe dangled from the man's blackened hand.

"Some possibly thirty thousand years old. Some two hundred thousand years old. Two are more recent."

"Unbelievable," Fletcher breathed, stepping up to one alcove. "They seem—" He gasped, staggering backwards.

"What is it?" Erin cried, staring wildly around.

"This one's alive!"

"They are all alive," Asim said.

Erin froze as a tremendous pressure built around them. *'It is time, K'zarz!'* cried a shrill voice in her head. *'It is our time again!'* A putrid stench assaulted her senses.

"What's that?" Fletcher exclaimed, eyes wide. "There's something else in here!"

Erin gaze snapped to the two alcoves at the end of the chamber, where a burgeoning sense of hatred swept out from the two figures within.

'We will rise again, my beloved!' came a distorted voice in Erin's head.

'And then we will wreak our vengeance on those who wronged us,' snarled another, hurling his voice through the ether in his rising fury. *'On them, on their families, on their offspring; on all of these deformed creatures who call themselves human.'*

'And on these accursed Warriors,' spat the first. *'And on this one who comes before us.'*

A tremendous pain lanced through Erin's mind, and she dropped to her knees, screaming. Her head afire, terror swept through her. *I'm going to die. I'm—*

A hand rested gently on her head, and the demonic fire vanished.

Gasping, she looked up and saw Asim's concerned face above her.

Fletcher rushed to her side. "Are you okay? What happened?"

Breathing hard, Erin rubbed her temple. "Something attacked me." *Something tried to kill me.* She glanced to the end of the chamber, where two tattered figures within the alcoves glared at her, their blackened, decaying teeth bared, their baleful power besieging her mind. "Those two are evil," she whispered as the figures glared at her with hooded eyes burning with hatred.

She pulled her eyes away, knowing now that these were the source of the malevolent presence she'd felt since first arriving at the ruins.

"Those two are shamans of a cursed god," Asim said. "And their chains are weakening."

Her head pounding, Erin slowly climbed to her feet. She glanced at the other ancient figures around them. "Then these others guard these shamans?" *But they're just corpses.*

"They are Warriors. They are the Wardens of this place."

Warriors? The horrors of the night at Mount Hope flashed back. A Warrior like the one called River, who'd protected them at the mountain? Another image swept by of a fearsome Beth striding past her with a blazing Axe. *Like my friend?*

Asim looked around the chamber, his eyes filled with sorrow. "But they weaken. They have guarded this place for a long time, and now little gold remains."

Erin walked slowly towards one of the ancient figures Asim had called Warriors. *Wardens.* She saw a gaunt man, thin strips of parched skin showing beneath the remains of his ragged clothing, his dead eyes staring into the distance. Stopping before the faintly glowing alcove, her skin suddenly tingled, and her muscles tensed as a vibrant feeling of hope coursed through her body and mind. She stared at the ancient man in astonishment. What power did this one wield?

Steadying herself, she ran her gaze around the chamber, now recognising the ripples of bright energy emanating from the other Warriors. From the Wardens. She glanced back at the two ravening shamans, their deep-socketed eyes still locked onto hers. "All this to contain those two?"

"They built this prison for one who lies elsewhere, but yes, it also binds these two."

Erin turned in confusion. "What else does this prison hold?"

A fell shadow crossed Asim's features. "The Geddon. This world's Armageddon."

"What!" Fletcher hissed, his eyes flitting around the chamber. "What do you mean? Where is—"

His gaze snapped to the entrance.

Erin heard footsteps in the stone corridor outside.

"The professor comes," Asim said softly. "Yet all is not lost. The portals must not be abandoned. Only one life is needed."

"What?" Erin said, bewildered. "What do—"

"Thank goodness," came a breathless voice behind them.

Erin spun around to see Robert – his shirt torn, a lens of his glasses broken – and the professor enter the chamber, each holding a torch.

"Thank goodness," Khaled repeated, sweat dripping from his brow, a look of concern on his face. "Are you okay? Do you know how dangerous that was, coming down here by yourself? What did you think you were doing?" He then looked around, his eyes widening. "Incredible," he whispered. "Truly incredible."

Erin saw a fell fire in his eyes. *A fire of destruction.*

"But tell them, Robert. How stupid to come down here by themselves – they could have been killed! What were they thinking?"

Robert scanned the chamber, his face unreadable. "Khaled is right, this was a crazy thing to do. I take it this was your idea, Asim?"

Asim nodded, tension in his stance. The young man then flicked a glance at Erin – she saw the despair within his eyes.

"Incredible," Khaled repeated as he moved further into the chamber, swinging his torch around its walls, its light casting eerie shadows over the recessed figures. "What do you think, Robert?"

Robert glanced at the rubble from the collapsed ceiling. "I think we should leave before the whole roof comes down on us."

"Come now, a moment; that is all I ask." Khaled gestured to one of the alcoves, a fervid desire on his face. "Look. What do you see?"

Robert swung his torch around, then peered over at the opposite wall. His eyes widened. "Axes! They carry Axes!" He turned to Erin. "Like those at the mountain. Like those carried by …" He stopped, casting a furtive glance at Khaled.

"So, Robert, there was more to your story than you told. You didn't say you'd met Warriors. A notable omission, wouldn't you say?"

Robert held Khaled's piercing stare. "A confusing and frightening time. I wasn't sure." He looked around. "But here there can be no doubt – these are Warriors." Casting his torchlight around the chamber, he frowned as the light landed on the hateful figures within the alcoves at the end of the chamber. "But these …" He walked to the end of the chamber, stopping before the two snarling figures …

Then he took a step back, holding his throat. "I can't breathe," he wheezed. "What evil is here?"

Asim quickly crossed to him and placed his hand on his head.

Robert immediately sucked in a deep lungful of air. His face pale, he faced them. "We have to leave," he said hoarsely. "Now. Something's not right. It—" His fearful gaze shifted to something beyond Erin's shoulder.

A chill settling on her, Erin turned …

Khaled stood facing them, the gun in his hand trained on them.

"What are you doing?" Robert breathed.

"Our master's work," Khaled replied, his eyes afire. "Tariq!"

Footsteps sounded in the corridor outside, then a man entered – a man wearing a black jacket. The thief from the hotel. He too carried a gun.

"Cover them," the professor ordered. "Kill anyone who moves." He faced Erin. "It seems you have brought me great luck in my search, and so I am most grateful that Tariq didn't kill you with the present he left in your hotel." He glanced at the hotel thief, smiling. "See, I told you killing them would be a mistake."

Tariq shrugged.

Still smiling, Khaled walked across to the two ancient shamans. "I wasn't sure, Robert, but I can see it now; these are the two I must save.

I thank you for your final service – you saved me from making a terrible mistake."

He swung his gun to the right and fired a single bullet into the head of the first Warrior beyond the shamans. The man cried out as a spray of blood splattered the alcove wall behind him, then he collapsed, falling forward into the chamber.

Erin retched.

Khaled gazed down at the twitching figure. "Far easier than I'd expected."

He stepped to the next alcove and fired another shot. Another Warrior fell. Twice more he repeated his deadly work, until four Warriors lay dead on the ground.

Erin flinched at bestial snarls behind her. She turned to see the torn, desiccated faces of the shamans twisted in manic rage as they glared out from their prisons, prisons that were failing as the Wardens died. *They* will *escape*.

"Why?" Robert whispered, his drawn face staring at the carnage before him.

The professor smiled. "For reasons similar to yours when you tried to steal the Staff."

Robert's eyes widened. "How do you know about that?"

Khaled stepped around the rubble from the collapsed ceiling to stand before the final two Warriors by the entrance. "It shouldn't be a surprise, Robert. We worked for the same god after all." He shook his head. "But unfortunately, you failed. A pity, the Staff would have been a great prize."

Robert gazed at the professor through tormented eyes. "To my enduring shame, I walked that path of deceit and treachery. But it is a false god that talks to us. An evil god. Do not do this."

A flicker of anger crossed the professor's face. "Kaos is the one true god. He is the holder of the Truths." He tilted his head. "And evil? No, people always misunderstand evil. They fail to see that this is where the true power lies." A fire burned in his eyes. "And I have worked my entire life searching for the root of all evil, for the one who holds the greatest power. And I found it in Kaos." He glared at Robert. "He is the one who will cleanse this world, bringing his Truths to the believers. And I will aid him in this glorious revolution."

The anger abruptly vanished from Khaled's face, and he smiled. "But we can discuss more of that later. First, I have a small surprise for you, my friend. I'm afraid it will be short-lived, but at least you can enjoy it while you can. Come. Come and see."

Seeing the flushed excitement on the man's face, Erin's gut wrenched. What evil did the man bring now?

The professor backed away, his gun trained on Robert as the bookseller walked towards him. "See!" Khaled cried, gesturing to the last two remaining Warriors. "See the joy I bring."

Robert turned to the Warriors beside the entrance …

Then he gasped and fell to his knees, staring in horror at the figures within. "Mother? Father?"

"A happy reunion, yes?" Khaled cried, a manic grin on his face.

Her mouth dry as desert sand, Erin saw only now what she had previously missed. Ravaged faces, yes, battle-scarred and gaunt, but not the features of these ancient others. Horrified, she saw tears rolling down the cheeks of the woman, and rage etched into the face of the man. She took a staggering step towards them. "Get out!" she cried. "Get out and fight!"

"My glorious god tells me that these Warriors may only be released by a shaman or another Warrior. Or if they are dead …" Erin cried out as Khaled fired his gun twice. Blood splattered on the wall behind the Warriors, and they collapsed, twitching, to the ground. "A fatal mistake, don't you think?"

Robert staggered, face frozen in terror. Then he rushed forward, dropping to his knees beside his mother. "No! No! I love you," he cried, tears streaming down his face. He collapsed onto her body, sobbing.

Shaking, a sickness twisting her stomach, Erin stared blindly at the horrific scene. *What can I do? I must do something.*

But she couldn't move.

"And now they are mine," Khaled rasped, turning and striding over to the ancient shamans, their faces contorted with primal savagery. "The culmination of—"

The shamans disappeared.

Khaled froze, staring at the empty space with an utter disbelief writ across his face.

They're what he wanted. He wanted those shamans to serve him.

A malign anger rose in Khaled's face, and he turned towards them, his eyes blazing. "What did you do?" he screamed. He looked around wildly as though the shamans might suddenly reappear, then swung his feral gaze to Asim. "You did this! It was you!"

"It seems you've been used," the young man murmured. "Welcome to the world of Kaos."

Khaled's expression twisted with rage – then he lifted his gun.

"Asim! Run!" Erin screamed.

She tried to move.

But her legs wouldn't respond.

She screamed as the sound of the gun exploded in the chamber.

With a heart-wrenching cry, Asim rocked back, holding his chest. Then he dropped to his knees, groaning, blood seeping through his fingers.

"No!" Erin cried out as Khaled walked up to the fallen young man, his teeth bared, his gun rising—

A harsh cry rent the air, and she spun around to see Fletcher's fist hammer into the black-coated thief's head, his knee thrusting into the man's groin. As the thief fell to the ground, howling in pain, Fletcher grabbed the man's gun and tore it out of his hand.

Out of the corner of her eye, Erin saw Khaled swinging his gun towards Fletcher.

"No!" she cried, rushing forward to grab the gun—

The pistol fired—

Vicious pain exploded in her left shoulder, and she spun around, falling facedown onto the ground. Fighting back tears, she tried to push herself up—

Terror gripped her as she heard two more shots behind her.

Fletcher!

Gritting her teeth, she pushed herself up with her good arm – then froze at the sound of someone approaching.

Shaking, unable to breathe, she slowly turned her head.

"Erin?" Fletcher whispered, his voice wavering. "Are you okay?"

She dropped her head, gulping in a lungful of air as a ferocious relief flooded through her.

"You're bleeding. Where did he hit you?"

She lifted her head. "My shoulder ... Help me sit up."

Fletcher stepped behind her and gently helped her up. She sat, breathing deeply, fighting the agonising pain in her shoulder.

Fletcher squatted down in front of her, his face pale and drawn.

"Asim?" she whispered.

He shook his head.

"And Khaled and the other?"

"Dead – I killed them."

Her stomach churned as she saw the pain in his eyes. She'd asked him to follow her to this place, to support her in this journey to aid her friends – and now he had blood on his hands. An emotion squirmed. Anger? Regret? *We should have tried to stop them. We left it too late.* She chilled at the thought. *I'm no killer. Fletch is no killer.* But even so ... *We left it too late.* "Is Robert alive?" she whispered, unable to stop her hands trembling.

431

"He's alive. He's with … with his mother and father." Fletcher glazed eyes seemed to refocus. "You're hurt, let me see what I can do."

'Erin.'

Erin froze. 'Asim? You're alive?'

'My heart has stopped beating. I must ask you: will you receive me?'

Hope surged. "Asim is alive! Quickly, help him!"

Fletcher's eyes widened. "How—"

"Go!"

His expression one of shock and confusion, Fletcher climbed to his feet and rushed over to Asim.

'Erin, all will be lost. Will you receive me?'

'I don't know what you mean, Asim. Fletcher will help you, then —'

'I can only ask once more. Will you receive me?'

Beset by a turbulent storm of dismay, grief, and rising panic, she answered him. 'Yes, I'll receive you. Now —'

She cried out as a chaotic kaleidoscope of tastes, colours, and sounds swamped her senses. She felt herself falling, tumbling and twisting through a vast, barren void. Deeper and deeper she fell, plummeting through the blackness of the void. Her mind warped, then fractured, sending rippling streams of colour cascading behind her as though she were a radiant comet hurtling through the night sky.

I'm losing my mind. I'm —

She gasped as a sudden warmth enveloped her. 'Calm. We will aid you.'

Her fall through the emptiness of the void slowed, and the majestic rainbow trailing in her wake arced through the darkness to sweep back into her healing mind, leaving only a faint, cool glow in the ether around her.

A strange calm settled on her, and she felt herself land softly on a hard ground.

Breathing easily, her mind, body, and soul now one, she looked out on a glistening white landscape, a barren flat plain seemingly with no end.

There was silence. Complete silence.

Where am I?

There was no answer.

She took a step. And then another.

She walked on through the bleak land, wondering how she came to be there, and who she was.

Aeons passed, and on she walked.

I wonder who I was, who I am, and what I will become?

And then a traveller, far in the distance. *Maybe they will know who I am.* She willed it; and she was there. By his side.

Who was I?

And he told her. For days, weeks, months, he talked, sharing her life, her Story.

Who am I?

"A shaman," he said.

And what will I become?

"That, only you will know," he answered.

Then the traveller raised his hand. In his palm sat a slim pillar of blue light, a coruscating web of delicate arcs of energy crisscrossing within. "Take the Kade."

Erin reached out—

A crushing – an annihilating – foreboding engulfed her. She snatched back her hand.

"Take it," the traveller said.

No. I cannot take this. She turned and ran.

An ear-shattering crack of thunder rent the air, and a redness fell across the sky as the horizon blazed with demonic fire. The ground beneath her rumbled, then split asunder, monstrous black fissures tearing across the barren plain. A towering wall, a cataclysmic inferno, roared across the land towards her.

"The Geddon comes," the traveller said at her side. "Wrong choices were made."

She quailed before the incoming storm. *What choices? What—*

"Erin! Erin!"

The horrific vision vanished, and her eyes shot open. Gasping, unable to speak, she saw Fletcher's strained face looking down at her. "Erin – are you okay?"

What just happened?

But she found nothing to latch on to, only faint whispers of a memory of a barren land – and of a traveller and a blue pillar of light.

And of fear. Of terror.

Yet within the hazy mist, one detail remained.

The traveller … *He called me a shaman.*

*

Throughout their eerie journey through the long-silent catacombs of the ancient ruins – the dancing shadows and claustrophobic weight of the ground above providing fuel for the mind's darkest imagination – Fletcher's dread at what they might find had grown to sheer terror. But when they'd arrived at that chamber of horrors, seen the decaying

433

bodies set around its walls, he doubted anything his mind could have created would have been worse than the sights encountered there. Sights – and feelings – he just didn't understand.

Then events had unfolded like a dream – a waking nightmare – leaving Fletcher numb, unable to move. But when the professor had shot Asim, Fletcher had found himself moving, launching himself at the thief beside him, grabbing the gun …

Then another single shot behind him.

Chilled to the core, he'd spun around to see Erin fall to the ground. The professor's rabid eyes had locked onto him, his gun following. With no hesitation, Fletcher had fired – blood gushed from the professor's head as he'd fallen to the ground. Shaking, Fletcher had moved towards Erin, but a hand had grabbed his leg. Without thinking, he'd turned and shot the thief in the head. The man had spasmed, then lain still.

I killed two men, Fletcher thought, his hands still shaking as he now sat beside Erin, giving her time to recover. *One in self-defence … But the other?* He tried to shake off the nauseating guilt. The thief had already tried to kill them at the hotel. *I had to protect Erin.*

But he still felt cold inside. The two men were dead. He couldn't bring them back.

He glanced at Erin, who sat, head bowed. She'd awoken from a trance but had since remained worryingly silent. He shifted, uneasy. As they'd moved through the catacombs, his admiration at Erin's resilience had grown. He'd thought he would be strong, but she'd proved stronger. But even with that strength, something had just happened to her, something even she'd not been able to brush off. He studied her, hesitant. Did he leave her, waiting until she spoke? *But we need to try to get out of here. We need to leave this evil place.* He reached out and tentatively placed his hand on her arm. "Erin," he said in a low voice. "We need to go."

For a moment, Erin didn't move. Then she lifted her head and looked into his eyes. "We failed," she whispered. "I failed … I failed my friends."

His relief at her breaking her silence was shattered by her simple words. Her friends remained lost. And so too Lanky. *Where are you, Lanky?* he thought, thinking of the young man and his heartbroken mother. *Where the hell are you?* He glanced at the bodies lying on the ground. *Hell?* No, this was hell.

And they needed to escape from it.

He drew his attention back to Erin.

She stared, open mouthed, at something over his shoulder.

Suddenly cold, he followed her gaze. In a faintly glowing alcove on the far wall of the chamber stood an unknown woman immersed in a shimmering, light mist. Dressed in light clothing, a belt of dark green around her waist, light strapping on her lower arms and legs, she stared out into the chamber. His hand tightly gripping the gun, he climbed to his feet and glanced around. Nothing else had changed; all other alcoves remained empty. He looked back to the ghostly woman. What threat had come upon them now?

"Help me up," Erin said behind him.

Shaken, he turned to see Erin holding out her hand. "You shouldn't move. We should—"

"We should get out of this foul place," Erin said, her face grim. "Help me up."

He grabbed her hand. "You are one stubborn woman."

"And you are one irritating man," she said as he pulled her up. She looked into his eyes. "But very welcome to have here right now." Then she shifted her gaze and walked across to the ghostly woman in the alcove.

"Not too close," Fletcher said, casting nervous glances to the other alcoves as he walked to her side.

Her brow furrowing, Erin peered into the light mist.

Still holding the gun, he studied the woman inside. *A severe face*, he thought, seeing the woman's features more clearly. *But striking. Late thirties, maybe? And those eyes …*

Erin reached into the mist.

"Hey! What are you doing?" he exclaimed, grabbing her arm and pulling it back.

"She needs our help."

"No. You don't know that. This place isn't safe. We need to—"

"Stand back," Erin commanded, and she reached out into the mist.

Fletcher watched, dumbfounded, as Erin's hand began to glow; brighter and brighter it shone before burning with such brilliance that he averted his eyes—

An explosion hurled him backwards with tremendous force. Staggering, the side of his face stinging, he steadied himself, then watched with amazement as the woman, her short, dark hair standing on end, walked out of the alcove and into the chamber.

"Shaman," the green-eyed woman said, brushing herself down. "Your timing was close. I am Paan."

Hesitating only a moment, Erin held out her hand. "Erin," she said, strength in her voice. The woman – Paan – grasped Erin's forearm,

435

then Fletcher watched, bewildered, as Erin glanced down and copied the gesture. Was this really happening?

"Call your Warriors," Paan said, scanning the chamber, her eyes narrowing as she rested them on the fallen Wardens. "We have little time. The bindings will soon break."

Erin's expression was suddenly uncertain. "We have no Warriors. I knew nothing."

Knew nothing? Of course we knew nothing. Fletcher wiped his brow. Who did this wild-haired woman think they were?

Fear flashed across Paan's face. "You have no one?"

Erin shook her head.

Features creased in thought, Paan ran her fingers through her hair, then walked a few paces away, studying the empty alcoves. She turned back, looking directly at Fletcher. "One single life may be enough."

Fletcher felt the woman's gaze bore into him. *She is a friend,* he thought, a warm feeling growing inside. *She can help us. I can help her. I can ...* He shook his head, blinking. What was he thinking? "Who are you?" he whispered, nerves stretched taut. "What do you want?"

"I am the Ensi, and I require your service to prevent your land's annihilation."

He heard her words, but they made no sense.

"There is little time, so enter quickly. But do not attempt to fight – you would be destroyed in an instant. Hide. Stay deep and stay silent. The presence of your life force is enough."

Fletcher stepped back, aghast. "You want me to climb into there?"

"There is no time left to explain. Take my place. Now!"

"No!" Erin said, a look of horror on her face. "He can't enter. He doesn't know anything about this."

Paan glared at Erin. "There is no choice. He *must* enter. We need a life within to preserve the last binding of the Geddon." Her eyes locked onto Erin's. "You know this. It must be done. Now."

"Know what?" Fletcher said, turning to Erin.

Erin was shaking, tears in her eyes. Tears and yet a sense of something more. A sense of another. Was this truly Erin before him?

"Erin?" he said, stepping towards her.

Erin, if that's who she still was, wiped her cheek. "I believe her," she whispered.

Fletcher gasped. What was happening here? "Hold on," he stammered. "You don't know this woman. What do you mean, 'you believe her'?"

An agonised look crossed Erin's face. "Somehow, I know ... the prison needs a life. I see no other way."

Fletcher recoiled as if struck. *I see no other way.* Her words battered his will, crushing his soul, as all he thought he knew shattered into dust. He stared blindly at her, unsure who – or what – this young woman before him had suddenly become. "You can't be asking me to go in there. You can't."

"The Geddon will destroy your land," Paan spat. "You must—"

"I will enter," came a strained voice behind them.

Fletcher turned to see Robert climbing to his feet, his mother's blood staining his torn shirt.

Paan's imperious eyes snapped to Robert. "Enter now," she commanded. "Quickly."

Robert walked towards the portal, head bowed, shoulders slumped, a broken and dejected figure. As he passed, Fletcher grasped the man's shoulder. "Don't do this, Robert."

Robert halted, his head still bowed.

"The prison needs a life," Paan hissed, "else the Geddon will be released."

"Well, you get back in there," Fletcher shouted, spinning around to face Paan, his face twisting in anger. "You who seems to know so much about this. You do it!"

"I cannot."

Fletcher glared at her. "And yet you ask this man to do it. You—"

Robert grasped his arm and pulled him around. "This is my choice, Fletcher," he said fiercely, his eyes ablaze. "*My* choice." He released Fletcher's arm and walked away. "It is my redemption."

Fletcher watched in despair as Robert walked towards the alcove. *It is your redemption, maybe, but what is it she asks of you?*

He flinched as a calm, ethereal voice sounded in his head. *'She asks him to save the world.'*

He fought a rising panic. *I know nothing of what's happening here, and now voices?* As the nightmare continued, he watched Robert step into the alcove. A sharp crackle cut through the air, and as Robert turned to look out into the chamber, the faint mist reappeared, bathing the bookseller with a soft, shimmering light.

"Where is the gold?" Paan asked behind him.

Fletcher glanced back to see Erin looking at him, a tortured sorrow in her eyes. "I'm so sorry, Fletcher," she said, her voice wavering.

The stabbing sense of betrayal cut deep. *You were going to let me go in there. How could —*

"The gold," Paan demanded. "He needs gold to sustain him."

Erin's anguished eyes held Fletcher for a moment, then she answered. "We saw no gold here."

"You," Paan said, facing Fletcher. "Find what gold you can from these alcoves – do not touch those polluted by the evil ones."

Fletcher turned immediately to the next alcove—

Then froze.

Anger flared. He'd reacted instinctively to her command. *She tried to coerce me.* He glared at the green-eyed woman. "I don't know who you are or what you're doing here, but don't try that again."

"This man will die if we don't help him," Paan said, holding his gaze. "And then so will your land and its people. Find gold – quickly."

Fletcher clenched and re-clenched his fist. Who was this woman? What was this place? And what had it done to Erin? But he had no answers those questions, and knew he had no choice – he couldn't stand there and do nothing. *Because what if she's right?*

Seething, he stepped to the alcove beside them and, avoiding the body of the fallen Warrior, knelt down to retrieve the few nuggets of gold lying in its base. *Gold? Why gold?* he thought as he collected the fragments. To preserve Robert, the wild-haired woman had said. But preserve him for what? What was Robert expected to do? As he moved on to the next alcove, the words of the woman, Paan, played back. "The prison needs a life, else the Geddon will be released." So, Robert was that life? Robert would save the world?

Gathering what little gold he could see, his anger slowly faded as a sense of hopelessness threatened to wash over him. So many questions, but so few answers. *I know nothing.* And yet deep inside him, that burgeoning wave of despair washed up against a stubborn belief. A battered and wavering belief, maybe, but one not yet broken. A belief that Erin was following the right path.

But she would have abandoned me to some unknown fate.

An image sprang into his mind, an image of Erin wrung by despair when Paan had asked him to enter the alcove. She hadn't wanted him to enter. *But she accepted it had to be.* Why? What did she know – what did she see – that he didn't? The realisation was sudden and stark. *I need to understand what she sees. I want to see what she sees.*

And why? Because he needed to understand this new world – this new storm that had blown in – else he'd simply be an autumn leaf, picked up and blown wherever the whims of the gale decided to take him. *But how do I understand this? What time do I have to learn? What else can I do but follow the wind?*

Uncertain, confused, he continued his search, placing all the scavenged gold before Paan, until she finally accepted there was nothing more to recover. She looked down at the small pile and scowled. "Not enough for a Warrior, but for this one? It may give us time. Throw it to his feet. Do not touch the portal."

"Time for what?" Fletcher said, throwing pieces of gold into the alcove, each triggering tiny sparks as they passed inside.

"Hurry," Paan commanded, ignoring his question. "We must leave this place. It is no longer secure."

"That's easier said than done," Fletcher muttered, continuing to add to the gold at Robert's feet. "The one who guided us here is dead."

"There is another way." Paan turned and strode away.

Dispersing the last of the gold, Fletcher stood back and studied the alcove, seeing the soft, shimmering light now tinged with gold. "I hope you find the redemption you seek, Robert," he whispered.

The sound of stone grating against stone echoed in the chamber. Paan had crossed to the far side of the chamber and stood to the right of the shamans' alcoves, heaving on something attached to the wall.

"Help me," she called, her voice strained.

Fletcher forced himself to move. Maybe Paan did know a way out of this hell. As he made his way across the chamber, Erin, her eyes averted, joined him. Reaching Paan, he saw she stood, legs slightly bent, her hands gripping the head of a small carved lion sitting atop a narrow pillar of stone. "Stuck," she grunted.

"What are you trying to do?"

"We need to pull up the locking stone – that will free the door."

He saw the pillar of stone – the locking stone, Paan had called it – was set in place through a hole in a rectangular block jutting out from the base of the curved wall. The pillar was obviously usually hidden beneath the lion's head, but Paan had managed to pull a short section free before it had become stuck. Grabbing the lion's head, he pulled hard.

The pillar came free.

"Good." Paan pushed against the stone wall, then stepped back as a section began to move. As Fletcher jumped clear, the door rotated about some concealed axle, the lower section rotating into the chamber, the upper into the darkness beyond. He watched in amazement as the door settled into place, hanging open horizontally, perfectly balanced.

"Pass me one of your torches," Paan commanded.

"Get it yourself," he growled, not yet ready to jump at her every command.

Paan's sharp gaze was scathing, but she spun away, heading back towards the centre of the chamber. Left with Erin, who watched him, her face drawn, a tension in her stance, he was caught between a deep sense of betrayal and the wish to understand her actions. He found he didn't know what to say.

Her eyes met his. "Will you still help me?" she said in a hushed voice.

A desperate ache rose, a fervid desire to hold her tightly in his arms. *But she would have let me go in there.* Steadying his breathing, he studied her face – and recognised beneath the strained features the Erin he knew. Her strength, her courage, her undying will to aid her friends. Yet what of the other he'd seen? "Who am I helping?" he asked.

She hesitated, seemingly uncertain.

She's unsure what to tell me. She—

"The echoes of a shaman," she said softly. "But also, Erin, one who still wants you for a friend ... and more."

A shaman? A shiver of fear ran through him as a rush of disparate thoughts tumbled through his mind. *Dark magic, mystic rituals, satanic sacrifices ...* "What do you mean 'shaman'?" he said, holding his voice steady.

A look of pain crossed her face. "That's not easy to answer." She ran her hand through her hair and looked away. "Something happened. I ... I hold memories. Fragments of memories. But nothing is clear." She hesitated, then shook her head. "Maybe nothing has changed," she whispered. "After all, I already speak with daemons ..."

He winced. And there lay an irrefutable truth. *I knew she spoke with daemons ... And I trusted her.*

A deep ache burned in his stomach. *And I still want to trust her.*

Erin turned back, a hardness in her eyes. "Yes, something happened, but I'm still who I was, Fletch. I'm Erin. And I'm someone who may be able to help Paan. Help my friends."

Fletcher glanced towards the centre of the chamber where Paan was examining a torch. "Who is she?"

Erin hesitated. "Someone Asim wanted safe. Someone who needs to be kept away from people like the professor."

"Is that enough to trust her?" *Can I trust you?*

"I'm not sure. But Asim was the Keeper and knew someone was coming who needed help. Asim is dead. I need to help her."

But who is she?

The self-challenge was immediate and raw. *Do you mean Paan? Or Erin?*

As Fletcher studied Erin's face, seeing her now familiar ice-blue eyes, and her short blonde hair, tangled strands plastered to her cheek, the tension eased from his shoulders. He knew who Erin was. *A woman with a heart of a lion, that's who she is. And one I care for deeply.* The

440

desperate ache in his stomach grew, but something remained unsaid. "You would have let me go in there," he whispered, gesturing to the softly glowing alcove.

She held his gaze, a tear appearing in her eye. She said nothing.

In the deathly silence, remembered voices echoed. "Only one life is needed," Asim had said. "The prison needs a life," Paan had said. The harsh reality swept in, dulling the sting of betrayal. *These people fight against forces beyond my comprehension. These people strive to save our world.*

He drew a deep breath. "I hope it was bloody important," he said softly.

Erin's eyes widened – then she rushed at him, throwing her hands around his neck.

"Your shoulder—"

"I don't give a damn about my shoulder. Keep hugging me."

He felt the fierce intensity of her embrace and drew her yet closer.

"I'm sorry," she breathed.

"It's not your fault. None of this your fault. It's—"

"There is a time and a place," came Paan's commanding voice, "and this is neither. Move!"

Fletcher broke away from Erin and was walking towards Paan before he realised what he was doing. Cursing, he forced himself to stop. He whirled around to face Paan, who had returned carrying a torch. "Stop doing that!"

Erin came to his side. "Yet she's right," she said softly, putting her hand on his arm. "We should go. Our presence here will draw attention. Robert must remain hidden."

Fletcher sucked in a deep breath. He turned to Erin, his expression softening. "I don't understand what's happening here … but I trust you."

She gave him a small smile.

He held her gaze for a moment, then looked back towards the alcoves. "Can we really leave him here?"

"His life preserves the binding of the Geddon," Paan said firmly. She glanced towards the glowing alcove. "His actions shall not be forgotten."

Fletcher hesitated, hating the decision he was about to take. But Robert had willingly stepped into the breach … *to save our world.* He shook his head. *I don't understand – but I can't intervene. My ignorance could kill us all.* His expression grim, he strode past Paan and walked back to the glowing alcove, seeing Robert bathed in a subtle yellow light. A drawn face now, but not before. No, in another time he'd

441

known this bookseller as friendly and kind, someone who'd always been happy to help others in need. *And you chose to help once more, but did you really know what choice you were making?*

His sigh was heavy. Where had all this gone wrong?

When Lanky had found that bloody Staff.

But that clearly wasn't true. All this had been a very long time in the making. *Millennia.* Or even longer. He glanced back to Robert, seeing his body glowing within the golden mist of the alcove. Whatever he'd done in the past, it seemed the bookseller had his most important work ahead of him. "My thoughts go with you, Robert, and may your god be with you."

Standing back, he glanced at the macabre sight around him: nine bodies lying dead on the floor. Seven murdered in cold blood by the crazed professor. *And two by me.* The loss of life was sickening. Guilt closed like a fist in his stomach. Should he have acted earlier? Should they have realised what the professor was doing? He glanced at the bodies of Robert's parents. How they'd gotten here he didn't know, but if somehow he'd acted sooner, maybe they'd still be alive.

Tormented by what might have been, Fletcher began to walk away … then stopped, frowning, as the light around him dimmed. He looked back. The light in the alcove was fading.

And so was Robert!

"No!" he exclaimed. "What's happening?" He heard the two women run to his side, and they watched together as Robert's body slowly disappeared within a darkening alcove.

"He's failed," Erin breathed.

"I think not," Paan murmured. She reached out, and Fletcher watched, dumbstruck, as her hand sparked as if striking a hidden barrier.

"He's still there, veiled," Paan said in a hushed voice, her emerald-green eyes glowing in the torchlight. "This man has done well. We need to repay him with our actions. Hurry, much remains to be done." She strode off towards the stone door.

Fletcher stared at the seemingly empty alcove in disbelief, a barrage of thoughts bombarding him. How had Robert done this? What did the bookseller now see? What did he feel? *Where is he?*

"I sense it now," Erin said, holding her hand close to the alcove. "But you would need to be standing this close to know it's there. This won't be easily discovered." She laid a gentle hand on his arm. "We have to leave."

Fletcher's gaze lingered on the empty alcove, then he reluctantly stepped away. With a heavy heart, he walked with Erin to join Paan.

As Erin and Paan ducked under the hanging stone door, he cast a final glance back. *Will I see you again, Robert?* The thought echoed for a moment, then, with the question unanswered, he sighed and followed the women through the doorway into the passageway beyond.

Behind them, the doorway slammed back into place, the horrors of the chamber finally out of sight. *But not out of my mind,* Fletcher thought grimly as he followed Paan and Erin. *I doubt I will ever forget this hellish place.*

*

The white-haired shaman stepped into the chamber and cast his gaze around the fallen Warriors. His gaunt face twisted into a smile. The servant, Khaled, had done well. The shaman lifted his gaze to the portal. A life had entered. His god must be told. *And I must bring Alkazar here. The daemon must understand—*

He flinched as a harsh energy flared around him. An energy of the Light. A most potent energy of a formidable enemy. This was another's fight.

'Alkazar! Here! Now!'

Knowing he could not stand against the might of the unknown arrival, the white-haired shaman reached for a Cord. His task now lay elsewhere. Follow the one who had arrived in this age. Follow the one the Keeper had awaited.

The shaman activated the Cord and vanished.

*

Light flared in the gloom of the empty chamber, and then the Guardian stood, her head tilted, facing the empty portal. She sensed the life within and wiped her sweat-drenched brow. "So, he was right. Robert entered here."

'Right place, wrong time,' a voice from the Staff pulsed. *'You must move him now. His energy is needed elsewhere.'*

"We condemn him."

'In this moment, we are all condemned,' the voice said. *'The Geddon breaks out in another time. This life must be there, not here. Act now.'*

Suddenly uncertain, the Guardian studied the portal for a moment longer. Should it be done? Should she move this bookseller from this time to the age of the Iyes? *He has been accepted by Taran. He has the chance to give us the time we need.* True, but what could a move like this do to the flow of the Continuum? What might they have missed?

'We have no choice,' the voice from the Staff said.

443

"We always have choices," the Guardian muttered. But the words rang hollow. They were failing. They needed more time to prevent the release of the Geddon.

'This will give us that time. This man chose to sacrifice his life to hold the last of the Geddon's bindings. Give him that chance.'

Wracked by uncertainty, the Guardian ran her hand through her long black hair. Could this truly be the way to change what had happened, to give her that invaluable time to understand? She reached out with her mind, feeling the life hidden beyond. Hidden from most prying eyes, but not yet hidden within the realm beyond. Taran's realm. *It is easy to move him now, but—*

A surge of energy flared in the chamber, then a putrid stench filled the air.

The stench of a daemon of the Dark.

'Alkazar comes!'

Eyes flashing with instant certainty, the Guardian swept a swathe of energy around the body and soul of the bookseller, then instantly connected with a Cord—

A flash of light. A shimmer. A transit through the Gate and the Void to an age before.

The Continuum adjusted, a subtle, imperceptible alignment.

And in a silent chamber of that past age, deep within the temple of Kaos in the Ka's thriving homeland, a single alcove briefly flared, then dimmed as the hidden life within withdrew to the realm of Taran.

Life within the Continuum continued.

And in another age, Alkazar raged at the barren, lifeless chamber he had been summoned to.

CHAPTER THIRTY-THREE

The Warrior had been in his grasp. Could it have ended then? Either way, the powerful servant of Kaos failed that day, thwarted by two brave Iyes.

*L*eaping down from the shimmering blue dragon, Bear quickly scanned the area. Flocks of startled birds scattered from the rangy trees and tall grasses, but he saw no immediate threat, confirming what they'd seen from the air.

"I must go," Hydrak rumbled, turning his massive head to the sky.

Bear hurried over to stand beside Scorpion and Stealth, then shielded his face as the Ancient's wings buffeted them with dust-laden gusts of the warm morning air.

"Good luck to you as well," Scorpion spluttered, spitting dust from his mouth as he watched the dragon rise, then fly off towards the Ka encampment, quickly picking up speed.

Bear glanced to the north, seeing a large plume of smoke billowing into the sky, evidence that Rakana had arrived at the camp.

Scorpion followed Bear's gaze. "So, we're here. Guess we now try to sneak into that hornet's nest." He rubbed his cheek. "But I'm still not happy with this, Bear. Spies? That feels as though we're abandoning our friends."

"Some of us must return to the tribe, Scorpion. The other Warriors need to know what is happening."

"Even so, I don't like it."

Neither do I, thought Bear, seeing the frustration written across the young man's face. The enormity of what had happened was hard to comprehend: their ancient enemy revealed as an ally of IY, and the Warrior and Guardian walking freely into the midst of the hated Ka. It

445

was all happening so quickly. He glanced to the departing dragon. And so little time to prepare.

Time. It escapes us.

It seemed only moments before that they'd walked out of the Ancient's mountain lair into the lacerating chill of the night, gathering in the windswept snow of the dragon's landing area. The silver dragon, Rakana, had spoken, her mighty voice cutting through the darkness: "Our time has come. We travel to the Ka homeland."

"What do we face?" Bear had asked.

Rakana's head had swung towards him. "We face our destiny, leader of the Iyes."

"Prepare to meet your ancestors!" Hydrak had snarled. "This will not be easily won."

A fiery glow had surrounded them as Rakana's great maw opened with a growl. "This is not their time for battle, Hydrak. That lies with us."

Hydrak had hissed, then fallen silent.

The darkness had returned as Rakana's great jaws closed. "No, leader of the Iyes, your task is to extract a Warrior and those with him. Those most precious must be saved." The Ancient's head had then risen to the sky. "We will talk more as we travel. Then we will see what must be done when we arrive."

Their journey south and east had been rapid, both dragons travelling low and flying straight, the sun slowly rising before them. They'd travelled over deep forests, through jagged mountain passes, and over a windswept sea before reaching the lands of the Ka.

Then, Rakana had spoken in his mind. *'Kaos's strength has grown.'* She angled alongside Hydrak as they flew down a mountain valley. *'He has worked unseen, in this time and others. A snake here and a clever jackal there, and millennia of our work undone in a day. The Land stands on the brink.'*

'You paint a bleak landscape, Ancient.'

'And beyond that ominous vista, loyal servant of IY, are visions so brutal and hopeless, you would cry in despair.'

'What can we do?'

'What we can,' Rakana had replied.

Bear blinked, and with Rakana's words echoing, he brought his attention back to the smoke-filled skyline above the Ka encampment. *My tribe is there. The Warrior is there.* Scorpion was right, they could not be mere observers.

He turned to the young Iyes sculptor. *But I must be sure of this decision.* He laid a hand on Scorpion's shoulder. "Know that you can

446

turn from here," he said, seeing the desperate fear hidden deep within the man's eyes. "You can walk away and find a new life for yourself – south, north, anywhere but here. And if you do, you will always carry with you the love of your tribe … and my blessing."

Scorpion held Bear's gaze, his flowing hair rippling in the breeze. Then his eyes glinted with ferocious intent. "My life has been for the Iyes, and theirs for mine. I will not abandon my people."

Bear studied him for a moment, then squeezed his shoulder. "Then shall we then try to be more than mere spies?"

A defiant smile grew on Scorpion lips. He nodded and looked north. "What shall we do?"

"What we can," Bear replied. "Only what we can."

He turned to the patiently waiting Stealth. "Are *you* ready?"

Stealth's staunch gaze locked onto Bear's. "Today, I follow you."

"Then let us see what awaits."

They set a determined pace north, skirting the swards of thick, spiky grasses, utilising the shade of scattered copses where they could. They encountered no one, but as they ran on, they soon saw a fiery glow in the sky ahead and heard the first cries of battle and the frantic cries of a panicked camp. Racing on, they approached the outskirts of the Ka encampment, the silver dragon circling overhead. Bear signalled to the left, and they veered towards the western end of a sprawling array of shelters, many ablaze. Skirting around the ravaged shelters, they entered a camp in total disarray. Gesturing for them to halt, he stood, surveying the mayhem. People were scattered everywhere across the smouldering grounds, some running, some standing nervously watching the dragon in the sky, others lying burnt on the ground. He grimaced. What could they hope to achieve here?

"Look!" Scorpion whispered fiercely. "The silver dragon is landing."

Bear glanced to his left to see the Ancient hovering above the ground. "We'll head over that way. Keep your movements as one who fears for their life, and hope they ignore us."

"Looking scared is not a problem," Scorpion whispered as they moved off.

As they ran on, Bear noticed a seemingly organised group assembling ahead. Clearly someone there had gathered their wits and had instilled some order. *Best to stay away from them.* "That way," he said sharply, angling his run to avoid the fighters. As they skirted the group, he caught a flash of blue in the sky. "Down!" He dropped, then lay flat to the ground as Hydrak swept over them, spraying plumes of fire over the enemy group to their left.

447

Breathing hard, he clambered to his feet, then signalled to the others. "Keep going," he shouted over the panicked cries of those fleeing the deadly inferno.

But as they raced on, he realised they were angling too far away from the silver dragon. *She landed over there. We—*

He instinctively protected his head as a series of massive blasts reverberated around the camp. Someone else was at work. "This way," he commanded, and sprinted towards a stand of trees.

The blasts grew louder as they ran through the copse. The Warrior? Or the enemy? Skirting the last few trees, he caught a glimpse of the silver dragon. She was climbing quickly into the sky. He cursed as they ran out into the open. What to do now? *We need to—*

He stifled a cry of alarm as they ran into a contingent of fighters emerging from the left.

"You!" barked a man at the front. "Fall in!"

*

Svana's heart raced as she watched Lanky and Rind running towards her, their silhouetted frames set against the torrent of roiling flames rolling across the Ka encampment as the blue dragon flashed past. *We didn't know who was here. We didn't know what to expect.*

A tear ran down her cheek. *But my sister lives!*

She saw the sudden recognition in Rind's face, and her sister veered towards her.

Her heart singing, Svana walked to greet her. "I—"

Rind flew into her, knocking her back a step as she grabbed her in a tight hug.

"Good to see you too, Sister," Svana whispered, wincing as a jolt of pain shot along her injured limb.

Rind looked up at Svana, tears in her eyes. "I thought I'd lost you."

Wiping her eye, Svana grinned. "Takes more than a dragon to kill me."

Rind laughed, then squeezed her tightly once more.

"Seems we each have a tale to tell," Svana said in a whisper. Rind nodded.

They stepped away from each other, both wiping their eyes. Svana looked Rind up and down. "Hair a mess, clothes torn – that's my sister!"

Rind punched her, sending another stab of pain through her arm.

"Knuckles. Shorty," Lanky said, greeting the two men standing beside a beaming Spider.

"Warrior," they acknowledged.

Lanky glanced at Knuckles, frowning. "What happened to your face?"

Knuckles grimaced, creasing his blistered face. "I'm not called Shield for nothing."

Rind glanced around. "Where are Bear and Scorpion?" Svana heard the nervous tension in her sister's voice.

"Alive and well, don't worry about that," Knuckles replied. "Dropped off just south of here with another. Needed to make sure someone took our story back home. Guess they'll be near the edge of the camp by now."

A flicker of relief crossed Rind's face. She turned to the old man and the girl with a fire in her eyes. "We meet again, Kapano. Inyana."

"We owe them, Rind," Spider said. "They helped save you."

Rind bowed her head briefly. "I thank you and look forward to your tale. But first, we need to escape this place." She frowned, then glanced around. "Where's Jessica?"

Svana saw Lanky's face darken. He nodded in the direction of the temple. "In there. But a hellish shaman lies between us and her."

"And that lot," Knuckles growled, looking into the distance.

Svana followed his gaze. A large group of fighters was heading towards them, seemingly led by a yellow-tunicked leader. They looked organised and well armed. Shorty and Knuckles immediately made to move past her.

"Stay behind me," Lanky ordered.

"No!" rumbled Rakana as the massive beast walked, swaying, towards them. "Stand back, Warrior. You are needed for another purpose. The time has come to make your peace with Fen."

The Ancient's shimmering bulk heaved past them, her fiery eyes burning below her gnarled brow ridges as she strode towards the approaching fighters. "You cannot pass!" rumbled the dragon's voice across the open ground ahead.

The enemy group paused, but with a command from the yellow-tunicked leader, walked on towards them.

Rakana's thick-scaled neck flexed, her ridged head lowering towards the ground.

Svana shielded her eyes as a roiling gout of fire rolled out across the parched ground towards the fighters. The flames roared and crackled, then died, falling well short of striking the enemy. Yet it seemed the Ancient's warning served its purpose – with a command from the yellow-tunicked leader, the company of fighters halted.

"Behind us!" came Spider's strident cry.

Quickly turning, Svana saw another group of fighters heading their way – a more ragged bunch, but three times the numbers of the first. Dismay twisted her gut. Even with the Ancient with them, this wouldn't be easy to escape without loss.

But as she readied herself for battle, the ragged group of fighters suddenly glanced to the sky, then dived to the ground as the blue dragon streaked in from the west. Unlike Rakana, Hydrak mercilessly engaged the enemy, streaming hellacious fire into the midst of the group. Many fighters scrambled to their feet, screaming, frantically trying to extinguish the rapacious flames engulfing them. Others were past screaming, their incinerated bodies scattered on the ground.

'The fool,' Rakana rumbled. 'He doesn't see.'

Hydrak suddenly screeched as if in pain, then banked away.

'I doubt any punishment will work today,' came Rakana's voice. 'And does it matter? The horrors yet to come will dwarf this.'

Svana heard Rakana's words but didn't understand.

"Time to get out of here," Knuckles growled. "Who's going on which dragon?"

"You forget yourself," Svana growled. "Jessica is still inside."

"I hadn't forgotten," Knuckles said evenly. "But how do you think we'll get to the temple without help?"

"The Guardian has left this place," Rakana declared.

"What!" Lanky and Rind exclaimed together.

"She lies beyond our reach. Beyond any of this Land."

Shaking his head, Lanky stepped towards the Ancient. "I don't believe she'd leave us."

"Did you remain with her?"

"That's not fair," Lanky hissed. "I only just got out of there with my life."

"But not with hers."

Lanky raised his Axe. "Rind tells me you're on our side, beast, but I don't trust you. And I'm not having a good day. Don't try to tell me I abandoned my friend. That would not end well."

A low rumble came from Rakana. "Even so. She lies beyond us. We must leave."

Svana saw the tension in the Warrior's stance. No, he wouldn't have simply abandoned Jessica. But where had the Guardian gone? The Warriors were needed here. *And the Guardian and the Staff.* She looked to the sky. *What are you doing, Guardian? We can't lose you again. We need you.*

Knuckles cleared his throat, breaking her reverie. "So, a group of eight here and two on the edge of camp. These dragons can't move ten of us."

The old man called Kapano shuffled forward, holding his bloodied chest with his hand. "We will stay. This is my home."

"No!" the girl beside him cried. "You cannot stay. We cannot risk the Song. We ..." She broke off, casting a worried glance at her grandfather.

Svana's eyes narrowed at the particular resonance of her words. *Song. What Song?* The faintest flicker of a memory glimmered – of a simple fireside tale told by Naga when she was a child ...

It vanished as the old man spoke. "We will be safe." He spoke quickly, wincing in obvious pain as he turned to the girl. "We have friends in high places. Even the Ensi could—"

"The Ensi!" Lanky growled. "You've no friend there, old man. Anyway, she's probably dead. Another now rules this place."

Kapano's expression showed shock, then dismay. His gaze sought out Spider. "Is this true?"

"If this Warrior says it's true, then it is." Spider stepped up to Kapano and laid his hand on the man's arm. "Come with us. We can get you to a safe place."

"That may prove difficult," came Knuckles's tense voice. "The Ka are regrouping. Someone out there knows what they're doing."

Svana looked out across the burning grounds, assessing the threat. Towards the temple, the regimented group of fighters still held their ground; Knuckles was right, it was a dangerous and disciplined group. Turning, she saw the scattered fighters in the killing field also regrouping.

"They're surrounding us," Shorty said. "But with the dragons here, they'll be reluctant to attack."

Svana's troubled gaze scanned the menacing sight around them. She wasn't so sure the dragons would keep them at bay. "It's not clear how we get out of this," she whispered to herself. She silently prayed to IY.

*

Lanky heard Svana's quiet words. *There is still a chance,* he thought, clenching his Axe as he watched the ravaged camp regrouping beneath the circling blue dragon above. With the dragons – *and me* – they had a chance. It would be a vicious battle, but they could force a path out and then ...

451

And then what? Fight a rearguard action all the way north? *No, we couldn't survive that.*

Rakana's voice sounded in his mind. *'There is another way, Warrior.'*

'And what's that?' Lanky growled.

'You need Fen.'

'I need Fen like I need a hole in the head. Next.'

'Fen can show you a way out, but you need to—'

'No. I don't need to do anything. Get out of my head!'

'It is the only—'

"I said, get out of my head!" Lanky roared, startling those around him. He saw Rind's eyes narrow. In his anger, he ignored her. No, it wasn't going to happen. No one was bonding with him. Not Fen. Not Dysam. This was his body, his mind, no one else's. He rubbed his beard, his frustration growing. Belligerent energies and belligerent beings – alien beings – strove for something that lay beyond his sight.

And a blind man didn't place his hand in the hand of one he didn't trust.

I don't trust you, Fen. Or you, Dysam.

A memory from the Ensi's throne room flashed back. Once again, Dysam had forced his way to the fore, attempting to wrench control. *He's getting stronger.* He clenched his fist. *But he is not me! He will not become me.*

He became aware of another watching him and glanced up to see Rind studying him.

"What did the Ancient say?" she asked softly.

"I don't want to talk about it."

Rind stepped up to him, a flash of anger in her eyes. "Be careful, Warrior. You may be a Warrior, but when you're in this group, I'm in command."

"That is—"

"Silence!" Rind shouted.

Lanky blinked in surprise.

She moved closer. "If there's something these Ancients advise," she said in a quieter voice, "I should hear it too. You can work with me and tell me – or I will ask them directly. You choose."

Her resolute face held firm as she looked up at him, her dark eyes scanning his. *Eyes I could look at forever.* His anger faded. *I may not trust the warg, but I trust this woman. More than trust.* "The Ancient thinks I should bond with a daemon. I think that daemon is a devious mutt."

He thought he saw a faint smile of satisfaction cross Rind's lip. But maybe not. "Can he get us out?"

"Maybe. Probably."

'It *is* you *who can save all those here,'* Rakana rumbled. *'But you need Fen to guide you. And you must leave now. The Song must be preserved.'*

Rind frowned. "What Song?"

Lanky looked at her in surprise. "You heard the beast?"

Rind nodded.

'Some things she must hear. As must you. Time escapes us. You need Fen."

Lanky bristled. *'I don't trust you, Ancient, and I don't trust the warg. But if this is the only way out, then —'*

"What's that?" Shorty exclaimed, pointing skyward.

Lanky spun around, scanning the sky – and saw three glistening red objects to the south, growing larger as he watched. *Dragons!*

'Our enemy approaches, Warrior. Those in the skies and those surrounding us.'

No sooner had the words been spoken than explosions shattered the silence on the ground. As Lanky turned towards the temple, the line of regimented fighters facing them parted, and three figures strode into view. He recognised the first: the fearsome shaven-headed shaman with the Black Staff. Beside him prowled two ragged figures. He sensed outwards – then recoiled at the waves of corrupting malice rolling off the two loping figures.

'The three most powerful shamans and daemons of the Dark,' Rakana rumbled. *'You need Fen, else you will die. I must go. Kaos's dragons have been released to the fight, but thank the Light, the Geddon has not. Hope remains for this world.'*

Rakana's immense scaled wings unfurled, then clouds of dust billowed towards them as she lifted from the ground. As Lanky shielded his face, cracks of thunder exploded above them. Squinting through the swirling dust, he saw the dragon assailed by lances of black lightning from the shaman's Black Staff.

Rakana slewed, her ascent stalled.

Reacting in an instant, Lanky shielded his mind, then unleashed a seething wave of power against the shaman. As the shaman snapped up a shield to protect himself, Rakana regained control, turned, then launched a deadly stream of shard-like flames towards all three shamans, transforming the scrubland into a wrathful blaze. The Ancient then banked and climbed, quickly gaining height. Lanky stared at the blaze, praying to any god listening that the three devils had been returned to the hell they came from …

But holding shields of black, the three shamans strode out of the inferno, licks of flames flickering harmlessly away from their wards as they cleared the wall of fire. *This isn't looking good,* Lanky thought as he snapped up a broad white shield between the approaching terror and the group around him. He glanced up and saw the silver dragon peel away, climbing steeply to join Hydrak, who had swept in from the west. The two dragons continued climbing, then arrowed away to meet the new threat racing towards them. As the blue and silver streaks met the red from the south, a great fireball erupted in the sky. The aerial battle was joined.

"They're attacking from behind," Rind shouted. "Pull Kapano and Inyana in and form a defensive wall. Now!"

That won't last a few seconds, Lanky thought as the group bravely gathered themselves into a defensive position behind him. He staggered as a frenzied onslaught assailed his shield, then a stream of fighters appeared around each end of his defensive wall. *'Fen!'* he cried in desperation.

'I am here,' came the warg's instant response as Lanky pulled back his shield and remoulded it, the white dome snapping into place above him and those behind.

'Who are these shamans?'

'Ones we could maybe defeat individually. Together they form a formidable force.'

Deafening explosions rocked him, and he saw – and felt – strands of the shield fracture.

'Krull and Angram,' Fen snarled. *'For Kaos, the deadliest combination he could have wished for. For us —'*

Another colossal strike rocked the shield.

"Warrior!" Rind shouted. "If that dragon had an option for you to take, take it! Being stuck within this shield doesn't give us many options."

'She's right,' Fen growled. *'I can help. But we must act now, else they will overrun us.'*

'What do you suggest?' Lanky growled, knowing now that he'd run out of options and was about to make the move he'd resisted for so long – a move he was sure he'd regret in the future. *But it will save lives now,* he thought as he felt another strip of energy torn off the shield.

'We must bond.'

'Of course,' Lanky said with a sardonic drawl.

'And then you can extract us.'

'How the hell do I do that? I thought only Jessica could travel!'

'Her power takes her outside the Continuum. We do not cross the boundary of time. Ready yourself.'

The ground shook, and the protective dome darkened.

"Get on with it!" Rind shouted. "I feel something bad out there, and it's not going to stay out there much longer."

Fen's head thrust into Lanky's mind, the black diamond shining on his forehead. *'We must work as one, Warrior. Touch the diamond!'*

"Damn it!" Lanky muttered, desperately seeking a final way out.

The ground shook again, and the dome turned black.

"Do something!" Rind yelled in despair.

Lanky saw there was only one choice. *To hell or the hangman.*

He reached out—

His shield shattered and he saw the three shamans beyond.

He touched the black diamond.

Dysam immediately stormed to the fore.

Time slowed.

'I will aid you, Dysam,' came a calm, ethereal voice. *'Use this Cord.'*

Dysam instantly snapped onto a Cord to a travelling Glade, then reached for the rich energy of the A'ven, drawing on the particular colours and vibrations needed. As he did so, someone unseen weaved those energies with razor-sharp precision around the life-forms surrounding him. *A skill beyond my imagining. A skill of the Guardian.* With the complex weave complete, Dysam activated the Cord, snapping them all into the Glade. Releasing himself from the energy weave, he focussed intently on their target destination and found the next Cord he needed. Activating it, the bound life-forms flicked from the Glade to the Iyes camp.

The ethereal voice spoke. *'There are others.'*

Images formed in Dysam's mind. Of the Ancient's servant and of two Iyes.

Dysam instantly locked onto the first target, the one called Stealth. Quickly activating a series of Cords, he transferred the stunned man to the safety of the Iyes camp.

And now the two Iyes. He reached for another Cord—

He cried out as a vicious pain ripped through him.

A triumphant face appeared before him.

The shaven-headed shaman had entered the Glade!

As Dysam vainly sought the A'ven, the smiling shaman pulled on a sizzling black coil now looped around the Warrior's neck. It was as though monstrous talons raked at Dysam's soul.

"We have the prize," Krull crooned. "Kaos will be most pleased to speak with you."

*

With no other choice, Bear, Scorpion, and Stealth had been swept into the vanguard of the company of fighters and on towards a raging firestorm ahead. Glancing to his left, Bear had seen Scorpion's fearful

455

eyes flick nervously around him as they had picked their way with the others across recently scorched ground, passing dead or dying fighters burnt beyond recognition. To his right, a grim-faced Stealth had strode on easily, quietly assessing the unfolding events around them. Together, they'd all been forced closer and closer to the battle raging ahead of them.

As they'd drawn nearer, with dawning horror Bear had finally seen it for what it was. A desperate defence by his own people! He'd looked on with cold dread, seeing Svana, Knuckles, and Rind amongst the huddled group facing the closing enemy fighters. And standing at the fore, the Warrior Lanky. Holding a blazing shield before the group, the Warrior protected them from baleful bolts of black lightning assailing them from the three demoniacal figures walking towards them, clearly shamans of terrifying strength. Beyond the shamans stood a well-organised array of fighters. Well organised, but fear was etched in many faces at the wanton power being wielded ahead of them.

Bear's gut had wrenched at the distressing scene. *Why did the dragon abandon them? What hope—*

"Attack!" a harsh voice had barked, and Bear, with Scorpion by his side, had found himself pushed forward by the men behind and forced to run towards his friends – in the melee he quickly lost sight of Stealth. Ahead, Lanky's white shield had snapped into a defensive dome, enclosing the Warrior and his group. Deafening blasts continued to rock the shield as the shamans closed in.

"Surround the enemy," had come the barked command from the Ka leader.

But as they moved on, Bear had found himself in danger of being pushed into the path of the oncoming shamans and their lethal fire. He'd grabbed Scorpion's arm and pushed back on the enemy fighters behind, attempting to slow their advance.

In that moment, the Ka leader had clearly seen the same danger. "Hold!" the Ka commanded.

The group had stopped a mere several arm-lengths from the tall, tattooed shaman, the blistering heat from Lanky's glowing shield stinging Bear's face as the merciless attack continued. Terrible nausea ripped through him. *How long can they hold against this?*

The answer came only moments later as the domed shield vanished. The tall shaman held up his hand, and the attack by all shamans ceased. The tall shaman then strode purposefully towards the Warrior's group, which was now partially shrouded by the swirling smoke rising from the scorched ground. *What hope remains now? They—*

His thoughts were shattered as the Warrior's group abruptly vanished.

Startled, he glanced to the tall shaman. Seeing the shock on the man's face, raw elation flooded him. *They've escaped. Somehow, they've escaped this hell.*

"What happened?" whispered a man behind him.

No one answered him, but Bear knew. Somehow, the Warrior had managed to get his people away. Somehow, he'd—

He froze as a figure appeared in the clearing haze, a lanky figure he now knew so very well. The Warrior Lanky stood alone, wisps of smoke drifting around him as he swayed slightly as though in a trance.

The tall, tattooed shaman smiled. "It seems the Warrior wishes to greet us."

Bear took an involuntary step, then stopped as he felt a hand on his arm.

"Don't," Scorpion whispered. "Not yet."

The tall shaman stepped forward.

Get out of there, Warrior! Bear cried to himself. *Flee!*

The shaman halted a short distance from Bear, then raised his Staff. Lanky cried out in pain as a thin black line appeared around his neck.

Why aren't you moving? Bear thought in despair, his elation at the others' escape now shattered. *He'll kill you!*

Shaking, he glanced at Scorpion.

The young Iyes was looking back at him, a savage intensity in his eyes, and a blade gripped tightly in his hand. *Now,* Scorpion mouthed.

A surge of fear-fuelled anticipation coursed through Bear as Scorpion's meaning hammered home.

They would try to save the Warrior.

And it would mean their death.

A flurry of evocative images flashed through his mind. Of River, of Sheba, of Ravine, of Naga; of so many wonderful people of his tribe. Of times past, and of a future he would never see. *But I must do what must be done. I am an Iyes. I must aid the Warriors.*

He held Scorpion's gaze. *But you don't need to do this.*

Scorpion's fierce and unwavering eyes held his.

At the certainty in the young man's face, sudden calmness descended. *We will make our ancestors proud.*

He gave a barely noticeable nod.

A ruthless set to his face, Scorpion levelled his gaze on the shaman.

Licking his dry lips, Bear slipped a blade into each hand. *We will get only one chance.* He noted the distance, shifted his weight ... "Now," he whispered.

He sprang forward and struck hard at the tattooed shaman's neck.

*

Krull's black eyes glared at Dysam. "Your trail was so easy to follow, Warrior," he said, tilting his head. "You disappoint me. I had expected more."

"Nothing is yet certain," Dysam growled.

Krull smiled. "Maybe ... but for you it is." He pulled again on the black coil, and a crippling pain ripped through Dysam's mind. "But now shall we return? Two shamans would be most pleased to meet you. They would like to thank you for imprisoning them. I think—"

The shaman's eyes shot wide open—

Then both he and the coil disappeared from the Glade.

*

The tattooed shaman reacted with lightning-fast speed, the blade only nicking the side of his neck as he recoiled from Bear's strike.

Bear cried out as searing pain exploded in his back.

As he fell, he saw Scorpion falling beside him, a spear driven into the young man's spine.

Unable to move, deep dread engulfed him. *No! We failed!*

"We did what we could," Scorpion breathed – then a spear pierced the back of the young man's neck.

Blood bubbling from his dying friend's mouth, Bear forced the words out. "We are Iyes," he whispered. "Your ancestors will be—"

Pain exploded in his head and back.

Disparate, chaotic visions swirled.

And then, all at once, calm serenity descended.

'You have served this Land well, my friend,' came an ethereal voice. *'And you have given the Warrior a chance. Leave in peace.'*

His mother and father appeared and stood beside him.

'Time to move,' said his father.

Bear smiled, then walked over to his wife, Ravine, and the two beautiful girls, River and Sheba, they had raised as their own. *'I—'*

He lost what he was about to say as a soft lassitude settled on him. Gentle hands lifted him up and carried him away ...

*

Released from Krull's lethal grip, Dysam instinctively reached for the Cord to the Iyes's homeland – but a part of him forced himself to hold. *I must bear witness.* Switching to another Cord, he partly activated it, allowing his mind to travel. He saw the two Iyes, Bear and Scorpion, lying on the ground, spears embedded deeply in their blood-drenched backs. Scorpion's long hair lay matted and twisted, trodden into the sickly-red ground.

They reached the shaman. They saved us.

He watched for a moment longer, acknowledging their selfless sacrifice, then fled back to the travelling Glade, severing the Cord behind him.

From within came Lanky's heartfelt plea. *'Save them.'*

'There is nothing that can be done,' Dysam said, reaching for the other Cord. *'But they saved us. Saved both our souls. They will be remembered.'*

Dysam snapped them to the Iyes camp.

*

Krull studied the two corpses lying on the ground before him. He saw nothing remarkable about either. Except these men had almost killed him. He had been lucky. Very lucky. He put his hand to his neck, feeling his fingers slide on the slippery, wet skin. If the assassin had been but a step closer …

His calculating eyes slid over the bodies. Who were they? Clearly assassins. Maybe brought here by the Ancient? If so, how was it possible they'd simply walked unchallenged to his side? Or had they already infiltrated the Ka and been in place for a while? Whatever the answers, it was clear that whilst the men of this Ka homeland had been growing weak and complacent, their enemy had been gaining in confidence and strength.

He flexed his neck, thick tendons straining, then stood tall. The Ka had served their time. A change was needed, a most drastic correction. The cleansing would now begin, and it would start with these people, these abject people who had failed Kaos. *These who almost failed me.* "Rathe!"

The blunt-nosed man detached from the temple guard behind him and walked to his side. "Return the Guard to the temple," Krull said in a low voice, "and remove all those peasants who entered. You and the Guard will remain inside. Find Xerses and repeat this order."

Rathe gave a curt bow. "Consider it done." He strode away, shouting a command to the Guard captain.

Krull looked around, seeing tense and nervous faces of the rabble around him. For a rabble they were, and not one amongst them he could trust. His eyes fell on K'zarz and Xehalla. And neither could they be trusted.

But I need them.

"These people are weak," K'zarz spat.

459

Krull smiled. "I agree." He turned and surveyed the ragged group of fighters massed beside the bodies of the two failed assassins. "You are failures before Kaos," he said in an icy voice, one that sliced through the air to all those around. "Your lives are thus forfeit."

As the fighters stood, bewildered, some of the smarter ones turning to flee, Xehalla leapt with glee, cackling madly. K'zarz, eyes gleaming with hate, strode towards them, unleashing a black swathe of energy, its power edged with the scent of Kaos. It swept around the stricken Ka, thickening quickly to an oily morass, trapping the now screaming fighters within. Xehalla joined K'zarz, and together they lanced bolt after bolt of blistering black lightning into their deadly trap – it was clear nothing would escape.

The killing had begun.

With the sounds of wanton slaughter and manic laughter raging behind him, Krull's smile fell away. He had been so close, so very close, to capturing the Warrior. *And his secrets of the ages.* Another breath only, and the knowledge of the Light would have been his.

But this was not the greatest blow.

He looked to the south, where the sky was afire with the titanic battle of the dragons. He bared his teeth. The red dragons had arrived, but of the Geddon, nothing had been seen. *'How was a Warden missed?'*

'No Wardens remain,' came Angram's reply.

'Then why can the seal not be broken?' Krull snarled.

'Contamination remains. Somewhere, some form of life remains, preserving the last of the bindings.'

'How can this be?'

'If we knew that, it would not be. But it will be found.'

Another life? How? Where? He was certain all Wardens of the prison had been found and destroyed – in two distant lands, and now here. And yet the seal remained unbroken. The Geddon was not yet unleashed to cleanse the weak from this world.

A life remains …

'Find it,' he snarled as he strode towards the temple. *'Find the life and destroy it. Release the Geddon!'*

The time of Kaos was here.

And the time of Krull!

CHAPTER THIRTY-FOUR

With some it took time. This was such a case.

$\mathcal{V}$oices. A melodic, persuasive voice inside his head, and strident voices outside. Why couldn't they just leave him alone? Shadow opened his eyes and waited for the fog to clear – and then wished it hadn't as he stared into the eyes of death. *Scar!* A man ready to avenge the deaths of two of his men. *As would I,* Shadow admitted wryly.

"Stand up," came a voice he recognised: the unkillable Warrior.

"That might be tricky," he muttered, lying on the ground, his head pounding.

"Get him up," Scar growled.

Rough hands grabbed his arms, hauling him up. *Focus, Shadow. You could die very quickly.* He focussed on a point on the ground before him, steadying his legs. *Okay, I'm standing. That has to be good, doesn't it?* Looking up, he scanned the chamber, the same chamber he and his group had attacked. *Where we failed. And where—*

His chest suddenly tightened at the memory. *And where I stood beside the unkillable Warrior, holding an axe …*

But I didn't strike.

No, he'd frozen.

Why?

Grimacing, he forced the memory away. That was then. *This is now. Focus.* He glanced at the people before him. Scar, the unkillable Warrior, the Iyes's shaman, and maybe six other armed men and women glaring at him in open hatred. *I guess I'll be paying you a visit, ancestors of mine. I hope you'll embrace me. I did what I could.*

"You killed two good men," the Warrior said coldly, "and for that, you will die."

Shadow calmed his breathing. "This is war," he said quietly.

461

"How did you free yourself?"

"A blade, kindly provided to me during my interrogation. And by the naivety of youth."

Scar surged forward, his face contorted with rage.

"Not yet," the Warrior said, holding Scar back.

Scar glared at him, eyes burning with hate.

Shadow breathed deeply. *Another few breaths to take. Another moment to feel alive.* And how exquisite that breath, how deliciously sharp this moment. *I like life. I enjoy life. And mine has not been wasted.* Unlike those fools who never truly understood how profoundly unique their time under the sun was until they were drawing their own last breath, too late then to correct their mistake, one chance and you missed it. He pitied them. What a waste. But not him. He was happy he'd lived life well, that he'd served the Ensi and her people well, and that his ancestors would be proud.

Wouldn't they?

They kill our children.

He staggered as crushing doubt descended like a hammer blow, a myriad of questions rushing into his mind, each a pitiless cut into the body of his life's endeavours, a body now stripped bare, open for all to see. Why? Why did you choose that path? How could one such as you follow the devil?

He fell to his knees, holding his head. What was happening to him?

"Get him up!" he heard Scar roar.

They dragged him back up to his feet.

'Calm,' came a deep, melodious voice, cutting through all others. A voice not of these lands. *'Calm yourself.'*

Hands shaking, he forced himself to draw deep, calming lungfuls of air.

His head cleared, and his legs steadied.

"Execute him now," Scar demanded, his voice wavering with anger. "He can give you nothing – we waste time."

The unkillable Warrior's regard was unwavering. "Why did you not strike?"

'Calm,' the deep voice said as he felt his throat tightening.

I stood next to her. I held the axe.

I held the Axe.

"I don't know," he murmured.

She glared at him for a moment, then nodded to Scar. A murderous smile crossed Scar's face, and he stepped forward, hand clenched around his spear.

Shadow readied himself to die.

The powerful, melodic voice swept into his mind. *'Do you wish to live?'*

'I love life.'

Scar drew back his spear.

'And what do you value most in life?'

'Truth. Friendship. And wine.'

'Then accept who you are ... and live.'

"Die, you Ka bastard!" Scar snarled.

As Scar's whole body tensed for the spear thrust, Shadow released his mind from life's shackles. *I am ready. I am Shadow and go to meet my ancestors—*

'No,' thundered a commanding voice in his mind. *'I am a Warrior.'*

Shadow cried out as every muscle in his body contracted with a mind-numbing explosion of pain. His body shaking violently, his whole being afire, he lifted his head to the sky and screamed, "I am Shaydu! I am a Warrior!"

The spasm ceased. The pain vanished.

He slumped to the ground, gasping. *What happened? What in Kaos's name happened?*

Drawing ragged breaths, he lifted his head.

He was still alive. *Why?*

He looked up to see Scar standing frozen, his spear arm still cocked, his arm tensed to throw.

As if in a dream, Shadow climbed unsteadily to his feet.

Scar bared his teeth and launched the spear.

Shadow blinked.

Time slowed.

"I am a Warrior," Shaydu said, catching the spear mid-flight, the tip of the arrowhead pricking his forehead as it came to rest.

He blinked again.

Shadow staggered, then steadied himself. He saw ten more spears cocked and ready to fly—

"Hold," the unkillable Warrior commanded, her fiery eyes locked onto his. "What did you say?"

"That wasn't me," Shadow said quickly. "I'm not a Warrior. I ... that ..."

"Who are you?" the Warrior grated, her eyes boring into his.

A roar of voices exploded in his head.

Go away!

The voices ceased.

"I am Shadow of the Ka, a Disciple of the Ensi. And a Warrior." He grimaced. "No, I am not a Warrior. I am a Disciple of the Ensi. I serve … I serve …" *Kef!* What was wrong with him? *Don't say anything!*

'With whom are you bonded?' the unkillable Warrior said in his mind.

'Balena,' Shaydu said. 'And Melapis.'

The unkillable Warrior's eyes widened.

Shadow's thoughts seemed bound by a cloying fog. What was he saying? What spell had these Iyes cast on him? "I'm not bonded with anything," he grunted through gritted teeth. "Don't listen to anything I say. I—"

There was a sudden commotion at the entrance to the chamber.

"Let me through!" came a woman's breathless voice.

The Warrior signalled to fighters by the chamber entrance. The fighters parted and the woman raced through. "Lanky, Rind, the others," she panted as she approached. "They're back."

The unkillable Warrior immediately walked away. But he heard her hissed command, "Bring him with us. I don't want him out of my sight."

Shadow grunted as two men roughly grabbed his arms, forcing one high up behind his back. He felt a spear point jab into his side. "Just give me a reason," a quiet, ice-cold voice said behind him.

As they walked out of the chamber and along a dimly lit tunnel, Shadow savoured each sweet breath. There was a madness within him, but he was still alive. He caught a glimmer of daylight ahead. *A glimmer of light, indeed. Head to it. Stay alive and live to fight on.*

Yet a whispered doubt pricked at his mind. *But what am I fighting?*

*

Spider fell to the ground from a height. Hitting hard, he cried out, pain radiating through his recently healed ribs, adding to the waves of nausea already racking his body. He rolled onto his side and retched, then lay still until the nausea passed. Opening his eyes and lifting his head, he saw the others scattered around him and heard shouts from nearby. Looking up to his left – and to his utter delight – he saw the familiar cliffs of the gorge rising before him. They were back with the tribe! *Krez! The Warrior did it!* He lay on his back and closed his eyes, allowing a savage relief to wash over him.

After a moment, he heard voices. He ignored them. *I think I will sleep for a while.*

"Spider!" Amber's worried voice shouted above him. "Can you hear me?"

"I'm sleeping." He felt a blow on his arm, which jolted his chest. "Aah, my ribs!"

"Serves you right for playing dead," came Knuckles's wry voice.

Spider opened his eyes and saw Knuckles smiling above him. Beside the Shield, the fiery-haired healer scowled.

Knuckles offered his hand. "You can't stay down there forever."

Spider took the man's hand and carefully levered himself up. "Sorry about that, Amber," he said, wincing in pain. "It's been a trying day."

Amber's scowl vanished, and she stepped to him, her face alight with joyous relief. "I expect it has," she said, wrapping her arms around him. "But you're back. You're safe." She stepped away, then turned to Knuckles, grinning. "And you – where have you been?" Without waiting for an answer, she rushed over to him and grabbed him in a tight hug. "We didn't think we'd see you all again." Her voice wavered as she wrapped her arms around the short man's head. Knuckles grinned as Amber released him. She ran to Shorty and grabbed him around the chest.

"I should be away more often," Shorty said, grinning. "I—"

With a blinding flash of light, the Warrior Lanky appeared. He too fell from the air, but landed, knees bent, rolling to the side. He climbed to his feet, then glanced around, uncertain. Then his face twisted into a snarl, and he growled unheard words as though another stood beside him.

Spider frowned. *Is this Lanky? It seems another haunts —*

The Warrior slumped to one knee, head bowed.

As Spider watched, unsure what to do, the Warrior looked up, his face drawn, a terrible pain in his eyes. He looked around, caught sight of Rind, then stood and slowly walked towards her, ignoring the greetings of others. Spider watched him in dismay. Clearly, something more than he'd seen had occurred back at the Ka camp. *But what?*

Before he could follow the Warrior, others of the tribe approached, and before long an excited crowd surrounded them, their cries of delight and scattered conversations filling the gorge as all tried to get news of what had been happening to them and to Bear's long-gone northern party.

Eventually, finding himself alone – Svana, Knuckles, and Shorty still being bombarded with questions – he glanced over towards the Warrior. Lanky spoke with Rind away from the others. His unease rekindled. What else had assailed them now? But he knew now wasn't the time to disturb them. *I'll find out soon enough.*

He shifted his gaze to the familiar sight of the gorge, the long-used, safe refuge for the tribe. *A safe refuge?* No, already the enemy had attacked this place. The tribe needed to move again. But where? Where was safe now? *We have to stop running and fight.* But what could they do against the might of the Ka shamans? *The Warriors can stand against them. The Warriors can defeat them.* And yet, even with the Warriors, so far, they had failed. Failed to retrieve the Kade, and the Guardian had once more vanished. *We are losing this war …*

Recognising the darkening spiral of his thoughts, he drew a calming breath. *Snap out of it, Spider. There has to be a way to win this.* The Warriors and the Guardian *would* somehow find a way. Glancing back over to Lanky and Rind, he saw them embrace. Despite the grave, uncertain mood of the moment, a small smile played on his lips. There was something between those two, he was sure. His smile faded. *And between me and River?* He reached into the pocket of his tunic and drew out the bone carving. Somehow, River had returned it to him. He looked down at the intricate carving, the horse seemingly racing ever faster on its unknown journey. *This saved me,* he thought, remembering the attack of the Ka and the blazing flash of light during his liberation of Rind. *River saved me.* Slipping the carving back into his pocket, he felt a glimmer of hope light inside. *I should speak with her. I should try again.*

Sighing, he glanced around him. He noticed the newcomers stood apart from the crowd of Iyes. Kapano and Inyana stood, faces strained, clearly uncertain what to do. And an older man with shoulder-length grey hair and a short white beard, who Spider hadn't seen before, calmly studied his surroundings. Spider set off towards Kapano and Inyana. *I need to thank them for …*

He frowned, his thoughts distracted, as he realised a sudden silence had fallen. Puzzled, he looked around. Walking out from the entrance to the Sacred Chamber was a strange procession. Headed by Beth and River, it was closely followed by Gravel and a group of warriors surrounding an unknown long-haired man, clearly a prisoner.

Spider watched as Lanky and Rind stepped forward to greet the group.

Beth strode directly to Lanky and hugged him. "It's great to see you back, Lanky," she said, a tired smile on her face.

"And it's good to be back," he said, his strained smile matching hers. Yet his eyes didn't smile. "It's been … difficult."

Beth stepped back and smiled at Rind. "And good to see you too, Rind."

Rind acknowledged her with a nod.

"Where's Jessica?" Beth asked, looking around.

Lanky winced. "Some things can't be told here."

Spider noticed River frown.

Beth's gaze lingered momentarily on Lanky, then turned to a quiet group to their right. "You've brought guests. Our recent guests have not been welcome."

"There is much to explain," Lanky said. He glanced at the prisoner. "But first, who's this?"

"Ka scum," Gravel spat. "A killer of our people – of Darius and Firuz."

Lanky's eyes hardened. He glanced at Beth. "Is this true?"

"It is. And yet—"

"And yet, nothing, Warrior," Gravel shouted. "He—"

"Silence, Shield!" Rind snapped, striding towards Gravel. "You will remember your place!"

Spider saw Gravel straining to hold himself back – but he remained silent.

Rind placed her hand on the Shield's shoulder and Spider heard her whisper, "I don't yet know what has happened here, but if it is as you say, we will avenge them. Of this you can be sure. But remember who you speak to. Friends. Allies."

Gravel nodded, yet his eyes burnt with a merciless rage.

Rind's piercing gaze flicked between Beth and River. "Why is this killer of our people still alive?" she said in a low, cold voice.

"Something here must be better understood," Beth murmured, glancing at the prisoner.

"Maybe I can help," came a gruff voice from the crowd behind.

They all turned to see one of the newcomers approaching: the older, grey-haired man.

"And who are you?" Beth said, little warmth in her voice.

"One who has met you before, Warrior. I am Stealth, the servant of the Ancient, who in turn serves IY. There is much to discuss."

*

Beth glared at the man, stark memories flashing into her mind: the dragon snatching her from the edge of the great canyon; a wretched, bone-chilling journey north through frozen lands; and … and what next? *I have no memory of what happened next.* "I don't know you," she said coldly. "And the Ancient is no adherent of IY."

The man held her gaze, his steely eyes unblinking. "Even so, I know you, Warrior. And I know this man." He tilted his head in the direction of the Ka assassin.

"That doesn't help your cause," she snarled.

"I can vouch for this man," came a familiar voice. "And for his words."

Beth spun around in astonishment. "Svana?" she breathed, seeing the tall woman walking up to her, Knuckles and Shorty close behind her. "I thought you lost." Shaking, she greeted her, wrapping her arms around the Iyes. "How? How is this possible?"

"That's not easy to answer," Svana murmured, holding her injured arm to her side.

Pulling back, Beth turned to Knuckles and Shorty. "Unbelievable," she said, joy rising within her. She hugged each of them in turn, then stood back, overwhelmed by what she was seeing. "You're back," she managed.

Knuckles's face was downcast as if he still carried guilt from the day she'd been taken by the dragon. "It was not an easy journey."

There was time enough to ease that guilt. "And Bear? Scorpion?"

"They were with us," Svana answered, glancing around. "Have they not—"

Lanky stepped forward. "Beth, we need to talk. But not here."

Beth heard the raw anguish in his voice.

"What happened to my father?" came River's wavering voice behind them.

Beth turned to see River walking towards them, the lines of her face drawn deep as though knowing the answer to her question.

"Give us a moment," Lanky said quietly to those around.

Svana's horrified expression betrayed her fear of what was about to be told. Beth heard her soft whisper to Knuckles and Shorty: "Let's give them space." As Svana walked away, she cast a fearful glance at Lanky.

The area around them quickly cleared, leaving Beth with Lanky, Rind, and River. She felt a stab of pain as she realised the stark truth. *Bear is dead.* The hurt deepened at the sudden image of the man. A determined yet approachable man. A good leader. One of the first Iyes she had met in the Land. Maybe the first. *And towards the end, a friend.*

And Scorpion? What of him?

She glanced at Lanky – and saw a dishevelled, bruised, and battered young man standing lost, uncertain of what to say.

"They died," Lanky said eventually. There was a gasp from Rind. "They both saved us, but ..." He shook his head, his expression distraught.

"What happened?" River asked in a whisper, a harrowing pain in her eyes.

"I … I don't know," Lanky said, his voice breaking. "The shaman had trapped me. Bear and Scorpion must have reached him somehow. But how they managed it, I just don't know."

There was a quiet sob from Rind.

"I am so sorry," Beth breathed.

"He has joined my mother," River said, her tear-filled eyes looking to the sky. "She will be happy. Her soulmate has returned to her side. But I will miss him. I will miss them both."

Rind stepped to Beth and Lanky's side and looked at them through tear-stained eyes. "Walk on," she murmured. "I'll spend a moment with River, then send for Sheba. Then I'll speak with Dune."

Beth gestured silently to Lanky, and they walked quietly away.

But after a few paces, Lanky stopped and glanced back. "I'm so very sorry, River."

River turned away without saying a word.

Lanky's shoulders slumped.

Beth took his hand and pulled him gently away. "Come on," she whispered. "She's got the right people with her." *And we've a lot to catch up on. On what has happened – and on what will be.*

CHAPTER THIRTY-FIVE

*Fen was a formidable and invaluable daemon, and
River a worthy shaman, Warrior, and Mother.
But both – or all – were flawed. Save Revri.*

*T*hey walked in silence down the well-trodden track towards the
gorge's entrance, then out into the bright afternoon sunlight
beyond. Beth veered to the left, following the ridge away from camp.
Lanky trudged on beside her. Approaching a group of scattered
boulders, she crossed to one and sat down. Lanky drew his Axe from
his holster, then sat, letting the Axe slip to the ground. He slumped
forward, his battle-scarred head in his hands.

Beth looked up at the sky and breathed in the rich, cool air. "This is
hard," she murmured. "Very hard."

Lanky said nothing.

She turned to him. "Where's Jessica?"

"That's not easy to answer," he said, head still bowed.

"Try me."

With a grimace, Lanky raised his head. "I'll tell you what I saw,
what I heard, but I can't tell you why it happened."

He then related a tale that left her aghast and bewildered.

"And so," Lanky finished, "I don't know where she is, and neither
does Fen. Nor IY."

"Why does she keep doing this?" Beth said, exasperated. "Isn't she
supposed to be *our* Guardian? It seems she's the one needing
guarded!" She picked up a stone and hurled it away. *What the hell are
you doing, Jess? We need you here.* Grimacing, she turned back to Lanky.
"I guess we have to assume Jess figured a way out. And that she's safe
and alive … somewhere."

Lanky rubbed his shoulder, torn skin showing beneath the ripped tunic. "I guess we do."

Her gaze lingering on him, she saw the desperate tiredness etched in his face. He'd clearly been lucky to escape with his life. *Thanks to Bear and Scorpion.* A heaviness weighing on her soul, she glanced to the distant camp, where scattered groups gathered to catch up on news from the recent arrivals. Bear had been one of the first she'd met here, one of those protecting her in those first few terrifying moments of their arrival to the Land. A murderous savage, she'd thought back then. How wrong had she'd been. *He knew things beyond my comprehension. He told me about the Continuum.*

And now he was dead.

And Scorpion. Dune would feel that loss deeply. *And Svana.*

'It is war,' came a voice within. *'Move on.'*

'Silence!' Beth snarled, fighting the instinctive urge to slam Bethusa back into the depths. But she knew she couldn't turn back. "The Land needs Bethusa. Forget Beth," the ancient Warrior had said. She knew she needed the strength of Bethusa for the battles ahead, despite her fear of where this would lead.

And Bethusa's words just now hit home. *Move on. Bear's words.* Had she chosen those particular words on purpose? Because despite the pain at the loss of those two brave men, that's what they needed to do.

She shifted her attention back to Lanky. "This Ensi, this leader of the Ka, she meets you, accuses you of being the destroyer of her lands, and then—"

"We. We are the destroyers of her lands."

"Okay, that *we* are the evil enemy. And then her own people attack her. A coup?"

Lanky nodded. "Led by a shaman I'm not in a hurry to meet again. With some pretty nasty friends too."

"So, what was she doing?"

"About the coup?"

"No, why did she invite you in? It makes no sense. She has you defenceless. She has her most feared adversary at her mercy. Why not kill you?"

"I don't know. Trying to get us to turn? Some perverse, vain effort to persuade us to believe her lies?"

Beth frowned. This didn't make sense. This Ensi had the Ka's most ancient enemy in her grasp. *And she talks to them?* No, it made no sense at all.

And yet it happened. Why?

With no clear answer, Beth sifted through the rest of his account. "So, no sign of the Kade?"

She saw a sudden tension in him, a disquieting uncertainty. He seemed reluctant to answer.

Her eyes narrowed. "Well?"

He ran his hand through his dishevelled hair, then held her gaze. "When the A'ven returned to me," he said slowly, as if questioning what he was saying, "I … I tasted something. An alien energy. But there was something more. When I faced the Ensi, Dysam tried to take over."

"I know that feeling," Beth muttered.

"Before I pushed him away, he shouted something. In the mayhem of the moment, I didn't take it in, but now …"

"What did he say?"

"Kill her. Destroy the Kade."

Beth stared at him in confusion – then she drew a sharp breath.

Lanky held her eyes. "Could it be?" he whispered. "Could the Ensi hold the Kade?"

'It seems she did,' Fen said, the daemon's voice clear in Beth's mind.

Beth's eyes widened. "Do you hear that?" But by the intense look in Lanky's eyes, she knew he had.

'What do you mean?' she heard him growl to Fen.

'She held the Kade. We missed the chance.'

Lanky climbed to his feet, his eyes blazing. 'Did you know?'

'No.'

'But you know more than you've said.'

'I know what I know, Warrior,' Fen snarled. 'Nothing more.'

'Then talk, damn you!'

There was a silence for a moment, then the voice of Fen in her mind: 'Follow me to a Glade. Here.'

Beth felt Fen's presence vanish. She glanced at Lanky and saw the anger in his face.

"Damn the warg," he rasped, turning away, tension in his stance.

She waited for his anger to cool. "We need to hear what the daemon has to say."

Lanky muttered something, then: "You know I bonded with him?"

"You what!" she exclaimed.

His expression darkened. "A pact with the devil. There was no choice, I had to get us out of there." He grimaced. "Me? No, Dysam got us out of there."

Fen *and* Dysam? *He must have faced hell.* She walked up to Lanky and laid her hand on his shoulder. "You saved many lives by those actions."

The tension eased a little from his shoulders. "I saw what Dysam did to travel the Land. I will show you."

I have seen it in Bethusa's thoughts.

"But how he moved Rind, Knuckles, and the others ..." Lanky exhaled softly. "There was a danger there, a great risk to their lives."

"Jess told us that only she had the skill to move others," Beth said, drawing back her hand. "That we shouldn't attempt it, or else ..." *Or else those others might vanish in the ether.* "But your need in that moment was great." She saw Lanky wince. The loss of Bear and Scorpion cut them all deeply.

Lanky seemed to look to another place. "I sensed something else ... someone else ... someone who aided Dysam."

"Fen?"

"Maybe. But I think not."

She studied his strained face. Then IY? Or merely a figment of the terror of the moment? She would let Lanky think more on that. "What now of Dysam?"

He seemed elsewhere for a moment, then turned to face her. "He is locked away. But I now have to live with the cursed warg beside me."

For better or for worse.

He frowned. "So, the Ensi had the Kade," he muttered as if to himself. "What the hell is going on?"

We're being told only what others want us to know, Beth thought grimly. That needed to change. "We can talk more in the Glade."

He nodded, then his keen eyes locked onto hers. "Before we go ... Jess told us there was a traitor here. Who?"

Beth's stomach twisted. *The one who betrayed me. The one—*

'Calm, Warrior,' came the voice of the lioness Afari. 'That time is behind us.'

"Who the hell is that?" Lanky said, jumping back to his feet.

Beth drew a calming breath. "Afari," she said, settling her thoughts. "My new daemon." *And one I trust.*

"Your new ..." His eyes widened. "Garrion! She was the traitor?"

Beth nodded. *She betrayed me. She abandoned a Warrior.*

Lanky sat back down, rubbing his temple. "What happened?"

She relayed the story of the shaman's attack and the ambush sprung by her, River, Fen, and IY.

"The conniving warg was in on this?" Lanky exclaimed. "This gets better and better." He paused, brow furrowing, then spoke as if to himself. "Then the Ensi was telling the truth about a traitor in our midst."

473

"Truths?" Beth murmured. "In this murky world, they aren't easy to see."

"Tell me about it," Lanky muttered. He released a long breath, then straightened. "So, these assassins who came here, where are they now?" She saw a dawning recognition in his eyes. "That prisoner is one of them?"

She nodded. "Three others escaped, including the Ka shaman, but this one we captured. He …" Movement in the distance caught her eye, and she saw the very man being led in a convoy of guards out of the gorge. "He is a killer and should die," she finished. But the memory of the shocking words he had spoken continued to haunt her. *He called himself a Warrior.* "Yes, he should pay for what he did, but there's something strange about this one – something hidden."

"If he killed our people, he's sealed his own death. Why would he be saved?"

'Because he is *a Warrior,'* came Fen's voice.

Both Beth and Lanky leapt to their feet. "What!"

'He is a Warrior of the Continuum. He is one of you.'

Beth saw her own stunned disbelief echoed in Lanky's face. "It can't be," she whispered, senses reeling as she turned to stare at the distant Ka. "He's an assassin. A killer of our people."

'And a loyal devotee of the Ensi. All true. But he met the Ancient's servant, who planted a seed of doubt. For a man seeking the truth, doubt can be a seed that quickly grows – then who knows what will blossom?'

Her chest tight, her body shaking, a visceral storm raged within her. How? How could this be? He was a Ka assassin, sent to kill her and River. A man who had killed two of the tribe. But beneath the vehement denial – beneath the turmoil of her pressured mind – Beth somehow knew it to be true. *I knew, but I couldn't accept it.* The smell, the taste, the colour of the energy about him. It was a touch she knew well, but she'd refused to allow the thought to settle.

"How can this be?" she whispered.

'Warriors of the Continuum can be born anywhere, anytime,' Fen said. *'If they follow the true path, then their fate is sealed. If—'*

"True path!" Beth exclaimed. "A Ka warrior, an enemy of IY, and killer of the Iyes. How is this the path of a Warrior?"

'Meet me at the Glade.' Fen's presence vanished.

"It just can't be," Beth whispered.

"Damn it!" Lanky exclaimed. "A Warrior from the Ka?" He reached for his Axe and holstered it on his back. "As if this wasn't hard enough without an enemy within."

474

Beth stood on a smooth white disk floating in a sea of blackness. The wolf daemon sat on his haunches, eyes gleaming like yellow topaz as a sleek lioness padded around the perimeter, powerful muscles rippling with each stride. There was a flash of light, and Lanky appeared by her side.

"We will be safer here from prying ears," Fen growled.

"That Glade wasn't that safe," Lanky grumbled. "What went wrong?"

A travelling Glade, came the instant thought in Beth's mind. Find the Cord with vibrations matched to the destination, latch on to the tight strands of intense energy, then travel. *The same way we get to the Gates,* came another thought seeming to rise from the depths of instinct. She tensed, wary of a quickening anticipation. The knowledge of a Warrior was rising to the fore.

"Krull has become a formidable shaman," Fen growled. "A shaman of no great age but one impressively skilled, and one who hid his true power well. He will have seen your actions and followed you to that Glade."

Lanky rubbed his beard, frowning. "I thought the Glades were protected."

"Finding one particular Glade within the myriad scattered through the Continuum would be impossible from afar: too many Cords, too many possible Glade sites. That is protection enough. But at the Ka camp, Krull stood close – he will have seen echoes of the Cord's activation."

Beth grunted. "But we're safe here. So talk."

"This Glade is safe from prying ears … Maybe."

"Maybe?"

"Of what I am about to tell, only a few have known." The daemon's menacing topaz eyes locked onto the lioness. "And only a few will know."

Afari emitted a low growl. "You want me to leave?"

"No," Beth interjected. "You stay."

Fen's penetrating gaze swung to her. "You trust this one? After the betrayal by Garrion?"

A sudden swirl of inner energy signalled Bethusa wished to speak.

Beth hesitated. She remained fearful of the dangers of releasing this ancient Warrior, but couldn't now deny Bethusa her time in the Land. She needed the skill, the knowledge, the power of this Warrior. *I need her on my side.*

She sighed. *A moment only.* Despite her trepidation, she relaxed her barriers—

Bethusa stormed to the fore. "The Dark one rises," she snarled in answer to Fen. "I cannot fight alone." She gestured to the lioness. "I chose this one, and in this one I trust."

The wolf's searching eyes studied Bethusa, then the daemon growled softly. "So be it. And maybe it matters not. That which was hidden is a secret no more."

"You talk again in riddles, warg," Lanky said with a frown. "You—"

"And your mind is riddled with fear," Bethusa snarled, glaring at Lanky. "A fear that weakens you, blinds you to what must be done."

Lanky eyes narrowed. "Who speaks?"

"I am Bethusa, Warrior of the Ages, and curse of the Dark." She bared her teeth. "And you are a distraction." Her Axe snapped into her hand. "Free Dysam. Free a true Warrior to aid this Land."

An Axe instantly appeared in Lanky's hand, and he readied himself. "I've bonded with the warg," he growled, "but I've gone as far as I'm going with the other."

"You don't have the strength," Bethusa snarled. "You—"

"Take another step and you'll find out just how wrong you are."

A snarling mass of muscle leapt between them. "This is not needed," Afari snarled. "Back off! Both of you."

Lanky glared at Bethusa.

Bethusa took a step forward—

'No! Stand down!' Sucking energy from the A'ven, Beth forced herself back to the fore. She felt the other resist, then, with a snarl, Bethusa retreated, leaving a simmering tension swirling in Beth's mind. She held up her hands. "It's okay. She's gone."

Lanky's eyes were sharp and unyielding as he peered into her face. Then the tension eased from his frame. "You should keep better control of that one," he muttered, taking a step back, his Axe vanishing into the ether of the Glade.

Beth grunted. *Control? No, that isn't the way,* she thought as Bethusa's anger simmered deep inside. What she needed was a truce. An alliance.

'I am Bethusa!' came the harsh voice from within.

'And I am Beth!' she responded fiercely.

An alliance? Maybe an uneasy alliance.

Lanky was still watching her closely. "I'm fine," she murmured.

He turned away to face Fen, a severe frown marking his brow. "You smell of lies, warg, of things obscured and unsaid. Secrets? Yes, I think you hold many secrets in your sly, cunning mind. Let's see what morsel you're willing to feed us today."

Low, vicious growls drifted through the ether as Fen rose from his haunches. "You are as a child in this place, Warrior, an innocent chasing the shimmering mirages before you, but unable to grasp what truly lies beyond." Ignoring Lanky's curse, the daemon spoke on. "Let me tell you a little of what you cannot see, Warrior. Let me tell of the Ensi."

"What of the Ensi?" Lanky said in a cold voice.

Fen uttered a low growl. "Though she is an enemy of the Iyes, the Ensi helped preserve the Land. She helped keep the Geddon from Kaos."

"What!" exclaimed Beth – and Bethusa.

Lanky stared at the wolf, eyes wide. "She hid the Geddon from Kaos?" His look of incredulity deepened. "How is that possible?"

Fen's hackles rose. "The Geddon is buried deeply, both within the Land and within the domain of the Spirits. Wardens protect it. Or at least, they did."

"Wardens?" Beth whispered, rocked by Bethusa's shocked reaction within.

"These were the Ensi's greatest secret. Hidden Warriors. Wardens concealed under the very nose of Kaos, their sole role to bind the Geddon."

"Hold on," Lanky said, staring at Fen in bewilderment. "Which Warriors? I saw no Warriors." Then he frowned, his gaze seeming to drift to another place. "In the throne room … they challenged the Ensi …" Stark realisation gripped his face. "Warriors … Her people mentioned Warriors."

Fen growled. "Part of the greatest secret of the Land – of the Continuum. Warriors like yourselves, but not those invoked to defend the Gates against the incursion of the Dark, or those needed to fight daemons roaming abroad. No, these Warriors were trained to bind the Geddon. These Warriors served as Wardens of the Geddon's prison."

The daemon's words sprang Beth's mind to another place. *Gates. I have defended the Gates.*

"But the Ensi?" Lanky stuttered. "The leader of the Ka holding enemy Warriors? How is that possible?"

"Because unknown to but a few, IY and the Ensi are allies. Of a sort."

"What!" Beth exclaimed, feeling the stunned reaction of Bethusa.

"You have to be kidding me," Lanky grated.

"I don't joke, human," Fen said, baring his teeth. "The line of the Ensi have honoured a sacred pact, first made millennia past when they discovered Kaos's plan."

Lanky put his hands to his head. "This makes no damn sense. Naga, Bear, all the Iyes have told us … What the hell is going on!"

"What you have been told is true, Warrior. The Ka are an ancient people, the first adherents of Kaos, the ferocious enemy of the Iyes. They are a people who believe in, and who follow, the misguided values and teachings of Kaos." Fen's fierce gaze followed Lanky as he walked away, shaking his head. "And the Ensi is the leader of the Ka. All this is true. But the Ensi and Kaos? She follows Kaos – but only so far. She sees things others don't – like his wish to release the Geddon."

"This is utter lunacy," Lanky stormed. "If she knows her god's aim is to wipe out all humanity, how can she support him? And why does she fight us? She stole the Staff. She attempted to kill Warriors. She …" He grunted and turned away in disgust.

"She is of her age. She is of her people. She can only act within the bounds of her knowledge. But like many great leaders, she has ambitions for herself, for her people, for her empire. And her god? She, and each Ensi before her, believed they could use Kaos, manipulate him, hide from him their true desires, their aspirations." Fen issued a low growl. "And for millennia it worked – for the Ensi and for IY, and for all peoples of the Land. The Geddon remained hidden … until today."

Beth – and Bethusa – stared at Fen, astounded by what they were hearing. What mad game was played here? *Manipulate a god?*

Lanky stood, head bowed, his anger spent. Then he sighed, and when he spoke his voice was subdued. "The Ensi was betrayed. By the snake allied to the shaman I fought. The snake said he'd seen the Warriors." He winced. "I didn't listen. But Jess did. She knew. Somehow, she knew. She told me we needed to take the Ensi, just before I …" He grimaced. "Before I abandoned her."

Abandoned? No, Beth had heard his tale of what had happened in the temple. "This isn't your fault, Lanky," she hissed. "You did what any of us would have done." She levelled a contemptuous gaze on Fen. "This is the fault of those who tell us nothing. Of those who hold secrets from us." She took a step towards the daemon, her eyes narrowing. "You knew all of this before Lanky and Jess went there, didn't you? You knew the Wardens were there."

"None could know of the Wardens," Fen growled. "None."

Beth clenched her fist with a rising fury. "You and IY held this secret for millennia. You withheld it from your own people. You let a war

478

between the Iyes and the Ka continue for millennia, condemning untold lives for generation after generation." Her eyes blazed. "Why didn't you stop it? Why the hell didn't you stop it!"

The daemon raised his massive head, glistening fangs bared. "We protected this world from Armageddon. That's what we did. And the war, the hatred? No, we didn't let this happen – humans let this happen."

"Humans led by Kaos," Lanky said in a cold voice. "And humans led by IY."

"Be careful where you go with this," Fen snarled. "IY has protected this Land for far longer than you could imagine. Kaos is the destroyer of life. The Dark is the evil."

Lanky glared at Fen, then strode off across the Glade.

Her anger simmering, Beth felt Bethusa's own rage burning deep within. *She didn't know.*

The daemon, hackles raised, swung his head to Beth. "You challenge what has been done to protect this Land, yet remember, if the Geddon is released, all life is lost. *All* life." His gaze held hers with unflinching ferocity. "What would *you* be prepared to do to preserve life when it is threatened with annihilation?"

Beth held the daemon's combative glare for a moment before turning away. That was too big a question to ask anyone, too vast to be comprehended. And yet … *I expect I'd do almost anything to preserve life.* Her anger cooling, she glanced around the glowing white Glade. Lanky stared out into the blackness beyond; Afari prowled the perimeter close by. *We each struggle with our own doubts and fears. Yet we all continue on.* She turned back to Fen. "The Wardens. What happened to them?"

"Killed. But not in this time."

Cold dread twisted her gut. "Then the Geddon is free?"

"Not yet. A life, somewhere – sometime – stepped into the breach. Not a Warrior but a life, nonetheless. And well hidden. That life feeds the prison bindings." A restless tension seemed to roll from the wolf. "But how long can they hold? Kaos will find this life – Kaos will terminate this life – *then* the Geddon will be released. We must preserve that life. And we must capture the Kade – remove the Dark's power."

"The Kade," Lanky muttered, turning around, his eyes narrowing. "We come back to the Kade." He walked slowly back towards them, his face grim. "When did you know the Ensi held it?"

"We sensed its presence as soon as the Ensi released her shield on the A'ven. Later, we felt its presence leave the Land – at precisely the time the Ensi vanished."

"So, the Ensi has the Kade," Beth said, shaking her head. "But now where the hell is she?"

Lanky's brow furrowed. "Maybe the same place as Jess? Is that why she went after the Ensi? Did Jess know the Ensi held the Kade?"

"You were the one there, not me."

"Jess had her eyes open. I didn't. I saw only an enemy."

She saw the pain in Lanky's eyes, but in this moment, there was no time for regrets. "Then Jess may be with the Ensi …"

Fen let out a low growl. "Maybe. Maybe not. But wherever the Ensi is now, she is vulnerable. The Kade is vulnerable. With the Kade, Kaos wins. He controls access to the A'ven; he controls the Continuum."

"And the Geddon?"

"Without the Kade, Kaos seeks to release the Geddon and destroy life. With the Kade, he has a choice. Destroy life or preserve the Geddon's bindings and seek to control life. It is not clear which would be worse."

Lanky's frown deepened. "And the Ensi? She holds the Kade. Why hasn't she used it for her own deadly purpose?"

"In her own way, she clearly has," Fen growled. "But she is weak. Small tricks, yes, but beyond that she has nothing that can threaten the strongest shamans. And to Kaos she is but a speck of sand in a desert storm."

Lanky rubbed his beard, his eyes hardening. "How come you seem to know so much about all this, warg? You, a simple daemon, a servant of the Spirits."

Fen said nothing.

Lanky's look was contemptuous. "I could have killed the Ensi. Killed the one protecting this world from Armageddon, the one carrying the Kade. Did you think about that in your damned scheming?"

Fen let out a low growl. "It was considered."

"And Dysam," Lanky continued, studying Fen intently. "Why did he want to destroy the Kade, when IY asks us to capture it?"

Beth frowned. Did she imagine it, or did she see a flicker of tension in the wolf's stance?

"He's mistaken, blinded by the past horrors inflicted on his family."

He hides something. What?

Afari growled. "Someone comes! One of the Iyes. The one you know as Knuckles."

"We will talk again, Warrior," Fen growled.

Fen and Afari vanished.

Lanky cursed, his eyes blazing. "Damn the cursed warg. What's he hiding?"

"What are they all hiding?" she muttered.

Lanky snorted and strode a few paces away.

Beth stood for a moment, striving to assimilate all that had been revealed this day. The prison of the Geddon beneath the temple of Kaos. The Ensi holding the Kade. The dragon an ally of IY. *And the Ka assassin.* She cursed. They'd had no time to interrogate Fen about the malicious twist of fate that had landed that into their midst.

Yes, so much revealed and yet so much seemingly still hidden.

And we failed to retrieve the Kade.

She squared her shoulders as if against an oncoming foe. They needed to regroup, because so far, they were being outmanoeuvred and outplayed. *By the enemy, or by friends?*

To Lanky, she said, "We need to go."

He nodded.

The Glade disappeared, and she found herself sitting on a boulder by the ridge.

"Hey!" Knuckles called as he approached. "You're needed at the meeting. No rest for the wicked, they say."

With Lanky muttering under his breath, Beth hauled herself to her feet. As they walked off with Knuckles, restless anger churned. *We need to act. We need to start winning some of these battles we fight.*

*

"He was a good man, a strong and trusted leader. We will honour his sacrifice, and I will carry him always in my heart." Rind's parting words to her and her sister echoed in River's mind as she made her way to the Sacred Chamber. Sheba had left with Rind to talk more with Svana and the others who had journeyed with their father, but River desperately needed time alone. As she entered the Sacred Chamber, she felt the warm embrace of the Spirits. "Thank you," she whispered as she sat, crossing her legs beneath her. She closed her eyes …

And saw an image of herself and Sheba laughing in the low branches of a sweet-smelling tree, looking down on her father, who was trying to coax them down, his face tired but happy after the end of a long day's hunt. As always, her father had to climb up after them, pretending to be a bear while they scrambled out to the lightest branches, squealing with delight. The scene ended with their return home, she tired and riding high on her father's broad shoulders.

Carefree and innocent times that she cherished.

And now he was gone.

"We feel your loss," came the gentle, lilting voice of IY into the chamber.

"It doesn't seem real," River said, welcoming her god's comforting presence. "But I feel the pain."

"He has joined your ancestors. And they are proud. He will be remembered as one of the greatest of the Iyes."

"He was my father …"

She felt the tears welling up, and the Spirits let her grieve, their whispering, ethereal caresses holding her in a gentle embrace.

"IY?" she said eventually.

"Yes," came IY's voice.

"Is this all worth it?" *The deaths of those I know. The death of my people. The fear.*

The loneliness.

River looked up as a woman appeared before her, wearing a dark green chiton tied off at the waist with a black sash, her hair cut short and spiky.

IY's face was grim. "To answer your question fully, there are things you must know. You may judge my actions wrong, but I have done what I can to preserve life in the Land."

"Does it relate to my father?" River breathed, a sense of foreboding sweeping over her.

"Let me start from the beginning," IY said, her voice even and steady.

As IY related the tale of an ancient pact between her, the Ensi, and the Ancient, her disciple listened in shocked silence, hearing a story that shattered her understanding of … everything. *The leader of the Ka protected the Land? Warriors stood guard within the temple of Kaos? The Ancient one who captured Beth and the Staff was an ally?* Finally, IY spoke the last of the tale, her final words drifting away into the silence of the chamber.

Lost and bewildered, River let her gaze wander blindly across the walls of the chamber until the wondrous images painted upon them swept into focus. Seeing the wealth of glorious drawings and paintings, her hands trembled with a burgeoning rage as IY's words ravaged her mind. How many artists, dedicated devotees of IY, had paid homage to the Spirits – and to their god – over countless generations, drawing energy from the Land and weaving it into their glorious work? And how many of these had been senselessly slaughtered by the Ka, the avowed enemy of IY?

For a lie.

"How many lives lost?" she whispered, glacial coldness to her voice.

IY looked at River, sadness in her eyes.

"How many lives?" River insisted, her voice growing louder.

The woman said nothing.

"How many lives?" she stormed, climbing to her feet. "And all the while, you stood by and watched them all die!"

Still, IY gave no reply.

River slumped, her head bowed, deep despair overwhelming her. *And still they die.* She looked up at IY. "You watched," she stammered, "and you let our people die." *You let my father die.*

"Kaos—"

"Forget Kaos!" River hissed. "Our people trusted you. The Ka were the enemy. This is what you told us. The Ka must be destroyed. The Warriors—"

"That I never said. The Iyes—"

"The Warriors – and the daemons – all supported to destroy the Ka!"

"No!" IY retorted, her eyes flaring. "All supported to stop Kaos. To destroy Kaos. All supported to save this Land and to save the Iyes. And fight? You had no choice but to fight, else you would have been destroyed, the Story lost … the Warriors lost."

River turned away, her chest tight. "Did the Spirits know?"

"No one knew," IY said, an edge to her voice.

Even the Spirits, mocked by the cloak of deception.

"The enmity between the peoples ran too deep," IY said. "The gulf between my values of the Light and those of the Dark, too great."

"You let us kill one another," River spat.

IY was silent for a moment, her expression unreadable. "Despite what they knew, despite the pact which imprisoned the Geddon, each Ensi believed in the way of the Ka. And they – and their people – believed the Iyes and the Warriors wished to destroy them." She shook her head gently. "This fed a cycle of enmity that could not, and would not, be stopped. And yes, in this, I failed."

Exhaustion sweeping over her, River's dulled gaze drifted around the chamber as though she might find this only a dream. "You could have led us away. Saved your people." *Saved my father.*

IY stepped to a scene painted on the wall of a herd of antelope pursued by hyenas. "The battle of this Land has been between Light and Dark, between preserving lands rich in life, or facing the bleak desolation of Kaos. And between the two has lain only the Iyes and the

Warriors, and the guile of the Ensi. Remove one and the pact would have failed." A harsh fatalism crossed her face. "As it has now done."

And yet how many untold dead? How many innocent lives lost, ignorant of the futility of their bravery? "I wish for time to grieve, for my father and for my people," River whispered.

"This I will respect. But you must know – the Guardian has left the Land, as has the Ensi."

River drew a sharp breath.

"Speak with the Warriors, they will share what they saw and heard. And in them you can trust."

Trust? I trusted you, but in a moment, it was lost.

"There is much I know," IY said quietly, "but much I do not. I serve the Light and have supported life in this Land since its very inception. But there may come a time when I fail. Because each day, Kaos is growing stronger. And each day, I fear the release of the Geddon. I need the help of the Warriors. I need your help."

With that, IY vanished.

Left gazing into the vacant distance, River felt lost and abandoned. Betrayed.

And where had Jessica gone? Had she left with the Ensi, and if so, did she know the Ensi carried the Kade? With no answers, she had no choice – *I must trust the Guardian.*

But what of IY? *She asks for my help, but why should I give it to one who misled us? And what is your vision for the future, IY? That was my first question to you. Is this all worth it? But you misunderstood.* A deep-rooted anger flared. *I have seen the future, and it's not what I want for my Land.*

It must change.

But how?

Understand what is happening, then look for the opportunity to change our path – to give my children's children a better future.

Watch. Listen. Then decide and act.

I will avenge your death, my father. That, I promise.

Still numbed by all that had been revealed by IY, she gave her thanks to the Spirits and walked out of the chamber.

CHAPTER THIRTY-SIX

Beth. Bethusa. A conundrum indeed.

*F*eeling the soft grass beneath her and the subtle yet welcome warmth of the low sun on her back, Rind relaxed her tense shoulders and let out a deep sigh. It was a rare moment of comfort within a dangerous and hard land.

And a momentary respite from Gravel's simmering rage.

He's struggling to understand. We're all struggling.

Because so much had been revealed.

With the tribe now reunited, they'd assembled at midday to share what they knew of the events of these last days, each given time to tell their story, their part played. And what horrific tidings. Bear and Scorpion dead; the Guardian lost; a traitor discovered amongst them; and demonic shamans released from the Ka's temple. But most stunning of all had been the telling of the secret pact between IY and the Ensi, a revelation that had rocked the tribe to the core, striking at the very heart of their Story.

Our Story.

Harsh, disquieting questions crowded her mind. How was it possible? How could the leader of their feared enemy be an ally of IY and the custodian of the Geddon's prison? Where was that in their Story? What else had been hidden from them? Grimacing, she pushed that chilling thought away. *Focus on what you can see, what you can truly comprehend. The rest is for the Warriors.*

Rind glanced around at those gathered. Close by stood Spider, Knuckles, and the simmering Gravel. Opposite, some distance away, stood the three Warriors, Lanky, Beth, and River. The three spoke in quiet voices, their words unheard. *Yes, it is their task to understand what we cannot see.*

She glanced at the final figure, one standing beside the Warriors and yet to Rind's eyes somehow apart, lost. *I'm still not sure why this one is here.* And yet, the traveller was here, one of the eight men and women of the tribe chosen to share what was known and discuss what was not. *And to decide our future.*

Looking back to the Warriors, Rind's gaze fell on Lanky. As with the others gathered, his face was wrung with bone-deep exhaustion. But he also carried scars from his battle with the enemy shaman. Brutal scorch marks crossed his face, slicing down across his torn tunic, and a red welt circled his neck, evidence of the shaman's noose. But despite the horrors he must have faced, his quiet strength still shone through. *He gives more than people see. And his eyes still sparkle; his smile draws you in.*

Lanky's gaze drifted, and their eyes met. He smiled. She smiled back, then instinctively looked away, fearing he would catch her thoughts. She steadied herself. *But why not? Why shouldn't he hear them?* She glanced back – but Lanky was talking with Beth as the Warriors headed back towards them. The moment had passed. She twisted a stone bead of her wrist bracelet. Life was short. Life was uncertain. *Don't waste it.* She would choose another time to follow her emerging and intriguing thoughts.

As the Warriors approached, she drew a deep breath and glanced over at Gravel. Tension hardened the Shield's stance, his cold, piercing eyes searching for someone foolish enough to challenge him. She'd never seen him so upset and angry. The deaths of those under his watch had been a crushing blow, a failure he would never forgive himself for. But there was more than this, she knew. He carried suspicions of a remaining traitor in the camp. "The enemy have eyes here, I'm sure," he'd said when catching her alone after dawn. "Those with access to the daemons should be watched. The Ka have a long reach."

He won't let this go, she thought as the Warriors rejoined the circle. *And do I blame him?*

She sighed. She didn't. He served as a Shield of the tribe, and those he protected had been slaughtered. Even so, she was wary of where this would lead.

As they all sat, Gravel climbed to his feet, beginning where he'd left off. "How certain can we be of what you've been told?" he said, glaring at the Warriors. "That this tale of a pact between IY and the Ensi is not more treachery of the Ka? The Ka shaman has proven his long and poisonous reach. Who can we trust?"

Knuckles sat forward. "Let me tell—"

"*You* have just returned from the Ka heartland," Gravel continued, ignoring Knuckles's interruption as he glared at Lanky, "and so may carry some hidden threat." As an angry muttering sounded from the group, Gravel gestured to Beth. "*You* were betrayed by one supposedly aiding us, one who none of the tribe had ever seen. And *you*, Mother," the Shield continued, turning to River, "are yet to be tested."

Spider leapt to his feet. "You will take that back, Gravel! Now!"

"Aye," Knuckles said, standing. "My long travels in the cold north have worn my patience and good humour very thin. Don't test what little is left by questioning our Mother."

Rind cleared her throat.

All eyes turned to her.

"And yet," Rind started carefully, "our *friend* makes a valid point, if not a little bluntly. Betrayal has already led the Ka against us." She faced the Warriors. *Gravel needs to hear their words. He must understand what we face.* "How certain are you of the daemons with whom you speak?" she said in an even voice. "And how certain are you that it was IY who spoke with you, Mother?"

Rind watched as Beth sauntered into the circle, her hand rubbing her shoulder. "So now you choose to doubt us?" she rasped, her dark eyes narrowing.

Rind hid her sudden unease. *We stand at a most dangerous moment. We need all aligned here.* She noted the Warrior's hand. *She itches to take her Axe. Is this Beth, or the other?* She glanced at Lanky, who was watching Beth carefully. *Good, we may need his help.* "I don't imply doubt on my part, Warrior," she said to Beth. "These are questions needing to be asked. Their answers will aid others' understanding."

Beth's fingers slowly flexed, but she held her position, glaring at Rind.

"It *was* IY," came River's voice. Rind turned to see River studying the group, her gaze settling on Gravel. "The Spirits were present when IY spoke with me in the Sacred Chamber. You have heard the truth of the deception."

Rind heard the suppressed anger in River's choice of words: "... the truth of the deception." The Ensi's deception? Or IY's? But that was for another moment. River had answered Gravel's challenge. No imposter could have passed the Spirits. It *had* been IY who spoke with River.

"And what I believe," came Lanky's quiet voice, "is that the Ensi had something hidden in that temple. I may have missed it at the time, but I remember what was said – her people talked of Warriors within the temple, Warriors they knew nothing about." He glanced at Rind. "You ask of daemons ..." His lips pursed. "For better or for worse, I'm a Warrior, and I'm aided by a daemon: the warg Fen. I suspect the warg secretly schemes for some unknown gain, but I believe he's terrified by the threat this Land faces. And *I* am terrified." His gaze fell on Gravel. "And so should you be."

"Words," Gravel said, his tone derisive. "Just words. What do you truly know? What can you truly trust from these daemons who speak with you? You're told the Ancient now fights for IY. You're told the devil Ensi has made a pact with IY. But what have you *seen*?" He faced Rind, his eyes blazing. "Well, I've seen the bloodied bodies of my people, killed by the Ka. I've seen the treachery of the daemon, aligned with the Ka. And I've seen the body of our Mother lying dead, slaughtered by the Ka." He spat. "The Ka – and the Ensi – are our enemy, and that will be true until the day I die."

"You don't understand—" started Knuckles.

"Have you been listening to anything here!" Spider cut in vehemently. "I saw the dragon, Gravel. I saw the supposed enemy dragon come to our aid! It helped save our lives! And the shamans that came out of the temple …" Spider shuddered. "I don't want to see what else lies in there, something even the Ka want locked away. Be glad that whatever it is, it has been hidden from Kaos."

"And whatever the truth of this pact with the Ensi of the Ka," Lanky growled, glaring at Gravel, "what I saw inside the temple – with *my* eyes – was a changing of the guard, a revolution. And these new leaders don't seem to me to be folk to make deals. The war that was coming has changed. The enemy – Ka or otherwise – has now massively upped its firepower. We need to be ready."

"But what of this Geddon?" Rind said. "That—"

"A lie," Gravel spat. "A ploy of the Ka."

A sudden sense of threat rolled into the circle as Beth strode forward. "Tell me," she snarled, her fiery eyes locked onto Gravel. "What if the Ensi of the Ka has indeed been hiding a weapon from Kaos – a weapon that can destroy this Land? What then?"

Gravel held the Warrior's gaze. "In that case, we need the support of true Warriors to aid us. We—"

A searing blast thumped into Rind, hurling her backwards. As she scrambled to her feet, she looked around to see a blazing white figure standing over Gravel, the sleek, rippling body of a lioness stalking behind her. "Doubter, you go too far!" the Warrior roared. She grasped Gravel by the throat, lifting him as though he were a child. "Do you think yourself ready to deal with this threat on your own? Then see how you fare!"

"Bethusa!" a voice thundered – an imposing voice of one who expected his commands to be obeyed. Lanky, a shimmering aura around him, strode up to Bethusa, his eyes burning, his face cast like granite. "Stand down!"

Bethusa glared at him, then threw Gravel to the ground. "We waste time with these children," she spat. "Time we do not have."

"All have to play their part, you know this," Lanky said, his voice glacial. "Stand down – this is not the right path."

"These fools do not listen. They—"

"None of you listen!" Knuckles yelled angrily, striding into the circle. "You are all fools!"

"Begone," Bethusa thundered, glaring down at Knuckles. "You—"

A bestial roar rent the air, and the growling fury of a fearsome white wolf appeared overhead, its fang-filled jaws thrusting towards the one called Bethusa …

Who took a step back.

Rind watched, horrified yet captivated, as Lanky turned to Knuckles. "Speak," the Warrior growled.

Standing bravely before the Warriors, Knuckles flicked a nervous glance to the eerie vision of the wolf that was now quickly fading. His gaze moved briefly to Beth, then to the scattered group, who watched on in alarm. And beyond this group, in the distance, others of the camp had gathered, unsure of what action they should take. Or could take.

Knuckles shifted, seemingly gathering himself, then spoke. "You are all fools," he began, his face betraying a frustrated rage that Rind had rarely seen. "So quickly do you judge others and decide for yourselves what is wrong and what is right, who to trust and who to ignore. Have you heard *all* the voices here?" He glowered at each one assembled. "Have you?" he challenged. His hands trembling, he shook his head. "What about me? Have you bothered to listen to me? Do I count so little that you ignore one who travelled with Bear and his party to recover the Warrior Beth? One who met the Ancient herself, Rakana, and her partner, Hydrak. One who listened to the story those Ancients told, a story of the pact between IY and the Ensi of the Ka, and of a destroyer of the Land straining for release from its binding." Knuckles's eyes raked them. "Bear died to allow the Warrior to escape, to allow them to help save this Land. And yet you disbelieve, and you mock." He studied them all, his gaze almost contemptuous. "Are we reduced to this? Scrabbling about searching for scraps of truths? Digging in the dirt hoping to find our lost soul?" He barked a harsh laugh. "Bear and Scorpion must be looking upon us and raging in their anger and despair."

In the depths of the silence that had fallen, Knuckles levelled his gaze on Gravel. "Do not turn away from the Warriors in the hour of their greatest need. And," he continued, turning to Bethusa, "do not abandon us to fight these battles alone."

The silence deepened.

And then mocking laughter. "Empty words, little man," Bethusa said in a bitter rasp. "They fall on deaf ears here."

"Not so, Warrior," Knuckles said, his eyes burning with anger. "I've dedicated my life to the Iyes – and to IY – and nothing I've heard or seen has changed that. But what I've seen, what I've heard from others today, is that the peril to this Land is upon us. And that this peril is immediate and dire. This is not the time to fight amongst ourselves – that way lies our doom."

"And what of you, doubter?" Bethusa snarled, glaring at Gravel. "What do you say in answer to this one's words?"

Gravel stood proudly defiant in the face of the Warrior. "You may not like it, but my statements remain. The Ka is the enemy. And I trust very few."

"Then you can leave this place," Bethusa roared. "You—"

"Beth!" a new voice shouted. Rind turned to see Tricia striding up to the Warrior. "You're not casting anyone out for expressing their honest views."

"Leave here, useless one, you—"

"Don't talk over me, Beth, you know that annoys me."

"Annoys you! Get out of—"

"And don't shout. I'm standing just here. I'm not deaf."

Bethusa turned to Lanky. "Remove this—"

"Hey, I'm still talking to you. That's right, pay attention. You need to wise up, girl, and quickly. Who's the boss here? You, or this big oaf pretending—"

"You go too far," Bethusa roared, grabbing Tricia by the throat.

Rind looked on, horrified, as Tricia's breathing became harsh rasps. "Help her, Lanky!"

"She doesn't need help," Lanky murmured, his voice suddenly weary.

As Lanky spoke, the blaze around Bethusa vanished … and *Beth* stood holding Tricia by the throat. Eyes widening, Beth released her hold on Tricia, then took a step back, confusion writ on her face. Lanky quickly stepped to Tricia's side and laid his arm around the young woman's shoulder, whispering a few quiet words in her ear. Glancing at Beth, Rind saw a simmering anger remaining beneath the Warrior's mask of confusion.

490

"You took a big risk," Beth said in a low voice.

Tricia glanced at Beth, waiting.

"But thank you."

Relief flooded Tricia's face. "It's what friends are for."

Rind hid her disquiet. *Friends? We're all at each other's throats. We have to change this, else the enemy has already won.*

*

As the terrible rage of Bethusa had washed over River, she'd fought a deep primal urge to call on Revri, and for them both to ready for battle. But her control was determined, and she and Revri had remained silent.

Not so Bethusa.

The raw power and ferocious aggression of the ancient Warrior was both stunning and chilling, and the new daemon, Afari, seemed unable to help Beth control the violent excesses of the battle-hardened Warrior. Bethusa still acted first and asked questions later.

As at the Mountain of Hope.

The mountain ...

For River it was suddenly as though silt had been swept from some long-undisturbed dream; a faint, fragmented dream of Beth killing a Staff-thieving traitor called Robert in cold blood. A dream? No, it had happened, she was sure of it – the enraged act of a formidable, short-tempered killer before the Guardian had intervened and reset the Continuum.

And yet, I shouldn't know this.

Because the Continuum was reset, and the killing undone. It never happened.

Yet, weak, ephemeral fragments of this man's execution remained.

How? Why?

All at once, everything shifted, a shocking thought hammering into River's mind. *If Jessica did this again, would we remember? Would we know it had been done?* Then, another stunning thought. *Had* she done it again? Had the Guardian attempted to correct some other tragic mistake, some other catastrophic failure?

She shivered. *I have other memories ... Could it be ...?*

Grimacing, she pushed the terrifying thoughts away. *Enough. There lies madness.*

She glanced back at Beth to see Bethusa's anger still lingering in the face of the Warrior. Who controlled whom? If Beth could harness Bethusa, then a most powerful Warrior walked beside them. *And if not?* Then the storm could shatter the unity of the tribe.

The thought echoed … *the unity of the tribe.*

There lay a festering source of many frustrations and deep indecision.

They had no tribe leader.

Her instinctive rebuttal was fierce and filled with regret. *We do. My father. He should be here. He is the true leader of the Iyes.* With a force of will, she forced back the pain and steadied herself. Her father was gone. The time for grieving would come. *In this moment, I must accept it.*

And we must decide on a new leader.

She glanced around the seated group, seeing uncertainty etched in the weary faces around her. Yes, they needed someone with the respect of all to stop the spiral of self-destruction, to somehow lift the tribe from the pit of despondency they had descended into. And they needed that leader now to prevent them stumbling into the claws of Kaos. Because for all her anger and resentment at the deceit IY had shown, she accepted her god's revelation. They faced a threat far beyond that of the Ka, an existential threat to all life of the Land.

A threat to my people, a threat to all peoples.

A threat to our future.

And despite her despair at the future she had seen, at least *a* future existed. *Preserve it. Preserve life.* Thereafter she could seek a way to change that future for the better.

"Mother," came Rind's voice, breaking her reverie.

River looked up.

Rind stood and stepped into the centre of the ragged circle, first glancing at Beth, and then looking down at River. "I request to be made leader of the tribe."

It is as if she read my mind. River instinctively glanced at Beth. The Warrior was glaring at Rind but remained silent. *Beth never wanted to be leader. But Bethusa?*

Steadying herself, River turned back to Rind. She studied the young woman, seeing the strength and confidence in her stance. Rind had served well as leader of the White Crags camp, and all there trusted her judgement. *She has proven her worth many times,* came the voice of the Mother within her. *But others here may wish to lead.*

She slid her gaze to those others, looking at each in turn. Spider, Knuckles, and Gravel. Three who Naga and her father had considered future leaders. "What say each of you?"

"Agreed," Spider and Knuckles said immediately, their faces both eager and relieved.

Her gaze shifted to Gravel.

"Agreed," Gravel growled. "I trust her."

"As do I," said all others around the circle.

Except Beth.

"Beth?" Lanky said quietly. "It makes sense."

River saw Beth's hands clench into fists, then quickly unclench. *She is fighting Bethusa. And if that one forces herself upon us, we may have a problem.*

She breathed a quiet sigh of relief as she saw Beth's curt nod. "But we need to act," the Warrior growled.

River turned to Rind. *My father is not here, but he is watching us. He would approve.* "Then it is agreed. May ..." She hesitated, unable to say the name. *But I can't abandon her. Not now.* "May IY travel with you."

"May IY travel with you," said the group.

Rind bowed a fraction, then she straightened, her impassioned eyes brooking no challenge. "First, forget the pacts, the deals, known or unknown. The Ka – and their empire – remain a threat. And today, they pose a far greater threat than yesterday. A new leader, new shamans, new dragons." She looked around the group. "Is this accepted by all?"

River saw all nod in agreement. "This was never in doubt," Gravel growled.

"Second," Rind continued, "if the Geddon is unleashed, it is likely that none of us will be here to worry about any of this. We have to find a way to prevent that. At all costs. Do all acknowledge this?"

River heard agreement from all, save Gravel. "I accept what Knuckles has told us," he said. "Whether the Ancient's words can be believed, that I cannot know."

"And third," Rind continued, "there must be trust between us." She looked pointedly at Beth, then Gravel. "Forget your petty squabbles, and start thinking with this," she said fiercely, tapping her head. She glanced around the group. "All of you."

Beth grunted but said nothing.

"Knuckles is the clearest headed of us all," Rind continued. "We *must* work together." She considered for a moment. "We've done what we can here, but there are new arrivals in camp who can tell us more – we'll use the rest of the day to interrogate them. Lanky and Gravel, you talk to Stealth; Knuckles and Svana ..."

Rind ran through assignments for the group, then reached for a waterskin, took a long draught, then wiped her mouth dry. "And so, to another matter. The Ka assassin."

"He dies," Gravel snarled.

River saw the fury in the Shield's eyes. *By his hand, if he gets the chance.*

Lanky leaned forward. "That can't happen," he said in a low voice.

493

"What!" Gravel hissed.

"It seems," Lanky continued, "that he's a Warrior of IY."

River sighed as Gravel exploded. This Ka was a problem. Many of the tribe would not accept him as a Warrior. *And if we are not careful, we will find him with a blade in his neck.*

A most difficult time lay ahead.

*

Lanky studied the grey-haired man called Stealth, the servant of the dragon, assimilating what the man had told them. Stealth sat relaxed, impressively calm, as though simply talking with friends. A stark contrast to the gathering they'd left, where heated debate and choleric clashes over the Ka assassin had left anger and frustration thick in the air. With no clear path to an answer, they'd called a halt, splitting up to interrogate the new arrivals. Rind had asked Lanky and Gravel to join her. *Keeping Gravel as far away from the Ka assassin as possible,* Lanky had thought wryly.

And now they'd heard Stealth's tale, a story repeating the same assertion they'd already heard – of a long-lasting pact between the ancient dragon, who was Stealth's master, and the Ensi of the Ka. More incredibly for Lanky, Stealth had added more background on the capture of Beth – with a twist that did little to dampen Gravel's dislike of the Ka assassin.

"So, the Ka scum was responsible for the capture of the Warrior," Gravel spat. "That might finally force *her* to see the truth. She—"

"No," Stealth said patiently. "Shadow had nothing to do with the Warrior's capture. He was there to deliver the Staff."

"Yes, the Staff," Gravel growled. "The litany of this devil's crimes goes on and on." He faced Rind, his eyes afire. "Do you not see what we have in our midst? He—"

"Yes," Rind said, holding up her hand. "He has clearly been an effective warrior of the Ka. He—"

"Effective! He has—"

"Strike, Gravel, I know!" Rind exclaimed. "You've made your point, and we've heard it. Now let's focus on what this man has to say. I don't want the cursed Ka mentioned here again."

Gravel was almost purple with rage, struggling to contain himself. Lanky grimaced. At some point, the man would explode and do something he would regret. *Maybe not now, but explode he will.* And Lanky didn't see how to stop him. *He won't listen to me right now.* And the irony? Gravel asked the right questions. *He's right to doubt. He just pushes it too far.*

They waited a moment, and to Lanky's relief, the seething Shield remained silent.

Stabbing a blade into the ground, Rind's attention shifted to Stealth. "What I don't understand is, if this dragon is an ally of IY – of the Warriors – why capture one, almost killing her in the process? And why steal the Staff in the first place?"

Stealth stroked the tip of his short white beard. "My master forgets the frailty of us humans," he said, a wry smile on his face. "For her, this was a Warrior, an unbending, tenacious Warrior. Not one to struggle with the biting cold of the air, oh no, but one who has the strength to fight against the might of the enemy for aeons. Robust, unbreakable … unfreezable! But my master had wanted her subdued on arrival. To keep unwanted attention away, she told me. To keep a daemon away, I think. She went a little far. The Warrior was lucky to survive the journey."

Daemon? And then Lanky saw it. *Garrion! It has to be.* With Beth subdued, the suspected daemon traitor wouldn't have been able to link with her, wouldn't have seen the events at the mountain lair. *Not seen the dragon's own treachery against Kaos.* He saw Rind staring at him. "I think I understand."

Rind nodded and looked back at Stealth. "But why capture her? And the Staff?"

"The Staff? To keep it from the Ka. To keep it from Kaos. And to keep it until the Guardian was ready. The Warrior? That's more difficult to answer. My master was told the Warrior was needed – or would be needed." A grim smile crossed Stealth's face. "I am not one who knows all the ways of the Warriors of the Continuum."

"Warriors of IY," Rind corrected.

"You repeat a simplification made by the Iyes and their Story, I expect. My master says the Warriors walk the Continuum." He gave a wry smile. "But remember, I only know what I know, and I don't know all the rest."

Rind frowned. "I leave that for Lanky to discuss with you." Her penetrating gaze searched his face. "What did you do with Beth?"

Here it was. The thing that Beth didn't remember and something Jessica refused to discuss.

"My job was to place her and the Staff in a portal. That's what I was told, and that's what I did. Beyond that …" He shrugged. "I don't know."

"What is this portal?" Rind asked, frowning.

Gates. Access to Gates. A vision of him staring into the Void flashed into Lanky's mind. Staring into a vast darkness at the frenzied hordes of Kaos striving to pass. Suddenly, he understood. "Beth," he said in a ragged whisper. "She was held in that portal for thirteen thousand years."

"What!" Rind exclaimed.

Lanky stared blindly at Rind as the mind-numbing realisation seared his mind. "She was at a Gate. She was defending a Gate." He suddenly felt cold. "I know it now." Or were those the memories of Dysam? "She fought at the Gate for generation after generation, for sun-cycle after sun-cycle. For thirteen thousand years."

"Why?" Rind breathed.

"To await the hour of Jessica's need. To help her return to this Land to aid you. To bring back the Staff to aid you. To bring back your tribe's Mother." Fractured visions flashed past. *And I too have stood at a Gate …*

"I didn't know," Stealth said, deep sadness in his eyes. "I truly didn't know."

There was a noise to the side of Lanky, and he glanced around to see Gravel walking away. *Damn him. He can't just walk from this.* He made to stand—

"Leave him," Rind said, grasping his arm. "He will return."

Lanky's frustrated gaze followed the retreating figure of Gravel. "We'll have words later," he growled as he sat back down.

Rind moved closer to him. "Why didn't she tell us?"

Lanky slow breath was pained. "She didn't know. She has no memory of it."

Yet that was not quite true, he realised, remembering her talk of lurid, fragmented visions seemingly not of her own. She hadn't understood, but a part of her had been traumatised by what she'd endured, preventing her re-engaging as a Warrior.

An inner voice cut into his thoughts. *You know the hell she will have faced during those millennia at the Gate. You know, because you've been there.* His lips thinned. Maybe he had – he was now certain he had – but this wasn't about him. It was about the hell Beth had faced. *And she had no choice.*

He turned sharp and unyielding eyes on Stealth. "Did you and your master explain what she would be facing?" he said in a quiet, cold voice. "Tell her how to prepare for this little adventure? Ask her very clearly if she was willing to accept the trial laid before her?" He stood and walked up to the dragon's servant. "Did you?"

Stealth sat, unmoving, looking at the ground before him.

"Look at me! Did you?"

Stealth lifted his head and held Lanky's raking gaze. He shook his head.

Lanky glared at him, then turned away before he did something he'd regret.

"You didn't know?" Rind whispered by his side.

Lanky fought to quell his anger. "No. I knew she'd suffered some trauma. But this? No, I knew nothing of this hell."

"Why doesn't Beth remember?"

"Would you like to remember that nightmare?" He frowned. "But I don't think this is her just blanking it out. Jess knew what had happened. Maybe she blocked Beth's memory."

"Why would she do that?"

"I don't know. But in all that happens here, I still trust Jess." He held Rind's eyes. "We remain silent on this until I find out more."

Rind nodded.

"Warrior," came Stealth's voice. "Some things remain untold."

Scowling, Lanky swung his gaze to the dragon's servant. "Go on," he said, his voice bitter.

For the first time, he saw fear in the man's eyes. "Other portals exist within the Ancient's lair, holding more Warriors concealed from Kaos. And more enemy shamans – ones that should never be released. If the Ancient should fall …"

Lanky's stomach lurched. "Talk. I'm listening."

CHAPTER THIRTY-SEVEN

The Continuum. A most wondrous creation of the Dark. And with the addition of Life, and the A'ven? And the evolution of the Guardian? A most wondrously complex creation, indeed.

*S*pider took a long draught, then passed the skin of water to River, who in turn passed it back to Svana. "Thanks, Svana, I needed that," he said, wiping his mouth.

Svana replaced the stopper and placed the skin on the ground. Brushing matted, dark curls from her face, she looked up at the two before her. "Nice feather."

The girl, Inyana, put her hand up to her hair – then dropped it quickly, with a scowl.

A feisty one then, Svana noted.

"She has worn them as a tribute to her mother," said Kapano, sitting beside his granddaughter and looking with pride at the crisp white feather in her tied-back hair. "She was the best bird catcher of the tribe. Isn't that so, Inyana?"

Inyana glanced at her grandfather. She gave a barely perceptible nod.

Svana could see that there was an enduring bond between the two. *They've seen much together,* she thought, noting the scars on the girl's face and arms. *And they've survived together.* The girl would die rather than see anyone harm her grandfather.

Spider cleared his throat. "Are you well, Kapano?"

The old man's hand went to his side. He smiled. "Your healer helped. She tells me I will live another day, and so for that, I am thankful."

The throb in her arm reminded Svana of her own visit to Amber. *She aids us all—*

"Why are we herded like prisoners?" Inyana hissed, her face darkening again as she glared at Spider. "We helped you."

"I'm sorry, Inyana, but the Ka …" Spider glanced at River.

"The Ka sent assassins to kill me and others of my tribe," River said. "We are cautious."

Inyana's eyes narrowed on River. "Just who are you?" she demanded.

"I am the Mother of the Iyes."

The old man gasped. Inyana stiffened, then spun to face Spider. "You are of the Iyes?"

He nodded.

"You lied!"

Spider held up his hands. "No, not so. I gave you no tribe. And remember, you offered to help me, I didn't request it." He studied her for a moment. "You saw the Warrior; you must have guessed."

Inyana scowled. "I saw shamans fighting. I didn't know one was a Warrior. Who was the one we rescued?"

"Rind – the leader of the Iyes."

Her eyes widened. "I rescued …" With a muttered curse, she turned away.

So, accidental allies, Svana thought, seeing the anger in Inyana's stance. She noticed Kapano staring at the guarded Ka assassin. "You know that one?"

He hesitated. "I do," he said, eventually, his voice guarded. "He helped us." His brow furrowed. "Why is he a prisoner here?"

"He is Ka assassin, sent to kill our Mother," Spider said evenly.

Inyana spun around. "So, we are prisoners!"

"No," River said. "You are free to go."

"Hah! Free to wander this barbaric land until one of the Iyes thrusts a spear in our back."

"If that is what you believe, then so be it, but what I have said remains true." River's attention shifted back to Kapano. "But I do have questions. Depending on your answers, it may be possible for you to stay with us. If not, you must go. Today."

"An old man and his granddaughter, free to go," Inyana growled. "And how long would we last?"

River's eyes remained focussed on Kapano. "We will provide supplies for five days. That will be sufficient. It is not difficult to survive in this land if you head south."

Kapano seemed to consider, then: "Ask your questions."

Inyana cast him a severe sidelong glance.

River tilted her head. "My first isn't so much a question as a request. The Warrior you met tells of a tale you told. I'd like to hear it."

Inyana bristled. "We are not—"

Kapano held up his hand, quietening his granddaughter. "I will tell. But on the condition I hear the tale of the Iyes."

Although hidden well, Svana saw it: an excitement in the old man's eyes. "Are you a storyteller?" she asked softly. Or something more? *A spy?* But as she studied the man's face, she felt no flicker of unease. Even so ... *What does he seek? Or what does he hide?*

"He is the best teller of tales in the Land," Inyana gloated.

Svana noticed the inflection in the girl's voice. *She speaks of the 'Land' as do we Iyes.*

Inyana turned to her grandfather, concern shadowing her face. "But you shouldn't do this, Patra."

Svana heard the raw emotion in her voice. *She doesn't want him to share their story. Why? What do they hide?*

"Do you agree?" Kapano asked, his sharp eyes studying River.

Inyana laid her hand on his arm. He shook his head. Svana saw the flash of anger in his granddaughter's eyes.

"I agree," River said.

Seemingly satisfied, Kapano settled himself – then he told his tribe's story.

Svana sat captivated by the man's telling, hearing the rich timbre to his voice, one exotically accented, drawing her into the man's warm embrace as he spoke of the birth of the light of Kaos, of the wonder of Kaos, and of the coming of their people's saviour.

A tale well told, but one twisted by the lies of Kaos.

"Kaos protects us from the death and destruction of the Iyes and their Warriors. He keeps our Land safe and protects our waters. He protects Life."

As Svana listened, she thought, *I'm sure now, something remains hidden.* The anger that had burned in Inyana's face had faded as Kapano progressed with his tale; instead, worry crept into the girl's eyes. When Kapano finished, Svana saw relief. Relief at what? The things her grandfather had chosen to say. *Or the things left unsaid?*

"That's wrong," Spider said as soon as the man finished. "The Iyes have no wish to destroy this Land. It is Kaos who strives to destroy us."

"Kaos is a great god," Inyana retorted. "IY misleads you. IY—"

"It is you who have been—"

"Hold, Spider," River said gently. "One will not convert the other with a few simple words; our beliefs are too deep." She faced Kapano. "As promised, I give you the Story of the Iyes—"

500

"Svana!"

Glancing around, Svana saw Knuckles striding towards them. "Warrior Beth wishes to talk with the Ka prisoner. She wants us both there. Now."

Svana looked at River, who nodded and said, "Go. We will speak later."

Standing, Svana faced the two strangers. "I thank you for your story," she said evenly. Her eyes lingered on the girl. *There is something more here. Something they hide.* "At the Ka encampment, you mentioned a Song." *We cannot risk the Song, she said.*

Inyana glared at her. "You are mistaken, Iyes."

She lies. They tell their story but omit this Song. She glanced at Kapano and caught a fleeting tension in his face before it was gone. *What do you hide?*

She regarded him for a moment, then turned away. Following Knuckles across open ground to the cordon of guards surrounding the Ka prisoner, she struggled to make sense of what she'd heard, what she'd felt. And was it important? She grimaced. In these times, everything was important. *But this Song?* Once again, the vague memory of a tale told by Naga returned. A tale of an old shaman Naga said she'd once met. A shaman who had told of a song, one that could save the Land in its time of direst need. But that had been just another simple tale of hope amongst the vast wealth of storytelling across the tribes of the Land.

Hadn't it?

Sighing, she walked on. She would discuss with River later. In these frantic times, how to know what was important and what was not?

Like my dream?

She shortened her stride, then came to a stop as a heartbreaking vision burned in her mind: her standing in a boat, staring through blurred, tear-filled eyes at a lone woman on the shore.

A woman she dreamt was her mother.

She stood, shaken, an unbearable ache twisting her gut. Why, after so long absent, had this dream so abruptly and painfully returned? This dream of the forlorn woman on the shore. This dream of … *of my mother?*

A bitter taste crept into her mouth. For sun-cycle after sun-cycle as a child, she had dreamed this dream. Of her leaving this woman by the shore. Of believing that this woman would return to her side. And yet beyond this, there was nothing more. Just this single scene, played out time after time. *Until I managed to dispel it, banish it, free my mind from the torment.*

501

Because the unknown woman never came.

I grew up.

And yet over these last days, this painful dream haunted her – taunted her – once more. She clenched her fist. She couldn't be distracted by bleak echoes of the past. *It is nothing. It means nothing.*

Dragging her focus to the reality around her, she hardened her heart and walked on.

As she and Knuckles approached the prisoner's cordon, she saw Beth standing on the far side, her expression unreadable. As they drew closer, the Warrior signalled to the guards. The men, fighters of the Mancs tribe, stepped back and withdrew, forming a defensive cordon to the rear of the Ka prisoner, who stood, hands bound. The man was not as Svana had left him earlier. His once tidy long hair hung dishevelled, loose across his swollen eye and blood-matted face. She saw several deep cuts had appeared on his body.

Revenge was being sought.

She glanced at Knuckles, who frowned. Not instigated by Knuckles then, she thought with relief. She looked back at the Ka and felt a moment of surprise. She saw no fear in his beaten face, nor resentful or vengeful anger. Only the confusion and bemusement of a man seemingly unsure of where he was, and what he was doing. She had never seen someone who looked less like an assassin.

"You spoke two names," Beth said. "Why?"

The Ka didn't respond.

"I'll ask you again, why speak those names?"

His eyes remained downcast.

"Look up," Knuckles said firmly. "And answer the question."

The man looked up – but remained silent.

"What are you afraid of?" Svana asked, surprising herself with the question, uttered aloud.

He looked at her through his one good eye. "Myself."

"What is your name?"

"Shadow. The Walk—" The man winced and looked down again.

Beth came to Svana's side. "Why didn't you strike when you had the chance?"

The man looked up. "I tried. But I couldn't."

"Why?"

"He stopped me."

"Who?"

The Ka shook his head. "It can't be," he breathed, looking up at Beth, his good eye glistening.

Svana was shocked. *Is the assassin crying?*

"How can it be?" he whispered. "It makes no sense. Am I mad?"

Svana turned to Beth. "What's wrong with him? Is this some sort of trick?"

"It's no trick, Svana. There's a truth here not easily accepted – by him or by us. This man is a Warrior. Of IY."

Svana stared at Beth in disbelief. Then she glanced at Knuckles. "Did you know?"

Knuckles nodded. "I heard earlier. As Warrior Beth says, this isn't easy to accept." His face creased into a frown. "Or straightforward to deal with."

"I am a Disciple of the Ensi of the Ka," the man murmured, straightening to stand proud and defiant. "Nothing more, nothing less."

Now there's the man I expected, thought Svana, seeing confidence rising within the man. The confidence of a deadly assassin.

Beth took a step closer to the Ka. "Well, it seems that position is no longer needed. Your Ensi has been deposed."

"What!" he exclaimed, quickly scanning their faces. "You lie!"

"I don't lie," Beth said, her voice hardening. She took another step to stand before him. "Take a look."

A look at what, thought Svana, seeing the man stare at Beth in confusion. As the Ka held Beth's gaze, his eyes widened. "That can't be. You couldn't know of that."

"Our Warrior, a guest of your Ensi, saw what happened. A snake in your midst."

"Cobra!" The Ka's face twisted in anger.

"He was aided. A shaman."

"But Growl was here. He—"

"Not that cursed one," Beth grated. "Another. Krull is his name, from the tribes of the Meso people."

"Krull? He is nothing. He—" He stopped and looked up at them. "What are you doing? What do you want from me?"

"What I want doesn't matter here. But what does is that you have become my problem. They call you a Warrior. A Warrior of IY." Beth studied his stunned face for a moment, then turned to Svana and Knuckles. "Allocate a hut for him. And guards." She lowered her voice. "Keep him safe. I choose you because I trust you. Don't let me down."

Svana and Knuckles nodded.

"I'll see you at the eastern hut shortly," Beth said as she walked away.

Knuckles stared after her, then glanced at Svana. "Azar! I need this day to finish, then I can sleep and do my best to forget it ever happened."

"You're getting old. Sleep is for when you're dead. Then you can have a nice long rest before some future descendant comes knocking on your grave for advice."

Knuckles laughed.

Not a sound I've heard for a while. I've missed it. Her attention swung back to the Ka. "It seems you're to be our guest for a while. You'll do well to avoid a blade in the back, but we'll see what we can do to delay that."

She signalled to the Mancs men, then turned to Knuckles. "After you, old man," she said, waving him forward. "Age before beauty."

"You know, Svana," Knuckles said as he walked ahead, "you seem to have warmed to me during our long trip together. My hut is—"

"Your hut can stay where it is. As can—"

"My wit?" Knuckles said, smiling.

She glared at him, then an intriguing thought eased to the fore. "Mind you," she murmured. "Your hut could be just what we need right now."

A while later, she stood outside Knuckles's hut, smiling as its owner stood glowering back at her. "It's only for tonight," she said. She nodded to the Ka standing bemused before them. "And what better way to keep him safe than under your caring and watchful eyes? See you at the meeting hut shortly."

She walked away, doubting that Knuckles would gain any peaceful sleep with a Ka assassin by his side. Her smile became a grin. In wretched times like these, you had to take the small victories where you could.

*

Where is Sy when I need him most? Shadow thought, flexing his bruised jaw and trying to clear his head of the voices – and of the persistent drone, an untouchable infestation driving him insane. *Ignore them, answer the question.*

That one was easy to answer. *He abandoned me.*

No, he tried to kill me, and then escaped with Growl, leaving me trapped.

His fraught mind sought a reason. *He tried to kill you because it looked as though you'd become a traitor.* The memory of that moment flashed back. He'd stood beside the unkillable Warrior with an axe in his hand, and he hadn't struck. He'd had the chance and hadn't taken it. What must that have looked like to Sy?

504

But Growl and Sy were planning to kill me, anyway. That look ... I was a dead man walking.

But why?

You questioned the Ensi. You were digging into places you shouldn't. They kill our children ...

Flexing his bound legs, Shadow eased them to a less stressed position. The Iyes healer had treated the worst of his wounds, but several still felt as though the blade cut anew. *The Iyes hurt me, but they didn't execute me.* He had the unkillable Warrior to thank for that.

She called me a Warrior. A Warrior of IY.

What twisted game were they playing?

'*You must accept the reality,*' came a deep, melodious voice cutting through the maddening, pervasive drone swarming though his head. A shimmering vision drifted at the edges of his mind: a glistening surface of a deep blue sea, the looming shape of an enormous, sleek whale cruising beneath.

He blinked to clear the vision. "Go away and take your buzzing friend with you," he growled, recognising the voice as the one who'd invaded his mind before.

"What did you say?" the Iyes said ominously – Knuckles they called him. The man had been gone most of the evening, at a meeting of the Iyes tribe from what Shadow had overheard, and he'd been left in the company of cold and forbidding guards. They'd unbound his hands and brought him food at least, a pleasant respite from their harsh regard.

And from the relentless heavy humming in his head.

"Not you," Shadow said to the Iyes. "It's ... I was talking to myself."

"Well don't. I don't want to hear anything from you, understand?"

Shadow glanced sidelong at the Iyes, who was seated in the light of the late evening's fire. A man with sharp eyes, intelligent eyes. *It's always the eyes*, he thought, *how they react when first engaged.* Do they hold yours and smile, or do they skip away at first glance? Or maybe they hold, but defend, scared to reveal what little is behind. Any number of quick movements revealing much of the mind veiled behind. And although assailed, Shadow's mind still absorbed and assessed what he saw – and it saw this man was not one to slide a blade in his back while he slept. *So, what about you?* he challenged himself. *You're a man who has slipped a blade into many a man. And woman.*

Yes, for good reasons.

Are you sure?

The swarm in his mind swept towards him. "Go away!"

"I warned you," the Iyes man grunted, quickly standing.

"No, I'm sorry," Shadow said quickly. "It … it's difficult. I—"

"No, it's easy. You stay quiet. What don't you understand?"

I have bees swarming in my head and a whale talking to me. Shadow suspected his Iyes friend wouldn't listen too long to that story. "I don't know," he said lamely.

The man scowled at him but didn't move any closer. But nor did he sit. "Who are you?" the Iyes asked, tilting his head, his eyes narrowing.

I am Shaydu, the Shadow Walker. A Warrior of the Continuum. And I am needed.

Shadow stifled a moan and dropped his head in his hands. He was possessed. But possessed by what?

'You are what you are,' the powerful, melodic voice said as the droning grew louder.

"What does that mean?" Shadow muttered. "That makes no sense."

"Warrior!" Knuckles commanded. "Who are you?"

The Ka Disciple blinked.

And the Warrior answered. "I am Shaydu, Warrior of the Continuum."

Silence fell as Shaydu watched the Iyes watch him.

"How can I believe that?"

Shaydu smiled. "Because you are still alive."

"I'm alive because you're bound and—"

Shaydu calmly watched as the Iyes fell to his knees, hands to his head, screaming. The guards rushed in, the fire's light revealing their startled bewilderment – then they too fell to the ground screaming. Flexing granite–hard muscles, Shaydu snapped his bonds. He saw others converging on their shelter. *I think the point has been made.* He released his hold on the men before him …

And immediately a guard – quicker than most, Shaydu noted, impressed – flashed her spear towards him. He swayed to the left, hearing it whistle past his right ear.

"Hold!" Knuckles shouted, climbing unsteadily back to his feet.

"I am the Shadow Walker," Shaydu said evenly.

"Give us space," Knuckles growled, and Shaydu watched, amused, as the guards reluctantly stepped back, holding their ground at the edge of the fire's light. The Iyes strode up to him, glaring up from his low height. "Don't attack my men again. Ever."

Short in stature, big in heart, Shaydu thought. *But foolish to challenge me.*

He hesitated, sudden uncertainty tickling the edges of his consciousness. Something was missing here, something he had not yet remembered. *I must let this play out.*

He nodded his acknowledgement to the Iyes.

Brow furrowed, the Iyes walked a few steps away, grumbling to himself. Then he turned back, the firelight casting a stark relief to his troubled face. "What is wrong with the assassin?"

"He resists his fate."

"He killed our people."

"You were enemies."

"And now?"

Shaydu paused. "Let him speak with the dragon's companion. We would hear more of what he has to say."

The Iyes studied him intently. "You may go."

Shadow blinked, and through the drone of the bees, he answered the Iyes. "I am Shadow, Disciple of the Ensi."

*

The full tribe meeting had not gone well, with many reacting with shock, distress, even anger, at the news being shared: their leader, Bear, confirmed dead; the Guardian lost; and demonic new threats emerging in the land of the Ka. But beyond what had been openly told, heated rumours abounded of assassins and traitors, and of long-hidden, nefarious deals with the Ka. Too much, too quickly, and too few answers; and those few answers not enough to satisfy the tribe. *These will be a dangerous few days*, Beth thought as she walked back to her hut.

"Beth."

She stopped, then waited as Tricia walked towards her.

"I'm sorry," Tricia said, her face drawn as she halted before Beth. "I didn't know what else to do."

Beth placed a gentle hand on her friend's shoulder. "It should be me apologising, Trish." *For the behaviour of Bethusa.* "You stopped me doing something I'd regret."

"I know it wasn't your fault," Tricia said. "Even so …"

Even so, Bethusa is now a part of me. And whatever I do – whatever we do – I shoulder the responsibility for our actions. "You did the right thing." Despite her friend's presence, Beth cast an involuntary glance to her hut. *I'm so tired.*

Tricia caught her glance. "I'd better get on." She half turned to go.

With a shiver of guilt, Beth gently, but firmly, held on to her friend's shoulder. "A moment, Trish." Tricia's eyebrows rose in question, and Beth was shaken by the hurt in her friend's gaze. *I've not given her my time. I've abandoned my friend.*

She dropped her hand and stood back. "I know this is hard for you …" She saw the flicker of doubt in Tricia's eyes. "I promise you, I do.

507

It's just …" *It's just I don't have the time for you.* Deep down, beneath layers of a Warrior's hardened emotions, she felt sick at the brutal reality of those words. "I know we never seem to get the chance to talk." *To talk as friends.* "It hurts me too."

"I do understand," Tricia whispered after a moment. "Well, I sort of understand. I should never have come here. I know that now." She glanced back towards the camp. "But there's nothing I can do about it until … until you Warriors do what you need to do."

Beth tensed. What they needed to do was prevent Armageddon. *Yet our true enemy remains hidden.* Kaos. The one who sought this world's destruction. "That may yet be some time. What else can we do to help you?"

A forced smile appeared on Tricia's lips. "Send me home? Get me pizza tonight?" The smile faded. "I know the stress you and the others must be under. I do know that." She ran her hand through the thick curls of her hair. "How you handle what you face is beyond anything I could do. I—"

"Don't say that," Beth said fiercely. "You've faced terrors of your own here, and with no aid from the energy of the Land. You've fled with others in the dead of night as an enemy descended on us. You've seen people killed." She grimaced. "And you've been abandoned by your friends."

Tricia said nothing.

Because I speak the truth.

Because you don't need her, came the strident voice from within.

Beth forced Bethusa back.

"The truth is, you don't really need me here," Tricia murmured, echoing Bethusa's words. "But while I'm here, I'll do what I can." Her face lightened a fraction as a faint smile touched her lips. "And working with Amber gives me a purpose. Maybe I'll even stave off insanity until we get out of here." The smile so quickly faded. "We will get home, won't we?"

Tell her, Beth. Tell her that Jessica could most likely have returned us home already if that's what we'd decided. But we are Warriors. We must prevent Armageddon. "We have to do what we must, Trish, then we'll see."

Tricia's face fell, as if her dreams had been shattered. Yet she nodded. Then she stepped closer to Beth, a deep yearning in her eyes. "All I ask is you stay my friend, Beth. I want us to get back to where we were."

So do I, Trish. Below the surface I wish it for all the world. She found she couldn't speak.

Tricia leaned forward and hugged her. Beth hugged her back.

Tricia stepped away and smiled. "You look awful. You need to rest. Why are you talking to me?"

Beth returned the smile. "Because you're my friend."

"Right answer." Tricia glanced towards Beth's hut. "Go on. I've unloaded my problems on you, so I'll be fine now. Let's just make sure we talk more."

Beth nodded.

Her face set with exaggerated determination, Tricia gestured to camp. "Right, before I turn in, I should catch Amber. She wants me to prepare some weird concoction for tomorrow's patient. I reckon either his wound will kill him or this noxious brew will." She stepped in and gave Beth another hug. "See you tomorrow."

"See you, Trish," Beth replied, then watched Tricia walk away to camp.

She stood for a moment in silence. It was true they'd been forced apart, but she was sure the bonds between them were unbreakable. Weren't they? Could the horrors of this world shatter a wondrous friendship built from their earliest childhood? Unsettled by the disturbing thoughts, she headed for her hut, craving the moment's rest she desperately needed.

As she approached the shelter, her heart sank as she saw the hunched figure sitting by the fire beside the entrance to her hut. *Gravel.* He'd not been at the full tribe meeting, but with how this day had gone, she'd been thankful for his absence. The Shield didn't turn as she walked towards him but continued to stare into the fire.

"Why didn't you tell us?" he asked as she neared, his voice unusually quiet.

She halted before him. "Tell you what?" she said, bemused.

"Of your capture by the dragon."

"What of it?"

"Why did you come back?"

"Gravel, what the hell are you talking about?"

He turned, his rugged profile silhouetted against the light of the fire. "How did you survive?" he whispered. "I didn't know."

Beth's heart pounded in her chest.

She felt the febrile anticipation of Bethusa!

Why?

"To be locked away for so long, a hell that no one should suffer. How did you—"

A cacophony of sounds and emotions flooded in, and she felt herself falling …

509

Beth opened her eyes, then lifted her head from the cold, hard ground beneath her and gazed into an expansive chamber. The tumultuous torrent of images, voices, smells, and tastes that had assailed her had slowed to a flowing stream – still terrifyingly shocking, but freeing part of her mind to function, to assess what had befallen her. She pushed herself up to a seated position, then, feeling no pain, she climbed to her feet—

She froze as she noticed the woman standing on a stone dais before her. Of no great height, of no great age, she wore a dark green chiton tied off at the waist with a black sash. Her hair was short and spiky. Scanning quickly around the chamber, Beth saw a golden glow emanating from beyond the stone pillars to her right; but she saw no obvious threats. Threats? Returning to the spiky-haired woman, she sensed shapeless swirls of restless energy radiating from her. Yes, this could be a most deadly threat indeed.

The woman laughed. A rich and deep laugh that gave Beth no comfort at all.

"Who are you?" Beth asked, taking a step forward.

"One who is aiding you, as you aid me."

"And how are you aiding me?"

"To have all you witnessed – all you endured – played back in but a heartbeat, well, that would destroy you. And that cannot be. I have … protected you."

Beth's eyes narrowed. "I know who you are." She ran her eyes over the woman. "I didn't expect this."

The woman laughed again. "It is simple and pleasing. And maybe more natural for you to converse with."

"The form doesn't matter," Beth growled. "But why I'm here does."

"Always straight to the crux of it," the woman said, her smile fading. "Why are you here? It is time to remember."

Remember? What was there to—

Something shifted inside, and she froze. Her startled gaze snapped to a place in the shadows beyond the woman. "It was there," she whispered, feeling as if she stood before a dam wall straining against the might of turbulent flood waters amassed against it. She reached out, tendrils of her mind sweeping into the darkness at the far side of the chamber and travelling along the passageway beyond …

She sensed the portal. The portal to a Gate.

I was there!

I was there for millennia!

The dam wall broke and she staggered as a tidal wave of displaced memories whirled out of the shadows to engulf her. Violent images, strident sounds, and vicious, brutal emotions crashed over her, while whispering voices spoke of things forgotten, of peoples cursed by history, of devils lurking in the shadows, all chilling her to the core. It was as though all she had truly known had been buried, denied.

"Take your time, Warrior. Let it come slowly. Don't fight it, just watch from afar."

Beth struggled to rise to the surface, to break free of the raging torrent, but it kept pulling her under, threatening to drown her beneath fell currents of insistent urgency demanding their pleas be heard.

"Here, I will help you."

Powerful arms wrapped around her, raising her up from the maelstrom. Gasping, she broke through the roiling surface of the screaming currents, rising above them – yet a lashing storm of images and sounds continuing to rage past.

She felt the energy of the A'ven flow into her, and the violent storm eased.

Yet the startling memories continued to stream past. And the lives. Countless lives. Some forgotten by history; most never witnessed or recorded.

But she remembered them.

"Remember, but move on. It is time."

Braced by the enriching power of the A'ven's energy, she managed to pull further and further away from the terrifying onslaught of the past.

"Let it flow by. It cannot harm you there. It will simply become part of you."

With a desperate effort of will, she drew further and further away, until finally, the torturous stream receded to a dark corner of her mind, still seen and heard, but now dying to a faint whisper.

Released from the delirious ordeal, she sank to her knees, shaking. Yet many memories remained stark and vivid. *Did I live through all that? Did I survive that hell?* Head bowed, she knew with grim certainty the answer was yes.

She looked up. "Why? Why do this?"

The spiky-haired woman walked to the edge of the dais. "Because it was needed."

Anger flared. "That's no answer."

The woman on the dais tilted her head. "Yet it is true." She held up her hand as Beth climbed to her feet, hefting her Axe. "It was needed.

511

We would have lost the Staff, left the Guardian stranded in time – that could not be."

Her mind feeling raw and bruised, Beth glared at the woman. "But this? You locked me away and threw away the key for an eternity!"

A resurgent flurry of images swept into her mind – of the savage yet despairing faces of condemned men fighting in an unknown battle for an unknown cause at the foot of the mountain; of a lone traveller caught in a blizzard, his last words, "I tried"; of a man burying his daughter, the last of his line.

"Why this way?" she breathed, swamped by the anguished final moments of innocent souls. "Why endure this? Why not send me straight to Jessica?"

The spiky-haired woman looked down on Beth from the dais. "You are Warriors of the Continuum, and may travel the Cords of the Land, but to enter the Void to travel its vast timelines? No, only the Guardian has such a skill and power. Without the Guardian, the Void would destroy you."

The Gates ... I fought at the Gate.

But I cannot pass the Threshold without the Guardian.

Forcing those despairing memories of innocents to the edges of her mind, Beth's hand curled tightly around the haft of her Axe. "You sent Jessica and River there," she insisted. "You could have pulled them back."

"I am no traveller of the Continuum. They were not sent from this Land by me. No, the Dark tricked the Guardian, banishing her with the aid of Garrion, removing her from the game." She stepped closer to Beth. "The Guardian was in danger. We needed a Warrior to search for her. We chose you."

Unsure, Beth wiped her brow, waiting for more.

"You – and the Staff – were placed in the portal, to be released when you sensed the Guardian. It took time, it took patience, but you found the right time."

"There was another," Beth said slowly, sensing a ghostly, shadowy figure standing at the edge of her mind. "But I can't see."

The woman said nothing.

Beth fought to bring the figure closer – but it remained obscure.

There was another.

She looked back at the spiky-haired woman, picking her way through the scattered detritus of her thoughts. Jessica had been banished. *Without the Staff.* Because it had been stolen. "Why did the dragon take the Staff?"

The spiky-haired woman took a few steps along the edge of the dais. "When Warriors first arrive, they are seldom prepared for what is to come. Until the Warriors understand – until the Guardian understands – the Staff must be secured." The woman sighed. "I hoped that the Iyes would give the Guardian time, but in this case, the Dark had the aid of a traitor. The Ka were waiting for you all at the Arrival Site. They stole the Staff." A faint smile crossed her lips. "Yet those same Ka, acting on an ancient alliance, delivered that prize to their ally, hoping for rewards in kind. The Ancient received the Staff. The Ancient protected that Staff until the Guardian was ready." She scowled. "Yet even so, the traitor almost succeeded a second time, allowing Krull into the Sacred Chamber. The Guardian fleeing this Land almost won him this world, this Continuum."

"I don't understand."

The woman drew a quiet breath. "Parts of this you will never understand. And why? You lived – and fought – at a Gate for thirteen thousand years, waiting to intersect the Guardian's timeline, waiting to find the Guardian to save her. The Staff was protected for those thirteen thousand years. And Kaos hunted for it for thirteen thousand years. The Continuum … continued. Life did not stop. The wheel of time turned."

"But what were the Ka doing all that time? What were the Iyes doing? What happened here when I was … gone?"

The woman's bright eyes locked onto Beth's. "Ah, now you see it. What *did* happen during that time? What *did* Kaos do? How was this place – your portal – protected for all that time? Who won the war while you were within the portal?"

Who won the war? "What happened?"

The woman walked back towards Beth, a thin smile on her face. "I don't know. None of us within the Continuum know. All we know is its state today. All we know is what we see, feel, and remember. *That* is what happened. That is *all* that happened." Beth stared at the spiky-haired woman in astonishment. The woman held her gaze. "The Continuum adjusts to preserve continuity, to preserve alignment. And you intervened. You modified the Continuum. What might have been is no more. Only what is."

Her words staggered Beth. She had heard Bear talk once of this Continuum – a conversation seeming an age past now – but never fully connected with what he'd said.

Until now.

And it horrified her.

We are Warriors of the Continuum. Everything we do ripples through the ages.

And yet we are blind. We cannot be sure that what we do is right.

The spiky-haired woman walked to the edge of the dais and spoke. "What I do know is this. Whatever is happening across the Continuum, Kaos has not won. The Geddon has not been released."

"Because life still exists," Beth whispered.

The woman nodded. "Kaos seeks to break the Geddon's bindings in this time, but once free, the Geddon destroys the whole span of the Continuum." A faint smile crossed the woman's lips. "And as you said, Life still exists. It exists here, and it exists in that other age in which you fought."

Her smile faded as she knelt at the edge of the dais. "You fought here and survived. You recovered the Guardian. Kaos did not win. But the Continuum moves on. Kaos is now close, so very close. Life in this Continuum hangs in the balance."

Kaos didn't win. I fought and survived for millennia. "You should have told me, prepared me for that hell. I was just a pawn in the game."

The woman said nothing.

In the silence, the churn of images continued to flow. Distracting, but tamed.

And fragments of some other forgotten dream. "Something else happened. Something I did. I … I can't remember."

The woman remained silent.

Beth took a deep breath. "Who is Bethusa?"

The woman hesitated, then: "Bethusa was a formidable Warrior, one of the bravest of her age. Driven by a zeal to protect the innocent, she became the leader in her time. A woman with a passionate heart, yet one flawed. But when she died, this Land wept."

"And yet, her soul lived on."

"Yes, her soul lives on. A restless soul that now resides beside yours."

"And she wishes to become me."

"She wishes to aid the Land. It is for you to find the way for you both to succeed."

"And if I refuse her?"

"Then you will both fail."

*

River watched Svana walk away into the night, the light of their fire slowly losing its shadowy hold on the Iyes scout. She hadn't noticed the reactions of Inyana herself, focussed as she was on the tale of her

514

grandfather, but had no reason to doubt Svana's suspicion – *there is a piece of the Land's energy in that one* – that the two held something back. But there were far bigger things at large than the family secrets of those two.

She pulled her shawl closer around her as the cold northerly breeze suddenly picked up. A myriad of stars swirled in the clear night sky, foretelling a light frost in the early morning, the first of the year, earlier this year than the last. *Again.*

She turned to Spider. "What did you think?"

Spider paused before replying, fidgeting with something in his hand. "I think life has gotten a little more complicated."

The firelight caught the edge of the object he held.

Tremendous elation – and relief – flooded her soul as she saw a flash of carved bone. *My carved horse.* The carving she had crafted in what seemed a lifetime ago. Her heart leapt. Jessica had passed it on to him. *And he holds it still.*

"But I guess this was never going to be easy," Spider murmured. "It's just not taking the path I expected."

She felt his gaze on her. *Is he talking about us?* "Meaning?"

"Meaning, I guess, that our tribe held tales of these fabled Warriors of IY – these all-powerful, all-conquering saviours of our people – arriving to our Land to protect the future for our children's children. But it seems, even with their might, we're barely surviving from one day to the next, and losing more of our friends – and family – as we go. It's harder than I expected."

She heard a flavour of Spider's emotions as he spoke: confusion, frustration, regret, even an emerging despair. Emotions she'd sensed throughout the tribe. But Spider? She had known him as a brother for most of her life, and this man never despaired.

A brother?

No, I wish for more.

The thought was instinctive, and the desire was raw. *But I can't. Now is not the right time.* She hid a stab of pain. *But when is ever the right time?* She saw Spider looking at her, a slight frown on his face. *What does he see?* "Am I a Warrior? One of these all-conquering heroes of which you speak?"

He fidgeted. "I didn't mean ... You are—"

"Or am I the tribe's Mother? Or their shaman?"

"I—"

"My problem is my tribe's problem; I can see that now. I must choose. Give clarity and focus. Else ..." *Else we self-destruct.*

515

Spider looked down at his hands, the carving still obscured. "Do you want my advice?"

Always, Spider. Always. She nodded.

"Rind is a good choice of leader. There's a clarity of purpose about her, and she holds an unassailable bond with the Islanders. A boon for our allies, and a boon for us – it keeps our wider alliance intact." He looked up and met her gaze. "Now all she needs is some space to organise things around her, ready the tribe for the days ahead, ready their weapons and their minds."

Studying her, Spider wiped his brow, a nervous act in the cool of the evening. "And you, River? It is time to bring the Warrior and the shaman to our side. Leave the tribe now to Rind. We need the Warriors united, prepared to face the threat before us now. Tomorrow is important, but only if we survive today."

All at once, a flurry of swirling emotions swept through her. Sadness. Relief. Regret. *He's moving on. He leaves the question of us for now.* She forced a smile. "Ever practical, Spider. Ever—"

"And you should follow your heart."

River froze.

"You should *listen* to your heart."

She couldn't move, but her heart beat faster.

"Follow your heart," Spider repeated softly. "Follow wherever it takes you before the path disappears from under our feet."

But many paths lie before me, she thought, her mind spinning. *How can I be sure?*

He held out his hand – her treasured carving lay in his palm. "It saved me," he whispered. "I don't know how, but it saved my life for a second time." He smiled, his eyes lighting up. "I owe you two lives."

You owe me nothing, Spider ... my love.

Unable to speak, she held out her hands and closed them around his, only the crackling of the fire breaking the silence ...

Until Revri heard Gravel's footsteps running towards them.

Allowing the other time alone, Revri came to the fore. She pulled her hands away and climbed to her feet. She looked down on Spider. "She needs you. And keep the Rivatsa carving close."

"What?" Spider said, his eyes widening in confusion.

Gravel raced into the firelight. "River! It's Beth. She's gone!"

Revri picked up her Axe from beside her. "Calm yourself, she will not be away long."

"Hold on, what's happening?" Spider exclaimed, confusion writ on his face as his eyes flicked between her and Gravel.

"There was something Beth was missing, which is now being returned," Revri said. "And she would have had many questions for her host."

*

Tricia was feeling down. Not quite down and out, but heading for the floor, and not looking forward to getting back up. Maybe it was because of the news of Jessica, missing again, with no one seeming to know where she'd gone. Or maybe it was her dismay of what was happening to Beth, someone increasingly difficult to recognise as her old friend. *Or maybe it's because I've been told the world could end any day soon?*

But actually, it was far simpler.

She missed home, and she missed her friends. Not just her three closest friends, but her other, day-to-day friends at college. And she missed speaking with her mum. She missed going out for a curry on a Friday night. She was a normal, everyday person, and she missed her normal, everyday things to do.

She missed her way of life.

And I hate the life here.

There, she'd finally admitted it.

She hated it, and she was sick of it. Sick of the horrors of the land, sick of the deaths, the killings. Deaths of those she'd known in camp, and deaths of those she'd never met killed in a faraway enemy land. A hated enemy, she'd been told. But an enemy who'd helped save the world. This was a world she struggled to understand. And she feared it was one that would be harder to survive in. For her, and for her friends. Friends who, more and more, she also struggled to understand.

Her high of a few days ago was now past. History. Flushed down the toilet along with the tidal wave of crap flung their way, gurgling down the pan with a garbled message of 'the end is nigh'.

But you bloody asked to come here.

And that had been a grave mistake. But what could she do? *Just keep doing what you're asked to do and help where you can.* She sighed and walked on through the camp, unable to escape the weary chains of her dark thoughts.

Approaching her hut, she saw the fire was dead, so clearly Beth was still out and about somewhere within the camp. *Great, my turn with the fire again.* Though, to be fair, it was not so much of a burden when you got the hang of it. 'Borrowing' suitable, handleable pieces of burning wood from your neighbour certainly speeded up the process. But it would have been nice, occasionally, if Beth did the stealing. *Let her reputation suffer for a while.*

As she reached the entrance to the shelter, she cast a weary glance to the cold ashes of the fire. *Sod the fire. I'm heading straight to bed.* She pulled back the entrance flap, crouched down, and entered—

A hand grabbed her round the shoulders, and another clamped over her mouth.

"Don't scream. Erin needs you. Get them to this place." A name and an image flashed into her mind. "I'm sorry, Trish."

She felt a blow on the head. And the world went black.

*

"This had become my favourite time," Rind murmured, sitting by her hut and looking up at the clear night sky. "All the day's tasks done, the camp quiet, and any troubles to be dealt with on the morrow."

"And now?" Lanky asked, pausing his quiet, reflective humming. He prodded the glowing embers with a stick, sending a fiery spray of sparks into the air. *I could do this forever,* he thought, enjoying this briefest moment of respite in this most hateful of times.

Hearing no answer to his question, he looked up.

Rind gazed to the night sky.

He watched the firelight playing on her rounded cheek, saw the gentle slope of her nose, watched her keen, glistening eyes studying the heavens.

"Do you ever wonder what other life may be out there?" she murmured, still not answering his question. "Whether two other people sit around a fire looking back at us?"

"I do," Lanky said, childhood memories flooding back. "I have."

"And do they understand this?" she said, waving her arm across the sky. "Do they understand this any better than we do?"

He lifted his gaze to the sky. A myriad of stars looked back at him. He reached for the energy of the A'ven and felt its comforting vibrations. If he could find the right Cord, could he travel out there? Could he travel the universe? Could he find those two other lives Rind spoke of? And *could* they explain what was happening? "I doubt it," he said quietly.

"Then it is down to us …"

He gazed up at the stars. He could travel the stars, he was sure of it. But navigate his way through the vastness of space to find those two people? He looked up at the brightest star in the sky. Out of the almost infinite number of Cords out there, how to find the right ones to visit that precise one? *Or that one,* he thought, looking at another star. No, if other life existed out there, they'd be no use to them here.

And yet …

The Continuum. A universe spanning the ages. A concept so vast that it was impossible to truly comprehend. *All I see is the narrowest snapshot of this Continuum, a single moment in time. I don't see the vast, almost incomprehensible realm from its primordial past to its unfolding future.*

And yet it existed. *Jessica travels it! She brought us here.*

It remained a staggering concept. The Continuum. Vast, alien, and yet one spoken of by Bear, a man millennia before their time. *And by this old man, Kapano, who holds his own ancient story of his people.*

The memory of that tale triggered a dread thought. *Destroyers.* Both the story of the Iyes and that of the old man spoke of destroyers. *Of the Geddon.* If released, could these destroyers travel the universe? He glanced back at the brightest star. *Can they travel there? Or there?* Did this Geddon threaten all life in this universe? In the Continuum?

Yes, came an answer from deep within.

"Lanky?"

Shaking himself from his reverie, he drew a deep breath. What had Rind said? All troubles would be dealt with on the morrow? *I doubt this one will.* "Sorry, what did you say?" he managed.

"I said, what do you think those two up there would be doing right now?"

He gave a mock frown. "Who are those people? You know them or something?"

She laughed. "No, just curious."

"Curiosity killed the cat …"

"Which cat?"

Lanky smiled. "Doesn't matter."

"You didn't answer my question. Do you think they are in love?"

He glanced at the distant stars. "If so, it's light years of love," he murmured absently.

He felt Rind's gaze on him.

Suddenly feeling warm, he poked the fire with the stick. "And I reckon they'll be heading off to bed, as it's late."

"A good idea," she said, slowly rising to her feet. She stretched. Lanky saw her lean profile against the simmering glow of the fire. She turned her head and caught his eyes. "It is late … I'm heading inside."

He felt a dryness in his mouth.

Her eyes held his. "I wish you to be with me tonight."

Lanky felt his heart leap. He nodded.

Rind held out her hand. Lanky climbed to his feet and reached out. A shiver ran through him as their hands touched. "Come," she said. "This night is for us."

CHAPTER THIRTY-EIGHT

*Krull's misunderstanding of Kaos – and of the Geddon –
led to the slaughter of the Ka. Whether he understood at
the end of things, I don't know. And maybe I don't need to.*

"What happened here?" Nefra whispered, standing horrified
beside Sy.

The Shade did not answer.

Nefra watched the red dragon rising higher as it arrowed south
towards the titanic battle raging in the fiery skies on the horizon.
Within the glowing clouds cut by blistering gouts of flame it was
impossible to distinguish friend from foe, or who held dominance over
another, if anyone. She cast her disbelieving gaze back to the gravel
plain before her. An eerie silence had descended in the wake of the
horrendous cacophony that had rolled across the plain from the Ka
homeland ahead. Screams of terror, desperation, and death that had
rent the air until mere moments ago as the red dragon's fire had
sprayed across the camp. And another evil had stalked the camp, one
unseen from their distant vantage, but revealed by the dense black
clouds that had thundered into being across the encampment.

And their Shade hadn't moved. *He's afraid.*

"What happened here?" she whispered again.

And yet again, the Shade did not answer.

"We can't just stand here and watch," Nefra said, anger creeping
into her voice. "We must help. We must act."

Beside her, Sy nodded. He started walking to the camp.

With a contemptuous glance at Growl, she turned to follow Sy. "You
can't abandon your people, Shade."

She walked on after Sy towards the distant encampment.

521

A moment later, she heard the crunch of the Shade's feet in the gravel behind her.

As she walked across the sandy gravel plain, she felt exhaustion sweeping over her. Their mission to the Iyes camp had been a disastrous failure, and only the Shade and his power of the Dark had got them out of that cursed place alive. And she'd suffered hell at the hands of the Iyes. Her anger flared. She'd done all she could – given all she had – to provide the others time to free themselves. *I gave Shadow time.* She scowled. But how had the cursed Disciple repaid her? She saw him again, standing meekly beside the Iyes Warrior, axe in hand. *Why didn't you strike? Why didn't you take the chance?* Her weariness deepening, a pained and bitter regret closed around her. *I helped you, Shadow. I gave you a chance.* She heard the Shade striding on behind her. *Which was more than others would have done.* For she'd seen clearly Growl's intent. He'd planned to kill the Disciple. A command from the Ensi? Or an action of the shaman himself?

Or his daemon?

Nefra cursed under her breath. These lands would be a better place without those shrouded creatures of the Dark, creatures who distorted even the strongest of minds. *We don't need them. We just need the might of unyielding people. People who can protect our tribes and our families.* The thought came unbidden. *People like Shadow.*

No! He is lost to me now.

She grimaced. *And yet …*

Cursing again, she slammed those thoughts aside. He would be dealt with at another time. Walking on, she fixed her attention on the burning camp seen through the shimmering haze ahead.

Before long they reached the Rim of the encampment and passed the first of the bodies. Scorched and burnt bodies of those who had tried – and failed – to escape the reach of the dragon and the other, still unknown, killers. She shuddered at the apocalyptic devastation laid bare before them: trees, huts, vegetation – and people – all burning. And with each step, another body. With each step, the sickening realisation that they were too late.

"They have killed them all," she whispered.

A hand touched her arm, and she turned to see Sy pointing towards the temple. Shielding her eyes from the bright sky, she saw distant figures standing on the rise by the temple entrance. It was impossible to make them out from afar.

"We must leave," Growl said behind her.

Fear lanced into her gut. "Why?"

"We are in danger."

Lithe muscles tensing, her eyes scanned around them. "From who?"

He didn't answer.

Nefra glanced at Sy – who gestured to the temple, then walked off.

Ignoring the fear settling in her stomach, she followed.

"This is a grave mistake," Growl said, but she heard him follow as well.

As they crossed the boundary ditch into the Flanks, she saw the charred remains of men, women, and children, many armed, but many not. Fighters mixed with fishers, mixed with weavers, mixed with … She pulled her horrified gaze away. The whole community had been slaughtered!

She almost walked into Sy, who'd stopped abruptly in front of her. He was studying a group of bodies off to the right, a slight frown on his face. She forced her gaze to the blackened bodies. "What is it?"

Sy pointed at the group of bodies to the right, and then at a scattered group to his left. And then she saw it. The bodies here were blackened in places, but – apart from the contorted faces, gruesome death masks reflecting their agonising last moments under the sun – there were no signs of mortal wounds. She glanced at Growl. "A shaman?"

He gave no answer.

They set off again, her unease growing. *What do we face here? And what is it you plan to do?* For both questions, she had no answer.

They crossed into the Core, where the body count dropped, but saw no sign of a living soul. *Apart from those up at the temple.*

Reaching the slopes of the temple rise, they began the ascent. She glanced up and saw a group of four figures walking along the wooden walkway towards them. Beyond them, another group of fighters stood silently at the temple entrance, looking out over the remnants of their homeland. *What were they doing whilst their comrades died?*

As they stepped onto the walkway, Nefra studied the group approaching. She recognised the two men in front: Xerses, one of the Disciples of the Ensi, and the tall, shaven-headed shaman beside him. *Krull.* Her father's shaman. Why was he here? *And who are these?* She stared in disgust at two ragged, corpselike figures standing behind Krull, manic grins on their withered faces, both twitching with barely suppressed rage, both glowering at her with hate-filled eyes. And both with Black Staffs in their hands.

"Nefra," Krull acknowledged with a smile. He ignored Growl and Sy.

"Krull. Xerses. What happened here?"

"A most brutal betrayal," Krull answered, his smile fading. "By the leader of the Ka."

His answer stole her breath.

"It is true," Xerses stated, the distress clear on his face. "The Ensi betrayed us. Brought the enemy upon us. Brought Warriors into our temple."

"And see where this has led," Krull rasped, sweeping his arm around the camp, his voice carrying to the group of fighters by the temple entrance. "The destruction of the Ka." He turned to the fighters. "See their work, brave defenders of Kaos. See the work of the devil Warriors and their dragons."

Nefra felt someone push past her. "I saw what happened, Krull," Growl said in a cold voice, his silver eyes glaring at the shaman. "Not quite as you would have us believe. I—"

"Silence!" Krull commanded, turning back to them. "I see you, Shade. I see your treachery, your alliance with the Iyes. You—"

"Treachery?" Nefra said, aghast at the shaman's words. "We barely escaped with our lives. Our mission—"

"Yes, your mission," Krull snarled, his eyes afire. "Sent by the traitorous Ensi to lead the enemy shamans to our door."

Nefra stared at the shaven-headed shaman in utter disbelief. "That's not true. Why do you say this? Xerses—"

A wall of blackness erupted before them, and Nefra stumbled backwards, dazed, as a series of violent blasts rocked the wooden platform. Sy grabbed her arm and hauled her to the ground. Crouched low beside him, she looked up, eyes wide, to see Growl backing towards them, firing bolt after bolt of sizzling energy at Krull, who stood before a cowering Xerses deflecting each vicious strike with his Staff.

A knot of terror twisted her gut. What had happened here? Who—

The two ragged shamans leapt forward—

There was a tremendous blast, a splintering crack—

Nefra hit the ground, striking her head on a rock.

Darkness descended.

*

Nefra lifted her head and retched. Her head hurt. Badly. *What happened? What in Kaos's name has happened?* She tried to move again—

An intense pain flashed through her head, and her stomach lurched. She heaved again, then rolled onto her back and lay still, the horrific images from the ravaged Ka homeland burning in her mind.

How long she lay there, she didn't know, but when the throbbing pain in her head finally eased, she opened her eyes and squinted up at a bright blue sky above, wafts of cold air sweeping across her face. *Cold air?* She tilted her head to the side and saw snowcapped mountains looming in the distance. *Kef! Where has he taken us now?*

Groaning, she pulled herself up and scrambled to her feet, ignoring the heaving wrench in her stomach. She stood on a broad ledge jutting from a mountain cliff, looking down into a verdant river valley below. There was silence, save for the alarmed twittering of birds in the treetops to her right. She turned to see Sy squatting on the ground, looking down at the supine form of the Shade, who lay still, eyes closed. Grimacing, she strode over to them. "Is he alive?"

Sy nodded.

"How badly hurt?"

Sy shrugged, but Nefra could see the concern on the man's face.

Kef! She scanned Growl's body but saw no obvious injury. "Just us here?"

Sy nodded again.

So, they had escaped. But escaped what?

Nefra sat back on her haunches. Xerses was no close friend of hers, but she knew his reputation as a principled man, a loyal supporter of the Ensi. And yet this same man had now accused the Ensi of betraying her people! And Krull – what was he doing there, with those crazed shamans beside him? *He serves my father. Why is he not by his side?*

Nefra climbed to her feet, dazed and confused.

And with a sudden, burgeoning anger at the thought of all she had done, all she'd sacrificed. All those sun-cycles of meticulous planning with her father to align the Meso tribes and the Ka. All those sun-cycles of patient engagement with the Ensi of the Ka to align their interests. All those sun-cycles of loneliness and abstinence.

All that to capture the one she desired.

Shadow.

And now it was gone! All destroyed before her unbelieving eyes.

She stormed to the edge of the rocky platform. "Who did this!" she roared, looking in fury to the sky. "Who!"

Shaking, she drew a ragged breath. After all that had been done, after all the sacrifices that had been made, it made no sense for anyone to destroy their plans ...

Unless ...

She whirled around, her eyes narrowing on the accursed shaman. "What have you done?" she hissed. She strode across to Growl, and grasped his scorched tunic, hauling his limp body towards her. "You've done something. What have you done!"

A hand rested on her shoulder, gentle yet insistent.

She released her hold on the shaman and pushed Sy away. "Leave me!" she hissed, climbing to her feet. "Don't touch me again!"

She strode angrily away. He would pay. She would—

There was a movement to her side, and she watched with wary eyes as the Shade's menacing black wolf padded out from the trees, dropping to its haunches beside him.

"Your wolf won't stop me, old man," Nefra threatened. "If you need to die, I can wait."

Two more black-coated wolves – then a third – padded out from the trees, coming to rest to form a cordon around the shaman.

"I will get my answers," she avowed, glaring at the beasts now lying by Growl's side. "And then someone will pay."

CHAPTER THIRTY-NINE

Some Warriors fight the roaming daemons. A very few serve as Wardens of the Geddon. Most fight at the Gates, protecting the Continuum from incursion of the Dark. So, was it unreasonable to use them this way? To save Life, I think not.

*B*eth groaned as she rose from her grass bed, her head thick with the fogged remnants of a disturbed night's sleep. She heard random mumblings from the other bed; Svana seemed to be suffering from her own sleepless night. "Welcome to the club," Beth muttered. The intense dreams – nightmares even – had continued unabated, her brain refusing to relent, churning through the heaving turmoil of the last days and the shocking revelations from Fen and IY.

IY. The one who had made the call to place her in stasis, to lock her away for millennia defending the Gate, whilst waiting for her path to cross the Guardian's. Trapped in relentless battle with the Dark, her world had moved on, countless lives coming and going, mere sparks in the firelight, no sooner starting their journey than gone forever, and forever forgotten. And yet on they came, those fleeting sparks of hope, driven on by their fiery creator; sometimes dimming, sometimes blazing brightly, those latter lucky few catching the attention of the watcher before, all too briefly, just another faded memory.

But at least witnessed.

And all the while, she'd fought on at the Gate, defending the Continuum, defending these precious embers of life, allowing them their fleeting moments of glory.

Glory? What glory? They know nothing! See nothing. Do nothing. Why do we still fight for them?

Beth pushed the embittered thoughts away, the thoughts of the other, a continuation of the unrelenting inner battle between her and Bethusa.

Wasn't this the clearest sign of madness?

It is madness you still remain. You are a distraction. Stand aside.

Beth reached out into the darkness and grabbed her clothes. She didn't care what time it was, she needed air; she needed to move.

To get away from herself.

To get away from the memories.

'No,' came the lilting voice of the spiky-haired woman. *'It is time for you to remember all. The battle must be joined. We must all work as one.'*

Beth's anger instantly flared. "You hold everything back from me for this long," she hissed under her breath, "and only now say I should remember?" 'No,' she pulsed. *'I remember enough. Thirteen millennia is enough.'*

'You both must understand. He needs your support. You must help the others accept him. It is time.'

Grimacing, Beth pulled on her leggings. *'Yet again, you talk in riddles. No more games. Leave me.'*

She slipped on her moccasins and jacket, then clambered out of the hut. *Games. Always games.* Scowling, she walked out into the silent camp.

*

Shadow rolled over and tried, yet again, to calm his racing thoughts, to bring back the controlled mind of a Disciple. But, at the nexus of his greatest crisis, he was failing. He couldn't kill the relentless droning in his head.

'Accept what you are,' came the deep, melodious voice of the one who'd spoken before. The image of the vast whale floated into his mind.

Shadow groaned. This couldn't go on. It was driving him mad. *I am mad.*

He sat up, rubbing his head. The voices were daemons, he knew that now. Why and how they were torturing him, he didn't know. But it had started with that cursed axe. *The Axe.* Somehow, that axe had drawn the daemons to him, infecting him, poisoning his mind. *And the unkillable Warrior knows this. She plays some hidden game.* Well, he was done with the game. It was time to escape the poisoned web she was weaving around him.

He glanced around in the dark. The Iyes called Knuckles was lost in the gloom, but he could hear the man's steady breathing, evidence of his deep sleep. Shadow stilled his own breathing, listening intently for any movement outside. Nothing. He glanced to the sealed doorway of the hut. This was his chance, maybe his only chance. But what about a weapon? Could he search the sleeping man? *I could search a dead man.* He pushed the thought away. This one was strong, and likely to awaken before he got close.

'*You can leave now,*' came the powerful voice. '*The guards are sleeping.*'

Shadow froze. '*What trick is this?*'

'*No trick. I can help you.*'

'*I don't believe you. Who are you anyway?*'

'*Balena. One who once walked your land. And the other, Melapis.*'

Walked? A whale? He cast that aside. '*This Melapis ... can't they be quieter?*'

The buzzing in his head eased to a low hum.

He frowned, surprised. And suspicious. '*Is the guard really sleeping?*'

'*Look for yourself. What do you have to lose?*'

'*My life?*' He'd killed two of their people. Eventually, an Iyes would kill him.

But maybe not in this moment.

Reaching for his tunic, he slipped it on, then rose and crept cautiously in the darkness to the hut entrance. Pulling back the hide, he glanced out into the gloom of the dawn's first light. There, around the glow of a small fire, lay three guards, sleeping.

'*This doesn't seem a people to tolerate sleeping guards – what have you done?*'

'*As I said, I can help you.*'

Shadow scowled. *The question is why?* But questions could come later. *Ignore all else. Move.* He stepped silently out into the cool morning air, and seeing only two distant figures, he walked quickly around the hut, keeping an eye on the sleeping guards. Not one of them moved. *Okay, walk on. And be confident.*

He veered away from the guards, lengthening his stride ...

And strode into someone coming the other way.

Hands instinctively raised, he collided with the other—

It was if a bolt of lightning lanced into his mind, and his head exploded into a cacophony of sound, of striking images, of familiar aromas ...

Of startling memories.

Memories of another time.

Bethusa!

'*I did say I could help you,*' came Balena's distant voice.

Beth pulled the cords of her jacket tighter around her neck to keep out the predawn chill as she trudged through the camp, no clear destination in mind.

And there is your problem! You don't know what you're doing here. You must depart this Land.

I defended the Gate. I survived that hell.

You did nothing! You are a child – a distraction who has lost us precious time. Leave before it is too late!

I won't relinquish control to you. IY brought me here to aid this Land, aid my world.

Hah – you are as ignorant as the boy. You —

Well, teach me, damn you! Work with me! Show me what —

It was because of you that Garrion turned. Disillusioned by the weakness of your people, by the state of your Land – by your future. Disillusioned by the Warriors. You —

That's a lie! Garrion wasn't there. She didn't travel.

Travel was not needed, when your mind shows all. Everything laid bare for the daemon to see. You —

You should have helped me, you fool! Together we can be strong!

Together? You wouldn't engage me or embrace me. You pushed me away, tried to suppress your own soul. Oh, you used me, yes, at those times when you most needed me. But understanding? There was none!

Beth shivered. Was that true? Had she failed to understand? Was it—

No. There is no we, only I. I am the Warrior. Stand aside, else I will fail.

I will not —

A figure strode into Beth's path.

Hands raised for impact, the man – the Ka – collided with her.

Their hands met—

She staggered as a blaze of white light exploded in her mind.

The other rose – *Bethusa* – and she felt their souls meet.

A blistering storm of vivid memories engulfed her.

The memories of Bethusa!

*

Stalking the snorting boar as it foraged through the forest's thick undergrowth, the girl heard faint cries in the distance by the river. Immediately abandoning the hunt, she locked on to the sounds, then ran, angling downriver of the cries, figuring that if the person was in the water, they'd be swept quickly through the rapids and emerge into the calmer flow below. Running easily, she glided through the oak forest, following the well-trodden animal trails she knew so well. She had only seen nine sun-cycles but was already a respected tracker and hunter – today had been a lucky escape for the boar.

Breaking through the cover of the trees, she arrived at the bank by the base of the rapids. The sporadic cries sounded louder now but came from upriver. And were not getting closer. Changing her plan, she set off upstream, following the bank and scanning the whitewater of the boulder-strewn rapids.

And then she saw him. A boy. Perched on a glistening boulder sitting in the midst of a raging torrent, occasional waves scurrying up the rock face and covering his feet. He faced away from her, looking at the opposite bank. She saw at once she'd no hope of reaching him and had no idea how he could get himself safely off the rock.

"Hello!" she shouted.

The boy turned on hearing her voice—

Then slipped.

He fell into the raging torrent and disappeared from view.

One problem gone. *He's off the rock.* She spun around and headed back downstream. As she raced along the riverbank, she caught no sight of the boy within the rapids. It was now in the hands of the Spirits. *I hope this boy gave them good reason to help him.*

Breathing easily, she reached the calmer waters beyond the rapids and waited. And waited. *It seems he didn't clear the—*

In that moment, she saw his body emerge from the rapids, floating facedown into the calmer waters. Without a moment's hesitation, she raced further downriver, stopping where she thought it best to intercept his body. She dropped her spear and pack, and discarding her tunic, she quickly undressed. Bracing herself for the icy waters, she clambered down the bank and into the river, and began swimming out.

She judged it to perfection. Treading water, she caught his floating body, then, floating on her back, kicked for the shore. Moments later, she hauled the body out of the water and onto the muddy bank. Remembering a tale told by her grandfather, she heaved the boy on to his chest, straddled his legs, then lifted him up by his hips, tilting his upper body forward. It had the effect of pushing the side of his face into the mud – *just watch he doesn't swallow it* – but she saw water pour out of his open mouth.

And then he coughed. And coughed again, spraying water into the mud.

With a great sigh, she dropped him, mud splattering her legs, and collapsed, exhausted, onto the grassy upper bank.

When she finally drew herself up to sit on her haunches, she found the boy sitting in the mud, staring at her. It was difficult to tell, but he looked slightly younger than her. She smiled. "Well, apart from being covered in mud, you look okay."

"Did you save my parents too?"

Her smile froze. Her heart sank. "I didn't ... there was no one else."

The boy looked down. And was silent.

She glanced to the river, tracking it down to the second set of rapids. And the falls beyond. There was no point searching.

But she did anyway.

She told the boy to wait up on the grassy bank to dry in the sun, and after recovering her clothes, pack, and spear, she searched downriver until the sun was low in the sky. Until she could finally accept the boy's parents were gone.

She made her way back to the boy. "What's your name?"

"Shaydu."

"Well, Shaydu, come with me to my camp. Tomorrow, we'll see if your parents have returned." A small lie, to ease his pain for now. *But who will ease mine?*

"Who are you?" the boy asked.

Who am I?

"Bethusa," she said.

But who am I?

*

Shadow's mind staggered under the fury of the images flooding past. *Memories,* he thought, fighting desperately to avoid being washed away by the torrent. *Mine, or another's?*

The torrent parted, and a single vivid vision hurtled towards him.

The vision engulfed him, and he entered the memory.

He stood over the body of a young woman lying still on the ground, blood dripping from a wound in her head.

"She fought well," a remembered voice said behind him. "Better than her family."

He spun around, and seeing the shadowy frame of the new arrival, stepped away from Bethusa's blood-spattered body, angling towards the other corpses strewn across the rocky ground.

"You arrived too late, Brother," the man said, stepping out from the shadows of the boulders, hefting his obsidian-headed axe in one hand, and holding a burnished black staff in the other. "But at least I flushed you out of the shadows."

Shaydu cast anguished eyes over the fallen of Bethusa's family, then slowly turned to his brother, seeing the hate in the man's eyes. "Why?" he asked. But he knew.

"You don't need to ask," the man said, stepping over Bethusa's body. "She is a devil. As are you."

And she turned down your brutal advances. "This could have been so different, K'zarz. We are no threat to this tribe. We—"

K'zarz spat. "You speak your foul words to the young, contaminating their souls and turning them away from the righteous path, taking them away from the protection of Kaos." He took a step towards him, baring his teeth. "And you speak to the elders, weaving your spiteful web of lies, swaying them to break from the Ka. And you say you are no threat? You and this devil woman are a mortal danger to our tribe."

"It's not the Ka I fear. It's those leading them. Those shamans—"

"You fool!" K'zarz stormed. "Those shamans are our protectors!" He took another step forward, his eyes afire with sudden fervour. "You speak from perilous innocence, Shaydu. A blasphemous ignorance. But soon, I will join the Ka and their shamans. I will bring them to our land. Then all will see the Truths. All will see the glory of Kaos! All will—"

"All will resist," Shaydu said quietly. "And I will be leading them."

With a snarl, K'zarz thrust out his staff.

Shaydu cried out as a bolt of blackness struck him in the chest, hurling him to the ground, his body afire.

"See what they teach me," K'zarz snarled. "See what I become."

Shaydu tried to pull himself up, but his legs refused to obey.

"Go back to your shadows, Shaydu." K'zarz raised his staff. "And stay there!"

A haze of darkness appeared around the staff, writhing tendrils reaching for him—

An explosion of light rocked K'zarz, and he staggered backwards.

Bethusa climbed to her feet, her Axe aloft, crackling streams of energy lancing towards K'zarz. Shaydu's brother stumbled, his face contorted with pain as he frantically tried to hold the searing strikes at bay. Then, with a hate-filled glare at Bethusa, he turned and ran.

Bethusa dropped to her knees.

Freed from whatever binding K'zarz had thrown at him, Shaydu scrambled to his feet and ran to Bethusa, who was kneeling on the ground, her hand held to her bloodied head.

"Let me see. How bad is it?" He winced as she removed her hand. "We need to treat this."

"I'll live," Bethusa muttered. Her breathing laboured, she looked up at him. "We have to get away, Shay. K'zarz will return."

"But the wound … and your family. We need to—"

"They … they will be avenged. And we need to survive." She climbed unsteadily to her feet. "Pass me the water."

Shaydu lifted the strap of his waterskin over his head, took out the stopper, and passed her the skin. She took a swig before pouring the rest over her head of short, unruly hair. Her chiselled face hardened. "We should move north. There is one I must meet. One we both must meet."

"Who?"

"She goes by the name of IY." Shaydu saw the fire in her eyes, of hope burning with hunger. "She can help us, Shay. Because I now know what we are, why we're different."

His unease was tempered by … anticipation. *How did you do what you did here, Bethusa? How did you release the power of the sacred Axe?* "What are we?"

"Warriors," Bethusa said. "We are Warriors."

*

Beth gasped as the shimmering vision of the young boy vanished.

Blackness descended.

Other shocking memories swept in. And so real …

The pressure surrounding her was immense, but she held … just. She scanned the blackness ahead, but there was nothing to see, no faint glimmer of hope. Instead, only another moment of deadly distraction, fatal for her and her partner if she succumbed.

She grasped for some point of reference to steady herself.

I feel the rock beneath my feet.

She forced herself to take a step. Just a step, but it was enough. She stood tall and steady, facing the daemon of the Dark that had assailed her.

Her face hardening, she hefted her Axe and allowed more of the A'ven's rich energy to flow through her, strengthening her hold on the rabid daemon beyond the Threshold of the Gate. A terrifying pressure ravaged her mind and her soul as she struggled to control the staggering power she wielded, while resisting the crushing forces of the Dark.

But she was Bethusa. Nothing would pass.

She felt Shaydu by her side. *Nothing will pass us!*

Nothing had passed.

How long now? How many turnings of the moon? And how many dread daemons come and gone? And yet still the servants of the Kaos assailed the Gate with a ferocious fury, each hurling themselves at the Warriors in their desperate attempts to enter the Continuum and achieve that demanded of them.

To reach the Geddon. To release the Geddon.

But though she didn't know how she'd arrived at this Gate – *but the stench of the Ancient lies on this* – this wasn't her first defence against the denizens of the Void.

They will not pass.

A voice pulsed deep within: *But it is my first time.*

Her lips curled. *I am Bethusa. Leave this fight to me.*

The other quietened.

But she would be back, Bethusa knew. *And the truth is, I may need her.* It was not clear how long the defence would be. *I will need to rest.*

No, she reprimanded herself. *I am Bethusa. I will survive.*

And on daemons came, and on Bethusa and Shaydu fought.

Until the glimmer of hope finally arrived.

Until the darkness cracked!

Pulling on the vast power of the Light, her very being stressed beyond that which any human could endure, Bethusa, with Shaydu by her side, channelled intense beams of energy into the newly formed fissures, forcing them wider, slicing deeper into the Void beyond the Threshold of the Gate—

The fractured daemon of the Dark shattered.

The darkness vanished as light flooded in.

They were left standing on their mountain peak, billowing white clouds below them, azure-blue sky above. And a shocking silence. A stunning silence after an eternity of savage fighting. She looked down and saw how close to the edge of the precipice she had stepped; her feet touched the edge of the vertical cliff, which plunged down into distant clouds below.

A step away from defeat.

Bethusa turned. Before her lay a rounded rocky platform, ten spears wide. In the centre, standing upright, lay a glowing golden ring. Large enough for a person to step through, it hovered a hand's width from the ground. Within the ring floated ghostly images from another place. From her Land. She looked to the other figure on the peak. Her beloved. Her partner. *Shaydu.* She smiled and stepped over to him. They embraced.

"How are you holding up?" Shaydu asked, stepping back, his dark, deep-set eyes looking over her with concern.

"I am Bethusa, I—"

"I know – you will survive. How are you really doing?"

A crack appeared in her defences. She immediately dammed it. "I'm fine."

Shaydu smiled. "You're a terrible liar, Beth. Are you hurt?"

"Just tired." She glanced to the clear blue sky. Clear for now, but … "How long do you think we'll be here this time?"

She saw the grimace before Shaydu managed to suppress it. "Let's take each day at a time. Maybe this time will be the last."

But it wasn't.

Moons passed.

The sun completed cycle after cycle.

And the ice pushed south.

"We're failing," Bethusa said, seated on the rocky ground, head in her hands after repelling another attack. "I'm failing."

"No. We're holding. Only one daemon made it through."

"But that's one too many. Kaos is winning. Maybe we're the only ones left. Maybe—"

"Don't go there, Beth. All we need to know is that life remains in the Land. We keep fighting, that's all we can do."

"I'm tired, Shay. So tired."

"So, give the other a chance. She's a survivor too."

And so, Bethusa stepped back and rested.

And the other refused to release her for millennia.

*

The brutal aftermath of K'zarz's senseless slaughter of Bethusa's family tainted Shadow's soul, but the whispering shadows of other displaced memories whirled out to engulf him.

One memory settled.

He stood at a gateway to the Void, Beth by his side, cursing the old man who'd tricked him all those millennia before. Just one more cup of wine, Stealth had said on that long-past fateful evening within the dragon's lair. Sy had warned him to stay alert, and as usual Shadow had ignored him, preferring instead to celebrate the success of their mission by enjoying Stealth's glorious wine. *And that one more cup of wine landed me at this Gate.* Because at some point he'd fallen into a drunken slumber … *Then that back-stabbing Stealth locked me in a portal.*

Back then, he'd understood nothing of what was happening to him, only finding himself thrust into a deranged nightmare where nothing made sense. He'd tried to shut himself away, withdrawing into the deepest recesses of his consciousness, but had seen only terrors looming in the darkness, cut by the briefest of respites on a godforsaken mountaintop in the sky. Then a voice had spoken to him: a beguiling, intelligent voice. Shaydu, a Warrior, it said. For so long, he refused to engage; it was not a voice he'd invited in. But later – how long, he didn't know – he'd finally responded to the glimmer of salvation the voice seemed to offer. It may have seemed a sign of the madness within, but it was better than the horrors without. The voice told him he stood at a Gate. That he must fight at the Gate. That he must fight for millennia to prevent the incursion of the Dark. And that he must ensure Bethusa reached the time of the Guardian. Shadow had ranted and railed at what had befallen him. It wasn't fair. It wasn't right. This couldn't be. But slowly, patiently, the voice had helped him understand where fate's roll of the knuckles had landed him.

He understood what was needed of Bethusa to save the Guardian.

And he came to understand himself and Shaydu.

We are as one.

Shaydu was as Shadow. Shadow was as Shaydu. There was no dichotomy here, no clash of being.

They were Warriors, and they strode on together.

Unlike Beth. *My wonderful Beth. My soulmate.*

Soulmate? An interesting choice of words. For Beth and Bethusa were most definitely soul enemies.

And there was nothing he could do about it.

Adding more of his power to bolster Beth's faltering defence of the Threshold, he glanced at her sweat-drenched face. "You should rest. Allow Bethusa to fight for a while."

Beth bristled. "I am Beth. Beth only. Bethusa had her time, and that time is long past."

"You need her, Beth. You know—"

"I know who I am, Shadow! And I know what she was to you. *Was.* No more. This is now." Her face brooked no challenge.

He sighed. Beth and Bethusa, so much alike.

And yet, so different.

Steadying the flow of energy to the shield, he glanced at Beth. *The unkillable Warrior.* He remembered his incredulity when, with Shaydu's help, he'd first arisen from the tortured shadows of his mind and seen the dark-haired woman beside him. He'd last seen her body icebound and frozen at the mountain lair of the Ancient. *Dead. Or so I thought.* Another subterfuge of Rakana and those of the Light who had need of the Warrior. She'd been placed in a portal by the cunning Stealth, and so also found herself at the Gate. *But nothing of this is simple.* As Shaydu walked beside him, Bethusa walked – strode – beside Beth. And for the first age of their defence, Bethusa's mind had ruled.

Only once Bethusa had finally released Beth to the battle had he seen the true character of the unkillable Warrior. He'd been amazed how quickly she had adapted to the terrors of the Dark, and had watched with growing admiration her tireless, selfless defence against the horrors assailing them from the Void. He'd admired her masterful wielding of the power of the Light, and the ease in which she conjured new and novel defences. And he'd admired her vulnerability. Her fierce determination. *Her companionship.* They'd fought ferociously side-by-side. They'd valiantly defended each other's back. They'd laughed and they'd cried.

And over the ages, they'd found a love grow between them.

I love her.

And I love her, came Shaydu's voice.

And this was said with no bitterness, no anger. Shadow and Shaydu had each found their own soulmate; there was no conflict between them. But Beth was not Bethusa, and Bethusa was jealous of Beth. And that conflict threatened their defence of the Gate.

For here they were, millennia later, Beth still refusing to allow Bethusa to aid them.

Shadow sighed and tried again. "This fight is not ended. Take a break. Please."

It took time.

It took until she almost collapsed.

But eventually Beth listened, and Bethusa returned.

Oh, how she returned.

*

Shadow staggered as the storm of memories raged on. His memories …

And those of Shaydu.

"Don't call me that! I've told you a thousand times, don't call me that," Bethusa stormed during a lull in the Dark's attacks. "My name is Bethusa, not Beth!"

"You've always been Beth to me," Shaydu murmured.

"I am Bethusa. I always have been, and always will be. Beth is no more."

Shaydu sighed. He knew she bore the relentless pressure of the other seeking a way out, an internal war as stressful as the war at the Gate. "You will need to rest, Beth … usa," he said. "Our fight is not over. I sense we're getting close, but—"

"It is endless," Bethusa spat. "Why do we do this? Why? Have you seen the Land out there? Look," she stormed, gesturing to the golden ring. "There. More armies. More innocents dying. And why? Because another weak-minded leader seeks their brief spark of gratification, their next step towards their imagined immortality. Another leader achieving nothing but the Land's destruction, condemning blameless lives to their graves." She walked to the very edge of the precipice – the edge of the protected Glade – her toes hanging in the air. "And we protect those mindless tyrants," she said in an icy voice.

Shaydu said nothing, waiting for her anger to pass.

Bethusa squatted down on her haunches, peering into the clouds below. "Why do this? It makes no sense."

"I have grown to like it – it soothes my mind. And prevents us stepping too far from the Gate."

"Not the mountain and clouds, you fool," Bethusa growled, standing, then stepping back. "These fools fighting these battles. Why do they continue to do what they do? It is as though the Dark already controls them."

Shaydu was silent.

Her eyes narrowing, Bethusa cast him a sidelong glance. "Did I speak a truth? Have you been holding something from me? Something you told the other, but not me?"

"I tell you both the same."

"Not true. You prefer her. This is why you want me to rest. You—"

Shaydu walked up to her and placed his hand on her cheek. "There is only one Bethusa – and you know I love you."

"But you also love her."

He was silent.

"She is not me," she murmured.

He said nothing.

"I cannot accept her. There will be a reckoning between us." She turned away from him. "But, for now, I will rest, and I pray to the Light that this Land heals."

*

The raging torrent of memories slowed.

Until only one remained.

Shaydu did not think he could continue much longer. How long could a Warrior survive and still retain a sense of self? The last attack had been the worst they'd endured; Bethusa still lay beside him, recovering her strength.

Whilst he hated himself for thinking it, he was glad of this brief moment of peace. For Bethusa had grown increasingly fractious since returning to the fold – what was it, a millennium ago? Angry with him, with the Light, with the battle – with the Land.

The Land. The main object of her ire when the lulls in battle came. Rants that would last for days as she vented her frustration. But despite the tirades, it was hard to argue with the core of what she said. The Land had cancerous growths that needed to be cut before they became an unstoppable corruption of ... of what?

Of everything life needs to survive.

So much of what he'd seen through the ages, he'd admired. The amazing profusion of incredible thinking, artistry, design, and drive. A drive for a better future, a drive to create the previously unthinkable. Thirteen thousand sun-cycles of astonishing and unimaginable progression, with pockets of stellar brilliance.

But all with one incredible oversight.

The health of their lands.

The health of the air; of the seas; of the soils of the earth.

The health of all animals.

Except humans, of course. And those that humans ate. These were protected.

But only for today. Tomorrow? No, live for today.

He grimaced. Millennia ago, Bethusa had asked whether she'd spoken a truth: "It is as though the Dark already controls them." He hadn't answered. For it was something he'd been unwilling to accept. But he knew now that she was right. The Dark *was* at work across the ages. Its insidious influence ran deep within those holding power. It would take much more than the defence of this single Gate to fight that wider war.

'You are correct, Shaydu,' came a calm, ethereal voice. *'But that is for another day. Wake Bethusa. Her time has come.'*

*

Shadow trembled as the memories swept by.

He and Bethusa stood within the bowels of the Mountain of Hope, the Staff lying on the dais before them. He had done what was needed, helping the Warrior survive through the millennia to arrive at this single, most critical moment in time.

To save the Guardian. To retrieve the Staff.

"We will find another way," Bethusa pledged. "The Light will not separate those souls who walk together."

540

He knew she would search for a way for them to stay together. To remember. But he didn't believe. He held a strength in his voice. "It is time. The Guardian needs you."

Bethusa held his gaze for a moment, then she turned and strode out of the chamber …

The memories flashed by: the immense presence of the Dark; the flaring of the power of the Light; the arrival of the traitor; the arrival of Bethusa. And something abhorrent beyond the edges of his mind. *What did Bethusa do?*

And then the parting. The sadness. The tears. The despair that had no shape.

We were returned to the Land.

But we didn't remember. We—

A searing flash rocked Shadow's mind, shattering the memories into jagged shards.

Staggering, he stared, unbelieving, into the eyes of the unkillable Warrior.

We fought side by side …

We defended the Gate …

But we didn't remember.

Until now.

*

Standing outside her hut, stunned by the mind-numbing echoes from a lost past, Beth found she couldn't move as she stared into the eyes of the dumbfounded Ka.

"It can't be," Shadow said in a whisper. "It just can't be."

Beth's hands trembled. "Why didn't she tell me? Why didn't IY tell me?"

Their hands remained locked.

And still, she didn't move.

Yet she yearned to grasp him in a fierce embrace and demand that he never leave her again. She yearned for them to run as far as they could from the Land, escaping the terrors threatening to engulf them. And she yearned to ask her soulmate to stand by her side. Forever.

"Beth?" Shadow whispered, so faintly she hardly heard him.

She nodded, her heart leaping.

Shadow looked into her eyes, a sudden aching hope in his own.

He remembers!

But as Beth forced herself to move, the light in his eyes died, clouded by a shadow of fear. Of doubt.

Pulling his hands away, Shadow took a step back.

541

Beth's heart shattered. *No, don't leave me again.*

He shook his head. "This can't be ... I don't understand ..."

"You don't understand what?" came a cold voice behind Beth.

Svana emerged into the morning gloom.

"Yes, I had the same question," Knuckles said, stepping around his hut.

"I ..." Shadow started, then fell silent.

Knuckles looked expectantly at Beth.

Wrung by a crippling dread, Beth couldn't speak.

Knuckles's eyes narrowed. He glanced at Shadow. "Well, I thought I heard someone outside, and am thankful you're still here. I wasn't sure you would be."

"I just needed air. Didn't sleep." Shadow's eyes never left Beth's.

Svana looked again at Beth. "Beth?"

Beth held Shadow's eyes. "You were there – at the mountain."

Shadow said nothing.

Svana raised an eyebrow.

Beth reached out her hand. "We—"

Shadow turned and walked back around the hut, disappearing from view.

Beth sank to her knees.

"Beth!" Svana cried, rushing to her side. "Are you hurt?"

Yes. I'm hurting. You can't imagine how much I'm hurting. And it's too much to bear.

"Beth?"

Beth looked up at Svana, tears in her eyes. "I have a story to tell, Svana. Will you hear it?"

"Of course," Svana whispered. "Of course I will."

"I'll see to the Ka," Knuckles said in a subdued voice. He walked away, heading back around his hut.

Svana helped Beth to her feet.

"Walk with me awhile," Beth murmured.

They walked slowly east towards the rising light of dawn, and as Beth told her tale, her incredulous companion listened in stunned silence.

*

The sun rose into a clear blue sky, its warming light angling across the tops of the distant trees and into the awakening camp. A select few rays settled on two women sitting beside a burbling stream, one cradling the other in her lap.

As the third figure watched from the shadows, the two women climbed to their feet, hugged, then slowly walked towards the camp, the sun on their backs.

The figure walked out of the shadows and watched them until they passed from view.

All knuckles were cast.

But where would they land?

She ran her fingers through her short, spiky hair.

The tale is still being spun, and no one, not even the gods, can say where it will end. But I have tried. And I have done what you asked.

CHAPTER FORTY

To truly understand, you must see through another's eyes.

A cool, dry breeze murmuring in her ear – the only sound breaking the eerie silence of the dusty landscape around her – Jessica surveyed the barren, red-hued desolation. Denuded hills lay in the distance, their broad, shattered scree slopes evidence of the unrelenting wear of the ages. The sun was high, dusk still hours away, but subtle shades of pink tinged the cloudless sky.

As the wild beating of her heart finally slowed, Jessica turned. Jalu, her dark hair and ragged tunic gently swaying in the breeze, stood waiting, her fierce silvery eyes watching her closely.

"This is a Glade," Jessica said. "But where is this land?"

"It is a reminder of a world I once knew," Jalu said, her eyes not leaving Jessica. "A world that died. A place where I should have remained."

"You were the Guardian here," Jessica breathed.

"I was. I failed … and yet I succeeded." Jalu glanced to the distant hills. "My time was done. This is where I should have lain. I should never have been taken from this land." Jessica caught the flash of pain – and anger – in Jalu's eyes before it was quickly hidden.

Jessica gazed out to the barren land. "It doesn't seem a place for life."

"In the end, it wasn't. It was the resting place for the dead."

Jessica held up her Staff. "Why didn't you show yourself to me when I first arrived? When we met the Iyes. Why didn't Naga speak of you?"

"Naga was a Keeper of the Story, one who could make the Request to call the Warriors, then aid them as she could. But the story of Life? Only the Guardian can know this."

"And you?"

Jalu stepped over to a red-crusted boulder, then sat, perched on the edge. *A powerful woman,* Jessica thought, noting the woman's relaxed poise, edged by a tension in the sleek curves of her arms. She studied the woman's strong, angular face. An intriguing face, youthful and proud, alive with radiant intelligence. Yet somehow also an ancient face sculpted by unknown storm-driven tides of an unrelenting history. *Just what has this woman seen?*

She tilted her head. *Woman? Or Spirit?*

"There are times I sleep," Jalu said, a veil of weariness crossing her face. "Long, tiring sleeps. Times when I wish for death." Jessica's intake of breath was sharp. "Then I am wakened," Jalu continued. "But it takes time – time to come back into the world, time to face yet another ..." She glanced at Jessica but said nothing more.

Another failure. That's what she was going to say.

"But I aid where I can. I aid *when* I can."

"You helped me protect the Ensi. And now I think you helped me save the bookseller." She studied Jalu's face. "What else?"

Jalu shook her head. "I only support you. The decisions are yours. You are the Guardian, not I." She frowned. "Although there was one I brought back from the shadows of your time. There, I ... borrowed you for a short while."

Jessica's eyes narrowed.

"Another time," Jalu murmured.

Jessica's gaze lingered, then she turned and looked around at the desolation around her. "Couldn't you have changed this? You – we – have that power." *Don't we? I did it once.* A flicker of uncertainty sparked. *Once?*

Jalu's brow furrowed. "Before I answer, know this. I was the Guardian of my world, but not of the ages. I did not have your strength. I could not travel the Continuum. But you are as other Guardians of this world, you carve a path through the Continuum. And that path is clear, well marked, with no hurdles to cross if you choose wisely. You travel and create your own timeline – a timeline you remember – and for each new path carved through time, the Continuum adjusts, adapts. All is aligned; all is remembered."

I carve a path through the Continuum ... Jessica glanced at her Staff. "And this aids my travel?"

"A myth of the Iyes. That Staff was birthed with Life in the Continuum. It is an artefact of the Light, the Staff of the Light." She scowled. "And my prison."

Jessica studied the Staff with a quizzical gaze. *A myth? And Jalu's prison?*

"You hold the power to carve these paths through the Continuum," Jalu continued. "No one else. Nothing else. But to strive to undo what has been done? To rewrite the timeline of the Continuum? There lies a great danger. To do this, you must cross your own timeline; you must cross your own soul. And the Continuum cannot allow this. If this is done, the Continuum will return to the first crossing of that time and place. You – and the Continuum – will be as you were, all paths between forgotten, your presence and influence through those times removed." Jalu's eyes locked onto Jessica's. "Is that something that you would be willing to risk?"

"I did it before," Jessica confessed. "At Mount Hope."

"You did, but what do you remember?"

"I remember ..." *I remember little.* Images, vague emotions, but all the details lost.

"The intervention made in that mountain was a mere drop in the ocean to the vastness of the Continuum. Yet you struggle to remember." Jalu's face hardened. "The power is there, but that is not a roll of the knuckles I would take." She hesitated. "But it has been tried, Guardian. I *know* it has been tried ... But I only hold faint senses of something said before, subtle feelings of places once visited."

With rising horror, Jessica recalled those fleeting, hazy moments of confusion when she'd felt she had walked the Land before, when it seemed she knew things she shouldn't have known. The Void. The burnt man. Standing before the Ensi in another time. Seeing the burnt man execute the Ensi. Other ghostly, incoherent memories swirled beyond her mind's eye. A coldness gripped her. Were these true memories? Lost memories of a Guardian she'd once been? Had she intervened in other turnings of this Land, with actions now forgotten, swept aside by the cold, brutal alignment of the Continuum?

She shivered at a terrifying thought. *How long have I been fighting this battle?*

Her chest suddenly tight, Jessica turned away, blindly looking out across the dry, barren landscape. How would she know? How would anyone know?

I wouldn't. They wouldn't.

"Why did the others fail?" she whispered. "Why did those Guardians before me fail?"

Jalu's answer was swift and sure. "They weren't determined enough. They weren't smart enough."

"But the Dark was defeated. The Geddon wasn't released."

Jalu scowled. "There is more to the guarding of Life than this. Life must be preserved for the future. Life must be protected." Her sharp, silvery eyes locked onto Jessica's. "A hope for the future, this is what you guard, Guardian. You preserve hope."

"The Seed of Life," Jessica whispered, the image of two intertwined coiled snakes snapping into her mind.

"Yes," Jalu said, tilting her head. "A Seed of Life. One that lies in so very few, yet is the genesis of Life beyond this world."

"And it lies within the Ensi."

"Yes. Seeds lie with her and her bloodline."

"Her daughters," Jessica said, remembering the Ensi's words. And those of the snake. "Who are they? Where are they?"

"That cannot yet be told. But know that the one named Cobra has led Krull to the wrong trail. That gives you time."

"Time for what? What can I do? What should I do?"

Jalu studied Jessica's face, then: "There are things you must see to truly understand, things that you must see to succeed where others before you have failed."

Her words lit up in Jessica's mind. *It has to be me ... I must not fail.*
Like the others?

"Why *did* those Guardians before me fail?"

"They failed because they fought the wrong battles. They fought the Ka, they fought the daemons of the Dark, they protected the Gates." Deep pain flashed in Jalu's eyes. "But they failed Life."

Jessica licked her dry lips. *Wrong battles?*

Jalu rose to her feet and walked across to her. "There is a war that we see, and there is a war that remains hidden." She gestured to the dusty, desolate land surrounding them. "You must try harder than I did on my world, Guardian. Some would say I succeeded, but I say I failed – failed because I couldn't see past those I ask you to face. I didn't have the strength."

Jessica studied Jalu with a creeping dread. "I still don't understand," she whispered.

Restless anger – or was that a savage anticipation? – blazed in Jalu's eyes. "Something lies beyond our sight. Something that plays an unknown game with Life. Something I was unable to reach. But you, Guardian, you hold a strength beyond all others before you. You hold a great strength in your soul."

"I ... I don't know what you ask."

"I ask you to understand, to step away from the path of all those before you. To see what truly lies in the darkness beyond."

The darkness. Long-ago words of Naga flashed back: "I think you will not finally understand what must be done until you have truly touched the darkness."

Dreadful, ranging fear swept over Jessica. But how? This imposing Warrior Jalu had served as the Guardian. But she had failed; she hadn't been strong enough. *What am I to one who has seen millennia – no, aeons – pass?* A wave of panic threatened to engulf her. *I can't push any further than I have already. I should get back to my friends. They need my help.*

But I am the Guardian, came an insurgent voice from the depths of her being.

No! I am Jessica. I am …

The Guardian! asserted the strident voice.

She staggered away, riotous doubts flooding into her mind. *Why me? Why was I chosen? I am nothing, nobody compared to these daemons, these gods.* She stood, shoulders slumped. *I can't be the one to protect life, to protect this Life of which they speak. I can't do it.*

Her innermost defences crumbled, releasing her deepest fear.

I can't do it alone.

I need someone by my side.

Someone who will hold me when I fall …

Through her pain, she realised that after all she had endured, after all she had survived, she was finally cracking. *And there is nothing I can do …*

But in this well of her deepest despair, a beautiful voice drifted in from afar.

A wondrously familiar voice.

A voice from another time.

When do we ever give up? came the beloved voice of her sister.

Eshe?

When do we ever give up? urged the remembered voice again.

A breathtaking image of her standing by her sister's side snapped into Jessica's mind. "We never give up," she whispered into the cold air, a tremendous surge of warmth filling her heart as her sister's smiling face turned to her.

What do we say? her sister said, her sparkling eyes filled with joy.

We say, 'Let's do it!' Jessica heard them shout together.

Her sister grinned.

Tears ran down Jessica's cheek.

I will be with you always, her sister promised. *We will walk together always.*

"Always," Jessica whispered.

Eshe's image began to slowly fade, drifting away in the ether. *Save Life*, came her sister's distant voice. *You have the strength, where others failed.*

And then the presence vanished.

Jessica's gaze lifted to the hazy horizon, the wondrous memory of her sister lingering. "I love you, Sis," she whispered. "I will love you always."

She stood for a moment, holding on to the glorious elation that had lifted her soul. *You are always by my heart, Sis. Always.*

Then she drew a deep breath and straightened. *I must try to understand.*

A fierce resolve welled. *I will understand!*

Casting aside the fearsome dread that had crippled her, she turned to Jalu. "I will do what is needed."

Jalu acknowledged her with the faintest of nods, her stern face unbreaking.

And then came another voice. A calm, ethereal voice.

'I thank you, Guardian.'

The desolate landscape around Jessica vanished, then her body exploded with pain as she was swept into a void.

The Void.

A dark horde rushed over her, raking at her mind.

Instinctively, she shielded herself, forcing the frenzied predators back.

Predators of the Dark.

Hazy memories of travelling this Void swirled wildly.

And flickers of understanding.

I enter the Void to travel the ages of the Continuum. But the creatures of the Kaos seek to destroy me, to prevent me reentering in another time.

But how do I do this? Who controls—

"Be ready," came the ethereal voice into the darkness. "And understand. Understand Pa'Andora. Understand Life."

A blaze of light.

Then a thunderous crack as she reentered the Continuum.

Then nothing.

*

Voices. Quiet voices.

Then silence.

Who am I?

A darkness swept over her.

549

Voices. Insistent voices.

And the feeling of others around her.

But she couldn't see. She couldn't feel.

Who am I?

A memory returned.

I am Jessica.

But where am I?

Darkness returned.

Voices. "Can you hear me?"

Voices she understood.

'Yes,' Jessica tried to answer. *'I can hear you. Where am I?'*

Silence.

Then an awareness of another soul.

And an awareness of being alive.

She took a sharp, involuntary breath and opened her eyes, then quickly closed them against the glare of the room.

"Thank God," a voice said.

Opening one eye a little, she saw a blurry figure standing over her. "Take it easy, Mar'Shi," came a voice. "You've had a tough few hours."

Mar'Shi?

She let both eyes gradually open, and as she adjusted to the light – not a bright light at all – the man's face came into view. She felt a momentary confusion as the fog of her dream cleared, then she recognised her brother. *P'Lan.*

"Can you understand me?" P'Lan said, reaching out and laying a hand on hers.

Mar'Shi nodded. "And I am alive," she whispered, pushing back the remnants of her crazy dream. *Who was Jessica?*

Me, Jessica tried to say from the deepest recesses of Mar'Shi's mind. But all she could do was watch. Observe.

"Well, that's just as well," came a woman's voice to her left. "You've work to do, remember. That ship can't head to the stars without you. What happened, Shi? You hit the bottle?"

Mar'Shi frowned. "I don't remember."

"Ha. Where did you hide the bottle? Must have been the last one in this godforsaken place."

She started to pull herself up, but P'Lan gently moved his hand to stop her. "Hey, not so fast. I may be just a dumb engineer, but even I can see you don't look well. Rest. I'll fetch some water."

"And something to eat. I'm suddenly starving."

"Water only," said the woman to her left. "What little food we have is stowed."

"I'll find something," P'Lan whispered softly. With a parting smile, he walked away. She heard his footsteps recede, then the sound of a door swishing open, then closing. Other footsteps softly approached, and a figure came into view.

Dro'Paan.

The woman leaned over her. "What happened, Shi?"

She winced. "I don't know. I ran through a final check of the mission procedures and then … then I remember nothing. Except …"

"Except what?"

"Strange dreams. Of other places. I … I don't know what happened." She shifted, suddenly uncomfortable. "I can't just lie here. Help me up."

With Dro'Paan's help, she sat up, swinging her legs over the side of the table. She mentally checked herself over. Slightly nauseous, but nothing serious.

"So, you remember nothing?"

Mar'Shi shook her head.

Dro'Paan frowned. "No one saw you fall. Nothing seen on the scanners. I don't like it. It may be a breach of the Wall. We'll run a check on the sensors and make sure the Safe remains secure." She studied Mar'Shi closely for a moment. "Let's hope you remember. It would tidy things up."

Mar'Shi grimaced. "I'd sure like to know what happened." But she recalled nothing.

Nothing but strange dreams. Of another woman. A woman with a Staff. *Jessica.*

She felt Dro'Paan's gaze on her. "Don't worry. I'm fine."

Doubt lingered on Dro'Paan's face, but she nodded. "You're back with us, Shi, that's the main thing. And if we're to leave tomorrow, we can't afford distractions. The new world awaits, and we can't afford to fail."

Mar'Shi knew the truth of her friend's words and saw the passion and desire for life – all life – in those bright eyes. Those shining green eyes of Dro'Paan.

EPILOGUE

It can be asked, why allow Fen to serve? The answer is because he served well. Are all who serve you perfect?

Tricia threw up – again – and then lay back down, placing her head onto the hard, cold ground. How long she had been there, she didn't know, and right now, couldn't care less. She closed her eyes, praying someone would come and remove her head and take it far, far away. Maybe then the pain would stop … and maybe also the hazy memory of vile alien creatures fighting to reach her.

And yet Jess somehow held them back.

With visions of the frenzied horde wracking her mind, she drifted into a restless sleep.

Sometime later, she cautiously opened her eyes to find her head had cleared and the day had gotten brighter. She gently raised her head and looked up.

A young girl carrying a schoolbag stared back at her. "Can we give her some money?" the girl asked the man beside her. "She doesn't look well."

The man gave Tricia a hard stare, but reaching into his pocket, he pulled out some change and threw a coin towards her. It clinked as it hit the pavement – for that was what she'd been sleeping on – then spun around a few times before rolling to a stop next to a cold pool of vomit. And many more coins.

"Thank you," Tricia mumbled to the girl, wishing she could curl up and vanish from their sight.

"Get a job," the man growled as he and the girl left.

Slowly pulling herself up, Tricia looked around her. A small village, early morning, and a cloudy sky looking like rain on the way. And plenty of people walking on by. She glanced down at herself. *Fairly clean. Seems I vomit with self-preservation in mind.* But she looked like the aftermath of a drunken fancy-dress party.

"Are you okay?" came a concerned voice from behind her.

Tricia clambered to her feet, fighting off the complaint from her stomach, and looked around. "I'm fine," she lied. "I … it … I'm sorry, I made a bit of a mess of …" She looked up at the building behind her. *Oh, no.* Of all the places to put on display your partially digested food. "… of your delicatessen."

"It happens," the woman said. "I'll deal with it. But are you sure you're alright?"

"I am …" *I am what?* The pain in her head had subsided, but a terrible foreboding was squirming in its place. *Heck, Jess, if you want me to find Erin, you could've done more than just abandon me here.* She looked back at the woman. "I'm okay," she lied again. "Where am I?"

The woman raised an eyebrow. "Cheda."

So the same place, different time. She glanced at the woman and her clothing, and then back to the street and its shops. It was her time, or close enough. "What year is it?" she said, squinting back up at the woman.

The woman's expression changed instantly. "Okay, I was willing to help, but I won't take any lip. Pick up your money and be on your way."

"Oh, that's not my—" *Hold on, girl, you'll need that.* "Thank you," Tricia said quickly, bending to pick up the coins. "A last question. Where is the closest charity shop?"

A short while later, dressed now in a blue shirt, black jacket, brown sandals, and the only pair of trousers that would fit – bright red tartan trousers – Tricia stood outside the charity shop, trying to figure out what to do next. Find a kind person who would let her make a free call, and then—

A police car drove past.

And her mind kicked into gear. *I'm a missing person here.*

Or worse if they found only her, but not Jess, Beth, or Lanky. A kidnapper? Murderer?

Then keep a low profile and move. Find Erin and tell her what she needs to know.

She grunted a slightly hysterical laugh. *Low profile? Dressed like this?*

<--->

"We waited too long."

Cyrene watched the distant lightning storm for a moment longer, then turned to her brother, the fitful light of the fire casting dancing shadows across her sharp face. "I agree."

"What now?"

Cyrene considered his question. What now, indeed. The Kade had gone from their land. *And so too the Ensi and the Guardian.* Coincidence? Taran thought not. And Taran believed he knew where – and when – they had gone. "Each of the Warriors of the Light arrived from the same time, a distant time in the future," Taran had told her. "That connection endures."

"For the Kade, we must wait," Cyrene said to Sylander. "A long time."

Sylander kicked the fire in anger, a glowing cloud of sparks flying into the air. "We should have moved when I said," he spat. He kicked another log from the fire. "Taran has grown complacent! Taran has—"

Sylander cried out as he flew backwards through the air and out into the darkness.

"Do not blaspheme against our god!" Cyrene admonished, lowering her arms. "Remember yourself, Sylander."

She heard her fellow mage get to his feet, and a dark shape emerged into the light. "I remember," Sylander growled. "But does Taran?"

Cyrene stood and raised her hands, vivid-blue light shimmering around them.

Sylander shook his head. "Do not fight me, Cyrene. You would not win."

She glared at him. But he was right. *And we shouldn't be fighting.* The blue light faded, and she relaxed her arms and sat back on the ground.

Tension eased from Sylander's shoulders. "I'm sorry, but you cannot deny we failed to take a chance we had."

Staring into the fire, she nodded.

"The Kade must be protected," Sylander said, his voice returning to its melodious lilt. "Protected from the Dark. Protected from the Light. It must lie with us."

"We all agree on this, Sylander."

"All? Fen does not."

"That one is mistaken."

"And the Seed of Life?"

"That is for the Guardian." A frown crossed Cyrene's face. "And yet ..."

Sylander's eyes narrowed.

"And yet, Taran asks us to be ready. Krull's shamans seek the Seed. They follow the Iyes."

This surprised him. "A Seed is with the Iyes?"

She faced him, her eyes glittering in the firelight. "Maybe. Or maybe those cursed shamans follow for another reason. Either way, we must observe the Iyes, and if they need our protection – if the Guardian fails – we must intervene."

"And IY and her daemons, they still know nothing of this Seed?"

"The daemons, no. IY?" She frowned. "The true IY remains veiled, and so what that one knows is uncertain."

"Then as you say, we must be ready to intervene."

"We will do what we can." She turned back to the storm and pulled her cloak tighter around her. *So few of us left,* she thought with a shiver. *But those few must be enough.*

<--->

Entering the clearing, Fen saw the Ancient turn a fiery eye to him, wisps of smoke drifting off her battle-scorched body, runnels of blood trickling through creases and tears in ruptured scales.

"You are late," Rakana rumbled. "The enemy is regrouping – I am needed."

"We're all needed," Fen growled.

He heard a deep grumble from the depths of the Ancient, then the beast swung her massive ridged head to a deep shadow in the trees at the edge of the clearing. "Is the Geddon still secure?"

The deep shadow flickered. "It is only a matter of time. Krull grows strong, and Kaos grows stronger. The Geddon's mind will be freed."

"That is your realm, Taran. You fail."

"It is my realm, but the binding of the Geddon belongs to others. In that, I cannot interfere."

"A pact with the Light that should never have been agreed," Rakana hissed.

"Even so," came the voice from the shadows. "One I cannot break."

"And if the Geddon is released?"

"Then we will all have failed, and I will mourn this Land's destruction."

"Life's destruction," Rakana rumbled.

"Yes," Taran murmured. "Life's destruction."

Rakana swung her massive head back to Fen. "If the Geddon's mind is freed, it will seek to reunite with its body."

"We will hold as we can."

The Ancient's eye burned with a volcanic fire. "It will not be enough."

"Even so, we will try."

The Ancient glowered at the white wolf. "And the Warriors? Did they secure the Kade?"

Fen emitted a low growl. "The Kade lay within our grasp, but another interfered. It has left this time."

"Good," Taran said from the shadows. "It is better away from the hands of Krull. And from you."

The Ancient issued a sharp hiss. "Of what do you speak?"

The shadows deepened, and Fen felt the quiet regard of Taran upon him. The god of the Islanders spoke: "Fen believes the Kade should be destroyed. Is that not so, servant of IY?"

A great rumble erupted from Rakana. "What! What treachery is this?"

Fen snarled and turned away.

"It has always been so, has it not?" the voice from the shadows murmured after the wolf. "You have always been against the path of your master. Your true master."

A wall of heat swept from Rakana as the dragon opened her massive jaws. "Destroy the Kade?" she rumbled. "What twisted reasoning would ever suggest this? The A'ven would be lost, the Warriors powerless. It would open the Gates and release the horde of Kaos upon us."

"Not true," Fen snarled. "No A'ven, no energy for those hordes of which you speak. Lands finally free from the corruption of the Dark. Lands free for life to thrive." His topaz eyes scanned the shadows. "The Kade should be destroyed."

"You forget the Geddon," Taran murmured from the shadows.

"I forget nothing. Everything I do is to rid these lands from that curse upon us. The Kade should be destroyed."

"You gamble with Life," Taran said quietly. "With the Kade gone, and the A'ven lost, what would then happen? You play with a raging fire. Leave the Kade. Leave—"

"Leave the Kade for you," Fen snarled. "No, that will not be. I trust no one to hold the Kade. Not even one such as you."

A rustle sounded high in a tree, then a bird flew from a branch, dislodging a leaf into the sudden harsh silence of the clearing. As the leaf fell, Rakana's penetrating gaze searched the depths of the shadows as though considering Taran's words. A tendril of smoke swirled into the air from a blackened scale on her back. The Ancient swung her head back to Fen. "Taran speaks true," she rumbled. "You play with something beyond our ken. And you play against the wishes of our master."

Fen growled. "How many Warriors have come and gone? How many Guardians? And still the Dark remains. Still the Geddon remains. This must change. Our master grows weak."

The formidable fanged maw of the Ancient swung open, and a wave of heat swept across Fen. As the ferocious heat faded, the intense glare of Rakana's fiery eye bore down on him. "Take care not to cross a line, daemon. You would not wish to feel my wrath."

Fen glared at the Ancient. *Even so, I am right. We are losing this war.* He said nothing.

Another swathe of heat swept from Rakana's jaws as the great beast turned away. "I have had enough of talk, and of these games," she thundered. "I go to fight. I go to defend your Warriors, to defend those fighting at the Gates."

The dragon lumbered into the open glade, and then with a thumping beat of her wings, lifted easily from the ground, quickly climbing. "Look to aid those who are dying," came the Ancient's voice, "and not merely those you serve."

Fen watched the dragon disappear beyond the tree line, then turned to the flickering darkness within the trees.

"For now, the Kade lies beyond all of us here," the voice from the shadows murmured. "And that is for the best."

Fen felt a ripple in the ether, and the midnight-black shadows vanished.

Fen glared into the now lightly dappled shade. "You're wrong," he growled. "Our master is wrong. The Kade is the bane of life in the Land. It must be destroyed." The daemon lifted his gaze to the skies. The Guardian was growing in strength. She would return to the Land, he was certain. The Kade would return. *And then we'll get our chance. Dysam will get his chance.* But first, the stubborn host needed to stand aside and let Dysam free. *Let Dysam free and let us do what is needed! Destroy the Kade!*

The daemon reached for the energy of the Dark. What needed to be done, would be done. *Because we cannot fail.*

A ripple in the ether, and then the glade lay empty.

Save for the brooding sense of an approaching storm.

This ends Part Two of
the Warriors of the Continuum Trilogy

GLOSSARY

The A'ven: an energy permeating the Land, an energy of the Void

Black Staff: a daemon-bound artefact carried by the chosen few of Kaos

The Continuum: a concept of the Iyes, a continuum of ages constantly in flux, yet all aligned, compatible, all changes adjusted unseen, no paradoxes allowed

Cords: energy strands allowing those with the power and skill to transfer mind (and body if possible) to Glades, Gates, or particular places within the Land

The Iyes daemons: allies of the Iyes Spirits, appearing in the form of venerated life of the age

The Dark: a hidden threat, a presence deemed to be linked to the god of the Ka, Kaos

Gates: gateways between the Continuum and the Void

The Geddon: a bound force of the Dark, a destroyer of worlds

Glades: warded sanctuaries for those of the Light

The Horizon: the transition between the Land and the Spirit realm

The Kade: an artefact essential for the presence of the diffuse energy in the Land

The Land: the Iyes tribe's known world, a world they strive to protect

Life: a little-understood concept to most, it encapsulates all life of the Continuum

The Light: an unseen force/presence deemed to be linked to the god of the Iyes, IY

The Spirits: the Iyes's collective name for their ancestors and other sentient life who aid them as they can from beyond the Horizon

The Story: the Iyes's ancestral story held by the tribe's Mother

The Threshold: attached to the Gate, it forms part of the ultimate boundary of the Continuum; not truly of the Continuum, but neither of the Void

The Void: the place beyond the Continuum, beyond its timeline, the realm of the Light and the Dark

ACKNOWLEDGEMENTS

No novel is ever completed in isolation, and I give thanks to my test readers of the books of this trilogy: Bish, Christy Howells, Cielo Bellerose, Daniel, Dave Wickenden, Grant, Kimberley Hunt, Willo, and eight anonymous people at Rowanvale Books. In particular, I also thank two other readers: Deb Rhodes for her uplifting positivity; and Gaby Michaelis for her deep focus, cutting insights, and unrelenting pressure on me to improve. I try.

I also express my gratitude to my line editor, author Tammy Salyer, whose rich and diverse feedback on each book of the trilogy aided the flow of the telling. And to the proofreaders at Pikko's House, who caught those infuriating errors that seem to slide from view as you seek them.

Finally, thanks to Paola Andreatta for her skill in transforming my frugal descriptions into the imaginative illustrations you see on the covers (and those illustrations you have yet to see), and to Ken Dawson for delivering the minimalist cover design I wanted.

BY ROGER P. HEATH

The Warriors of the Continuum Trilogy

ARRIVAL
DECEPTION

Coming soon

LIFE